The Fields of Death

The Fields of Death

SIMON SCARROW

headline
review

First published in 2010 by HEADLINE REVIEW
An imprint of HEADLINE PUBLISHING GROUP

1

Cataloguing in Publication Data is available from the British Library

ISBN 978 0 7553 2439 2 (Hardback)
ISBN 978 0 7553 3918 1 (Trade paperback)

Typeset in Bembo by Avon DataSet Ltd,
Bidford-on-Avon, Warwickshire

Printed and bound in Great Britain by
Clays Ltd, St Ives plc

Headline's policy is to use papers that are natural, renewable and recyclable
products and made from wood grown in sustainable forests. The logging
and manufacturing processes are expected to conform to the environmental
regulations of the country of origin.

HEADLINE PUBLISHING GROUP
An Hachette UK Company
338 Euston Road
London NW1 3BH

www.headline.co.uk
www.hachette.co.uk

For James and Bob, for their unstinting
dedication to the team.

Chapter 1

Napoleon

The Danube, April 1809

The defences of the Bohemian town of Ratisbon looked formidable indeed, Napoleon silently conceded as he swept his telescope along the aged walls and ditches confronting him. The retreating Austrian army had hastily thrown up more earthworks to bolster the existing defences and cannon muzzles were discernible in the embrasures of each redoubt, with more cannon mounted on the thick, squat towers of the old town. Here and there, the white-uniformed figures of the enemy regarded the French host approaching the town. Beyond the walls the pitched roofs and church spires were vague in the last vestiges of the early morning mist that had risen up from the Danube. On the far side of the river Napoleon could just pick out the faint trails of smoke rising up from the Austrian camp on the far bank.

He frowned as he lowered the telescope and snapped it shut. Archduke Charles and his men had escaped the trap Napoleon had set for them. Ratisbon had been in French hands until a few days before, and the enemy had been caught with their backs to the river. But the commander of the garrison had surrendered after a brief resistance, leaving the bridge across the Danube intact. So the Austrians had crossed to the north bank and left a strong force behind to defy their pursuers. Archduke Charles had surprised him, Napoleon reflected. He had fully expected the Austrians to fall back towards Vienna to protect their supply lines and defend their capital. Instead, the enemy general had crossed the river into Bohemia, leaving the road to Vienna open. Only it was not as simple as that, Napoleon realised well enough. If he led his army towards Vienna, he would be inviting the Austrians to fall on his supply lines in turn. That might be an unavoidable risk.

Napoleon turned round to face his staff officers. 'Gentlemen,

Ratisbon must be taken if we are to cross the Danube and force the enemy to face us on the battlefield.'

General Berthier, Napoleon's chief of staff, briefly raised his eyebrows as he glanced past his Emperor towards the defences of the town, barely a mile away. He swallowed as his gaze switched back to Napoleon.

'Very well, sire. Shall I give the order for the army to prepare for a siege?'

Napoleon shook his head. 'There is no time for a siege. The moment we settle down to dig trenches and construct batteries the Austrians have the initiative. Moreover, you can be sure that our other enemies . . .' Napoleon paused and smiled bitterly, 'and even some of those who call us friends will take great comfort from the delay. It would not take much prompting for them to side with Austria.'

The more astute of the officers readily understood his point. Several of the small states of the German Confederation were sympathetic to Austria's cause. But by far the biggest danger came from Russia. Even though Napoleon and Tsar Alexander were bound by treaty there had been a marked cooling of their relationship over the past months, and it was possible that the Russian army might intervene on either side of the present war between France and Austria.

Napoleon had been surprised by the temerity of the Austrians when they had opened hostilities in April, without a formal declaration of war. Before then there had been many reports from spies that the Austrian army had been reorganised and expanded, and equipped with new cannon and modern muskets. The signs that Emperor Francis intended to begin another war were unmistakable, and Napoleon had given orders for the concentration of a powerful army ready to meet the threat. Once the campaign had begun, the usual plodding progress of the enemy columns had allowed the French to outmarch them and force the Austrians to fight on Napoleon's terms. The performance of his army had been most gratifying, Napoleon considered. Most of the soldiers who had engaged the enemy so far had been fresh recruits, yet they had fought superbly. But for the failure to prevent the Austrians from escaping across the Danube, the war would already be as good as won.

Napoleon turned towards one of his officers. 'Marshal Lannes.'

The officer stiffened. 'Sire?'

'Your men will take the town, whatever the cost. Understand?'

'Yes, sire.' Lannes nodded, and casually adjusted his plumed bicorne over his brown curls. 'The lads will soon chase the Austrians out.'

'They'd better,' Napoleon replied curtly. Then he stepped closer to Lannes and fixed his gaze on the marshal. 'I am depending on you. Do not let me down.'

Lannes smiled softly. 'Have I ever, sire?'

'No. No, you haven't.' Napoleon returned the smile. 'Good fortune be with you, my dear Jean.'

Lannes saluted, then turned to stride swiftly towards the orderly who was holding his horse. Swinging himself up into the saddle, Lannes touched his spurs in and trotted his mount forward, riding down from the small knoll towards the columns of his leading infantry division as they formed up out of range of the Austrian guns. A brief lull settled over the French positions and then a trumpet signalled the advance and with a rattle of drums the infantry columns tramped towards the enemy fortifications. Ahead of them a screen of skirmishers advanced in loose order, muskets lowered as they looked for individual targets along the line of the Austrian defences.

Napoleon felt his heart harden at the sight of the blue-coated columns closing on the enemy-held town. At any moment the Austrians would open fire and cones of case shot would tear bloody holes in the brave ranks of his men. But Ratisbon had to be taken.

'For what we are about to receive,' Berthier muttered as he strained his eyes to observe the leading elements of the division closing on the enemy defences.

The Austrians held their fire until the French skirmishers had almost reached the wide ditch in front of the town's walls. Then hundreds of tiny puffs of smoke pricked out along the walls as bright tongues of flame stabbed from the guns mounted on the towers and redoubts. Napoleon raised his telescope and saw that scores of the skirmishers had been cut down, and behind them the leading ranks of Lannes's columns reeled as they were subjected to a storm of lead musket balls and the iron shot of the guns. The officers raised their swords high, some placing their hats over the points to make them more visible, and urged their men on. The soldiers surged over the lip of the ditch and were lost to view for a moment before they reappeared, scrambling up the far slope and running on towards the wall. Above them, the battlements of the town were lined with the white uniforms of the Austrians, barely visible through the drifting banks of smoke that hung in the air like a tattered shroud. All the while, the attackers were being whittled down as they tried to reach the wall.

Then, quite abruptly, the forward impetus died as the soldiers went to ground, huddling behind whatever cover they could find as they desperately exchanged shots with the enemy. Still more men entered the ditch, crowding those on the far slope who refused to advance any further. The dense mass of humanity presented an irresistible target to the enemy, who swept the ditch with case shot while grenades were lobbed down from the walls. They detonated with bright flashes, shooting shards of jagged iron in every direction, mutilating the men of Marshal Lannes's first wave.

'Damn.' Napoleon frowned irritably. 'Damn them. Why do they sit there, and die in that ditch? If they want to live, then they must go forward.'

His frustration grew as the slaughter continued. At length the inevitable happened as the men of the first wave slowly began to give ground, and then the pace increased as the urge to retreat spread through the soldiers like an invisible wave rippling out through their ranks. Within minutes the last of the survivors sheltering in the ditch was hurrying away from the town, leaving the dead and wounded sprawled and heaped before the wall. As the men streamed back the Austrians continued to fire after them until the French were out of musket range, and then only the cannon continued, firing several more rounds of case shot before they too fell silent.

Abruptly, Napoleon dug his spurs in and urged his mount down the gentle slope of the knoll before galloping towards Lannes's forward command point in the ruins of a small chapel. The emperor's body-guards and staff officers hurried after him, anxiously trying to keep up. Marshal Lannes strode forward to confront the first of the fugitives as soon as he was aware that the attack had failed. By the time Napoleon reached him he was berating a large group of sheepish-looking soldiers.

'Call yourself men?' Lannes bellowed at the top of his voice. 'Running like bloody rabbits the first time we come up against some Austrians who have the balls to stand and fight. Sweet Jesus Christ, you shame me! You shame your uniforms, and you shame the Emperor.' Lannes indicated Napoleon as he approached and reined in. 'And now the enemy are laughing at you. They mock you for being cowards. Listen!'

Sure enough, the faint sound of jeers and whistles came from the defenders of Ratisbon and some of the men looked down at the ground, not daring to meet the eyes of their commander.

Napoleon dismounted and stared coldly at the men gathered in front of Lannes. He remained silent for a moment before he shook his head wearily. 'Soldiers, I am not angry with you. How could I be? You obeyed your orders and made your attack. You advanced into fire and continued forward until your nerve failed. And then you retreated. You have done no less than any other man in any army in Europe.' Napoleon paused briefly to let his next words carry their full weight. 'But you are not in any army in Europe. You are in the French army. You march under standards entrusted to you by your Emperor. The same standards that were carried to victory at Austerlitz. At Jena and Auerstadt. Eylau and Friedland. Together, we have beaten the armies of the King of Prussia and the Tsar. We have humiliated the Austrians – the very same Austrians who now taunt you from the walls of Ratisbon. They think that the men of France have grown weak and fearful, that the fire in their bellies has died. They think that the enemy they once faced, and feared with good cause, is now as meek as a lamb. They shame you. They laugh at you. They ridicule you . . .' Napoleon looked round and saw the glowering expressions of anger on the faces of some of his men, just as he had hoped. He pressed home his advantage. 'How can a man endure this? How can a soldier of France not feel his heart burn with rage at the scorn poured on him by those whom he knows to be his inferiors?' Napoleon thrust his arm out in the direction of Ratisbon. 'Soldiers! Your enemy awaits you. Show them what it means to be a Frenchman. Neither shot nor shell can shake your courage, or make your resolution waver. Remember those who have fought for your Emperor before you. Remember the eternal glory that they have won. Remember the gratitude and gifts that their Emperor has bestowed on them.'

'Long live Napoleon!' Marshal Lannes punched his fist into the air. 'Long live France!'

The cry was instantly taken up by the nearest men and swept through the ranks of those gathered around. Other soldiers, further off, turned to stare, and then joined in so that the taunts of the Austrians were drowned out by the tumultuous acclaim sweeping through the men of Lannes's division. Lannes continued leading the cheering for a moment before he raised his arms and bellowed for his men to still their tongues. As the cheers died away the marshal drew a deep breath and pointed to the first of the soldiers rallying to their regimental standards.

'To your colours! Form up and make ready to show those Austrian dogs how real soldiers fight!'

As the men hurried off Napoleon could see the renewed determination in their expressions and nodded with satisfaction. 'Their blood is up. I just hope they can take the wall this time.' He turned his gaze back towards the enemy's defences. They were less than half a mile from the nearest enemy guns. 'We are still within range here. And so are the men.'

'It would take a lucky shot indeed to hit anyone at this range, sire,' Lannes replied dismissively. 'Waste of good powder.'

'I hope you are right.'

An instant later there was a puff of smoke from an embrasure in the nearest Austrian redoubt and both men traced the faint dark smear of the shot as it curved through the morning air, angling slightly to one side of their position. The ball grounded a hundred yards ahead, kicking up dust and dirt before it landed again another fifty paces further on, and then again before carving a furrow through the calf-length grass and coming to rest a short distance from the front rank of the nearest French battalion.

'Good conditions for artillery,' Napoleon mused. 'Firm ground – the effective range will increase, and the ricochet of the enemy shot is going to cost us dear.'

More Austrian guns opened fire and a shot from one of the heavier pieces grounded just short of one of the French battalions before slicing a deep path through the ranks, felling men like skittles.

Lannes cleared his throat. 'Sire, it occurs to me that we are also in range of the enemy guns.'

'True, but as you pointed out the chances of their hitting us are negligible.'

'Nevertheless, sire, it would be prudent for you to withdraw beyond effective range.'

Napoleon glanced towards the redoubt, noting that the muzzle of one of the guns was foreshortened to a black dot. Abruptly the gun was obscured by a swirl of smoke and a moment later a puff of dirt kicked up just ahead of them.

'Look out!' Lannes yelled a warning.

But before Napoleon could react, the ball grounded much closer, and then again right at their feet. Grit and soil sprayed in their faces as Napoleon felt a blow, like a savage kick, slam into his right ankle. The shock of the impact stunned him and he stood rigidly, not daring to look down, as Lannes dusted down his uniform jacket with a chuckle. 'As I said . . .'

Napoleon felt his ankle give way, and stumbled to the side, thrusting out his arms to break his fall as he went down.

'Sire!' Lannes hurried to kneel at his side. 'You've been hit?'

The pain in Napoleon's leg was agonisingly sharp and he gritted his teeth as he replied. 'Of course I've been hit, you fool.'

'Where?' Lannes glanced over him anxiously. 'I can't see the wound.'

'My right leg.' Napoleon winced. 'The ankle.'

Lannes shuffled down and saw that Napoleon's boot had been badly scuffed. He felt tenderly for signs of injury. Napoleon gasped and forced himself to sit up. Over Lannes's shoulder he could see several staff officers and orderlies running towards them. Beyond, the men of the nearest battalion were falling out of line as they stared towards their Emperor with shocked expressions.

'The Emperor is wounded!' a voice cried out.

The cry was repeated and a chorus of despairing groans rippled through the ranks of the division forming to launch the second attack. Napoleon could see that he must act swiftly to restore the men's morale, before the chance to seize Ratisbon slipped away.

'Get me on my feet,' he muttered to Lannes.

The marshal shook his head. 'You are injured, sire. I'll have you carried to safety and send for your physician.'

'You'll do no such thing,' Napoleon snapped. 'Get me up. Bring me my horse.'

'As you command.'

The marshal was a powerfully built man and he grasped his Emperor's arm and raised him up easily. Napoleon stood with all his weight on his left foot and fought to hide any sign of the shooting pain that made an agony of any movement of his right leg. He rested his hand on Lannes's shoulder as the latter called for his horse. While one of the Emperor's bodyguard held the reins Lannes carefully lifted Napoleon up into the saddle and placed his right foot into its stirrup. Napoleon took the reins and breathed in deeply.

'Your orders, sire?' Lannes looked up at him.

'Continue the attack, until Ratisbon is taken.' Napoleon clicked his tongue and touched his heels in as tenderly as he could, wincing at the fiery stab in his right ankle as he did so. The horse walked forward and Napoleon steered it along the front of the regiments forming up for another attack on the enemy defences. Berthier trotted up and drew alongside.

'Do you wish me to have your carriage brought forward?'

'No. I will stay on my horse. Where the men can see me.' Napoleon held up his hand to greet the nearest battalion, and a cheer rose up, loud and prolonged. It was taken up by the next formation and continued down the line of Morand's division. Napoleon continued riding along the front rank, forcing himself to smile at his men, and exchanging greetings with their commanders as he passed by.

He reached the far end and turned to make his way back. Marshal Lannes had remounted his horse and trotted it forward so that he stood in full view of his soldiers. Napoleon reined in alongside, and forced himself to keep his expression impassive as another cannon ball grounded a short distance from the division's band, took the head off a young drummer boy and smashed through the chest of the one behind.

Lannes took off his plumed hat and raised it high as he filled his lungs and bellowed, 'Volunteers for the ladder party step forward!'

His voice resonated briefly in the warm air, then died away, but not a man moved. Those in the front rank stared ahead, refusing to meet the gaze of their marshal or their Emperor. Those who volunteered to carry the ladders would be advancing right behind the skirmishers and the enemy would be sure to concentrate their fire on such easy targets. The ground in front of the Austrian defences was already littered with the dead and wounded of the previous attack and the memory of the storm of fire from the walls was still fresh in the minds of the survivors.

Lannes stared at the silent, still ranks with a surprised look on his face, which swiftly turned to scorn. 'Is there no man amongst you willing to have the honour of being the first to scale the walls? Well?'

No one moved and Napoleon was aware of a terrible tension building between the marshal and his men. If it was not resolved, and quickly, there would be no second attack. Lannes must have shared the realisation, for he glanced anxiously at his Emperor and then suddenly dismounted and strode towards the nearest of the ladders. As the soldiers looked on, Lannes picked it up and adjusted his position so that he could carry it by himself. He turned towards the men and called out contemptuously, 'If no man here has the stomach for it, then I'll do it alone. Before I was a marshal I was a grenadier – and I am still!'

With that, he turned away and began to march towards Ratisbon, the unwieldy ladder held in a firm grip.

'Good God,' Berthier muttered. 'What on earth does he think he's doing?'

Napoleon could not help smiling. 'What else? His duty.'

For a moment no man stirred, then one of Lannes's staff officers ran forward and stood in his commander's path.

'Sir! You can't do this. Who will command the corps if you are killed?'

'What do I care?' Lannes growled. 'Out of my way, damn you.'

He brushed the officer aside and continued towards the waiting

Austrians. The other man stared after him, aghast. Then, recovering his wits, he hurried to catch up, took hold of the end of the ladder and fell into step with Lannes.

'Wait, sir!' one of the other staff officers called out as he and his companions ran forward, snatched up the nearest ladders and hurried after Lannes.

There was a brief pause before the colonel of the nearest battalion turned to his astonished men and bellowed, 'What are you waiting for? I'll be damned if I let a marshal of France take a bullet that's meant for me! Advance!' He drew his sword and swept it towards the town. 'Long live France!'

The cry was taken up by his men and they lurched into movement, running down to pick up the ladders and surging after Lannes and his officers. In an uneven tide of cheering soldiers the rest of Morand's division swept forward, snatching up the remaining ladders as they went. Napoleon felt his blood quicken at the sight and he urged his horse to advance with the rest of the men. The defenders reacted swiftly to the new threat and every gun that could be brought to bear opened fire on the wave of men rushing across the open ground towards the ditch and the wall beyond. A roundshot briefly droned close overhead and Berthier instinctively ducked his head.

'Sire, is this wise? You've already been wounded. I implore you to have your leg attended to.'

'Later. All that matters now is taking Ratisbon.'

'With respect, sire, Marshal Lannes can handle the attack.'

'Really?' Napoleon glanced at his chief of staff. 'You saw the men. You saw how fickle their mood is. If their Emperor is with them, they will not lose heart.'

Berthier bowed his head wearily. 'I am sure you are right, sire. But what if you are killed? Right here, before the men? Not only would the attack fail but it would be a blow to the morale of the whole army.'

Napoleon forced himself to smile. 'My dear Berthier, I can assure you that the bullet that will kill me has not yet been cast. Now, enough of this. We remain with our soldiers.'

'Yes, sire,' Berthier replied meekly and did his best to look unperturbed as they rode on.

Ahead of them, Napoleon could make out the gold-laced uniforms of Lannes and his officers, still leading the attack as they hurried forward. They reached the ditch, half running, half slithering down the near slope before they ran at the far side and scrambled up to cross the last stretch of open ground before the wall. Above them the battlements were lined with Austrian soldiers, firing and reloading their muskets as quickly as possible as the tide of blue uniforms surged towards them. On either flank of Morand's division, the cannon in the enemy redoubts blasted case shot into the French ranks, sweeping several men away at a time in bloody tatters. Napoleon and Berthier reined in a short distance from the ditch and watched as Lannes and his officers reached the wall. They hurriedly raised the ladder and the marshal sprang on to the lowest rungs and started to climb. On either side other ladders were thrust against the wall and the men of Morand's division streamed up, clambering over the breastworks and falling on the defenders.

Most had fired their muskets as they closed on the wall, and now went in with the cold steel of the bayonet, or used their weapons like clubs as they fought at brutal close quarters with the Austrians. The same fate befell the defenders of the flanking redoubts as the French fought their way in through the gun embrasures and fell on the enemy gunners within. After the death wreaked by their cannon, Napoleon knew that none of the artillery crews would be spared the vengeful wrath of the attackers.

As more men climbed over the walls there was a cheer from those still outside the town as the gates began to open. For an instant Napoleon tensed, wondering if the enemy were about to launch a counter-attack, but as the gates swung back a hatless figure in an elaborate gold-laced uniform emerged from within the town.

'That's Lannes!' Berthier cried out.

'Yes.' Napoleon grinned in relief, and nudged his horse forward towards the ditch. As the horse cautiously stepped down the slope Napoleon saw for the first time the bodies heaped along the bottom of the ditch, some badly torn up by the heavy iron balls of case shot. The horse whinnied until Napoleon leaned forward to pat its flank soothingly and urge it up the far side. Lannes was waving his men through the gate and bellowing encouragement as Napoleon and Berthier rode up to him. Napoleon noted the tear in the marshal's uniform jacket, and the smear of blood on his neck.

'It seems that you are the reckless one now, my dear Jean.'

Lannes looked up, then touched a gloved hand to his neck. It came away with a smear of fresh blood. 'A scratch, sire. Nothing more.'

Napoleon glanced back over the ditch and out across the approaches to the town. He estimated that nearly a thousand Frenchmen had fallen before the walls of Ratisbon. He turned back to Lannes. 'It would seem that you lead something of a charmed life.'

'As do we all, sire, until the day we die.'

They shared a laugh, and Berthier joined in a little uncertainly. Then Napoleon leaned forward to give his marshal fresh instructions. 'Pass the order for your men to clear the town. Meanwhile I want you, and every other grenadier that you can find, to make directly for the bridge. We must capture it intact. Stop for nothing, and having taken it, hold on at all costs. Clear?'

'Yes, sire.'

'Then go.'

As Lannes trotted back into the city and called his staff officers to him, Napoleon and Berthier remained by the gate and the Emperor acknowledged the greetings of the soldiers of the follow-up regiments of the division as they marched into Ratisbon. Many, particularly the young recruits, had only ever seen their Emperor from afar, if at all, and now regarded him with excited curiosity and not a little awe. Some of the older men, with campaign stripes on their sleeves, shouted out informal greetings to Napoleon in order to impress their younger comrades. Napoleon knew that they would be holding court over the camp fires that night, telling tales about the times they had fought at the side of the Emperor when he had still been a young officer.

He waited until the first two regiments had entered the town before following them through the gate. The sounds of fighting had receded towards the river and the faint crackle of musket shots was punctuated by the occasional dull boom of a cannon from the Austrian-held bank of the Danube. There were bodies strewn along the street leading from the gates, both French and Austrian. The dead and wounded had been hurriedly dragged aside so as not to hold up the troops marching through. The living sat propped up against the walls, waiting to be helped to the rear where their injuries would eventually be treated. Some raised a cheer as Napoleon rode by, others stared blankly, too shocked or in too much pain to care.

Ahead of them the street opened out into a square which the enemy had been using as a vehicle park. The space was lined with the ornately decorated facades that Napoleon had grown used to seeing in the small villages and towns on the banks of the Danube. Artillery limbers, ammunition caissons and supply wagons were packed tightly together in the middle of the square.

On the far side, Napoleon could see the broad route that led to the bridge that crossed the great river. A throng of blue-coated soldiers was pressing across the bridge. Napoleon spurred his horse forward. As he approached the end of the bridge he saw Lannes and his officers on a landing stage to one side. Beyond them the water of the Danube

11

stretched out for over a hundred paces to the first of the small islands that lay between the two banks. The bridge, built on massive stone buttresses, extended right across the great river, passing over the islands to the far side. Napoleon could see that it was so solid that it could not easily be destroyed by gunpowder charges. Dense formations of enemy soldiers and several artillery batteries were clearly visible covering the far end of the bridge. Beyond them, on the slope rising up from the river, sprawled the camp of Archduke Charles's army. Even as Napoleon watched, the French troops on the bridge began to give way under the vicious fusillade of musket balls and grapeshot sweeping the length of the bridge. The men fell back, the more resolute amongst them pausing to fire a last shot from cover before scurrying back to the shelter of the buildings lining the river.

At the sound of hooves approaching over the cobbled road, Lannes turned and he and his officers bowed their heads in greeting.

'Make your report,' Napoleon ordered as he reined in. The pain in his ankle had subsided into a steady throb and he had to force himself to pay full attention to the marshal.

'The town is ours, sire. Most of the enemy managed to escape across the river, but we have a few hundred prisoners, and have taken twenty guns. A handful of the Austrians are still holding some buildings in the eastern quarter of Ratisbon, but they'll be dealt with shortly. As for our losses—'

'That's not important now. Is the bridge safe?'

Lannes nodded. 'Major Dubarry of the engineers has checked for charges. It seems the Austrians had no intention of trying to destroy the bridge.'

'Good. Then we still have a chance to pursue Archduke Charles.'

Lannes raised his eyebrows momentarily. 'Sire, as you can see, the enemy holds the far bank. We cannot force a crossing here. The enemy has escaped us, for the present.'

Napoleon pressed his lips together and fought to contain his temper. It had been over ten days since he had had a good night's rest and in the sudden surge of anger he recognised the symptoms of exhaustion. Lannes was not to blame. As he stared across the river Napoleon could see for himself that any further attempts to cross the bridge would only lead to a bloody massacre. He felt a sudden heaviness in his heart as he contemplated the impasse. The Austrians had managed to put the Danube between them and their pursuers. If they moved parallel to the French army then they could block any attempt to cross the river and bring them to battle.

He sighed bitterly. 'It seems that the enemy have learned their lesson from the last war. Archduke Charles will think twice before accepting a battle on my terms.'

'We can find another crossing point, sire,' Berthier replied. 'Masséna is marching on Straubing. If he crosses the river before the Austrians stop him, then he can attack their flank.'

'On his own?' Napoleon shook his head. 'Even if Masséna did manage to surprise the Austrians they can simply retreat into the German states to the north, and try to win over their allegiance while drawing us after them, and away from Vienna.' He paused a moment and gently scratched the stubble on his chin. 'No. We'll not play Archduke Charles's game. Instead, we must try to make him follow us.'

'How, sire?'

'We march on Vienna. I doubt the Austrians will be prepared to let us occupy their capital a second time.'

Lannes gestured to the enemy forces massed on the far bank. 'And what if they cross back over and try to cut our communications?'

Napoleon smiled. 'Then we turn on them and force them to fight. My guess is that they will not have the stomach to risk that for a while yet. So, we take the war to Vienna, my friends. Then we shall have our battle.'

Chapter 2

The Austrian army withdrew during the night and Napoleon sent Davout and his corps across the Danube to keep in contact with the enemy, and harass them. Meanwhile, the main army marched east, towards Vienna, pushing the remaining Austrian forces ahead of them. The spring weather remained fine and the soldiers of the French army tramped across the enemy's lands in high spirits.

All the while Napoleon carefully scrutinised the regular intelligence reports sent to him by Davout. As soon as the threat to Vienna became clear Archduke Charles had turned his army round and set off along the north bank of the Danube in a bid to reach his capital city before the French. There was little chance of that, Napoleon calculated, since the Austrian army had always marched at a ponderous pace. The only news that concerned him came from Italy, where Archduke Charles's brother, Archduke John, had bested the French army there. It was possible that John might march back towards Vienna in an attempt to combine the Austrian armies against Napoleon.

Early in May, the spires and roofs of the Austrian capital came within sight of the French army and Napoleon gave the order for the artillery to prepare to bombard Vienna. Before the guns could open fire the gates of the city opened and a small party of civilians rode out.

'I wonder what they want?' Berthier mused as he raised his telescope and watched them cautiously approach the French pickets. He turned to his Emperor. 'Maybe they want to sue for peace already.'

'I would hope so,' Napoleon replied. 'But if they intend to defend Vienna, then this time I will not hesitate to flatten the city. There will be no third chance for Emperor Francis to defy me.' Napoleon gestured for the telescope and squinted through the eyepiece. There were five men in civilian clothes, together with a small mounted escort from the city's militia.

'Have them brought to the main battery,' Napoleon instructed Berthier. 'I'll meet them there. Might as well let them see what they can expect if they fail to meet my demands.'

'Yes, sire.' Berthier nodded and wheeled his horse away to carry out the order. Napoleon turned his gaze from the approaching horsemen to the defences of the city beyond. There were a handful of forts guarding the approaches to Vienna, and then the walls. However, there were no signs of life in any of the forts, and no flags or regimental standards flying over them. He lowered the telescope with a slight frown and muttered, 'What the hell are they playing at?'

Half an hour later Napoleon, together with Berthier and a squadron of Guard cavalry, rode into the main battery to meet the enemy deputation. On either side the line of twelve-pounders stretched out across the Austrian countryside. Fifty yards behind them lay the caissons, loaded with powder and shot, ready to feed the guns when they opened fire on Vienna. The gun crews had completed their preparations and stood close by their weapons, watching the Austrians curiously. At Napoleon's approach the gunners cheered and he indulged it a moment as he slowed his mount to a slow walk and fixed the Austrians with a hard stare. They removed their hats and bowed their heads curtly as the French Emperor raised a hand to quieten his men. Once the cheers had died away Napoleon cleared his throat and addressed the man at the head of the Austrian deputation. The official was tall and thin, and his dark curls were streaked with grey. His coat was finely embroidered with gold lace and a broad red ribbon hung across his shoulder. Napoleon spoke curtly.

'What is the purpose of your presence here?'

'Sire, I represent the mayor of Vienna. His honour respectfully requests an audience with you.'

'Your name?'

'Baron Karinsky, sire.'

'Tell me what your master wants.'

'Yes, sire. He wishes to discuss terms for the surrender of Vienna.'

'Vienna? I see.' Napoleon paused. 'And has Emperor Francis agreed to the surrender of his capital?'

'As far as I understand, sire.'

'What does that mean?'

'His imperial majesty and the court have left the city, sire. The mayor was left in charge with orders to defend it for as long as is practicable.'

'Then this offer relates to Vienna alone?' asked Berthier.

'Indeed, sir.'

'There is no intention on the part of Emperor Francis to discuss an armistice?'

'Not as far as I am aware.'

Berthier exchanged a look with Napoleon, who let out a brief sigh of frustration before he continued addressing Karinsky.

'So why is the mayor preparing to discuss surrender before we have fired a single shot?'

The Austrian gestured towards the city. 'The garrison has already withdrawn from the walls, sire. On the orders of Archduke Charles. All that remains is the militia. Accordingly, the mayor has determined that he cannot defend the city. Out of compassion for the inhabitants of Vienna he believes it would be better to surrender rather than waste lives in a pointless attempt to resist you, sire.'

'Where is the garrison now?' Napoleon snapped.

'They have retreated across the Danube.'

Napoleon stared at the man briefly. 'And the bridges are intact?'

The man lowered his eyes as he replied. 'They were when I left the city, sire.'

Napoleon turned to Berthier. 'Send a cavalry division forward. Tell Bessières I want his men to take those bridges at once. We must have access to the far bank if we are to—'

He was interrupted by a faint roar and looked towards Vienna. Beyond the city skyline he could see a billowing column of smoke rising up into the clear sky. A moment later there was a second explosion and more smoke, followed by two more blasts that echoed across the landscape towards the startled leading elements of the French army.

'They've blown the bridges,' Berthier said quietly.

Napoleon nodded, and glared at Baron Karinsky. 'Tell the mayor Vienna is to surrender unconditionally. If he does not surrender the city within the hour, then I will order my guns to pulverise your capital. Is that clear?'

Karinsky shook his head. 'Sire, I am not authorised to negotiate with you. My master simply sent me here to invite you to speak with him.'

'There is nothing to say. There will be no negotiations. Tell him that I demand he surrender, and that if he fails to do so then the death and destruction that I will rain down on Vienna will be his responsibility.'

The Austrian opened his mouth to protest but Napoleon took out his watch and glanced down briefly. 'It is now just gone eleven o'clock. If the city has not surrendered by noon I will order the guns to open fire. It would be wise of you to waste no time in informing the mayor of my terms.'

Karinsky frowned and then abruptly turned his horse about and spurred it into a gallop as he headed back down the road to Vienna.

★ ★ ★

As soon as the gates of Vienna were thrown open to the French army, Napoleon and his chief engineer, General Bertrand, rode through the city to assess the condition of the demolished bridges. The Austrian engineers had done a thorough job. The central spans of each bridge had been blown, and the buttressed piles were little more than heaps of masonry in the swiftly flowing current of the Danube. On the far side of the river the enemy was busy building barricades across the ends of the ruined bridges. On the flanks artillery batteries were being constructed to cover the river in case the French engineers attempted to make any repairs to the blown spans.

Napoleon gazed at the bridges with a heavy heart. The enemy would be safe until the French could find another way across the river.

General Bertrand had finished surveying the bridges and the Austrian forces beyond, and clicked his tongue. 'It would be suicide to attempt any repairs, sire.'

'I can see that for myself,' Napoleon replied testily. 'If we can't cross here, then we must find somewhere else.'

'Yes, sire.' Bertand nodded thoughtfully as he removed his hat and scratched the thin strands of hair plastered to his skull. 'The main problem is the current. As you can see, the river flows quickly, particularly at this time of year. Any sudden storms can only make matters worse. If there is a sudden flood, then our pontoons could be carried away.'

'Very well, then. Where do you suggest?'

'I've considered a few possibilities already, sire, having questioned the local people.' Bertrand delved into his saddlebag and unrolled a map. He pointed a gloved finger at the map where it indicated the banks of the river, downstream from Vienna. 'I think this looks promising, sire. Here, opposite the island of Lobau. It's over eight hundred yards from our bank to the island, but from there to the far bank it's only another hundred yards. And the width of the river means that the current is slower there than elsewhere as well.'

Napoleon nodded approvingly. 'Good. Assuming this site is suitable you are to begin work the moment the bridging train reaches the army. The wagons carrying the pontoons are to have priority over all other vehicles on the road. Issue orders for that in my name.'

'Yes, sire.'

'I want the river bridged as quickly as possible. Understand? There's no time to waste. The army must be across the Danube in less than a week if we are to defeat Archduke Charles.'

Bertrand puffed his cheeks. 'As you order, sire.'

Smiling coldly Napoleon turned his attention back to the enemy troops on the far bank. The latest reports from Davout indicated that Archduke Charles and his army were still some distance from Vienna, on the far bank. If Bertrand could bridge the Danube quickly the Austrians would be caught between Napoleon and Davout and be forced to give battle. The odds would be in Napoleon's favour, as further reinforcements under Marshal Bernadotte were marching from Dresden to join him. Provided the French army kept up its momentum Archduke Charles should be defeated before his brother arrived to help him.

Five days after the fall of Vienna, the wagons carrying the pontoons arrived and Bertrand began work on the bridge. Napoleon joined his senior engineer to watch the progress as each raft was manhandled down into the river and rowed out into the current with long oars, until it was in position to drop a heavy anchor upstream. The engineers paid off the cable until the pontoon was in line with those already secured in place; then the pontoon was linked with lengths of timber and covered in decking. A covering force of infantry had been landed on the island and they quickly flushed out the handful of Austrian defenders. General Bertrand drove his men hard and the Danube was bridged in little over a day and a half. The moment the task was complete, the first of the cavalry units began to cross.

'Fine work!' Napoleon congratulated the general when he reported the news to the Emperor in person, just after midday. The forward headquarters had been established in a small village close to the end of the bridge, and the countryside around was crowded with men, horses, cannon and their limbers and wagons, as the army massed ready to cross.

'Thank you, sire.' Bertrand bowed his head. He had not slept for nearly three days and his exhaustion was evident.

'What of the last stage?' Berthier asked. 'The crossing from Lobau island to the far bank?'

'The pontoons will cross to the island this afternoon, and we'll bridge the final gap tonight.'

'Excellent.' Napoleon smiled warmly. 'Then by dawn we'll have our bridgehead. Masséna's corps will take the villages of Essling and Aspern and then the rest of the army can cross.'

Marshal Lannes leaned forward in his chair and cleared his throat. 'That's all very well, sire, but can we be sure that the enemy will not contest our landing on the far bank?'

'Rest assured, my dear Lannes, the Austrian army is still many days' march away. The first they'll know about our crossing the Danube is when the cannon announce our presence. By then, it will be too late to do anything but give battle.'

'But if the Austrians are closer than you have calculated, then we could be advancing into a trap of our own making. Sire, I urge caution. We are advancing over a fast-flowing river on a single bridge. What if this span broke, or was destroyed? Then the army would be cut in half. The vanguard would be at the mercy of the enemy if they could gather sufficient forces to oppose us. Sire, it is too much of a risk.'

'The enemy are not strong enough to hamper the river crossing, I assure you. War is the realm of risk, chance and opportunity. In this case it is my judgement that the opportunity outweighs the risk.' Napoleon's tone hardened. 'Gentlemen, the orders are given and the army begins to cross the Danube tonight.'

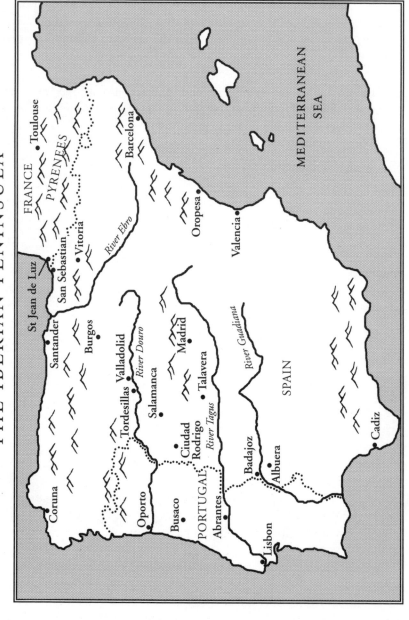

THE IBERIAN PENINSULA

FRANCE

Toulouse

PYRENEES

Barcelona

St Jean de Luz

San Sebastian

Vitoria

River Ebro

Oropesa

Valencia

MEDITERRANEAN SEA

Santander

Burgos

Valladolid

River Douro

Madrid

Talavera

River Guadiana

SPAIN

Coruna

Tordesillas

Salamanca

Ciudad Rodrigo

River Tagus

Badajoz

Cadiz

Oporto

Busaco

PORTUGAL

Abrantes

Albuera

Lisbon

Chapter 3

Arthur

Abrantes, Portugal, June 1809

General Sir Arthur Wellesley lowered the letter with a frustrated sigh and leaned back in his chair. Even though he sat in the shade outside the small tavern the noon heat was stifling. Not so bad as India, he recalled, but beyond reasonable comfort all the same. He had taken off his coat and sat bareheaded at a plain trestle table as he dealt with the morning's reports and correspondence. The army had halted at the Portuguese town of Abrantes several days earlier as it waited for supplies and money. The latter was Arthur's most pressing concern. Not only had his men not been paid for over two months, but there were also numerous bills that required settling with Portuguese grain merchants and horse dealers, as well as the need for twenty thousand pairs of boots to replace those worn out by his men. It was Arthur's policy that the British army must pay its way in the Peninsula if it was to enjoy the continued support of the Portuguese and Spanish people. His army was outnumbered at least five to one as things stood and the British could not afford the enmity of the people across whose land they campaigned.

Arthur knew that the French took a less enlightened view regarding their supplies, and lived off the land with no regard for the consequent attitude of the local people. As a result the French had incurred the wrath of the Spanish and Portuguese peasants who now waged a pitiless war of resistance, ambushing French patrols, harassing their columns and butchering any stragglers left behind.

Arthur looked down the steep slope towards the river Tagus. The water flowed with a serene grace through hills planted with groves of olive and fruit trees and the men of the British army were enjoying a hard-earned rest as they waited for their commander to decide on his next steps. Hundreds of soldiers were lining the bank, taking the chance to wash their clothes, while the more adventurous had stripped and were splashing in the shallows.

Arthur permitted himself a small smile as he regarded them. The men had performed well at Oporto a month earlier, where they had surprised Marshal Soult and sent him fleeing towards Spain, abandoning all his artillery and wagons in the process. Besides proving that they could march hard, the redcoats had shown that they could stand up to the fanatical attacks of the French at the earlier battle of Vimeiro. Arthur was confident that his army, even outnumbered as it was, had the beating of all the marshals and men of Napoleon's forces in the Peninsula, provided that the French were prevented from concentrating their armies. That was the trick of it, Arthur reflected. He must defeat them in detail until the Peninsula was liberated. Conversely, he dare not let his army suffer a single setback.

He commanded the largest British army in the field and there were many at home in England who loudly questioned the sagacity of supporting such a large force in the Peninsula, far from the vital battlefields of central Europe, where Arthur's men could be better used. He disagreed. It was best to deploy valuable British soldiers where they stood a good chance of tipping the scales. Even so, Arthur's political masters had proved reluctant to allow him to take risks. Or they had been until the victory at Oporto. Then, true to form, the politicians had veered from caution to opportunism in an instant.

Before Oporto Arthur had been forbidden from entering Spain without the express permission of the British government. Now that the news of the victory had arrived in London, together with Arthur's report of his pursuit of Soult as far as the Spanish border, the Prime Minister had sent him a despatch expressing his disappointment that Arthur had not fully exploited his success. The Prime Minister now urged Arthur to invade Spain, capture Madrid and drive the French out.

Arthur heard footsteps approaching the table and looked up to see his senior aide de camp approaching. Lord Fitzroy Somerset was a handsome youth, but unlike many of the other younger officers in the army he dedicated himself to his duties with a high degree of organisation and intelligence. He had proved to be a valuable member of Arthur's small team of staff officers and the general had come to rely on him and, on occasion, seek his opinion.

'Good morning, sir,' Somerset smiled, proffering a small bundle of letters.

'Put them there, on the corner of the table. You can deal with them in a moment. For now, read this.' Arthur pushed the despatch he had been reading across the table to Somerset as the latter pulled up a stool and sat down.

Somerset picked up the document and read through it quickly, his expression settling into an irritated frown as his gaze flitted across the text. He looked up as he lowered the letter.

'He must be joking.'

'Only at my expense,' Arthur muttered.

'Sir, this is preposterous. They get one whiff of victory and then want the impossible.'

Arthur sighed. 'You are right, of course. It is impossible. We have barely twenty-five thousand men under arms, and another fifteen if you include Beresford and his Portuguese troops. Against us Joseph Bonaparte has perhaps as many as a quarter of a million men. It is true that many of the enemy are tied down in garrisons but they must still be marched upon and destroyed, and any siege is a costly affair.' He paused briefly. 'Speaking of cost, it appears that His Majesty's treasury has declined to send me the four hundred thousand pounds I requested to fund our operations here. I am told that they have decided that the hundred and twenty thousand already sent is sufficient for the foreseeable future. It barely covers our existing debts.'

'At least we should be able to pay those off soon enough, sir,' Somerset responded, as he began to open and read the morning's despatches. 'Once Cradock returns from Cadiz.'

Arthur nodded. Cradock was one of his senior officers, entrusted with a hundred thousand pounds' worth of captured bullion to be converted into Portuguese dollars. He was due back any day, and once there was money in the army's war chest Arthur would be able to lead his men against the French once more and enter Spain. The Spanish junta, the government opposed to the regime of Joseph Bonaparte in Madrid, had offered to co-operate with the British and Arthur was bidden to join forces with General Cuesta to the west of the capital. Britain's ally promised to provide ample supplies of food and ammunition to the redcoat army marching to their aid. Arthur had been promised much by the Portuguese government and received little, and feared that he could only expect the same from the Spanish.

Somerset cleared his throat as he looked at a lengthy list of names on a sheet of paper. 'More bad news, sir. A score at least of our officers have requested reappointment to the Portuguese army.'

Arthur's heart sank at the news. 'How many is that so far?'

Somerset paused a moment to think. 'Must be over a hundred by now.'

Dearth of supplies was not the only difficulty facing the army, Arthur mused ruefully. The men were in good enough spirits, despite the frustration of watching Soult escape when they reached the border, but the mood amongst many of the officers was far less encouraging. In an army where commissions were bought and sold like any other commodity, those without a family fortune or access to large loans were often destined to spend the whole of their careers as junior officers. So it came as little surprise when many of them requested a transfer to the Portuguese army where they would be assured of swift promotion and far better pay. Beresford, charged with training and leading the Portuguese army, had already been promoted to the rank of marshal, technically outranking Arthur himself. It was frustrating to lose good officers this way, but at least they would be helping to improve the performance of Britain's allies. Besides, Arthur could not begrudge the unfortunate officers unable to buy their chance of advancement in the British army. If only some of his more incompetent subordinates could be induced to transfer to the colours of Portugal along with the others, Arthur mused briefly.

He nodded wearily. 'Very well. Have their applications approved in my name. Then send a memo to the War Office to notify them of the relevant vacancies in our ranks.'

'Yes, sir.' Somerset continued working through the morning's paperwork and then paused as he came across a small, neatly addressed bundle of letters. He cleared his throat and held the bundle up. 'Correspondence from Lady Wellesley, sir.'

Arthur glanced up briefly. 'Put it with the rest. I'll attend to it when I have the time.'

Somerset was still for an instant, as if considering adding some further comment, and then put the bundle in the wooden tray reserved for low priority papers. Arthur felt a flicker of irritation at the imputed reproach of his aide. After all, he had an army to command, with all the duties that came with the post. His wife was back in London in a comfortable house, surrounded by servants. Yet Kitty contrived to drag him into making decisions about the pettiest issues of domestic management. While he found her news of friends, family and society mildly diverting, his heart began to sink when Kitty turned to the more substantial issues that consumed her thoughts: how to end the service of a difficult or incompetent maid, or whether to redecorate a room, or her latest choice of school for their sons, even though they were little more than infants. Despite his polite efforts to encourage her to take charge of the family's affairs whilst he was away on campaign, thus far she had proved to have little faith in her ability to do so. Privately, it infuriated Arthur, just as it did when one of his officers failed to show the initiative required of his rank and responsibilities. It occurred to him that a wife and a subordinate might not be quite the same thing, but he dismissed the notion. A wife had duties, just the same as a man, and should be measured by how well she carried them out.

Marrying Kitty had been a mistake, he accepted. Nevertheless, the deed was done, though for all the wrong reasons save one: that he had given his word that he would marry her before he set off for India. She had waited for his return and so Arthur had dutifully married her, though her looks and youthful charms had long since faded. Now, if he were honest, he was glad to be away from her.

As he shook thoughts of Kitty aside, Arthur spied a movement on the far side of the river. A small convoy of wagons was snaking through the olive trees down towards the bridge that crossed the Tagus. A thin gauze of dust hung about the wagons as they rattled along the crude roadway. Two squadrons of cavalry escorted the convoy, one at its head and the other guarding the rear.

'Somerset.'

'Sir?'

'See those wagons down there, on the far bank, approaching the bridge?'

Somerset looked in the direction indicated. 'Yes, sir.'

'Ride down there and see if it's Cradock. If it is, send him directly to me.'

'Yes, sir.' Somerset lowered the document he was reading, saluted and made his way over to the horse line where several mounts waited in the shade of some cedar trees, their tails flicking at the flies that buzzed round them in a constant cloud. He unhitched the reins and swung himself up on to the saddle of the nearest horse, then spurred it towards the track that led down to the bridge.

While he waited, Arthur pulled a blank sheet of paper towards him and took up a pen. He paused a moment as he composed the arguments necessary to try to squeeze more money and men from the government. Try as he might, Arthur could think of no new way to state the obvious. If the politicians in London were serious about winning the war then they would provide the means to see it through. If they were not serious, then whatever Arthur said would not sway them from the path to defeat. All that he could do was lay the facts in front of his political masters and trust to their good sense. With a deep, weary sigh, he flipped open the cap of the inkwell, dipped his pen and began to write.

'Cradock!' Arthur looked up as Somerset returned with another officer. He lowered his pen and rose from his chair, leaving the table to greet the new arrival. Cradock's short jacket and bicorne hat were covered with dust, which had also settled into the creases of his face, making him look far older than he was. 'Good to see you!'

Cradock saluted briefly and grinned. 'And you, sir.'

'How was the journey?' Arthur asked, and then shook his head apologetically. 'By God, where are my manners? You must be hot and thirsty. Somerset, get you to the innkeeper and have some refreshment brought here.'

Somerset nodded and hurried away. Arthur turned his attention back to Cradock and lowered his voice. 'I'll ask about the journey later. First, tell me that you have changed the Spanish gold.'

'Yes, sir. It's locked away in pay chests in the wagons. Though I'll admit that a hundred thousand in gold doesn't buy as much Portuguese currency as one would like.'

Arthur looked sharply at him. 'Explain yourself.'

'It's the money changers, sir. They knew how much we needed the money and charged a somewhat higher commission than we were expecting. I did what I could to get the best deal.'

Arthur frowned. 'Damn them! The Spanish are fighting to survive, and we're putting our heads on the block to try to help them, yet those blasted bankers still try to get their claws on every last penny that passes before them. By God, sometimes they forget whose side they're on.'

'Alas, sir.' Cradock shook his head. ' 'Tis a well-known fact that bankers are a nation unto themselves and damned be the rest.'

'Amen to that,' Arthur said with feeling. 'Anyway, the greed of bankers notwithstanding, at least the army can move forward again.' He nodded down towards the river where twenty or thirty men were spraying handfuls of glittering water at each other. 'It will do the men good to remember that we are here to fight the French, not play like children.'

Cradock gazed longingly down towards the river. 'I suppose so, sir. But I have to say they've earned their pleasure.'

'Maybe.' Arthur pursed his lips. 'But there's a long road ahead of us, Cradock.'

Somerset emerged from the inn, followed by a teenage boy carrying a tray with some old chipped glasses and a bottle of white wine. He set it down on the table, bowed his head and withdrew.

Arthur nodded to Somerset. 'You do the honours.'

'Yes, sir.'

Somerset pulled out the cork stopper and half filled each glass before handing one to Arthur and Cradock. Arthur raised his and smiled. 'Gentlemen, the toast is death to the French, and an end to tyranny!'

'Aye!' Cradock agreed and the three officers downed the wine. It was cooler than Arthur anticipated and he guessed that the owner of the inn kept a deep cellar beneath his house. He set his glass down with a sharp tap on the table and turned to Somerset.

'Right then, pass the word to all the senior officers. The army is to prepare to march.'

'Yes, sir.' Somerset smiled. 'In case I am asked, might I enquire in which direction the army will advance?'

'Why, towards Spain, of course. Towards Spain, and glory.'

Chapter 4

The early days of June brought renewed heat that beat down on the columns of the British army as it tramped along the dusty road towards Madrid. The hearty spirit that had upheld the men as they crossed the Portuguese border had soon faded as they settled into the exhausting routine of rising before dawn to break camp and begin the day's marching in the coolest hours of the morning. The infantry trudged forward, bent under the load they carried in their wooden-framed backpacks. The cavalry rode half a mile out on each flank, their kit hung behind the saddle, tightly stuffed forage nets slung across the pommel. A screen of light horse fanned out some distance ahead of the army, watching for signs of the enemy, and the outriders of General Cuesta.

As the sun rose across the barren Spanish landscape it washed a warm ruddy glow over the British soldiers and suffused the choking dust kicked up by boots, wheels and hooves with a fiery hue. As Arthur and his small staff rode to the side of the main column, far enough away not to be bothered by the dust, he was amused to think that any Englishman at home who might suddenly be transported to Spain would hardly recognise these soldiers as his compatriots. Most of the men had sprouted beards and their uniforms were worn and patched, their shakos battered and badly misshapen. The red woollen cloth in which British soldiers were normally dressed was almost unknown in Portugal and the men had to make do with the cheap local material, which seemed to be available in brown only. After the first months of campaigning the makeshift repairs to uniforms and the accumulation of dust meant that the British army appeared to be predominantly clothed in a murky brown.

By late morning the sun was overhead and its harsh glare seemed to bleach the colour out of the landscape and send a silvery shimmer squirming along the horizon of the flat plain ahead of the army. Now the men began to suffer most from thirst as the dust dried out their throats and parched their lips. Their sergeants and officers, mindful of the need to conserve water in this dry land, watched their men closely to make sure that they did not consume too much from their canteens during the day's march.

Once noon had come the army had usually advanced fifteen or so miles and was ready to halt and make camp. After the battalions had been dismissed, the men set up their makeshift tents and shelters and rested in the shade until late in the afternoon, when they ventured out to find wood for the cooking fires, and see if the local people had any food or drink to sell. Arthur had made sure that every soldier was aware that he would not countenance any looting. The least a man could expect was a public flogging if he was caught in the act.

At dusk the first fires were lit and the men cooked a stew of their pooled rations, and any game or fresh meat they had been able to buy, all added into the large pot suspended over the flames. After they had eaten, they would sit and talk. Some broke into song, accompanied by a fiddle or a flute as darkness gathered over the camp. Then the fires were built up and the men turned to their bedrolls and settled down to sleep. Those on sentry duty would be roused when their turn came during the night, while their comrades slumbered, resting before being roused to begin the whole process all over again – the timeless routine of an army on the march.

As the British advanced along the banks of the Tagus towards Madrid, Arthur began to be concerned over the lack of news from General Cuesta. Then one evening, as the army settled for the night some ten miles from the foothills of the Sierra de Gredos, Somerset brought a Spanish officer to Arthur's tent. Stepping through the flaps, the aide saluted.

'Sir, beg to report, there's a messenger from General Cuesta outside.'

'Ah, at last!' Arthur nodded. 'Please, bring him in.'

Somerset drew the flap aside and beckoned to the waiting officer. A moment later a short, swarthy man entered and stood in the glow of the lamp hanging from the central tent post. Arthur and the Spaniard regarded each other briefly in silence. Arthur took in the other's dark eyes and thin moustache, and the elaborate braiding that all but covered his green coat and tasselled hat.

'I bid you welcome, sir.' Arthur bowed his head. 'I am Lieutenant-General Sir Arthur Wellesley. I have the honour to command his majesty's forces in the Peninsula.' He gestured towards Somerset. 'I take it you have already been introduced to my aide.'

The Spaniard nodded curtly and then presented his right leg and bowed deeply before he rose again and spoke in fluent English. 'I am General Juan O'Donoju, of the army of Andalusia.'

Arthur cocked an eyebrow. 'Did you say O'Donohue?'

The other man smiled faintly. 'That was the name of my forefathers, sir. When the family was obliged to leave Ireland we took on a Spanish form of the name.'

'Bless my soul,' Arthur muttered before he recovered his equanimity. 'I apologise, sir. I had not expected to find an Irishman serving as a general in the army of Spain.'

'I hardly consider myself to be Irish, Sir Arthur. I was born in Seville and have never set foot in Ireland. So you may rest assured that I harbour no ill will towards you on account of the shameful manner in which the British have treated my ancestors.'

'What?' Arthur glared at him. 'Oh, I see. That's just as well then, since we are allies.'

'As the fortunes of war would have it, sir.' O'Donoju flashed his teeth again. 'For the present.'

'Er, yes.' Arthur cleared his throat. 'Now then, General. I take it you have a message for me from Cuesta.'

'From his excellency, General Gregorio García de la Cuesta, yes,' O'Donoju corrected Arthur with heavy emphasis. He paused briefly before he continued. 'He told me to convey to you his great joy that his brave soldiers will be fighting at the side of our British allies. He is certain that together we will soon put an end to the French cowards skulking in Madrid. Before the summer is out we will have won a glorious victory that will be an everlasting tribute to the alliance between Spain and Britain.' The Spanish officer paused briefly before he concluded, 'His excellency is most gratified to hear that Spain's new ally has sent you and your men to reinforce our army in this endeavour.'

Arthur exchanged a quick look with Somerset before he responded, 'I fear that his excellency is misinformed concerning my purpose here. I am under orders to co-operate with Spanish forces, not to reinforce them as such.'

O'Donoju shrugged his shoulders. 'It is merely a form of words, sir. His excellency is the senior officer and has sent me to offer greetings to his new subordinate.'

Arthur saw Somerset stiffen out of the corner of his eye, but nevertheless managed to keep his expression neutral as he responded in a reasonable tone. 'And I, of course, send greetings to him and look forward to working with him to defeat our common enemy. Before we can achieve that it is necessary that I confer with his excellency to determine our common strategy. May I enquire as to his present location?'

O'Donoju nodded. 'His excellency has informed me that he will meet you at the fort of Miravete, near Almaraz, on the tenth of July. Do you know the fort, sir?'

Arthur thought a moment. 'I can't recall seeing it on our maps.'

'It is some sixty miles from here,' O'Donoju explained. 'I will send you a guide when I report back to his excellency.'

'The tenth of July?' Somerset intervened. 'That's three days from now. The army can't possibly march so far in that time.'

O'Donoju shrugged. 'That is his excellency's order.'

Arthur cleared his throat with a quick warning glance at Somerset to hold his tongue. 'Tell General Cuesta that I will be there. I shall take a small escort and ride ahead of my army. Your guide can meet me on the road and take me to this fort of yours. In the meantime, I would be grateful if you would inform the general—'

'His excellency,' O'Donoju intervened. 'That is his correct title, sir.'

'Of course. Please inform his excellency that my men will require supplies of food and ammunition, which the junta in Cadiz has promised us. I take it that his excellency has made the necessary arrangements in that regard?'

'Naturally. A Spanish gentleman's word is his bond, sir.'

'I am delighted to hear it. Now then.' Arthur adopted a friendly tone. 'I take it that you will be remaining with us tonight. Somerset can escort you to the officers' mess and find you a bed for the night.'

'Alas, I will not be able to enjoy your hospitality, sir. I must return at once.'

'In the dark?'

'I know the road well, sir. If there are any enemy patrols, I can avoid them easily enough.'

'As you wish. I will see you again on the tenth.'

They exchanged a bow and then O'Donoju left the tent, to be shown back to his horse by Somerset. Arthur eased himself forward in his seat and folded his hands together as a rest for his chin as he stared at the canvas wall of the tent opposite his campaign desk. He was under orders to co-operate with the Spanish yet he could not help a degree of anxiety at the prospect of relying on their promise to supply his army. When Somerset returned to the tent, Arthur sat up and sighed wearily.

'What do you make of our Spanish friend?'

Somerset hurriedly composed a tactful response. 'He seemed keen enough to take the fight to the enemy, sir.'

'That may be so.' Arthur rubbed his forehead. 'The fact is that our Spanish allies have won all too few victories over the French. Cuesta himself was badly beaten at Medellin back in April. Still, if we combine our strengths we should be able to give a decent account of ourselves when we meet the enemy. The latest intelligence reports say that Marshal Victor's corps is defending the approaches to Madrid. I am told he has little more than twenty thousand men. If that's true, then if we combine with Cuesta we should outnumber Victor two to one. That should be enough to guarantee us a victory.'

Somerset tilted his head to one side. 'I hope so, sir. Provided General Cuesta knows his business.'

Arthur shrugged. 'Well, I shall only be in a position to judge that once I have had the chance to meet the man.' He paused. 'Pardon me. I meant to say his excellency.'

Somerset chuckled for a moment before he asked, 'Do you intend to accept Cuesta's claim to overall command of our combined forces?'

Arthur's eyes widened. 'By God, man, are you quite mad? Of course not. We have a common enemy, that is all. I command this army, not Cuesta. That we are here in the Peninsula is down to the pursuit of the British interest in this war. At present it suits us to assist the Spanish, but we have written them no blank cheque. On that account you can rest assured.'

'Yes, sir.' Somerset looked relieved.

'Now then, the interruption is over.' Arthur gestured to the paperwork on the table. 'Come, let us finish this and get some rest. I suspect we will need it sorely in the days to come.'

Arthur sat in his saddle in silence. Behind him the thirty dragoons of his escort were halted, under strict orders not to make a sound as they waited in the darkness for the Spanish guide to return. He had reached the army in the morning, presenting his credentials from General O'Donoju, and been escorted into Arthur's presence. The guide was a young peasant, dressed in a crude jerkin and filthy shirt and trousers. He wore a straw sun hat and rode on a mule which was accompanied by a swirling cloud of insects. The boy spoke only a few words of English and Arthur had been obliged to summon one of his Castilian-speaking staff officers to interpret. Despite promising that he could take Arthur to the fort, the youth had lost his way at dusk and the small party had been led up one path after another into the hills, before backtracking and trying yet another. The map that Arthur had brought with him was useless, with little reliable detail beyond the course of the river and the towns and villages lining the route to Madrid.

There was a sudden scrape of gravel on the track ahead and Arthur felt his muscles tense. His mount sensed the change and raised its head, ears twitching. The sound came again, stopped, and then a low voice sounded from the shadows.

'English . . . English, where you?'

Arthur felt the tension drain from his muscles as swiftly as it had come. 'Here!'

The guide clicked his tongue and flicked a cane on his mule's rump as he came forward and then reined in a short distance from Arthur.

'I find the fort! You come. This way.'

'Are you certain?'

'Come, come.'

Arthur held up his hand to stop the guide and turned back to the column. 'Lieutenant, I'd be obliged if you translated.'

When the dragoon officer had joined him Arthur nodded towards the guide. 'Ask him if he is certain he has found the right path this time.'

There was a brief exchange before the lieutenant turned back to Arthur. 'He says it is. He also says that General Cuesta is not pleased that you failed to arrive at the appointed time.'

'Really? Perhaps if he had provided us with a proper guide instead of this halfwit then I would have been there long ago . . . No, don't translate that, you fool. Just tell him to lead us to the fort without any further delay.'

The youth beckoned to Arthur and turned his mule back up the track and Arthur hurriedly spurred his horse into a walk before he could lose sight of the guide. The track wound its way between two hills and then began to climb a steep incline. At length Arthur could see a glow at the top of the slope above them and then, as the track evened out, he saw the walls of an old fort ahead of them, brilliantly illuminated by the torches that flickered along the battlements. As the guide led them towards the gate Arthur could see that a company of soldiers had formed up on either side of the track, muskets resting on shoulders as they waited. A figure on horseback sat before the gate, watching and waiting. He shouted an order over his shoulder and there was further commotion within the fort as men hurried to take up their places. Arthur recognised the officer as General O'Donoju and offered a salute as he rode up.

O'Donoju's sword rasped from his scabbard and the men of what Arthur realised was an honour guard shuffled one foot out and presented their muskets to greet the English general.

Arthur bowed his head to either side and then smiled at O'Donoju. 'My thanks for such a fine greeting.'

The Spaniard shrugged. 'His excellency gave the order to welcome you formally, some five hours ago.'

Arthur took a sharp breath. 'And I would have been here five hours ago if I had been provided with a guide who knew the route.' Arthur gestured to the boy, who smiled uncertainly as the two officers conversed in English.

O'Donoju glanced at the boy. 'He claimed to know the area well enough. He lied and I'll have him flogged.'

'There's no need for that. The fault is with the man who hired him.'

The Spaniard stiffened indignantly before he replied. 'I will punish all those I hold responsible, señor. Now, if you would follow me I will take you into the presence of his excellency.'

Without waiting for a reply he wheeled his thin mount round and trotted through the gate into the fort, while Arthur led his escort between the ranks of the Spanish soldiers. He examined them closely by the flickering light cast by the torches on the wall. They seemed to know their drill well enough, but they looked lean and hungry and their uniforms were worn and dirty and the barrels and bayonets of many of the muskets were spotted with rust.

The horses' hooves echoed off the walls of the arched gateway and then Arthur emerged into the courtyard of the fort. Three sides of the paved area were lined with ranks of soldiers, save for a gap directly opposite the gate where steps climbed up to the inner keep. In front of the steps stood a crowd of gaudily uniformed officers, and before them a large, very overweight officer sat on a horse. His uniform coat seemed to be so smothered with bejewelled decorations, ribbons and gold lace that Arthur wondered how his horse could endure such a burden. Two men stood either side of the horse, firmly grasping the rider's boots, and Arthur realised that they were there to hold him in place and stop him toppling out of his saddle.

An order was shouted and the soldiers stamped to attention and presented their muskets. A quick glance showed that these men were in the same sorry condition as those outside the gate. Arthur gestured to the lieutenant to halt the escort and then continued across the courtyard alone, stopping his horse a short distance in front of the other man. O'Donoju had wheeled his horse round and stood by his commander's side, ready to interpret.

Arthur cleared his throat. 'I am Sir Arthur Wellesley, commander of his majesty's army in the Peninsula. I take it that I am addressing his excellency General Cuesta?'

The man nodded his heavy jowls and spoke curtly.

'His excellency wants to know why you are late, Sir Arthur,' said O'Donoju.

'You know why, but just tell his excellency that we lost our way in the dark.'

Cuesta's lips lifted in a slight sneer as he spoke to his interpreter.

'His excellency trusts that you will not make a habit of leading your men in the wrong direction.'

'Assure him that it will not happen again, and that I hope that we might both lead our men in the direction of victory from now on.'

The answer seemed to gratify the old officer, who Arthur guessed must be in his sixties at least. He muttered to O'Donoju and then growled an order at the two men propping him up. At once they began to help him down from his saddle with much grunting of effort as O'Donoju bowed to Arthur.

'His excellency will wait for you in his office, while you are introduced to his staff.'

Arthur glanced at the crowd of officers. 'What? All of them?'

O'Donoju smiled and waved Arthur towards the first of the waiting men. As General Cuesta was manhandled up the steps and into the keep Arthur began exchanging bows with a series of colonels and generals, each of whom was laden down with long lists of titles and honours. Arthur endured it for a while before he leaned towards O'Donoju and spoke quietly. 'Look, since the hour is late and there is much to discuss, might we dispense with the full title of each man and just use their name and rank?'

The Spaniard's eyebrows knitted for a moment before he replied. 'As you wish, sir. We will abandon the usual courtesies in the interests of brevity.'

Arthur smiled. 'That would be appreciated.'

As soon as the last officer had been introduced, Arthur followed his host up the steps and into the keep. When they were shown into General Cuesta's office Arthur saw that the Spanish commander was sitting propped up on a couch. Before him, spread out across the floor and weighted down with bottles of wine, was a map of Spain. One of Cuesta's orderlies brought a chair for Arthur and placed it on the opposite side of the map. O'Donoju took up his position beside the couch and translated Cuesta's first comment.

'His excellency hopes that you were impressed by the men parading in the courtyard. They are the finest battalion in our army.'

'Really? Good God . . .' Arthur quickly forced a smile. 'Why yes, as fine a body of men as I have seen in a long time.'

The comment seemed to be appreciated and Cuesta continued.

'His excellency wishes you to join forces with him and march directly on Madrid.'

'Ah, yes, a most laudable ambition, but surely we must prepare the ground for such an advance? I suggest that before we can even entertain such a notion, it is vital to clear the approaches to Madrid of all enemy forces, in case we are obliged to retreat.'

Cuesta shook his head.

'His excellency does not agree. He says that we must be bold and strike at the heart of the enemy. He says that a fierce patriotic fire burns in the hearts of our men and it can only be quenched by the blood of Frenchmen.'

'I see. Tell him that I am full of admiration for the patriotic zeal he demonstrates, but such zeal must be tempered by the realities of the situation. My sources tell me that Marshal Victor and his army protect the route to Madrid. It would be wise for us to fall on him while he is outnumbered by our combined strength, would it not?'

Cuesta considered this for a moment and nodded.

'In which case then, I suggest we join our forces at . . .' Arthur leaned over the map and saw that it was depressingly lacking in detail. The Tagus was marked, together with the road that ran beside it, and a few topographical features. 'There. At Oropesa, ten days from now. Can his excellency move his army there by the appointed date?'

'Of course. The Spanish army marches as swiftly as any.'

'Delighted to hear it.' Arthur eased himself back in his chair. 'Now then, I have been told by the junta at Cadiz that his excellency has been instructed to arrange for my army to be provisioned.'

Cuesta frowned as Arthur's words were translated.

'His excellency is not obliged to act on the instructions of the junta.' said O'Donoju. 'Nevertheless he will provide your soldiers with whatever is necessary.'

'I am grateful to him. Could you let me know where and when we will receive the supplies?'

Cuesta raised his hands and shrugged as he responded to O'Donoju.

'His excellency says that his staff officers will deal with the matter. As soon as the supplies are ready a message will be sent to you.'

Arthur puffed his cheeks. 'It would greatly aid the close co-operation of our armies if I could be given the precise date and time now.'

'That is not possible. But his excellency says that you need not fear going hungry. He gives his word that your needs will be satisfied.'

Arthur looked levelly at Cuesta for a moment. There was little enough gold in the British army's war chest. In a matter of days he would be obliged to order a cut in rations. A week on from that there would be nothing to eat. He was depending on Cuesta. If the man had given his word, then that would have to be good enough. After all, what could the Spanish gain from starving their ally?

'Very well. I will advance to Oropesa and meet his excellency there. Meanwhile I will await instructions concerning the supplies you have promised. If that is agreed, then I am afraid I must now depart to re-join my army. We will need to waste no time getting on the road to Oropesa, and victory thereafter.'

Cuesta nodded, then clicked his fingers.

'His excellency will provide a guide to lead you and your escort back to the main road.'

Arthur raised a hand. 'I offer him my thanks, but I am sure we can find our own way.'

'As you wish.'

Arthur rose from his chair and bowed to Cuesta, who responded with a brief bob of his head, and then turned to leave the room and make his way back outside to the waiting escort. As he strode down the steps Arthur glanced at the Spanish officers and the soldiers lining the courtyard. His heart filled with foreboding at the prospect of co-operating with his allies in the coming campaign to find and crush Marshal Victor.

Chapter 5

Oropesa, 21 July 1809

'Not a damn thing!' Arthur snapped at Somerset as he threw down his riding crop and sat down heavily in his chair. 'There is not one wagon of supplies, not even one cart. And no remounts for the cavalry, nor spare mules for our own vehicles.'

He shut his eyes and breathed in deeply to calm his irritation. The two armies had met on the appointed date and Arthur had at once ridden across to the Spanish headquarters to arrange for the distribution of supplies to his men. The army had been on half-rations for two days already and he was determined that they would march to battle with Marshal Victor on full stomachs. General Cuesta and his staff were at lunch when Arthur arrived. Several long tables had been arranged in the shade beneath the boughs of some Mediterranean oak trees. The table was piled with racks of roast mutton, freshly baked bread and bottles of wine. Arthur was ushered to the side of Cuesta, who sat on a large, cushioned seat, jaws working furiously as he hurried to finish his mouthful of meat. General O'Donoju had caught sight of the new arrival and rose from his bench, dabbing at his mouth as he came to interpret for the two commanders.

Arthur was covered with a fine layer of dust from the road and Cuesta gestured to the nearest bottle as he spoke.

'His excellency says that you must be thirsty after the day's march. He bids you refresh yourself.'

'Please tell General Cuesta that I thank him for his offer and will have a drink, once he confirms that the supplies he has promised me are ready for my men to collect.'

O'Donoju did not translate the remark and simply shrugged his shoulders. 'There are no supplies, sir.'

'No supplies,' Arthur repeated leadenly. 'How can this be? General Cuesta gave me his word that the supplies would be here. Where are they?'

O'Donoju turned to his commander. Cuesta waved his hands

dismissively, then stabbed another chunk of mutton with his fork and raised it to his mouth.

'His excellency says that he gave orders to the local mayors for the supplies to be gathered, and that the local people have failed him. He regrets this and suggests that if you supply him with sufficient gold he will see that his best staff officers are sent out to buy what is needed.'

Arthur glanced round the tables. The men he could see, despite their finery, seemed to be the very last men he would entrust with what remained in the British army's war chest. He turned back to O'Donoju and shook his head.

'No. I will not pay for what I was promised by my ally. If General Cuesta would have the British as his allies then he is obliged to live up to the obligations of an ally.' Arthur gestured to the sweep of the Tagus valley as he continued. 'This is rich farmland. For the last few days we have marched through fields of crops, and orchards filled with fruit. There is more than enough to feed my army here.'

Cuesta chewed slowly on his fresh mouthful of meat and then made his reply.

'His excellency says that if that is the case, why did your men not help themselves to supplies as they passed through?'

'Because we are not the French,' Arthur replied as evenly as he could. 'If I permitted my men to forage freely across your lands it would very soon place a terrible strain on the alliance between our two nations.'

O'Donoju listened to his master's reply and turned to Arthur. 'His excellency says that if you will not take the trouble to feed yourselves then he does not see why he should do it for you.'

'I will not have my army be seen as some horde of looters. It would be better if General Cuesta demanded that the local landowners hand over what I require. At least that would have the virtue of not turning the local people against us.'

'Sir,' O'Donoju gestured to the officers around the table. 'Most of these men are local landowners, or at least they are related to them. They would not countenance offending against their family's interests.'

Arthur felt his temper rising dangerously and closed his eyes for a moment to force himself to remain calm. He spoke in a low, hard tone when he continued. 'Tell him that I am astonished that men could act so selfishly when their nation is threatened by tyranny. Is there no sense of honour amongst the nobles of Spain?'

O'Donoju was about to translate when Arthur took his arm. 'No. Don't bother. It would serve no purpose to impugn the integrity of the general and his staff. I just need to know what is the latest news of Marshal Victor.'

'Victor is not thirty miles from here,' O'Donoju replied. 'A short distance to the east of the town of Talavera. He has taken up a defensive position behind one of the tributaries of the Tagus.'

Arthur felt his heart quicken. 'Two days' march. Has he been reinforced yet?'

'No. The garrison of Madrid is still in the capital, or was when we last heard.'

'Then Victor has some twenty thousand men in the field. I have almost the same. What is your present strength?'

'Twenty-eight thousand infantry, and six thousand cavalry.'

'Then we have him, by God!' Arthur smiled. 'It is likely that the French do not know that my army is here. If we can strike at Victor before he can retreat, or is reinforced, we can beat him. Tell your general that there is no time to waste. We must march east as soon as possible. We can both attack him on the morning of the twenty-third.'

Cuesta heard the translation and thought for a moment before he nodded and made his reply to O'Donoju.

'It is agreed. We will attack Marshal Victor in two days' time. His excellency says that you may help yourself to the French supplies after the battle is won.'

Back at his headquarters, in a small barn outside Oropesa, Arthur opened his eyes and glanced towards Somerset. He explained the intention to attack Marshal Victor and called for any maps featuring Talavera and the ground to the east of the town. With the map spread out across his campaign table Arthur stabbed his finger at the line marking the course of the river Alberche.

'There. That's where he is. That's where he will be caught by us and our Spanish friends. I want the word passed down to all brigade commanders. We will be engaging the enemy in two days from now. We will outnumber Victor by nearly three to one. Have the men told that they will no longer have to tighten their belts once we have captured the enemy's supplies. I'm sure that will please them.'

'Yes, sir.' Somerset nodded. 'Provided that Marshal Victor holds his ground and does not decide to retreat.'

'Why should he?' Arthur smiled. 'At the moment he assumes that he is faced by General Cuesta. I'm sure that Victor considers his twenty thousand more than a match for Cuesta's thirty. He will welcome a battle. With luck he has no idea that we have added our strength to

Cuesta's. I think Marshal Victor may be in for the surprise of his life.'

'I hope you are right, sir,' Somerset replied. 'For I fear that if we do not take Victor's supplies then our men may well starve before they ever see Madrid.'

A thin sliver of moon hung in the star-speckled night sky and by its wan light Arthur surveyed the lines of his men, visible as the more uniform features in a landscape composed of little more than dark shades. The only spark of colour came from the sprinkling of camp fires on the far side of the Alberche river that marked the French picket line. Arthur felt a warm satisfaction in his heart that they had succeeded in closing on Marshal Victor without his being aware of the danger. Perhaps he had misjudged his Spanish allies, Arthur reflected. Following the meeting at Oropesa the two armies had advanced in parallel and made good time in their approach to the enemy position. As night had fallen, Arthur had led the British forward the last few miles to take up position opposite the enemy's right flank. At the same time, General Cuesta would advance towards the opposite flank and make his headquarters at a small inn at Salcidas. Both armies should be in position by two in the morning and Arthur had conceded the honour of opening the attack to Cuesta. Three guns would be the signal for the attack to begin.

There was the clop of hooves as Somerset came up to report. 'All our men are in position, sir. The guns are deployed to cover the fords and General Hill sends his compliments and says the Second Division are champing at the bit.'

Arthur smiled. 'Very good.' He took out his watch, raised it close to his face and squinted to make out the hands. 'Just after midnight. Send a message to Cuesta and tell him we are ready and waiting for his signal. Make sure that he confirms his army is in position. I don't want our men to be facing Marshal Victor's army on our own.'

'Yes, sir.'

'Oh, and tell him that all Spain will rejoice in today's victory and that the name of Cuesta will be remembered for ever in the hearts of his people.'

Somerset was silent for a moment. 'Isn't that a bit vainglorious, sir?'

'Of course, but if it helps to spur the old man into action then it's worth it.'

'Yes, sir. I'll send the message at once.'

'Thank you, Somerset.'

When his aide had left him Arthur again surveyed the lines of his men, and once more he recalled the ground he had seen late in the afternoon, when he had ridden forward in a plain brown coat and broad-brimmed hat to inspect the lie of the land. Leaving his small escort out of sight in a small grove of olive trees he had approached the bank of the river and casually trotted along its length to the junction with the Tagus. The French sentries on the far side had watched him, but paid no great attention to the lone horseman. Once he had identified the location of some of the fords, as well as the best routes to approach them without being detected, Arthur returned to the army and drew up his plan of attack.

Now, in the cool night air, all was calm and still. It was hard to believe that nearly twenty thousand men were poised to fight. At the moment they would be sitting in their companies, with their unloaded muskets at their sides. There was no talking as the order had been given for them to wait in complete silence so as not to alert the enemy as to their presence. The corporals and sergeants paced quietly up and down the lines ready to pounce on any man who uttered a word. Elsewhere the cavalry would be standing by their mounts, and aside from the odd scuffle of hooves and faint whinny, they too waited in quiet anticipation. The gunners, still hot and sweaty from their effort to wheel the guns into place as noiselessly as they could manage, stacked their ammunition a short distance from their cannon and carefully loaded the first round. Most men found the waiting intolerable, as every faint sound and movement of a shadow seemed threatening, and wore away at their nerves. Only a handful of fatalistic veterans, and a small number of men who had managed to suppress their nerves through surreptitious consumption of spirits, waited calmly.

Half an hour had passed when Arthur next checked his watch. With a click of his tongue he turned his horse to his right flank and made his way down the line, pausing every so often to exchange a quiet greeting with one of his officers and offer them a few words of encouragement. There was still no sign of the orderly who had been sent to find General Cuesta by the time Arthur reached the end of his battle line. He stopped his horse and strained his eyes to try to detect any sign of movement from the direction of Salcidas, but there was not enough light to make out anything more than the vaguest detail.

'Damn, where is he?' Arthur muttered. 'Has the fool lost his way, I wonder?'

'I doubt that, sir,' Somerset replied. 'I chose a good man to deliver the message. Cornet Davidson was confident he knew the ground well enough.' He paused a moment. 'It's possible that General Cuesta may not have reached his position.'

Arthur turned to his aide. 'By God, I hope you're wrong. General Cuesta would have to be a consummate fool to let such an opportunity come to naught.'

He was about to continue when both men heard a distant clop of hooves and they turned to stare into the night. A figure on horseback emerged from the shadows.

'Ours?' Somerset whispered.

'Only one way to tell,' Arthur replied. He cleared his throat and called out, 'Halt. Who goes there?'

The other rider reined in and hurriedly responded. 'Cornet Davidson, of the Light Dragoons.'

'Davidson, come here, man!' Arthur called back.

The cornet spurred his horse forward and a moment later he reined in before his commander and saluted.

'Did you find Cuesta?'

'No, sir. I looked for him at Salcidas, but there was no one there, not even one of his advance patrols. So I tracked across the route he should be taking for a mile, perhaps two, and still saw no sign of him, sir. That's when I decided I had better report back to you.'

Arthur's jaw tightened with frustration. Where the hell was the Spanish army? By this time they should have completed deploying for their attack. He lowered his head for a moment and thought. Even if Cuesta was still moving up towards Salcidas he could not possibly be ready for at least another three hours. That would mean delaying the attack until four in the morning. It would still be dark then, and there was still a chance of surprising Marshal Victor's men in their camp. Arthur looked up.

'Davidson, I want you to go back and try to find Cuesta. Tell him that I have decided to delay the attack until four. He is still to give the signal we agreed on. Make sure that he understands the urgency with which he must act if we are to succeed.'

'Yes, sir.' Davidson nodded.

'Off you go then.'

Davidson turned his mount and spurred it into a trot as he headed off in search of the Spanish army.

Somerset let out a weary sigh. 'Our Spanish friends are proving to be somewhat unreliable, sir.'

'Indeed.' Arthur was furious, and it took some effort to keep his tone neutral as he continued. 'There are times when one might think that they actually pose more of a danger to us than the French do. Anyway, we are where we are, Somerset. We must return to the army and pass the word for the men to stand down for a few hours. I need them alert and fresh for when the fighting starts.'

They made their way back to the flank of the British army, and were challenged by the pickets before passing on and returning to the command post behind the centre of the British line. As they arrived an officer hurried up to Arthur and saluted.

'Sir, we have visitors. General O'Donoju and some of his staff are waiting for you, down by the headquarters tent.'

Arthur turned to look down the hillock into the small depression where a handful of lamps glimmered, hidden from French view. 'Did he explain why he is here?'

'No, sir. I asked, but he said his message was for you, and not your underlings.'

'He said that?' Arthur shook his head. 'Come, Somerset.'

They continued down the slope to the tent and dismounted alongside the Spanish horses being held by some of Arthur's orderlies. O'Donoju was waiting inside, with four of his officers. He rose to his feet when he saw Arthur and bowed his head.

'It is a pleasure to see you again, General Wellesley.'

'Where is Cuesta?' Arthur cut in. 'He should have been at Salcidas hours ago.'

O'Donoju frowned at the informal use of his superior's name. 'His excellency has sent me to inform you that he has been delayed.'

'Delayed? Why?'

The Spaniard shrugged. 'The men were slow to break camp. The night is dark, and they do not march as fast as they do during the day.'

'Then why did your general not take account of that, and start out earlier?'

'I do not presume to know the mind of my commander, sir.'

Arthur puffed his cheeks irritably. 'Where is he now?'

'Perhaps three miles east of Salcidas. His excellency says that he will be in position to attack at six in the morning.'

'Dawn will have broken by then. The French will be aware of our presence. We will have lost any element of surprise.'

'Perhaps, sir,' O'Donoju countered. 'Even so, we can still proceed with the attack. After all, the odds are vastly in our favour.'

Arthur thought a moment. The Spaniard was right. Provided Victor did not react swiftly and break camp before the attack began, he would be obliged to stand and fight.

'Very well then. General Cuesta must begin his attack at six. No later. Is that clear?'

O'Donoju stared back defiantly. 'If that is the wish of his excellency, then yes. Now, I bid you farewell, sir. My officers and I must return to our army.'

'Yes, you must, as swiftly as you can. There must be no further delay.'

The rest of the night passed slowly, and as the sun fringed the eastern horizon in a pale orange glow Arthur gave the order for his army to stand to. All along the line, the men wearily rose to their feet, stretching their muscles before forming ranks. As the light strengthened the French sentries on the other side saw the massed ranks of the British army and at once a warning shot was fired to alert the main camp.

'There goes our surprise,' Somerset said bitterly.

'That can't be helped,' Arthur responded. 'We just have to hope that Cuesta begins the attack before Victor can break camp.'

'Sir, what is to stop us beginning the attack ourselves?'

Arthur turned to his aide. 'My dear Somerset, if we attack across a river against defensive positions without support then we will suffer grievously. So much so that I doubt we could continue offensive operations in Spain. I would be obliged to fall back, and if we were pursued then I dare say we would be forced to repeat General Moore's retreat to Corunna. England can endure only so many such defeats before being forced to kneel to Bonaparte.' He paused to let his words sink in. 'We must wait for Cuesta.'

Now even the minutes seemed to drag by, and as the first brilliant rays of the sun broke across the eastern horizon the first French battalions hurriedly marched forward to cover the fords, together with several guns. The opportunity to attack was fast slipping away and Arthur forced himself to remain still in his saddle, ears straining for the first sound of cannon fire that would announce Cuesta's attack. Out of the corner of his eye he saw Somerset discreetly draw out his pocket watch, glance at it with a raised eyebrow, and then slip it back into his waistcoat.

'You might as well tell me the time,' Arthur muttered.

'Ten minutes gone six, sir.'

Both men were still for a moment, then Arthur took up his reins and slowly turned his horse. 'The army is not to move until I return. If the enemy opens fire, then have our fellows fall back to cover and leave our guns to their work. Is that clear?'

'Yes, sir. Might I ask where you are going?'

'To find Cuesta. It is time to speak plainly to his excellency.'

★ ★ ★

45

General Cuesta was taking his breakfast in a large open carriage when Arthur rode up to him near Salcidas. The leading units of the Spanish army had downed their packs and some were already busy foraging across the surrounding countryside for the day's meal. The following columns were still strung out along the road, cloaked in the dust kicked up ahead of them. Arthur regarded the scene in a cold rage for a moment before he approached Cuesta. The Spanish commander regarded him warily. He bowed his head briefly in greeting and called for O'Donoju to attend him.

Arthur touched his hand to the brim of his hat. 'Good day, sir. Or at least it would have been, had the battle begun. It was my understanding that we should attack at two in the morning. Where were you, sir?'

Cuesta shrugged and then made a curt comment to his translator.

'His excellency says that you asked the impossible of our soldiers. The distance was too great to march in the darkness. Your plan was flawed.'

'Nevertheless, my army has been in position since midnight. After having marched through the night to take up its appointed position. If my men could do it, then why not yours? It was not the fault of the plan.'

General Cuesta lurched forward as Arthur's comments were passed on to him. He stabbed a fleshy finger towards Arthur and launched into a bitter tirade which O'Donoju struggled to keep up with.

'His excellency says that he tires of the demands you make of him and his army . . . Who do you think you are to order him to provide you with food? To tell him where and when to wage his battles? The English are every bit as arrogant as he had heard. He will not endure this any longer.'

'Enough!' Arthur raised a hand. He drew himself up to his full height on his saddle and tilted his head slightly to look down his nose at Cuesta before he continued. 'I'd be obliged if you tell General Cuesta that I have never heard of a situation where an ally has been so ill-treated. You gave me your word that my army would receive supplies and yet my men are forced to march on half-rations thanks to your broken promises. And now you have failed to grasp the chance to strike a humiliating blow at the enemy. Hear me clearly, O'Donoju. As soon as Marshal Victor realises that he is outnumbered he will fall back. I tell you now that I will not lead my men one step further towards Madrid until you hold good to your word, and give me the supplies I was promised. Moreover, I am not prepared to extend any further military co-operation until General Cuesta concedes overall command to me.'

Cuesta's mouth sagged open as O'Donoju translated. Then his thick eyebrows knitted together and his expression tightened into a scowl. When the last of Arthur's remarks had been heard he made his reply in an umistakably furious tone.

'His excellency says that you and your soldiers can stay here and rot for all he cares. Why should he feed you? You are parasites. The Army of Extremadura does not need you. We can defeat the French on our own. While you sit here, his excellency will pursue Marshal Victor alone. The glory will be his and you will be left to wallow in your mire of shame.'

Once the Spaniard had finished Arthur nodded. 'It seems I am done here. I will return to my army and await your general's apology at my headquarters.'

Arthur clicked his tongue, and turned his horse round before spurring it into a trot, anxious to quit the presence of General Cuesta. It would be rash in the extreme for Cuesta to act without support. Only a fool would contemplate such a course of action, Arthur mused bitterly. He had said his piece. Hopefully there were enough wise heads amongst the general's staff officers to persuade him against the folly of advancing alone. If not, then disaster threatened and Arthur feared that he would not be able to do anything to prevent it.

Chapter 6

Talavera, 27 July 1809

Arthur watched as the long column of Spanish troops trudged into the town. Many were wounded and blood seeped through their hastily applied dressings and bandages. Hundreds of them carried no weapons, having thrown them aside as they fled back down the road from the direction of Madrid. There was little sense of order as men from different battalions blended into one long stream of rabble fleeing from the pursuing French army. A handful of guns had been saved and moved steadily along the column as a squadron of blue-jacketed hussars cleared the way ahead of them. Only a handful of senior officers were in evidence, marching with their men. The rest had accompanied General Cuesta as his mule-drawn carriage had led the retreat back to the banks of the Alberche where he had decided to rally his men and make a stand.

'Not a pretty sight, is it?'

Somerset shook his head. 'A beaten army never is, sir. All the more unfortunate that this was avoidable in the first place.'

'That it was,' Arthur replied with feeling.

Having failed to make a co-ordinated attack on Marshal Victor six days earlier, General Cuesta had waited three days before continuing the advance alone to try to run down the French. The result was predict-able, Arthur mused. The garrison of Madrid had advanced to join forces with Victor and the French had turned on Cuesta and broken his army, sending it reeling back in confusion. The crisis had almost turned into a complete disaster when the Spanish commander had ordered his men to turn and fight with a river at their back. On hearing this Arthur had galloped forward from the British camp outside Talavera to persuade Cuesta to fall back to a less dangerous position. The old general, still bitter over their previous confrontation, had at first refused to listen. Fearing that Cuesta's obstinacy would allow the French to destroy each army in turn, Arthur had swallowed his pride and begged Cuesta to reconsider.

Cuesta had sneered as he had made his reply via O'Donoju.

'On your knees, Sir Arthur.'

Arthur could not hide his astonishment. 'What?'

'His excellency wants you to beg on your knees. You have humiliated him enough by refusing to accept his command. Now he wants to see you humiliated.'

At first Arthur was too surprised to react. Surely the man must be mad. With his army facing certain defeat if it stayed where it was, and a powerful French army only hours away, Cuesta was wasting time settling such a petty score. For the first time Arthur fully appreciated the depths of the man's vanity, selfishness and arrogance. If Arthur refused to do as the Spaniard demanded then thousands of his men would die unnecessarily, and the British army would be left hopelessly exposed in the heart of Spain with almost no supplies left to sustain the men as they were pursued back into Portugal. He swallowed his distaste for the Spanish general. What did it matter if he suffered a moment of humiliation if it saved the men of two armies?

He swallowed bitterly and eased himself down on one knee as he stared straight into Cuesta's mocking eyes and spoke steadily. 'Tell his excellency that I beg him to fall back to defend Talavera with my army.'

The memory of that moment burned in Arthur's soul. It was only partly shame; the rest was anger and disgust at his ally. But at least his humiliation had bought time for the men of the Spanish and British armies as they prepared to turn and make a stand against the French.

Arthur had chosen the ground carefully. Between the Tagus and the steep hills of the Sierra de Segurilla stretched an undulating plain. Closer to the hills there were two large ridges that created a narrow valley on the far side before rising up again into hills. A small stream, called the Portina, running from the hills cut across the plain to the Tagus and formed a natural line for the combined army. With the flanks secured by the Tagus and the hills all that the allies had to do was hold their line.

Mindful of the rough handling the Spanish had recently endured Arthur had left the right of the line to Cuesta. Here the Spanish would be protected by a line of ditches and walls stretching out from the town. More fortifications in the form of barricades of felled trees had been constructed by British troops. The defences were formidable enough to deter the enemy and therefore could be safely entrusted to Cuesta's badly shaken troops. That left the more exposed part of the line to the British.

Once he was certain that the Spanish were indeed taking up the positions allotted to them, Arthur gestured to Somerset to follow him. They trotted across the plain towards the small force sent forward towards the Alberche river to cover the retreat of the Spanish. The twin towers of an old fortified manor house rose above the olive groves and small oak trees that grew along the near bank of the Alberche and Arthur followed the road that ran through the trees towards the building. He passed through one of the brigades spread out through the trees and nodded a quick greeting to their commander, General Mackenzie, as he saw him in a clearing. When they reached the manor house Arthur saw a number of his men resting around the walls, with their muskets stacked as they talked quietly. More men were visible, spread out through the trees. Those closest to the entrance to the manor hurriedly rose and stood to attention when they spied their general and his aide approaching. Arthur dismounted and went inside.

The manor was built round a courtyard, and seated on the edge of a small pool into which a fountain trickled was the officer charged with guarding the route through the surrounding olive groves.

'Good morning, Donkin,' Arthur nodded as he strode up. 'How is it with you?'

Major Donkin stood smartly and brushed away the crumbs of a pie he had been breakfasting on. 'All's well, sir. No sign of the French yet, but my lads will send 'em packing the moment they show up.'

'Glad to hear it.' Arthur pointed to the nearest tower. 'Come, let's see what's happening.'

Stuffing the last morsel of the pie into his mouth and chewing ferociously, Donkin followed Arthur to the narrow staircase that ascended inside the tower. At the top they climbed out through the narrow opening into a square room with open arches on each side that afforded good views across the olive groves. A mile to the west Arthur could see the narrow course of the Alberche river, and on the far bank some swirling black clouds of smoke where several buildings were on fire. The smoke made it hard to see the river at that point and Arthur glanced further to the south, towards where the road from Madrid crossed a bridge. Clouds of dust indicated where the main French columns were closing on the river and with an anxious twist in his stomach Arthur estimated that the enemy must have some fifty thousand men.

He pointed towards the burning buildings. 'What happened there?'

'Mackenzie's men set fire to them before they retreated back through my line.'

'Why?'

'To prevent the French from using them as strongpoints, sir.'

'And what is the point of that?' Arthur responded tersely. 'Our line is over two miles back from the Alberche. All that he has done is deprived the local people of their homes. For which they will not be inclined to thank us.'

'No, sir. I imagine not.'

Suddenly Arthur saw a movement through the distant smoke. A file of enemy soldiers was making its way down the bank and into the river, where they crossed and filtered into the trees. He turned to Donkin. 'Best have your command stand to. The French will be on your pickets soon.'

'Pickets?' Donkin frowned, and then looked alarmed.

'Good God, man, you must have posted them?'

'Well, no, sir. I mean not yet.'

Arthur glared coldly at the major and was about to berate him for his reckless inattention to his duties when there was a shout from below the tower and a moment later a musket cracked amid the trees. Some of Donkin's men sprang to their feet and peered into the nearest olive groves. As Arthur followed the direction of their gaze he saw blue-coated figures swiftly passing through the trees. He cupped a hand to his mouth and leaned over the parapet and bellowed down at Donkin's men.

'To arms! To arms! The enemy's here!'

More shots were fired, and Arthur saw jabs of flame and puffs of smoke on three sides of the manor house. One of the British soldiers below doubled over and collapsed on the ground with a deep groan. The quicker-witted of the redcoats were sprinting for their stacked muskets, but several were cut down before they could take up their weapons. There was a crack and plaster exploded off the tower wall just below the parapet.

'Damn!' Arthur stepped back. 'We're in a damned bad fix, Donkin.'

'Yes, sir.'

Without another word Arthur hurried back down the steps, the sound of boots ringing off the hard walls. At the bottom he ran through the courtyard and out of the main entrance. From the ground the position looked ever more desperate. French skirmishers were rushing out from the trees, shooting down Donkin's men who had no chance to form ranks, or look to their officers for orders. Most had gone to ground, and those without weapons crouched down low with fearful expressions as the enemy closed round them.

'Sir!' Somerset had grabbed the reins of Arthur's mount and was riding towards his commander, ducking low over his saddle.

Arthur glanced round. 'Donkin, get your men out of here at once. Get back to our line as best you can.'

'Yes, sir.' Donkin nodded, crouching and holding his hat down on his head as if that would prevent it from being shot off. There was no time for any more words, and Arthur sprinted towards Somerset. Seeing a prize target the nearest enemy skirmishers took aim and fired. A bullet whipped past Arthur's head, while another spat up a divot of earth a yard in front of him. As soon as he reached his horse, he placed a boot in the stirrup and heaved himself into the saddle with a grunt, taking the reins from his aide.

'Get you gone, sir!' Somerset called out, drawing one of the pistols from his saddle holsters. He glanced down to ensure the percussion cap was in place and thumbed back the hammer.

Arthur dug his spurs in and wheeled his horse round, urging it into a gallop down the road leading back through the trees. Glancing back he saw Somerset steady his horse, raise his pistol and take aim. There was a flash and the dull detonation and then Somerset thrust the weapon back in his holster and galloped after his general. Behind them, Major Donkin was bellowing orders for his men to fall back on him and make for the road.

Keeping his head down, Arthur rose up in his saddle as his horse thundered down the dry track. The sound of firing steadily faded behind them but Arthur continued riding as fast as his mount would carry him. Then, a half-mile from the manor house, he came across the first of Mackenzie's pickets at the side of the road and reined in.

'Stand to! The enemy's coming. Take care not to fire on Donkin's men!'

A sergeant nodded and saluted, and then turned to relay the order down the line in a parade ground bellow. Arthur waved Somerset on and the two of them continued at a less breathless pace down the road until they came to the clearing where Mackenzie still sat with a handful of his officers. Arthur reined in and thrust his arm back down the track.

'The French have surprised Donkin's men! Have your brigade formed up at once. We have to stop them here, or they'll press on right up to our main line. You must drive them off before re-joining the main army.'

'Yes, sir!' Mackenzie was on his feet at once, shouting out his orders. As they were repeated Arthur saw figures scrambling from under the low boughs of the olive trees and taking up their positions in each company. The sergeants paced down each line, dressing the ranks and shouting threats at those who were slow in joining their comrades in the line. Within five minutes the men of Mackenzie's brigade stood ready, watching the trees ahead for sign of the French.

Arthur trotted over to Mackenzie's side. 'Make sure your men don't fire until they are certain they see the enemy. Donkin, and what's left of his men, will appear first.'

'Yes, sir.' Mackenzie hurriedly briefed two officers and sent them down the line in each direction to pass on the instruction. There was not long to wait. The uneven crackle of muskets quickly drew closer and then the first British soldiers could be seen, some helping wounded comrades while others fired their muskets and fell back to take cover behind trees where they reloaded and fired again at their pursuers. The first of the French skirmishers were not far behind, flitting through the sunlit shafts of powder smoke that hung in the still air of the olive groves. As the last of Donkin's men passed though the gaps in the line, Mackenzie bellowed out the order.

'Present arms! Make ready to fire!'

There was a muted shuffling as his men raised their muskets and waited for the next command.

'Cock your weapons!'

A sharp clatter passed down the line as the men thumbed back the firing hammers of their primed muskets.

'Take aim!'

Up came the muzzles as the soldiers pointed them in the direction of the enemy soldiers who had halted and now flinched as they faced the first volley.

'Fire!'

The command merged with the crash of volleys fired by each company along the length of the British line. A dense cloud of smoke instantly filled the air beneath the trees. From his vantage point in the saddle Arthur saw the withering hail of lead slash the French ranks, cutting down a score of men and sending others reeling, while leaves, twigs and bark exploded off the trees.

'Reload!' Mackenzie shouted. 'Fire by companies!'

The shaken French fired a few hurried shots in return before a second British volley struck home, and then Mackenzie gave the order to fix bayonets. There was a brief clatter as the men slid the bayonets over the end of their muskets and twisted them into the locked position.

'Advance!'

The British line paced forward into the slowly dispersing powder smoke and became spectral figures in the gloom before they emerged on the far side, scarcely twenty paces from the nearest Frenchmen. The grim faces of the redcoats and the deadly glimmer of their bayonets were enough to send a ripple of mortal terror through the enemy ranks, and those nearest edged back, then turned and hurried away, despite the shouted encouragement and threats of their officers and sergeants.

Satisfied that Mackenzie had the situation in hand, Arthur let out a deep sigh of relief and nodded with satisfaction. 'That will do for now. Come, Somerset.'

They turned away and spurred their horses down the track, through the groves and back on to open ground. Ahead of them the allied armies had almost finished forming up between the Tagus and the hills and Arthur was struck by the thinly stretched British line, two men deep, that stood ready to hold their ground against the French without the benefit of the field defences afforded to Cuesta's men. There was little doubt in Arthur's mind where the main weight of the French attack would be launched. Leaving a small force to occupy the Spanish the French commander would send in upwards of forty thousand men against Arthur's twenty thousand.

Arthur slowed his horse to a walk as he contemplated the coming fight. 'This is not the battle I would choose to fight, Somerset.'

'Indeed, sir?' His aide urged his horse alongside. 'Our position seems strong enough, and the French cannot outflank us. It will be our line against their column, just as it was at Vimeiro, and we won that day.'

'Vimeiro was different. Junot's army was no stronger than ours. If we had been worsted then the coast was a few miles away and the Royal Navy would have covered the shore while the army embarked.' Arthur paused a moment. 'If the Spanish break, or give up their position, then we will be outflanked and cut to pieces. If we attempt to retreat then the enemy cavalry will harry us all the way. The men are half starved as it is. If they are not able to forage, then any retreat will degenerate into a rout. So, my dear Somerset, we must fight here, and we must win. That is the only road open to us now.'

Chapter 7

In the thin light of the first hour of dawn Arthur gazed steadily towards the east as, column after column, the French army formed up ready to begin their attack. The Portina divided the two armies as it flowed, almost straight, across the plain to the Tagus and the pickets of both sides were already withdrawing, with a few men exchanging final, fatalistic farewells with their opposite numbers. The sight briefly moved Arthur, who could not help wondering at the nature of men that they could be so civil to each other one moment, and intent on each other's destruction the next. His body felt stiff after sleeping the last few hours on the open ground, covered in his cloak. He stretched his back with a slight groan as he surveyed the enemy's dispositions with grim satisfaction.

As Arthur had hoped, the main strength of the French army had been drawn opposite the British. Over forty thousand of them, he estimated, while a few thousand faced the Spanish. It was an odd thing to have wished for, he mused, but the situation was such that the battle could only be won if the French were persuaded to concentrate their efforts on the British alone. Cuesta's army was largely a spent force, and most of his men would only be onlookers in the day's fighting.

'Sir?'

He turned and saw Somerset approaching with a stoppered jug and a loaf of bread.

'Thought you might like some breakfast, sir.'

'Yes, yes I would. Thank you.'

As he watched the French gunners bring forward the first rounds of ammunition Arthur tore off small chunks of bread and chewed quickly. He swallowed, pulled the stopper out of the jug and took a swig. Instantly his face screwed up and he spat to one side. 'By God, what is this?'

'Wine, sir. I found it in a tavern outside the town. The French must have overlooked it when they passed through.'

'Small wonder.' Arthur put the jug down and nodded towards the enemy. 'This is going to be a hard-fought battle, and the men know it.' He glanced at Somerset. 'I've seen their faces. They know the odds are against us.'

'Then they will fight all the harder for it, sir.'

Arthur looked at him again and smiled. 'I only hope they have as much spirit as you do. We shall know soon enough.'

A dull thud sounded and both men stared across the battlefield to where a plume of smoke eddied in the faint morning breeze as the French fired a signal gun. A moment later the main battery of enemy cannon sited opposite the ridge opened up, spitting flame and smoke before the roar carried up the slope like an uneven peal of thunder. The ridge was defended by General Hill's division, formed up across the slope in two lines. The first shots began to strike home, smashing men into bloody fragments as they tore through the British ranks. The outnumbered British guns fired back, exacting a smaller toll of their own amongst the French infantry massed on the far side of the Portina. Arthur watched for a moment before he turned to Somerset.

'Ride over to Hill and tell him to withdraw his men back over the crest of the ridge. Have them lie down, but be ready to rise up and advance at once.'

'Yes, sir.'

While Somerset rode off with his orders for Hill, Arthur watched the French advance begin. As usual, the three dense columns of the attacking division were preceded by a wave of skirmishers who scurried from cover to cover as they exchanged fire with their British counterparts. As the enemy numbers began to tell, a shrill bugle signal recalled the defenders, and they began to give ground as they made their way back up the ridge. It was clear that the ridge was about to become the most vital part of the battlefield and Arthur decided that it would be best if he was at the heart of the fight, where he could control and inspire his men. He mounted his horse and rode forward to join Hill by the colours of the Twenty-ninth Foot. Besides the colour party, the only men between the officers and the approaching enemy were the skirmishers, and the French artillery was still firing over the attacking columns. Roundshot smashed into the ground, kicking up bursts of earth and stone, and Arthur had to steel himself not to flinch as a ball took the head off a sergeant standing at the end of the colour party line. The body collapsed like a sack of wet sand, the spontoon slipping from the lifeless fingers and clattering on the stony ground. An ensign who had been standing close to the sergeant grimaced as he wiped the man's blood and brains from his cheek.

'It might be as well for you to retire to a safer distance, sir,' Somerset said quietly.

'No. This will do. Besides, we must all lead by example today.'

General Hill nodded. 'Aye, sir. The men will expect nothing less.'

The British skirmishers had reached the crest and were falling back to cover. A moment later the French guns ceased fire. Their skirmishers also fell back, between the dense columns climbing up the slope. The colour party, standing defiant on the crest, seemed to act as a beacon, and the centre column of the advancing French division made straight for the handful of redcoats.

Arthur cleared his throat and spoke calmly to Hill. 'I think the time has come to bring your fellows forward.'

'Yes, sir.' Hill smiled and wheeled his horse about. Cupping a hand to his mouth, he bellowed over the crest of the ridge. 'The brigade will advance, at the double!'

The three battalions of Stewart's brigade that had been lying down just behind the crest rose up at once, as if out of the ground, and trotted forward in a line that stretched across the crest. They swept on, past Arthur and Somerset, and drew up a short distance in front of the colour party. Less than a hundred yards beyond, the head of the French column hesitated, and Arthur heard an officer shout an order to deploy into line. But even as the first men began to shuffle to the side, Stewart's brigade levelled their muskets, aiming straight into the dense ranks of the enemy.

General Hill raised his hat to attract the attention of his officers, paused a moment and then swept it down as he bellowed, 'Fire!'

At close range, over fifteen hundred muskets poured their bullets into the head of the French column. To Arthur it seemed as if the front rank simply collapsed as men toppled forward or crumpled to the side, leaving a narrow fringe of blue and white uniformed bodies sprawled in the dry grass. A second, and a third, volley cut down scores more of the enemy so that the dead and wounded now lay heaped one upon the other. By now the French were firing back, at will, since there was too much chaos in their leading ranks for the officers to organise a proper firing line. Despite outnumbering the British, they could bring only a limited number of muskets to bear and all the time fresh casualties added to those piled in the grass.

Arthur saw the column begin to give ground, slowly edging back down the slope. To the right and left the other French columns were being given similar punishment and endured little longer before they too were in retreat. Squinting through the powder smoke engulfing his line, General Hill saw that the gap between his men and the enemy had widened and gave the order to cease fire and advance. As the brigade moved on, they left their own dead and injured scattered across the crest, but no more than thirty or forty men, Arthur estimated. An acceptable loss when compared to the hundreds of Frenchmen who had been shot down.

Hill pursued the enemy with his brigade at a measured pace, stopping every so often to pour another volley into their ranks and press them back down towards the thin band of the Portina. As they reached the bottom of the slope Hill gave the order to charge, and with a hearty roar the men lowered their bayonets and ran towards the battered French column. Most of the enemy turned and fled across the stream, splashing through the water to the far bank and then back towards their guns. Before the British soldiers lost their heads a bugle sounded the withdrawal and the men hurriedly re-formed their line, then turned about and climbed back up the slope. General Hill urged his mount ahead of his men and rode back up to Arthur, greeting him with a barely suppressed smile and an amiable nod of the head.

'The lads have seen 'em off, sir. But hot work indeed! Never seen them fire and move so smoothly.'

'A fine performance, Hill,' Arthur agreed. 'But you can be sure that we have repulsed only the first attack.' He drew out his pocket watch and glanced at it briefly. 'Just gone eight. The day is young, gentlemen, and the enemy is still far from beaten.'

As the sun edged higher into a clear blue sky the slight breeze faded and the air began to feel hot and heavy. A lull had settled over the battlefield and Hill gave the order for his dead to be buried at once, so the heat would not corrupt the bodies. Lower down the slope, the British skirmishers had once again gone forward, but they held their fire as small parties of the French waded across the Portina to retrieve their wounded and the bodies of their dead officers. Once again, warily at first, the fraternisation resumed. Those who had little knowledge of each other's language made signs and mimed to communicate, while others sat and talked, sharing drink and food, amid the dead and wounded of the earlier fighting.

'Ought we to stop that, sir?' Somerset gestured towards the Portina.

'Why?'

'One wouldn't want the men to become too fond of their enemy, surely? Otherwise it might predispose them to be merciful when they should be ruthless?'

Arthur briefly removed his hat and scratched at his close-cropped hair. The heat was making him perspire freely and his scalp itched. He regarded Somerset thoughtfully. His aide was still young enough to have rather fixed opinions about the nature of war and experience had not yet tempered his judgement with a wider understanding of military life.

'Somerset, those men down there know their trade and can be trusted to act as they must when called upon. War is a cruel, brutal business. If we are not to make brutes of those who are obliged to practise it, then we must indulge the better side of their natures whenever we can.'

Somerset was still for a moment and then nodded. Arthur sensed that his aide had not fully accepted the point. Perhaps he would one day, if he lived long enough. Arthur replaced his hat and resumed his consideration of the enemy's intentions. The first attack had been repelled. The question was, would they repeat the attempt? If not, where would they press next? For the moment, the enemy's formations stood their ground under the baking sun and waited for orders. Arthur pulled out his telescope from his saddlebag and began to scan the enemy's positions until he located their senior officers.

He found them easily enough, a gathering of figures in neat blue jackets heavy with gold lace and bullion epaulettes, with feathered bicornes. Some of them were examining the British line through their telescopes and Arthur was briefly amused by the thought that they might well be trying to divine his intentions in turn. A cluster of senior officers seemed to be engaged in a heated debate, with much gesturing towards the British line. Arthur watched them a moment longer, then lowered his telescope and sent Somerset to tell Hill that he could stand his men down for a while and encourage them to find what shade they could for the present.

The lull in the fighting continued for the rest of the morning, and both sides took the chance to send small parties of men, loaded with canteens, down to the Portina to refill them. Elsewhere men, stripped down to their shirts, continued to dig graves and remove as many bodies from the field as possible. Arthur moved to the shade of a small grove of olive trees close to the crest of the ridge and sat and rested in the shade, leaving strict orders that he was to be disturbed if necessary. Overhead, the sun climbed to its zenith and the battlefield became a stifling cauldron of hot air and painfully bright light, infused with the irritating drone of flies as they swarmed over the corpses still awaiting the burial parties.

Arthur stirred as he became aware of a presence close by, and he blinked his eyes open to see Somerset standing over him. 'What is it?'

'Sir, the French are on the move.'

Arthur was on his feet at once, quickly rolling his head to ease the stiffness in his neck. He looked down the slope. Sure enough the French army was spreading out across a wider front as more cannon were brought forward from the reserve and manoeuvred into position a short distance beyond the Portina, ready to bombard the British line.

'They mean to attack along the entire front,' Somerset commented.

'I have eyes and a brain of my own,' Arthur replied tersely. As his embarrassed aide kept his silence Arthur quickly thought through the coming phase of the battle. The French were doing the right thing, he realised. Their earlier attempt to seize the ridge had allowed Arthur to redeploy men to meet the threat, but an attack along the entire line of his army would mean that there would be little chance to shift his outnumbered forces about to bolster weakened points. As before, the defences manned by the Spanish were being avoided as the enemy was determined to shatter the British army first. The hour of gravest danger was swiftly approaching.

Shortly after noon the massed artillery of the French army opened fire. Over eighty guns were answered by Arthur's thirty in a one-sided duel. Once again, bloody gaps were torn in the thin red lines waiting to receive the enemy attack. The French generals were clearly impatient, since the bombardment was mercifully short. As the guns fell silent the drums of the French infantry rolled out, signalling the advance. The skirmishers waded across the Portina and fell in with their British counterparts in a brief exchange of crackling musket fire. Beyond the Portina Arthur saw that the main enemy formations were advancing with broader fronts, as he had expected. There was to be no repeat of a narrow frontal attack this time. The survival of his men would depend on their rigorous training. They would have to fire and reload faster than the French in a bludgeoning exchange of massed volleys.

Campbell's Guards brigade, on the extreme right of the line, was the first in action, waiting until the French had closed to within eighty yards before unleashing their first volley. A moment later the enemy halted and returned fire. After the first few exchanges, the space between the opposing sides was filled with smoke and the combatants were obliged to fire blindly at each other. Watching through his telescope Arthur could see that the enemy were having the worst of it, firing no more than two volleys to the redcoats' three.

Closer to the ridge, the French line closed up on Cameron's brigade and the men of the King's German Legion. Seemingly not to be outdone by the Guards, Cameron allowed the French to close to within fifty yards before unleashing his first volley. With a clear view of the target, and at such close range, nearly every bullet struck home and the French line stopped dead in its tracks as the front ranks were annihilated by the withering fire. Without waiting to let off another volley, Cameron's men fixed bayonets and briskly advanced through the thin screen of smoke and charged at the disorganised French line.

'That's the spirit!' Arthur clenched his fist.

The mêlée was brief, and then the French gave ground and began to retreat across the Portina. Cameron's men, overcome by the excitement of breaking the attack, streamed after them, thrusting their bayonets into the fleeing enemy, or clubbing them down with the heavy butts of their muskets. Some cooler heads paused to reload and fire on the enemy, thereby inadvertently contributing to the loss of cohesion of the brigade.

Somerset sniffed with derision. 'What do those bloody fools think they're doing? They can't take on the whole French army by themselves.'

Arthur's jubilation of a moment earlier turned to dread as he watched the tiny figures in red dissolve into a formless swarm as they crossed the brook and pursued the French into their own lines. Already another enemy line was moving forward to counter the British charge, and their beaten comrades flowed round them to the rear, where their surviving officers began to steady them, and re-form their units. As the screen of fleeing Frenchmen thinned out, the soldiers of Cameron's brigade suddenly found themselves confronted by a new enemy force. While Arthur watched with a sinking heart, the French halted, made ready and unleashed a lethal volley. The redcoats were cut down in swathes, and while a few men returned fire it was clear that most were momentarily stunned by the sharp reversal of fortune. Another volley sealed their fate, and leaving their stricken comrades on the far bank of the Portina the survivors hurried back over the brook, losing more men as the French skirmishers rushed forward to pursue the broken British formation.

It was clear that there was no question of Cameron's rallying his men, and their foolhardiness had left a gaping hole in the centre of the British line. Arthur turned to Somerset.

'We must fill the gap at once! Get you to Mackenzie and order him to move his men across and stop the French. Go!'

While his aide spurred his horse down the slope towards the brigade waiting in reserve, Arthur galloped across the crest and reined in at General Hill's side. The sudden spray of dirt startled Hill's mount.

'What the devil?' The general looked round irritably until he saw his commander.

'Hill, Cameron's brigade has broken. I need your men.' Arthur gestured to the Forty-eighth Foot, on the right of Hill's command. 'Whatever happens you must hold your ground here.'

'I will, sir. Have no fear of that.'

'Thank you.' Arthur touched the brim of his hat and turned his horse to the south, thundering along the rear of Hill's brigade until he reached the colonel in command of the Forty-eighth, where he gave his orders breathlessly. 'Double your men to the right. I want them in a line to take the French in the flank.' He pointed out the French pushing Cameron's chaotic brigade across the Portina. 'If they are not stopped and sent back, then the battle is lost.'

'I understand, sir.' The colonel saluted and turned to shout the necessary orders. Arthur stayed with him and led the regiment down the side of the ridge at a steady trot, the men's knapsacks and bayonet scabbards slapping and jingling as their nailed boots trampled down the dry grass. As he watched the French attack press forward, into the British line, Arthur willed his men on. The enemy had to be stopped swiftly before they managed to cut his army in two. To the right he saw the two thousand men of Mackenzie's brigade trotting across the plain to head off the French column.

'Not enough,' he muttered softly to himself.

Mackenzie's men faced at least a division of the enemy, ten thousand of them, as the French, scenting victory, marched more men into the breach. Mackenzie's brigade halted, and turned from column to line as they prepared to face the onslaught. Cameron's survivors flowed through the gaps between the companies ahead of them and paused a safe distance beyond, breathless and shaken as their officers rallied them. The British line fell silent as the French came on, drums beating while the men in the rear ranks sang lustily. Those at the front held their muskets ready as they paced towards the waiting redcoats, who were standing still, muskets grounded, as if they were on parade. As the enemy closed, the order to make ready echoed down the line and with well-drilled precision the muskets came up, the weapons were cocked and the men took aim. As the first volley was fired, Arthur halted the Forty-eighth and wheeled the formation into line, perpendicular to the head of the attacking French column.

'Advance!' he ordered and the men, two deep, marched forward to add the weight of their fire to that of Mackenzie's brigade.

The first volleys had caused the French to stop and now they began to fill out their flanks as they formed a firing line. The quicker they could do it, the quicker they could overwhelm the firepower of the last line of British infantry standing between them and victory.

'Keep moving there!' Arthur called to his right as one of the companies began to lag slightly behind the others. The men obediently quickened their pace and pulled back into position. Ahead of the regiment Arthur could see the faces of the men on the right of the French column, glancing anxiously towards the new threat closing on their flank. He had time to reflect that this was further proof of the inferiority of the French system. Once their columns were unleashed they were unwieldy giants lumbering forward and unable to manoeuvre freely enough to cope with threats from either flank or the rear.

The two sides closed, and all the while Mackenzie's brigade continued to exchange fire with the head of the column, pinning the French in place while Arthur came up with the Forty-eighth Foot. A handful of French skirmishers had run forward to interpose themselves between the column and the approaching British line, and opened fire. A handful of men went down, one after another, and Arthur heard the faint whip of a bullet close by as they closed to within a hundred yards of the enemy. This was the moment, he decided, and filled his lungs.

'Forty-eighth will halt! Make ready to fire!'

The line ceased its advance and the front line shifted a pace to the right to present a staggered wall of men, all of whom could now bring their muskets to bear. As soon as he saw they were ready Arthur called out, 'Take aim! Fire!'

Those skirmishers still standing were struck down, and then their comrades in the flank of the French column, wheeling round under the impact, toppled. As the redcoats hurriedly lowered their muskets and reached for the next round, Arthur heard a faint groan of dismay and fear from the French ranks.

'Pour it on, boys!' shouted the colonel of the Forty-eighth. 'Pour it on!'

The flank companies of the French column began to shuffle round, their progress being held up by the bodies underfoot, but another volley swept into them, striking down more men and creating further chaos, and the attempt to present a firing line to Arthur and his men collapsed. The men of the Forty-eighth methodically loaded and fired with a ruthless efficiency, cutting down swathes of Frenchmen with each volley. Yet the column stood its ground, hemmed in by the bodies of its fallen. At the front their losses had been grievous, but then so had the losses amongst Mackenzie's brigade, Arthur saw. Perhaps a third of his men were down already and Arthur knew they could not stand much more punishment. If the French could hold their nerve for a few more minutes then victory was surely theirs. Behind Mackenzie's men the remains of Cameron's brigade were still re-forming, and could play no part in the action at this critical moment. Arthur was seized by frustration at his powerlessness to affect the outcome. All now depended on which soldiers endured this terrible punishment for longest.

Then a movement caught his eye. From the saddle he could just see over the mass of the French column to the ground beyond. Through the thin smoke wafting back from the men firing along the front, something flashed. And then again, and more – sunlight reflecting off polished steel, he realised. Fresh hope stirred in his heart as he saw a line of cavalry sweeping in against the far side of the column.

'By God, it's the Light Dragoons!' he exclaimed through gritted teeth. 'Ride on. Ride on and break them!'

Attacked from three sides now, the less spirited of the Frenchmen began to back away, seeking escape from the sweep of British bullets and the slashing of the dragoons' swords as they carved at the enemy's left flank. More men backed away, and despite the frenzied encouragement and fury of their officers the contagion spread and the column lost what little cohesion it had left as the men broke, falling back in a frightened mass towards the Portina and the greater safety of the far bank. The battered regiments of Mackenzie's brigade followed up, pausing to fire volleys whenever the enemy retreat showed any sign of slowing. The sight of the fleeing enemy gave heart to Cameron's survivors, who hurried forward to join the flanks of Mackenzie's line.

Arthur left orders for the Forty-eighth to remain on the plain and then, when he was satisfied that the danger had passed, turned and galloped back up to his vantage point on top of the ridge. The rest of the line had held off the French, who had pulled back to re-form their savaged columns. Looking over his own men, Arthur was shocked to see how many had fallen. Almost every battalion had closed its ranks, leaving large gaps along the line. If the French launched another attack then it would surely smash through the exhausted and bloodied redcoats.

When he returned to the crest he heard the sounds of fresh fighting coming from the valley on the other side of the ridge. Fearing a new threat Arthur anxiously rode forward until he had a clear view of the fighting below. Three large squares of French infantry were slowly picking their way back towards the Portina, followed up by the cavalry of the King's German Legion, and a Spanish regiment that Cuesta must have sent to aid the British. The artillery further down the slope was taking advantage of the large targets being presented by the enemy and firing roundshot through their ranks as they retreated, leaving a scatter of blue-uniformed bodies in their wake.

As the French passed out of range of the British guns, they fell silent one after another and the cavalry withdrew and re-formed further down the valley to wait for the next French attack. Somerset joined his commander shortly afterwards, his face ashen and streaked with grime from the powder smoke of the desperate fight down on the plain.

Arthur greeted him with a faint smile. 'I was beginning to fear you might have become a casualty. Where have you been?'

'I stayed with Mackenzie's brigade through the attack, sir.'

'Ah, yes, I must remember to tender my thanks to him. That was a fine stand he and his men made.'

'Mackenzie is dead, sir.'

'Dead?' Arthur's expression hardened. 'A pity.'

Somerset cleared his throat and continued hoarsely. 'Together with seven hundred of his men. Cameron is dead as well. He was shot on the other side of the Portina.'

'I see.' Arthur nodded sadly. 'This is only the start of a long list, I fear. But we have no time to mourn them now. Later, after the battle. The French may still be game enough for another attempt to break us.'

'Yes, sir.' Somerset stiffened his spine and sat as erect as he could in his saddle. 'I understand.'

As he spoke there was a ripple of flashes along the French line as their cannon fired again, bombarding the men on the ridge and spread across the plain towards Talavera. It was late in the afternoon, and Arthur was reeling with exhaustion and a blinding headache from the glare of the day's sunlight. He knew that his men must share his condition and would be in poor shape to continue the fight. As the sun sank towards the horizon behind the British, the shadow of the ridge stretched across the rolling landscape and over the French troops massed opposite. Even though the enemy guns continued firing, there was no sign of another attack. The enemy simply stood and waited as the light started to fail.

'Do you think they will make another attempt tonight?' asked Somerset.

'It is likely,' Arthur replied. 'Hill's division must stay in position in case they do. I'd be obliged if you would ride to him and let him know that he may stand his men down, but they must be ready to fight again at a moment's notice.'

'Very well, sir.' Somerset saluted and turned his horse down the slope to Hill's command post.

The French guns continued firing while there was light, and then fell silent. An uneasy stillness fell across the battlefield, and men whose ears had rung with the sound of cannon and muskets all day seemed stunned by the quiet of the gathering night. Only the faint cries of the wounded and the occasional whinny of stricken horses broke the spell. Then, as the men of the British army sat on the ground in their regiments, a faint glow flickered into life at the bottom of the ridge. Flames licked up amid the dry grass, and the fire quickly spread across the lower slopes. Some wadding from one of the French guns must have caused the blaze, Arthur realised. At first he welcomed the fire. It would show up any attempt by the enemy to take the ridge under cover of darkness, and possibly impede them. But then a thin wail of terror reached his ears. There were more cries for help and then screams of agony from lower down the slope.

'It's the wounded,' Somerset said quietly. 'There must be hundreds of men out there, ours and theirs. We have to send men to save them, sir.'

'No,' Arthur said firmly, and then swallowed to try to ease the dryness in his throat. 'We cannot afford to have men looking for the wounded if there is another attack. There's nothing we can do for them.'

As the fire spread the screams increased and cut through the night so that, even as exhausted as they were, few of the men on the ridge could sleep. Satisfied that there were no signs of a new attack being prepared by the enemy, Arthur made a quick tour of his command and offered words of encouragement to the gaunt figures he came across. Most of the men seemed too numb to continue the battle and when he returned to the ridge Arthur lay down on the ground and tried to rest. But his mind would not be still. When the morning came he had little doubt that his army would face another onslaught such as the one they had endured that day.

He rose just before dawn and stood, straining his eyes and ears for any indication that the French were preparing for another attack. As the eastern horizon grew more distinct the first bugles sounded from the French camp, and then the faint cries of command and the crack of whips as the artillery crews moved their guns.

The light continued to strengthen as Arthur tried to concentrate his thoughts on what needed to be done to prepare for the first attack. Then, as he stared towards the French positions, he frowned. The artillery batteries had gone. There were no lines of infantry and cavalry massing for attack. Only a handful of enemy horsemen remained on the far side of the Portina, keeping watch on the British line.

'What the devil?' For a moment Arthur was struck by a terrible anxiety as he wondered if the French were attempting to move through the hills to the north to try to cut him off from his lines of communication back to Portugal. Then, as the first rays of the sun filtered out across the landscape, he saw the French army. Dense columns of men, horses, cannon and wagons, marching to the east, back in the direction of Madrid. It was a while before his mind, dulled with exhaustion, finally grasped the truth.

'They're retreating . . . By God, they're retreating,' he muttered to himself. The British had won the battle after all. There was no elation in his heart. None. Only relief, and that soon faded as the morning light revealed the terrible cost of victory spread across the still smouldering lower slopes of the ridge and out on to the plain towards Talavera.

THE BATTLE OF WAGRAM

THE BISSAM

River Danube

MARCHFELD

Aderklaa •

Wagram •

River Russbach

Grosshofen •

Essling •

Aspern •

Mühlau •

Lobau Island

Wittau •

VIENNA

Schönbrunn

Arrows indicate
French break out attack
from Lobau Island

Chapter 8

Napoleon

Lobau island, July 1809

'This will do,' Napoleon nodded. 'Mark it down, Masséna.'

'Yes, sire.' Masséna took his pencil from behind his ear and carefully noted the location on the folded map he was holding, then quickly tucked it away again before they attracted the attention of the Austrian sentries on the opposite bank, scarcely a hundred paces away. Napoleon and Masséna had borrowed the jackets and caps of two sergeants and set out without an escort in order not to provoke scrutiny of their reconnaissance work.

They were selecting the sites for the series of pontoon bridges that were to be thrown across the final stretch of the Danube. The first attempt to cross at the end of May had ended in a humiliating reverse that had cost thousands of lives, including that of Marshal Lannes. Napoleon's enemies across Europe had been greatly encouraged by the news from Austria. The only way to retrieve the situation was to deliver a crushing blow against Archduke Charles and his army.

The difficulty was that the Danube separated Napoleon from his prey. In addition, the Austrian army had erected a formidable array of field fortifications in a wide arc that stretched across most of the bank that faced Lobau. The enemy had made no moves to carry the fight to Napoleon and seemed content to sit and wait for him.

With all Europe watching the conflict, Napoleon was determined to make another attempt to cross the river, and this time the result would be very different.

Every soldier that could be spared had been summoned to Vienna, where the army steadily increased in size until over a hundred and sixty thousand men had gathered to take part in the attack on Archduke Charles. The troops left to guard the army's communications with France were thinly stretched and if only one more of the European powers chose to intervene on the side of Austria then there would be little to stand in their way.

Meanwhile Lobau was turned into a fortress. By the end of June over a hundred and thirty cannon were sited in batteries covering the far bank. Two strong bridges had been constructed across the main channel of the Danube as well as three new pontoon bridges. Stakes had been driven into the river bed upstream of the bridges to ensure that they would be protected from any Austrian fireships or floating rams. There was to be no dependence on a single, vulnerable bridge across the river this time.

The enemy had made no attempt to intervene. The French had even managed to land a force across the river to seize the salient on which the hamlet of Mühlau stood. Within hours the French engineers had thoroughly fortified the village and mounted powerful batteries in redoubts to cover the approaches. The enemy had reacted with their usual plodding deliberation and by the time a column had arrived to retake the village it was clear to Archduke Charles that it would cost him far more men than the village was worth and he opted to enclose the salient within the wider system of fieldworks designed to contain any French attempt to break out on to the Marchfeld. Napoleon had been careful to ensure that the Austrians saw the construction of the elaborate series of batteries to cover a landing between Aspern and Essling. Moreover, the elite Imperial Guard had loudly paraded opposite Mühlau, and two additional bridges had been constructed to the salient. The enemy could hardly be in any doubt where Napoleon's blow would fall.

Which was as well, he mused to himself as he strolled further along the bank of Lobau island with Masséna. For it was all an elaborate ruse, calculated to draw the enemy's attention away from the true direction in which the French would strike. Already, ten pontoon bridges had been constructed out of sight of the Austrians, ready to be towed into position on the night of the attack. It was these bridges that Napoleon and Masséna were choosing positions for as they made their way along the eastern end of the island in their borrowed jackets.

Napoleon paused to survey the opposite bank once again. A party of Austrian soldiers were bathing in the shallows, their laughter and sound of splashing carrying clearly across the water. Beyond the Austrians the bank sloped gently up to higher ground.

'What do you think?'

Masséna stared across the river for a moment before he nodded.

'Looks good to me, sire. The river bed must be firm there, and our guns will be able to negotiate the far bank easily enough.'

'I agree. Mark the position.'

They worked their way steadily along the bank, choosing the points where the ground was most solid and the bank posed no obstacle to the swift crossing of the river. When the last site had been marked on the map they turned to make their way back across the island to the Emperor's forward headquarters. Behind the screen of forests that surrounded the heart of the island sprawled a vast camp. Marshal Oudinot's corps had joined Masséna's men, and once night came Davout's thirty-five thousand soldiers would swell the ranks of the army waiting to be unleashed on the unsuspecting Archduke Charles. Obedient to their strict orders the men had not lit camp fires, and sat quietly resting. Some were stretched out asleep, others were cleaning their weapons, the cavalry rasping whetstones along the edges of their sabres. Although no orders had been issued for any attack, the concentration of so many men was evidence enough that their Emperor was preparing for an imminent battle.

As they walked through the camp Napoleon felt the keen sense of anticipation amongst his soldiers. So different from little over a month earlier when the army had been thrust back on to the island by the Austrians. Napoleon's brow creased into a frown as he recalled the scene. The survivors of the battle had slumped on the ground in exhaustion. Thousands of injured men had been forced to spend two nights in the open, and hundreds had died from their wounds and been buried in a mass grave on the south of the island.

Eventually the wounded had been evacuated to Vienna, including Marshal Lannes, whose legs had been smashed by a cannon ball. With both legs shattered the imperial surgeon, Dr Larrey, had no choice but amputation. Napoleon had gone to his friend's side after the operation and found the veteran of many campaigns lying on a bed in a small chapel. A thin sheet covered Lannes and his arms lay at his sides. The sheet fell flat to the bed from his thighs down. Lannes was in a troubled sleep, his face slick with perspiration, as Napoleon and Dr Larrey entered the room.

Napoleon turned to Dr Larrey and asked quietly, 'What are his chances of surviving?'

'Good enough. The marshal has a strong constitution. Provided there is no corruption of the wound, the stumps will heal in time.'

Napoleon nodded. 'Keep me informed of his progress.'

'Yes, sir.'

Napoleon glanced back through the door and felt a great sadness over the knowledge that the courageous and utterly dependable Lannes would never again be at his side during a battle. It would be hard for a man so full of vitality to accept life as a cripple, Napoleon realised. As he closed the door, he wondered if it might not have been kinder if Lannes had been killed outright.

Marshal Jean Lannes died eight days after he had been wounded. The pain of his loss still burned in Napoleon's heart. He had wept at the news, and the army had been stunned. Many had seen Lannes in the front rank in battle and had been steadied by his example. He had risen from amongst their ranks and had shared their perils and their wounds, and they openly grieved for him as the news spread through the ranks.

Jean Lannes would be avenged, Napoleon vowed silently as they approached a group of sergeants sitting beside the track running across the camp. The men had a small keg of brandy with them and a haunch of cured venison. One of them looked up as Masséna and Napoleon passed by.

'Hey, friends, join us for a drink?'

Masséna was about to refuse the offer when Napoleon nudged him and smiled a greeting. 'Why, yes. Thank you.'

Masséna shot him a surprised glance, but Napoleon simply pulled his cap down a bit further as he sat on the crushed grass. After a moment's hesitation Masséna joined him. The sergeant who had invited them held out two battered copper cups and lifted the keg to pour a small measure into each. Napoleon raised his cup. 'Good health!'

The other sergeants, ten or so of them, raised their cups to return the toast and then, after a sip of the fiery liquid, Napoleon wiped his lips and asked, 'So what unit is this, then?'

'First battalion, Eighty-second regiment of the line. In Friant's division.'

Napoleon nodded. 'Davout's corps, then. Only just arrived.'

'Not only that,' the sergeant continued, 'but only just formed. The battalion's marched here from the depot at Lyons.'

Another sergeant cleared his throat and spat on to the ground beside him. 'Most of the recruits are just boys.'

'And what about you lot?' asked Masséna. 'What's your service record?'

'Us?' The first sergeant laughed. 'Up until a couple of months ago we were just customs officers. Then the call-up comes from Paris. The

Emperor needs a new army and his recruiters are scouring France for discharged veterans, National Guard officers and NCOs, and finally, at the bottom of the barrel, us. That's why I asked you to join us.' He pointed at their jackets. 'You're from the Imperial Guard. You must have seen a thing or two.'

Masséna nodded.

'Then you must have been here when the army last went up against the Austrians.'

'Yes.'

'The army newspapers say that it was a tactical withdrawal after the enemy had been given a good hiding. Of course, no one believes a word of it. From what we've heard, it was a bloody disaster. Is that true?'

Masséna glanced at Napoleon, who was still for a moment before he nodded discreetly. This was a rare chance to hear what his soldiers really thought. Freshly arrived from Lyons, it was likely that none of them had ever set eyes on their Emperor. Most of the paintings and prints that were to be found around the country had him bedecked in glittering uniforms. They would not guess his identity, for now at least.

Masséna looked at the sergeant and nodded. 'It was a hard fight, and yes, they drove us from the field. We lost good men, thousands of them.'

'How did that happen?'

Masséna shrugged. 'We advanced too far too quickly and the reconnaissance was sloppy, and somehow the cavalry patrols managed to miss spotting the Austrian army. That's how.'

'Then it's like we were told,' one of the others intervened. 'The Emperor fucked up.'

Napoleon sensed Masséna freeze by his side, and he coughed and leaned forward. 'Careful, that's dangerous talk. I wouldn't let any officers overhear such an opinion. But, for what it's worth, the Emperor made a mistake. I doubt he'll make the same one again.'

'Really?' The sergeant raised his eyebrows. 'What makes you think so?'

Napoleon gestured at the vast camp surrounding them. 'Every preparation has been made. I doubt there's any army in the whole of Europe that could beat us now.'

'I'm not worried about other armies. I'm worried about the one that's waiting for us on the other side of the river. They've beaten us once. They'll be thinking they can do it again.'

'Then they're wrong,' Napoleon replied, and jerked his thumb at Masséna. 'We've fought 'em before. Trust me, the Austrians can be beaten, and they will be beaten.'

The sergeant still seemed doubtful. 'Well, I hope you're right. God knows we need to beat them and end this war. Let's hope this time we can have a real peace at the end of it all. Perhaps we'll live to see the day when the Emperor has finally had his fill of war. All I want is peace, and the chance to go home to my family.'

'Peace, and the chance to go home?' Napoleon shrugged. 'I'm sure that's what the Emperor wants as much as the next Frenchman. The question is, will the other nations let us have peace?'

'No chance,' the sergeant replied bitterly. 'War is all that kings, tsars and emperors understand. They love the uniforms, and pushing tokens round on maps, and all the time it's the lot of common people to die. I thought the Revolution was supposed to put an end to all of that. We got rid of the King, and the aristos. Now look at us. Dukes, princes and barons as far as the eye can see, and Napoleon sitting on top of it all with his crown. What's changed, tell me that?'

The first sergeant laughed. 'Ignore him. Pierre's just an old-fashioned Jacobin. He's always grumbling. I wonder . . .' He looked eagerly at Masséna and Napoleon. 'You must have seen him. What's he like?'

'The Emperor?' Masséna puffed his cheeks at the awkward situation. 'Well, he's just a man, like any of us here. He may be Emperor when he's in the palace in Paris, but here, in the field? Here, he's a soldier. He takes his risks with the rest of us.'

'And what about you?' asked the sergeant called Pierre, staring directly at Napoleon. 'What do you think?'

Napoleon stared back at him for a moment, tempted to reveal his identity, but at the same time loath to break the illusion that they were all comrades. He set down his cup and stood up, punching Masséna lightly on the shoulder. 'I think it's time we got back to our battalion. It's going to be a busy night.'

Masséna handed back his cup and stood up. 'Good luck to you all.'

'And you,' the first man nodded back.

'What do you think?' Napoleon asked quietly, as he and Masséna strode off.

Masséna glanced at him. 'Sire?'

'Don't be a fool, Masséna. I'm talking about what those men said. Are they right? Have I betrayed the Revolution and simply created a new form of tyranny?'

'You are talking about politics, sire, and I am a soldier. It's not my field.'

'You are evading the issue.' Napoleon laughed softly. 'When a man fears to speak the truth then he does indeed live in a tyranny. It seems that the sergeant was right.'

'King or emperor, what difference does it make?' Masséna responded. 'The fact is, France is at war and it is the duty of every soldier to fight for his country. When the fighting begins there is no place for questioning the cause of it.' He was quiet for a moment. 'Besides, what use have I for peace? It would do me out of a fine living.'

Napoleon looked at him and shook his head. 'Marshal Masséna, you have a brutally practical way of looking at life. Even so, I must admit I had hoped that a little idealism burned in your heart.'

Masséna shrugged. 'I'll leave idealism to the philosophers, sire. As long as there's fighting, fucking and fortunes to be made, I am your man.'

'And what if I make peace? What of your allegiance to me then?'

'Sire, that sergeant was right about one thing. While you are Emperor there cannot be peace in Europe, whether you will it or not. And that suits me perfectly.'

They returned their borrowed jackets when they reached headquarters and made their way into the map room. Berthier was leaning across the table with a pair of dividers as he calculated the march timetables for the remaining columns still moving forward to join the army. He straightened up and bowed his head as the Emperor and Masséna entered.

'Everything proceeding to plan?' asked Napoleon.

'Yes, sire. The entire army should be over the river by the second day. One hundred and eighty thousand men, less the garrison to cover the bridges.'

'What's the latest intelligence on Archduke Charles?'

'According to the reports from the cavalry corps, the Austrians have something in the order of one hundred and fifty thousand men concentrated against us. Of course, we are still unsure of the precise location of Archduke John's army. He began his withdrawal from Italy two weeks ago, and might be close enough to intervene.'

'What's his strength?'

'No more than fifteen thousand, sire.'

'Then he is of little consequence to us,' Napoleon decided. He clicked his fingers. 'Masséna, the map.'

Masséna took out the diagram of the river crossings and unfolded it beside the larger-scale map that Berthier had been working on. Napoleon tapped his finger on the pencilled markings on the eastern side of Lobau island. 'This is where we cross. Have the map copied and sent to the commander of the engineers. He is to have the pontoon bridges ready to move into position at nightfall.'

'Yes, sire.'

Napoleon studied the map in silence for a moment before he nodded with satisfaction. All the pieces were in place. Archduke Charles had concentrated his army around the French troops in the Mühlau salient. It appeared that he had taken the bait and was waiting to meet the French attack over the same ground as where they had attempted to force a crossing just over a month earlier. Instead, Napoleon would strike two miles to the east, towards the village of Wittau. In overwhelming strength the French would pour across the Danube and immediately wheel round to take the Austrians in the flank and rear and crush them. Napoleon looked up at Marshal Masséna and smiled.

'We have the enemy precisely where we want them. Tonight, you will have the honour of leading the army across the Danube and on to victory.'

Chapter 9

The storm broke just after night fell over the Danube. Lightning illuminated the landscape in brilliant flashes of dazzling white which caught thousands of men, horses, guns and silvery streaks of rain in a frozen tableau for an instant before plunging the world back into darkness. Then, as the men marched forward through the mud towards the pontoon bridges, the thunder crackled and boomed like a vast cannonade in the heavens.

'It could hardly be better,' Napoleon commented to Berthier as they sat on their horses, watching the first columns of Masséna's corps move forward to the river bank, ready to cross over the moment the bridges were swung into place. Napoleon gestured towards the western side of the island, nearly two miles away. 'This storm, and the diversionary attack from Mühlau, will provide perfect cover for Masséna's assault.'

Berthier nodded, and reached for his pocket watch. He waited a moment, and then read the time as lightning flashed overhead.

'Just gone nine o'clock, sire. Less than ten minutes to go now.'

They waited in the darkness while the rain hissed down, pattering off the flat tops of the soldiers' shakos and soaking through their greatcoats and the uniform jackets beneath. Around them, the trees that lined the river bank swayed in the gusts of wind that sounded like the sea as it swept through the leafy boughs. Every time the lightning burst across the landscape the soldiers looked like statues, Napoleon mused as he hunched his neck down into his collar to try to keep the water from trickling down his neck. Then, at the appointed time, there was a deep roar from the west that echoed across the island as the guns massed opposite Mühlau blasted the Austrian lines. At the same time General Legrand would be launching his diversionary attack, engaging the enemy outposts as aggressively as he could to draw Archduke Charles's attention away from his left flank.

As soon as the cannonade began, the five hundred grenadiers of Masséna's assault force rushed the small boats they had been issued down the bank and into the river, before clambering aboard and paddling across the current as swiftly as possible. No shots were fired from the Austrian sentries, who were either sheltering from the storm or distracted by the furious sounds of battle away to the west. In the darkness, Napoleon could just make out the boats surging across the river, the men landing and then heading cautiously up the far bank, muskets at the ready.

As soon as the assault force was across, the first of the pontoon bridges was towed into position. Behind it came the other nine, emerging from the small channel where they had been waiting, hidden from Austrian eyes. The engineers hauled them into position and fastened them to the posts already driven into the bank of Lobau island. Napoleon urged his mount forward to the nearest of the pontoon bridges and sent for the officer in charge.

'How long will it take you to get the bridge into position, Lieutenant?'

'Fifteen minutes, sire,' the engineer replied at once.

'I will give you five minutes,' said Napoleon as he reached for his pocket watch. 'I'll be timing you.'

'Yes, sire.' The engineer saluted and turned to run down the bank to his men, already shouting his orders to get a boat across the river with a cable and some stout stakes to drive into the far bank. As soon as the stakes were pounded into position the engineers pulled the cable attached to the end of the bridge and with ponderous grace the line of pontoons and trestles angled across the current until it extended from bank to bank. As soon as the last cables had been tied securely to the stakes the engineering officer sprinted up to his Emperor and saluted as he stood to attention, chest heaving from his exertions.

'Beg to report, the bridge is ready, sire.'

Napoleon thrust his pocket watch back inside his coat. 'With nearly half a minute to spare. Fine work.'

'Thank you, sire.'

'Now, I'd be obliged if you would get the first of Masséna's men across that bridge of yours.'

'Yes, sire.' The engineer saluted smartly and hurried off to the head of the bridge and waved the first company forward. The soldiers broke step as they reached the first trestle and then strode as quickly as they could across to the far bank. Further downriver Napoleon could just discern the outlines of the other bridges being swung into position across the current, and more of Masséna's corps quickly crossed to the far bank. A few hundred paces inland, individual muskets flared as those enemy soldiers on watch who had managed to keep their powder dry opened fire on the assault party. Once the first division was across it marched off along the bank of the river to the north, making for the fortified village of Gross-Enzerdorff before pressing on to Essling.

To the right, Oudinot and Davout led their men across and drove the enemy back as they fanned out across the plain and formed their corps up on Masséna's right flank. By the early hours of the morning half of the Grand Army was already over the Danube. Napoleon and his staff crossed the river and set up headquarters in the hamlet of Uferhaus, where the Emperor's bodyguard unceremoniously turfed out the owner of a small estate and surrounded the walls with pickets. Inside Napoleon sat at a hastily arranged map table and took a bowl of soup as Berthier eagerly read over the reports sent back from each of the three corps which had already crossed the river.

'No reports of any serious opposition, sire. The Austrians seem to be retreating right across our front.' Berthier sifted through a few more sheets of paper before he looked up again. 'Casualties are minimal.'

'Good. And what of the bridges? Are they still in one piece?'

'As far as I know, sir. At least, there have been no reports to the contrary.'

Napoleon stared at his subordinate for a moment, wondering if he could trust his junior officers to keep him fully informed of the army's progress across the river. After the debacle of the last attempt to force a crossing of the Danube, Napoleon was determined to ensure that the army's lines of communication were unhindered. He pushed the bowl to one side. 'Berthier, send an officer to the river bank. I want to know the instant anything happens that might frustrate our plans, in any way. Is that clear?'

'Yes, sire.'

Napoleon gazed at the map, deep in concentration. By dawn three army corps and the Imperial Guard would be drawn up in a line facing north across a six-mile front from the bank of the Danube across the plain to the east. A hundred thousand men. Opposed to them would be a hundred and fifty thousand Austrians. Napoleon was confident that his men could hold their line, even though outnumbered, until the last formations of the Grand Army crossed the Danube and swelled the total to over a hundred and eighty thousand men. If Archduke Charles retreated, then the Grand Army would be obliged to pursue him, all the time stretching their lines of communication, and being forced to leave behind men tasked with guarding vital supply routes.

Very well, then, Napoleon resolved, the enemy must not be given any chance to break contact. At first light, the first three corps must be launched against the Austrians, forcing them to stand and fight.

When the sun rose across the plain in the morning, it was clear that the Austrians had been caught by surprise. Through his looking glass Napoleon could see enemy lines scattered across the landscape. The largest concentration of Austrian forces was between the villáges of Aspern and Essling where the diversionary attack had struck the previous evening. Elsewhere individual units were hurriedly forming up into lines to face the coming onslaught. As the light strengthened across the drenched fields, he saw that some of the enemy formations were already pulling back, heading for the Russbach river. The bank was raised on the far side of the river and would provide the Austrians with some defence against a French attack.

During the first hours of the morning there was no attempt to counter-attack and most of the French soldiers had the chance to chew on some bread and sip some water. They stood in the muddy fields, muskets slung over their shoulders as thin wisps of steam rose from their uniforms into the warm air. As they waited a steady stream of infantry, cavalry and artillery hurried across the river. Three more corps were due to cross the Danube during the day, and the last, commanded by Marmont, would join them on the morrow. In little over a day, almost all the army would have reached the far bank. It was an achievement to be proud of, Napoleon mused to himself as he stretched his shoulders and watched the men of Prince Eugène's corps stepping out across the pontoon bridges.

His heart warmed at the thought of his stepson. Eugène had proved himself to be an able commander and, more important, a loyal subordinate – unlike the commander of the corps that was waiting to cross after Eugène's men. Marshal Bernadotte had become increasingly arrogant in the years since Napoleon had been crowned Emperor. Recently, there had been reports from some of his officers that Bernadotte had been speaking very openly of his superiority to the Emperor in military affairs. While it was tempting to dismiss the marshal and be done with him, the fact was that Bernadotte was popular with his men, and well connected amongst the politicians in Paris. He would present more of a danger if left to his own devices in the capital than here in the field, where Napoleon could keep a close eye on him. Even so, there was a limit to how far the Emperor would tolerate such a troublesome officer.

He thrust Bernadotte from his mind and returned to his consideration of Eugène. It was a shame that he had not fathered such a fine man, Napoleon reflected sadly. That had been a fond hope and ambition of his marriage to Josephine. But there was no chance of her bearing another child now. She was too old for that, and even if she had still been fertile she would not be prepared to risk another childbirth. Yet France needed an heir to the imperial throne. Without a son to succeed him, Napoleon could not give his empire the stability it so desperately needed. Since he had fathered a son by the Polish Countess Walewska, he knew that his own fertility was not at fault. If there was to be an heir, then he must find himself a new wife. Yet he shrank from the consequences of that knowledge. Despite the discovery of Josephine's numerous affairs, and her failure to give him a son, Napoleon loved her more deeply and surely than any woman he had ever known.

He sighed heavily. Once the campaign was over, and Austria had been humbled, then he would have to deal with the matter of providing his empire with a successor, no matter how much pain that would cause him, and Josephine. Duty and destiny must prevail over emotion, he resolved.

He was disturbed by the arrival of a young dragoon officer who stood to attention and saluted as he stood before his Emperor.

'What is it?' Napoleon snapped.

'Sire, Marshal Masséna sends his compliments and begs to inform you that the Austrians are beginning to withdraw from Essling.'

'Are they now?' Napoleon frowned. It seemed that Archduke Charles had finally realised the danger of his situation and was starting to extricate his army. 'Tell Masséna that he is to press forward at once. He is to push the enemy back, and stay in contact with them. They must not be allowed to escape, or be given any respite. Masséna must drive all before him. Now go!'

'Yes, sire!'

Throughout the afternoon the French soldiers pressed forward, driving the enemy back across the plain. The last clouds had long since gone and the sun blazed down from a clear blue sky. But while there was serenity in the heavens, the Marchfeld was marked by great banks of rolling gunpowder smoke and the litter of war. Bodies of the dead and wounded lay strewn in the trampled grass, together with discarded equipment, shattered gun carriages and lame or abandoned horses that grazed between the corpses. The air was heavy from the heat, and reverberated with the sounds of cannon and the lighter crackle of musket fire.

Late in the afternoon Napoleon and his escort rode forward to assess the situation. He stopped by a small church on a dusty road heading north from Aspern, and climbed its tower with Berthier. There was little space at the top, and they had to squeeze past the old bronze bell before they could open the shutters and look out over the battlefield. Both men raised their telescopes and slowly swept them along the French line, taking in the formations of men and horses advancing under their tricolour and imperial eagle banners. They were dark against the shimmering gold of wheat fields, and the verdant green of meadows.

Napoleon could see that his army formed a giant wedge, driven into the centre of the Austrian line. He felt the familiar excitement tingle in his scalp as he viewed the over-extended enemy.

'Berthier, do you see?'

'Sire?' Berthier lowered his looking glass and waited patiently while his Emperor briefly examined the battlefield once again before he lowered his own glass and turned round with a cold smile.

'Berthier, we have them, provided we strike swiftly. Come!'

Napoleon led the way back down the narrow steps of the tower and they emerged in the cool plastered nave. Striding across to the altar, Napoleon swept the ornaments aside.

'Let me see the map.'

Berthier unfasted the strap of the leather document case hanging from his shoulder. He took out the map, unfolded it and spread it across the altar. Napoleon leaned forward and stared at it a moment, eyes darting across the features, and then he nodded.

'Our line extends thus.' He drew his finger east from the Danube, towards Wagram, and then angled it south, along the length of the Russbach river. 'The enemy's right wing hinges on Wagram. Masséna can pin their right, Oudinot and Davout can strike against their left, and then we use our reserves to punch through, here.' He tapped the map. 'At Wagram. If we succeed, then we can turn and trap their right flank against the Danube and annihilate a third of Archduke Charles's army.' His eyes glittered.

Berthier studied the map a moment. 'But what of Archduke John, sire? What if he appears on our flank? It could be dangerous.'

Napoleon shook his head. 'Send a cavalry division to screen our flank. If he nears the battlefield before we have dealt with his brother, they can hold him off while we defeat Archduke Charles.'

'Very well, sire. What time shall we begin the attack?'

Napoleon took out his watch. 'It's five o'clock. We should begin no later than seven. That gives us the best part of three hours of daylight to break the Austrians. The orders have to be sent out no later than six.' Napoleon took off his jacket and threw it to the side of the altar. 'To work, Berthier!'

The massed guns of the Grand Army opened fire on the enemy just after seven that evening. Napoleon watched with satisfaction as solid shot ploughed through the dense enemy formations. Then their own guns replied, smashing gaps in the French columns waiting for the order to advance. Once he judged the Austrian centre was beginning to waver under the intense bombardment, Napoleon gave the order for the attack to begin. As the French guns fell silent, the drums began a deep rolling beat and the infantry closed up on the waiting Austrians. Again, the long smears of dense smoke spread across the landscape, shrouding the battle, and Napoleon waited with the Imperial Guard, just behind Eugène's corps.

As the sounds of the assault rose in a crescendo Napoleon rose up on his stirrups and strained his eyes to see how the leading division was progressing. Eugène had chosen General MacDonald, the descendant of an exiled Scottish aristocrat, to lead the way with his division of Italian soldiers. In the fading evening light, Napoleon could just make out the distant figures of his men beginning to enter the streets of Wagram. He nodded approvingly.

'I have misjudged MacDonald's men. I had feared they might lack the elan of French men, but look at them now. Charging in like lions!'

'Yes, sire,' Berthier replied, looking up from the first reports that had arrived from the other sectors of the battle line. He cleared his throat nervously and addressed his Emperor. 'Sire, Oudinot and Davout are taking heavy losses.'

'Of course they are. It's to be expected in a frontal attack.'

'But the enemy are holding their ground, sire. Our columns have been stopped in their tracks. And they're losing men.'

Napoleon's brow creased and he thought for a moment before responding. 'It does not matter. The battle will be decided at Wagram. Once we have that, the enemy's spirit will break. I know it.'

As he watched MacDonald's men advance into the town Napoleon felt a glow of triumph kindle in his breast. The Grand Army was on the cusp of another great victory. Once Austria was defeated he would make sure that they would never again dare to defy France and her Emperor. But harsh terms in any treaty would not be enough. Napoleon intended to find a way of tying the destiny of both nations together.

A sudden intensification of musket fire from the direction of Wagram broke into his thoughts.

'Sounds like MacDonald has run into some determined opposition,' Berthier commented.

'Archduke Charles must have reinforced Wagram. Even he isn't so stupid that he does not see a danger when it stares him right in the face. Still, it's of no consequence. Eugène will reinforce his leading division in turn. The Austrians will run out of reserves before we do.'

'You are right, of course, sire.'

Napoleon raised his nose and continued to gaze towards Wagram, trying to discern how the battle was going. Then the first Italian casualties began to limp out of the town, making their way back towards the rest of Eugène's corps formed up a short distance ahead of Napoleon and his staff. After the walking wounded came those who were being helped to the rear by their comrades and Napoleon regarded them coldly, always suspicious of unwounded men who fell out of the battle line, for any reason. There were always men who took advantage of a comrade's injury to duck out of the fight. Soon the trickle emerging from the town became a flood; some had even abandoned their weapons in their haste to get away.

'Bloody cowards!' a voice called out from the front rank of the nearest battalion of the Old Guard.

'Silence there!' a sergeant bellowed. 'I'll have the balls of the next man who opens his mouth!'

The veterans stood and watched as hundreds of men from MacDonald's division streamed out of Wagram. The sounds of fighting began to diminish, and a faint cheer rose up in the distance.

Berthier glanced anxiously at his Emperor. 'Sire, it seems that they have broken.'

'Nonsense!'

And yet still they came, running back towards the rest of their division. Napoleon felt his temper rise at the sight of such mass indiscipline and cowardice. 'Why doesn't somebody rally those bastards? Before they disrupt the rest of the corps.' Napoleon craned his neck towards the cluster of standards that marked the position of Prince Eugène and his staff. 'For God's sake do something!'

The remnants of MacDonald's division emerged from Wagram,

closely pursued by the jubilant Austrians, who shot down the fleeing Italians, or bayoneted them on the ground, without a shred of mercy. Mad with fear, the Italians raced towards the safety of their steadier comrades, pushing aside the leading ranks and breaking up the formation. Berthier nodded towards the scattered figures fanning out as they fled from Wagram.

'They're coming this way, sire. We should order the Guard to open ranks and let them through.'

'No,' Napoleon said firmly. 'We cannot afford to let that rabble throw the Guard into chaos. Order the men to fix bayonets.'

'Sire?'

'Do it!' Napoleon snapped. 'At once.'

'Yes, sire.'

As the command was relayed through the battalions of the Old Guard standing in the front rank, the long triangular spikes of steel rasped from their sheaths and clattered into the locked position over the musket muzzles. Napoleon and his officers retired behind the leading battalion and watched as the sergeants gave the order to advance bayonets. A wall of lethal points was presented to the Italians fleeing towards the Guard. At the sight of the threat, and the cold and contemptuous expressions on the faces of the veterans, they turned aside and ran for the gaps between the French units. As the last men of MacDonald's division hurried by, the pursuing Austrians drew up at the sight of fresh enemy units.

With parade-ground precision the Imperial Guard unleashed several volleys that cut the leading enemy wave to shreds. A handful of gallant Austrian officers attempted to rally their men and re-form their ranks to return fire, but they were swiftly struck down and lay with the rest of their men in heaps scattered across the bloody ground. The Austrian soldiers began to fall back, and soon they were running to the shelter of the houses on the edge of Wagram. In the failing light those French battalions that had been disrupted by the men of MacDonald's division had re-formed, and stood ready to advance once again.

'Shall I order Prince Eugène to counter-attack?' asked Berthier.

Napoleon shook his head. 'It's too late. It will be dark within half an hour.' He puffed his cheeks in frustration. 'Call off the attack. Order all formations to fall back and make camp for the night.'

Once the last of the fighting had died away and an uneasy quiet fell across the plain, Napoleon summoned his marshals to his headquarters to discuss his plans for the next day. First, however, the Emperor made a last visit to the bridges to ensure that the supply trains had begun to cross from Lobau island. The pontoon bridges sagged under the weight of the long, heavy artillery caissons, and the lines of wagons carrying ammunition for the men of the infantry and cavalry. The engineers had placed lanterns along the length of each bridge and the flickering glows undulated up and down as the vehicles passed by.

Satisfied that the men of the Grand Army would not be short of supplies for the next day, Napoleon returned to his field headquarters at the church. The cluster of staff officers and escorts that stood around the entrance revealed that his senior officers had already arrived. Dismounting, Napoleon handed the reins to a groom and hurriedly returned the salutes of the men on either side of the church doors before entering the building. The sound of voices came from the altar, and by the light of a handful of candles burning in brackets on the walls Napoleon saw his marshals gathered there. Marshal Bernadotte's voice carried clearly over the subdued talk of the others.

'I'm telling you, it was a wasted opportunity. The Emperor delayed his attack for too long, and he should not have attempted to attack along the whole line.'

'Really?' Davout responded drily. 'And what would you have done in his place, I wonder?'

There was a pause and the other marshals stopped talking. Bernadotte cleared his throat and replied, 'If I had been in command of the army, we would be celebrating a great victory at this moment. I would have used a special manoeuvre that would have defeated the enemy. I would have . . .'

Napoleon decided he had heard enough, and strode towards the altar. As the marshals stood to attention, he waved them down. 'No time for formalities, gentlemen. We have a battle to plan.'

Everyone clustered around the altar and Napoleon stared at the map before them as he gathered his thoughts. 'We have every reason to be pleased with today's achievements, my friends. The Grand Army's crossing of the Danube caught our enemy by complete surprise. All that remains is for us to deliver the final blow and crush Archduke Charles.'

There was a brief silence before Davout cleared his throat and tapped the line of the Russbach river. 'Sire, what is the latest intelligence of Archduke John's position?'

'Our cavalry patrols report no sign of him for twenty miles, south and east of here. He need not concern us.'

'What if Archduke John does reach the battlefield, and attacks our flank?'

'If, if, if.' Napoleon frowned. 'I told you, Archduke John does not concern us. He is not near enough to intervene.'

Davout nodded slightly. 'If you say so, sire.'

Napoleon felt a slight giddiness as he struggled to contain his fraying temper. It had been some days since he had had a proper night's sleep. He had been constantly awake for almost all that time, and his limbs were heavy. It took some effort to think clearly. He rubbed his eyes and then looked round at his officers. 'Gentlemen, you may return to your commands. Berthier will issue your orders during the night.'

After the marshals had left the church Napoleon decided to move his headquarters closer to the decisive sector of the coming battle. Leaving Berthier to arrange for his staff to follow on, Napoleon mounted his horse and rode north of the village of Raasdorf to stop on a small knoll a short distance behind Masséna's right flank. In the darkness, he could just make out the faint outline of columns of men massing in readiness for the coming attack. When the first battalion of the Old Guard arrived to secure the Emperor's new command post, Napoleon had the drummers stack their instruments to make a shelter for him. Then, with a rolled greatcoat for a pillow, he lay down to snatch a few hours' sleep.

Berthier gently shook his shoulder at three in the morning and Napoleon blinked his eyes open, his mind still vague with exhaustion. A guardsman holding a lantern stood behind Berthier.

'What time is it?'

'It's past the third hour, sire.'

Napoleon eased himself up and then rose stiffly to his feet, pressing his fists into the small of the back as he stretched his spine. 'Is the army in position?'

'Yes, sire. All corps headquarters report that they will be ready to attack by four.'

Napoleon glanced round. Even though it was still dark he could make out the vague masses of men slowly forming their ranks. The cool night air was restless with their muted conversation and the shuffling tramp of their boots. He could feel their tense excitement at the prospect of the coming battle. There was some anxiety and fear there too: a certain edge in their voices. Napoleon turned back to Berthier and forced a smile.

'All goes well. Our leading divisions will fall upon the enemy while they're still eating their breakfast, eh?'

Berthier nodded, with a nervous chuckle. 'Yes, sire.'

'I wish I could see Archduke Charles's face when he realises we have stolen a march on him a second time in as many days.'

Napoleon called for some bread and water and sat on a pile of firewood as the army continued to form up around him. Over to the east a faint glow presaged the coming dawn. Moment by moment Napoleon began to see more and more detail of the surrounding countryside, and the tens of thousands of men standing ready. He rose to his feet, brushing the crumbs from his jacket, and took out his watch.

'Ten minutes to four,' he muttered.

There was a sudden thud of cannon fire to the south-east and Napoleon and his staff officers turned to look.

'That comes from the direction of Davout's corps.' Napoleon frowned. 'What the devil is he up to? The orders were for the attack to begin at four. This is the work of some glory-hunter with an itchy trigger finger. Well, whoever it is, he'll have to answer to me when the day is over.' He turned abruptly to Berthier. 'No point in waiting for four now. Send orders to all corps to begin the attack at once.'

'Yes, sire.'

The distant cannon fire quickly swelled into a continuous rumble as the skirmish line began to filter forward towards the enemy. Then, with a deafening crash, the guns of Masséna's corps opened fire on the Austrian centre, pounding the village of Aderklaa, a short distance from Wagram in the blue-hued light of the predawn. As the bombardment continued, Napoleon watched the officers of the leading infantry columns ride up and down their ranks, shouting encouragement to the men.

Berthier appeared at his side with a nervous expression.

'What is it?'

'Sire, a message from Davout. He is under attack.'

'Under attack?'

'Yes, sire. The enemy have fallen on his right flank. He is being driven back.'

'No, Davout must be mistaken. It's probably just a local counter-attack. Nothing more.'

'His messenger says the Austrians are attacking in force, sire.'

'Rubbish!'

Before Napoleon could give further vent to his anger, he was aware of a sudden increase in the sound of gunfire to his right. He turned to stare towards the flank, unable to comprehend the obvious at first. Then he smiled ruefully. 'Who would have guessed it? Archduke Charles has finally learned to take the initiative.' He turned to Berthier. 'The enemy have got their attack in before us.'

Chapter 10

'Tell all corps commanders to hold their positions, until I discover exactly what is going on.' Napoleon listened again to the cannonade to his right and made another decision. 'We must be ready to reinforce Davout. Send the cavalry reserve and all the horse artillery to cover the end of our right flank.'

'Yes, sire. Do you wish me to order Masséna to suspend his bombardment?'

'No. It may help to unsettle the enemy. Let him continue.' Napoleon scratched his chin anxiously for a moment. The situation between the two armies had changed completely. Instead of launching a decisive attack to break the Austrians, the Grand Army was itself under attack. He dared not proceed with his original plan until he had discerned the intentions of Archduke Charles. 'I'm riding over to Davout. I have to see what is happening for myself. The rest of the army is to hold its ground and be ready to receive new orders. One other thing: have the Imperial Guard moved two miles to our right, in case I need to call on them in a hurry.'

Napoleon saw Berthier's brief look of surprise. The order to shift the position of the Guard was a clear admission that the Emperor was anxious about the fate of Davout and his corps.

'What if it is Archduke John?' Berthier asked quietly.

'It isn't.'

Napoleon strode towards the white mare being held by one of his grooms. 'Make a step!'

The groom obediently released the reins and cupped both hands as he bent down. Once Napoleon was hoisted into the saddle he took the reins and called out to Berthier. 'If anything happens, if the enemy make any further movements, send word to me at once!'

'Yes, sire.'

Napoleon turned his horse away and spurred it into a gallop across the heart of the plain towards the Grand Army's right flank. As he rode he was deep in thought and ignored the cheers of the men he passed by. Despite what he had said to Berthier, he feared that the attack on Davout might well herald the arrival of Archduke John. The right flank of the Grand Army would be vulnerable to the Austrian re-inforcements.

Ahead of him clouds of gunpowder smoke billowed across the eastern horizon, blotting out the first rays of the sun. Napoleon raced to the corps headquarters on the edge of the village of Glinzendorf, where he found Marshal Davout's staff hurriedly packing their document chests on to wagons. The crack of muskets and thud of guns came from less than half a mile to the east.

'You!' Napoleon pointed at the nearest staff officer. 'Where is Davout?'

'The marshal has gone to the flank, sire. Some of our units broke when the enemy attacked. Davout went to rally the men.'

Napoleon wheeled his horse round and rode on through the reserve formations of Davout's corps until he passed over a small rise and saw the battle on the flank raging across the landscape before him. The edge of the sun had risen over the rim of the distant hills and by its light Napoleon could see the dark columns of the enemy tramping forward. They had crossed the Russbach and struck Davout's men as the latter were forming up for their own attack. Tiny figures of fleeing soldiers were still spreading about across the plain as they ran from the enemy. The second French line had held firm and was now locked in an exchange of volleys with the Austrians. To the right of the line Napoleon could make out a group of officers, and he spurred his horse on.

As he rode up to Davout the marshal was busy issuing orders to his subordinates to steady their men and hold their ground. Some distance to the rear Napoleon saw the horse artillery and the cavalry he had sent to cover the army's flank.

'Sire.' Davout greeted him with an anxious look. 'I didn't expect to see you here.'

'No?'

'I thought you'd be leading the attack.'

'The attack is delayed until this flank is safe. What is your situation?'

'They caught us by surprise, sire. Their guns opened fire shortly before dawn, breaking up my leading formations. Then they sent their infantry across the river.'

'What about their cavalry?'

'No sign so far, sire. My guess is they are holding them back to mount a pursuit if their infantry break through my line. However,' Davout gestured to the rolling smoke along the firing line, 'we have stopped them, for now.'

Napoleon stared across the smoke and saw more enemy units marching to support their attack. Davout was right. His corps could hold their own. But that was not good enough. Napoleon needed them to retake the initiative and attack.

'Hold your position here, Davout. Once the enemy start giving ground, you follow them up and keep pushing them back. Understand?'

'Yes, sire.'

Napoleon nodded curtly, turned his horse towards the distant batteries of horse artillery and galloped towards them. The commander of the guns, General Nansouty, was as surprised as Davout to see the Emperor so far from the centre of operations and he stammered a greeting before Napoleon cut him short.

'Nansouty, take your guns over to the right of Davout's line. You see that stand of trees along the track there?'

Nansouty followed the direction the Emperor indicated. A mile away some poplars stretched out, shading a country road. 'Yes, sire.'

'That will be your firing line. The range should be good enough for case shot. You are to fire into the enemy flank as they close up on Davout. Keep firing until they break.'

'Yes, sire.'

'There's no time to waste. Go!'

As the horse guns rumbled into a trot, the chains of their traces jingling, Napoleon returned to Davout and his officers. He indicated Nansouty's column thundering out to the flank. 'You'll have some support from that direction soon enough. Make it count.'

'Yes, sire.'

They watched as Nansouty's batteries deployed just in front of the line of trees. The gunners hurriedly loaded the weapons and a moment later there was a flash and puff of smoke as the first gun fired, quickly followed by the others. Napoleon turned his gaze on the approaching Austrian columns and saw several men suddenly smashed aside, then some more, and soon the side of the enemy attack was marked by a trail of bodies. The Austrians' progress slowed as the battered flank battalions halted to re-dress their ranks, filling the gaps, before tramping forward again until they were hit by another salvo from Nansouty's guns.

As the losses mounted Davout's infantry began to counter-attack, advancing between each volley of musket fire. Caught from two directions, the left flank of the enemy attack began to crumble as the more fearful of the men started to give ground, falling back at first and then turning to run. For a moment the Austrian attack wavered, and then fear swept through it like a torrent. Battalion after battalion fell back, and all the time Nansouty's guns poured lethal cones of case shot into their scattering ranks.

Napoleon turned to Davout. 'I'm returning to headquarters. You know what you have to do.'

'Yes, sire.'

'Then good luck, Marshal.'

Napoleon pulled on his reins and turned his mount to race back to the west, while Davout's drummers beat the advance and his soldiers let out a great cheer as they began their pursuit of the retreating Austrians.

The moment he arrived back at the forward command position Napoleon sensed something was wrong, as Berthier hurried towards him with a relieved expression.

'What's happened?'

'Aderklaa is in enemy hands.'

'How is that possible? Bernadotte has the best part of a division in the village. They'd turned the place into a fortress.' Napoleon felt a leaden despair in his guts. 'What happened?'

'Marshal Bernadotte ordered his men to quit the village, sire. He informed me that he was obliged to shorten his battle line by pulling his men back between Masséna and Prince Eugène.'

Napoleon closed his eyes briefly as he took a sharp intake of breath. The village was intended to be the base for his attack on the centre of the Austrian line. Now it had to be retaken, at the cost of the lives of many of his men. Because of Marshal Bernadotte. He breathed out through clenched teeth and opened his eyes.

'Send orders to Bernadotte. He must retake Aderklaa. At any cost.'

'Yes, sire.'

While Berthier hurriedly prepared the orders, Napoleon dismounted. As he landed, a terrible giddiness struck him so that he had to hold on to the pommel of the saddle for fear that he might fall. He raged at his body for this moment of weakness. He knew that he was suffering from exhaustion. Ten years earlier he would have endured this without a thought, and Napoleon realised that age was creeping up on him. He stood a moment until his head had cleared and then walked carefully to the map table and sat down heavily. He snapped his fingers at the nearest orderly. 'I want something to eat. Something to drink. Now.'

'Yes, sire.'

The orderly returned with a lump of hard cheese, some bread and a jug of beer. Napoleon did not care for ale and only sipped at it as he forced himself to eat.

Shortly after six in the morning, Bernadotte's division of Saxon soldiers began their attack on Aderklaa. Napoleon abandoned his meal and called for his horse. Ordering Berthier to accompany him with a small escort of staff officers and lancers from the Imperial Guard, he rode forward to view the action more closely.

Marshal Bernadotte was close to the front, encouraging his Saxon infantry forward as they were met with a withering hail of fire from the Austrian defenders. The enemy had made good use of all the defences prepared by Bernadotte's men only hours before, and fired from behind walls and loopholes in the houses on the edge of the village. Even so, the Saxons advanced steadily, the leading battalions closing ranks as their men were whittled down by enemy bullets. As he watched, Napoleon could see more enemy forces approaching from behind the village. He willed Bernadotte to throw his men forward, before the Austrian defenders could be reinforced.

There was a final flurry of musket fire at point-blank range before the Saxons charged home and attacked the enemy with bayonets. Napoleon raised his telescope, and through the dispersing gunpowder smoke he caught glimpses of the bloody close-quarters skirmishing on the outskirts of the village. A gallant young officer urged his men over a garden wall. Several men went down like skittles as they burst through a gate, straight into the muskets of the men waiting within. Two men were helping a comrade with a shattered leg to the rear. A sergeant smashed down an Austrian soldier with the butt of his musket before reversing the weapon and thrusting his bayonet home into the enemy's throat.

Napoleon lowered his telescope. Bernadotte's attack seemed to be succeeding. Once the village was back in French hands, then the rest of the army's assault on the Austrian line could begin. At last, the morning's crises had been contained. He turned to Berthier.

'The moment Bernadotte confirms that Aderklaa has been cleared of the enemy, send the order to all commands to begin their attacks.'

'Yes, sir.' Berthier nodded, and then glanced past Napoleon with a curious expression.

'What is it now?' Napoleon grumbled, turning round.

The Saxon columns entering the village had halted. On either side, flowing back round them, were the men from the leading battalions. Some of the officers and sergeants tried to stop them, but were quickly thrust aside or knocked down as the Saxon troops fled. Napoleon raised his looking glass again and saw more flashes of gunfire and smoke amid the buildings, then the green of Austrian uniforms, and over them the standard of Austria, waving from side to side. A volley smashed into the leading ranks of one of the Saxon columns stalled just outside the village. That was enough to break their wavering spirit and they too turned and ran. In a short space of time the entire Saxon division was on the run.

A horseman raced out ahead of the fleeing infantry, cutting diagonally across their path and straight towards Napoleon and his entourage.

'That's Bernadotte,' said Berthier, lowering his telescope. 'Must be trying to cut ahead of his men to rally them.'

'Ah, leading from the front, as usual,' Napoleon sneered. 'Even in retreat.'

Berthier glanced at the emperor and spoke quietly. 'Sire, the marshal is a brave man, even if he is inclined to self-aggrandisement.'

'Inclined to it?' Napoleon smiled coldly. 'Why, the man is utterly devoted to himself.'

Berthier seemed about to respond, but thought better of it and clamped his jaw shut instead.

They watched as Bernadotte reined in his mount in front of a group of soldiers and began to berate them, thrusting his arm out towards the village. A handful of those closest to the marshal stopped and regarded him briefly before warily turning aside and hurrying on after their comrades. Bernadotte called after them, then spurred his horse into a gallop to attempt to get in front of his men again. Ahead of him the plain was covered with thousands of his Saxons, the foremost of whom were coming close to Napoleon and his staff. Berthier turned to the commander of the escort and ordered him to send his men forward to screen the Emperor. The lancers walked their mounts up and halted ten paces in front of Napoleon, in a loose line, and lowered the tips of their weapons. The fleeing Saxons began to flow to the sides to avoid the new danger. Marshal Bernadotte stopped a hundred paces away and drew his sword, turning on the Saxons.

'Cowards!' he shouted. 'Stand your ground! Rally to me, damn you!'

He edged over towards the nearest of his men and slapped him across the shoulder with the flat of his sword. 'Stand! Stand with me!'

Napoleon regarded him in a cold fury. Bernadotte had not only failed to stem the tide of his broken division, he had been the cause of the debacle in the first place by abandoning the village and obliging his men to attempt to retake it, with disastrous results. He had endangered not only his men but also the army's battle plan. Taking a sharp intake of breath, Napoleon clicked his tongue and urged his horse forward.

'Berthier, come with me. I want you to witness this.'

They walked their mounts between the lancers and on towards Bernadotte. The moment the marshal saw them, he sheathed his sword, took up his reins and trotted up to Napoleon. He saluted as he reined in.

'Sire, I regret to inform you that the attack has failed.' Bernadotte swept his arm up to indicate the fleeing Saxons. 'As you can see, my men have failed me.'

'Really?' Napoleon folded his hands over the saddle pommel as he glared at Bernadotte in contempt. 'Tell me, Marshal, is this the special manoeuvre you were going to use to force Archduke Charles to lay down his arms?'

Bernadotte's mouth sagged open, and then surprise gave way to anxiety as he recalled his bragging to the other marshals the night before and realised that Napoleon must have heard him. 'Sire, I . . .'

'Silence, Bernadotte!' Napoleon snapped. 'You have failed me for the last time. You are herewith dismissed from command of your corps, which you have handled with such incompetence.'

'Sire, no,' Bernadotte protested, but Napoleon continued.

'You are to leave this battlefield at once. You are to leave the Grand Army before the day is out and return to France. I will decide your fate in due course. Now leave my presence.'

'You cannot do this!' Bernadotte blustered. 'I am a Marshal of France!'

'Not any longer. You are disgraced. I will say it once more. Leave my presence, before I have you arrested and taken to the rear in chains.'

Bernadotte straightened to his full height in his saddle and opened his mouth to speak, but Napoleon turned away and trotted back through his escort to re-join his staff officers. 'Do not permit that man to approach me,' he ordered loudly with a nod back towards Bernadotte. For a moment Bernadotte stared helplessly after Napoleon, then looked to Berthier questioningly. The latter shook his head faintly. With a tap of his heels Bernadotte turned his horse towards the pontoon bridge nearest Essling and walked his mount away, urging it into a trot after a little distance, and then a gallop – so stung by the shame of his treatment at Napoleon's hands that he was compelled to leave the field as swiftly as possible.

Napoleon spared him a brief glance and muttered, 'Good riddance.'

Berthier cleared his throat. 'Is that wise, sire? In the middle of a battle?'

Napoleon nodded. 'I could hardly afford to have Bernadotte fouling things up any more at such a critical moment, wouldn't you agree?' He turned to his chief of staff with a penetrating glare.

'Yes, sire. Of course.'

'Good. Then we shall have to try to struggle on without the tactical brilliance of Bernadotte to help us. Now then, send an order to Masséna. He is to retake Aderklaa immediately. Masséna at least will not fail me.'

'Yes, sire.'

'And let us hope that there will be no further surprises this morning.'

Within the hour, just after the church clock in Aderklaa chimed nine, the tricolour was flying from the church tower. Napoleon had just sent an orderly forward to express his congratulations and gratitude to Masséna when a messenger arrived from General Boudet, commander of the division guarding the army's left flank.

'What is it now?' Napoleon asked wearily.

'General Boudet begs to report that he has been forced back into the Mühlau bridgehead, sire.'

'Forced back?' Napoleon frowned. 'What has happened? Speak up, man!'

'Sire, we are under attack from two army corps. We are a single division. We were driven back.'

Napoleon was about to give vent to his anger at this new frustration when the full significance of the report suddenly hit him. This was part of Archduke Charles's plan. The enemy commander must have intended to envelop both flanks of the Grand Army, but, for whatever reason, the attack on Napoleon's left flank had been delayed until some hours after the attack on his right. It was bad timing for the French, Napoleon reflected bitterly. With Masséna's attention directed towards the recapture of Aderklaa, a gap had opened between the Danube and the left flank of the Grand Army. Now, Archduke Charles was attempting to seize or destroy the bridges that crossed to Lobau island. If he succeeded, then he would sever the supply lines that fed the Grand Army.

'How far have the enemy advanced?'

'When I left General Boudet the Austrians were approaching Essling, sire.'

'Essling!' Berthier turned to Napoleon with a look of horror. Glancing round at his staff officers he saw that the news had stunned them. There was fear in some expressions too. He had to steady their nerves. He must set the example, or all was lost. Forcing a calm expression on to his face, Napoleon addressed Berthier. 'We have two options. We ignore this attack and continue with the plan, and hope that Davout successfully crushes the enemy's left flank. Or we send Masséna to block their advance, hold the bridges and then force them back.'

'But Masséna is already engaged, sire. Besides, even if he could break contact, he would have to march across the face of the Austrians on our left. If they can bring their guns to bear then Masséna's men will be mauled.'

'That's possible,' Napoleon conceded. 'My conviction is that the Austrians will not be able to bring their guns into action fast enough to do much harm to Masséna. Everything will depend on our speed. Firstly we must extricate Masséna and prevent the enemy from trying to maintain contact. The reserve cavalry are to charge the enemy forming to the west of Aderklaa. They must pin them in place long enough for Masséna to reach Essling and form his line there.'

Berthier nodded.

'If Bessières fails, then our centre cannot possibly be held. The Grand Army will be cut in two. Make sure Bessières understands the danger we are in.'

'Yes, sire.'

The situation was critical, Napoleon realised. As at Eylau, his battle line was in danger of shattering under enemy pressure. If the cavalry could relieve the strain on the rest of the army there was some chance that the line could re-form and hold off the enemy. While he watched the cavalry come forward and form lines ready to charge the enemy centre, Napoleon saw movement behind Masséna's corps as a division from Eugène's corps and some batteries of artillery crossed the rear of the formation and formed a line facing the enemy columns advancing along the bank of the Danube. With a nod of approval and relief, Napoleon realised that his stepson had acted on his own initiative to attack the enemy's flank. The crews hurriedly unlimbered their cannon and loaded case shot. Within minutes the first of them was in action, belching flame and smoke as the gun carriage leaped back on the recoil. More guns joined in and soon began to tear holes in the Austrian columns passing by their front. As the enemy soldiers were scythed down, each battalion had to slow to step over the bodies and re-form their ranks, buying vital time for Masséna.

Masséna's formations pulled back, apart from one division left behind to defend Aderklaa. As soon as they were a safe distance from the enemy, the French soldiers turned about and began to quick-march across the plain towards Essling. The race was on, Napoleon realised, his stomach knotted by anxiety. If the enemy captured Essling and moved swiftly enough, they would take the bridges over the Danube. He could see Masséna riding up and down the columns of blue-coated infantry, urging them on. Despite having had little sleep for nearly three days the men stepped out in a lively fashion, kicking up a thin haze of dust from the dry ground.

A series of sharp bugle notes pierced the morning air and Napoleon turned to see the first of Bessières's charges ripple forward towards the Austrian centre. A line of cuirassiers trotted across the plain, breastplates and helmets shimmering as their crests swished from side to side. Half a mile in front of them the nearest units of Austrian infantry began to form squares while the gun crews trained their cannon on the new threat.

'A brave sight,' Napoleon commented. As the horsemen closed on the Austrians and increased their pace to a gentle canter, there seemed to be a pause in the fighting on either side of the battlefield as the two armies watched the wave of men and horses thundering over the flattened grass and crops of the plain. The brief spell was broken as the first of the enemy batteries opened fire, scouring the leading ranks of one of the cuirassier regiments. Scores of men and horses went tumbling over as if they had been tripped, and the succeeding lines had to swerve round them like eddies in a stream. More guns joined in, decimating the ranks of the French heavy cavalry. The bugles sounded again, ordering the charge, and the riders dug their spurs in, extended their sword arms and let out an exuberant cheer that could be clearly heard by Napoleon and his staff officers as they watched.

The Austrian gunners turned away from their weapons and ran for the shelter of the nearest squares, throwing themselves flat at the feet of the kneeling front rank as the latter's muskets came up, ready to fire into the approaching cavalry. The face of the closest Austrian square abruptly disappeared behind a line of gunpowder smoke and several more of the cuirassiers were cut down. The rest plunged on, riding into the smoke.

The squares of the enemy's front line held firm, and the French horsemen were forced to flow round them, fired on as they galloped past. Some tried to lean from the saddles and slash at the Austrians with their swords. Others, more cool-headed, sheathed their blades and drew out their pistols, firing back at point-blank range. All the time, the Frenchmen were steadily cut down and the wounded trickled back across the body-strewn fields towards the French lines. The second wave of horsemen opened ranks to let them pass through, and then moved forward to add their weight to the survivors of the first charge.

'They're being cut to pieces,' Berthier said. 'They can't break those squares.'

'No. But that is not necessary,' Napoleon responded coolly. 'Just as long as they pin those Austrians in place, long enough for us to reorganise our lines.' He looked round at his reserve formations. 'We'll need all the guns from the Imperial Guard. Line them up with Eugène's batteries. That'll give us over a hundred pieces to blast the enemy with. See to it at once.'

As soon as the guns were in place, Bessières withdrew his battered cavalry divisions and there was another brief lull as the enemy squares formed back into lines and then advanced, en masse, towards the waiting Italians of Prince Eugène, and the hurriedly assembled battery defending the centre of the Grand Army. With a thunderous roar the guns tore into the enemy lines, carving bloody paths through the leading ranks. Napoleon could only wonder at their discipline as the Austrians closed up the gaps and continued at a steady pace, muskets sloped.

'My God, Berthier, those men are fearless.'

Berthier nodded, eyes fixed on the terrible carnage being wrought by the continuous blasts of the French guns. Over a thousand men must have been cut down before they came within musket range of the French line. Still their discipline held as their officers gave the order to shoulder their weapons and take aim on the French. Their first volley whirred through the dense smoke hanging in front of the cannon, striking down scores of the gunners. A second volley did as much damage, and there was a brief pause before the first company of Imperial Guardsmen were ordered forward to serve the guns. They slung their muskets over their shoulders and did as they were bid by the artillerymen who had survived the initial volleys.

The two lines stood their ground, the French guns and muskets of Eugène's men answered by the massed volleys of the Austrians. Napoleon watched the mutual slaughter without expression. Thousands had fallen, and all the time more were struck down, falling upon the heaped bodies of their comrades. It was a small mercy that the smoke became so thick that it hid the true scale of the horror from the men locked into a mechanical ritual of firing and reloading as swiftly as they could. The carnage amongst the gun crews in front of Napoleon's position numbed his staff officers, who sat in their saddles and watched the bloody spectacle in silence.

For nearly an hour the firing continued. In that time Napoleon had news that Masséna had managed to form his men up in front of Essling and was starting to push the Austrians back. The cannon on Lobau island were firing across the river into the enemy's flank, and under attack on three sides they could only endure so much before falling back. On the other side of the battlefield Marshal Davout was also steadily pushing the enemy back. Napoleon glanced at his watch and saw that it was almost noon. He turned to Berthier.

'It seems that the enemy's attacks have been checked, and the last of their reserves are committed to the battle. Now is the time for us to mount our own assault, break the Austrian line and defeat the army of Archduke Charles.'

The Emperor's chief of staff looked round the battlefield. 'Sire, we have few enough reserves of our own. Would an attack be prudent?'

'Prudent?' Napoleon shook his head in pity. 'Have you no faith in me, Berthier?'

Berthier lowered his gaze.

Napoleon continued. 'Send orders for the army to attack along the entire line. The main blow will be delivered there.' He raised his hand and pointed to the ground west of Aderklaa.

'Yes, sire. And who is to have that task?'

Napoleon thought a moment. 'General MacDonald. His men are the freshest troops we have on the field.'

'They are also some of the most inexperienced,' Berthier countered.

'Even so, they will win the battle for me. What greater glory could a new soldier ask for? Tell MacDonald to form his men up to attack.'

Hundreds of cannon rumbled along a battle line that stretched from the Danube to Wagram, and then down the line of the Russbach river, a distance of nearly eight miles. Opposite the Austrian centre, General MacDonald led his men forward. Eight thousand of them, their battalions arranged in a huge square formation. As soon as the drums beat the advance, the formation marched forward. The men were sweating freely in their stifling uniforms. The ground before them was a patchwork of trampled fields, strewn with bodies and abandoned equipment from two days of fighting. The dead had begun to corrupt in the midsummer heat and the air was thick with the stench of decaying flesh, blood and shit. Clouds of flies and other insects created a steady drone as they gorged themselves.

Ahead, the leading ranks could see the enemy artillery crews hurriedly repositioning their guns as they spied the new threat through the thinning clouds of gunpowder smoke.

'MacDonald's men will make a fine target, sire,' said Berthier. 'That square of his will be impossible to miss.'

Napoleon did not respond, but just continued to watch intently as the first of the Austrian batteries opened fire. The range was long, and they had loaded the guns with roundshot. The heavy iron balls grounded with a puff of dry soil a short distance in front of the leading battalion before ricocheting through the ranks, mowing down every soldier in their path. More guns opened up and MacDonald's division began to lose scores of men with each minute that passed. Their progress across the plain was marked by a bloody trail of dead and wounded. As they came within range of case shot the nearest guns unleashed a devastating hail that wreaked even more slaughter on the diminishing French ranks.

Berthier shook his head in wonder. 'My God, they can't take much more of this.'

Napoleon sucked in a breath through his teeth. 'Pray that they do.'

The square staggered on, coming in range of the Austrian skirmishers, who added their fire to the cannon. MacDonald had already lost half his men, Napoleon estimated, yet still they advanced into the teeth of the enemy's cannon and muskets. At last the survivors were close enough to the enemy line to fire their first volley in reply. The leading battalions deployed, loaded and raised their muskets, and fired at the nearest enemy guns and infantry formations. Napoleon felt a moment of blissful vengeance as the distant figures of Austrian artillerymen were cut down beside their guns.

MacDonald ordered the square to advance again and it pressed on, pausing to fire another volley before bayonets were fixed and they charged into the line of Austrian infantry waiting beyond.

The terrible tension of waiting for the division to get into action gave way to anxiety that MacDonald's men had suffered too many casualties to carry the day. Napoleon nodded to himself as he made a decision. 'Berthier, we need every available man to support MacDonald! We must send forward what is left of Eugène's reserves, and also the Imperial Guard.'

Berthier raised his eyebrows. 'But sire, then we will have no reserves left. Nothing to face Archduke John should he reach the field.'

Napoleon gestured towards the two battalions assigned to guard the headquarters. 'That will be our reserve. Send them to cover our right, and order the rest forward to save MacDonald, before it is too late.'

As the reinforcements swiftly advanced over the torn-up plain, Napoleon read through the latest reports from the other sectors of the battlefield. Davout and Masséna were driving back the Austrian flanks and Wagram had been taken by Prince Eugène and his men. Satisfied that the battle was tilting in his favour, he turned his attention back to the centre. With the aid of the fresh troops Napoleon had sent him, MacDonald was pushing steadily through the Austrian centre. Both sides were exchanging volleys at point-blank range and bodies lay in heaps across the battlefield. The arrival of the Imperial Guard proved to be decisive. After delivering one volley, they charged the Austrian line. There was a brief and bitter struggle and then the enemy broke, thousands of their men scrambling away towards the shelter of the hills running along the edge of the plain to the north.

At long last the Austrian army had been broken in two.

Napoleon stared at the fleeing enemy, too exhausted and too bitter at the cost of the battle to feel any triumph. As the enemy began to pull back the French battalions did not pursue them. The men's strength had gone. The heat of the two days and the numbing slaughter they had witnessed meant that they had reached the end of their endurance. There was nothing further that could be done with them, Napoleon realised. Any pursuit of the Austrians was out of the question, especially with Archduke John's army at large. He could only sit on his horse and watch the enemy make their escape, all the while burning with frustration.

Berthier spoke tonelessly. 'A victory then. My congratulations, sire.'

'Victory?' Napoleon blinked his aching eyes and scanned a landscape of shattered buildings, heaps of bodies and the mangled remains of those caught by the full blast of artillery fire. Amid the carnage, the survivors stood, or sat, in a daze, some drinking from their canteens as they slaked their day-long thirst. 'If this is victory, then I wonder can France ever afford such a victory again?'

Chapter 11

Schönbrunn, 23 October 1809

A chill wind was blowing across the parade ground outside the yellow and cream walls of the palace, a short distance from Vienna. Overhead the sky was grey and threatened rain. Even so, the display had attracted the usual crowd of people from the city who had paid for tickets to view the spectacle of the Imperial Guard marching in formation, to the tunes struck up by their bandsmen. Some had come to see Napoleon, curious to gaze upon the great man of the day. For most it was the only chance they had to see him since the French Emperor rarely ventured out in public, and then only to attend the opera or theatre, where he sat to the rear of his private box, giving the audience no more than an occasional glimpse of him.

Napoleon stood on the steps of the parade ground, watching his troops march past. It was ten days since the Austrians had finally signed a peace treaty with France. The negotiations had dragged on for months following the battle at Wagram. Emperor Francis had cavilled over every point, playing for time. Napoleon decided that Austria had to be punished, and the eventual agreement forced Emperor Francis to hand portions of his land to France, the Grand Duchy of Warsaw, Bavaria and Russia. Emperor Francis was also required to recognise Joseph as the legitimate King of Spain and to restrict the size of the Austrian army to no more than one hundred and fifty thousand men.

That, Napoleon smiled to himself, had done much to diminish any future threat that might be posed by Austria. As a final reminder to Emperor Francis of the new balance of power that existed between Austria and France, Napoleon had delayed his withdrawal from Vienna. Today's parade was to be one of the last reviews before the Grand Army began its march back to the Rhine.

The last company of guardsmen stamped to a halt at the end of the line and then a silence fell across the parade ground as Napoleon surveyed the men before him. Four regiments of the Old Guard, the finest soldiers in his army. He gazed fondly at them, even though he kept his severe expression fixed. Many of these men had fought for him at Marengo and Austerlitz. To join their ranks a man had to have served a minimum of five years and fought in two campaigns. That was before they were even considered for selection. The men stared directly ahead, many sporting extravagant moustaches and beards. Their uniforms were clean, their white cross-straps a brilliant white, and their buttons gleamed, due to long hours of careful application of tripoli powder. Their tall bearskin hats and proud bearing made the men seem larger than other soldiers and Napoleon knew that their appearance alone on the battlefield was enough to unsettle an enemy. When they went into action they were utterly fearless and ferocious and only the finest of their foes ever dared to hold their ground against the Imperial Guard.

Napoleon slowly paced down the stairs, followed by Berthier and General Rapp, the commander of the brigade being reviewed. Approaching the guardsmen, Napoleon began his inspection as he strode along each line, occasionally stopping to exchange a word with one of the veterans, conspicuous thanks to the chevrons on their sleeves denoting the number of campaigns they had fought in.

Once the inspection was over, Napoleon returned to the stairs and began to award the promotions, decorations and prizes to each of the recipients called out from the ranks. Each man approached the Emperor smartly, stood to attention while his citation was bellowed out by General Rapp, and then received the appropriate reward, together with the profuse congratulations of his Emperor. But all the time, Napoleon's mind flitted from one preoccupation to another.

Foremost in his mind was the coming confrontation with the Empress Josephine. His heart felt heavy with remorse at what he must do when he returned to Paris. France needed an heir to the throne. Only royal blood would do, since it would make it impossible for rival rulers to deny that a child of Napoleon lacked the breeding required to rule as the equal of any other emperor, king or tsar. Even though the logic of his decision to divorce Josephine was unassailable, still he felt the sour grief of being forced to act contrary to his will. Despite all the infidelities on both sides, and his frequent despair over her profligacy, Napoleon loved her as no other. It was as if their hearts and minds were bound together, and the prospect of her enforced rejection crushed almost any notion of pleasure in his life.

Once the last of the guardsmen had received his award, General Rapp ordered the soldiers to shoulder their muskets and then, as the band struck up, the battalions marched off the parade ground. As the last company passed by the civilian sightseers began to spill out across the parade ground. Napoleon turned to Berthier.

'How are preparations for the army's departure progressing?'

'The last two corps are ready to march. The imperial baggage train is packed and can leave at any time. There's only one issue to resolve.' Berthier paused. 'That's the sale of surplus supplies, ammunition and equipment we captured from the Austrians.'

'What's the problem?'

'The Austrians refuse to pay the price agreed when we signed the treaty.'

'What are they saying?'

'They'll pay thirty million francs, sire.'

Napoleon shook his head with a dry laugh. 'Thirty million! They must think me a fool. No, the price is fifty million, as we agreed. If they don't pay up then tell that fool, Prince Metternich, that we will not leave Vienna until they do.' Napoleon's resolve hardened even as he spoke and he thrust a finger into Berthier's chest. 'You also tell him that if we are not paid in full by the end of the year then I will regard the treaty as having been broken, and that means war. You tell him that!'

'Yes, sire. As you wish.'

'Austrian bastards,' Napoleon hissed through gritted teeth. 'They brought this war on themselves. Emperor Francis is in no position to change the peace terms. I will bring them to heel, whatever it takes.'

He turned away and made his way down the steps to head back across the parade ground to his quarters in the palace. As he did so a young man stepped forward from the milling crowd of awed sightseers and strode towards him. Napoleon noticed him at the last moment and drew up with a scowl.

'What's this?'

'Sire,' the man said, eyes wide and staring. 'I bring you a petition from all Germans.'

Napoleon glanced over the youth. He was blond-haired, blue-eyed, and broad-shouldered beneath his plain black coat. Napoleon shook his head. 'You must take it to my clerks. They deal with such matters. Now, then, if you would step away.'

'No, sire. You will deal with it now!'

The youth lurched forward. There was a dull gleam and General Rapp cried out, 'Sire! He has a knife!'

Napoleon stared at the youth, frozen where he stood. Then Berthier grabbed his arm and pulled him back, stepping in between his Emperor and the youth. There was a blur of blue uniform and gold lace as Rapp threw himself at the assassin and both crashed down on to the parade ground. Rapp clasped both hands around the wrist of the young man's knife hand and bellowed, 'Guards! On me! On me!'

The soldiers who had stood guard on the staircase came dashing over. The youth balled his free hand into a fist and smashed it into Rapp's face, at the same time kicking out at the general with his feet. But Rapp rolled his weight over the youth's chest, pinning him down as he held the weapon hand away from them both. A moment later the guardsmen reached the spot, and while one forced the youth's hand open and took away the knife, the others dragged him to his feet. General Rapp rose to his feet, hatless and breathing heavily as he glared at the youth.

Napoleon pressed Berthier aside and took a step towards the German. 'You mean to kill me.'

'Yes!' the assassin shot back.

Napoleon shook his head. 'Why?'

'You are a tyrant. Enemy of liberty. Enemy of the German people.'

'Enough of that claptrap!' roared Rapp as he threw a punch into the youth's midriff. The young man doubled over, as far as the soldiers holding him allowed, and groaned as he gasped for breath. Rapp turned to Napoleon. 'What shall I do with him, sire?'

Napoleon stared at the youth for a moment, still stunned by the suddenness and surprise of the attack. It was not the first time that someone had tried to kill him, but in the past his would-be assassins had used bombs, poisons and other methods of the coward. This was different. A direct attack on him with a knife, by an assailant little more than a boy who had no hope of escape whether he succeeded or failed in his attempt.

Napoleon cleared his throat nervously. 'Take him away. Have him questioned. Find out who else is involved in this conspiracy. They will all be made to pay dearly for it.'

Rapp nodded, and gestured to the guardsmen. 'You four, take him to the cellars and wait for me there. The rest, stay close to the Emperor. If anyone else comes too close before you reach the palace, then shoot 'em.'

Napoleon set off, his guardsmen closed up around him, cautiously watching the civilians milling around the parade ground. Those who had witnessed the assassination attempt looked on in silence as the French Emperor and his escort hurried by, and then turned their attention to General Rapp and his small party as they dragged the young man away.

'Death to tyrants!' the youth cried out. 'Death to Napoleon!'

Rapp leaped to his side and smashed his fist into his jaw, silencing him.

A short distance away, Napoleon glanced back at his assailant, and then noticed that his hands were trembling. With an angry frown he clasped them together behind his back and strode towards the palace.

Late in the evening Napoleon descended into the cellars of the palace. General Rapp had taken his prisoner to one of the empty storerooms beneath a little-used section of the palace. There Napoleon found him, with three burly sergeants of the Old Guard, stripped to the waist as they sat on stools around the youth, who was tied into a chair. His coat had been removed, and his white shirt and breeches were spattered with his blood. Rapp's men had beaten him severely about the face, and by the light of a lantern hanging from a beam above him Napoleon could not recognise the features of the man who had tried to kill him earlier in the day. His lips were cut and swollen, his nose was broken and bloody and his forehead was grazed and cut in places.

Rapp and the sergeants rose to their feet as their Emperor crossed the room towards them, his footsteps echoing off the cold flagstones.

'Well? What have you got from him?'

'Not much, sire.' Rapp pursed his lips. 'My boys had to work him over before we began to loosen his tongue.'

'So I can see.'

'He says his name is Friedrich Staps. He's from Saxony.'

'Who sent him to kill me?'

Rapp shrugged. 'He says he was acting by himself.'

'A likely story!' Napoleon snorted. 'Someone sent him. Someone who was too cowardly to face me in person. This boy must have had accomplices. I must have their names.'

'He denied there was anyone else, sire.'

'Then he's lying.'

'I don't think so, sire. He was questioned for over eight hours. If he was trying to hide anything he would have said something by now that would have given the truth away.' Rapp paused and regarded the youth frankly. 'He stuck to his story through it all. He says he acted alone.'

'I see,' Napoleon mused. 'What else did he say?'

'He is a clerk in a trading company. He believes in a greater union of the German states, and he accuses you of standing in the way of the destiny of the German people.'

'What about his family? Did he confess any links to the Prussian court?'

'Hardly, sire. Staps says that his father is a parson.'

'Then he did a bad job of teaching his son the ten commandments.' Napoleon stood in front of the youth and shook his head slowly. 'Whatever happened to "Thou shalt not kill", eh?'

Staps swallowed the blood in his mouth and raised his head to look squarely at the French Emperor. 'You tell me, sire. After all, I have attempted to kill one man. You have killed tens of thousands.'

Napoleon was silent for a moment. 'That is different. That is war. What you tried to do was murder.'

'That's a matter of perspective,' Staps replied.

'Really?' Napoleon smiled faintly. His curiosity was aroused by the young Saxon. He turned to Rapp. 'Is he securely bound?'

'Yes, sire. I checked his bonds myself.'

'Then I want your men to wait outside. You stay.'

'Yes, sire.'

The sergeants picked up their jackets and bowed their heads before marching across the room to the door of the storeroom. Napoleon waited until the door had closed behind them and then took one of the stools and dragged it round and sat directly in front of Staps. General Rapp stood to one side, behind the prisoner, ready to intervene should he try anything, even tightly bound as he was.

Napoleon stretched his shoulders, easing the strain, and then leaned forward, resting his elbows on his thighs and clasping his fingers together. 'Young man, surely you can see that what you attempted was evil. Not only evil, but irrational. You could not hope to escape.'

'I was not concerned by that,' Staps replied, licking his lips and wincing at the pain this provoked. 'I merely wanted to kill you. Nothing else mattered.'

'That is absurd,' Napoleon countered. 'You were prepared to commit suicide?'

'I am still alive.'

'For now. But not for much longer.' Napoleon tilted his head slightly to get a better view of Staps's eyes. 'You must know that you face execution for what you tried to do.'

Staps shrugged. 'Of course. I expect nothing less.'

'Then why do it? Suicide is not the act of a sane man.'

'I beg to disagree, sire.' Staps eased himself up, straightening his back so he could face the Emperor squarely. 'I did not happen upon this course of action by chance. I am not inspired by madness. I believe that the German people must be freed from the shackles imposed on them by you. I considered how best this might be achieved. Clearly one man alone cannot take on an empire and win. However, one man might take on an emperor alone, and vanquish him.'

'And if you had murdered me, do you think that would have won you freedom for your people?' Napoleon shook his head. 'If I had been killed, France would still hold sway over your German states.'

Staps smiled. 'It seems to me that France is a monster with but one head. Remove that and the beast is beaten.'

'You flatter me.'

'No. I see things clearly enough, sire. You are a great man. Like all tyrants. That is why killing you would have changed everything.'

'But you did not kill me. Nothing has changed, and you have wasted your life without purpose.'

'Perhaps. But there is a chance that my death might inspire others.'

'Inspire them to suicidal attacks?' Napoleon laughed drily. 'What makes you think that I have not learned from today's attempt? In future it will be impossible for a man like you to get close to me.'

'Impossible?' Staps pursed his swollen lips. 'Not impossible. Only more difficult. In time, another man . . .' he paused and smiled faintly, 'or woman will get close enough to you to make another attempt, and succeed where I failed. The odds are against you in the long run, sire. Surely you must see that?'

'Supposing it is not a question of odds, but of fate,' Napoleon countered. 'Some men are chosen by fate for greatness, and fate alone decides when their time is over.'

'If you believe that, then what need have you of bodyguards? I suspect that you have no wish to put it to the test.' Staps looked at the Emperor shrewdly. 'There's something else that worries you, sire.'

'Oh?'

'The fear that stalks all great men. You believe in your greatness, and the thought that a man of no consequence, such as I, could put an end to your life is an effrontery to your sense of that greatness.'

Napoleon stared at him fixedly for a moment, and Staps stared back, unblinking. After a moment Napoleon smiled and patted the young man on the knee. 'There's some truth in what you say. Yet now it is you who diminish yourself.'

'Me?'

'My dear Staps, you are no common man. What you did took great courage. I recognise that. Surely such dedication to your cause must be most uncommon amongst your kind.'

Staps narrowed his eyes momentarily. 'My kind?'

'Those who believe as you do. The comrades who share your beliefs and work with you to oppose me.'

Staps shook his head wearily. 'I told your interrogators, there is no one else. What I did, I did alone.'

'But you say you did it for all Germans?'

'One man may act for the benefit of all.'

'But surely it is arrogant for you to assume you know what is of benefit to all? That is if you are speaking the truth about acting alone.'

'It is no more arrogant for me to assume that than for you to assume that you rule for the benefit of your subjects, and all those who live under the sway of France. Who is to say that one man knows better than another, be he an emperor or a humble clerk?'

Rapp stirred at the last remark and bunched his fists as he took a step towards the prisoner. Napoleon glanced at him and waved him away, then leaned back and thought for a moment.

'If I accept that you did act alone, now that you have been apprehended the threat to me has ended. Provided that I do not make a martyr of you.'

Staps looked at Napoleon curiously. 'You would let me live?'

'I could,' Napoleon replied. 'Provided that you made a public apology for your act.'

'An apology?'

'You would have to admit that what you did was wrong. An act of temporary madness perhaps. And now you have seen things more clearly you realise that your action was foolhardy and without just cause. If you would say that in public then I would spare your life and have you returned to your home to live out your life in peace.'

Staps laughed, then winced and coughed, spraying flecks of blood across Napoleon's breeches. A minute passed before the pain subsided enough for him to speak again. 'And you would make an example of me. Living proof of your magnanimity.'

'Why not? That's what it is,' Napoleon replied tersely. 'I offer you life.'

'You offer me shame, sire. You offer me the coward's way out. I would rather die.'

'Then you are a fool indeed. Where is the logic in choosing death over life?'

'I did not act from logic, sire, but principle. Where is the value of principle if a man refuses to place his faith in it, come what may?'

Napoleon raised his hands. 'Enough!' He paused and took a deep breath before he continued in as calm a tone as he could manage. 'Staps, I must tell you that you have impressed me. You have as much courage as the bravest of my soldiers. I do not want to put an end to a life with as much promise as yours. It would be a waste. All I require is an apology. Here and now. I will not even ask for you to make it in public. Then you can return to your home.'

'Sire, I am honour bound to tell you that I cannot return home. Not while you live. I do not want your pardon. I only regret having failed in my attempt to kill you.'

'Then you leave me no choice,' Napoleon replied in frustration. 'I must have you executed. But know this, it is by your will that you shall die. If you truly desire death, then death you shall have.'

Staps leaned forward with an earnest expression and a fierce light burned in his eyes. 'Sire, you must believe that I want to live. I want to live, and find love, and marry and have children, and die in peaceful old age. As do other men. I can assure you I choose death as a last resort.'

'Then choose life instead, you young fool! I offer it to you, here and now. What more would you have of me?'

Staps leaned back in his chair and was silent a moment before he continued in a flat tone. 'I will choose life, if you promise to free the German states. If you swear, by all that is holy to you, to end your wars in Europe.' Staps raised his chin. 'If you agree to that, then I will accept your pardon.'

Napoleon's jaw sagged for an instant before he recovered from the young man's hubris. 'You will accept my pardon? Well, that's uncommonly generous of you, I must say.' He turned to Rapp and asked rhetorically, 'Did you hear that?'

'I heard, sire. Obviously my lads have failed to beat the spirit out of him. Let me try to teach him some manners, sire.'

'What is the point? He is mad. Quite mad.'

Staps shook his head. 'Not mad, sire. What other reasonable course of action is left to a man when he is opposed by such might as you command? I have committed my life to ending yours. Nothing will change that.'

Napoleon sat back and stroked his cheek wearily. He could not help admiring the strength of the young man's convictions, however much he disagreed with them. The youth was attractive and obviously thoughtful and intelligent. Not so intelligent, however, that he could be swayed by Napoleon's offer to spare him. It was a tragedy that the qualities that most recommended him were the very ones that now condemned him. Napoleon sighed.

'Very well, take him away. Have him put in a secure cell and kept under watch. Make sure that he is made comfortable and fed well.'

Rapp looked surprised for an instant before he shrugged and stepped forward to haul the youth to his feet. Grasping him by the arm, the French officer marched him to the door, opened it and thrust him into the hands of the waiting sergeants. When the orders had been given he shut the door and returned to his Emperor, who was staring at the blood-spattered paving slabs under the chair that Staps had been sitting on. At length he looked up at the general.

'Do you believe him?'

'Sire?'

'That he was acting alone?'

'I don't know, sire. He says he was.'

Napoleon thought for a moment. 'I cannot believe it. There are other conspirators . . . there must be. Staps is the product of all those secret societies that I am told infest the German states. Men like him are under the influence of religious zealots and political schemers. They make young men into assassins and fill their heads with false ideologies. But how can we fight against false ideas? They cannot be destroyed by cannon balls.'

Rapp pursed his lips. 'Force has its uses in keeping people under control, sire.'

'I know that. But it is at best an expedient. We must rule their minds and their hearts if we are to rule without living on the whim of maniacs like Staps.'

'Yes, sire.'

Napoleon stared at the empty chair. He had escaped the knife of an assassin this time, but how many more men like Staps were out there, waiting for their opportunity? If he died now, then that would be an end to any dream of a new dynasty of Bonapartes. The need for an heir was more pressing than ever and Napoleon steeled his heart to do what was necessary the moment he returned to Paris.

'Sire?'

'What is it?'

'What are your orders concerning the prisoner? How long do you want him held?'

'Held?' Napoleon frowned. 'I don't want him held. Draw up the paperwork for a military court. Have him charged, and convicted, of attempted murder.'

Rapp nodded. 'Yes, sire. I'll select the necessary officers in the morning. We can try him straight away.'

'There's no need for that. We just need the appearance of a fair trial. Draft the paperwork as soon as you can.' Napoleon rose from his stool and stretched. 'Meanwhile, Staps is to be shot. At dawn. Find him an unmarked grave and have the body covered in quicklime. Is that clear?'

'Yes, sire.'

'I will not permit Friedrich Staps to become a martyr, or his grave to become a shrine. He is to be obliterated. Erased from history.'

Chapter 12

Fontainebleau, December 1810

'Her imperial majesty is not happy with the new arrangements,' Baron Bausset muttered as he escorted Napoleon up the steps to the chateau. A light rain fell from leaden skies and a keen breeze drove it into the faces of the soldiers and household staff who had formed up to greet the emperor. He had returned from Austria shortly before noon, tired and cold after several days in his carriage. He had sent word to Bausset a few weeks before that all the staircases and doors that linked his apartments with those of the Empress were to be sealed up. In view of the coming confrontation, Napoleon had no wish to provide Josephine with any more access to him than possible. He well knew the hold she had over him. Over the next few weeks he must be strong. He must resist her tears and her pleas. For the good of France, he reminded himself.

Bausset cleared his throat as they reached the top of the curved staircase that led to the entrance. 'Sire, the Empress has asked me repeatedly for an explanation for blocking the access between her apartments and yours.'

'I can imagine,' Napoleon replied. 'What have you told her?'

'I told her that I was only obeying your orders and had not been informed of the reasons behind your instructions.'

'Good.'

As he entered the hall, Napoleon paused and undid the buttons of his coat and then eased his shoulders as a footman stepped forward and helped slip it from his back. Napoleon removed his hat and thrust it towards the man as he continued addressing Bausset.

'Does she know I have returned?'

Bausset paused a moment before replying. 'I received notice of your arrival some two hours ago, sire. As you instructed, the staff were told not to say anything to her imperial majesty.'

'Some hope,' Napoleon sniffed. 'She's bound to have a few of them in her pocket. Now then, I need some soup, and some coffee. Send them to my office. Has the fire been made up?'

'Of course, sire.'

'I sent orders to Paris for despatches to be sent here. I want them brought to me the moment they arrive.'

'Yes, sire.'

'Very well, then.' Napoleon waved Bausset away, but before he could turn towards the wing of the chateau where his office was situated, there was a shrill cry of delight from the top of the staircase in the hall.

'My darling! My dearest Napoleon!'

He looked up and saw Josephine smiling as she clasped the rail in her hand and leaned slightly forward. Even at this distance Napoleon could see her small stained teeth clearly and could not help making an unflattering contrast with the neat, white smile of Marie Walewska, waiting to be reunited with him in the suite of rooms that had been provided for her at the Tuileries. As soon as he made the comparison Napoleon felt the sickening burden of guilt and betrayal settle on his heart. He felt a flicker of self-loathing, then swiftly upbraided himself. There was no need to blame himself for anything. His duty to his country must come before personal feelings. Josephine would understand that. After all, she had hardly comported herself as the wife of the most powerful man in Europe should do. Her profligacy was a public scandal, and her past affairs had embarrassed him with a shame that still smouldered in his breast. He swallowed nervously and pressed his lips together in a thin, cold expression as he stared back at his wife.

A flicker of concern crossed her face, then Josephine ran down the stairs, her slippered feet pattering lightly on the steps as she descended. Napoleon watched her with a sense of dread and then hardened his heart as he drew himself up and folded his hands behind his back. She hurried across the hall and folded her arms around his shoulders as she kissed him on the cheek.

'My love, I have missed you,' she whispered into his ear, and then froze, sensing the unyielding stillness of his body. She drew back with a slight frown and stared into his eyes. 'My dear, what is the matter with you? Have you no kiss, no embrace for your wife?'

'Later,' Napoleon said harshly. 'I have work to attend to. If I have time, we may talk later. Excuse me.'

Without a kiss, or any other sign of affection, the Emperor turned away and walked towards his suite of offices. He did not falter or look back once, knowing that she would be gazing after him in that forlorn, helpless manner that she knew would melt his heart. When he reached the study, Napoleon ordered the footman standing outside to admit no one, on any pretext, unless they were carrying a bowl of soup. He closed the door firmly behind him and immediately crossed to his desk. A small pile of documents and letters lay on a salver, and with a heavy sigh Napoleon tried to banish all thought of Josephine from his mind as he slumped into his chair and began to deal with the correspondence.

Breaking the seal of the first document, he opened it out and glanced over the contents. It was from a senior treasury official requesting an interview to discuss the looming monetary crisis. Napoleon was aware that France's coffers were running low, but had hoped that the new peace would restore the flow of taxes and other revenue. However, the treasury reported that the economy was suffering from the trade embargo with England, which was affecting the whole continent. That, coupled with the costs of maintaining the armies in Spain, was bleeding France dry. Napoleon penned a few hurried comments on the document and moved on to the next, a reply from his brother, King Louis of Holland, to his request for Dutch reinforcements to be sent to Spain. Louis claimed to be fearful that his subjects might rise in revolt if he attempted to send troops to the aid of King Joseph. To add to his grievances, he claimed that he could not enforce the embargo on English trade for the same reasons.

'Fool,' Napoleon muttered as he scribbled a terse response at the bottom of his brother's letter. 'Does he not understand that unless we break England, no Bonaparte is safe on his throne?'

The next letter contained a politely worded request that the Emperor might be kind enough to settle the debt owed by Josephine to a Parisian dressmaker. Napoleon's eyes widened at the sum she owed. Over ten thousand francs. He glared at the letter, then thrust it to one side.

There was a soft click as the door opened and a servant entered the room bearing a tray with a small steaming bowl, some bread, a small decanter of watered wine and a glass.

'Here, on the desk.' Napoleon tapped the gleaming wooden surface to his right. The servant crossed the room and carefully lowered the tray before bowing his head and backing away. Napoleon finished his notes and set the pen down. The pleasant odour of onion soup curled into his nostrils, and he eased the tray across the desk in front of him. Outside the rain rattled against the window panes in an irregular rhythm as the wind moaned over the chateau. Taking up the spoon he began to sip carefully, his mind soon moving back to the most pressing of the issues weighing on his mind – the matter of how to break the news to Josephine.

★ ★ ★

A week later Napoleon ate alone with his wife. The last of the dinner service had been cleared away, with most of the food lying untouched on the fine chinaware. At length a steward served them coffee and then retired from the small salon where the Emperor and Empress had taken their supper. It was bitterly cold outside and night had long since closed over the chateau. Hardly a word had been spoken over the meal, beyond mere pleasantries. Napoleon's stomach was too knotted with anxiety to allow him to eat and he had had to force himself to eat a few mouthfuls of chicken before poking at the rest of the meal and finally laying aside his cutlery and clicking his fingers for the servants to clear the table.

'It will soon be Christmas,' Josephine observed at length.

'Yes.'

Josephine raised her cup and sipped carefully. 'Nothing has been arranged.'

'No.'

'Well, don't you think we should organise an event of some kind? A celebration?'

Napoleon looked at her, feeling sick at the imminence of his betrayal. 'There will be nothing for us to celebrate.'

'What?' Josephine lowered her cup slightly. 'Why do you say that? What is wrong, my love? You have been so cold with me from the moment you returned.'

'I . . . I have something to tell you.' Napoleon swallowed nervously and found that he could not continue. Josephine saw the pained look in his face and began to rise from her chair to come and comfort him. 'Sit down,' he ordered. Then, aware of the harshness of his tone, he forced himself to soften his voice. 'Please, sit, my love.'

After a moment, she did as she was told and stared back at him. 'What is it? Tell me.'

There was no longer any means of avoiding the moment and Napoleon took a calming breath before he spoke. 'I must divorce you.'

'What?'

'I have to divorce you. I must have an heir. So I must find a new wife.'

She stared at him and then laughed nervously. 'You are joking. That's it. You are teasing me.'

'No. It's true.' Napoleon felt the relief begin to flow through his body now that he could finally explain the situation. 'This is not about you and me, it is about France. I love you, I always have. But we must be brave and put the needs of our people before our own.' He watched her dumbstruck expression closely. 'Do you understand?'

Josephine shook her head faintly, her lips trembling. 'No . . . No . . .'

'I wish, with every fibre in my body, that we could avoid this situation,' Napoleon continued gently. 'But it has to be done.'

Josephine clenched her fists. 'Don't. Please don't.'

'I have to. If we are to be divorced then we cannot be together. It would be unseemly.'

'Don't do this, my darling.' Her voice quavered. 'I beg you.'

'It has already been done. The senate ratified the decree earlier today. I will announce it in Paris tomorrow, and we will both sign the formal agreement before the imperial court. It is best for it all to be done as swiftly as possible.' Napoleon smiled. 'To ease our suffering, you understand.'

'NO! NO! NO!' Josephine screamed, sweeping her arm out across the table, knocking her coffee cup and saucer flying towards the fireplace, where it exploded into fragments with a sharp crash. She rose to her feet and lurched round the table towards him, then stopped and stared at him, eyes wild.

'NO!' She suddenly raised her fist and Napoleon instinctively flinched. Instead of striking him, she struck her breast, hard, again and again.

'Don't do that!' Napoleon stretched a hand towards her. 'Please don't, my love.'

A sob racked her body, and then her legs gave way and she fell on to the thick rug underneath the table and curled up on the floor as she screamed and wept. Napoleon stared at her for a moment, knowing that he must not weaken this time. Her tears had undone his anger many times in the past, and caused him to change his mind. But not this time, he told himself. He pushed his chair back and stood over her.

'Get up, Josephine. Stop crying.'

She shook her head and continued sobbing, adding a grief-stricken shriek every now and then as Napoleon stared at her, helpless as pity and irritation vied to control his thoughts. Behind him the door opened and there was a footman, holding a lamp, and beside him stood Baron Bausset.

'Sire? I heard cries. Is anything the matter?'

Napoleon gestured towards Josephine. 'What do you think? Come here, I need your help.'

'Yes, sire.'

As Bausset hurried across to the table, Josephine reached out and grasped Napoleon's leg. 'Help me up,' she muttered. 'I don't want to be seen like this.'

He leaned down and grasped her shoulder, slipping the other hand round her waist as he eased her on to her feet. Her eyes were puffy and red, her cheeks streaked with tears, and her bottom lip trembled. Napoleon felt a terrible guilt burning in his veins and a compulsion to hold her in his arms. Then Bausset arrived at his side and the spell was broken.

'Here, you help the Empress.' Napoleon tried to pull himself free but Josephine clung to his arm desperately.

'Don't leave me!'

'I'm not leaving you. I'll help you to your apartments.'

Her eyes glittered for an instant. 'Yes. That would be kind of you.'

She eased her grip and Napoleon slipped free, taking a quick pace back. 'Here, Bausset, you hold the Empress. Tightly, don't let her fall. I'll light the way.'

Bausset quickly stepped in and took his place. Josephine forced a smile and thanked the imperial official frostily as her husband carefully took a candle from the holder on the table. Cupping his spare hand round the flame to shield it from any draught, he led the way to the door. With Bausset supporting the Empress, the small party made their way to a small rear staircase and began climbing the steps to Josephine's apartments on the floor above. As they reached the top step she suddenly went limp in Bausset's arms and started weeping again.

'Don't do it, Napoleon. For pity's sake don't divorce me.'

Napoleon turned round. 'Quiet!' he hissed. 'Bausset, for God's sake, keep a firm grip on her.'

With Bausset half carrying and half dragging Josephine, the three of them made their way down the corridor to the door of her sleeping chamber. Napoleon opened the door and stood to one side, holding the candle high.

'Get her over there on the bed. Quickly.'

Bausset did as he was ordered and gently laid the Empress down on her silken quilt, before retiring towards his master.

Napoleon felt a sudden burning on his wrist. 'Shit!' He snatched the candle down to brush away the molten wax with his spare hand and the little flame flickered wildly.

'Don't leave me!' Josephine rose up on her elbow, her other hand stretched out towards him.

'Out!' Napoleon ordered Bausset. 'Now.'

The two men hurried into the corridor and Napoleon shut the door firmly behind them, cutting off a fresh bout of tears and cries of anguish. He puffed his cheeks with relief before he looked at Bausset.

'Stay here. The Empress is distraught and needs to rest. She is not to be permitted to leave her apartments until I say. She may receive visitors if she desires, but it would be . . . inappropriate for her to encounter me in the present circumstances, you understand.'

'Yes, sire. I will see to it.'

'Good.' Napoleon patted him on the shoulder and then turned back towards the staircase, being careful not to let the wax drip on to his hand again. Once he was out of earshot of Bausset he shook his head. He felt worn out. His heart was leaden and yet he was grateful for the sense of release and relief that washed over him. He sniffed wryly to himself.

'That went well, then.'

Chapter 13

The members of the imperial court entered the throne room of the Tuileries palace in silence. They filed to their assigned places and waited for the sombre ceremony to begin. The previous night had been bitterly cold and the roofs of the capital gleamed under a coating of frost, while jagged crystals of ice had formed in the corners of each pane of glass in the throne room. The sky was a leaden grey, adding to the gloom of the mood of those assembled to await the arrival of the Emperor.

At length, some hour or so after the members of the court had gathered in the chamber, the tramp of soldiers' boots in the corridor outside announced the arrival of the Emperor and his bodyguards. The doors of the room opened with a light creak and Napoleon entered. He strode across to the elaborately carved gold leaf and velvet cushioned throne positioned on a raised dais. The throne of the Empress had been removed the previous evening and carried off to a storeroom. When he had taken his seat there was a short pause before more footsteps announced the arrival of the Empress. Josephine wore a simple dark blue gown, as if she was going to a funeral, Napoleon reflected. She crossed the room and stood a short distance in front of the dais, facing him. He could see that she had been crying again, and her skin seemed even more pale than usual.

Napoleon cleared his throat and looked round the chamber at the members of his family, his ministers, the members of the senate, scores of his marshals and generals, and representatives from the church. Josephine was the only woman in the room.

'My lords, I have summoned you here to bear witness to a sad, but necessary, day in our lives. For reasons of state, I am compelled to end my marriage to the Empress Josephine. The senate has ratified the required decree and today both I and my wife will sign the civil register acknowledging the end of our marriage.' He paused, not daring to look at her, and fixed his gaze on a ceiling moulding near the top of the opposite wall. Despite all his intentions to keep the formalities brief and without emotion, he could feel his throat constricting painfully. He coughed.

'Before the decree is signed, I wish it to be known that I impute no fault, nor lack of love, to the Empress; nor do I mean her any disfavour. The only fault that has brought us to this unfortunate decision lies in the failure of nature to provide us with an heir to succeed me to the imperial throne.'

He could no longer deny the need to look at her, and his gaze fixed on hers. Fresh tears glistened in her eyes. She quickly raised a hand and dabbed them away.

Napoleon breathed in deeply, then stood up and signalled to Fouché, the Minister of Police and one of Napoleon's closest advisors, to bring forward the decree. Fouché strode up on to the dais with a small writing case. Flipping it open, he revealed the document, and held the case in front of Napoleon. Taking up the pen inside the case, Napoleon opened the inkwell, dipped the nib inside and then moved his hand towards the bottom of the decree. He paused for a moment, looking past his brother towards Josephine. She gave the faintest shake of the head as she stared at him pleadingly. He looked down and quickly signed his name before returning the pen to its holder.

Fouché retreated two paces and turned to approach Josephine. He addressed her coldly.

'If you would sign the decree, your imperial majesty, then it is all over.'

Josephine stared at the document as if it were a poisonous snake, and then slowly raised a trembling hand to reach for the pen. She picked it up and charged the nib before preparing to sign her name next to Napoleon's. She started to write, and then shook her head.

'I–I can't.' Her voice caught on a sob. 'I can't do this.'

'You must,' Fouché urged her quietly. 'You have no choice.'

She shook her head, blinking back more tears.

Napoleon could bear it no more and rose from his throne and crossed to her side. 'Josephine, my dearest love, you must sign the decree, or all that I have worked for can come to nothing. Sign it, I beg you, for me. Sign it out of the love you have for me.'

Josephine nodded, held the pen ready again and then, slowly and deliberately, signed her name. As soon as she had finished, Fouché took the pen from her hand and closed the writing case.

'It is done,' he announced to the people standing in the audience chamber. 'The decree is signed and the divorce is official.'

His words were greeted with silence, the only sound in the room the sobbing of Josephine as she clutched her arms around herself. Napoleon raised a hand to comfort her, then withdrew it, and made himself return to the throne. No one spoke, unsure how to react, and nervously watching for a cue from the Emperor, but Napoleon sat still and silent, staring straight ahead. Then he rose abruptly and left the chamber.

Early the following morning Napoleon was woken by his personal valet, Roustam, and he dressed and ate a hurried breakfast before making his way down into the courtyard of the palace. It was not quite eight o'clock and the light was thin and pale. A convoy of carriages and wagons waited to carry Josephine and her retinue and belongings to Malmaison, the country chateau that Napoleon had decided to grant her, amongst other gifts and riches, that would ensure that she lived comfortably for the rest of her life. The horses pawed at the cobbles and the servants stamped their boots and rubbed their hands to try to stay warm as they waited for their mistress. Napoleon saw that her carriage was empty and called one of her ladies-in-waiting over to him.

'Where is your mistress? She is supposed to leave on the hour.'

'I'm sorry, sire. She sent word that she would be here at the appointed time. I last saw her in her bedchamber.'

'I see.' Napoleon lowered his voice. 'And how is her imperial majesty?'

'Tired, sire, for weeping most of the night. She was sitting on her bed when I last saw her, looking at your portrait.'

'You'd better get into your carriage. No sense in you getting cold while we wait.'

She backed away and turned towards the carriage, and Napoleon looked up at the clock above the arch of the courtyard. The large hand notched forward another minute and he suddenly felt a familiar irritation with Josephine, who had always contrived to be late for events, keeping him waiting. His mood continued to sour as the eighth hour approached. Then, as the clock struck, a door opened and Josephine emerged from the palace, wrapped in fur and coolly elegant as she strode gracefully across to her carriage. Her step did not falter as she recognised Napoleon and she held out her gloved hands to him. With only the slightest of reservation he took her hands, and leaned forward to kiss her on both cheeks before drawing back. A pained look flickered across her face and he felt her hands gently attempt to draw him closer.

'No, Josephine.' He smiled softly. 'That would not be a good idea.'

'Is it so easy for you to resist my love?'

'It is never easy.'

'So?' Her eyes invited him. 'If you should ever want to visit me, I would not breathe a word of it to anyone else.'

'That will not happen. We must both be strong in this.'

She bit her lip and then nodded. 'Very well. Then I must go.'

'Yes.'

She released her grip on his hands and turned away, taking the hand of a footman as he helped her up into the carriage. The door closed behind her and all along the small convoy of vehicles men clambered aboard and drivers took up their reins and whips. An order was shouted from the front and the convoy lurched forward, iron-rimmed wheels and iron-shod horses filling the chilly air with a clattering cacophony. As Josephine's carriage started forward and headed towards the arch, Napoleon stared after it for a moment. The window did not open. There was no sign of her face at the small panel at the rear, and a moment later it passed through the arch and turned into the avenue beyond and out of sight.

Two weeks later, on the first day of the new year, Napoleon convened a meeting of his family and closest advisors. The clouds and rain that had seemed to hang over the capital for all of December had departed and left a clear blue sky. However, the Emperor had begun to brood over the loss of his wife, and his mood was not helped by the need to make a decision about her replacement. After consulting with his diplomats and sending messages to France's ambassadors to put forward the names of suitable women a list of candidates was drawn up.

In the end there were only two that matched Napoleon's aspirations, and he had called the meeting to help him choose between them. Once everyone was settled at the long table in the briefing room of his private apartments, Napoleon rapped his knuckles on the table.

'Quiet, gentlemen.' He paused until the others had fixed their attention on him. 'We need to decide who is to be my wife, and the new Empress of France. You will be aware that I have been considering a number of women, and it is my belief that our interests will be best served by either the Grand Duchess Anna of Russia, or Princess Marie-Louise of Austria. As most of you will know, the Grand Duchess is the sister of Tsar Alexander. With relations between Russia and France as they are at present, a marriage into the Tsar's family would help us to repair some of the damage that has been done to our alliance. In time, when there are children, they can only help to strengthen the union of our two powers.'

'Sire,' Joseph interrupted. 'There is no guarantee that the Grand Duchess will be fertile. The most pressing need is to produce an heir to the throne. At fifteen, she will be somewhat on the young side to bear children. There might be a risk to her health that would not apply to an older, stronger woman.'

'She is old enough,' Napoleon replied. 'There are many women who are capable of bearing children at such an age. Besides, if she proves to be fertile then we can be guaranteed an extended period of child-bearing age. The Grand Duchess may well provide us with a good many heirs to the throne over the years.'

'That is true,' Joseph conceded. 'However, we must consider her stock. The Romanovs are renowned for producing many sickly offspring, as well as a small number afflicted with insanity. We would not want to risk contaminating your bloodline with such specimens.'

'No, we would not.' Napoleon nodded thoughtfully. 'Even so, we must bear in mind the political advantages of a union between France and Russia. Particularly now when England is so close to collapse. Fouché's agents report that the embargo on English trade is causing goods to pile up in their ports. Factories are closing and their workers are going hungry. Soon they will begin to starve, and when the people starve, they begin to demand change.'

'We have heard this all before from the Minister of Police,' Joseph said wearily. 'How long is it that he has been promising us that the common people of England are close to revolt? Two years? Three?'

Minister Fouché pursed his lips and shrugged. 'I trust what my agents say. The problem is that the English have a distressing capacity for endurance, and a lack of appetite for revolution. But trade is their Achilles' heel. Cut that and they are hobbled.'

'And still they fight on,' Talleyrand intervened from the far end of the table. Despite the deepening rift between them, Napoleon had summoned his former Foreign Minister with the rest. Talleyrand's advice was too precious to overlook. 'Indeed, far from showing any sign of weakening, their influence grows from strength to strength in the Peninsula. They defeated us at Talavera.' He raised a hand as he saw Napoleon lean forward to protest. 'I know that Marshal Jourdan and Victor claim it was a victory, and that is how you ordered it to be represented in our newspapers, but the truth is that our forces were repelled by the English.'

'Really?' Napoleon's lips curled into a faint sneer. 'Then how do you explain why General Wellesley felt compelled to retreat all the way back to Portugal, if he won the battle?'

'Strategic necessity, sire. All the English have to do is maintain an army in the Peninsula in order to tie down French forces many times their number.'

'Enough!' Napoleon slapped his hand down. 'The situation in the Peninsula is moving in our favour. Victory there is inevitable. In the spring I shall send more men to Spain, together with Masséna, and the English will be routed once and for all. So let us not waste another moment thinking on it. We are here to choose a bride. As I pointed out, a marriage would do much to strengthen our ties with Russia. The risk lies with the ability of the Tsar's sister to present us with an heir.' He paused. 'On the other hand, Princess Marie-Louise is nineteen, a ripe enough age to produce children. The pity of it is that she is no beauty.' He recalled the long Hapsburg face she had inherited from Emperor Francis, together with a narrow nose and bulging eyes. 'I admit that the thought of bedding her appeals more to my sense of duty than to my desire as a man.'

'Sometimes great men are called on to make great sacrifices,' Talleyrand shrugged. 'Do not forget, sire, that it is your duty to provide France with an heir.'

'True, but in this case I wish there was an easier way to achieve that end.'

Louis, who had not yet spoken, or even seemed terribly interested, stirred and caught his brother's eye. 'If you'll pardon me, I seem to recall hearing that one of her forebears, a great-aunt I think, gave birth to twenty-six children. That answers to her suitability for marriage on one ground.'

Napoleon stared at Louis. 'Twenty-six children? Astonishing. That is just the kind of womb I want to marry.' He turned to Champagny, Talleyrand's successor as minister for foreign affairs. 'Do we know how the Austrians will react to the offer?'

'Indeed, sire. When I discussed the matter with their ambassador, he said that Prince Metternich had suggested a similar form of alliance between France and Austria. Apparently he had even mentioned Marie-Louise by name.'

'That's good,' Napoleon mused. If Metternich could smooth the path for the marriage proposal then it stood every chance of success. However, he reflected, if Metternich was for such a marriage, then he was sure to be playing some kind of long game. Be that as it may, marriage to Princess Marie-Louise served France's immediate interests, and if she proved fruitful, France's long-term interests as well. He looked round the table and nodded.

'All right, then, Princess Marie-Louise it is. Champagny, you must place our offer before the Austrians as soon as possible. If they agree, then we will need to move swiftly. I want to give the Russians as little time as possible to register any kind of protest about closer ties between France and Austria.'

'Yes, sire.'

'Inform Emperor Francis that I wish the marriage to take place no later than spring. Affairs of state will make it impossible for me to leave Paris for some months, so I will send an envoy to make the offer on my behalf. If Emperor Francis agrees, then the envoy can act as my proxy and the marriage can take place at once, and Marie-Louise can travel to Paris as my bride.'

'A proxy marriage?' Joseph raised his eyebrows. 'Would that not seem a bit rushed? Surely if we are to give the impression of a union of our two powers, a state wedding would be more emphatic?'

Napoleon waved the objection aside. 'We can put something on later, if necessary, to keep the people happy. What matters is that we tie things up swiftly and that I endeavour to make my new Empress pregnant as soon as possible. Are all agreed then, gentlemen?'

His advisors nodded, except Louis who stroked his jaw with a rueful expression.

'What is it, brother? You wish to raise an objection?'

'No, sire, not as such. I am only concerned about the damage this will do to the French reputation for romance.'

The other men smiled and a few laughed, but Napoleon's expression remained humourless. 'There is no place for romance in the affairs of state.' He frowned and hardened his voice. 'Not any more.'

Chapter 14

Arthur

Lisbon, February 1810

'The government is making a fine mess of things.' Henry Wellesley shook his head as he helped himself to another glass of Arthur's Madeira. The two brothers were seated in front of a fire in the country house Arthur rented from a local noble. Outside night had fallen and rain lashed the shutters. The army was in winter quarters along the border with Spain and he had taken the opportunity to visit Lisbon to arrange for provisions to be sent forward. He was also taking stock of the progress of the network of defences he had ordered to be constructed across the strip of land north of the city, between the sea and the river Tagus. Tens of thousands of Portuguese peasants had been conscripted to build the forts, redoubts and trenches on either side of the town of Torres Vedras that were intended to hold back the onslaught of the French army when it next attempted to sweep the English out of the Peninsula.

Henry had arrived from Cadiz in a packet ship, bearing the latest despatches from London. It was a source of considerable infuriation to Arthur that his political masters informed the British representative at Cadiz of developments at home, before such news was passed on to the commander of the English forces in the Peninsula. There was some small cheer on this day at least since Henry had brought the despatches in person, together with letters from friends and family.

'By God,' Arthur growled. 'Those fools back in London. Anyone would think they would rather dish their political opponents than the enemy.'

'But Arthur, as far as they are concerned their political opponents *are* their enemy. The French are merely an inconvenience.'

'Precisely. I thought I'd heard it all when news arrived of that ridiculous duel between Castlereagh and Canning. It's a miracle only

129

Canning was wounded. Now both men are in disgrace and out of government, precisely at the time when all Englishmen should be putting country above all else. Meanwhile, we have that religious zealot, Spencer Perceval, as Prime Minister. At least in Lord Liverpool we have a cool head as War Minister. He at least appreciates the need to keep an army here in Spain.'

'That he does, but Liverpool is struggling to defend that point of view. There are men in the cabinet who are quite open in their calls to either have you replaced, or have the army evacuated and returned to England.'

Arthur stared into the heart of the fire and asked quietly, 'Why would they want to replace me? What reason could they have?'

'Reason? You are a Wellesley; Richard's brother. That is reason enough as far as they are concerned.'

'You forget.' Arthur smiled. 'I am not Wellesley any more.'

'I know. You now serve under the name of Wellington. A silly choice, if you ask me. Typical of brother William.'

'Wellington will suffice for the present,' Arthur replied, briefly reflecting on his ennoblement following the battle at Talavera the previous year. The King had agreed to confer a peerage on Arthur to reward his victory. William had taken charge of the process of finding a title and he had discovered a small village named Welleslie in the west country. But rather than risk confusion with Richard's name and title, the College of Heralds had chosen the name of the nearby town of Wellington instead. And so, from September, Arthur had become Viscount Wellington of Talavera. An awkward-sounding title, he had decided.

'We cannot afford to abandon our hold here,' Arthur continued. 'Our presence forces Bonaparte to keep a quarter of a million men tied down in the Peninsula. Every day costs the enemy dearly in lives and gold. France is slowly, but surely, bleeding itself dry. And while that continues it weakens Bonaparte's ability to field powerful armies in the rest of the continent.' Arthur leaned forward and tapped his brother's knee. 'Henry, I need you to press the case in London. You must make sure that the government does not abandon the only strategy that can defeat the French.'

Henry sighed. 'I will do what I can, Arthur. You have my word. The trouble is that our Spanish allies are not helping the cause. Their generals seem to be incapable of mastering their French opponents.'

'Indeed.' Arthur shook his head sadly. 'But we need not abandon all hope. If the rulers of Spain have failed us the same cannot be said for the common people. Their hearts are made of sterner stuff and they will fight on.'

'What good will that do them, or us? The rebels are no match for Bonaparte's regulars. They will be massacred if they try to resist.'

'I think not. Say what you will about the junta, and the army, but the war of the partisans will continue for some time yet. In that you may find the seeds of our eventual victory in the Peninsula.'

'I hope you are right.' Henry picked up his glass and turned it slowly in his hands for a while before he continued. 'Arthur, I must ask you to take me into your confidence, if I am to help persuade the government to continue backing your work here. I must know precisely how you plan to wage this war.'

'There is little I can do at present,' Arthur responded flatly. 'I am outnumbered ten to one. The men we lost at Talavera have only recently been replaced by fresh recruits. Many of the men who survived the battle are worn out, and some have been broken by sickness following our retreat to Portugal. What is true of the men is also true of my officers, with the additional complication that some are disloyal, some are incompetent and some are a downright danger to our own side. Even supposing that the army was ready to strike deep into Spain, I have not yet solved the problem of supply. The government's parsimony means I can barely afford to feed and equip our soldiers here in Portugal. I will not be able to rely on our Spanish friends for supplies, and so if I am to wage war in Spain I shall need far more gold to pay our way.' He gave a weary smile. 'So, Henry, you see how I am constrained from taking the fight to the enemy.'

'I understand that well enough, but then what is your plan?'

'If we cannot attack the enemy then we must lure him into attacking us. That is why I have given orders for the construction of the defence lines to the north of Lisbon. For the moment Napoleon has fashioned a peace with the other powers on the continent. That means he will be able to concentrate a large army in Spain, tasked with crushing my forces here in Portugal. So, I will make a show of preparing to fight the French, while the land in front of the lines is cleared of people and stripped of food, shelter and forage. Then I will fall back into the defences and wait there for the enemy. The French will face the choice of trying to starve us out, or retreating back into Spain. Since we can be readily supplied by sea we shall not go hungry. The enemy on the other hand will begin to starve, yet they will not retreat for fear of incurring the Emperor's wrath. That dilemma will destroy them.' Arthur eased himself back into his chair. 'That, Henry, is my strategy. We may not be able to win the war here, but we certainly won't lose it, provided England is patient and generous with its supplies of men and money. It may seem perverse, but I would welcome a French attack. I only hope it arrives before the government in London loses its nerve and orders me to withdraw.'

Henry was silent for a moment and then nodded. 'I will do what I can to prevent that, but you must realise that England expects victories, sooner rather than later.'

'Victories we will have, when I am ready to deliver them.' Arthur refilled their glasses and looked closely at his brother. Henry's face was lined and his hair was streaked with grey. His duties in the service of his nation had aged him.

There was a tap on the door and Arthur twisted round towards the noise. 'Come!'

The door opened and Somerset entered. Behind him, in the corridor, stood another junior officer, waiting in the shadows.

'What is it, Somerset?'

'Sir, I have to report that Captain Devere has returned.'

'Ah, good! Show the man in.'

Somerset stood aside and beckoned to the officer outside. He strode into the room, the firelight gleaming off the braid adorning the pelisse of his hussar's uniform. Devere was a recent arrival. He had been assigned a position on Arthur's staff as a favour to one of Richard's allies in Parliament. He was competent enough, but his arrogance was yet to be tempered by experience. Arthur had sent him out at dawn to negotiate the sale of a herd of cattle from a Portuguese landowner. The sound of his footsteps echoed off the walls as he strode across the tiled floor and halted in front of Arthur with an elaborate salute.

'Sir, beg to report that I have returned from my assignment.'

'Good. How many head of cattle did you manage to buy?'

'None, sir.' Devere stared straight ahead.

'None?' Arthur frowned. 'What is the meaning of this? Explain fully, man! I assume you found his estate? The directions were clear enough.'

'Yes, sir. I reached the house just after noon, and presented your terms to him for the purchase of his herd.'

'And?'

Devere's steadfast gaze faltered and he could not help glancing warily at his commander before snapping his eyes front once again. 'Sir, I told him our price and how many we required, and he seemed somewhat put out by my direct manner. After we agreed a price, he told me he would not complete the transaction unless I begged him to sell me the cattle.'

'Begged?'

'Yes, sir. Don Roberto Lopez ordered me to go down on one knee and beg.'

Arthur rubbed his brow. 'I assume that you refused his request?'

'Yes, sir. Of course. I'm an English gentleman and I'll be damned if I'll go down on bended knee to some dago.'

Arthur shut his eyes and winced. 'And did you actually say that to him?'

'In as many words, yes sir. Through my translator, naturally. After all, I don't speak the lingo and the bloody man refused to speak any English.'

'I see.' Arthur looked up. 'And what happened then?'

'Then?' Devere frowned. 'Nothing, sir. Don Roberto said that he refused to sell me the cattle. Not until I went down on my knee. I told him his cattle could go to hell and that we would find another seller. After that I took my leave and came back here to report. I've returned the gold to the clerk in charge of the war chest, sir.'

Arthur stared at the young officer. 'Tell me, Devere, do you have any idea how much trouble I have been to in order to locate such a quantity of meat for our troops? There is hardly a herd left within twenty miles of Lisbon. Our men need to be fed. Now, thanks to your petulant display of hubris, they will go hungry.'

Captain Devere instinctively opened his mouth to protest, then thought better of it and clamped it shut instead as he stood stiffly and stared straight ahead.

'Look here, Devere, you're a cavalry officer. What is the maxim of such officers? It seems that you need to be reminded: you look after the horses before the men, and the men before yourself. That means you put aside all other considerations until horses and men are properly fed. Correct?'

'Yes, sir.'

Arthur gazed levelly at Devere for a moment. 'See here, Captain. We are a small army of which a great deal is expected by our country. We need every ally we can get. In future let that thought be your guide in all your dealings with the Portuguese and the Spanish. Is that understood?'

'Yes, sir.'

'Very well, dismissed.'

The officer saluted, turned and marched from the room as swiftly as he could, shutting the door behind him. Henry cocked an eyebrow at his brother.

'The man is not a natural diplomat, it would appear.'

'He is young.' Arthur shrugged. 'And that melancholy affliction will soon pass. If Devere lives long enough I think he will do good service for his country. But for now, alas, he has left me with yet one more problem to resolve.' Arthur pulled out his watch and glanced at the hands. 'Nearly eleven. The hour is late, my dear Henry. Forgive me, but I have some work to do before turning in. I am sure you are tired after your voyage from Cadiz. We can continue our conversation in the morning.'

Henry smiled. 'As you wish.' He drained his glass and rose from his chair. 'I'll bid you good night then.'

Arthur nodded, and sat staring into the fire as Henry left the room. He waited a few minutes before making for the door and ordering the duty orderly to bring Somerset to him. Somerset entered, stifling a yawn, a few minutes later.

'You sent for me, sir.'

'Yes. I want two squadrons of dragoons in their saddles, immediately. And I'll want some gold from the war chest.'

'Gold?' Somerset blinked. 'You intend to buy something at this hour, sir?'

Arthur stifled a yawn and smiled wearily. 'Merely some goodwill.'

The estate was two hours' ride from Lisbon. The route was hard to follow in the dark, made worse by the rain clouds that obscured the stars and moon. Three times they lost their way, and were obliged to find a farmhouse and wake the occupants to get directions to put them back on the right path, but finally, at two in the morning, the column passed through the gates of the estate belonging to Don Roberto Lopez. A long drive weaved through groves of fruit trees, bare-limbed in the winter, and stretches of pasture where the dark humps of cattle and goats clustered for shelter beside ancient walls. At length Arthur spied a single lantern burning in a portico. Around it loomed the barely visible mass of a large house.

The column halted by the portico and Arthur dismounted. He beckoned to his translator and strode stiffly towards the door and rapped the heavy iron ring against the stout timber. There was no reply and he waited a moment before rapping again, more insistently. The hiss of the rain and the low moan of the wind made it impossible to hear any sound from within. After a brief delay, the bolts on the inside of the door suddenly rattled back and the door opened wide enough for a man to peer suspiciously through the gap.

'Good evening.' Arthur smiled. 'Please inform Don Roberto Lopez that he has a visitor.'

The translator spoke and there was a brief exchange before he turned to Arthur.

'He says his master is asleep, sir.'

'I should imagine so. Tell this man that I am General Lord Wellington, Marshal of Portugal and commander of the allied army. I must speak to his master on a matter of some urgency.'

The introduction was translated and the servant looked at Arthur closely and then opened the door and waved him inside. There was a large hall within, and Arthur could just make out the forms of picture frames and tapestries adorning the walls. The servant indicated some benches on either side of the door and muttered a few words.

'He tells us to wait here, sir,' said the translator, 'while he wakes his master.'

'Very well.'

Arthur sat on one side, and the Portuguese translator respectfully took the other bench. Removing his hat, Arthur wiped his sodden locks of hair aside and made a mental note to have his hair cut short again, as soon as opportunity permitted. He unbuttoned his coat, setting it to one side so that his uniform jacket would be visible, with the star of his knighthood and other decorations pinned to his breast.

Don Roberto did not keep his unexpected visitors waiting long. The loom of a lamp appeared in a corridor off to one side of the entrance hall, and a moment later the servant returned, holding the lantern high to light the way for his master. Arthur and the translator rose to their feet and bowed their heads in greeting.

The Portuguese landowner was an elderly man with a thin, haughty face. A neatly trimmed beard of snowy white lined his jaw and he regarded Arthur with piercing brown eyes. He gestured to the bench and muttered to the translator.

'His honour bids you sit down, while his servant fetches a chair.'

The servant put the lantern on the floor and hurried to the side of the hall, returning a moment later with a heavy oak chair, inlaid with ivory in a geometric Moorish design. Arthur waited for his host to sit before taking his place on the bench again. The translator remained standing.

'The hour is late,' Arthur began, 'so please excuse me if I speak to the point.'

Don Roberto inclined his head in assent as he heard the translation.

'I have come to apologise for the behaviour of the officer I sent to buy your cattle. Captain Devere is newly arrived from England. He is unused to the ways of foreign people, and he is young enough to not consider the impression he creates. I would have you know that he is not typical of English officers. I have also come to ask that you reconsider your refusal to sell your cattle.'

As the translator began to convey Arthur's words, Don Roberto held up his hand.

'That is not necessary. I understand perfectly well, thank you.'

Arthur could not help letting a brief look of surprise cross his face, and the Portuguese noble smiled. 'What? Did you think that I only spoke the local . . . lingo?'

Arthur laughed. 'By God, you have me, sir.'

'Not as much as I had your Captain Devere,' Don Roberto continued with only the faintest of accents. 'I would have conversed in your tongue, but his demeanour so affronted me that I decided I was under no obligation to make the encounter easy for him. Tell me, do all English speak louder in order to make themselves understood by foreigners?'

Arthur smiled. 'Alas, it is a common affliction.'

'It is not the only affliction that we Portuguese have had to endure since your army arrived, my lord.'

'The presence of my men is less onerous than that of the French,' Arthur protested. 'I will not tolerate looting or mistreatment of non-combatants. Any looting that occurs is the work of camp followers. They are not wholly respectful of military discipline, but I have ordered my provosts to deal with any camp followers they catch stealing. In time, even they will understand the importance I attach to good relations with those over whose land I am obliged to make war.'

Don Roberto regarded him thoughtfully. 'It is a shame that you did not come here to buy the cattle in Captain Devere's place. I would have received you generously. As it is, I was not treated with the respect due to me, particularly by so junior an officer. Your army is not here as an army of occupation. That is why I demanded that your officer went down on his knees to request the purchase of my herd.'

'That is true. We are here to guarantee the liberty of your people, and to fight for the liberation of the people of Spain.' Arthur spoke frankly. 'However, the army cannot continue to defend its allies on an empty stomach. So I would ask you to reconsider your decision, and sell me the cattle.'

'I see. Tell me, General, how long do you think your army will remain in our land? I ask since I see little indication of your willingness to engage the French.'

'I will attack when I am ready. Until then I must maintain my army and ensure that it is fit and ready to fight when the time comes.'

'And when will that be?'

'I cannot say. All I can do is give you my word that I will do everything in my power to beat the French here in the Peninsula.'

'Everything?' Don Roberto raised an eyebrow.

'Yes. The fall of Bonaparte will begin here, or it will not happen at all. That is my conviction. That is all that matters to me.'

'I wonder. I am impressed by your dedication to your duty, my lord. But as I said before, my honour has been offended. Expiation is required. Do you still wish to buy the cattle?'

'Yes.'

'Then I demand that you go on your knees and beg for them.'

'You require me to beg you to sell the cattle?'

'Yes.'

Arthur felt a wave of anger swell up inside. He was tired, cold and wet, and furious with Devere for putting him in this position. The thought of begging stuck in his throat like a rock. Then he took a deep breath and forced himself to calm down. It would not be the first time, after all. He had gone down on his knees to Cuesta. But that had been to save both their armies from the madness of the Spanish commander's decision to turn and fight with a river at his back. This new humiliation related to a week's rations for his men. He could refuse. But then he would simply be reinforcing the damage done by Devere.

'Very well.' Arthur eased himself off the bench and went down on one knee in front of his host. 'Don Roberto, I beg you to allow me to buy your cattle.'

'On both knees, General, and please, add an apology.'

Arthur bowed his head to hide his dark expression, and slid his leading foot back so that he was on both knees on the hard paved floor. 'Don Roberto, I apologise for the behaviour of my officer, and I beg you to let me buy your cattle.'

There was a brief silence before Don Roberto smiled faintly. 'I accept your apology, and I give my permission for the purchase of the herd. You may get off your knees, my lord.'

When Arthur had returned to the bench he saw that the other man was regarding him curiously. 'General, not many of your compatriots would have acted as you did. Even fewer of my countrymen, and certainly no Spaniard.'

'I told you, sir. There is nothing more important than victory. For any of us. We do what we must, or we are lost.'

'That is true. Very true.' Don Roberto rose to his feet and held out his hand. 'The herd is yours, General. I will tell my steward to rouse my people to drive them to your camp.'

'I thank you.'

'If I may presume, I would be greatly honoured if you would dine here as my guest one day.'

Arthur took his hand and smiled. 'The honour would be mine.'

Don Roberto lowered his hand and turned away, and then paused to look back at Arthur as the latter made for the door. 'One last thing, General. Please ensure that you pay for the herd before you take delivery, eh?'

Chapter 15

April 1810

'It seems that Bonaparte has chosen Marshal Masséna to crush us,' Arthur informed his senior officers. They had been summoned to his headquarters and now sat in the shaded courtyard, cooled by a late afternoon breeze. He held up a copy of *Le Moniteur*. 'This was taken one week ago, together with other documents, by partisans north of Madrid. Masséna is appointed commander of the Army of Portugal, a force of some one hundred and fifty thousand men. Even allowing for garrisoning his supply lines, that means Masséna will still outnumber us by some margin.'

Arthur paused as his officers exchanged glances at the size of the host opposed to them. The British army, together with the Portuguese regiments raised and trained under the command of General Beresford, numbered less than sixty thousand. After the retreat from Talavera the exhausted army had been ravaged by malaria and the blistering heat of the Mediterranean summer. It had taken the whole winter for the survivors to build up their strength, and for the new drafts of replacements to be trained for the next campaign. Yet Arthur was content that his army would be able to hold the enemy at bay. The men were more than a match for their opponents and they would have the advantage of a formidable line of defences at their back, should they be obliged to retreat.

Having permitted his officers to reflect on the odds arrayed against them, Arthur continued his briefing. 'Our latest intelligence reports indicate that the enemy is concentrating at Salamanca. Their forward elements have been probing General Craufurd's outposts along the Portuguese frontier near Almeida since the first days of March. It is my judgement that Marshal Masséna will attempt to invade Portugal from the north. It is the best route. The alternative direction of attack is from the east, towards Elvas, but the roads there are atrocious. Bad enough for infantry, but impossible for artillery and wagon trains. Accordingly, I have ordered General Hill to march his corps to join the main army.'

'Excuse me, sir,' General Hamilton interrupted. 'But that leaves the eastern frontier unguarded.'

'If you had permitted me to finish,' Arthur responded coldly, 'I would have said that Elvas will be defended by General Leite's brigade. He's one of the best of the Portuguese officers and I am confident that he will stand his ground – if the enemy should be unwise enough to attempt any attack from the east. The enemy will come from the north. Have no doubt about that. However, before Masséna can invade Portugal he will need to take the fortresses at Ciudad Rodrigo and Almeida as they guard the route along which he will advance. General Herrasti, the governor of Ciudad Rodrigo, has written to inform me that he has a strong garrison and plenty of supplies. He can hold out until he is relieved by a Spanish army.' Arthur smiled. 'I know we have not had the best of experiences at the hands of our Spanish allies . . .'

Several of the officers who had served at Talavera muttered their agreement.

'However,' Arthur continued, 'they may act with a greater sense of urgency since their compatriots will be in danger. But let us assume the worst. Ciudad Rodrigo will fall. We can only hope that it delays the French advance long enough for us to improve Almeida's defences. There too we must attempt to delay Masséna, until we have cleared the land in front of the defensive lines at Torres Vedras and completed the fortifications.' Arthur looked round the courtyard to make sure he had every officer's close attention. 'The opening stages of this campaign require us to buy as much time as possible. Every day we can delay the enemy is a day gained for the improvement of our defences. Every French soldier lost in assaults on the frontier fortresses is one fewer that our men will have to face. I will be blunt with you, gentlemen: we cannot win this campaign in the conventional sense. We cannot march to battle and face Masséna on an open field and hope to defeat him. He outnumbers us, and his cavalry are some of the finest in Europe. We could not stop them flanking us. Our cavalry is far too weak to oppose the enemy horse.

'Our goal is not to lose the campaign. If we achieve that, then we win.' Arthur smiled sardonically. 'Though the newspapers and other croakers in England may not be quite so accepting of this definition of victory. Do not expect to be the recipient of fine titles, pensions and other such spoils of war, gentlemen.'

His audience responded with a mixture of smiles and laughter. The newspapers and letters from England that reached the Peninsula were all too full of the opinion that Lord Wellington's army was doing nothing in Portugal, and the soldiers should be withdrawn.

'So, I am resolved that we will only fight on advantageous terms. When we come to face Marshal Masséna in battle you will all be required to move your men swiftly so that we may be strong where the enemy is weak, and that we quickly reinforce any points on our line that come under pressure.' Arthur paused. 'Any questions, gentlemen?'

One of the officers raised a hand, a stocky man in his early thirties, with piercing brown eyes and an almost completely bald pate.

'Yes, Colonel Cox?'

'Have you decided where to face Marshal Masséna, sir?'

Arthur was silent for a moment, wondering if he should take his senior officers into his confidence. If anything should happen to him, then it might be as well for them to know his mind, and adapt to his strategy for facing the enemy. On the other hand, Arthur realised that much as it might benefit them to carry on his plan, they would be handicapped by constantly attempting to pursue his intentions too strictly and thus lack the flexibility that characterised effective leadership. He fixed Colonel Cox with a steady look.

'I have a location in mind.'

There was a brief, expectant silence, but Arthur said no more.

'Where might that be, sir?' Cox persisted.

'All in good time, Colonel. You will find out soon enough.'

Two days later, Arthur was riding in the company of Somerset and a squadron of light cavalry scouting the landscape north of the Mondego river, the route along which Masséna was likely to advance, once he had disposed of the frontier fortresses. Most of Arthur's army had already crossed the river and was camped around the town of Coimbra. The officers and men were in high spirits, almost eager to close with the enemy after so many months of waiting in camp, with the unending routine of exercise and drilling that their commander insisted on. Arthur was well aware that the army was spoiling for a fight, but so far Masséna had defied his expectations. The French had invested Ciudad Rodrigo slowly and the latest report from Arthur's scouts revealed that the enemy had not even begun to dig any approach trenches, or establish any siege batteries. It would be some weeks before Masséna was ready to assault the fortress. The danger was, by that time the English soldiers might have lost some of their edge. The greater danger was that the longer it took for the invasion of Portugal to begin, the greater the chance that the government back in London might lose its nerve and issue orders for the evacuation of Arthur and his army.

As the small party reached the crest of a ridge on the road to Mortágua they came upon the whitewashed walls of a convent. Arthur turned to Somerset.

'What is this place?'

Somerset twisted round and fumbled for the map in his saddlebag. Drawing it out he unfolded the map and ran a gloved finger over it. 'Ah, here we are. The convent of Busaco, sir.'

'Busaco, eh?' Arthur muttered as he raised a hand to shield his eyes and examined the surrounding landscape. Ahead of him the road crossed the crest of the ridge and then descended along a curved spur. The slopes on either side of the route were covered with copses of pine trees interspersed with heather. To the left the ridge continued for two miles or so to the north before dropping very steeply to the valley floor. To the right the ridge ran almost straight, in the direction of the Mondego, nearly eight miles away. The crest of the ridge hardly varied in height and afforded a clear view along its length.

'A good position to defend, I'd say.' Somerset nodded as he gazed round. 'We've a good view of the approaches to the ridge, sir, and any attacker is going to face a pretty tiring approach up the slope.'

'Yes, so I imagine.' Arthur took another quick look over the position. The steep slopes would cancel out the enemy's superiority in cavalry since they could neither charge up the rising ground, nor easily flank Arthur's battle line and fall on the rear. He nodded with satisfaction and then turned back to his aide. 'Make a note, Somerset.'

Somerset folded his map and tucked it back in his saddlebag before fishing out a pencil and his notebook. 'Ready, sir.'

Arthur raised his arm and pointed along the ridge to the south. 'I want our engineers to construct a road along there, in case we have need to move our men along the line to reinforce weak points. The route will have to be cleared of rocks so we can move the guns and ammunition wagons easily. Make sure that the road runs along the reverse slope. No sense in making our men a target for enemy guns.' He turned to Somerset. 'Got all that?'

'Yes, sir,' his aide replied as he finished writing the final words and looked up. 'Do you think we can beat Marshal Masséna on this ground, sir?'

Arthur pursed his lips briefly. 'We may not win a decisive victory, Somerset, but we shall certainly give him a sharp and costly rebuff.' He smiled. 'That'll be something to still the tongues of the croakers back in England, eh?'

'Let's hope so, sir.'

The siege of Ciudad Rodrigo proceeded as the spring gave way to summer. Arthur received regular reports of the enemy's progress as the French sappers slowly dug their zig-zag trenches towards the walls of the fortress. Masséna's siege guns began a steady bombardment of the outer works, gradually battering a series of breaches in the defences. Once the French came within mortar range, they began to construct a well-protected earthwork for a battery of the snub-barrelled weapons, which soon began to lob shells over the walls with deadly effect, cutting down swathes of General Herrasti's men.

Towards the end of June one of the defenders succeeded in slipping out of the fortress on a moonless night. Picking his way carefully through the French lines, he made good his escape and was picked up by a British cavalry patrol a day later. The Spanish officer was at once escorted to Arthur's headquarters in a tavern, arriving two nights after his escape. By the light of the lanterns hanging from the solid beams of the tavern the man's exhaustion was evident to Arthur. He swayed slightly as he stood to attention and saluted. His uniform was filthy and torn and his face smeared with grime and scratches, incurred as he crawled through the siege lines.

Arthur bowed his head in greeting and glanced at Somerset who was standing at the Spaniard's shoulder. 'From Ciudad Rodrigo, you say?'

'Yes, sir.'

'By God,' Arthur mused as he looked the officer over again, admiringly. 'That's fine work. Somerset, I'll need a translator. Send for Captain Hastings.'

'Señor,' the officer interrupted, 'I speak English. So my general send me.'

'Ah, good. Good!' Arthur smiled warmly. 'Might I know your name?'

'Captain Juan Cerillo de Alimanca y Pederosa, sir.'

'Yes, well, Captain, what news do you bring from General Herrasti?'

'The general, he says that he asks you to bring your army and raise the siege. The French, they make a breach. The fortress will fall in no more than a week, if no help comes.'

'I see.' Arthur nodded. He leaned back in his chair and folded his arms as he regarded the Spanish officer frankly. 'I must ask you to tell your general that there is little I can do to help him. My army is not strong enough to relieve Ciudad Rodrigo. The country around the fortress is open and flat. Perfect for the French cavalry, and I have too few mounted men to counter them. I am sorry, but I cannot afford to risk my army by coming to the aid of General Herrasti.'

The Spanish officer's eyes narrowed. 'If you are truly an ally of my country, then you would help us, señor. Even so, my general has sent for help from the army of Andalucia. General Alvarez, he promise to send his cavalry to help the English raise the siege. You need not have fear of the French horse, señor. General Alvarez deal with them.'

'Is that so?' Arthur's expression hardened. 'And what is the strength of General Alvarez's cavalry?'

'Five thousand sabres, señor.' The captain stiffened his weary back and stared at Arthur haughtily. 'The finest cavalry in Europe.'

Arthur did not respond immediately. He had been promised much by Spanish generals in the past, only to be disappointed when their promises had proved worthless. Their bad faith had cost the British army dearly during the Talavera campaign and he had vowed not to make the mistake of taking them at their word again. It grieved him that the Spanish people, and the common soldiers, were patriots and prepared to defy Bonaparte whatever the cost, yet their senior officers were utterly unreliable. In all likelihood, General Alvarez would never make any attempt to raise the siege. Even if, by some miracle, they did march on Ciudad Rodrigo his men would be scattered by the first enemy formation that barred their way.

Taking a deep breath, Arthur leaned forward and met the Spanish officer's contemptuous gaze directly. 'I would ask you to convey my profound regret to General Herrasti. Tell him that I am unable to lift the siege. Tell him that if I were to attempt it, then it is possible that our enemy would inflict a defeat on the one allied army in the Peninsula that stands any chance of defying Bonaparte. I cannot afford to squander what slim hope we have of driving French troops from Spain in the future. Is that understood?'

'Yes, señor. I understand that perhaps the English are as Napoleon says – you cannot trust them. And that they will fight to the very last drop of Spanish blood.'

Somerset gasped. 'Now, that's—'

'Quiet!' Arthur snapped. He glared at his aide for a moment before turning his attention back to the Spaniard. 'I apologise for my subordinate's lack of self-discipline.' He rose coolly and offered his hand. 'There is nothing more I can say, Captain, except good luck, to you and your general.'

The Spaniard did not take his hand, but bowed his head briefly and turned to stride out of the tavern, stumbling slightly at the entrance as exhaustion got the better of his haughty demeanour. Then he was gone, and Arthur immediately rounded on Somerset. 'What the devil did you think you were doing? British officers have a reputation for imperturbability and discipline, Somerset. I'd be obliged if you reflected on that and make sure that you do not damage that reputation.'

'Yes, sir.' Somerset shuffled uncomfortably. 'Is that all, sir?'

'Yes. Dismissed.'

Alone in the tavern, Arthur sighed wearily and then reached for the sheaf of maps on one side of the table. Fanning through them, he selected the map depicting the Portuguese border with Spain and tapped his finger on Ciudad Rodrigo. General Herrasti had done a fine job of delaying the French. He had bought Arthur several weeks in which to complete the system of defences defending the approaches to Lisbon. It was a pity that Arthur could do nothing to assist the Spanish commander. Except honour his sacrifice by defeating Marshal Masséna.

The French siege guns battered a practicable breach in the walls of Ciudad Rodrigo on the tenth day of July. Rather than subject the townspeople to all the horrors of having their city sacked, General Herrasti surrendered. It was a sad end to a valiant effort, Arthur reflected as he read the report, but there was no time for regret, as the French were already advancing on the border town of Almeida. General Craufurd's division did what they could to hold them, but the enemy's vanguard steadily forced the British back. Two weeks after the fall of Ciudad Rodrigo the French army reached Almeida. Craufurd had left behind one of his ablest officers, Colonel Cox, to command the Portuguese garrison. The town had been well provisioned and there was plenty of ammunition for the cannon that lined its walls. Arthur was confident that Cox would hold out for at least as long as General Herrasti, and so he turned his attention to the problem of persuading the Portuguese civilians in the line of Masséna's advance to pack up their valuables and seek protection behind the lines of Torres Vedras.

Many had heard of the fate of those who had fallen victim to Soult's army as it retreated from Oporto two years earlier, and willingly took their families south to Lisbon. Some refused, to defend their homes, and there were those who felt they could make a living out of selling their produce to the French just as easily as to the English. Arthur, still haunted by the memories of the burned villages and mutilated bodies of men, women and children that he had seen in his pursuit of Soult, tried his best to persuade the civilians to leave. However, there were still some who refused, placing the prospect of making money above the risk of being robbed and butchered by Masséna's soldiers.

Three days after the enemy began their siege of Almeida, Arthur was in the small square of a village on the road to the town. The Portuguese officer who had been sent to tell the villagers to flee had failed to impress upon them the dangers of remaining in their home, so Arthur had decided to persuade them himself. The peril facing them all had been made clear to the local priest, who had rung the church bell to summon the inhabitants to the square. It was mid-afternoon and Arthur and Somerset sat on a bench in the shade of a dusty tree in front of the church. A short distance from them their translator sat cross-legged on the ground. The people were slow to emerge, disgruntled at the interruption to their siesta, and trickled into the square to squat down in whatever shade they could find as they waited for the priest to address them. They showed little interest in the two British officers, or in the six dragoons of Arthur's escort, resting in the shade to one side of the square.

Somerset pulled the stopper from his canteen and took a swig as he glanced over the local people. 'Hope our priest is a good performer, or this lot will be fast asleep before he speaks to them.'

'Oh, they'll listen all right,' Arthur replied evenly. 'I've spared the priest none of the details. I suspect he is more fearful over the fate of the church's fittings and fixtures than he is for the people.'

Somerset smiled.

They waited a little longer. Somerset stoppered his canteen and eased himself back to rest against the peeling white paint on the wall. Arthur closed his eyes and tried to ignore the stifling heat and the irritating drone of insects as they hovered around his head, occasionally alighting and causing him to twitch or raise a hand to swat them away. After ten minutes he gave up and rose to his feet impatiently. The translator, the son of a Lisbon wine merchant, stirred as he saw Arthur stand up.

'We've waited long enough,' Arthur snapped, and nodded his head towards the priest sitting in the entrance of his church. 'Tell him that he must begin.'

The translator hurried across to the priest and respectfully bowed his head before he passed on Arthur's order. The priest looked round the square, where no more than fifty people had gathered, and shrugged. He stood up and strode over to join Arthur, followed by the translator.

'Tell him to let his people know they are in the path of the French army. They will be advancing right up this road.' Arthur gestured along the street that led through the heart of the village. 'Tell the villagers that I am the commander of all the Portuguese and British forces in Portugal, and I have seen with my own eyes the fate that the French visit upon those whose lands they pass through. Tell the priest to repeat what I described to him earlier.' As the priest turned to his people and began to speak, Arthur murmured to Somerset, 'If that doesn't persuade them, nothing will, and then God help them.'

The local people listened to the priest in silence, but as he continued some of them began to shake their heads, and Arthur felt his heart sink at the gesture. His gloom was interrupted when he noticed a rider entering the village, an officer, whose red jacket had become dulled by exposure to the elements and a liberal coating of dust. The man reined in beside the dragoons and dismounted, then handed the reins to one of the troopers and strode up the street towards Arthur.

'Somerset, see that fellow?' Arthur nodded discreetly.

'Yes, sir.'

'I don't want him distracting attention. Intercept him and see what he wants.'

'Yes, sir.'

Somerset backed away and made his way at an easy pace round the small crowd and down the street towards the approaching officer. While Arthur stood still and listened calmly, but uncomprehendingly, to the priest, he watched as Somerset reached the officer and took him off to one side, out of sight of those in the square. A short time later they reappeared, and the officer hurried back to his mount, swung himself into the saddle and rode back down the road. Somerset came to the edge of the square and gestured to Arthur.

Arthur leaned towards his translator and muttered, 'Tell the priest to get to the conclusion. Swiftly.'

The translator nodded and then whispered close to the priest's ear. The latter glanced at Arthur with a frown, then shrugged and raised his voice, spoke quickly, and ended with a brief incantation and the sign of the cross. The local people were still for a moment and then some turned away while a handful clustered together to converse in low voices. Arthur thanked the priest and made his way across the square to Somerset.

'Well?'

'Bad news, sir. One of Craufurd's patrols reported that Almeida has fallen.'

'Fallen?' Arthur's eyebrows rose. 'How? Cox should have been able to hold out for weeks. What happened?'

'The patrol was watching the French guns open their bombardment. Nothing untoward happened for the first few hours, and then there was an explosion.'

'Explosion?'

'Yes, sir. Seems that a lucky shot must have found a way into the garrison's arsenal, and set their powder reserves off. Apparently the blast destroyed much of the town and damaged the fortifications. Can't have done much for the defenders' morale either. In any case, they surrendered before the day was out. Our men saw the French flag raised over the fortress.'

Arthur considered the news quickly. Masséna had taken Almeida. Nothing now stood in his way. The road into Portugal was open.

'By God, the enemy could already be advancing on us,' he said softly. 'Somerset, there's not a moment to waste. Send word to every element of the army. They are to fall back and concentrate on the ridge at Busaco.'

'Busaco. Yes, sir.'

As Somerset dashed towards his horse, Arthur took a last look around the village. In a matter of days the French would be here. They would devastate this place, and bring hunger and death to its people. Then they would march on Lisbon, and only the outnumbered men of the allied army would stand in their way.

Chapter 16

Busaco Ridge, 27 September 1810

'Damn this mist,' Arthur grumbled as he stared down the slope. Even though it was past six in the morning and the sun had risen well above the horizon, a thick mist shrouded the foot of the ridge, concealing the French camp below. The allied army had moved to their appointed positions along the ridge the evening before and had slept in the open. They had stirred and formed before dawn and were now in an extended line that ran just below the crest of the ridge, out of sight of the enemy. The only troops visible to the French were the riflemen of Craufurd's division, and a battery of six-pounders covering the road that climbed to the ridge and passed along the walls of Busaco convent. Arthur and Somerset had ridden forward to the riflemen who had occupied the village of Sula. Resting his telescope on a crumbling wall, Arthur surveyed the point where the road dissolved into the mist. Only a handful of French soldiers were visible. Pickets most likely, Arthur decided.

'Can't see anything of their main force.' Arthur lowered his telescope and slowly tapped his fingers on the top of the wall.

'May I?' Somerset gestured towards the telescope and Arthur passed it to him. 'If Masséna intends to fight his way over the Mondego, then he will have to take Busaco first, sir.'

'True enough,' Arthur conceded. The French army was down there somewhere, in any case. Shortly after the British and Portuguese soldiers had stirred, the enemy drums had beaten the reveille and the bellowed orders of the sergeants had carried clearly up the slope. Since then, the only other sounds had been the rumble of iron-rimmed wheels, and the occasional neigh of a horse and crack of a whip as the French guns were moved forward. Now all was quiet, and it was hard to believe that Masséna's army was formed up somewhere along the base of the ridge, ready to assault the British line. The latest intelligence put the size of the French forces at over sixty thousand. As Arthur had hoped, the enemy's initial strength had been eroded by the sieges and the need to leave strong garrisons behind to protect Masséna's communication lines.

Arthur was silent for a moment before he nodded his head and muttered, 'Masséna will attack us here, I am sure of it. I dare say that he will see our riflemen and assume that there is nothing but a rearguard at Busaco. A force that he will be able to brush aside before continuing his advance into Portugal.' Arthur smiled. 'It is my intention to disabuse Masséna of that perception.'

Somerset returned the smile briefly. 'As long as the men stay out of sight, sir.'

'That is so. But I shall only reveal them when I must.'

'Let us keep our French friends guessing for as long as we can, eh, sir?'

'That is the idea,' Arthur replied, and then gestured towards the mist obscuring the low ground in front of the ridge. 'However, it plays both ways, Somerset. We have too few men to cover the entire length of the ridge. Until the French reveal the direction of their attack, I cannot know where to concentrate our fellows in order to repel the enemy. Still, I'm sure we will not have much longer to wait before Marshal Masséna reveals his hand.'

A faint popping of musket fire away to the right drew their attention. There was no sign of any movement above the edge of the mist. Arthur held out his hand.

'My telescope, if you please. Quickly now.'

He raised it and squinted into the eyepiece. A mile or so away the forward slope of the ridge was covered with sparse patches of heather between small outcrops of rock. At first he could see little sign of life, apart from a handful of riflemen dotted amongst the rocks. Then, a figure in a dark uniform emerged from the mist and scurried a short distance uphill before taking cover behind a boulder and reloading his weapon. Others followed suit, and then a few moments passed as the first of the French skirmishers cautiously picked their way up the slope in pairs, one man shooting while his comrade reloaded. Craufurd's riflemen returned fire and tiny puffs of smoke instantly blossomed across the slope. Every so often a man on either side would topple over and disappear from sight amid the grass and heather. As the exchange of fire continued the French worked their way forward, pressing in on the riflemen until the latter fell back to a new position.

A movement at the edge of the bank of mist caught Arthur's eye as a French column emerged into view, a standard swirling slowly above the leading ranks. There was a brief sparkle of light as the sun caught the gilded eagle atop the standard. Arthur lowered his telescope.

'The first attack of the day, I think. Masséna intends to turn our flank.'

Somerset nodded. 'Yes, sir. But they'll not get far. If they continue to advance in that direction then they'll run into Mackinnon's brigade. And there are at least a dozen guns that can be brought to bear on the French column.'

Arthur continued to watch as the British skirmishers fell back towards the crest, keeping up a harassing fire as they did so. He was pleased to note that they were careful to target the officers leading the French column, and every so often a figure urging his men on with a gleaming sword held high would fall. As they reached the crest the riflemen ceased fire and hurried back to join the neat lines of their comrades on the reverse slope. No doubt sensing victory, the head of the French column surged towards the crest.

'There they go,' Somerset muttered as the allied line advanced up on to the crest; a battalion of redcoats with Portugese battalions on either flank. Arthur watched keenly. This was the first major action for the Portuguese infantry, recruited and trained by General Beresford and his officers. They had every advantage over the Frenchmen before them and if they survived their baptism of fire, then they would be confident enough to hold their place in the line on any battlefield. A battery of cannon was positioned just beyond each flank of the brigade and the crews made ready to fire.

The head of the French column hesitated as the three allied battalions appeared over the crest of the ridge, halted, and then lowered their muskets to deliver the first volley of the battle. With a crash that carried clearly along the ridge to Arthur, the brigade struck down the leading ranks of the attacking column, leaving bodies heaped and writhing along the front. Then the guns on each flank blasted out. Grapeshot swept through the densely packed ranks, cutting down scores of men as heavy lead balls smashed their way through flesh and bone.

Despite this savage punishment the French soldiers in the rear ranks edged forward as sergeants and officers desperately ordered them to form line. Under fire from three battalions and the cannon, there was little chance of the change in formation being carried out with any sense of order. Instead, those at the front continued to fire and load as quickly as possible, shooting blind into the bank of gunpowder smoke that hung in the air between the two sides.

'Those fellows are made of sterner stuff than most of the Frenchmen

I've seen in action,' Arthur commented. 'By God, they can take everything that Mackinnon's brigade are giving them.'

'Aye, sir.' Somerset nodded. 'They're bearing up to it, for the present. But they'll break, soon enough.' He paused, then squinted at the slope, closer to their position, before thrusting his arm out. 'Sir, look there! Another column, I think.'

Arthur's gaze followed the direction indicated and he saw the enemy, a screen of skirmishers emerging from the mist. They were headed up at an angle from their comrades, following a shallow gully up towards the crest of the ridge, halfway between Mackinnon's brigade and the track leading towards Busaco convent. A quick glance told him all he needed to know.

'There's no one to turn them back if they don't change direction.'

Somerset glanced at the crest, and saw that there was no sign of any allied officers to indicate the presence of their men on the reverse slope. 'You're right, sir.'

'There isn't much time.' Arthur turned away from the wall and hurried towards the orderly holding the horses. With a lithe step up into the stirrup he swung his leg over the saddle. Somerset scrambled after him as Arthur spurred his horse into a gallop. They headed out of Sula and made their way along the crude road that had been cleared along the ridge by Arthur's engineers. As they rode, Arthur kept glancing to his left to keep track of the approaching column. No doubt Masséna had sent both columns forward to take the crest, but they had become separated in the mist, and had continued up the slope in widely diverging directions. Now, by sheer bad luck, the second column was heading for an undefended stretch of the ridge.

The route veered off towards the reverse slope and a quarter of a mile ahead of them Arthur saw a company of redcoats, then the rest of the battalion, in an uneven line, spread across the undulating side of the ridge. The nearest men turned to look as their commander and his aide came galloping up. One of the soldiers raised his shako and gave a hoarse cheer, taken up by a handful of others as Arthur thundered by. There was little more than ten minutes before the French skirmishers reached the crest and realised the opportunity that was there to be grasped. If they could break through the allied line then each half could be destroyed in turn. Even though Busaco was as fine a defensive position as Arthur had seen in the Peninsula, that had always been the danger in trying to defend the ridge: too few men to hold its ten-mile length.

The colonel of the Eighty-eighth Foot, Alexander Wallace, saw the two riders approaching and trotted his mount forward to meet them.

'Good day to you, my lord.' He bowed his head. 'And to you, Somerset.'

Arthur nodded briefly and pointed back along the crest. 'There's a French column coming up from the mist. They threaten to cut through our line. I need your men half a mile to the north there. At the double.'

'At the double, yes, sir.'

Arthur fixed him with a steady look. 'You must hold them at all costs. There may be an entire division of them. Do you think your fellows can do their duty?'

'Aye, sir. They will,' Wallace replied soberly.

'Good, then see to it, as swiftly as you can.'

They exchanged a salute and Arthur wheeled his horse round and galloped back along the ridge towards the point threatened by the French column tramping steadily up the slope. At first they could see nothing of the enemy as they rode, and Arthur wondered if they had withdrawn, or changed direction. Then he saw the fold in the slope where the gully dropped away, concealing a wide breadth of ground within. The first pairs of skirmishers were already in view, cautiously moving up the slope, looking for the first sign of their opposite numbers, but the ridge ahead of them was empty beneath a warm morning sky as larks flitted low over the heather.

'My lord, over there!' Somerset called out from behind.

'I see them.'

Arthur reined in and stared at the French skirmishers, then twisted round to look along the track. The leading company of the Eighty-eighth was still nearly half a mile back, musket barrels chinking from side to side as they trotted along the rear of the crest, kicking up a faint haze of dust in their wake. It would take them at least another ten minutes to reach their new position, directly in front of the French. Turning back, Arthur saw that the skirmishers were less than a quarter of a mile from the crest. Ahead of them, the steepness of the slope increased before abruptly flattening out a short distance from the top of the ridge.

There was still time, he decided. Just enough time, if Wallace's men kept up their pace.

'Somerset!'

'Sir?'

'Ride back to Wallace. Tell him to form the centre of his line some two hundred yards on from my position. His light company is to contest the ground in front of the enemy column to buy some time for the rest of the regiment to form up. Go!'

Somerset tipped his gloved hand to the brim of his hat, swerved his horse round and spurred it down the track. Arthur turned his attention back to the enemy. The glint of a gilded eagle revealed the position of the main column, following in the wake of the skirmishers. The sound of hooves pounding over the ground caused Arthur to turn. Somerset was returning, and beyond him Wallace rode at the head of the men of his light company. The men were breathing hard, sweat dripping from underneath the brims of their shakos.

Wallace judged the spot where he should be, then ordered the men to fan out over a hundred yards behind the crest. When they were ready, he sent them forward. Arthur watched as they crested the ridge and came in view of the French skirmishers, not fifty paces below them. An enemy officer shouted, muskets rose up and several shots cracked out. None of them hit their targets and the light breeze that had picked up along the ridge quickly dispersed the puffs of gunpowder smoke. The light company began to fire back and the air filled with a steady crackle of muskets. The skirmishers halted, and behind them the head of the column slowed momentarily as the leading ranks anticipated the coming action.

The following companies of the Eighty-eighth began to file past. Wallace stopped the second company further down the track and the rest of the regiment took up their position in the line, shuffling into place, two ranks deep, facing the crest. Arthur urged his horse into a trot down on to the track, and rode up to join Wallace's men.

Wallace edged his horse out in front of the line and took a deep breath. He shouted above the sounds of musket fire, slightly dampened by the crest of the ridge. 'Now, men! Mind what you have to do. It is as I trained you. Don't just poke your bayonets at 'em, but push them home, right up to the muzzle!'

His soldiers grinned and some let out a bloodthirsty cheer, until Wallace walked his horse into a gap between the companies at the centre of the line and drew his sword. 'Fix bayonets!'

The sergeants repeated the order and the deadly lengths of steel clattered out, to be fixed over the ends of the muzzles and twisted to lock them in place.

'The Eighty-eighth will advance!' Wallace swept his sword towards the crest and the line stepped forward, pacing up the last few yards before revealing themselves to the enemy. Arthur and Somerset followed the line as far as the crest. A short distance ahead of them Wallace halted his men, then ordered them to fire their first volley. The enemy skirmishers were falling back, and as the muzzles of the redcoats swept up and foreshortened they went to ground, leaving their comrades in the main column anxiously staring into the face of over five hundred weapons.

'Fire!'

The range was close, and despite their recent exertions the aim of the redcoats was steady. More than fifty of the leading Frenchmen went down, knocked back into the ranks of their comrades and bringing the column to a halt. Before the French officers could give the order to fire a volley in return, Wallace leaped down from his saddle and cupping his spare hand to his mouth he bellowed, 'Charge!'

The cry was instantly taken up and with a savage roar the Eighty-eighth dashed forward, trampling over the heather, down the slope, directly at the waiting Frenchmen. Some of the latter had the presence of mind to discharge their muskets into the oncoming attackers, while a handful of others hurriedly fixed their bayonets. Then the redcoats were in amongst them, stabbing out, or clubbing with the butts of their muskets. The momentum of their charge carried them deep into the leading ranks of the column, and they fell on the enemy in a wild frenzy. Arthur could see Wallace, still wearing his cocked hat, at the head of the charge, slashing out with his sword and grasping the barrel of his pistol as he used the heavy butt as a club. In less than a minute the first French battalion broke, turning back and scrambling down the slope. The following formation had halted and Arthur watched as the officers and sergeants began to extend the line, in readiness to open fire. The real test of Wallace and his men was about to come, and Arthur felt his pulse quicken as he watched the tangle of men fighting across the slope directly in front of him. If they blundered into a volley fired by the second French regiment, the charge would be stopped in its tracks and there was every risk that the men of the Eighty-eighth would be flung back.

As the men of the broken regiment fled down the slope, Wallace halted and shouted an order to his men to halt and form ranks. To Arthur's relief the other British officers and their sergeants and corporals echoed the order and within moments the redcoats had stopped their pursuit and hurried back to re-join their companies. As soon as the men of the Eighty-eighth had formed up Wallace gave the order to reload, and then advance down the slope to within fifty paces of the second French regiment. Despite standing their ground, the enemy ranks had become disordered as the fugitives from the first charge thrust their way through. With their view of the British obscured there was little that the second battalion could do to bring their muskets to bear, and only a handful of men fired their shots before they faced the full fury of the second massed British volley.

Again the muskets blasted their hail of lead, and again bloody carnage tore through the leading French companies, dropping them on the spot. With a hoarse cry, Wallace again charged with his men. This time Arthur saw that the fighting was more desperate, more confused, and the two sides were soon mixed up in a mad flurry of stabbing bayonets and swinging muskets. It was an insane, savage fight, but once more the British had the uphill advantage and Wallace and his men pushed the French back until they too could take no more, and turned to run, streaming down the slope, deaf to the enraged shouts of their officers attempting to rally them.

With the leading formations in chaos the commander of the French division had little choice but to halt his attack. The remaining battalions began to give ground, retreating back down the slope towards the rapidly thinning mist that obscured the foot of the ridge. Wallace re-formed his men again, and as they watched the enemy division recoil they let out a triumphant cheer. Wallace indulged them briefly before calling for silence once again. Arthur clicked his tongue and edged his horse down the slope towards the Eighty-eighth. The ground was covered with bodies, sprawled in the grass and heather. Most were alive, and many of the injured lay groaning and writhing pathetically as they clutched hands to their wounds. They would have to be tended to later, Arthur reminded himself. Once the battle was over.

He reined in beside Colonel Wallace and nodded his head. Wallace was still breathing hard and the edge of his sword was streaked with blood. Arthur smiled.

'By God, Wallace, I tell you, I have never witnessed a more gallant charge.'

Wallace cleared his throat. 'Thank you, sir. My boys did well enough. What are your orders?'

'You've done your work here, for now.' Arthur briefly surveyed the foot of the ridge where the mist had all but dispersed. The beaten division was re-forming well back from the slope, while a battery of guns was trundling forward on to a slight rise, opposite Wallace's position. 'Best pull back to the reverse slope or the enemy guns will use the Eighty-eighth for target practice.'

Wallace glanced at the guns and pursed his lips. 'The range is long, and it might serve the men well to face up to a small dose of artillery fire.'

'I think they have proved their mettle well enough. Pull 'em back, Wallace, directly.'

'Yes, sir.'

Arthur wheeled his horse round and headed back in the direction of Busaco. Below, to the east of the brow of the hill on which the convent stood, he could see more enemy columns making for the road that led up the slope. This would be the main attack, he realised. The assault on the ridge to the south of Busaco was a diversion. Masséna intended to draw off allied forces to protect their flank, before throwing his main blow at the convent.

By the time Arthur and Somerset returned to the brow of the hill overlooking the village of Sula, the riflemen and the battery positioned there were already engaging the French skirmishers advancing up the road. Puffs of smoke from the scattered trees and boulders on either side of the road marked their advance as they picked their way towards the village. The British returned fire from the buildings they had fortified on the edge of Sula and every so often one of the guns would boom out as their crew spotted a cluster of enemy skirmishers that merited a blast of case shot. Even as Arthur watched he saw that the French were steadily advancing and would soon reach the village.

'Those men cannot hold position, sir,' said Somerset.

'No, I suppose not.'

There was a brief pause before Somerset cleared his throat and continued. 'Shall I order Craufurd to send men to reinforce Sula, sir?'

Arthur shook his head. 'Craufurd knows his business. He will act in good time.'

Arthur had spoken confidently, but he hoped that he had not misjudged the commander of the Light Division. While generally a fine officer, Craufurd had an unnerving tendency towards over-confidence on occasion. Fortunately, the gun crews had ceased firing, and they begun to limber their cannon as the riflemen intensified their covering fire to slow down the enemy skirmishers. Then, as the horse teams trundled out of the village and up the road towards the convent, the green-jacketed riflemen fell back in pairs to re-join their division. From where he sat on his horse Arthur could see the men of the Fifty-second lying down just behind the crest of the ridge as they waited for orders. Before them stood Craufurd on horseback, calmly watching as the French skirmishers swept through the village and then waited as the main column climbed up to join them. There was a pause before Arthur heard the faint rumble of thousands of boots scraping over the dried ruts of the road, and then the main body of the enemy emerged from

157

the trees a short distance from Sula. There were three columns in the attacking force, each advancing on a company frontage of little more than a hundred men.

With standards held high, but breathing heavily from their effort to ascend the ridge, the French marched steadily over the open ground just before the crest. Ahead of the middle column Craufurd held his ground, defiantly facing the enemy.

'By God,' Somerset murmured. 'He'd better do something soon, or the Frogs will skewer him where he stands.'

Arthur did not reply and remained still as he watched the spectacle. Some of the French officers had placed their hats over the ends of the swords and were waving them high overhead as they shouted encouragement to their men. There was a band at the head of the nearest column and they struck up as they approached the crest, the strident trill of brass instruments accompanied by the pounding rhythm of drums. And still Craufurd did not flinch, even as the leading enemy ranks closed to within no more than thirty paces. Arthur felt his pulse quicken and willed Craufurd to act.

Then, when the enemy was within pistol range, Craufurd snatched off his hat and twisted round to bellow at his men. 'Now, lads! Avenge the death of Sir John Moore!'

Arthur could not help smiling faintly. The Fifty-second had been Moore's regiment for a long time, and Craufurd's words were bound to fire their hearts. All along the crest of the ridge the men of that regiment, and the others of Craufurd's division, scrambled to their feet and stood ready, muskets grasped firmly in their hands. Before them, close enough to read the steely expression in the British soldiers' eyes, the French columns stumbled to an abrupt halt. The jaunty tune that the band had been playing broke down into a cacophony before it died away completely. The officers stood frozen, their swords slipping down to their sides as they stared at the ranks of their foe that had sprung up right in front of their eyes.

A few simple commands echoed down the British line and the muskets swung up, the firing hammers clicked back, and then the order to fire instantaneously dissolved into the roar of the first volley as thousands of tiny flames darted from the muzzles of the Light Division's muskets and rifles. The effect was even more devastating than the one that had repulsed the attack along the ridge a short time earlier. At such a close range, far more shots struck home, cutting down the heads of all three columns like a well-honed scythe slashing through stalks of wheat. Craufurd did not order another volley, but immediately commanded his men to charge. With a bloodthirsty roar the Light Division swept across the crest, the bayonets of the leading rank lowered towards the reeling Frenchmen. Then they were in amongst the enemy, stabbing, clubbing and kicking like savage furies, sparing no one as they drove Masséna's soldiers before them. Some fought back, but they were too few and too isolated to stem the flow of redcoats, and were swiftly struck down and killed where they lay on the ground.

It took less than a minute for the charge to break the enemy attack. As Arthur watched, the enemy columns crumbled as one formation after another dissolved and the men fell back down the slope, desperate to escape the wrath of the British soldiers sweeping towards them.

'So much for Masséna,' Somerset grinned. 'He won't be trying that again in a hurry, sir.'

'Perhaps not,' Arthur agreed. 'He has been taught a lesson sure enough. But if he doesn't attack the ridge again today, then you can be sure he will move to outflank us, there to the north.' He nodded towards the end of the ridge.

Somerset turned to examine the clear ground beyond. 'Then we will be forced to fall back, sir.'

'Of course we will.'

Somerset looked at his commander with a surprised expression. 'Was that always your plan, sir? Then why face the enemy here?'

'I felt it would do our men good to see the French run. Certainly, it will have stiffened the backs of our Portuguese troops, eh?' Arthur smiled. 'Not to mention shaken the confidence of Masséna and his army.'

Somerset pursed his lips and nodded as he turned to watch the Light Division pursuing the broken enemy columns down the slope. Craufurd let his men continue for some distance before he had the recall sounded. Such was the ferocious discipline of their commander that his men responded to the trumpet's shrill notes at once, and began to climb back towards the crest where they re-formed their companies in high spirits, slapping each other on the arm, and jeering after the enemy, until their sergeants shouted at them to still their tongues and stand to attention.

For the rest of the day Arthur watched the French lines at the bottom of the ridge, but there was no further attempt to attack. Instead he observed a column begin snaking away to his left and knew that his position on the ridge would have to be abandoned. He turned to Somerset.

'Pass the word to the army. We fall back across the Mondego and march towards the lines of Torres Vedras.'

'Yes, sir.'

Arthur detected a note of disappointment in Somerset's response and offered him a smile. 'We have done our work here.' He gestured towards the French bodies littering the slope. 'Masséna's nose has been bloodied, and there's something else.'

'Sir?'

Arthur's smiled faded a little. 'Now the newspapers in London will have proof that the army has the measure of the French. There is no question that, man for man, we have the advantage.'

'And yet we must retreat, sir.'

'Retreat? Yes, that is how some will see it. But I am content to give ground to Masséna for now. He will be brought to a halt before our defences, and there he will starve, until he is forced to retreat.' Arthur was silent for a moment before he nodded with satisfaction. 'I have not the slightest doubt that it is now only a question of time before the tide turns in our favour.'

Chapter 17

Lisbon, January 1811

'Amateur dramatics?' Arthur frowned. 'What the devil is Masséna playing at?'

He sat back in his chair by the fireplace and folded his hands together, tapping his index fingers against his lips as he considered the news Somerset had brought him from one of the outposts on the first line of defences. 'Tell me again, what exactly did Masséna's officer have to say?'

Somerset was standing just inside the door to the office, and he quickly recalled the note he had received. 'Masséna conveyed an invitation to our officers to attend a performance of *Candide* being staged at Marshal Masséna's headquarters in five days' time. Any of our gentlemen who accept are assured of free passage through the French lines.'

'By God.' Arthur shook his head. 'One could be forgiven for thinking that England and France had been at war for the best part of eighteen years.'

'Yes, sir.' Somerset nodded, used by now to his superior's sense of irony. 'Would you like me to send orders to decline the invitation?'

Arthur thought for a moment. There had already been some criticism of his actions following the battle at Busaco. *The Times* had wondered why the British army had not followed up its victory over Masséna and hounded the French back into Spain. Despite that, Arthur was confident that he had the advantage over the enemy. After one bloody assault on the lines of Torres Vedras the French had been forced to camp on the bare ground before the British defences while Masséna pondered his next move. The French had managed to survive on dwindling rations for the last three months, but soon they would be forced to retreat or starve.

It might not be the most glorious manner of inflicting a reverse on the enemy, Arthur mused, but it was certainly the least costly. He would have to hope that the more enlightened politicians back in England appreciated his strategy and gave him the time and support that he needed to erode and then crush the French forces in the Peninsula.

He lowered his hands and smiled at Somerset. 'We must indulge Masséna. The longer he remains in Portugal, the more his army will wither. Pass the word to all commands in the first line of the defences that their officers may accept the invitation. I will, however, be expecting full reports from any man who crosses into French lines for social purposes. They are under strict orders not to get drunk and to keep their wits about them. Tell them to keep their eyes and ears open for any information that might be useful to us.'

'Yes, sir.'

'If there are any further attempts to fraternise then I will need to approve them. Make sure that is understood.'

'Indeed, sir. And what if our officers should wish to reciprocate?'

Arthur frowned slightly. 'It would not be wise to allow Masséna's men to investigate our defences too closely. Tell our gentlemen that they may arrange hunts, dinners and other entertainments, as long as they take place beyond the limits of our front line.'

'Yes, sir.' Somerset paused an instant before he continued. 'Will that be all, sir?'

Arthur nodded, and then tapped his hand on his thigh. 'Oh, one thing. Have the latest despatches arrived from London yet?'

'They reached headquarters at noon, sir. I haven't had a chance to open them. Do you wish me to see to it now?'

'No, bring them in as they are, then start drafting my orders concerning that invitation from Masséna.'

Somerset bowed his head and left the office. Arthur stared blankly into the hearth for a moment and then laughed drily. 'A play indeed! Strange fellows, these French.'

He built the fire up while he waited for Somerset to return. Outside, the winter sky was grey over Lisbon, and through the long windows Arthur could see the harbour below, packed with cargo ships plying their trade between the Portuguese capital and their colonies and customers scattered across the world. There was also a convoy of ships from England unloading military supplies for the army. The supplies were welcome enough, Arthur mused, but he needed reinforcements far more urgently. More men, as well as more money. The army's pay was already three months in arrears, and the debt owed to Portuguese farmers and grain merchants continued to grow. The Portuguese civilians regarded their redcoat guests with guarded enthusiasm. The same ships that brought supplies to the army could just as easily be used to evacuate the soldiers if the French broke through the lines, or the British government lost heart and ordered their army home.

The latter was a very real possibility, Arthur knew. The Prince of Wales and his Whig friends were all for abandoning Portugal, arguing that it was a waste of thinly stretched resources and did little to unseat Bonaparte. The thought made Arthur feel weary and frustrated. While his army held its ground in Portugal, and offered inspiration to the Portuguese and the Spanish, the enemy was obliged to commit over two hundred thousand soldiers in the Peninsula – soldiers who would not be available for Bonaparte to use elsewhere. The constant erosion of his forces by partisans, disease, hunger and battle required a steady flow of replacements, slowly bleeding the enemy to death. It was a long-term strategy, and Arthur prayed that the British government was wise enough to understand its efficacy.

The door to the office opened again and Somerset entered, clutching a thick leather folder under his arm. Arthur nodded to the low table in front of him and Somerset crossed the room to lay the folder down. Flipping it open, he cleared his throat and briefly summarised the contents.

'Correspondence from London, official and personal – unopened; the latest reports from our cavalry patrols, weekly strength returns from each brigade, and more requests for payment from Portuguese suppliers. Will that be all?'

'For now.' Arthur nodded towards the door. Once his aide had left and quietly closed the door behind him Arthur briefly glanced over the bills presented by the Portuguese. There was sufficient gold in the army's war chest to pay a proportion of the bills, enough to keep the suppliers happy for another month. He dipped his pen into the inkwell and made a note at the bottom of the first bill, then placed them to one side. The strength returns offered some good news. Despite the winter, many of the sick and injured from the last season's campaign had recovered and re-joined the ranks, bringing his army up to thirty thousand effectives. With his Portuguese units, Arthur had over fifty thousand men ready to take the fight to the enemy the moment the opportunity arose.

He turned his attention to the correspondence, opening those letters marked official first. These were from the various departments dealing with the provision of engineers, supplies and artillery, all of whom claimed to be doing their utmost to meet his requisitions. While they recognised the urgency of his situation, they reminded the general that his was not the only call on their resources and his needs would have to be weighed against those of other commanders. Arthur shook his head irritably. It should be clear to the dunderheads in England that his army was the vanguard of the entire nation's effort against the Corsican Tyrant. Resources should flow to the very tip of the sword that was lodged in Bonaparte's side, not languish in warehouses far from the field of battle. He made a note to Somerset to send more requests, couched in far more robust language, and then turned his attention to the last letter.

As he picked it up he felt his heart sink. It was from Kitty. On the eve of Busaco he had written her a terse note detailing his finances back in England. He had come to have little faith in her ability to manage the family's affairs and had spelled out what she must do if he was killed. Since then he had received a steady flow of letters asking his advice on all manner of minutiae. This time, she wanted to know if she could buy new curtains for their house in London.

'Curtains?' Arthur muttered. 'Bloody curtains be damned!'

His hand spasmed momentarily as he clutched the letter, threatening to crumple the paper with its spidery writing into a tight ball. He took a deep breath, smoothed the paper out and laid it down on the table. Thoughts of Kitty and her inability to cope with the household in his absence weighed on his heart with the dull mass of a lead ingot. Their marriage was the gravest mistake he had ever made, Arthur accepted. But it had been his choice, and he could not reverse the decision, nor indeed was he prepared to admit to his error in public. Therefore he was bound to her while they both lived, for better or worse. He sighed. Then he reached for a fresh sheet of paper, dipped his pen in the ink, and composed his reply.

Through the rest of the month, and on into February, the officers of both armies met frequently, enjoying their social and sporting events. Arthur kept his distance from such activities as he deemed it inappropriate for the commander of the British army to become involved. It took little imagination to picture the scandal that would result in London if it was reported that Arthur and Masséna had met socially. Accordingly, Arthur limited himself to offering an exchange of newspapers with the enemy general. The pages of the Paris press were filled with accounts of the activities of the imperial court as Bonaparte showed off his new bride to his people and to dignitaries from across Europe. At first Arthur had been surprised by the news of the marriage. Then he realised that the Austrians had little choice in the matter, following their humiliating defeat by Bonaparte at Wagram. Now it was rumoured that Bonaparte might be expecting an heir in the spring. That was ill news, Arthur reflected. If Bonaparte could establish a dynasty then there was no knowing how long his poisonous influence would endure on the continent.

The temperature rose in the first days of March and thick fog and mists lingered over the Portuguese landscape. Arthur rode to the front line to inspect the forts and lost his way several times as he struggled to follow the crude communication roads prepared by the engineers to link them. Most of the forts were garrisoned by Portuguese troops commanded by British officers. The British infantry were in camp a few miles behind the first line, ready to respond to any attack the enemy made. A short distance to the east of Torres Vedras he stopped at a post commanded by an officer in his forties. Colonel Cameron was typical of those who had transferred to the Portuguese army. Previously, he had been a British captain without any useful connections or enough income to buy promotion. By taking the transfer he had rank and a higher income, as long as the war lasted. He saluted as Arthur entered the fort, and Arthur touched the brim of his hat in response. 'Good day to you. Colonel Cameron, isn't it?'

'Aye, sir. My apologies for the lack of protocol, sir.'

'It is no matter,' Arthur replied as he dismounted. 'The visit is informal. How many men have you here, Colonel?'

'A battalion, sir. Almost at full strength. The lads are in good spirits, though they'd be happier if the Frogs had some fight in 'em and tested our defences.'

'That decision is down to Marshal Masséna, alas. After Busaco I suspect that he is in no hurry to be repulsed again.'

Colonel Cameron grinned. 'If he comes, the lads will send him on his way soon enough, sir. They're game all right.'

He gestured proudly round the interior of the fort and Arthur noted that his men were well turned out and their wooden shelters were neatly set out by companies. Most were clustered around their camp fires quietly talking or cleaning their kit. Up on the ramparts and in the towers those on duty were keeping watch on the dense banks of fog below for any sign of the enemy.

'Your battalion looks like a fine body of men, Colonel.'

'Thank you, sir.' Cameron smiled proudly.

'Anything to report?'

'Sir?'

'Have you noticed any sign of any unusual activity by the enemy?'

'No, sir. In fact they've been quiet today. Usually, our pickets exchange greetings in the morning, but there was no sign of them this morning. Either they've been ordered to keep silent, or they have been posted further back.'

Arthur felt a vague twinge of anxiety at the colonel's words. Cameron's explanations might be sound enough, but the failure to contact the enemy's pickets could equally well indicate something else.

'Colonel, I want you to send a patrol towards the French lines. They are not to engage anyone, but keep going until they see some sign of the enemy, then report back.'

'Yes, sir.'

'Somerset!' Arthur turned round and strode towards his aide. 'What's the nearest cavalry unit to here?'

Somerset thought briefly. 'The Light Dragoons, sir. At Mafra.'

'Ride to them. I want them out across the lines as soon as possible. They are to confirm the location of the French and report back here at once. And send a messenger to headquarters. I want the order to go out to the army to be ready to concentrate and advance directly.'

'Yes, sir. But in this fog we're going to find it hard to manoeuvre.'

'That may be,' Arthur conceded. 'However, if Masséna has stolen a march on us then the army will need to move swiftly to close up on him. Let's hope that it's a false alarm and that the French have merely fallen back a short distance. My concern is that Masséna may elude us and retreat to Spain.'

'Surely, if he retreats, then we have won our victory without having to shed a drop of blood, sir?'

Arthur looked at him sharply. 'You fail to understand the wider strategy, Somerset. If we allow Masséna to retreat then we merely prolong the struggle. It was my intention to starve his army before our lines and then attack him when I judged that the moment was right. If Masséna has begun to retreat, then that means that his men have reached the end of their endurance. We must not let him escape. We must pursue him and defeat his army utterly. Then we will have a victory that will shorten the war. Is that clear?'

'Yes, sir.'

'Good. It is important that you grasp the need for speed in our reaction to Masséna's moves. You must impress that on the commanders of every brigade in the army. Now go.'

Once Somerset had left, Arthur made his way up into one of the watchtowers, together with Cameron. From their elevated position the view over the ground in front of the fort was still obscured by fog, above which only the tops of hills were visible, like great leviathans rising from a milky sea. Arthur strained his eyes and ears but there was no movement, and not even the faintest sounds from the enemy camp. Where he might expect to hear the sounds of horses, farrier's hammers or the thud of axes, there was silence, broken only by the cawing of crows.

He turned to Cameron. 'I can't see a thing in this fog. Assemble your Light Company. By the way, do you have a pocket compass?'

'A compass, sir? Why yes.'

'Good; we shall need it. Leave word for my aide that we have headed due north. If he returns before we get back he is to follow on and report to me.'

'Yes, sir.'

A quarter of an hour later Arthur, Cameron and the men of the Light Company filed quietly out of the fort and down the slope of the rise on which it had been constructed. All unnecessary kit had been left behind and each man carried only his musket and ammunition in a haversack. Ten men spread out ahead of the rest of the company as they advanced into the fog, keeping in sight of each other. They advanced cautiously, alert to any sound or movement ahead as they crept over the ground that had been cleared the previous year to deny any cover to the enemy. They had gone perhaps a mile when the grey outline of a burned farmhouse emerged from the fog. The company halted while two men went forward to investigate. They were gone for a few minutes before they returned and reported to Cameron. He listened, nodding, and then translated for Arthur.

'The farm has been abandoned. There are the remains of a fire there, but it appears to have been built up and then allowed to burn itself out. They left a wagon to burn as well.'

'A wagon, you say.' Arthur thought briefly. The wagon might have been awaiting repair, or it might have been abandoned if there were insufficient draught animals to pull it. The fact that it had been burned meant that the enemy did not want the vehicle to fall into the hands of the British. 'Let's continue forward.'

Cameron struggled to contain his anxiety and nodded. As they passed through the farm Arthur noted that the fire in the yard between the buildings was fringed by the charred remains of other equipment: the spokes and timbers of a gun carriage, and what looked like the carcass of a horse, or a mule. Further on they came across a deserted camp site. Flattened grass gave way to latrine ditches and then a broad expanse of muddy ground, churned up by nailed boots, horseshoes and heavy iron-rimmed wheels. There were the remains of more fires where the remnants of equipment and looted furniture still smouldered.

Arthur turned to Cameron. 'I've seen enough. Masséna is retreating. There's no question of it.'

'Yes, sir.' Cameron paused a moment before he continued. 'What will you do, sir?'

'I shall pursue him. I shall outmarch him and then, by God, I will destroy him.'

Marshal Masséna had gained over a day's march by the time Arthur's army took up the pursuit. The cavalry raced on ahead of the main column, tracking the line of retreat. The passage of the French army was not difficult to trace since they had left a now familiar trail of abandoned equipment and small bands of stragglers and wounded eagerly waiting to be taken into captivity rather than face the wrath of the local peasants. Further on the allied army came across the first of the villages devastated by the retreating French. Everything of value that could be carried away had been stripped from the houses. All the food was gone. Mutilated bodies lay sprawled in the streets. Three blackened bodies, a woman and two children, still hung from a tree over the remains of the fire that had been lit beneath them. The only survivor, an old man, bleakly informed Arthur that the dead had been tortured by the French in an attempt to discover any hidden supplies of food.

Thereafter the Portuguese battalions stopped taking French prisoners, and their British officers stood by in silence as the enemy's throats were cut and their bodies left for the buzzards.

As the pursuit continued both armies crossed the frontier. Ahead lay the fortress town of Salamanca, where Masséna would be safe from his pursuers. That night, Arthur and Somerset rode to a small hill and surveyed the twinkling fires of the enemy sprawling across the rolling landscape half a day's march to the east.

'Frustrating, is it not?' Arthur muttered as he stared towards the enemy. 'To have chased them so far, but not quickly enough to force them to turn and fight.'

'I suppose so, sir,' Somerset replied. 'But Masséna's army is a spent force. It is a victory all the same.'

'Victory?' Arthur rubbed the bristles on his jaw. 'No. Just a step on a very long road. But we shall reach the end by and by. Now we have to take the war into Spain. To do that we need to take the frontier fortresses of Ciudad Rodrigo, Badajoz and Almeida. It will be a bloody business, Somerset. Laying siege will take some time, and cost many lives.'

Arthur was about to turn his horse back towards the British camp when a cannon boomed out from the direction of the French camp, followed a moment later by another gun, and then more in a regular series of thuds that carried clearly to the ears of the British general and his aide. Arthur's weary eyes scoured the ground between the two armies but there was no tell-tale flicker of shots to indicate a fight, just the steady report of French guns, firing into the night, one after another.

'What the devil are they up to?'

Chapter 18

Napoleon

The Tuileries, Paris, 20 March 1811

'Sire?' The doctor stood away from the bed where the Empress lay moaning through gritted teeth. 'May we talk?'

'There is no time for talk,' Napoleon said tersely as he sat on the edge of the bed, holding his wife's hand. 'Just do your duty. See to it that my wife delivers the baby safely.'

The doctor glanced anxiously at Marie-Louise. She lay on her back, knees raised and arms flung out to each side. While Napoleon held one hand, one of her ladies in waiting held the other. Her face was waxen and gleamed in the shaft of light that entered the chamber through a tall window. Perspiration had matted her fair hair to her scalp, and as the doctor watched she let out another prolonged cry of agony before the contraction passed.

The doctor cleared his throat and then spoke softly. 'Sire, her imperial majesty has been in labour for nearly twenty hours. She is growing weaker all the time, and there is little sign of dilation. I must speak to you about the possible complications that may arise from a protracted labour.'

Napoleon stared at him for a moment and then nodded. He leaned across the bed and kissed his wife's clenched brow. 'My dearest, I must talk to the doctor. I'll return in a moment.'

Following the doctor to the window Napoleon stood to one side, out of sight of the crowd that had been swelling outside the palace all day. Rumours concerning the Empress's labour had swept through the capital all afternoon and now tens of thousands waited expectantly for the signal that a birth had occurred. Already a battery stood ready on Montmartre waiting for the pre-arranged signal. The guns would fire a steady salute to announce the birth. If it was a girl there would be twenty-one rounds fired; if a boy, then one hundred. If there was a tragedy there would just be silence.

The doctor took a quick look across the room to the bed and then spoke in a low urgent tone. 'Sire, I have to tell you that there is a danger that you may lose both your wife and the child if the labour continues much longer. If it comes to the crisis we may still be able to save one or the other. But I must know now which it is to be: the mother or the child.'

Napoleon raised a hand and clasped it to his forehead as he considered the doctor's words. He had risen early the day before to deal with state business, and shortly before noon a breathless servant had arrived in his office with the news that the Empress had gone into labour. Napoleon had rushed to her side at once and remained there through the rest of the day, and on through the long night into the next morning. He was exhausted, and it took some effort to marshal his thoughts. The main purpose of his marriage to Marie-Louise was to secure an heir. Now he was on the cusp of achieving that goal. If it came to a choice he knew that he should put the child before the mother, in the interests of France.

And yet, he hesitated. It was true that he had married her out of cold-blooded self-interest, but since they had met, and he had bedded her on that first occasion, a genuine affection for her had grown in his heart. She was not beautiful, but she had an innocent grace about her. The first night the sex had been strained and functional, but she had quickly surrendered herself to the pleasure of the act. For his part, Napoleon enjoyed the thrill of bedding a virgin. Not just any virgin, but the flower of one of the oldest royal families in Europe. Now, finally, he had taken a wife worthy of an emperor and with good fortune there would one day be a prince who would unite the interests of France and Austria. For that reason, as much as any, he loved her.

And if he chose the child and let the mother die, then the damage to relations with Austria would be incalculable. At present, Napoleon was cultivating an alliance with Austria against the day when he would finally be forced to confront the Russians on the battlefield. That thought settled his calculations and he looked up at the doctor.

'If it comes to a choice, save the mother.'

The doctor bowed his head. 'Yes, sire.'

They returned to the bed just as Marie-Louise had another agonising contraction and the doctor examined her again, this time nodding with satisfaction. 'The dilation has increased. The child is coming, sire.'

Napoleon resumed his place beside his wife and took her hand, and gently stroked her head with his spare hand as he spoke gently. 'Did you hear? The child is coming. Be strong, my love; it will be over soon and the pain will pass.'

She gritted her teeth and nodded, then strained again.

'The child is coming, sire,' said the doctor. 'I can see the crown emerging now.'

Marie-Louise suddenly screamed and arched her back and a sudden, glutinous rush of liquids soaked the sheet covering her knees.

The crowd outside the palace stirred as the signal flag was hoisted up the mast above the Tuileries. There was a brief roar of relief and delight that the Emperor's child had been born, then the cheers subsided as they waited to discover if it was a boy or a girl. A distant thud sounded from the battery at Montmarte, then another, and the crowd counted each discharge as it rolled across Paris like thunder. As the twentieth gun sounded the crowd fell absolutely silent, and waited.

Another gun fired, and some muttered to themselves, 'Twenty-one.'

The sound died away and then there was a pause. No more than the regulation interval between shots, but the moment seemed to stretch out intolerably.

The boom of the next gun was instantly swallowed up by a roar of joyous exultation as the crowd waved their arms, and some threw their hats into the air. In amongst them were members of the Paris militia, and they stuck their cocked hats on the ends of their muskets and raised them high, the red plumes dancing above the crowd. Bottles and jars of wine were uncorked and passed around as the mob celebrated the arrival of the Emperor's heir.

In the palace, Napoleon waited as the doctor and the midwife carefully swaddled the cleaned child. On the bed, Marie-Louise sat propped up. Now that the delivery was over she looked exhausted but radiantly happy, and she smiled at her husband.

'Show him to the people, but not for too long. It is cold outside.'

'Yes, my dear.' Spontaneously, Napoleon rushed across the room and held her gently as he kissed her on the lips. 'You have made me the happiest man in all Europe.'

'That pleases me.'

He looked down at her fondly. 'This means everything to me. My son, our child, marks the true union of France and Austria, and our own.'

She touched his cheek. 'I am glad. I am also tired, my dear husband. I must sleep. But you must show our son to your people. Go now.'

Napoleon kissed her again and crossed to the midwife who was holding his child. As he took the small bundle in his arms and gazed down at the tiny wrinkled face he felt a surge of tenderness and love that he had never experienced before in his life. Then the doctor opened the long glazed door on to the balcony, and Napoleon emerged with his child. The cheers of the crowd reached a deafening climax as they beheld the Emperor and his heir. Napoleon turned slowly so that all the people who had gathered in the Place du Carrousel, tens of thousands of his subjects, could see the child as the guns continued to thunder out across the capital. Already the signal stations that stretched across France would be carrying the news to every city, town and village. Soon the guns of every French army would be echoing the salute across the empire, from the cold expanse of Poland to the hills and plains of Spain and Portugal.

The celebrations for the birth of the emperor's son, whom Napoleon named François Charles Joseph, soon abated and Napoleon turned his mind back to the growing number of problems besetting his empire. When his advisory council met in the palace on a clear spring day there was little sense of any good cheer that the change of seasons had brought to the capital. Looking down the table Napoleon was struck by how few men of genuine talent remained for him to call on. Talleyrand remained in disgrace. Fouché had been removed from office after rumours had reached Napoleon's ear that the Minister of Police was plotting against his master yet again. Fouché had been attempting to negotiate with the English to discover what terms they would consider, if anything happened to the Emperor. It had been tempting to have Fouché imprisoned, but the minister had many supporters in the capital, as well as a network of agents across the country. Napoleon could not risk becoming a victim of his vengeance.

Talleyrand had been implicated in the same plot, and had been stripped of his office as the Emperor's Grand Chamberlain. There was no question that Talleyrand could ever be trusted, but his intelligence and peerless diplomatic connections meant that Napoleon did not dare dispense with his services completely. For the moment Talleyrand must be shunned, to teach him a lesson. In time Napoleon would readmit him to his close circle of advisors, but only when Talleyrand had come to appreciate that his influence and power were at the whim of his Emperor.

Napoleon had replaced Fouché with General Savary, a man whose loyalty was unquestionable. Sadly, his ability was somewhat more uncertain, and he was neither as well connected as his predecessor, nor as clever and cunning. As a consequence government officials had returned to their old vices and were as corruptible as they had ever been under the Bourbons. The Minister of Finance, Cordet, was equally second rate and relied too heavily on the advice of his subordinates. Lastly, the new Foreign Minister, Maret, had no opinions of his own and merely deferred to everything that the Emperor said.

The members of the council, and two of the imperial secretaries, had arrived first, as protocol dictated, and stood beside the table as they waited for their master to appear. Napoleon arrived promptly at the scheduled time and took his seat. Once he had made himself comfortable he waved a hand at the others. 'Sit down, gentlemen.'

Their chairs scraped as the officials took their seats, and the secretaries settled at their desks, set to one side. They hurriedly took out inkwells, pens and notebooks from their satchels and prepared to take notes. When he could see that they were ready, Napoleon began.

'Gentlemen, we have a considerable number of difficulties to resolve, foremost of which is the need to increase the flow of revenue to the treasury. Even allowing for the corruption of sundry officials, our receipts continue to fall. This is not acceptable at a time when it is essential to expand the army and the navy to meet current and future threats. Cordet, you speak for the treasury. What are your plans to deal with the situation?'

Cordet swallowed as he flipped open his folder and quickly consulted his notes. 'Sire, my officials are doing all that they can to collect taxes efficiently. I am told that a drop in tax raised from trading activities is the area where our loss of income is most pronounced.'

'And why is that?'

'Sire, trade is increasingly restricted right across Europe, due to the Continental Blockade,' he ventured warily. 'The embargo on trade with England is stifling all of the economies of Europe, including ours.'

'I am aware of that,' Napoleon cut in tersely. 'But we are at war with England. If we are to defeat them then we must strike at their weak spot. England needs to trade with other nations, or die. There is no question of lifting the restrictions on trade with our enemy.'

'All nations need to trade with England, sire, or their economies will wither. We and our allies have suffered enough already. In fact, I would argue that the Continental Blockade is doing far more to harm France's cause than to assist it.'

Napoleon frowned. He knew that Cordet spoke the truth. In Holland, Napoleon's brother, King Louis, had all but abandoned any adherence to the system and the Emperor had been forced to annex the country and run it as a province of France. Louis had fled and gone into hiding, eventually resurfacing in the court of a Bohemian prince. Napoleon had been furious at first, but in the end he put his brother's resistance to his will down to weakness of mind, and insanity.

Cordet continued. 'Sire, for the good of France, it would be better to dismantle the system at once. Allow free trading to resume and tax revenues will rise.'

Napoleon shook his head. 'We have almost brought England to her knees. I know it. All it requires is one last push. If we can bind Europe to the system just a little longer England must sue for peace.'

'With respect, sire, the Continental Blockade is failing. It is openly flouted right across Europe. Why, our ambassador to St Petersburg reports that English goods are freely available in the shops and markets there. English ships come and go from the port without the slightest hindrance. Is that not so?' Cordet turned to the Foreign Minister.

Maret looked pained, and shrugged. 'That is what Ambassador Lauriston says. However, he is relatively new in his post and he may have been responding to hearsay. I shall write to him to ask for a more detailed report, sire.'

Cordet shook his head in derision. 'You do that, Maret. Anything but make a decision, eh?'

'Silence!' Napoleon intervened. He stared round the table, daring anyone to defy him. Then he continued. 'While we are at war with England, while our soldiers are needed to subdue Spain and Portugal, and while Russia seems intent on provoking us into a war, then the needs of our economy must serve the needs of our army, and our navy. Therefore we need to raise sufficient funds to pay for them. That is the problem we need to resolve, gentlemen.'

There was a brief silence. Cordet shifted uneasily in his chair.

'Sire. We have no choice but to cut back on our spending. Since military costs consume such a high proportion of government expenditure, they must be cut back.'

'No,' Napoleon responded sharply. 'There is no question of cutting military expenditure. It would be madness to do that now, on the very cusp of victory.'

'But, sire, the nation will be in debt for generations to come if you continue spending as you are.'

'If a country is at war, then it must spend whatever is required to achieve victory. We can worry about the debt when we have achieved peace.'

'And if we don't have peace?' Cordet countered. 'Our economy will be crippled. Sire, might I remind you that it was the debt of the last of the Bourbon kings that brought on the Revolution. Would you risk a similar fate?'

'There will not be another revolution. King Louis was weak. He gave too much ground to his opponents and his reign slipped from his fingers. I will not repeat his mistake. I rule with an iron fist.' He nodded towards Savary. 'My Minister of Police will ensure that the newspapers report what I want them to report. His agents will ensure that even the smallest hint of conspiracy will be investigated and any plotters eradicated. Is that not so, General?'

Savary nodded. 'As my Emperor wishes.'

'Indeed. As I wish,' Napoleon repeated emphatically. 'Very well, then. Now that we all understand how things stand, let me relate my military requirements to you. Cordet, take note.' Napoleon continued without any need to refer to his notes. 'One: the Army of Germany requires eighteen thousand more horses. These must be bought and delivered to training depots before the end of the year. Two: I will need another fifty thousand recruits to bring the armies of Germany and Spain up to full strength. Masséna's reverses in Portugal have cost France dearly. He must be reinforced so that he can crush Lord Wellington and his army before the year is out. Three: the navy must be expanded as soon as possible. We must make good the losses of Trafalgar and then shift the balance in our favour sufficiently to overwhelm the Royal Navy. To that end I will issue orders for the construction of a hundred new ships of the line, together with seventy-five frigates.'

He looked round the table. Cordet looked stunned.

'Sire, you ask the impossible. We cannot possibly afford such an expense.'

'Nevertheless, it will be done. We must be ready for war with Russia, when it comes. I shall expect a report from you within the month explaining to me how these requirements will be financed.'

'A war with Russia is not inevitable,' said Maret. 'We should be concentrating our energies on finding an accommodation with them. It is by far the least costly option, in gold as well as lives.'

'There can only be one great power in Europe,' Napoleon said firmly. 'It must be France, whatever the cost. As things stand, the situation is propitious for striking at Russia next year. At present the Tsar is engaged in a war with Turkey and a large army is tied down in that conflict. For the moment we enjoy good relations with most of the lands bordering Russia and they can be persuaded to contribute men towards the armies we deploy against the Tsar. Now Bernadotte has been called on by the Swedes to be their Crown Prince, we have a united front running from the Baltic to the Black Sea. The time is ripe, gentlemen. We have but to seize the opportunity afforded to us by fate.'

There was another silence before General Savary cleared his throat and spoke up. 'Sire, I have no doubt that you are right about the timing. However, we are heavily committed in Spain. Is it wise to fight two campaigns at once?'

'I have considered that,' Napoleon replied, and then smiled faintly. 'You are right, my dear general. We must deal with Spain. To that end I have already sent word to my brother, King Joseph, to come to Paris to confer. Once our remaining difficulties in Spain are resolved then nothing shall stand in the way of humbling the Tsar.'

Chapter 19

The baptism of the new prince was set for June and the Emperor summoned his family, the leading aristocrats of the empire and foreign dignitaries to witness the ceremony. When King Joseph arrived towards the end of May, the Paris newspapers reported that he had travelled from Madrid to celebrate the arrival of his brother's heir. The other purpose of his visit – to brief Napoleon on the situation in Spain – was kept secret from the people, particularly since Joseph was the bearer of bad news.

'Masséna failed to relieve the fortess at Almeida,' Joseph explained as he walked round the garden at Fontainebleau. It was a fine early summer day, and the new leaves gleamed a vibrant green on the trees, while the last of the cherry blossom floated down on the light breeze. On the lawn, in front of the orangery, the Empress and her ladies in waiting were fussing round the infant boy as he lay in his cot. Napoleon spared them a quick glance as he continued listening to his brother's report. 'He was turned back by the British army at Fuentes de Oñoro and was forced to retreat. The last message I received from the garrison at Almeida said that the food had run out and their ammunition was almost exhausted. If they were not relieved within ten days the commander said that he would be forced to surrender. There was nothing I could do. Almeida has fallen to Wellington's army.'

'Yes. But it can be retaken in due course.'

Joseph paused in mid-stride and turned to his brother. 'You think it is that simple, brother? I think you overestimate the soundness of our position in Spain. We are fighting a new kind of war in the Peninsula. In order to control the country we have to disperse our troops to police every town, village and road. It is the only way to keep the people in check. Yet whenever Wellington advances we are forced to concentrate our forces and abandon control over the countryside. And if we advance against Wellington with an army large enough to overwhelm him, he simply gives ground, luring us on, to the limit of our supply lines, until we are forced to give up the pursuit. And then we have to pacify the countryside all over again. I tell you, we will lose the war in Spain. While our numbers are whittled away, the enemy grows ever stronger. Our soldiers have been pushed out of Portugal and the British are poised to seize all the frontier fortresses and invade Spain.'

Napoleon shook his head. 'Wellington is not strong enough to launch an invasion. He has no more than a fifth of the number of men available to you. Besides, I think you overrate his ability. He is the same as all the other British generals – too cautious to cause us much trouble. He cannot afford to lose any men. The longer the war goes on, the more certainly the English army will be frittered away. Besides, he lacks the experience of my marshals. Before he arrived in Portugal he commanded very modest forces out in India. I hardly think that a general of sepoys would be capable of besting the commanders of the finest army in Europe.'

'Yet that is precisely what Wellington has done,' Joseph countered. 'He has beaten Junot, Jourdan, Soult and now Masséna. He is a man to be reckoned with.'

'As I said, you overrate him. I have read the reports of those battles Wellington claims as his victories. He did not win them, he simply allowed our commanders to lose them through their reck-lessness. That is all. Hardly a firm basis upon which to build such a reputation as you would ascribe to him, Joseph. I tell you he can, and will, be beaten.'

'Then why don't you test yourself against him?' Joseph stared at his brother intently. 'The Army of Spain needs you, Napoleon. The men's spirits are low. They have suffered too many reverses at the hands of that cursed English fox and their nerves are worn down by the bands of peasants that dog them wherever they march. The men are a long way from France, from home, and they can see no end to the war they wage in the Peninsula. They say that they have been forgotten by their Emperor.'

'Forgotten?' Napoleon exhaled irritably. 'Who do they think sends the convoys of gold to keep them paid? Do I not make them plenty of awards for bravery and fine performances? Well?'

'It is not enough. They need you to lead them. To fill their hearts with inspiration once again. Then we could be sure of crushing Wellington once and for all. After that the Spanish will give up the fight and we will have peace.'

Napoleon considered his brother's words for a moment. He did not deny it was tempting to teach his marshals in Spain that the redcoats were not invincible, as some of them seemed inclined to believe. But then, defeating Wellington would hardly be an achievement worthy of him, he concluded.

'Joseph, I cannot afford to leave Paris. There are matters here that demand my attention.'

'More than settling the issue in Spain?'

'Even more important than that.' Napoleon turned and continued walking along the path between the flowerbeds, head down and hands clasped behind his back. He had grown heavy from taking too little exercise in the past year and after a moment the discomfort of his arms pressing round his portly body made him release his hands and fold them across his chest instead. Joseph took a few quick steps to resume his place at his brother's side. They walked in silence for a moment, and the only sounds were the gravel that crunched under their boots, the occasional cry of a peacock, and the laughter and faint snatches of high-spirited conversation of the Empress and her coterie. High above, puffy clouds floated across the sky, serene and unblemished.

'It is a fine day,' Joseph said. 'I had almost forgotten that a man could feel peace like this. It has been such a long time. I would give up the Spanish throne in an instant – if I was permitted to.'

'You shall do no such thing,' Napoleon responded without looking up. 'I have already removed one brother from a throne. I dare not risk the same happening to another Bonaparte. You will remain in Spain, on the throne, and we will win the war there.'

'And if we don't win? If we can't win? Then what? You would leave me there to be torn apart by the mob? Have you not read of what they do to the French officers they capture? Why, the bastards sawed one of our generals in half, and they boiled another alive. Can you imagine that?' Joseph shook his head in horror. 'We should cut our losses and abandon Spain completely. That's my advice, brother.'

'And that is why you are not Emperor,' Napoleon replied curtly. 'You lack the necessary appreciation of the wider situation. Spain is but one theatre of war. However, what happens there influences the rest of Europe. If you fail me in Spain, then our enemies will be emboldened to defy us elsewhere.'

'Then find another king. I am finished with Spain.'

'Another king?' Napoleon looked at his brother with a bitter expression. 'Do you imagine that kings grow on trees that I might just pluck down another whenever I wish it?'

'I find it hard to believe that you will struggle to find any man who would not wish to be a king.'

'I will struggle to find one whom I can trust implicitly.' Napoleon cast his arm wide. 'I am surrounded by ambitious men who would be king, and most of them would betray me without a moment's thought.

Men like Bernadotte. For the moment he relishes the prospect of the crown of Sweden, but how long before he covets my throne?' He turned and placed his hands on his brother's shoulders. 'That is why I depend on you, Joseph, as I always have. Will you abandon my cause now?'

Joseph did not reply, but stared mutely at his younger brother.

'My brother.' Napoleon softened his tone and there was a pleading edge to it when he spoke. 'Please, I need you. Now as never before.'

Joseph tried to pull away, but Napoleon held his shoulders firmly and refused to let him move. 'I need to know you are with me.'

'I must think.' Joseph glanced down at his brother's hands. 'Please, release me.'

Napoleon pursed his lips, then nodded, and his arms fell to his sides. Joseph walked a little further and then sat down on a bench. Napoleon joined him. For a while neither spoke, until Joseph broke the silence.

'You made me King of Spain, yet the marshals of the Army of Spain refuse to obey my orders. When I have issued commands to them they refer to Paris for permission to carry the orders out. Some have openly said that they will only answer to you, Napoleon. Soult does not even reply to my letters.'

'They are only carrying out their orders.'

'*Your* orders. So you don't trust me to rule my own kingdom, then?'

'You are a fine administrator,' Napoleon said patiently. 'But you have had little chance to develop your military skills. I decided that it would be most effective to entrust the governance of Spain to you, and the command of my troops there to experienced soldiers. Besides, I have certain plans for the northern provinces of Spain.'

Joseph stared at him. 'Plans? What plans?'

'France needs secure frontiers,' Napoleon explained. 'It is my intention to annex the territory to the south of the Pyrenees. It will provide me with secure routes into Spain, and it will remove some of the burden from you.'

'I see.' Joseph shook his head sadly. 'And you did not think to consult me over this . . . small matter?'

Napoleon pressed his lips together briefly. He was pricked by guilt, and then a wave of self-justification swept the sentiment away. Had he not given his brother every privilege and opportunity that he now enjoyed? Had he not placed Joseph on the throne himself? Had he not given him ample military power to enforce his rule and bring peace to the turbulent Spaniards? What had Joseph given him in return? Incompetence and failure.

'I am not obliged to refer my decisions to anyone. If I choose to seek advice then I will. In any case, I need to secure peace in Spain as swiftly as possible. So far you, and my marshals, have failed me. Which is all the more galling bearing in mind that I have provided you with such rich rewards.'

'The Spanish throne is not a reward, it is a curse.'

Napoleon struck him on the shoulder, hard. 'Ungrateful fool! Is that how you repay me?'

Joseph stared hard at his brother, eyes narrowing slightly. He took a deep breath to calm himself and spoke in an undertone. 'Did I ask for the crown of Spain? No. You forced it on me. And I forced it on the people of Spain. Now they revile me for it, almost as much as they revile you.' Joseph's shoulders drooped as he clasped his hands together. 'It is hopeless, I tell you.'

'It is never hopeless. Those are the words of a coward,' Napoleon replied coldly.

'No, they are the words of a reasonable man who knows when the game is up.' Joseph stiffened his posture. 'I have made my decision, my brother. I will abdicate from the throne. I will leave Spain and retire to my estates in France.'

There was a brief silence before Napoleon turned away and clasped his hands behind his back. When he spoke again it was in a strained voice. 'You will not abdicate. I forbid it.'

'You cannot forbid it.'

'I forbid it. What is more I will have you treated as a deserter if you ever leave Spain again without my express permission.'

'A deserter?' Joseph could not help smiling thinly. 'You would have me shot?'

'That is the fate of deserters,' Napoleon replied coldly. 'Though you are my brother, and I love you, I would have you put up against a wall and shot without the slightest compunction.'

'I don't believe you.'

Napoleon turned round, his stare piercing and merciless. 'Believe it.'

Before Joseph could reply, his brother's face creased in a sudden expression of agony and he staggered a pace towards Joseph before sinking slowly on to the path, propping himself up on one hand as he gasped for air.

'Napoleon!' Joseph crouched down beside him, supporting his shoulder. 'What is it? What's the matter?'

'My stomach . . .' Napoleon hissed through clenched teeth. 'Christ, it hurts.'

His brother glanced up, but could see no one in the grounds around them. The imperial staff were keeping a discreet distance from their Emperor and the Spanish King.

'I'll get help,' Joseph said, then looked down at his brother anxiously.

Napoleon nodded, gritting his teeth as he fought off another wave of burning agony from low down in his abdomen. 'Go.'

He slumped back on to his elbows as Joseph hurried off in search of assistance. The pain in his stomach felt as if a heated iron bar had been pressed into his groin. It was not the first time that he had experienced the pain. Over the last year it had struck him down on several occasions – usually when he was exhausted by the demands placed on him by the endless calls on his time and strength.

'What is wrong with me?' he growled bitterly. Ten years before he could have endured such strains on his constitution without any complaint when he had campaigned in Italy. He had marched, eaten and slept in the open with his soldiers, even in the depths of winter. Many times they had forsaken sleep for days as they dashed to confront yet another Austrian army.

Napoleon closed his eyes and sank down on to the path, curling slightly on his side. 'So many battles,' he murmured wearily. 'I am growing old.'

His heart felt heavy and he wondered at the process by which time had laid the years upon him so subtly that he had not really noticed their effects until recently. In the last two years he had grown heavy, fat even, and now there was this pain in his stomach. With a stab of fear Napoleon wondered if this was how his life might end, struck down by a common malady. He had always imagined he was most likely to die on the battlefield, like Desaix or Lannes. A death with some dignity. The thought of dying in agony from some ignoble sickness, before his life's work was complete, terrified him.

He heard the sound of boots crunching on the gravel of a nearby path and blinked his eyes open.

'This way!' Joseph yelled. 'Quickly, now.'

Napoleon rolled slowly on to his back and waited a moment before Joseph knelt beside him, breathing hard and looking anxious. Other men appeared around him.

'Take me inside,' Napoleon commanded.

'I've sent for the doctor,' Joseph panted. 'He's coming directly.'

'Take me into the house,' Napoleon replied firmly. 'I don't want to be seen lying out here like an invalid. Get me inside.'

For a moment Joseph looked as if he might protest; then he nodded.

He rose up and turned to the servants he had fetched from the house. 'Pick his majesty up. Gently as you can. Take him to the couch in his study.'

Napoleon felt their arms slip beneath his shoulders and legs and a moment later he was carefully hoisted off the ground. He grimaced. 'Does the Empress know?'

'Not yet.'

'Then don't tell her. No need to cause her any concern. Let her enjoy the day.'

Joseph nodded.

'Besides, I don't want her to see me like this. Weak. If word of this got back to the Austrian court . . .'

'I understand.'

The little party skirted round some neatly clipped bushes to keep out of sight of the Empress and her guests and made their way through the long glazed doors into Napoleon's private study. Once he had been placed on the couch he dismissed all the others except Joseph as they waited for his personal surgeon to arrive.

'Where the hell is he?' Napoleon groaned.

'He went for a ride. I've sent one of your staff officers after him.'

'Damn the man.'

Joseph pulled up a small chair and sat beside his brother, and hesitantly patted his shoulder. 'You need to rest. You look exhausted.'

'I am exhausted.' Napoleon breathed deeply, fighting the pain as it began to recede, very slowly. 'But there's so much for me to do. All the time.'

'Indeed.' Joseph nodded. 'But you cannot do it all. No man can.'

'No ordinary man.'

'Ordinary or extraordinary, you are still just a man,' Joseph countered. 'And you must look after yourself. You have a duty to your people, and your family. They need you, Napoleon. Now more than ever.'

Napoleon looked up at his brother with a calculating expression. 'And I need you, more than ever. In Spain.'

The door to the study opened and the imperial surgeon came hurrying in, flushed from his ride. Joseph rose up and stood aside for him.

'What happened to his majesty?'

'I can speak for myself,' Napoleon grumbled, easing himself up. 'It's my stomach.'

'Again?' The surgeon felt for his pulse, and while he counted he glanced over his Emperor. 'Sire, you have not been heeding my advice. You need a rest. We have spoken of this. You must rest, before you work yourself into the grave.'

Napoleon frowned and glanced towards his brother and sniffed. 'Doctors! Nothing but a pestilence.'

Joseph forced a smile, and Napoleon beckoned to him to come closer, suddenly taking his hand as Joseph reached the couch.

'Swear to me that you'll stay in Spain!'

'What?' Joseph tried to back away, but his brother's grip was too tight.

'Swear to me, now, that you will keep the crown. Swear to me!' Napoleon stared intently at his brother. 'I need your answer.'

Joseph lowered his head, and then nodded. 'I will not give up the throne. There. You have my word.'

Napoleon breathed deeply. 'I thank you. And you have my word that I will do all that I can to help you defeat Wellington. You'll see. A year from now, the British army will be broken. Besides, I doubt that the rest of Europe will care much about our affairs in Spain by then.'

'Why not?'

Napoleon gave his brother's hand a squeeze and then released it. 'All in good time. Now, I must thank you, Joseph, and ask you to leave, so that I might rest.'

'Hmph.' The doctor snorted. 'I'll believe that when I see it.'

Joseph nodded and turned towards the door. Napoleon watched him leave, and then smiled contentedly to himself. As long as a Bonaparte remained on the throne in Madrid, then he could proceed with other plans. Perhaps the greatest plan of them all.

Chapter 20

Arthur

Albuera, 21 May 1811

Arthur reined his horse in as he and his small escort reached the top of the ridge above the town. Even though General Beresford and his army had fought their battle five days ago, the ground was still covered with the bodies of the dead. The camp followers of both sides, as well as the local peasants, had stripped most of the corpses of anything of value and now the battlefield was abandoned to a handful of allied patrols, and the predations of carrion, wild dogs and buzzing swarms of flies.

Somerset walked his mount forward, instinctively raising the back of his gloved hand towards his nose as the stench of corruption struck him. 'Good God, what a sight,' he muttered. 'What a bloodbath.'

Arthur nodded distractedly. His eyes were covering the salient features of the battlefield as he tried to make sense of the reports he had received of the encounter. General Beresford had been sent south with a third of the army to take the fortress of Badajoz while Arthur and the main army set about the defences of Ciudad Rodrigo. The antique artillery of the nearby town of Elvas had been stripped to supply Beresford with a siege train but it had made little impression on French defences. Then news came that Marshal Soult was marching to relieve the garrison. Beresford had been obliged to abandon the siege and turn to face the threat. Outnumbered, he had chosen to fight a defensive battle of the kind Arthur had found so effective on previous occasions.

Only this time the French had succeeded in turning the allied flank. In the ensuing confusion battalion after battalion had been thrown into the fight piecemeal. It had been a decidedly chaotic and desperate affair and only the raw courage and professionalism of the common soldiers had prevented disaster. Even so, Beresford had suffered grievous losses, nearly five thousand men, most of whom had been British.

Arthur felt numbed by the sight that lay before him. Across the length of the ridge that had formed Beresford's right flank, the trampled grass and rough heather was covered with the mottled flesh of the dead, still half clad in uniform after the looters had sated their appetite for the bloody harvest of the battlefield. He clicked his tongue and walked his horse on towards the point where the heaviest fighting had occurred. Here the bodies were heaped in places, possibly where some of the British battalions had been caught by the enemy's lancers before they could form square. Small groups of men had clustered together to try to fight off the lancers before they were overwhelmed and cut down. Elsewhere, two long lines of men lay where they had been blasted by muskets and cannon. Arthur estimated that the best part of a battalion lay dead on the ground. Men who had held firm, steadily firing and reloading even as their comrades had been shot down either side of them, until they too were hit. Arthur regarded the scene with a great sadness weighing on his heart, but pride in these men too. They had served their country with unshakable dedication, and paid the supreme price.

The French had suffered grievously in turn, and small piles and rough lines of blue-coated bodies marked their position on the battlefield. Soult's losses were even greater than Beresford's, and it was the French marshal who had first baulked at the carnage being wrought in the thick banks of powder smoke drifting across the ridge. Soult had called off the attack and retreated back towards Madrid.

'And Beresford calls this a victory?' Somerset mused as he stared round the battlefield.

'It is a victory of sorts. He fought off Soult and forced the French to give up their attempt to relieve Badajoz. However,' Arthur paused and gestured towards the bodies littering the surrounding area, 'another such victory would ruin us.'

Beresford's army was camped a short distance outside Elvas. The general had fallen back beyond Badajoz to give his men time to recover from their ordeal at Albuera. Only a token force remained outside Badajoz to continue the siege, digging a handful of approach trenches. The motley collection of cannon fired occasional shots at the sturdy defences of San Cristobal, the outlying fort that dominated Badajoz from the high ground on the far side of the Guadiana river. A distant tricolour rippled in lazy defiance above the walls of the fort.

Of all the forts that guarded the routes leading from Portugal into Spain, Badajoz was the most formidable by some margin, Arthur reflected as he rode past. Protected on two sides by the wide Guadiana and one of its tributaries, the city was surrounded by a massive curtain wall, with powerful bastions at regular intervals. On a rock, in one corner of the city, the citadel was defended by yet another tough wall. The choice facing the British was whether to reduce San Cristobal and then use that as a platform to bombard the city, or to attempt to breach the walls from the other side, and then assault the defences. Either would be a costly affair. Casting his eye over the fort across the river, Arthur considered that it was all but impregnable and decided that he must instruct Beresford to abandon his designs on San Cristobal and concentrate his efforts directly on Badajoz.

The subdued spirits of the men of Beresford's column were readily apparent. The pickets covering the approaches to the camp made little effort to patrol their ground, but sat in the shade, muskets leaning against the trunks of the nearest tree. Further on, the tents and shelters sprawled across the rolling hills in makeshift clusters, rather than the neat lines that Arthur insisted on. The men, stripped down to shirtsleeves, patched trousers and felt caps, were resting in small groups as they talked quietly or slept. The lively ambience of a normal camp was absent.

As some of the men spied the new arrivals a handful stood up.

'Why, it's Nosey!' a voice cried out. 'It's Nosey! He's 'ere! Hurrah for old Nosey!'

Scores more of the men rose to their feet and most of them cheered. Others, Arthur noted sadly, did nothing but stare as their commander in chief and his escort rode through the camp.

Arthur sensed Somerset stiffening by his side. The aide cleared his throat. 'Er, want me to shut them up, my lord?'

'No. It's not necessary. If it pleases them, then it serves my purpose, for the present.'

'Yes, sir.'

They rode on through the camp, accompanied by a ripple of cheers so that by the time they reached the farmhouse that served as Beresford's headquarters several officers had stirred to witness his approach. Arthur's heart sank a little further as he saw that some still wore the bloodied and dirty uniforms they had on the day of the battle. None the less, they made an effort to stand to attention as he rode up and dismounted, handing the reins over to one of Beresford's grooms.

'Good day, gentlemen.' Arthur touched the brim of his hat and the officers saluted in return. There was a brief silence as Arthur glanced round, and then he continued in a neutral tone. 'It would seem to me that you could use a change of clothes, and in some cases a shave, gentlemen. Please see to it before I have the honour of dining with you tonight.' Arthur nodded towards a face he recognised. 'Major Templeton, where is General Beresford?'

'Within, my lord.'

'Then I will see him directly. If you would see to the needs of my escort?'

'Of course, my lord.' The major bowed his head.

With a gesture to Somerset to accompany him, Arthur went through the farm gate and crossed the courtyard towards the house. A narrow colonnade ran round the inside of the whitewashed walls and a trellis with a leafy vine offered shelter from the sun. A sentry snapped to attention outside the open doorway, and Arthur paused in front of him, then tapped him gently on the breast with his riding crop.

'Where is your stock?' he asked mildly.

'Dunno, sir,' the soldier replied, staring straight ahead over Arthur's shoulder. 'Must 'ave lorst it in the battle, sir.'

'I think not. Even so, I would expect a good soldier to find a replacement within a day or so. See to it.'

'Yes, sir!' The soldier nodded and started to move off.

'Not now! You're bloody well on duty, man! See to it the moment you are relieved. Somerset!'

'Sir?'

'Make a note to pass that on to this fellow's company sergeant. I will not have headquarters sentries stand their duty out of uniform.'

'Yes, sir.'

Arthur stared hard at the soldier a moment longer and then trotted up the small flight of stairs leading into the house. A large hall was well lit by a series of arched windows running along the rear of the building and a handful of Beresford's staff were busy compiling casualty lists to be sent back to London. There was a scraping of chairs as they hurriedly rose to their feet.

'Easy, gentlemen. Pray continue with your work. Where is your general?'

'In there, sir.' A corporal indicated a closed door to one side of the hall.

Arthur crossed to the door and rapped on the weathered surface.

'I left orders not to be disturbed, damn your eyes!' Beresford's voice bellowed from within.

Arthur and Somerset exchanged a brief look, then Arthur grasped the handle and opened the door. The room was dimly lit; a single narrow shaft of light entered through a window. Adjusting his eyes to the gloom Arthur saw that they were in the dining room. Beresford sat on a plain wooden chair on the far side of a long, sturdy table. A pile of reports and other papers lay to one side. To the other side were two bottles of claret and a glass. Beresford sat in his shirt and breeches, pen in hand as he leaned over a document on the table. He stared at Arthur for a moment and frowned.

'I wasn't expecting you, my lord.'

'Evidently.' Arthur crossed the room, drew up a chair and sat opposite General Beresford. 'I was on my way to assess the progress of the siege when we received the first report of the battle. I take it that you have written a full account for me?'

Beresford nodded towards the papers immediately before him. 'I was just writing the conclusion. Rather, I was rewriting it. It's been hard to relate precisely what happened. They will not understand back in London. Nor forgive.'

'That remains to be seen, my dear Beresford.' Arthur smiled gently. 'Now then, if I may read your report, while Somerset finds us something to eat. It's been a long, hard ride and I am famished. See to it, Somerset.'

'Yes, sir.'

Once the aide had left them, Arthur gestured towards the report. 'I'll look at it while I wait.'

Beresford glanced down at the slim sheaf of papers and bit his lip. Then he lowered his pen and slid his report across to Arthur. 'Yes, of course.'

Arthur turned in his chair to let the light fall across his lap and began to read. It was as he feared. Beresford had been badly shaken by the mauling he and his men had endured. It was evident in the dark tone that pervaded his description of the conflict and Arthur could readily imagine the stir it would cause if the document reached the London papers in its current form. Especially the conclusion, where Beresford dwelt on the heavy losses he had endured, and the large number of men who had been injured, and the savage blow that had been dealt to the men's spirits.

Somerset returned with a servant carrying a tray of cold chicken, bread and a jug of watered wine which he set down at one end of the table before quitting the presence of his superiors. Arthur finished reading the report as the others waited in silence. He placed the papers on the table and eased himself back in his chair as he stared across at Beresford.

'You had a hard fight of it, that much is clear. But you won the day, and that is what counts.'

'Won the day?' Beresford sniffed. 'I hardly think that is of any comfort to the families of the dead men, nor those who will have a cripple return home from the war.'

'We must make up our minds to affairs of this kind sometimes, or give up the game. That is the price of war, my dear Beresford. It is a necessary evil if the world is to be free of bloodthirsty tyrants like Bonaparte. You must accept that, just as you must accept that the army has won a victory. England needs victories. Her people need to believe that we are slowly but surely progressing towards a successful outcome to the war. What England does not need is despondent descriptions of the efforts and sacrifices of her soldiers.' Arthur tapped the report. 'This will not do, Beresford. You must write me down a victory.'

'I have written the truth, my lord. I owe nothing less to the men who fell at Albuera.'

'You have written a truth, that is all. One of many truths that could be told about the battle. The trick of it is to write the most effective one. Let the English people know that our men fought like heroes and died with the contentment of knowing that they had done their duty. Tell England that we sent the enemy reeling and once again we have proved, before Europe, that our army has no peer.' Arthur folded his arms. 'That is the tale you must tell.'

Beresford continued his commander's words for a moment and then sadly shook his head. 'That is not a tale that would sit easy on my heart, or my conscience.'

'Damn your conscience!' Arthur suddenly snapped. 'Do you think you have a monopoly on the suffering that we have endured during the years that we have fought here? Do you not think that I, and every British general, feels the loss of his men in battle like a great weight on his soul?' He paused and took a calming breath. 'Look, Beresford, the war in the Peninsula is broadly going in our favour. I wish that were true of the wider conflict but our allies come and go, beaten again and again. Yet still they come back to the fight. Do you know why? Because we provide them with hope. As long as England endures. As long as her army prevails, then Bonaparte is denied his ultimate victory.'

He leaned closer to his subordinate. 'Your report is a self-indulgence. You have allowed yourself to be too much the man, and too little the general. I cannot afford such self-indulgence in my senior officers. It undermines the morale of the men. A general must stand above the passions of ordinary men. He must be the rock upon which his army is founded. When men have endured as much as they think they can it is to the general that they look for the will to endure more.'

Beresford lowered his head in thought and sat silently for a moment. In truth, Arthur was bitterly disappointed with the man. He was a fine trainer of men and had fashioned his Portuguese battalions as well as Arthur could have hoped, but he lacked the necessary ambition and confidence to act independently.

With a sudden insight, Arthur realised that this was part of the price of being a successful commander. The more he achieved, the greater the degree to which his men depended on him and came to distrust their own abilities.

He cleared his throat. 'Well, Beresford? What's it to be?'

The other man looked up, staring into his commander's eyes, and then nodded. 'I'll do as you wish. If it helps our cause.'

'Good man,' Arthur replied warmly, and then before Beresford could speak again he rose to his feet. 'I will leave you to compose your report again, then. Be sure to send a fair copy to me to read before you return to Lisbon.'

'Return to Lisbon? I don't understand, sir. Are you relieving me of my command?'

'Your skills are needed elsewhere. I need more men. You are to return to Lisbon to recruit and train more Portuguese battalions to fill out our ranks.'

Beresford stared at him a moment. 'Sir, I do not deny that I am weary, and my heart is heavy with the thought of all those who were lost at Albuera, but I beg you, do not humiliate me in this way.'

'That is not my purpose. I no more desire to humiliate you than I would thrash a horse who had stumbled beneath me. It is clear to me that you require a rest from the strains of command. That is all. Once you have made me some more soldiers you shall return to the campaign. You have my word.'

'I see. And what of my army? Who will command it?'

'I shall. Since I am here. I will continue the good work that you have begun here, my dear Beresford.'

Beresford considered the situation for a moment and then nodded. 'As you wish, sir. Thank you.'

It pained Arthur to see the pathetic look of gratitude that Beresford shot at him but he nodded anyway and turned towards the door. 'Send the report to me as soon as it is rewritten.'

'Yes, sir. Where will you be?'

'I'll see the wounded. Where were your casualties taken?'

'They're in Elvas, sir. Being well cared for at a Franciscan monastery.'

'Then that is a small mercy.' Arthur nodded. 'Send the report to me at Elvas.'

The monastery was on the edge of the town, set into the sturdy wall that ringed the town. General Beresford's chief surgeon commanded a small team of overworked orderlies who did what they could for over a thousand of their comrades wounded at Albuera. As Arthur and Somerset entered the refectory they saw that the long tables and benches had been pushed to the sides and the vast open space was now crowded with row upon row of wounded British soldiers. Their limbs were wrapped with soiled bandages and hundreds of them had suffered amputation of an arm or a leg, and now lay in miserable contemplation of a life of begging and reliance on others. Many were groaning or crying out in pain, or were tormented by hunger and thirst, since the medical orderlies had no time to see to their needs as they dealt with the more seriously wounded.

'This is a disgrace,' Somerset muttered as he scanned the dim interior of the monastery, and wrinkled his nose at the smell of the soldiers who had soiled themselves and now lay in their own filth. 'Why aren't there more men assisting the surgeon's team?'

'I suspect that our friend Beresford has been too preoccupied to consider these men's needs. That must change.'

'My lord . . . sir . . .' a voice called hoarsely. Arthur turned and saw a young corporal staring at him from one of the few mattresses the monks had been able to spare for the soldiers imposed on them. 'Sir, a drink. For pity's sake.'

Arthur nodded and turned to Somerset. 'Find this man some water, or small beer.'

'Yes, sir.'

Arthur found a stool and eased himself down beside the corporal. For a moment he said nothing, and then, as the soldier turned his head slowly to face him, he saw that a blast of grape had mutilated the other half of his face, which was now a mass of dried blood and purple flesh.

'What is your regiment?' Arthur asked.

The corporal licked his lips. 'Twenty-ninth Foot, my lord.'

'How did the Twenty-ninth fare?'

The corporal gestured to the rows of men surrounding him.

'Most of 'em are from the same regiment, sir. We were pretty badly cut about.'

Arthur looked round at the casualties before he continued in a muted voice, 'By God, I am so sorry to see so many of you wounded.'

The corporal nodded. 'If *you* had been commanding us, my lord, then there wouldn't have been so many of us lying here.'

Chapter 21

Badajoz, 9 June 1811

Once Beresford's rewritten report was safely on its way to London and the general had returned to Lisbon, Arthur directed his attention to the siege of Badajoz. On first hearing the news of the battle at Albuera he had sent for the main column, ordering that a small covering force be left behind to keep the defenders of Ciudad Rodrigo bottled up behind their walls for as long as possible. Due to the heavy losses at Albuera, Beresford's command was too weak to continue the siege on its own and Arthur was reluctantly compelled to concentrate all his strength against Badajoz.

General Beresford and his engineers had bungled their initial attempt to capture Fort San Cristobal. The approach trenches crossed open ground and had not been dug deeply enough, so that they filled with water and mud every time it rained. They also provided inadequate shelter from enemy fire and Beresford had lost hundreds of men to the blasts of grapeshot and bursts of mortar shells as they laboured to dig their way towards the fort. The difficulties facing the allied army were compounded by the lack of decent siege guns. The guns stripped from the walls of Elvas dated back two centuries and lacked accuracy, calibre and ammunition. The batteries that had been constructed for the guns were too far from the fort and as a result it was a chance shot that ever actually struck the areas targeted for breaches.

Had there been sufficient time Arthur would have given the order to abandon the attempt on the fort and turned the army's efforts towards the walls of Badajoz itself. However, the network of spies run by his quartermaster general, John Waters, had reported that Marshal Masséna had been replaced by Marshal Marmont, who was already marching his army south to join forces with Soult for another attempt to relieve the garrison at Badajoz. The French would be able to muster more than sixty thousand men against Arthur's fifty thousand, a third of whom were Portuguese and Spanish. Such odds were not favourable, and unless

Badajoz could be reduced quickly then the allied army would be obliged to withdraw.

As the sun rose over the rolling Spanish countryside, bathing it in a dusty orange hue, Arthur glanced down at his pocket watch.

'Ten to six,' he muttered.

Around him a small cluster of staff officers nervously glanced at their watches and some adjusted them to synchronise with their general. Arthur clambered up on to an upturned gunner's tub to peer out of the embrasure. Ahead of him the trenches zig-zagged across the bare ground, scored by heavy iron shot. Only a handful of heads and hats bobbed up occasionally as the engineers risked a quick glance towards the fort. The men of the assault party, and the brigade assigned to follow them up if they succeeded in clearing the breach, remained out of sight, crouched down in the churned mud at the bottom of the closest length of trench. Arthur raised his telescope and scrutinised the defences the small force would have to overcome. There was perhaps a hundred yards of open ground to be crossed before the men would reach the base of the hillock upon which the fort stood. Then they would have to clamber up the slope, negotiating the abattis that had been placed at all angles to break up any assault. Then there was the fort itself, protected by thick walls twenty feet high. Expending the last of the ammunition, the siege batteries had succeeded in battering a small gap that ran most of the way down the wall. Arthur estimated that the breach was perhaps ten feet wide. Barely enough to be considered practicable for an assault, yet there was no choice in the matter. Arthur was running out of time. A few days from now Marmont would join forces with Soult and the combined French army could arrive before the walls of Badajoz in less than a week.

'Let us hope that your men succeed this time, señor.'

Arthur turned to the neatly uniformed Spanish officer standing at his shoulder. General Alava was a slight man with a ready smile who had been assigned by the junta in Cadiz to act as Arthur's liaison officer. Although Alava had only been on Arthur's staff for a brief time he had already begun to win Arthur's respect by offering a considered opinion when he was asked for one. He was also honest about the shortcomings of those who commanded the Spanish armies and the politicians who were supposed to pay and supply their soldiers. In short, General Alava was exactly the sort of man Arthur required to mediate between himself and the Spanish authorities, who promised so much and delivered so little. It was a great pity, Arthur mused, that the patriotic fervour of the common soldiers and people of Spain was so ill served by many of their leaders.

Arthur puffed his cheeks as he considered Alava's remark. Three days earlier he had given orders for the first attempt on the breach. A hundred and forty men, weighed down by ladders, had dashed towards the fort, into the face of a withering fire of musket balls and case shot. They had not even reached the wall before half of them had been cut down and the rest had gone to ground. Neither their officers nor their sergeants and corporals could get the men moving again and Arthur had been obliged to have the recall sounded. Since then the aged siege guns had managed to widen the breach and the bottom of the gap was now within easy reach of the base of the wall. However, the enemy would be expecting another attack and casualties were bound to be high again. Arthur lowered his telescope.

'They have a decent chance of success, General. Otherwise I would not have given the order to attack.'

Alava nodded, then glanced round the battery. The guns were well served with powder, but the racks of iron shot at the rear of the battery were nearly empty. He cleared his throat. 'I would imagine that the guns will be forced to fall silent within a day for want of shot, señor. Is that not so?'

Arthur was silent for a moment before he replied. 'You are right. There is little more damage we can do to the walls of the fort. My men will settle the issue by cold steel.'

'And if they fail to take the breach?'

Just beyond Alava, Somerset stirred irritably. 'They will take the breach. Our men are amongst the best in Europe, and certainly the best in Spain.'

Alava did not react to the implied slight to his countrymen and nodded sombrely before he replied. 'Of course. But, for the sake of argument, what would your intentions be if the attack failed?'

'Then we will be obliged to give up the siege. Without ammunition for the guns we can do nothing, and by the time any more could be found Marmont and Soult would be upon us. Our only hope is to take the fort and turn its guns on the town to blast our way through the walls.'

'I see.' Alava nodded. 'Then we had better pray for success.'

'Pray if you like,' Arthur said quietly. 'But this matter will be settled by cold steel and stout hearts.'

The blast of a whistle pierced the cold dawn air. At once the volunteers of the Forlorn Hope clambered out of the trench and began to dash towards the wall, burdened down by their ladders. Their distant cheers carried thinly as they ran forward over the torn-up ground.

Arthur felt his pulse quicken as he stared towards the fort, waiting for the inevitable reaction. Already a drum was sounding the alarm, a tinny rattle that brought the tiny figures of men scrambling up from inside the fort to man the wall. A tongue of flame leaped from the muzzle of a cannon mounted in the nearest bastion. Arthur saw a patch of earth ripped up as the blast of case shot tore up the soil and felled one of the attackers, who was slammed back on to the ground as if he had been kicked by some invisible titan. Another gun opened up, cutting down another two men. Then a series of small stabs of flame and puffs of smoke rippled along the wall as the defenders opened fire with muskets, adding the crackle of their shots to the booming roar of the cannon. More of the redcoats were struck down, some killed outright, while others lay wounded and a few began to crawl back towards the British trenches, desperate to escape the enemy fire that flayed the approaches to the fort.

'Keep going forward,' Somerset muttered through clenched teeth. 'Forward, by God.'

The scattered figures of the assault party dashed on, gaining the foot of the slope leading up to the fort. There they bent forward, using one hand for support as they struggled up the steep incline. All around them were the abattis with their savagely sharpened wooden points waiting to impale the unwary. Arthur felt a surge of relief that the French guns could no longer be brought to bear on his men. But now the wall either side of the breach was bristling with muskets as the defenders continued to pour their fire on to the hapless figures struggling up towards the bottom of the breach. Arthur estimated that a score of men had fallen on the slope, in addition to another thirty or so who had been cut down after leaving the safety of the trench.

Those that remained had reached the foot of the wall, clustering against it for shelter while the lieutenant commanding the party helped to plant one of the ladders below the breach. Drawing his pistol he scrambled up the rungs. As he reached the breach he heaved himself on to the crumbling masonry filling the gap, only to be shot down the moment he stretched up to his full height. The body fell back, arms outstretched, and landed in a crumpled heap to one side of the ladder. But there was already another man on his way up, musket slung across his shoulders as he mounted the rungs. He was shot down even before he reached the breach. Five men were lost in this way before the rest refused to climb the ladder and crouched against the wall, occasionally risking a shot at the defenders above.

'Damn them!' Somerset balled his hands into fists. 'Don't just stand there. Get up the bloody ladder, you fools . . . you cowards.'

Arthur frowned. He turned to look at his aide with a flash of anger in his eyes. 'I'll thank you not to accuse our men of such a base sentiment. Especially as we are standing well out of range of their guns.'

'Yes, my lord.'

'In future you might care to endure what they do before you pass judgement on them. Now be so good as to have the recall sounded.'

Somerset saluted and hurried away down the communication trench leading towards the fort. Arthur watched him for a moment, until he disappeared from view. Then he raised his telescope and examined the situation of his men at the foot of the wall. For the moment they were relatively sheltered from enemy fire, since the defenders had to lean out from the top of the wall to take aim on those below, and thus expose themselves to fire. Then Arthur saw one of the French near the breach drop something. A moment later there was the flash of an explosion close to the ladder and three of the redcoats were flung back down the slope, where they lay motionless.

'Grenades,' Arthur muttered distastefully. 'Infernal devices.'

'None the less effective, señor,' Alvara replied. 'Let us hope your aide orders the recall before too many more men are lost.'

Arthur nodded and watched as two more grenades burst close to the wall. A short time later the shrill notes of the bugle signalled the recall and the men at the wall fell back, half running and half sliding down the slope as they sought to escape the renewed firing from the defenders. Several more were lost before they reached the bottom of the slope and began to sprint back across the open ground towards the shelter of the trench, pursued by renewed blasts of case shot from the guns mounted on the bastion. The last of the survivors of the attack dropped out of sight and the enemy guns fell silent, not deeming it worth the powder to kill the handful of wounded men who were still staggering or crawling back to the allied lines.

Arthur snapped his telescope shut and turned away from the scene. He strode through the battery towards the horse lines, swung himself up into the saddle and spurred the mount back towards his headquarters.

'What was the butcher's bill this time?' Arthur folded his hands together as he looked up at Somerset.

The latter glanced down at his open notebook. 'A hundred and forty men this time, my lord.'

'A hundred and forty? With the ninety casualties of the first attack and the two hundred and fifty that we lost while the men were digging the trenches, that's nearly five hundred men.' He sucked in a quick breath. 'We have lost the best part of a battalion and achieved nothing here.'

Somerset kept silent. It was not his place to criticise Beresford's plans for the siege.

There was little choice in the matter, Arthur reflected. The attempt to take Badajoz had failed. There was no shot for the siege guns, and without them the outwork of San Cristobal would continue to defy any attacks Arthur launched. Finally, a report from a cavalry patrol revealed that Marmont and Soult's force was no more three days' march away. Their combined armies outnumbered Arthur's. No choice then. He looked up at his aide.

'The army will break camp at first light. We will withdraw to the north. Have the orders drawn up, and make sure that the head of the commissary sends his men ahead to purchase rations.'

'Yes, my lord.'

'One final thing. I want the siege guns returned to Elvas. If they are moved quickly they should reach Elvas before the French can catch up with them.'

'Why take the risk?' Somerset shrugged. 'We could roll them into the river, to ensure that the French don't capture them.'

'I cannot guarantee that they would not be retrieved. Besides, the guns belong to our Portuguese allies. It would be unseemly for us to allow them to fall into French hands.'

'Why not let the French have them, my lord? They are more of a hindrance than a help. Let the enemy have the burden of them.'

'No.' Arthur shook his head. 'We shall return the guns to their proper owners, if only as a token of our goodwill. Make sure the appropriate orders are given.'

Somerset nodded and made a note with his pencil.

Arthur sat back and wearily eased a hand through his close-cropped hair. 'Next time I will be my own engineer, by God. There will be no more hasty decisions and half-measures. I will have a proper siege train, and when we lay siege to a fortress we will pound it to pieces and make damned sure that we take it. Once we have all the frontier forts securely in our grasp there is nothing that the French can do to force us out of Spain.' He smiled at his aide. 'Every small step matters, Somerset. No matter how long it takes, we will wear our enemy down and drive him back across the Pyrenees.'

'Yes, my lord.'

Arthur picked up the report from the cavalry patrol. 'For now, we are obliged to retreat from Badajoz. Once we have rested the men and gathered enough force together we will turn and face the enemy.'

For the rest of summer, and on into the autumn, Arthur was powerless to intervene as the French resupplied and reinforced their frontier forts. The months passed in frustration for Arthur. While he was free to threaten the enemy at any point along the frontier between Spain and Portugal he was still obliged to retreat when the French gathered superior forces to repel the allied army. To add to his frustration the enemy seemed to have learned the lessons of earlier battles and now refused to attack whenever Arthur found a good defensive position and turned to fight.

Even as the series of marches and counter-marches and bloodless confrontations became a source of discontent for the rank and file, Arthur was steadily preparing the ground for the following year's campaign. His requests for more reinforcements, particularly cavalry, had been agreed by the government. A siege train of good-quality heavy guns was landed at Oporto and then laboriously hauled overland to Almeida where supplies of ammunition and rations were being stockpiled. When the time came for the allied army to advance again, they would be properly supplied, and ready to batter down the defences of any fortress that stood in their way.

Chapter 22

Paris, 2 December 1811

Even though the night was raw and cold, much of the population of the city had turned out to celebrate the anniversary of the emperor's coronation. The crowds lined the banks of the Seine, waiting in excited anticipation for the fireworks display to begin. Three barges had been anchored in the middle of the river, opposite the Tuileries palace. By the light of carefully shielded lanterns the crowds could make out the dim figures making the final preparations. The display marked the end of the day-long celebrations to mark the eighth year of Napoleon's reign. At dawn a battery of twelve-pounders had thundered out a salute from the heights of Montmartre. Each boom had echoed across the roofs of Paris, slick and glistening in the light mist that coated every surface with damp.

Early that morning, the battalions of the Imperial Guard had begun to march into the city from their billets in the suburbs. Their route was lined with crowds, cheering proudly as the elite soldiers in their towering bearskins marched past in neat ranks to the rhythm of the patriotic music played by each battalion's band. Interspersed between the infantry were squadrons of Guard cavalry, large men in shining high boots and breastplates, mounted on powerful horses whose coats were brushed to a satin gleam.

A reviewing platform had been erected in the great courtyard of the Tuileries where a more select audience had been permitted into the palace grounds to witness the military parades that took place in the afternoon. On the platform sat Napoleon, his Empress, and senior members of the court, as well as guests from the courts of the other Euopean powers.

One by one the battalions of the Old Guard marched past with their muskets shouldered, campaign stripes adorning their immaculate uniforms and medals pinned to their breasts. After the guardsmen came a small party of junior officers, each man carrying one of the Prussian, Austrian and Russian standards captured in the campaigns of the previous years.

Napoleon turned his head slightly to glance at Prince Metternich, the Austrian Foreign Minister. Metternich's normally curly hair was plastered to his head by the faint drizzle, yet his expression of resentment was clear to see and it warmed Napoleon's heart. Never let the Austrians forget that they had been humbled by Napoleon whenever they had dared to wage war on France. Beyond Metternich sat the Russian ambassador, Kurakin, his head inclined towards Talleyrand as the two exchanged a few muttered comments. The Russian turned at that moment, and met Napoleon's stare. He smiled faintly and bowed his head to the French Emperor before turning his eyes back to the captured standards passing by. Talleyrand pursed his lips and looked directly ahead as he slowly twisted his walking stick.

Napoleon turned his face back towards the passing flags, acknowledging the salutes of his officers automatically, but his mood had been soured by the sight of the two men conversing. What was that devil, Talleyrand, up to now, he wondered. It was possible their exchange of comments was innocent enough, but with the steadily growing rift between France and Russia Napoleon was inclined to be suspicious of every Russian, and those they chose to associate with. Only a few months earlier the Tsar had increased the import duties on French goods yet again, at the same time as he continued to turn a blind eye to the English goods that were being landed at Russian ports. And now the Tsar was protesting about the presence of French troops in Poland, and demanding that Napoleon agree to his annexation of some Polish territories that bordered Russia. This, on top of his demand that Napoleon give him a free hand in the crumbling Turkish empire. The reports from the ambassador to St Petersburg spoke ominously of the growing anti-French feeling at the Russian court. Increasingly, there was talk of war with France and a new alliance with England.

Napoleon felt his stomach clench tightly as he was gripped by a familiar rage at the thought of his old enemy, defying him from behind the wooden walls of the Royal Navy. It was a perverse freak of geography that had separated England from the rest of the continent by that narrow, unbridgeable channel. From behind that cursed channel, England, a nation of petty businessmen, mocked him. But for that strip of water, it would all be over. England would be occupied, its fleets broken up, and Europe would be enjoying peace under the leadership of France, and Napoleon, and his heirs. Instead, the war continued, slowly eating away at the flower of French manhood down in Spain.

There was scarcely any good news from Madrid. Just endless lists of casualties and demands for more men, supplies and gold. Spain was like an open festering wound in the side of his empire, Napoleon decided. Worst of all, his marshals seemed to have got it into their heads that their English opponent was some kind of military genius. It was clear from their reports that they had begun to fear Lord Wellington. Even though the forces commanded by the marshals outnumbered the English, and could outmarch them, it seemed that when the English general was forced to fight the courage of Napoleon's marshals withered and they were too nervous to finish off the fox that they had successfully cornered. If only there was time for him to go to Spain and face this English aristocrat himself, Napoleon thought bitterly. He would manoeuvre Wellington into a trap and crush him in short order. The thought of proving to his marshals how groundless their fears were was most appealing. He would triumph where they had wavered, and he would prove before all Europe that he was the finest general of the age, or indeed any age.

But there was little chance of finding the time to campaign in the Peninsula, Napoleon realised. There was an empire to rule, and enemies to be faced here in Paris, as well as the other great capitals of Europe. If there was going to be a war between France and Russia then he would need to bend his full concentration towards preparing for that conflict. It would be a struggle on a gigantic scale. As his mind grappled once again with the complexities involved in an invasion of Russia, Napoleon briefly wondered if it could be done. The distances concerned were greater than any he had led an army before. There would be a huge wastage of men, horses and wagons, long before he could engage the Tsar's armies, or, failing that, seize St Petersburg or Moscow and dictate his terms for peace from one of the Tsar's palaces.

Napoleon knew that there would not be enough men in France to fill out the ranks of the army he would need. He would be forced to depend upon contributions from his allies. Meanwhile, over a quarter of a million of his soldiers were tied down in Spain. It was maddening. Napoleon clenched his fist and frowned, and then he felt his stomach knot again, tightly, and the now familiar pain stabbed into his guts. Overwork and too much anxiety – that's what caused the stomach pains, according to the imperial surgeon.

The last of the captured colours passed by the reviewing stand and the parade was over. He thrust all thought of war from his mind and turned to his Empress. He took her hand and squeezed it gently, smiling as she turned to look at him with a questioning arch in her finely shaped eyebrows.

'I hope you are not cold, my dear. You have been sitting here for over two hours.'

'I am warm enough.' She smiled sweetly. 'It pleases me to be at your side.'

'Really?' Napoleon shook his head. 'I suspect you are being kind to me. I should think only soldiers, and those who want to be soldiers, enjoy such parades.' He leaned closer to her and nodded in the direction of Kurakin and Talleyrand. 'Others, however, evidently find such occasions a bore.' Napoleon suddenly released her hand and straightened up. 'Is that not right, Talleyrand?'

Talleyrand turned quickly, his face wearing its usual neutral expression. 'Pardon, sire?'

Napoleon rose from his seat and gestured to Marie-Louise. 'I was explaining to the Empress that not all men feel comfortable in the presence of soldiers. Men like yourself, and Ambassador Kurakin there.'

'I am not uncomfortable, sire.' Talleyrand gave the faintest of shrugs. 'It is just that I find that my tastes, and manner of conversation, have little in common with the sentiments of those in the military.'

'Is that so?' Napoleon enquired frostily, then pointed towards Talleyrand's deformed foot. 'But for that I am sure you could have served your country in a more useful capacity than you have endured.'

'I think the word is enjoyed rather than endured, sire.' Talleyrand bowed his head. 'In either case, I am sure that soldiers and statesmen alike would prefer to repair to the palace than remain here in the cold.'

'Soldiers are hardened to such temperatures,' Napoleon responded with contempt. 'As are Russians, eh, Kurakin?'

The ambassador nodded. 'Indeed, sire. The winters are so harsh in Russia that only those born and bred to it will ever survive there.'

Napoleon stared at him. 'You think so?'

'I am sure of it, sire. A man would be a fool to fight a campaign in the depths of a Russian winter.'

He held the Emperor's gaze and both men were silent for a moment before Napoleon suddenly smiled and turned back to Talleyrand. 'The mere mention of Russia is making me feel cold. Come, let's go inside.'

With the Empress on his arm, Napoleon led his guests from the reviewing platform across the courtyard to the doors leading into one of the reception chambers. A long dining table had been laid for the guests and polished cutlery, crystal and porcelain gleamed from end to end. Napoleon took his place at the head of the table, the Empress at the foot, and once they were seated the rest moved towards their assigned places. Footmen stood behind each chair, smoothly pulling them out and easing them back under the guests as they sat down. Talleyrand, Metternich and Kurakin had been placed close to the top of the table and as several imperial servants entered carrying steaming tureens Napoleon lifted his nose and sniffed.

'Onion soup! Now there's a hearty dish to warm a man through.'

'That, or a rare brandy,' commented Talleyrand.

Napoleon wagged his finger. 'Your fondness for fine things is a weakness, my friend.'

Talleyrand smiled, and no more was said until the soup had been served and a good-natured hubbub of conversation gradually rose around the table. Napoleon waited until he could be sure that his words would not easily be overheard by any but the intended recipients, and then turned to Kurakin.

'Tell me, Ambassador, does the Tsar really think that I do not know that he has all but abandoned the trade blockade against England?'

Kurakin slowly lowered his spoon as he composed a reply. 'Sire, you can rest assured that the Tsar is aware of his obligations. However, he wonders how you can insist on Russia's keeping faith with an agreement when you yourself break it when it suits the needs of France. There is something of a double standard being applied here, is there not?'

Napoleon felt his veins burn with irritation at the man's bold exposition of the tensions between the two rulers. Yet it would be hard to defend the trade deals in boots and uniform cloth that had been conducted between France and England, two nations implacably at war.

'It was a question of expediency. France benefited more from the arrangement than England. And if it was to the benefit of France, then it is also to the benefit of her allies.'

'That is an argument that applies equally to Russia, sire. Or, indeed, any of the other nations that count themselves amongst your allies. On that basis, one might ask what is the purpose of maintaining the blockade? Since it is an open secret that the blockade is flouted by every nation in Europe.'

'You are wrong, Kurakin. I have tens of thousands of customs officials enforcing the blockade in every port in France. Elsewhere, my soldiers enforce it. If only my cousin, the Tsar, would enforce the blockade as diligently, we could force England to sue for peace within the year. Once there is peace, there will be no further need for the blockade and we can all reap the rewards of unrestricted trade again.' Napoleon leaned forward and emphasised his next words. 'But we must bring England down first. That is all that matters. All that stands between us and an age of prosperity for both our nations. You tell him that.'

'I will tell him, sire.'

'See that you do. And remind him that when we first met, at Tilsit, it was I who offered the hand of friendship. I could have chosen to continue the war and crush the Tsar's armies, but I was merciful. I chose peace and offered to share the spoils of Europe. For that, Alexander owes me a debt of gratitude.' Napoleon's tone hardened. 'Instead, he insults me. He lies to my face, while all the time conspiring to steal away my lands piece by piece. Like a common thief.'

Talleyrand cleared his throat. 'Sire, I hardly think this is the place to broach such matters. Later, in private, would be better.'

Napoleon shook his head. 'No. I want the matter settled as soon as possible. I've spoken my mind; now let the ambassador carry the message back to his master.'

'Sire,' Talleyrand turned in his chair so that he could face his Emperor more directly, 'it would be wiser to confer with your advisors before agreeing on the form of any message to be sent to the Tsar. That would reduce the impact of any . . . inflammatory language, before it does any harm.'

'Damn your diplomatic niceties!' Napoleon snapped. 'This has gone on long enough. Either the Tsar is a friend and ally, or he isn't. I demand to know which path Alexander chooses.'

'I am sure the Tsar wants peace,' Talleyrand continued calmly. 'Isn't that so, Kurakin?'

The ambassador nodded, keeping a wary eye on Napoleon's darkening expression as he did so. 'Sire, with your permission, may I try to explain the Russian view of the situation?'

Napoleon took a calming breath and folded his arms. 'By all means.'

'Very well. When Russia looks towards Europe she sees an unbroken line of nations under the sway of France. She sees French troops in towns and fortresses along much of the frontier. We are not blind to the aspirations of the Poles towards becoming a fully fledged nation, with French encouragement. The antipathy between the Poles and Russia is as old as history and you would place a bitter enemy on our doorstep, sire.'

Kurakin paused and gently pushed his unfinished soup away from him. A servant nimbly reached round to remove the bowl as he continued, 'Then there is the matter of the damage the Continental Blockade is causing to our economy. Every day the Tsar is deluged with petitions from merchants who are suffering because of France's efforts to strangle trade with England. Even if the Tsar turns a blind eye to those who flout the blockade, our trade still suffers as French officials intervene further down the chain. Sire, it seems that you would beggar the whole of Europe to defeat the English. While I am confident that your imperial majesty will succeed in humbling England, we in Russia are looking to the future. With England reduced, what then will France aspire to? There are Bonapartes and Bonapartists on thrones across Europe. Your majesty is a man of ambition. We ask ourselves if such a man can ever be satisfied with what he already holds.' Kurakin leaned back in his chair, his explanation concluded.

Talleyrand and Metternich glanced from the Russian to Napoleon, nervously trying to read his reaction.

Napoleon felt the blood drain from his face, and a cold rage seized his body, making his hands tremble. How dare the Russian accuse him so boldly? How could the Tsar betray the amity that Napoleon had so carefully contrived between the two of them? It was clear that every concession made to Russia had been taken as a matter of right. This was no alliance of mutual interest. It was the Tsar whose ambition was unbridled. He took everything and gave nothing. Why, when France had last faced Austria the campaign was over and peace declared long before the Tsar's army had marched to assist his ally. Even then, the Tsar had taken the opportunity to snap up some of the Austrian lands bordering Russia. The fruits of a victory paid for by French blood, Napoleon concluded bitterly. He glared at Kurakin, tempted almost beyond endurance to explode and expose the duplicity of the Tsar, and those who lied on his behalf . . .

With a great effort, Napoleon held back his anger. This was not the time. His tirades were a weapon to be deployed with care. More often than not they were calculated to have a specific effect. Uncontained rage could be as dangerous to himself as it was frightening to others, if it then caused advisors to be restrained, and provoked enemies to revenge.

Napoleon glanced outside. Dusk was falling over the city and soon it would be dark enough for the fireworks. They were scheduled to begin after the dinner was over, but Napoleon's suppression of his anger had left him feeling brittle and impatient. Abruptly, he waved to the chamberlain in charge of the entertainments and the man came hurrying over.

'The dinner is over,' Napoleon announced.

'Over?' The chamberlain raised his eyebrows. 'What of the other courses, sire?'

'They will not be needed. Pass the word to the officer in charge of the fireworks. I want the display to begin in thirty minutes.'

'Yes, sire, but—'

'But?' Napoleon frowned at him and the chamberlain lowered his gaze nervously.

'Yes, sire. As you command.'

The man bowed and backed away the regulation number of steps before turning to issue the orders to the staff waiting the tables. As soon as the Emperor's guests had finished their soup the bowls were whisked away, and when the last of the waiters had filed out of the room the footmen stepped up behind the chairs. The chamberlain rapped his rod on the tiled floor and the conversation quickly died away.

'At his majesty's command, the banquet is over and his majesty is pleased to request that his guests now repair to the river terrace in preparation for the fireworks.'

The guests glanced at each other, surprised that the banquet to celebrate the coronation of the Emperor amounted to no more than a bowl of soup. At the head of the table, Napoleon abruptly rose to his feet, sweeping the napkin from his lap. The footman behind him just caught hold of the chair in time to prevent it from falling back, or scraping in an undignified manner. The Empress rose quickly and then the rest of the guests got to their feet. Napoleon turned to the footman.

'Bring me my coat and hat.'

'Yes, sire.'

As soon as he was well wrapped against the cold of the evening Napoleon led the way through the palace to the long wide terrace overlooking the Seine. Guardsmen were spaced at regular intervals overseeing the braziers that provided a little light and warmth for the small crowd filing out on to the terrace. As the crowds packed along the river bank saw the figures emerging from the Tuileries they let out a great cheer and the sound continued along the river, far beyond the range of those who could see the imperial party.

The Emperor and Empress took their seats, and once the other guests were in place he pulled out his pocket watch. Angling the face towards the nearest brazier he read the time, and then he replaced the watch in its fob. There were still ten minutes to go before the half-hour was up.

Napoleon coughed at the sharpness of the night air. 'Tell them to start.'

The chamberlain opened his mouth slightly, then quickly nodded and hurried away. There was a band just below the terrace and a sudden beating of drums silenced the guests and the crowds. The pounding rhythm echoed off the surrounding buildings as tens of thousands of people waited excitedly for the spectacle to begin. Then the drums stopped, and a moment later the band struck up the *Marseillaise*. Along the river the people joined in and sang with full hearts as they were caught up in the thrill of the occasion. As the last note faded away there was a brief flicker out on one of the barges, then a flare of sparks and a brilliant thread of light as a rocket shot up towards the overcast sky with a harsh hiss. It exploded in a cloud of star-like sparks that briefly illuminated the scene below, and the crowd let out a collective sigh of pleasure. More rockets whooshed into the sky and burst overhead. On the two flanking barges, carefully arranged combinations of fireworks gushed fountains of red and white sparks into the air to accompany the rockets, and all the while the band continued to play patriotic tunes, competing with the crackle and detonations of the fireworks.

Napoleon watched the display with little pleasure. His mind was still concentrated on the accusations that the Russian ambassador had made against him. Every now and then, he glanced to his left and saw the profile of Kurakin, lit up by the lurid glare from the display. The Russian had overstepped the mark. In doing so, he was clearly repeating the views of his master back in St Petersburg. If that was the case, then Alexander was spoiling for war, despite any protestations to the contrary. In that light, every slight and snub that Napoleon had received at the hands of the Russians, every breach of the terms of their alliance, every expansion of Russian power over new tracts of land, was all calculated to provoke France into open conflict.

He felt a moment's sadness at the memory of the friendship he had shared with the Tsar at Tilsit. For a time there he had felt a fondness for the Russian ruler, as an elder brother might feel for a sibling in need of guidance and a good example. Now he had been rejected, and, worse, the Tsar seemed bent on becoming the dominant voice in Europe, brooking no rival.

Across the water on the centre barge, a giant N flared into life and the Emperor's guests applauded appreciatively. On the opposite side of the river, the letter was reflected in the water of the Seine and the crowd lifted their voices in a vast, deafening cheer.

Napoleon shifted in his chair and turned towards the Russian ambassador. 'Kurakin!'

The man looked towards him, and Napoleon raised his voice so that as many as possible of his guests would hear. He stabbed his finger towards the ambassador. 'You have enjoyed the spectacle?'

'Yes, sire.'

'Good. I want you to tell your master, the Tsar, that it is clear to me that he wants war with France. That is the only explanation behind all that he has done to undermine our alliance. He has proved himself a false friend. You tell him that if he wants war with France then he will have his war. I swear by all that is holy that I will wage it on a scale beyond anything that Europe has ever seen.'

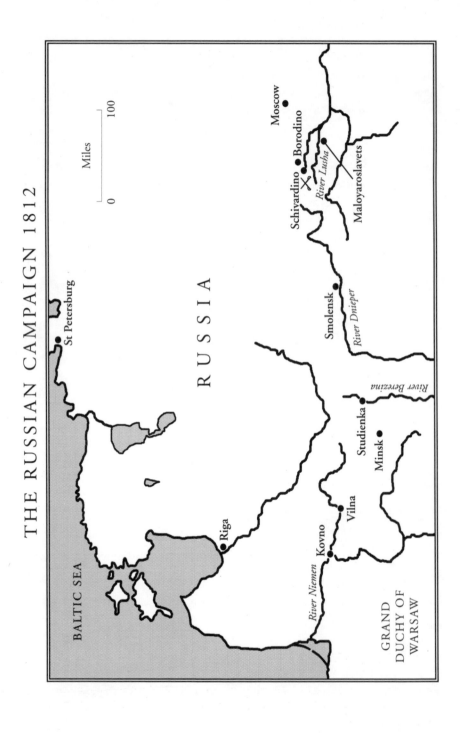

THE RUSSIAN CAMPAIGN 1812

BALTIC SEA

St Petersburg

Riga

RUSSIA

Moscow

Borodino
Schivardino

River Lusha

Maloyaroslavets

Smolensk

River Dnieper

River Berezina

Studienka

Minsk

Vilna

Kovno

River Niemen

GRAND
DUCHY OF
WARSAW

Miles

0   100

212

Chapter 23

Paris, January 1812

Talleyrand looked up from the document and gently stroked his chin with the tips of his fingers while he digested the information.

'Well?' Napoleon's voice broke into his thoughts. The Emperor was seated on the other side of the large table in the planning room of the Tuileries palace. A built-up fire blazed in the grate, casting a warm glow about the room, but not enough warmth for Talleyrand, sitting on the far side of the table. Behind him the tall windows overlooked the courtyard. Snow had fallen and blanketed the cobbles with an even layer, broken up now by the ruts of a handful of carriages and the footsteps of sentries. An icy wind was blowing across the city, occasionally rattling the windows and moaning across the chimney, causing the fire to flare and flicker.

'What do you think?' Napoleon pressed.

'This list.' Talleyrand tapped the document lightly. 'This list of grievances, sire. What do you hope to achieve by presenting this to the Tsar?'

'It will serve to remind him of all the agreements he has broken. It will provide the basis for a new agenda when we meet to renew our alliance.'

Talleyrand looked up. 'A meeting has been arranged, then?'

'No. Not yet. It is my hope that when the Tsar reads through the list of grievances and realises that the likelihood of war is very real, he will come to his senses and agree to negotiate.'

'On these terms?' Talleyrand nodded at the document. 'You say here that you demand that Russia enforces the Continental Blockade to the fullest extent. Our ambassador in St Petersburg says that there is a great deal of anger over the issue. Moreover, there are many in the Tsar's court, and also officers in his army, who are openly demanding war with France. I suspect that Alexander is living in daily fear that some coterie of malcontents is already plotting his murder and preparing the way for a more belligerent ruler. Either way, war is a distinct possibility.'

'It is more than possible, Talleyrand. It is inevitable, unless the Tsar bows to my demands.'

'I see. Then this document is designed to provoke him into declaring war.'

'I suspect that he will choose war as the lesser of two evils.'

Talleyrand stared at him. 'In my experience war is always the greatest of evils.'

'You say that because you are not a soldier. There is more to war than death.'

'Oh, yes, so I have heard. In addition to death, there is the devastation and despoiling that follows in the wake of an army. Hunger, looting, rape, torture and massacre. Not to mention the huge cost in gold that it takes to wage war on the scale that you envisage.'

Napoleon stared back at him. 'You speak like the consummate civilian you are. If it were left to the likes of you, then every nation would be crawling on its belly, prostrating itself to its neighbours.'

'If international affairs were left to my kind, I suspect that there might be an end to the curse of war that has blighted humanity throughout history, sire.'

'Then you are a fool, Talleyrand. The history of mankind *is* the history of warfare. Men have always fought each other. They always will. Which means that the primary quality in all men is their adeptness at war. Anything else is subordinate to that need. You speak of diplomacy as if it were an art in itself. It is not.' Napoleon leaned forward as he continued. 'Diplomacy can only succeed in so far as it is backed up by force. For all your fine words, do you really think that you could persuade other nations to do as we wish if they did not fear the military consequences of defying us? Your kind merely provide the illusion that the affairs of nations are governed by discussion. Such delusion merely flatters the weak and undermines the strong. Any man who cannot see through such a charade fails to grasp the fundamental reality. Power defines progress. Nothing else.'

'Then why do you have need of men like me, sire? Why waste time with diplomacy if you have such contempt for it?'

Napoleon smiled thinly. 'Even if we are little more than brawling barbarians wrapped in fine clothes, the idea that we might be something better than that is a comforting solace to the common man. If it serves my purpose to indulge such an idea then I will do so without hesitation.'

Talleyrand considered this for a moment and shook his head. 'There we differ, sire. You see, I believe that we are not barbarians. That we are capable of barbaric acts is beyond question. Therefore, it behoves the best of men to persuade the rest to embrace civilised values, for the long-term good of all. That is the sacred duty of the good and the great, in my view.'

'No doubt you feel that I am not of that class?'

'On the contrary, sire. I have always known that you possessed one of the most brilliant minds of our age, despite the disadvantage of humble origins. I do not mean that as a slight on your character. I admire you for what you have achieved. When I first met you, before your campaign in Egypt, I counted it a blessing for France that young men of such promise were available to serve her interests and see that the ideals of the Revolution lived on. Then, when you became First Consul, you dragged the governance of France into the modern age, as well as securing her safety from foreign powers on the battlefield. Your achievements were prodigious, sire. When the Peace of Amiens began I felt sure that you were about to lead us into a new golden age. But then the war resumed, and has plagued France ever since.'

Talleyrand paused and a look of sadness crossed his features. A rare expression of feeling, Napoleon noted, as the other continued. 'It is my fear that you have lost the sensibility of a just ruler, and that you have been seduced by the glory and power of military command. At present it seems that France is being ruled according to one principle – that of facilitating the waging of war. That, sire, is a perversion of power.'

The two men stared at each other. Napoleon was quite motionless as he considered this astonishing interpretation of his character and motives. It would be easy to dismiss Talleyrand from his presence, and yet Napoleon said nothing. There was much to despise about this aristocrat, yet he had always proved to be an effective and useful sounding board to refine Napoleon's thinking. But there was something more. Despite all the treachery of the past, the Emperor still felt an affection of sorts for Talleyrand. They were both products of the Revolution. Talleyrand had as much of a hand in Napoleon's rise to power as any man, and he in turn had benefited from the generosity of Napoleon, first as Consul and then as Emperor.

Talleyrand broke the tense silence. 'Sire, do you remember Tilsit?'

'Of course. It has been much on my mind lately.'

'Then you will remember the high hopes we had for the future. The war with the Tsar was over. Better still, when you and he met, man to man, there was a mutual regard for each other, was there not? I recall how he looked up to you, as a man of destiny. On your part, there was a certain fondness.'

'What of it?' Napoleon cut in tersely. 'What is your point?'

'You must reach an accommodation with the Tsar. You must do everything that you can to rekindle that mutual regard, and affection. There must be peace between you. Great nations must find ways to live alongside each other, or they will surely tear each other to pieces.'

'You speak of compromise,' Napoleon replied with disdain. 'Compromise is nothing but the death of a thousand cuts. It bleeds a great man of his determination, of his sense of direction, of his sense of purpose, until he is nothing but a petty schemer hanging on to power by his fingertips. When that happens he is no longer great, but a figure of ridicule, and finally pity. That much I understand, Talleyrand. As does Alexander. And only one of us can be permitted to dominate the rest of Europe.'

Talleyrand settled back in his chair and his expression resolved into its usual inscrutability. 'Then there will be war between you and the Tsar. You have resolved to carry it through. I can see that now. So what is the point of this list of grievances? If Alexander agreed to answer them, it would change nothing. You would still be determined to wage war on him.'

'Of course. But this way, it forces him to accept the blame for the war.'

'He is the Tsar. What does he care about the moral burden of such a responsibility?'

'Nothing. The list of grievances is not for his eyes alone. I intend to have it published in every newspaper across Europe. I want no one to doubt that the coming war is being instigated by the Tsar. I want all Europe to see Alexander as a relentless threat to their existence. And when they do, then all the kings and princes of Europe will unite behind me, and we shall combine our strength into a vast army that will lay waste to Russia and put an end to the threat that she poses.'

'I see.' Talleyrand nodded. 'I see it all.' His chair ground faintly on the polished floorboards and he rose to his feet. 'I must take my leave of you, sire. There is nothing more I can say. There is no point in our conversing on matters of policy again, for I can see now that you will lead France to ruin and you will not heed any opinion that runs counter to your will.' He bowed his head. 'I bid you goodbye.'

'You will not leave,' Napoleon said coldly. 'I have not dismissed you.'

'You have dismissed reason, sire. So what is the purpose of any further dialogue between us?'

'You will not leave until I say!'

Talleyrand gazed back and Napoleon could not discern a trace of fear in either his eyes or his voice as he replied, 'As you command, sire.'

He remained standing and Napoleon lowered his hands below the edge of the table so that Talleyrand would not see them clenching and unclenching, as if they were already clamped around the man's throat.

'Damn you,' Napoleon growled. 'Get out. Go. Out of my sight!'

'Yes, sire.' Talleyrand bowed his head, backed away and then turned to make his way out of the room, walking in the studied manner that he had developed to help conceal his deformed foot. The footman outside the Emperor's study had a practised ear, and opened the door at the sound of approaching footsteps. Talleyrand passed through and turned out of sight without once looking back.

'Send for my chief clerk!' Napoleon shouted.

As he waited, Napoleon turned to the fire and gazed into the flames. He knew that he had lost Talleyrand's ear for ever. There was nothing between them now but open enmity. The man would have to be placed under close watch in future, and if there was any proof of treachery, dealt with.

The sound of footsteps drew Napoleon's attention to the approaching clerk and he turned away from the fire and indicated the document on the table.

'Take that. Have it copied and sent to every newspaper in France. Have more copies sent to every court in Europe. Every newspaper. Every division headquarters in the army. Is that clear?'

'Yes, sir.' The clerk swallowed nervously. 'I shall have to call in every available man on my staff, sire.'

'Then do it. At once. Now take it and go.'

Once he was alone, Napoleon stood up and crossed to the window. He clasped his hands behind his back as he reflected on his plans for the coming war with Russia. Outside the snow was falling again, thick swirling flakes that soon blotted out his view of Paris, and then of the soldiers on guard down in the courtyard.

Chapter 24

Throughout the winter long columns of wagons had been carrying supplies to forward depots in eastern Europe. With the first buds of spring battalion after battalion marched across Europe to join the army building up in the lands of the Duchy of Warsaw and Pomerania, a Swedish territory which Napoleon had occupied in preparation for any war with Russia. In addition to the long columns of infantry there were brigades of cavalry and artillery teams dragging their lumbering burdens along the primitive roads and the tracks that were thick with mud from the thaw and rains of the season.

Napoleon had not waited for the Tsar's response to his list of grievances before giving the order to mobilise his forces. Despite the protests of his marshals in Spain, some of the best divisions were withdrawn from the Peninsula. The soldiers were glad to leave Spain. Any other posting had to be preferred to that land of heat, hunger and thirst, where every rock could conceal a peasant with a musket ready to blow the brains out of any hapless straggler or forager who wandered even a short distance from his comrades. Although their destination was a secret, by the time the men had marched through Prussia it was clear where their next campaign would take them and they viewed the coming test of arms with eager excitement.

Even though large numbers of French troops were concentrating around Warsaw they soon discovered that they would not be the only nation represented in the host gathering to humiliate the Russians. The Emperor had compelled his Austrian allies to provide forty thousand men. Another twenty thousand came from Prussia, viewed with great suspicion by the French troops. Then there were contingents from the German principalities as well as Swiss, Dutch, Belgian and Polish troops, and men sent from Napoleon's domains in Italy.

It was April before the response from Moscow reached the Tuileries. Ambassador Kurakin presented himself at the palace and requested to deliver the message to the French Emperor in person. Napoleon was closeted with his senior military planners in the room where the final confrontation with Talleyrand had taken place. Kurakin was made to stand in the doorway while a footman carried the letter to Napoleon.

The Emperor broke the seal, which bore the impression of an eagle, and quickly read through the contents of the Tsar's letter before rapping his knuckles on the table to silence his officers.

'Gentlemen, your attention.' He raised the letter and began to summarise the contents. 'The Tsar says he has considered and rejected my complaints. He tells me that while he wishes for peace between France and Russia, that peace is conditional upon certain demands. One, that France is to withdraw all of its forces from Prussia. Two, that France will compensate the relations of the Tsar whose lands were lost when the Confederation of the Rhine was created. Three, that our forces will leave Polish lands in order to create a non-aligned territory between French territory and that of the Tsar. If I comply with his wishes then the Tsar says that he might . . . might . . . consider reviewing the high tariffs imposed on French imports. If I do not comply then he regrets to inform me that he may be obliged to enforce his demands.' He lowered the letter and looked towards Kurakin. 'I take it this letter is meant to be an ultimatum?'

'I was merely instructed to deliver it to you, sire.'

'Nevertheless, you are aware of its contents, and no doubt you have been informed of your master's intentions in a separate message.'

Kurakin did not reply, but stood and returned Napoleon's gaze with a blank expression.

'Your silence betrays you, Kurakin. The Tsar well knows that his demands are unacceptable. Indeed, they are an affront to the aspirations of every Pole, as well as an insult to me. Does he think that the Emperor of France will meekly obey his whims? He knows that I cannot possibly agree to this nonsense and retain one shred of my honour and integrity. I will not abandon my Polish allies, and I will not withdraw my troops from Prussia. Does he think that I would trust Frederick William to continue to pay his indemnity to France without French troops there to remind him of his obligations? Well? Speak up, Kurakin.'

The Russian cleared his throat. 'Sire, I am merely an ambassador. I only speak for the Tsar when expressly instructed to do so. In this instance I was merely ordered to deliver the letter.'

'Nevertheless, you fully appreciate the import of its contents?'

'I believe the letter speaks for itself.'

'Weasel words, Kurakin. Be sure that this letter will be printed and circulated to every court in Europe so that they may see for themselves how the Tsar covets Europe.' Napoleon paused. 'Does your master wish to know my response?'

Kurakin looked surprised for a moment before he recovered his wits and replied, 'Surely your imperial majesty needs time to consider the letter and formulate his response?'

'No. I already know my response,' Napoleon said menacingly. 'You can tell the Tsar that he will regret his insults, when I next see him in Russia. Now leave us.'

Kurakin bowed and left the room. Once the door was closed behind him Napoleon turned to his planning staff and cleared his throat.

'We know precisely where we stand now, gentlemen. The Tsar has decided on war. Now we have to determine the best way to deliver one to him.' The officers chuckled. 'Back to work, gentlemen. There is much to do. Berthier!'

'Yes, sire?'

'You have the list of formation commanders? Then send word to them. I want to see them all, here, before they join their commands for the campaign. Given the scale of the task we are undertaking it would be well to ensure that they understand the part they must play.'

That evening Napoleon returned to his private quarters with his mind full of the myriad details of planning so vast a military enterprise. Together with Berthier, he had calculated the requirements of an army of over half a million men: the number he deemed necessary to ensure a decisive result. In addition to the men, there would be over eighty thousand cavalry mounts, nearly fifteen hundred cannon and eight thousand wagons to carry spare ammunition, powder, and sacks of biscuit and rice, all drawn by another two hundred thousand mules and oxen. Some fresh meat would be provided by the herds of cattle that were to be driven along in the wake of the army. Once they were eaten the army would start working its way through the oxen as the supplies in the wagons were exhausted. The need to scrape together every available soldier for the campaign meant that there would have to be another wave of conscripts taken on to defend France's borders and garrison the reserve areas of the invading army.

Napoleon had dismissed his valet and was slipping into his sleeping gown when there was a gentle knock at the door that linked his quarters with those of the Empress.

'Come in,' he called.

The handle turned and the door swung in to reveal Marie-Louise in her nightgown. Her long light brown hair hung down across her shoulders and she smiled at him.

'I had hoped to see you earlier. You said we could spend the evening together.'

'I know.' Napoleon crossed the room and took her hands. 'I am sorry. There is so much to do. Time is the one thing I will never conquer.'

He leaned forward to kiss her cheek, and then kissed her again, on her lips. She was not as beautiful as some of the women he had bedded, but she was young, and had developed a certain fondness for the pleasures of the flesh once she had got over the anxiety of her first experience.

She responded to his kiss with urgency, folding her arms round his back and drawing him closer. They remained there by the door for a moment before Napoleon drew his head back and nodded towards his bed. 'Over there. We'll be more comfortable.'

She flashed a smile and let him lead her by the hand to the wide bed. Warming pans had recently been taken out and there was a comforting heat beneath the heavy covers. Napoleon lay on his back, head propped up on a bolster, his arm around her shoulder as she rested her head on his chest.

'You have been planning for another war, I suppose,' she said softly.

'Yes.'

'When will you be leaving Paris?'

'In May. The campaign will start in June.'

There was a short silence before she spoke again. 'How long will you be gone, my dearest?'

'Some months. If all goes to plan the Tsar will be defeated and we will have peace before winter arrives. Then the army returns to winter quarters in Poland, and I return to you.'

'Make sure that you do,' she replied, twisting her little finger into the curls of the small patch of hair on Napoleon's chest. 'I was thinking. Could I accompany you on campaign?'

'No.'

'Why? I know that many of your officers are accompanied by their wives.'

'They are not in command of the army. I am. And I cannot afford to be distracted in any way until victory is mine.' Napoleon reached his hand down over her shoulder, beneath the gown and on to the warm smoothness of her breast. 'And you, my dear, are a terrible distraction.'

As she laughed lightly at the comment, Napoleon was already thinking that he might arrange for Marie Walewska to accompany the army, for the first part of the campaign at least. It was some time since he had enjoyed her charms and he felt his lust stirring. The Empress sensed his arousal and raised her head to kiss him on the cheek. 'Not so exhausted by the work, then?'

Napoleon looked at her and smiled. 'It seems not.'

'Then let's create another heir for the Emperor,' she said mischievously.

Napoleon rolled over, on top of her, and began to nuzzle her neck. 'You know, for a finely bred young woman, you have certain earthy tendencies.' He pulled her gown open and continued to trace his lips down her shoulder and on to her breast, taking her nipple into his mouth and giving it a tweak.

'Yes!' she gasped. 'Do that again.'

Napoleon obliged, and the corners of his mouth lifted in a smile at the thought of returning to the arms of his Polish mistress. Fantasies of her would add a certain spice to his present experience, he decided, as he eased himself forward and entered Marie-Louise.

Two weeks later the planning room was filled with marshals and generals, dressed in their blue frock coats adorned with gold epaulettes and lace, and the ribbons, stars and medals they had been awarded. Some of the officers had already been in Paris, but many had been called from their commands to attend the meeting. Napoleon wore his favoured uniform of a colonel of the chasseurs of the Guard, without any decorations. Several tables had been pushed together to accommodate the large numbers in the room, and a map depicting the vast sprawl of territory between Warsaw and Moscow lay across them.

Napoleon regarded the officers carefully. These were the finest men in his army, seasoned by many years of hard campaigning. They had proved their courage, and their ability to inspire the men who served under them. He had little doubt of their personal loyalty to him: after all, in most cases they owed rank, title and fortune directly to their Emperor. Only two issues concerned him: the rivalry between some of his commanders and then the more worrying fact that they would be required to act independently due to the scale of the coming campaign. In the past he had led smaller armies directly, and over lesser expanses of land.

When the last of the officers had arrived, Napoleon nodded at the guardsmen on the door and they pulled the door closed behind them, standing guard to ensure that there would be no interruption or eavesdropping.

Napoleon rose to his feet and his officers fell silent. He waited a moment longer to end a greater sense of gravity to the occasion, and then began.

'For some months now you will have been aware of the build-up of our forces in the east of Europe. It is well known that there are tensions between the empires of France and Russia and that both the Tsar and I have been engaged in spats of sabre-rattling. Well, the time has come to unsheathe the sword and thrust it into the heart of our enemy. Despite every effort that I have made to avoid war, the Tsar has been determined to force one upon me. I am sure you have all read the list of his demands, and I am certain that you share my sense of outrage that Alexander thinks he can humiliate me, you, and all of France. It is with reluctance that I am obliged to answer his demands with force, but nothing more can be gained from diplomacy, and the time has come to settle the question of which power commands Europe.' Napoleon paused to let his senior officers take stock of his opening words, then continued, 'You have all served me before, so you will know that I believe in seizing the initiative. Therefore we are obliged to invade Russia. As ever, our aim is to find, fix and destroy the enemy's field armies and thereby compel Alexander to sue for peace. Then we will make him eat his demands,' Napoleon added with relish. 'By the time the invasion begins we shall be able to field over six hundred thousand men, half of whom will be French.'

The officers looked at each other in astonishment. They had known about the build-up of forces, but this was the first time that they had been given the number of soldiers involved. Three times the size of any army that Napoleon had ever commanded before.

Marshal Davout raised a hand.

Napoleon nodded at him. 'Speak, Davout.'

'Have we accurate intelligence on the size of the Tsar's armies, sire?'

'Our agents report that Russia has somewhere in the order of four hundred thousand men under arms. However, many are deployed in garrisons spread across his lands. Only two hundred thousand will be standing between us and Moscow. At present they are divided into two armies. The main army, a hundred and fifty thousand men, under the command of General Barclay de Tolly, is presently dispersed between Riga and the Niemen river. The second army, under General Bagration, is to the south of the Pripet marshes.' Napoleon lifted the long cane that lay on the table and indicated the vast sprawl of wetlands, small lakes and swampy forests that stretched across the middle of the western expanse of Russia. 'Our primary target is the northern army. We will need to force them to fight before Bagration can march his men to join them. Once the northern army is crushed, we will deal with Bagration. When that is done, the Tsar will have no choice but to admit defeat.'

Prince Jérôme spoke up. 'Surely if we have six hundred thousand to their two hundred thousand, then we could face their combined army and still win easily. Why not encourage them to link up? It would surely shorten the campaign and make our task easier, sire.'

Napoleon looked at his younger brother and forced himself to respond patiently. 'Look at the map again. It is seven hundred miles from Warsaw to Moscow. The reason why I need so vast an army is because we will need to leave tens of thousands of men in our wake just to protect our lines of communication back to Warsaw. We can also count on losing more men along the route, due to injury and sickness. By the time we force the Russians to fight the chances are that we will only have a small advantage in numbers. That is why we must do all that we can to defeat them in detail. Is that clear, Jérôme?'

'Perfectly, sire.' Jérôme smiled. 'Though I am certain that we can defeat those Russian peasants, even if they outnumber us.'

'Oho!' Marshal Ney snorted, sitting opposite Jérôme. 'And do tell us why that is.'

'Certainly. I have heard that the Russian soldiers are little more than dumb brutes, conscripted from their farms. Their officers are drunkards and imbeciles. How can such a rabble stand before the might of France?'

'You were not at Eylau, were you, boy?'

'As you well know.'

'Then you have never faced the Russian soldiers. I have, like many others in this room who were also at Eylau. Yes, some of them were roaring drunk, but drunk or not, they feared nothing and fought like bears and died like men I would have been proud to command.' Ney leaned back and regarded Jérôme with a hard smile. 'So before you come over all cocksure, it would be as well to know of what you speak.'

Jérôme flushed angrily and leaned forward to reply, but Napoleon cut him short. 'That's enough!' He glared at both men for a moment, then took a deep breath and continued the briefing. 'My intention is to destroy each army in turn. We will make every effort to keep Barclay de Tolly and Bagration apart. That means that we will need to manoeuvre as swiftly as possible. However, due to the sparse population of the steppes, it is doubtful that we can resort to our usual practice of living off the land. That is why I have ordered the build-up of rations at our forward supply depots, and gathered the wagons necessary to carry the rations with us from there. Once we are over the Niemen, we can feed our army for twenty-four days on the march. With such resources we shall devour all distances. Within that time I aim to have defeated both armies.' Napoleon rested the stick against his shoulder. 'Any questions? Davout, you look as if you have something else to say.'

The marshal nodded. 'Sire, what if the enemy decide to trade space for time? Look at the map. They could fall back for months before they risked exposing Moscow, or even St Petersburg. Our rations would have expired long before then, and if there isn't much to be had by foraging, then the army might well starve before it ever reached the battlefield. And there's something else that concerns me. We both know the appalling conditions of the roads in Poland. It would seem reasonable to assume that the roads in Russia will be as bad, if not worse. If that is so then we can expect to lose a high percentage of our supply vehicles due to broken wheels and axles. I know they can be repaired, but the key point is they will be delayed. I fear that our supply convoys will start to fall behind our soldiers in a matter of days. Once that happens, then our ranks will start to thin out, slowly at first, and then more and more swiftly the further we advance.'

When Davout finished, the other officers remained silent. No one sought to contradict him and Napoleon felt his anger rise at the lack of confidence Davout had inspired amongst his peers.

'Thank you, Davout. Your concerns are duly noted. However, I can assure you that no army has been better prepared for such a campaign.'

'No army has ever attempted such a campaign, sire.'

'Then the fame and glory we shall win will be all the greater, Davout. Think on that.' Napoleon looked round at his officers to gather their attention for his concluding remarks.

'As I said, our aim is to destroy the Tsar's armies. If they refuse to fight then we will occupy Moscow and St Petersburg. Either way, the Russians' will to continue the fight will collapse and we will have our victory. Marshal Davout is right. Nothing like this has ever been attempted before. Once it is over, the whole world will know that there is no limit to what the armies of France can achieve. We will finally be able to enforce the Continental Blockade to the utmost. I predict that within a year, England will at last be starved into submission. When that happens, gentlemen, then this war of wars will be at an end, and France, our France, will hold dominion over the whole world. In years to come, you, and all of our soldiers, will be able to tell your grandchildren about the day you entered Moscow at the side of your Emperor. Think on that as you ride to join your commands.'

He sat down, and an instant later Ney was on his feet, thrusting his fist into the air as he called out, 'Long live Napoleon! Long live France!'

Jérôme rose and repeated the cheer, along with the others. Even Davout eventually rose to his feet and joined the cheering, but Napoleon saw the concern and doubt still lingering in his expression.

Davout was wrong, he told himself. With so many men at his command, so many fine officers, the best cavalry in Europe and enough artillery to equip a fleet, how could there be any other outcome than a triumphant victory that would eclipse those of every other general throughout history? Napoleon eased himself back in his chair and smiled.

Chapter 25

Arthur

Badajoz, 6 April 1812

'This time we'll have the place,' Arthur concluded as he finished surveying the three breaches that had been opened in the wall between two of the most powerful bastions of Badajoz. The new siege guns had proved their worth and in the space of two weeks the heavy shot of the twenty-four-pounder cannon had battered down the defences of the outlying fort of Picuriña before being turned on the formidable walls of the town itself. 'Those breaches will be practicable before nightfall.'

Somerset took a last long look through his telescope before he lowered it and nodded. 'Yes, sir. Shall I issue the orders for the attack to take place tonight?'

'Indeed. Tonight.' Arthur's cheerfulness faded. This was the point of greatest risk and loss of life. All sieges built towards it – the assault – and even if the assault were successful the cost could be heavy. Still, the army was in high spirits, and had been so since the start of the year when Arthur had led them back into Spain to take the fortress of Ciudad Rodrigo. Despite the gruelling cold of January, the army had besieged the town efficiently, digging the approach trenches, constructing batteries, smashing down the walls and assaulting the fortress in the space of ten days. All at a cost of six hundred casualties, a fifth of whom had been killed, including General Craufurd. Arthur had felt his loss keenly. Although Craufurd had been a prickly character, and prone to occasional acts of rashness, he had been an inspired commander of the Light Division. There were too few officers like him in the army, Arthur reflected. Men who could make the difference in an assault on a fortress as powerful as Badajoz.

The capture of Ciudad Rodrigo had been rewarded by elevation to an earldom back in England, while the Spanish junta had conferred the title of Duque de Ciudad Rodrigo upon him. More important, the army's success had prompted the government to promise more reinforcements, especially the cavalry that Arthur had been pressing for since he had taken command. The first of seven fresh mounted regiments had already joined the army and the others would soon arrive. With a strong force of cavalry Arthur would be able to operate against the French with far more flexibility. No longer would he be tied to fighting defensive battles on terrain that negated the enemy's superiority in cavalry. Now his army could go on the offensive and risk battle in the open.

But that was work for the future, Arthur reflected. First he must take Badajoz. He raised his telescope to inspect the fortress once more. The side facing the open ground to the west and south was protected by a formidable wall, and other defences put in place by the garrison commander. General Philippon was a veteran, some years older than Arthur, grey hair tied back above a lined face with piercing brown eyes. Arthur had met him briefly at the opening of the siege, when he had approached the fortress town under a flag of truce to demand its surrender. Philippon had emerged from the main gate, by the river, to decline the demand and Arthur, according to protocol, had reminded the defender that he would be able to come to terms until such time as a practicable breach had been opened in the walls of Badajoz. After that the fortress would be assaulted and, according to the customs of war, the defenders would be at the mercy of the British soldiers.

'We'll use four divisions for the assault,' Arthur announced to his officers at the midday briefing. He was standing before a detailed map of the town's defences pinned to the wall of the tavern that served as the army's headquarters, and now raised his cane and pointed to the south-eastern corner of the walls of Badajoz. 'Alten's Light Division and Cole's Fourth Division will assault the breaches at ten o'clock tonight. At the same time there will be two diversionary attacks.' He pointed out the eastern sector of the town. 'Picton's Third Division will cross the Rivillas stream, climb the cliff to the east and attempt to escalade the castle. The walls there are sufficiently low to enable our ladders to reach the battlements. Meanwhile, on the other side of Badajoz, Leith's Fifth Division will assault the main gate. Leith?'

'Sir?' General Leith leaned forward.

'The enemy have mined the approaches to the gate. Your fellows will need to be careful. Let the enemy explode the mines before you close on the wall, understood?'

'Yes, sir.'

Arthur looked round at his officers. 'I fully expect that this will be a much harder nut to crack than Ciudad Rodrigo. We can expect a greater number of casualties, but it is important to bear in mind the strategic purpose of this operation. With Ciudad Rodrigo and Badajoz in our hands the initiative passes to our side for the remainder of the campaign in the Peninsula. As you will know, Bonaparte is almost certain to attack Russia later this year. It is my conviction that he is about to make a mistake that may well be the turning point of the long war we have been engaged in. His campaign in Russia will exhaust his armies, and if we are lucky he may be defeated on the battlefield into the bargain. Our intelligence has shown that the best French formations are in the process of withdrawing from Spain in order to swell the ranks of the Grand Army. Gentlemen, this is precisely the opportunity I have been waiting for and I intend to seize it as firmly as possible. With the frontier fortresses in our hands, we will take the war to the French on our terms from now on.' He paused. 'Let that prospect fill your hearts and stiffen your sinews for this night's work.'

His senior officers clapped their hands on the table to applaud the sentiment and then Arthur raised a hand to quell the racket. 'Any questions?'

There were none, and he dismissed them to return to their commands and prepare for the attack. For the rest of the afternoon, until dusk, the divisions assigned to the attack rested in their bivouacs. The siege batteries shifted their fire to fresh sections of the wall in the faint hope that the defenders would think that the British required more breaches before launching an assault. Arthur doubted that Philippon would fall for such a ruse, but it was worth trying.

From the terrace garden of the tavern Arthur scanned the lines of the Light Division with his telescope and saw that some of them were reading, a few – more literate – were writing letters or diaries, and most were sitting in loose circles around their camp fires cooking up the daily ration of meat and biscuit into a thick broth. A handful of men had produced fiddles or flutes and were entertaining their comrades with jaunty tunes. Arthur was pleased. The men seemed to be in good humour. Then his gaze caught a small group of men, a hundred or so, kneeling before a chaplain, heads bent in prayer. Those were the volunteers of the Forlorn Hope, the assault party. They would lead the attack in an almost suicidal attempt to rush the breach selected for the Division and hold it open until the follow-up troops arrived to break into the town.

As he watched, Arthur could not help wondering at the nature of men who would volunteer for such a task. To be sure, there were rewards for those who survived. Promotion for the officer, sergeant and corporals, and the privates who distinguished themselves. But with the odds so stacked against them, those men would have to be so desperate for promotion that they valued it above life itself. Then there was the darker possibility, Arthur realised. Some of those men might be motivated by a lust for blood, a sickness he had seen in a few soldiers during his career. They craved battle and found such elation in the experience that it became an addiction, until death or a crippling wound cured them. If there were any men like that in the assaulting units then God help the people and garrison of Badajoz when the walls fell, Arthur thought, shuddering.

When night had fallen across the Spanish countryside Arthur, General Alava and Somerset, together with some of the staff officers, made their way up on to the ramparts of the Picuriña fort where they would have a good view of the attack on the three breaches. To the left of the fort the men of the Light Division were stealing forward along the shallow banks of the Rivillas. They had been ordered to advance in strict silence and Arthur could barely discern any sign of life in the shadows below the fort. To the right, the men of the Fourth Division had entered their approach trenches and begun to creep forward until they were halted a short distance behind the men of the assault parties.

At nine o'clock the siege batteries fired their final round, as ordered. Arthur had not wanted to risk the flare from their discharges illuminating any of the preparations for the assault. As the firing ceased there was a tense quiet that felt strange after the din of the bombardment, the silence broken only by the occasional challenges of sentries and the croak of frogs along the banks of the stream.

Arthur turned to General Alava and muttered. 'This time you shall see us take the town.'

'I have every confidence, my lord.'

As they waited for the attack to begin the officers around Arthur grew increasingly tense, and while some fidgeted nervously others talked in low tones until Arthur turned round to glare at them in the dim glow of the lanterns hung inside the fort. They fell silent and he turned his gaze back towards Badajoz. Torches burned along the walls and here and there he could make out the dim figures of sentries patrolling the battlements. Every so often a sentry, suspicious of some sound or movement in front of the wall, would lob a torch in a fiery arc into the dead ground and perhaps startle a dog or some other small animal.

The minutes dragged by. Arthur kept himself as still as possible, in order to set a calm example to his subordinates and ensure that his reputation for being unflappable endured. At length he discreetly took out his fob watch and angled the face towards one of the lanterns down in the fort. Almost quarter of an hour remained. Down below, within the fort, a handful of artillery men stood in one corner, ready to launch a rocket that would be the signal for the main attack to begin.

At that moment a voice called out from the direction of the trenches.

'Pick that bloody ladder up, you lazy Irish bastard!'

Arthur felt his heart jump. Around him the other officers froze, waiting for the alarm to be given up on the wall. The seconds passed, but there was no reaction from the enemy and no more shouts from below as the frogs continued their rhythmic croaking. The tension eased and Somerset let out a long low sigh.

'That was close. Someone should have that man on fatigues for the rest of the year.'

'I dare say there will be time for recriminations later,' Arthur responded evenly.

He concentrated his gaze on the approaches to the breaches, knowing that the Forlorn Hopes of each division would be creeping stealthily forward at that moment. After a delay of a minute the assault parties would begin to follow them, while those behind gripped their muskets and awaited the signal for the general attack. Arthur saw a movement in the shadows perhaps fifty yards from the breach, then another, then more, as the Forlorn Hope crawled through the rocks and scrub in front of the wall.

A French voice called out, a challenge, then an instant later there was a muzzle flash on the wall. The crack carried to Arthur a second later.

'Up lads and at 'em!' shouted the ensign in command of the Forlorn Hope, and figures rose and sprinted towards the breach. The cry was taken up to the left and right as the other volunteers dashed for the other breaches. Arthur turned to Somerset. 'Kindly give the signal.'

Somerset cupped a hand to his mouth. 'Rocket crew! Fire!'

There was a brief glow as the sergeant blew on his slow fuse and then applied the end to the tail of the rocket. Sparks pricked out and then with a whoosh the rocket soared into the night sky leaving a brief trail of fire in its wake. High above Badajoz it burst in a brilliant explosion of white, and the detonation echoed back from the town walls. There were more shouts along the wall now and more muskets crackled as they saw the attackers rushing towards them. There was no need for stealth any longer and the English soldiers shouted their battle cries as they broke cover and charged for the ditch in front of the wall. Arthur felt his muscles tense as he watched the Light Division's Forlorn Hope begin to scramble across, and then up to the debris below their breach. The walls on either side flickered with musket fire and the ensign in command dropped before he was even halfway up the pile of rubble. His sergeant went down within feet of him and then several more were cut down as they struggled over the difficult ground. The remainder charged forward regardless of the slaughter, and they too fell as they scrambled towards the breach. Not a single man from the Forlorn Hope got even as far as the tangle of abattis spread just below the breach.

'Good God,' Arthur muttered under his breath.

The leading men of the assault party reached the ditch, but now the first of the cannon on the bastions joined in with the musket fire, the blast of flame briefly illuminating the walls in a lurid orange glow as the grapeshot lashed the ground in front of the ditch, dashing several men on to the grass. More figures emerged from the darkness, some carrying plank-covered ladders which they threw over the ditch and rushed on towards the breach. Soon over a hundred men were struggling up the rubble and some were on the verge of gaining the breach, under a storm of musket fire that was cutting them down all the time. Then, as the first redcoat clambered into the breach, there was a brilliant flash of light close to the foot of the wall which sent rocks and men and body parts flying through the air as the walls and approaches were briefly lit up for hundreds of yards, freezing thousands of men in a tableau of destruction. The concussion and roar of the explosion struck the officers in the fort a moment later. Despite the shock, the assault continued without any pause.

'A mine!' Somerset exclaimed in horror. 'They hid a mine in the rubble.'

'Thank you, Somerset,' Arthur snapped tersely. 'I am following events, you know.'

The assault party was now swarming across the ditch and the fire from the walls was reaching a new intensity, cutting down the attackers in swathes, all in full view of Arthur and his staff as the lurid flare of artillery and muskets continuously illuminated the scene. But the horror of the assault was not yet complete. As the first of the attackers climbed into the breach they were confronted by a screen of *chevaux de frise*, wooden beams pierced with sharpened sword blades and supported by trestles at each end. In front of them were planks with six-inch nails protruding from the surface, and behind them a barricade lined with French marksmen. Dozens of redcoats stumbled on to the nails in agony before being shot down or impaled on the sword blades and left to hang there, screaming as they bled to death.

The assault party died in the breach, and now the following wave of the Light Division came forward, the men throwing themselves into the attack, determined to succeed where their comrades had failed. They charged over the ditch, their ranks thinned by grapeshot, and then on to the breach where they faltered, unable to find any way over the savage obstacles waiting for them.

For an hour one attempt after another was made to take the breach, and then Arthur watched in despair as the men started to go to ground, pressing themselves into the soil, or sheltering behind rocks and down in the ditch. Now the French began to lob grenades down from the wall and each burst caused more casualties amongst the men taking cover. Arthur knew that the crisis of the assault had been reached. If the men could not go forward then they would die where they were. The only chance of success was to keep attacking.

'Somerset, send a message down to Alten. He must keep his men going forward.'

'Yes, sir.'

'Also, send word to Cole and the other divisional commanders. I have to know how their attacks are proceeding. See to it.'

The second assault began at eleven thirty as a fresh battalion moved forward towards the breach. They fared no better than their predecessors and the slaughter continued as before. It was now impossible to see the gap or the debris slope leading up to it through the heaps of redcoats, and yet still the officers rallied their men and made one attempt after another.

General Alava could not help marvelling at the terrible spectacle. 'My lord, I have never seen such gallantry in any body of soldiers.' He paused a moment. 'Surely they have sacrificed enough this night? They have proved their gallantry. Yet they cannot take the breach. Spare your men. Recall them and end this butchery, I implore you.'

Arthur resisted the urge to turn and meet the Spaniard's gaze. He felt consumed by anguish over the decimation of those fine men down in front of the breach. Alava was right. They had no peer in terms of their courage and determination. That was why they would, why they must, surely succeed. He swallowed to make sure his voice did not betray him when he responded. 'I will not recall them.'

The attackers' nerve did not fail them for another two hours. Only then did they pull back from the wall, just far enough to be out of the range of the French muskets, and hidden from the cannon by the darkness. Even so, the French regularly fired blind in an effort to discomfort their attackers.

In that time Somerset had returned to inform Arthur that the Fourth Division had also failed to take the two breaches to its front and had suffered grievous losses. Shortly after two in the morning a runner arrived from General Alten. The corporal had a bandage around his head, and one arm hung uselessly in a sling as he made his report to Arthur.

'The general's compliments, sir. He begs to inform you that his first two battalions have failed to take the breach. They have suffered heavy casualties, most of them dead, as those who fell wounded were struck again by the defenders' fire where they lay. The general wishes to know if you require him to continue the attack, sir.'

Arthur stared at the man, momentarily unable to issue any orders. Then he summoned the will to harden his heart. He spoke as gently as he could. 'Tell your general that he knows my will as well as I know his courage. Tell him to rally his men and reorganise his leading formations in readiness to resume the attack as soon as possible. Is that understood?'

'Yes, my lord,' the corporal replied bitterly. 'Perfectly.'

'Once you have given him my reply, I would be grateful if you would go to the rear and have your wounds seen to. Ask for my surgeon.'

The corporal stared at him and then shook his head. 'If it's all the same to you, my lord, I'd prefer to remain with my mates than with your surgeon.'

The corporal turned and trotted away, leaving Arthur to stare after him, his stomach sick with guilt. Then he turned back towards Badajoz, not daring to meet the eye of any of his officers.

A pounding of hooves sounded from down in the fort and a voice cried out, 'Where's Wellington?'

'Up there, sir.' One of the artillery crew pointed to the rampart. A moment later an officer came running up to Arthur and the others.

'My lord, I come from Picton's division. He sent me to find you as soon as he was sure of our success.'

'Success?'

'My lord, the castle is yours.'

'What? Tell me more!'

'The escalade succeeded, sir. Only after heavy losses, but the division has control of the castle.'

Arthur felt hope rekindle in his heart, and a familiar alertness to the possibilities of the situation. The sacrifice of the men in the breaches might have had some purpose after all if, as seemed likely, the enemy had been obliged to draw men from the other sectors of the town to defend the breaches. If Picton's division had succeeded then there was a chance that Leith might as well.

'Has Picton enough men left to attack the breach from behind?'

'Surely, but he cannot break out of the castle, sir. The French have blocked all the gateways.'

'Damn.' Arthur frowned. 'Very well, ride to Leith. Tell him what you have told me. Tell him that the French have sent every available man to defend the breaches. If he is bold he can take the wall in front of him.'

Picton's officer saluted and ran back down the stairs to his horse. Within twenty minutes there was a ferocious fusillade of shots to the north and then the shrill notes of bugles as the Fifth Division stormed into the streets of Badajoz. The fire from the French soldiers around the breaches quickly died away and then there was only sporadic shooting, fading slowly as the enemy pulled back to the northern sector of the town. Below the fort, the Light Division was warily advancing towards the breach again. This time the walls were silent, the ramparts and bastions abandoned by the enemy. Arthur watched as the leading company clambered over the bodies in the breach and then disappeared into the town, followed by the rest of the battalion.

'Come, Somerset, Alava!' He turned and hurried out of the fort, striding swiftly over the open ground towards the breach. They came across the first bodies a short distance from the ditch, sprawled and twisted on the ground. The rear formations of the division were standing formed up in front of the ditch waiting their turn to enter the town. General Alten was on the far side ensuring that his men did not advance in a mad rush. Until the lethal obstacles were removed it would be too perilous. Alten saw Arthur and the others approaching and turned to salute his commander.

'A very bloody business, my lord.'

'Indeed. But we have the town.'

'Yes. There is that.'

For a moment there was elation in Arthur's heart. Then his gaze travelled up the pile of bodies, rising to the breach where yet more lay heaped. A company of Alten's men had stacked their muskets and were busy clearing away the spiked planks and the *chevaux de frise* while other men searched amongst the bodies for the living. Here and there a voice called out for help, or groaned in agony, and the dead were pulled away so that the wounded could be freed from the tangle of limbs.

Meanwhile, the companies entering the breach were obliged to climb over the bodies of their comrades.

'What is that smell?' asked Somerset.

Arthur sniffed. It was like roasting meat and his stomach lurched as he realised it came from the men who had died when the mine had exploded. He pressed a gloved hand to his nose as he stared at the hellish scene.

'What was it you said, General Alava? You had never before seen such gallantry?'

'Yes, my lord.'

'I hope that I shall never again be the instrument of putting them to such a test as that to which they were put tonight.'

As he gazed at the dead there was a woman's scream from somewhere in the town, then a harsh chorus of laughter. Elsewhere a shot rang out. The British army had paid a high price to take Badajoz and now they would be sure to slake their thirst for revenge on the people of the town, regardless of whether they had aided the French or not.

Chapter 26

Badajoz was thoroughly sacked over the following days. The soldiers broke into every house and stole all that they could, killing those who stood in their way. Many sought out wine and spirits and their drunkenness served to strip away what was left of their self-control. The terrified cries of women filled the streets. Rape became simply one of the vices through which the soldiers vented their rage against the town that had cost them so many comrades. Once the thirst for revenge had been sated, they turned to looting, and when the townspeople's gold and valuables were exhausted the soldiers began to turn on each other, clubbing men down to steal their loot.

Arthur knew what was going on within the walls of the town but was powerless to act. The officers had simply lost control of their men and some of those who had tried to enforce discipline had been shot at, or violently thrust aside and forced to flee the city. The only soldiers still under Arthur's control were those who had been ordered to remain outside the walls, and they looked on with a degree of envy as the other men indulged in an orgy of theft and destruction.

The final act of the siege occurred the day after the assault, when Fort San Cristobal surrendered. With the breaches taken, General Philippon had gathered the survivors of his garrison and led them across the bridge over the Guadiana, and fought his way along the bank to reach the fort.

Having given orders for the burial of the dead, and viewed the harrowing list of casualties, Arthur crossed the river and approached the fort together with an ensign bearing a flag of truce. Riding up the steep ramp to the gate he halted and demanded to speak to General Philippon.

After a brief delay the locking beams rumbled behind the thick timbers of the gate and one of the doors swung inwards. Three men emerged, two soldiers supporting the general as he limped painfully between them. Philippon's breeches were cut away below the right thigh and there were splints on his leg, tied round with bandages through which blood had oozed in a series of dark round patches. He was bareheaded, and his face was streaked with dried blood from a tear across the top of his scalp. Nevertheless he managed to smile as he greeted Arthur.

'My congratulations on the swift and successful resolution of the siege, my lord.'

Arthur swallowed bitterly. 'It is hard to derive any satisfaction from the outcome when so many men have been lost. Over three thousand of my soldiers fell before your defences.'

For a moment the Frenchman's composure slipped as he recalled the ferocity of the previous night's battle. 'I never before saw such slaughter . . .' He cleared his throat and raised his head. 'My men and I did our duty, just as your men did. That is the cost of war.'

'An avoidable cost. You could never have held the town. There is no honour in fighting to postpone inevitable defeat.'

'Is there not?'

'No. Not for you here at Badajoz, nor for the rest of the French army in Spain. Nor for your master, Bonaparte. He cannot win the war. All Europe is against him, despite the sham treaties and alliances he has forced on France's neighbours. There is only one outcome, I am sure of it. Bonaparte can't win. He can only put off losing.'

Philippon smiled sadly. 'My lord, that is half the reason why men go to war, to postpone inevitable defeat, as you put it.'

'Then such men are bloody fools,' Arthur replied tersely. 'Now then, I have no desire to prolong this discussion. I am here to offer you terms for the immediate surrender of San Cristobal. I do not desire to lose any more men in assaulting this fort, so if you refuse to surrender I will have my siege guns ranged against the fort and they will pound it to pieces. I will not take any prisoners.'

Philippon scrutinised Arthur's unflinching expression. 'You wish to discuss terms? Then I will surrender the fort, and my men's arms, in exchange for free passage to Madrid.'

Arthur shook his head. 'You misunderstand. I am not here to discuss terms, but to state them. In short, you will surrender the fort unconditionally. Your men will be disarmed and marched to Lisbon where you will be shipped to England as prisoners until the end of the war, or such time as his majesty's government decides to exchange you. If you will not agree to these terms then you and your garrison will be destroyed along with the fort.'

'I need time to consider.'

'No. You accept or reject my terms now.'

Philippon frowned and looked down to conceal his anguished

indecision. He shook his head slightly, then paused and looked up, resigned to his fate. 'Very well. I accept.'

'Good. Then your men will leave the fort within the hour and form up there to surrender their arms.' Arthur pointed to the flat expanse of ground below the fort, close to the camp of Beresford's Portuguese battalions. 'You will make no attempt to destroy any supplies or equipment within the fort, is that understood?'

'Yes, my lord.' Philippon nodded as he stared at the Portuguese soldiers in their camp. 'But I would rather surrender to English soldiers than the Portuguese. In view of the . . . barbarity with which they have treated French prisoners before.'

'I recall little difference between the barbarity of the Portuguese and that of the French under whom they were forced to suffer. In any case, I cannot afford to despatch one of my battalions to escort your men to Lisbon. I think you will find that the Portuguese, thanks to our training and example, will treat you with greater mercy than you have shown to many of their compatriots,' Arthur concluded coldly. He lifted his hat. 'I bid you good day, General. We shall not meet again. Make sure that the last of your men leaves the fort within the hour.'

Arthur turned his horse away and spurred it into a trot, a sour taste in his mouth.

It took four days for the soldiers to recover their senses and start drifting out of the city, nursing hangovers and clutching their spoils in loose bundles. The army's provost general was all for disciplining them for being absent without leave, but Arthur ordered that no action be taken. Instead, fresh toops were sent into the town to fish out the last of the looters and eject them. Then the work of repairing the damage began. The sick and injured of Arthur's army were carried into the castle's barracks to be looked after by the surgeons of the units assigned to garrison the town.

A steady trickle of those who died from their wounds was added to the corpses laid out in a series of long graves a short distance from the walls. When each grave was filled, men wearing gin-soaked cloths about their faces to overcome the stench of the corpses shovelled earth over the bodies and then piled heavy stones on top to discourage wild dogs, carrion and human scavengers.

With Badajoz in English hands Arthur began to plan his next course of action as he waited for the latest reinforcements to reach the army. Despite the losses, his strength, when the fresh regiments and replacement drafts arrived, rose to over sixty thousand men. Enough to take his campaign into the heart of Spain, but – frustratingly – not enough to contemplate facing a combination of French armies. Therein lay the irony of his situation. The more successful the allied army became the more likely it was to provoke the French into concentrating their forces to march on Arthur and destroy him and his army once and for all.

There was another, constant, cause for concern. Having reinforced the Peninsular army the government back in England would expect him to take the war to the French. It was evident that only a small number of wiser heads in the government appreciated the game of cat and mouse that Arthur was obliged to play with his more numerous opponents.

The most obvious enemy force for his army to engage was the army of Marshal Marmont. The latest intelligence suggested that Marmont commanded fewer than thirty-five thousand men, and that decided Arthur.

Early in May, he left General Hill and eighteen thousand men at Badajoz, in case Soult decided to venture out of Andalucia, and marched back to Ciudad Rodrigo to organise his offensive against Marmont. As he waited for the final reinforcements to reach him from Oporto, he gave orders for his wagons to be repaired and loaded with marching rations from the fortress's depot. The soldiers were rested, and given the chance to repair their kit in readiness for the campaign.

Late in the month, as Arthur was putting the final touches to the campaign plan, Somerset entered his office with the latest packet of despatches from London.

'Left London on the twelfth. They've made good time,' Arthur noted with satisfaction. He broke the seal, opened out the waterproofed covering and extracted the documents within. At the top of the pile was a small note from Lord Liverpool marked *Most urgent – read at once.*

Arthur raised his eyebrows, then with a slight shrug he pushed the rest of the letters towards Somerset. 'Prioritise those for me, if you please.'

His aide nodded, pulled up a chair and began to open and sort through the documents, ensuring, as was customary, that personal and administrative missives were placed below more vital communications. Arthur sat back in his chair and broke the wafer seal on Liverpool's letter, unfolded it and began to read. At length he folded the letter up.

'The Prime Minister is dead,' he announced evenly.

Somerset looked up from the latest document he had been glancing through. 'I'm sorry, my lord, I missed that.'

'I said the Prime Minister is dead.'

'Good God. Dead? How? Accident or illness?'

'Neither. He was assassinated. Shot in the lobby of the House of Commons. Some madman named Bellingham who blamed Perceval and the government for ruining his business, apparently.'

'I say, that's a bit much.'

Arthur raised his eyebrows. ' "A bit much" is hardly the apposite reaction, Somerset. The man has deprived us of a Prime Minister.'

'Sorry, sir. I'm just shocked by the news. It's not the sort of thing that happens in England. France or Russia yes. But England?'

'Well, yes, quite.' Arthur raised his arms, folded his hands together and rested his chin on them. 'The question is, what impact does this have on the government's policies here in the Peninsula? However parsimonious Perceval might have been in supporting our campaigns, he at least had the virtue of understanding their necessity. The danger is that his replacement may not share his views, just as we are on the brink of changing the balance of power here. Worse still, the government is weak and its opponents may seize on this as a chance to topple the Tories and push the Prince Regent to appoint a Whig administration. If that happens . . .' Arthur did not need to finish the sentence. Somerset, and indeed most of the army, knew that any Whig government would seek to withdraw the army from the Peninsula as a matter of priority.

'The government, any government, would be mad to abandon the campaign when it is showing such promise, my lord,' Somerset responded, then he smiled. 'It may take a little while for a new Prime Minister to emerge, or even a new government. Whether it be the Tories or the Whigs, you must use the time to inflict as many reverses as you can on the French, my lord. Make it politically inexpedient to recall the army.'

Arthur nodded. 'By God, you are right. Somerset, for a fine staff officer, you make a decidedly formidable politician.'

His aide sat back in his chair with a shocked expression. 'Sir! I hardly think my suggestion merits such a slur on my character!'

'Indeed.' Arthur laughed. 'I have to apologise, Somerset, else I am sure that you would call me out, and the army cannot afford to lose either of us.'

Somerset nodded, satisfied.

'So then,' Arthur stood up and looked out of the window, over the camp of his army. 'While we await word of poor Perceval's replacement, we march against the French.'

Early in June, as the allied army set off from Ciudad Rodrigo, Arthur received news that Marmont had been reinforced and now slightly outnumbered the allies. On past French showing Arthur was prepared to accept the odds and the army continued marching into Spain, making for Salamanca, the enemy's nearest base of operations.

There Arthur found that the French garrison had abandoned the city, leaving behind a few hundred men to fortify the convents that dominated the bridge over the river Tormes. While the main bulk of the army made camp on the hills to the north of the city, the engineers set to work besieging the convents by digging approach trenches and constructing batteries for the small number of siege guns that Arthur had brought with the army.

As Arthur had hoped, Marmont advanced towards Salamanca to attempt to relieve the defenders, but the allied troops on the hills barred his way. There followed a few wearing days when Arthur had the army stood to in the dust and the heat, waiting for a French attack that never came. For his part, Marshal Marmont contented himself with regularly sending a few batteries of horse guns together with some skirmishers to fire on any allied troops who were exposed on the forward slope. Arthur responded by ordering the greenjackets forward, and after a short duel the skirmish broke off and the two armies sat and watched each other as before.

The convents quickly surrendered once the siege guns began to pound the walls to pieces, and as soon as the last of them had been taken Marmont began to withdraw north, towards the protection of the river Douro. The allied army followed, camping on the southern bank. Arthur inspected the enemy through his telescope in frustration. A thin screen of pickets patrolled the far bank and the main enemy camp, its position marked by trails of smoke from camp fires, was beyond a low ridge that ran along the river for some way. His spies had told him that Marmont had already been joined by another division and was waiting for yet further reinforcements.

Then, on 15 July, a band of Spanish resistance fighters rode into the allied camp in an excited state, demanding to speak to the English general. They wore bandannas, short-cut jackets over their shirts and breeches, which were buttoned below the knee, and heavy boots. A formidable selection of carbines and pistols were visible in their saddle buckets, and swords, clubs and knives hung from their belts. The two sentries on duty outside Arthur's headquarters, a disused barn, eyed the new arrivals warily as Somerset brought General Alava out to speak to them. After a few words, Alava beckoned their leader to dismount and follow him and Somerset into the barn.

He rapped on the weathered doorpost and Arthur looked up from the map he had been studying. 'What is it?'

'One of the local fighters, my lord. He says he has captured some enemy despatches and wishes to sell them to us.'

Arthur puffed his cheeks. 'Very well. I can spare him a few minutes. Bring him in.'

A moment later the leader entered, carrying a saddlebag over one arm. Arthur rose to exchange a bow with him as Alava made the introductions. 'Señor Jose Ramirez, or El Cuchillo, as he claims to be known along this stretch of the Douro.'

'What has El Cuchillo,' Arthur smiled at the man, 'got for me, exactly?'

Once Alava had translated, the resistance leader stepped forward and laid the saddlebag over Arthur's map. Arthur noted a dark smear on the casing and assumed that it was the blood of the hapless courier who had been intercepted by El Cuchillo and his men. With a flamboyant gesture the Spaniard unfastened the strap and flipped the bag open. Inside were a number of sealed documents. One immediately caught Arthur's eye – larger and bearing a more ornate seal than the others. He gestured towards the bag and the Spaniard nodded. Arthur drew the document out and saw that it carried the seal of King Joseph and was addressed to Marshal Marmont. He broke the seal and opened it, quickly scanning the contents before he looked up.

'King Joseph is marching to join Marmont with thirteen thousand men.'

Somerset shifted uncomfortably. 'That will give Marmont nearly twenty thousand men more than us, my lord.'

Arthur nodded. 'More than enough to make a difference, I fear. The question is, has Marmont had a copy of this message? It is possible he may not know that Joseph is marching to join him.'

'It's possible, I suppose,' Somerset said doubtfully. 'Though the French tend to send out two or three couriers by different routes, given the danger presented by the partisans.'

Arthur folded the despatch and tapped it on the table. 'General Alava, please ask our friend if he has seen anything of the enemy recently. Any sign of a column on the move.'

The general translated the question and El Cuchillo nodded, and then there was a lively exchange of comments before Alava turned back to Arthur with an excited glint in his eye. 'He says that he saw a large force crossing the Douro at Tordesillas. They could not get close enough to estimate the number because of the enemy's cavalry pickets.'

'I see,' Arthur responded. He was wary of any amateur's estimation of an enemy force and needed to have a more accurate assessment of what

243

the Spaniard had seen. 'He says it was a large force. Does he mean a brigade, or a division, or something bigger?'

The general questioned the man and turned back. 'He says it was a host. He has never seen so many men.'

'It'll be King Joseph and his reinforcements, my lord,' Somerset suggested.

'I don't think so,' Arthur responded with a frown. 'That would mean they were right on the heels of the messenger bearing the news of their coming. Alava, ask him from which direction this host was crossing the Douro.'

'They were coming from the north bank,' Alava translated.

Arthur's eyes widened for an instant. 'By God, it's Marmont. He's over the river and trying to outflank us!'

Somerset nodded. 'He must know about Joseph. Why else take the the risk?'

Arthur pushed the saddlebag aside and examined the map, before crossing to an empty window frame and staring across the river at the thin haze of smoke above the ridge opposite. 'That scoundrel Marmont has tricked me. And now he aims to slip round our flank and cut us off from Salamanca. Well, whether he knows about the message or not, it makes little difference now.' He turned to Somerset. 'Pass the word to all divisional commanders: we're breaking camp and marching back to Salamanca immediately. Oh, and reward this fine fellow generously for his services. A hundred guineas in gold.'

Alava cleared his throat and rocked his hand discreetly.

'Second thoughts,' Arthur muttered. 'Make that fifty.'

'Yes, sir,' Somerset nodded and gestured for El Cuchillo to follow him. Arthur looked down at the map again with a leaden feeling of disappointment. It was as he had feared. The enemy had taken enough notice of his successes to gather together a force sufficient to turn him back. It would be a heavy blow to the army's morale, Arthur realised. To begin a retreat so soon after setting out from Ciudad Rodrigo. It would also play into the hands of his political enemies in London, who would be sure to use this latest setback as proof that the army in the Peninsula was achieving little but marching up and down the length of Spain at the taxpayer's expense.

Arthur breathed in sharply. 'Damn that fellow Marmont. He may ruin our fortunes yet.'

Chapter 27

Salamanca, 22 July 1812

'Typical of those underhand American rascals.' Somerset spoke with acid contempt as he read the despatch that had reached the army at first light. Just over a month earlier President Madison had declared war on Britain. Since Britain had only a handful of soldiers in Canada at the time the opportunist nature of the war was clear to all. 'I tell you, my lord, this is a day that will live in infamy. They attack us when our back is turned and we are fighting to save the world from a tyrant.'

'Yes, yes, a pox on them all,' Arthur muttered, doing his best to ignore his aide's ire as he contemplated the implications of the news. 'You can be sure that the army in Canada will now have first call on reinforcements. An ill day for us here in Spain, that is for certain. But for now we have other matters upon which to concentrate our minds.' Arthur nodded across the valley to the opposite ridge where Marmont's soldiers were exchanging fire with a handful of riflemen defending a small chapel beside the road to Salamanca.

For most of the last five days the two armies had been marching alongside each other, sometimes separated by no more than two hundred yards, as if they were in a race. And it had been a race of sorts, Arthur reflected. Marmont had been driving his men on in an attempt to pull ahead of the allies and then turn to cut them off from Salamanca, on ground of Marmont's choosing. For his part, Arthur had been urging his men to reach Salamanca first, and keep open their line of communication to Ciudad Rodrigo.

In the end, the allies had won the race, crossing the river Tormes some miles east of Salamanca the day before. After a night's rest, Arthur had given the order for the baggage train to take the road to Ciudad Rodrigo while the army covered the retreat. Escorted by a Portuguese cavalry unit, the baggage train was obscured by a haze of dust as it headed away. Arthur had given orders for his men to form up on the reverse slope of a roughly horseshoe-shaped hill overlooking a valley, on the far side of which was a corresponding hill formation that curved round the first. In between was a tall free-standing hill known as the Greater Arapil, as it was marginally taller than the hill upon which Arthur sat with his staff observing the movements of Marmont's army. Earlier that morning a French division had seized the hill and now, as they saw the English commander and his staff, some of them waved.

Arthur did not feel in any mood for levity. The most recent report from his scouts revealed that King Joseph was little more than a day's march to the east of Marmont, and another column of reinforcements was a similar distance to the north. Today would be the last chance to fight on roughly equivalent terms. After that, the allied army would have no choice but to retreat to the fortress of Ciudad Rodrigo. So far Marshal Marmont had shown no sign of wanting to fight and Arthur's men looked like spending the whole day without shade on the reverse slope of the ridge.

A movement caught Somerset's eye and he turned towards a nearby farmhouse, surrounded by a low wall. One of the junior staff officers was waving his hat. Somerset raised his in reply and then prepared to address his commander, somewhat unnerved by Arthur's irascible mood.

'My lord, Lieutenant Henderson has managed to secure a light meal for us.'

'What?' Arthur glanced round. 'What's that?'

Somerset pointed to the farm. 'I sent Henderson to organise some food, my lord. Neither you nor the staff officers have eaten today, and it's nearly two in the afternoon. We can eat and still keep an eye on the enemy from there.'

Arthur thought a moment and then nodded. 'Very well, but mind the food is eaten quickly. I'll not be caught napping by Marmont simply because my officers have decided to have a picnic.'

The small party trotted across the ridge towards the farmhouse. Inside the wall two long trestle tables and benches had been set out. A large platter of cooked chicken, some baskets of bread, and jugs of wine with clay cups had been laid out by the farmer and he smiled as he waved his guests towards the table. Somerset and the others slid down from their saddles and eagerly took a seat and began to eat. Arthur did not dismount, but took out his telescope from the saddle bucket to take another look at the enemy. The French were still deploying on the other ridge but seemed to have made no attempt to prepare for an attack on the division straddling the road to Salamanca, the only large formation that the enemy could see.

'Would you care for something to eat, my lord?'

Arthur lowered his telescope and saw that Somerset had brought him a chicken quarter and the end of a loaf of bread. He did not feel hungry, but knew that he needed to eat, and besides, he did not want to spoil the appetite of his subordinates by his example.

'Just the chicken, if you please.'

Somerset passed it up and Arthur forced himself to take a bite out of the cold joint. It had been hurriedly fried and the meat was slippery in his gloved hand. Somerset returned to the table and helped himself to a cup of wine as he joined the other officers happily satisfying their hunger and slaking their thirst after sitting in the saddle, under the sun, for the last few hours. Arthur watched them for a moment, mechanically biting at the chicken, chewing and swallowing. Then he walked his horse towards the wall so that he would have a better view of the enemy-held ridge to the south, opposite the centre of his line.

At first he was not certain what he was seeing. It made little sense. He raised his telescope with his spare hand and trained it on the ridge. Sun-browned grass swam across his field of vision, then he carefully tracked up the slope until he could make out an enemy division marching hurriedly along to the west. Beyond them marched a regiment of cavalry, the sun glinting off their helmets.

'What the devil is Marmont up to?' Arthur muttered to himself. He swept his telescope along the line of march and saw that it continued all the way back to the main French position. All told it looked as if three divisions were making their way across the front of the allied position. Such was the enemy's hurry that their formations were dangerously extended. Then Arthur grasped what was going through his opponent's mind. Marmont could only see a handful of men on the Lesser Arapil and the division blocking the Salamanca road. He had mistaken the great cloud of dust being kicked up by the baggage train for the allied army in full retreat, and now he was hoping to outflank, cut off and destroy what he took to be Arthur's rearguard.

Arthur felt an icy flush of excitement in his veins as he realised that the battle on advantageous terms that he had been seeking was upon him, but only if he acted swiftly. Hurling the chicken aside he turned to his staff officers.

'Mount up, gentlemen! At once!'

The imperative tone of his command had the desired effect and they jumped up from the benches, abandoning their food and wine. As they climbed into their saddles Arthur was already calling out his orders, as calmly as he could to ensure that there were no mistakes.

'The French are on the move.' He gestured towards the far ridge. 'Marmont aims to work round our position. The army is to prepare to attack as soon as possible. Gentlemen, ride out to every division and have them make ready. Somerset!'

'Sir?'

'Stay here and be ready to report to me the moment I return.'

'Where are you going, my lord?' Somerset asked anxiously.

'Why, to close the trap, of course!' Arthur grinned exuberantly, and then spurred his mount into a gallop as he raced along the ridge, heading towards the extreme right of the allied line. The Third Division, now commanded by Kitty's younger brother Edward Pakenham, had been tasked with holding the flank and was perfectly positioned for what Arthur had in mind. As the track leading towards the Salamanca road began to angle to the right and down the reverse slope, Arthur glanced to his left to make sure that the French were still advancing to the south, and was gratified by the glint as the sun caught their polished accoutrements in a shimmering sparkle.

He rode on, angling down the slope until he emerged from a vale and out on to the dusty plain behind the hills. Ahead of him was a column of redcoats, and a regiment of Portuguese dragoons, tramping south along the Salamanca road and kicking up a cloud of dust as they took up their position to cover the flank. He saw the colours of the division's battalions marching in a cluster behind a small group of horsemen. At their head was the tall, elegant figure of their general. Arthur urged his horse on, and approached the column fast, hooves pounding over the hard, dry ground beneath him. Faces turned towards him as he approached and he heard a voice cry out, 'It's our Arty!' A cheer sounded from some of the men, but they were too tired and too thirsty for any more. He slowed the horse as he reached the divisional staff officers and then reined in behind his brother-in-law.

'Edward!' he called out, and Kitty's brother turned round with a quizzical look that turned to a smile as he saw Arthur. 'Edward, I want you to continue advancing with your division. Beyond this ridge there is another. Take it and then drive back the French you will see to your front. Go in hard, and keep pushing them back for all you are worth, is that clear?'

'Perfectly, my lord.'

'Good. Then before the day is out we shall have Marshal Marmont caught in a vice of his own making. Good luck!'

Arthur turned and spurred his horse back up the slope to the ridge. The Third Division had two more miles to advance before it took the hills Arthur had described. Most of the time they would be shielded from French view by the Lesser Arapil, so that their attack would come as a surprise to the enemy. If Packenham struck swiftly he would smash into the French vanguard and start rolling their line up.

As soon as he reached the ridge Arthur rode to the two divisions waiting on the reverse slope, and ordered them to advance into the enemy's flank strung out before them. With Pakenham driving Marmont from the right, the French advance would be halted in its tracks, and then there would be chaos, and easy pickings for the Fifth and Fourth Divisions as they joined the assault. If all went well, the enemy's line would be shattered. All that remained was for the left flank of the allied line to advance and finish the job.

By the time he returned to the farmhouse the roar of cannon echoed across the left flank of the battlefield as the British and French artillery fought a duel across the valley that separated them. It was of little immediate concern to Arthur. As long as the French guns concentrated their fire in that direction they could not intervene at the decisive point.

Already the Fourth and Fifth Divisions were advancing, marching over the crest and down the forward slope towards the flank of the extended French line. Each division was formed up in a long line two men deep. It seemed like an impossibly slender formation, but it made the most of the firepower that could be brought to bear on the French when the two sides engaged.

A faint shrill call of trumpets caused Arthur and his staff to turn to their right where they saw the Portuguese dragoons attached to Pakenham's division charging towards the flank of the leading French division. Beyond the dust kicked up by the cavalry Arthur could see the infantry of the Third Division doubling forward to form a line across the head of the French advance.

The enemy were not slow to react and thousands of Marmont's soldiers rushed forward, drums beating, as they fired freely down the slope at the silent redcoats. As the dragoons began to withdraw the infantry advanced up the slope and, on reaching the crest, loosed off the first volley into the milling ranks of the leading French division. There was a brief exchange of fire, the French responding with an ill-disciplined rolling musketry, while Pakenham's men fired in volleys, discharging over a thousand muskets at a time. Arthur knew the morale effect of such a devastating blow. The leading ranks of both sides were obscured by smoke and dust, and then Arthur saw the first of the French break away, running back along the ridge to the east. Moments later he saw the redcoats emerging from the smoke as they charged and shattered the leading French division.

General Alava clapped his hands together with delight. 'Fine work! Ah, Marmont has already lost! I know it.'

Arthur kept his concentration on the action as his forces closed on the French line. The second enemy division had begun to move down from the ridge to avoid being thrown into confusion by their comrades fleeing back towards them. As they reached the floor of the valley they halted and began to adjust their formation.

'What on earth?' Somerset sat up straight in his saddle and squinted as he watched with growing disbelief. 'They're forming squares. Madness . . .'

Arthur felt a brief sense of pity for the men of the French division as the long lines of the redcoats closed on them. The key to winning a battle was using the correct formation to counter the enemy's moves. Infantry in square might well be invulnerable to cavalry but they provided an easy target for artillery and muskets. Having seen the dragoons savage the flank of the division ahead of him, the French general had decided to be cautious, and now his caution was about to be punished.

The men of the Fourth and Fifth Divisions approached to within effective musket range and halted. Opposite them, the densely packed French squares stood their ground, and Arthur was impressed by their self-discipline: not one shot had been fired. A moment later, as the redcoats lowered their muskets to take aim, the foremost sides of the French squares spat flame and smoke and after a short delay the crash of the massed volley carried up the slope to Arthur. Scores of men went down along the British line, but the casualties were far fewer than they would have been if they had been more closely formed up, as were the French.

When the British fired back, it was hard to miss, and hundreds of the enemy were cut down in the first discharge. The following volleys tore the nearest faces of the French squares to pieces, and as smoke and dust engulfed the battered formations the redcoats charged home. The struggle was brief as the badly shaken French infantry suddenly saw faint figures rushing through the haze towards them, bursting into view with a deafening roar, eyes wide and wild, bayonets gleaming as they cut their way into the ruined French squares, stabbing and beating down all who stood in their path. Having already suffered murderous losses from musket fire and now faced with the savagery of a bayonet charge the French spirit broke and the squares fell apart as the men turned and ran back up the slope towards the ridge.

However, their suffering had only just begun. Into the gap between the Third and Fifth Divisions streamed the heavy cavalry of General Le Marchant. A thousand sabres glittered in the hot sunlight as the horsemen charged at full tilt in amongst the fleeing French. It was the ideal opportunity that every cavalryman hoped for and they set about their broken enemy with ferocious slashes and thrusts, cutting hundreds of them down as they struggled up the slope.

'Glorious work!' General Alava exclaimed. 'Simply glorious.'

'For now,' Arthur replied evenly. 'But unless they are reined in, Le Marchant's men will be a spent force.'

The cavalry continued their pursuit in a swirling cloud of dust, cutting the second French division to pieces, until they came up against the third enemy formation. This time the French squares came into their own and the British cavalry were stopped in their tracks by the massed volleys of the enemy infantry. Arthur gritted his teeth in frustration at yet another example of his cavalry's propensity to lose their heads. As the dragoons began to fall back Arthur quickly surveyed the battlefield. Already, two French divisions had been shattered, and now the three British divisions were closing in on the front and flank of the next enemy formation. Arthur frowned as he watched the Fourth Division advancing, its left just starting to pass the slope of the Greater Arapil. Arthur could see a French unit on top of the hill.

'What is Cole doing?' Arthur muttered. 'Why doesn't he cover his flank?' He turned hurriedly to Somerset. 'Send a message to General Cole and warn him to watch his left flank. And tell Pack to send one of his brigades forward to take the hill.'

'Yes, sir!'

As Somerset wheeled away Arthur watched anxiously as the Fourth Division halted and began to exchange fire with the third of the French formations. So intent was Cole's concentration on the target to his front that he had clearly missed the danger to his left. Arthur could see that the enemy had realised the chance they had to take sweet revenge on the redcoats in precisely the same manner as they had suffered. But before they could strike, General Pack's Portuguese doubled forward and began to clamber up the slope towards the crest of the Greater Aparil. It was a desperate attempt to win time for their British comrades, and they were outnumbered by an enemy who held the high ground. The attack stalled as the French skirmishers unleashed a withering fire down the slope. Arthur watched with growing anguish as Pack's men stopped and went to ground, and then started to fall back.

'Time for the reserves,' he decided. Wheeling his horse about, he galloped across the ridge to where the men of the Sixth Division were waiting on the reverse slope, hidden from the battle. General Clinton sat on his horse at the head of his men and tipped his hat as Arthur rode up and reined in breathlessly.

'Clinton, I want your fellows to advance directly. They are to take the large hill to your front. The enemy must be driven from it and across the valley.'

'Yes, sir.' Clinton nodded. 'You can rely on us. The boys have missed enough of the excitement as it is.'

'Then I am glad to be of service,' Arthur smiled. Then his expression hardened. 'Remember, drive the enemy off the hill.'

By the time he had returned to his command post Arthur was shocked to see that fresh French formations were descending from the Greater Arapil, directly towards the left flank of the Fourth Division. General Cole was finally alert to the danger and had begun to wheel the battalion at the end of his line to face the danger. But one battalion would not be enough, Arthur could see at once. Within the next few minutes his fears were borne out as the French line halted and opened fire, cutting down swathes of men in the thin red line opposing them.

Arthur felt his stomach tighten as he watched. The battalion could not possibly hold its ground for long, and when it gave way the French could charge into Cole's flank and begin to roll up the allied line. Another French volley ripped through the battalion, cutting down scores of redcoats. Now it seemed that more lay crumpled on the ground than still stood, steadily reloading and firing into the oncoming French formation.

Arthur was aware that General Alava was watching him, trying to gauge his reaction, and he determined not to show the Spaniard any sign of the anxiety that gnawed at his heart. He looked to his left and saw that Clinton's men had reached the crest and begun to descend the slope. But they would not reach the hill in time to prevent the collapse of Cole's division.

'Who's that?' Somerset asked, then hurriedly lifted his telescope to examine a formation approaching the hill. It had been hidden from Arthur and his staff by a spur reaching out from the Lesser Arapil. 'It's a Portuguese brigade! Must be from the reserves, sir.'

Arthur was watching them now, and saw a general in a heavily gold-braided uniform leading them from the front. He smiled. 'Good for you, Beresford.'

The fresh Portuguese brigade marched swiftly across the intervening ground and formed a firing line on the flank of the French division that had been poised to crush General Cole and his men. With a dull crash the brigade fired into the the French flank, cutting it down almost to a man. The French advance abruptly stopped, and hurriedly began to swing back the right of its line to face the new threat.

Cole's division had been saved and Arthur breathed a sigh of relief as he exchanged a quick glance with General Alava. 'That was close.'

'Indeed?' Alava laughed. 'I would never have guessed it from your demeanour, my lord.'

Arthur turned back to observe the battle and saw that Cole had withdrawn one of his brigades from the crumbling French line to his front and sent it to reinforce his flank, stabilising his position. Caught in the angle between two allied brigades, the French began to pull back towards the protection of the hill's summit. Clinton's men began to climb the hill, the red line wavering slightly as the soldiers struggled across the boulders and patches of scrub that covered the slope. Above them the enemy re-formed, and such was the gradient that Arthur could see that the rear ranks would have a clear shot over the heads of those before them.

'General Clinton will find the going hard,' Alava mused as he watched the redcoats slowly advancing upon the waiting French men.

'We shall see,' Arthur responded quietly as he glanced at his watch. It was nearly six. Less than three hours had passed since the first shots had been fired and the sun hung low to the west, bathing the dust and smoke of the battlefield in a ruddy red-brown glow. To the south Arthur could see thousands of the French fleeing over the crest of the ridge, pursued by cavalry. The British infantry had all but given up the pursuit, and were wearily re-forming their ranks amid the enemy bodies that littered the rising ground.

A sudden crackle of gunfire from the Greater Arapil drew all eyes to its slopes as the French opened fire on Clinton's division. For once, the French firepower was massed in such a way as to permit more than just the front rank sight of the enemy, and Arthur saw the leading British brigade stagger to a halt as the leading ranks were decimated by enemy musket balls. The men steadily dressed to the right, lowered their bayonets and continued forward, closing the last hundred or so paces to the enemy. Another French volley ripped out, cutting down more men, and then Clinton swept his sword forward and with a harsh roar his men charged through the smoke and threw themselves at the French. There was a short struggle before the French fell back and retreated down the far side of the hill, closely pursued by Clinton and his men, who were intent on driving them from the battlefield.

Arthur nodded his satisfaction. There was just one section of the

French army remaining now, still covering the road leading from Salamanca, where the first skirmishes of the day had taken place. Leaving Somerset with orders to organise the pursuit of the rest of the French army until midnight, Arthur and General Alava rode across the hill to the Light Division, which had not moved since the battle had begun. General Alten was forward of his front line watching his skirmishers exchange fire with the enemy as Arthur and Alava rode up. Occasional musket balls passed by with a dull whirr before they slapped into the ground.

'How goes the battle?' asked Alten.

'It is won,' Arthur replied. 'All that remains is for your division to follow the French up. Engage the rearguard and drive it back.'

'That will be a pleasure, sir.'

Arthur reached his hand up to touch the brim of his hat. 'You have your orders, General. Hang on their heels. Give them no respite. We have Marmont beaten; now we must ensure that his army is destroyed.'

Arthur stayed to watch the Light Division begin to advance, and as soon as he saw the enemy begin to fall back, leaving a screen of light infantry to cover the retreat, he turned away and returned to headquarters with a feeling of exultation. That morning, he had been resigned to a wearisome retreat towards Ciudad Rodrigo. Now, at a stroke, and scarcely five hours later, the army of Marmont was scattered and little stood between the allied army and the Spanish capital of Madrid.

Chapter 28

Napoleon

Kovno, 24 June 1812

As the sun set on the first day of the invasion Napoleon sat in his campaign wagon reading through the latest intelligence reports. It had been a sweltering day and he was stripped to his shirt as he leaned forward over the small desk. The doors of the wagon were open and a lantern hung from an iron loop in the roof of the vehicle. Berthier sat at another table further into the wagon, busy collating the reports so that he could pass on only pertinent information to his Emperor. A cloud of mosquitoes and gnats had been drawn to the glow of the lantern and Napoleon continually swatted them away as he read. Outside the wagon a company of the Old Guard formed a cordon to keep the area clear of the long lines of soldiers tramping forward on the road to Vilna. A squadron of chasseurs had been detailed to carry messages and stood quietly in their horse lines waiting to be called forward. The wagon had stopped temporarily while the general in charge of the Emperor's campaign staff arranged for the field head-quarters to be set up in the chambers of the merchants' guild of Kovno.

Napoleon finished reading the first batch of selected reports and pushed them aside before leaning back on his bench and rubbing his eyes. There had been no sleep the night before. The first troops had crossed the Niemen in the early hours, followed by the engineers who immediately began construction of the three pontoon bridges over which the main thrust of the Grand Army was to pass, a quarter of a million men, under the Emperor's direct control. To the north, another army of eighty thousand Bavarians and Italians under Napoleon's stepson Prince Eugène was advancing to cover the left flank of the main force. On the right flank, heading towards the south of the Pripet marshes, was another army of seventy thousand men drawn from a variety of German states, as well as a contingent of Poles, commanded by Prince Jérôme. Their task was to force General Bagration east, and prevent him from linking up with the main Russian army. Still to the west of the Niemen were the last two formations of the invading army. Marshal Victor was in charge of the reserves, a hundred and fifty thousand men, ready to be sent forward to replace the losses of Napoleon's army. Behind Victor marched Marshal Augereau with sixty thousand men, tasked with guarding the supply depots to be established in the wake of the army, and keep the lines of communication with Warsaw and thence to Paris open. Even though Napoleon was commanding the largest army that Europe had ever seen, he was also the ruler of an empire and needed to ensure that messages continued to flow to and from his capital city. Ahead of the entire army rode Marshal Murat's cavalry screen, nearly twenty thousand men, probing ahead of the army, searching for the enemy while at the same time preventing enemy scouts from observing the advance of the French armies.

Napoleon lowered his hands and turned to Berthier. 'Still no sign of Bagration's army?'

'No, sire.' Berthier shook his head. 'Nothing in the reports so far.'

'Hm.' Napoleon shut his eyes again and concentrated his mind on visualising the disposition of the French columns snaking across the Russian frontier. The fact that Murat's cavalry had not fallen in with any of the enemy's outposts was strange, unless General Bagration was already retreating, in which case it was vital to discover the direction he was taking.

'Sire.' Berthier broke into his thoughts.

'What is it?'

'There's a new message here from Davout. His cavalry scouts captured some stragglers from Bagration's army. It seems that they began to march north two weeks ago.'

Napoleon blinked his eyes open and sat up. 'North? Pass me the map.'

Berthier reached towards the rack of map cases and pulled out a large-scale representation of the west of Russia. He unrolled the map across a board and fixed it in place with some pegs before passing it across to his Emperor. Napoleon glanced at the map, then traced his finger north from the last reported position of Bagration's army. 'Minsk. He's heading for Minsk.' He smiled thinly. 'It seems that the Russians are not so easily fooled. They've guessed that our main line of advance is to the north of the Pripet. Very well then, inform Jérôme that his feint is over. He's to pursue Bagration, and drive him away from the main Russian army. Let him know at once.'

'Yes, sire.'

'One day into the campaign, and already things are starting to go awry,' Napoleon sighed wearily. 'If the Russians are already attempting to link up then it is more than likely that the main army will be retreating on Vilna. Send an order to Murat. He is to take two divisions of cavalry from the reserve and ride to Vilna. He must not occupy the town. He is to observe only and report back if he encounters the main Russian army. Is that clear?'

Berthier nodded and reached for a fresh sheet of paper to write the orders.

'Good, that's done,' Napoleon muttered. 'Now I must get some sleep. Wake me when the headquarters is ready.' Rising from his desk, he squeezed past Berthier's table and climbed into the cot at the end of the wagon and pulled the netting curtain closed to keep the insects out. Rolling on to his side, away from the interior, Napoleon banished further thought from his mind and closed his eyes. A minute later, his light snores rumbled in the background as Berthier dabbed at his brow, and picked his pen up again, dipped it in the ink, and continued scratching away.

The main column of the French army marched swiftly on Vilna, where Napoleon hoped for a decisive encounter. Intercepted despatches revealed that the Tsar himself had joined the main Russian army. The news raised Napoleon's hopes of a swift end to the campaign. The prospect of his capturing the Tsar as well as defeating the army would surely compel the enemy to submit, and Napoleon ordered his army to advance as speedily as possible, even if that meant outpacing the ponderous convoys of supply wagons. But when the French army reached Vilna, they found that the Russians had gone, leaving their supply depot in flames and destroying the bridge over the Vilia river behind them.

There was still one chance to achieve an early blow against the Russians and Napoleon ordered Davout to take his corps to intercept Bagration, while Jérôme pursued him from the south. Then in early July, while Napoleon waited at Vilna for news of the positions of the Russian armies, Berthier brought him a despatch from Jérôme.

'What does my brother have to say?' Napoleon asked as he lay in a bath in the town's finest hotel.

Berthier scanned the report and then looked up nervously. 'Sire, Jérôme says that his cavalry patrols lost contact with the Russians two days ago, on the third.'

Napoleon sat up. 'Lost contact? How can they lose contact? Where is Jérôme?'

'The despatch was sent from Grodno, sire.'

'Grodno?' Napoleon recalled the name from the map and his brow knitted angrily. 'What the hell is Jérôme doing? Why is his army moving so slowly? That young fool is going to cost us dear. Berthier, take this down. Tell him that it would be impossible to lead his men in a worse manner. He should have been harassing Bagration at every step. Then he might have driven the Russians into Davout's path. We could have crushed one of the Tsar's armies. Instead he has let it escape. You tell him that he has robbed me of all that I had hoped to achieve. We have lost the best opportunity ever presented in this war, all because he has failed to learn the most fundamental principles of warfare. Did you get all that?'

'Yes, sire.'

'Send it at once. With luck that might spur the fool into activity. Too late to do much good now, though. Let's hope he responds with greater alacrity next time.'

There was not to be a next time. The next despatch from Jérôme's headquarters was written by Marshal Davout. The Emperor's letter had caused his younger brother so much offence that he had abandoned the army to return to his kingdom of Westphalia, leaving Davout to assume temporary command of his corps. Despite his anger, Napoleon considered the news a blessing of sorts as he continued his pursuit of the main Russian army.

July brought with it several days of rainstorms that lashed the columns of the Grand Army as it tramped eastwards, driven on by its commander in his desire to find the Tsar and his soldiers and bring them to battle. Within hours every rutted track was turned into a muddy morass that sucked at the boots of the men and the horses' hooves and slowed the speed of the artillery trains and supply wagons to a crawl. The Emperor's marshals, aware of his orders to press on at all costs, left a small guard behind to escort the wagons and continued the advance.

When the rains had passed, the sun blazed down on the Grand Army. The roads dried out, and then in place of mud there were choking clouds of dust that clogged the lungs and stung the men's eyes. Despite the season the nights were cool and the men huddled around their camp fires. Many of the soldiers were unseasoned and the long marches quickly exhausted them. When the rations started to run out they lacked the experience of veterans in foraging and began to starve.

Before July came to an end a long line of graves stretched back behind the army, and here and there lay an occasional naked body: stragglers killed and stripped by the bands of Cossacks that began to shadow and harass the French columns like jackals.

Nor were the men alone in their suffering. The horses were equally exhausted, and once the feed had been consumed they were forced to eat whatever green corn they could find as they passed through the sparsely inhabited Russian landscape. At the end of July Napoleon halted the army at Vitebsk to allow the supply convoys to catch up. There, Berthier updated the notebooks that recorded the strength of every regiment in the army. Nearly a hundred thousand men were absent from the lists of effectives. Many of these were sick, some were stragglers, and the rest had died on the march.

After eight days the army continued the advance, and still the Russians fell back, burning crops and destroying farms and villages in the path of the French columns. Then, at last, in the middle of August, the enemy made a stand at Smolensk. For two days Ney's infantry fought their way into the suburbs of the city, only to see the bridge over the Dnieper river blown up in their faces. The army had to wait another day while the bridge was repaired. By then the Russians were again in retreat towards Moscow.

Napoleon gave the order for the army to halt and rest while reinforcements and supplies came forward. While the weary soldiers scoured the city for food and plunder, Napoleon summoned his marshals to his temporary headquarters to consider the situation. The Russian summer was at its height and the windows of the mansion overlooking the Dnieper were wide open to admit what little breeze there was. The commanders of the central army group were as tired as their Emperor and when Berthier spread the campaign map before them Napoleon could see the dull despair in their eyes as they contemplated the two hundred and eighty miles that still stretched between Smolensk and Moscow.

An orderly served wine, chilled in the mansion's ice house, and Napoleon waited for him to leave the room before he addressed the others.

'My friends, we have been obliged to advance far deeper into Russia than I had anticipated. It seems that the Tsar is prepared to sacrifice his entire country rather than face us in battle. The army has been on the march for two months and every day we lose more men and horses to sickness, starvation and exhaustion. The main strike force has been reduced to little over a hundred and fifty thousand men. Today, our scouts have confirmed that General Bagration has succeeded in uniting with the main Russian army. Murat estimates that the Tsar now has a hundred and twenty-five thousand men between us and Moscow.'

Napoleon looked round the table at Berthier, Ney, Murat and Davout. There was a time, when he was younger and unburdened by the duties of an emperor, when Napoleon would have continued the advance without hesitation. And these men would have followed him on the instant. Now? He was no longer so sure of them.

He leaned back, raised his glass and took a quick sip before he continued. 'A number of choices lie before us. At present the army is reaching the end of its endurance. It is imperative that the men are rested if we are to continue to advance on the road to Moscow, where I am sure the Tsar will turn to fight us. At the same time it would provide us with the chance for our supply convoys to reach us. We will need them to sustain us for the final march to Moscow, as we can be certain the Russians will destroy any stocks of food or forage in our path.' He paused a moment. 'There is little doubt that continuing our advance entails a number of risks. Which brings me to a second course of action. We halt now and winter in Smolensk. It would give us time to reorganise our supplies and rest the men so that we can renew the campaign in the spring in easy striking range of Moscow. However, I will not pretend that it will be easy to maintain such a large army as ours through the winter. The last choice is the most difficult. We retreat back over the Niemen and winter in Poland and reconsider the strategic situation next spring.' Napoleon folded his hands together and looked round at the others. 'Well?'

'Retreat is out of the question, sire,' Ney replied at once. 'Our enemies would say that we had been defeated. They are already parading our reverses in Spain as proof that France is starting to crumble. I say we press on. One great victory is all we need. Then we can afford to rest and feed our men.'

Murat nodded. 'Ney is right. We need to end this affair as soon as possible. Even if we did not retreat, and remained in Smolensk, the Russians would portray it as a defeat. Continue the advance, what-ever the cost. As long as we chase down the Tsar and crush his army.'

Napoleon nodded as he considered their advice, and then turned to Davout. 'How about you?'

Davout ran a hand over his thinning hair. 'As you can see from the map, we are still nearly three hundred miles short of Moscow. The attrition of our men will only increase the further we march. Given our current rate of losses, we will be lucky if we reach Moscow with a third of the men we started out with.'

'A third is all we need, if we take Moscow,' Ney intervened. 'And a third is sufficient to beat the Russian army, if they have the stomach to stand and fight us.'

A frown flitted across Davout's features. 'Why should they stand and fight? They haven't so far. What if they let us take Moscow and refuse to sue for peace? They could continue to draw us on, biding their time while our strength diminishes, and then strike once the odds are on their side. There's something else to consider, sire. If we suffer a reverse and we're compelled to retreat, then given the distance involved we might well face a disaster. It is my view that our priority must be to keep the army in being as best we can. It might be prudent to winter here.'

'Thank you for your honesty, Davout.' Napoleon put a finger inside his collar to wipe the sweat from his neck. 'Is there anything you wish to add, Berthier?'

The chief of staff pursed his lips briefly. 'I fear that Davout is right, sire. Every step we take towards Moscow increases the risk of catastrophe, particularly with the onset of winter. I have spoken to some of our local guides. The Russian winter could kill us all.'

Napoleon considered the situation in silence for a moment. Besides his immediate difficulties there were other concerns. He was far from Paris, and the bad news from Spain concerned him greatly. Worse still, his enemies in France were becoming more outspoken in the absence of the Emperor. The sooner he could return to the capital the better. The fingers of his right hand drummed on the table as he weighed each factor up. In the end it was clear to him that he had more to lose by delaying action than by embracing it. He took another sip of the cooled wine and made his decision.

'If we continue the advance, I cannot believe that the Tsar would abandon Moscow to us. I am convinced that he will make a stand somewhere on the road from Smolensk. If he refuses to fight then his own people will kill him and find themselves a new Tsar. So he will fight. I will stake the army on that. He will fight and we shall defeat him and take Moscow within a month. Then the Tsar will make peace. What else can he do?'

Chapter 29

Schivardino, 6 September 1812

'It is a good likeness, is it not?' Napoleon examined the portrait of his son, then pulled out his handkerchief and cleared his nose as he muttered, 'Damned cold.'

Around him the headquarters staff and his marshals nodded approvingly as they looked at the painting they had been summoned to view. It had arrived with the latest government despatches and letters in an escorted carriage. Napoleon put his handkerchief away, sniffed, and stepped up to the painting, in its slim gilt frame. He stared at the infant's face and for a moment the eyes seemed to come alive, gazing fondly at him. Napoleon felt a pang of longing, even though he knew it was a trick of artistic technique. He reached forward and brushed the cheek with his finger. The coarse surface of paint and canvas that met his touch broke the illusion and he stepped back.

'Take it to my quarters. Hang it by the bed.'

The two servants holding the frame bowed their heads and carefully carried the painting out of the room. When they had gone, Napoleon turned to face his officers. 'I've had bad news from Spain. Marshal Marmont was defeated by Wellington outside Salamanca six weeks ago. It is possible that Madrid has already fallen. Our position in Spain is dangerous. Which means that we must conclude our business in Russia as swiftly as possible, gentlemen.'

He crossed to the large open doors that led out on to a wide balcony. The view from the summer lodge on the edge of the village faced east. Just over a mile away lay the hills where the Russian army blocked the road to Moscow. 'Out here, if you please.' The officers filed out into the afternoon sunshine. The sky was cloudless and the azure depths inspired a sense of serenity that was not in keeping with the preparations for battle on the earth below.

'I told you the Tsar would fight.' Napoleon smiled grimly as he surveyed the Russian lines before him. It was a strong position, and the enemy had made good use of the time to prepare some formidable earthworks to protect the centre of their line. Their right flank was protected by the Kalatsha river, and the town of Borodino on the far bank, and the left by a dense wood and the town of Utitsa beyond. Solid blocks of infantry and cavalry were clearly visible on the slopes over-looking Schivardino and a thin line of skirmishers dotted the brown grass at the foot of the slope, a short distance from their French counter-parts. All morning, a group of priests had been parading religious artefacts up and down the ranks of the Russian army and the distant formations had shimmered in the sunlight as they went down on their knees and bowed their heads as the priests passed by.

Even with the latest replacements the French army was now only a hundred and thirty thousand strong. The Russians were estimated to be fielding almost as many men, but still Napoleon felt confident of another triumph for the Grand Army. The Tsar had already handed the initiative to Napoleon by choosing to defend this ground rather than continue his retreat.

Raising his arm, Napoleon pointed towards the centre of the Russian line. 'That's where we will strike at dawn tomorrow. We'll mass our guns in front of those earthworks and pound them to pieces before sending the infantry forward. Prince Eugène's corps will drive in their right flank while Poniatowski deals with the left.' He turned to face his officers. 'That is the battle plan.'

His subordinates glanced at each other in surprise and Napoleon could not help frowning. The heavy cold of the last few days had left him feeling even more weary than usual. His head was throbbing painfully. He clasped his hands behind his back and tapped a foot impatiently. 'Comments?'

Eugène nodded. 'A frontal attack on those earthworks is going to be bloody work, sire.'

'Of course. But once we have the redoubts we can crush the Russian centre and destroy each flank in turn.'

'Sire.' Davout spoke up. 'A frontal attack is too dangerous. If we lose too many men then there won't be any chance of a breakthrough. Even if we did achieve that, there is a danger that we would be too weak to mount an effective pursuit.'

'I see. Then what would you suggest, Davout? That we wait for the Tsar to attack us? He has shown little sign of any offensive spirit so far.'

Davout shook his head. 'No, sire. Of course we must attack. But the ground is open to the south. There is nothing to stop us outflanking the Russians beyond Utitsa. Let Murat take his cavalry round the flank and attack the rear of their line while the main assault goes in.'

'Against any other commander I would agree with you, but not the Tsar. We have him before us. He is willing to give battle and I do not want to give him any excuse to break off and continue his retreat. We must do all that we can to encourage him to remain in front of us. Is that clear?'

Davout shook his head. 'Sire, our cavalry is the finest in Europe. Why did we bring so many of them with us if you are not prepared to use them? This is a heaven-sent opportunity to trap the Tsar.'

'He's right, sire.' Murat nodded. 'Let my cavalry settle the issue.'

Napoleon raised a hand to his brow. He had decided on a plan, and balanced the risk of heavy losses against the fear that the Tsar would slip away once again. It was too late to change his mind. His head was pounding now, and despite the warmth of the day he felt cold and his body started to tremble. As Murat began to speak again Napoleon raised his hand to stop him. 'Enough! The Grand Army has its orders, and you have yours. All that remains is to deploy your men in readiness for tomorrow. You are dismissed. Go.'

The rising sun was still hidden behind the hills upon which sprawled battalion upon battalion of Russian troops. The silhouettes and standards of the men on the crests were black against the soft orange hue of the eastern sky. The redoubts bulked huge and ominous in the shadowed side of the hills. The largest was on the right of the line commanding the bridge across the river to Borodino. A ditch lay to the front, then high earth ramparts and scores of embrasures through which the barrels of cannon pointed towards the French lines. The other earthworks took the form of two huge chevrons, their tips thrusting towards the enemy. Napoleon knew that when his infantry advanced the crossfire between the chevrons would be murderous.

He had not slept well. His cold had made it difficult to breathe easily and kept waking him. Now he struggled to think clearly as he beheld the final preparations for the battle. The corps of Ney and Davout stood ready to advance. Ahead of them lay over four hundred cannon, massed in batteries to bombard the Russian earthworks. They had been protected by hastily erected earthworks of their own, but the previous evening Napoleon's artillery commander, General Lariboisière, had informed him that they were out of effective range of the Russian defences. So the guns had been dragged forward in the early hours and now stood out in the open. The reserve, the Imperial Guard, was formed up just outside Schivardino.

The air was still and a few swifts darted low over the trampled grass, sweeping up the first of the day's insects. Most of the soldiers of both sides stood in sombre silence. A few had got hold of some spirits and attempted to raise a cheer or start some singing, but the sounds soon died away. Napoleon had given orders for the French bands to advance to the first rank, ready to strike up some rousing tunes when the attack began.

Berthier glanced down at his watch and coughed. 'It's time, sire.'

'Give the order.'

Berthier turned to the waiting artillery lieutenant and nodded. The gunner cupped a hand to his mouth and shouted towards the headquarters signal gun. 'Fire!'

The sergeant in command of the gun leaned forward to apply the portfire to the fuse. Sparks sputtered momentarily and then the barrel shimmered as a long tongue of flame leaped from the muzzle, followed at once by a swirling cloud of powder smoke and a detonation like a thunderclap. There was a short delay and then the first of the batteries opened up with a roar. The others fired moments later and soon the sound was almost continuous as it carried back to the church tower of Schivardino where Napoleon and Berthier had climbed to look out over the battlefield.

On the slopes of the Russian position the heavy iron shot ploughed into the earthworks, kicking up spouts of loose soil. Some shots struck the embrasures, loosening the wicker fascines that sheltered the gun crews beyond. The Russian guns started to return fire and quickly began to score hits on the unprotected French artillerymen. Napoleon saw a gun carriage shatter, the timber spraying splinters all around and felling the six men either side of the weapon. Soon, the batteries of both sides were shrouded in thick smoke and they were firing blind.

To the continuous roar of the cannon was added a new sound: the sharp rattle of drums sounding the *pas-de-charge* as the French infantry began to advance along the entire length of the line. To the north Napoleon could see the dark blocks of men from Eugène's corps converging on Borodino, on the far side of the Kalatsha. In front of him the leading divisions of Ney and Davout had started up the slopes. Ahead of them advanced the *voltigeurs*, taking shots at the Russian skirmishers falling back towards the main Russian line.

The batteries in the redoubts ceased firing on the French guns and reloaded with case shot before switching their aim to the dense lines of infantry climbing up towards them. A moment later the first blasts of iron shot ripped through the leading French formations, striking down several men at a time. The fire from the Russian cannon intensified and the infantry hunched down as their officers waved them forward and the drums continued to beat, frantically urging the soldiers on into the hail of destruction sweeping the slopes.

From the church tower Napoleon and Berthier watched the attack's progress through their telescopes, until Ney and Davout's men had passed into the gently rolling banks of smoke surrounding the redoubts and out of sight. Below the smoke they could now see hundreds of blue-coated bodies flecking the slope. Napoleon took a deep breath and snapped his telescope shut.

'Come, there's little to see here. We can follow the battle better from downstairs.' He led the way down into the nave of the church, which had been cleared to make way for the imperial staff. A map table had been set up and a handful of junior officers were busy tracking the movements of the army using small blocks of coloured wood as messengers hurried in and out of the entrance bearing hastily written despatches.

Despite the familiar anxiety and excitement whenever he was involved in a battle, the fatigue and illness of recent days weighed heavily on Napoleon. He slumped down on a small bench set into an alcove along the wall of the nave and rested his head in his hands. Outside the thunder of guns continued, and the concussion could be felt even where he sat. An hour after the attack began Berthier came up to him.

'Sire, there are reports from all corps now.'

'Well?'

'Prince Eugène has taken Borodino and has sent a division across the river to take the Gorki Heights.'

'No.' Napoleon looked up. 'One division is not enough. He must support it, or have them fall back.'

'Yes, sire.'

'What else?'

'Davout is attacking the two earthworks to the right of the village of Semenowska. Once they are taken he will turn and attack the largest redoubt on the other side of the village.'

'Good. And what of Prince Poniatowski?'

'He has taken Utitsa, sire. However, he reports that there are a large number of enemy infantry and some guns in the woods close to the town. He is sending skirmishers forward to drive them out.'

Napoleon nodded. So far all was going to plan. Once Davout had control of Semenowska and the redoubts he could wheel to the left and drive the Russians back against the river. He glanced at Berthier. 'What have we lost?'

'First reports say that the leading formations have suffered badly. One of Davout's divisions has been cut to pieces and the survivors have fallen back.'

Napoleon pursed his lips. He had expected to lose many men; their sacrifice would be worthwhile if the Russian army were destroyed. 'Very well, Berthier. Notify me of any further developments.'

'Yes, sire.' Berthier bowed and turned to hurry back to re-join his aides. Napoleon thought about ascending the tower again, but there was little point. The smoke would obscure his vision. He was not well enough to mount his horse and ride forward, so he would have to follow the battle on the map. He sat in the nave and waited. An hour later there was a fresh flurry of reports and Berthier read through them with a concerned expression before he approached the Emperor again.

'The Russians have counter-attacked, sire. Eugène's division has been driven from the Heights, and Davout has lost control of Semenowska. He has re-formed his men and is preparing for another assault, with Ney in support. Poniatowski has been halted just beyond Utitsa. The Russians have hundreds of guns covering the road.'

'Very well. Tell Murat to have one of his cavalry corps ready to support Davout, and order Eugène to send three of his divisions across the river to attack the main redoubt.'

As the next hour passed sporadic reports continued to reach imperial headquarters. The fighting around the Russian centre sucked in more and more of Davout's and Ney's men. Several of the French generals were lost, and Davout was injured, but he had the wound dressed quickly so that he could continue to lead his men. Still, the Russians held on to the village of Semenowska and the earthworks. Before the third hour of the battle had passed Napoleon was obliged to send Junot's reserve corps forward to support the attack. Every formation was now committed to the battle, with the exception of the twenty-five thousand men of the Imperial Guard, drawn up on a knoll a short distance from the church.

Napoleon picked up his telescope and gathering his strength he climbed back into the tower to try to gauge the progess of the latest attack on the Russian centre. The entire strength of three infantry corps together with ten thousand horsemen pressed forward, supported by two hundred and fifty cannon. The enemy had also concentrated their artillery in the centre, and more guns savaged the French flank from the largest redoubt. The hills opposite the church were now heaped with bodies and a steady stream of walking wounded limped down the slope to escape the maelstrom of cannon and musket fire around Semenowska and the two smaller earthworks. Slowly, the smoke cleared from the Russian centre and Napoleon realised that the enemy were starting to give ground. Now was the time for the cavalry to push forward and break the Russian line.

He returned to the nave to issue the order and then pulled up a chair so that he could sit by the map table to wait for further news. Surely Murat's cavalry would scatter the Russians, he thought. After the earlier cannonade and the assaults by the French infantry, the Russians would be badly shaken. The sight of thousands of heavy cavalry charging towards them would be the final straw. Yet the minutes passed and there was no report of a breakthrough. Then, nearly an hour later, a message came from Murat. Incredibly, the Russians had not run. Instead, they had formed squares and steadily retreated to a ridge nearly two miles beyond their initial position. Murat asked for the Old Guard to be sent forward to settle the matter. Napoleon finished reading the note and handed it to Berthier.

'The Imperial Guard is the only reserve that remains,' he grumbled. 'Murat wants to throw them against the Russian cannon. Tell Murat that he and my other marshals must make do with what they have. The enemy are still holding out in the strongest redoubt. We must have that before we advance any further. Bring every spare gun to bear on the redoubt. Eugène's corps will make the attack from the front, while Caulaincourt's cavalry advance round the flank to take the redoubt from the rear.'

Berthier nodded.

Napoleon stared blankly at the map and muttered, 'I will not destroy the Guard. They are the last fresh formation in the army. We are too far from home to risk everything.'

The middle of the day passed as Eugène gathered his forces for the assault on the redoubt. It was two o'clock before four hundred guns opened fire, pounding the embrasures to pieces, dismounting dozens of guns and killing their crews. As Eugène's men closed on the redoubt the dazed defenders opened fire with the remaining guns while the Russian infantry lined the battered fortifications and fired into the approaching mass. As the French drums beat, the leading ranks surged forward, clambering up the steep sides of the earthwork, and engaged the defenders in a ferocious hand to hand struggle with cold steel and the butts of their muskets.

The shrill call of trumpets added to the sound of the drums as the French cavalry surged round the side of the redoubt and swept aside the line of infantry guarding the open entrances to the rear of the fortification. The garrison was caught between the two forces, and before the hour was out the last of them had been cut down. Not a single prisoner was taken.

Napoleon nodded in satisfaction when he heard the news from one of Ney's staff officers. 'Good. The time for one last assault is upon us. Tell Ney to advance and the day is his.'

'Sire, Marshal Ney says that his corps is too exhausted to advance, and he has lost too many men.'

'Ney said that?' Napoleon was shocked. Had even his bravest and most aggressive marshal lost heart? 'Ney?'

'Yes, sire,' the officer replied nervously. 'And he begs you to send forward the Guard. He said to assure you that if they attack now, then what is left of the Russian line will break.'

'No! No! No!' Napoleon hammered his fist on the table. 'The Guard stays where it is! Tell Ney, Davout and Murat that they must go forward.'

It was late in the afternoon before the exhausted French soldiers had re-formed their columns. They were grimly resolved to obey the Emperor's order. All around them lay tens of thousands of dead and wounded men and horses. Before them, on the next ridge, thousands of Russian cavalry stood waiting, screening the remains of the Tsar's army as it too re-formed its ranks. Once more the French guns belched flame and smoke and heavy iron balls arced across the battlefield to plough through the lines of Russian horsemen. They stood their ground with stolid courage as the French came on. Then the sound of trumpets called out, and the enemy cavalry turned about and trotted away to catch up with their infantry and guns as they left the battlefield.

Ney gave the order to halt, and as the daylight began to fade his men wearily spread out along the crest of the ridge that had been drenched in the blood of so many French and enemy soldiers. Once he was certain there was no danger of any counter-attack, Ney rode back to headquarters to confront his Emperor.

'The Guard would have made all the difference!' Ney glared at the Emperor.

Napoleon looked back, pale and sweating from his sickness. Ney had a dressing around his head, darkly stained where his skull had been creased by a spent musket ball. He had also been hit in the thigh and twice in the arm by chips of stone when cannon balls had grounded close to his horse.

'One final assault by fresh troops would have put the seal on a great victory.' Ney shook his head. 'Now they have escaped.'

'You are wrong,' Napoleon replied evenly. 'We have won a great victory today. That is what I have told Berthier to report to Paris. We have met the enemy and swept them aside.'

'What?' Ney's lips curled in contempt. 'Only a fool would believe that. Some victory.' He gestured towards the ruined enemy earthworks. 'We have won a few piles of dirt and the ruins of two villages. The Tsar's army is still intact and now we will have to fight it again. All because the Guard refused to muddy their uniforms.'

'The order was mine,' Napoleon replied coldly as he rubbed his brow. The headache had returned with a vengeance. 'I take full responsibility for the consequences.'

'That's good of you, sire.'

Napoleon ignored the mocking tone and continued, 'The fact is, we have defeated the Tsar's army. Even if he has managed to save most of his men, there is nothing that can stop us reaching Moscow now.'

Chapter 30

Moscow, 15 September 1812

Napoleon stood at the window of the Tsar's private study in the Kremlin gazing out at the historic Russian capital with an expression of horrified awe. His face was lit in the blood-red hue as he stared towards the great swathe of Moscow that was on fire.

He had reached the city shortly after noon, a day after the first of Murat's cavalry had cautiously made their way through the abandoned streets. The road junctions had been plastered with copies of a proclamation issued by Moscow's governor ordering the population to evacuate, or face arrest and possible execution for treason. Naturally, many had refused to leave and had gone into hiding, emerging later to enjoy the freedom to break into the wealthiest houses and steal whatever valuables they could find. They had scuttled away, back into concealment, the moment they caught sight of the French troops entering the city. For their part, the hungry, tattered figures of the Grand Army took over where the native looters had left off.

'Who started the fires?' Napoleon asked.

'We haven't discovered that yet, sire,' Murat replied. 'None of the infantry had penetrated that part of the city before the fires broke out, so it might have been the work of some of the cavalry patrols. Or it could have been the Russians.'

'The Russians?'

'Why not, sire? They've been busy burning crops, villages and bridges behind them as they have retreated.'

'That's one thing. But to destroy the most sacred city of your country is quite another. I can't believe Alexander could do such a thing. Such an act of barbarism.'

Murat shrugged. 'Perhaps you have underestimated the Tsar.'

Napoleon frowned. Had he misjudged Alexander? Was his opponent a far more ruthless man than he had assumed? If that was the case, then Napoleon had erred more profoundly than ever before. It was an unsettling thought and he hurriedly banished it from his mind as he turned to Murat. 'What is being done to contain the fires?'

Murat looked surprised. 'Why, nothing, sire. It's not our problem.'

'It will be unless something is done. The army needs billets and food, which they won't have unless something is done about the fire.'

Murat thought quickly. 'We'd better use the Guard. Most of the other divisions are looting. The Guard is about the only disciplined unit left at the moment. That is, if you can spare them.'

'Take them,' Napoleon replied at once. 'The fire must be contained.'

Murat nodded. 'At the moment it's confined to the poorest quarter of the city. Most of the houses there are small affairs, made of wood. We should be able to destroy enough of them to create a fire break.'

'Very well then, deal with it, Murat.' Napoleon waved a hand to dismiss his cavalry commander. The door closed loudly and Napoleon was alone again. He turned away from the window and began to examine the room, curious to see what it revealed about the Tsar.

The study was lit by a handful of candles burning in a chandelier. Paintings of family members and illustrious ancestors adorned the walls, though not, Napoleon noted, Alexander's father, Nicholas, who had been murdered by the men who had placed Alexander on the throne. The vast desk, with its ornate marquetry, was empty, as were the document cupboards throughout the Tsar's suite. Piles of ashes and scorch marks defiled the brilliant marble tiles of the floor where confidential documents had been burned. A long row of bookcases lined the wall opposite the windows and Napoleon ran his finger along the spines of the books. A few shelves contained works in Russian and others contained texts in Latin and German, but the majority of the books were in French. Napoleon smiled at the eclectic range of writings, everything from obscure philosophical tracts to the works of Rousseau and Voltaire. So, the Tsar was a man interested in liberal politics, Napoleon mused. A pity; he might have made a good Frenchman. Then he paused, stared and smiled. On one of the top shelves he had spied some racy romantic novels of the kind hawked around the less salubrious neighbourhoods of Paris.

'A man of the people as well, then.' Smiling, Napoleon stretched up an arm to pluck out one of the books. He idly flicked through the opening pages and then placed the book in the pocket of his coat and strode across the room to sit down in the finely carved and upholstered chair behind the desk. Directly opposite him, on the far wall, hung a portrait of Alexander in military uniform, his gloved hand resting on the handle of a curved sword. Napoleon stared at the portrait for a long

272

time before he muttered, 'Why don't you surrender? Why? Your army has been beaten. Your greatest city has fallen and now burns. What more can you endure? It is madness to continue the war. You will sue for peace. I know it.'

The fire burned for another three days, consuming most of the city before it died out, or was stopped by the firebreaks the French soldiers had created by blasting entire streets to pieces with powder charges. The air over the city was filled with the acrid stench of burning and smoke still curled into the clear skies for many days afterwards. Only a quarter of the city, including the Kremlin, had escaped the flames, but it was more than enough to accommodate the men of the Grand Army.

After the initial orgy of looting the soldiers were content to make their billets as comfortable as possible while they rested, and enjoyed whatever food they found in the abandoned city. It was an opportunity for the wounded to recover in the comfort of proper beds and not on the overcrowded, jolting bed of an army wagon. Many men used the time to patch their worn uniforms, repair their boots, or find more comfortable replacements. They were happy to believe the proclamations issued from the Emperor's headquarters that congratulated them on having fought the campaign to a glorious and successful conclusion. All that remained was for the Emperor and the Tsar to negotiate a peace and then the men of the Grand Army could return home, laden with the spoils of war and tall tales of having fought and bested the wild Cossacks of the steppes.

The days passed, and there was no sign of any Russian officials approaching the city to discuss peace terms. Despite the lack of an armistice Murat's cavalry patrols reported that their Cossack counterparts were happy to fraternise and exchange spirits and other gifts. The only worrying intelligence was that the Russian officer appointed to command the Tsar's forces, General Kutusov, was marching his men to the west of Moscow, threatening the Grand Army's communications.

September drifted into October and there was a noticeable drop in the temperature as the end of autumn drew near. Napoleon instructed Berthier to prepare the army to march once more. There was a distant possibility that the Russian army might have to be fought again to shatter whatever was left of the Tsar's desire to continue the struggle. Still the Emperor waited for the Russians. He expected them hourly, and spent most of his time in the Tsar's study, waiting to receive the war-weary and dispirited representatives of the Tsar. It was difficult to concentrate his mind on anything else, and in order to cope with the wait Napoleon began to read the romantic novels in Alexander's private collection, numbingly banal as they were. At mealtimes, his closest comrades were surprised to see the Emperor lingering over his food, picking at it carefully where before he had treated a meal as a necessary waste of time.

On the fifth day of the month Napoleon abruptly gave orders for a delegation headed by General Delacorte, who had once served in the Russian embassy, to be sent to Kutusov to request an audience with Alexander. They returned six days later and Delacorte was brought before the Emperor to make his report. Napoleon greeted him warmly.

'I am glad to see you have returned safely.'

'Thank you, sire.' Delacorte bowed his head.

'So tell me what happened.'

'We found Kutusov's army easily enough and were escorted through his picket lines and on to his field headquarters. He welcomed us, insisting that we dine with him and his officers before we discussed the purpose of our mission. I gave him your letter first, sire, asking that an armistice be agreed while I was given safe conduct and taken to the Tsar. Kutusov refused to let me proceed. He took your letter and said that he would ensure that it was delivered safely into the Tsar's hands.'

Napoleon frowned. 'I gave you strict orders to deliver that letter in person.'

Delacorte shrugged. 'I didn't see what else I could do, sire.'

Napoleon stared at him for a moment. 'Very well. Continue.'

'Yes, sire. We were kept at Kutusov's headquarters while we waited for the reply. He continued to treat us well, and claimed that he and his men would like nothing more than peace between Russia and France. Then, yesterday morning, there was a reply from the Tsar.'

'A reply? Then where is it?'

Delacorte hesitated, and then reached into his jacket and extracted a single sheet of paper, folded, without any seal. He handed it to Napoleon, who opened it out and read the short message, written in French in a neat small hand.

To his imperial majesty, Napoleon of France, greetings.

I thank you for your letter requesting me to state my preliminary terms for discussing a peace treaty between our nations. However, I am resolved not to discontinue the state of war between us, and therefore I regret that I must refuse your request. Sadly, I refute your claim that the campaign is concluded. Indeed, this is the moment when my campaign begins. Alexander, Tsar of Russia.

Napoleon lowered the note. 'Is that all there is? Is there nothing more?'

'No, sire.'

Napoleon read the note again. 'This must be a joke.'

'I don't think so, sire. I recognise the Tsar's hand from my days in the embassy. That's his signature, I am sure of it.'

Napoleon shook his head. 'Then he mocks me . . . Or his mind is troubled. Yes, perhaps that's it. After all, his father was reputed to be insane. He must have written this in haste. After the defeat at Borodino and the loss of Moscow his mind is bound to be disturbed. When he has had time to think it over he will write again and accept my offer.'

Delacorte looked at his Emperor in surprise for a moment, then nodded. 'Yes, sire. I imagine you are right. Will that be all?'

'What?' Napoleon looked directly at him. 'Yes, you may go. And I thank you for your efforts, Delacorte.'

The general left the study, closing the door softly behind him. Napoleon read the letter once again, then smiled faintly before screwing it up and tossing it into the fire.

There was still no further word from the Tsar three days later and Napoleon summoned Delacorte again and tasked him with leading another delegation to Kutusov. This time they were not permitted to hand over any letters, and Kutusov brusquely informed them that no further delegations would be received. Once he had dismissed the officer Napoleon sank into his chair and stared down the room towards the portrait of Alexander. He had spent many hours gazing at it already, trying to read the expression the artist had caught.

Napoleon knew that portraits rewarded close study. The sitter would be conscious of how they wished to be presented to those who would view the completed portrait down the years. So they crafted a pose which would embody their virtues, as they saw them. It was the task of the artist to study and amplify his subject's qualities, yet at the same time a good artist could not resist subtly inflecting his depiction according to his opinion of the person sitting before him.

It might have been a trick of the light, but for the first time Napoleon saw a glint of cruelty in the eyes of Alexander, and the lips were not set in a faint smile of beneficence any more. It was another man who stood before him, no longer the impressionable young ruler who had only recently taken the throne and wanted to improve the lot of his people and be loved by them. An icy chill rose up in the nape of Napoleon's neck and he shuddered.

A knock at the door startled him out of his thoughts and he sat forward and called out, 'Come!'

The door clicked open. Berthier entered and crossed the room to stand before the Emperor's desk.

'What is it?' Napoleon asked hopefully.

Berthier pulled out a loose leaf folder from under his arm and flicked it open. 'There are a few issues that I need to bring to your attention, in accordance with your order to prepare the army to march, sire.'

'Oh?' Napoleon sank back in his chair.

'I've spoken with the cartography staff, sire, and they calculate that it will take a minimum of fifty days to return to the Niemen.'

'I did not say that we would be retreating to Poland,' Napoleon cut in.

'No, sire, but as chief of staff it is my duty to prepare for all contingencies.'

Napoleon was silent for a moment before he nodded. 'You are right. Continue.'

'Yes, sire. Even if we were to leave Moscow at once, we cannot reach the Niemen before the winter sets in. The first snow will fall in November, and the temperatures will drop far below freezing. Our men are still in the uniforms they were wearing for a summer campaign. They need warm clothing, sire. Thick coats, gloves, scarves and boots.'

'Then see to it. Have them issued with whatever they need from stores.'

'Sire, I have already spoken to the chief of the commissary. Dumas has hardly any stock of winter clothing. If your majesty recalls, it was decided not to overburden the supply wagons with unnecessary equipment. It was anticipated that the campaign would be over in time for the army to return to winter quarters in Poland.'

'Yes. I remember.'

'Whatever clothing Dumas has now has been picked up along the route, as the wagons emptied of rations.'

'A wise precaution.' Napoleon nodded vaguely. 'Dumas is a clever fellow.'

'The problem is that there is not nearly enough winter clothing for the entire army. Our latest strength returns give us ninety-five thousand men. Dumas can provide for no more than twenty thousand.'

'Then requisition some more coats, and whatever else is needed.'

'Where from, sire?'

'I cannot believe there is not enough winter clothing to be had in Moscow.'

'The fire destroyed the shopping and warehouse districts,' Berthier explained evenly. 'The only clothing that is left is whatever is in the houses that survived. Even then, the Russians took nearly everything with them when they evacuated the city.'

'Then do what you can,' Napoleon replied tersely. 'Anything else?'

'Yes, sire. Murat reports that he has fewer than ten thousand cavalry mounts remaining and many of those are lame, and all of them are short of forage. The same is true for the artillery. The city's stock of feed was also lost in the fire.'

'Then we must have fresh horses. An army is nothing without cavalry and artillery. Tell Murat to send his men out to buy horses from the towns and villages around Moscow.'

Berthier took a deep breath. 'Sire, the city is surrounded by Cossacks. In any case, Murat's patrols report that every settlement within twenty miles of Moscow has been evacuated and torched. There are no horses to be had.'

'Why do you tell me this? What can I do?' Napoleon waved his arms wide. 'I can't just make horses appear!'

Berthier kept his mouth shut, closed his file and tucked it back under his arm and then stared straight ahead, refusing to meet the Emperor's eyes. Napoleon tilted his head back and stared at the intricate ceiling mouldings, painted with gold leaf. He smiled grimly. He had a fortune in gold in the army's war chest, enough to buy all the coats and horses he needed. Now the gold would be little more than a burden if the army was forced to retreat through the harsh Russian winter. He leaned forward and looked across at Berthier.

'Send for my marshals.'

A servant built up the fire before drawing the long curtains across the window and leaving the study. Outside the night was cold and a chilly wind moaned down the streets of Moscow, bringing with it brief squalls of rain that drove those men of the Grand Army still searching for spoils into the shelter of their billets.

Inside the room in the Kremlin, Napoleon faced his marshals, bracing himself to admit the truth.

'The Tsar does not want peace. He refuses to even contemplate it.' Napoleon frowned. 'It seems that he will not admit defeat, in spite of all that he has lost.'

'Why would he?' asked Davout. 'Every day that we sit in Moscow and wait on events, his army grows stronger. By now, he will have gathered in men from his garrisons, and from the army that was facing

Turkey. Sire, if we are not careful, Moscow will turn from a trophy into a trap.'

'Then what do you suggest we do?'

'There's no question about it. We must retreat, while we still can.'

'Retreat?' Ney snorted. 'When we have won all that we have? Kutusov is still too afraid to fight. That's why he sits out there and does nothing.'

'He doesn't have to do anything,' Davout replied, 'but sit and wait for the winter to do his work for him. Soon this city will run out of food, and then wood for the fires. We shall have to start eating the horses. When spring comes whatever is left of the Grand Army will not be fit to fight.'

'Then we don't stay here,' Ney responded. 'If the Tsar won't sue for peace when we have taken Moscow, then I say we march on St Petersburg instead. Let's see how reluctant he is to talk when we burn down the most prized of his palaces.'

Napoleon smiled sourly. 'I suspect that it would make no difference to his resolve. Besides, our communications are already stretched enough and it is four hundred miles from here to St Petersburg. It is out of the question.' He drew a breath. 'Our position in Moscow is already growing tenuous. The Cossacks have started attacking Murat's patrols and they are gradually closing in around the city. The road to Smolensk was cut three days ago, and has only today been cleared by General Sulpice . . . The danger is clear enough. I have made my decision. We will quit Moscow and fall back to Smolensk. There are enough rations there to last the army through the winter. It is possible that General Kutusov might feel bold enough to try to block our retreat. If so, he will hand us another chance to crush his army. In any case, that must be the explanation that we give to the army. They must not be allowed to think of this as a retreat. As far as the soldiers are concerned, we are marching out to find and destroy Kutusov. Is that clear?'

The marshals nodded. Then Davout spoke.

'Sire, whatever the soldiers believe, we can be sure that our enemies in Europe will present this as a defeat. We have to be careful that defeat is not turned into catastrophe.'

'What do you mean?'

Davout folded his hands and stared down at them thoughtfully. 'It is no secret that many of our allies contributed their contingents under duress. We know that we can't trust the Prussians. If this campaign goes against us, then I fear that Frederick William may well change sides and join the Tsar. If he does, then he will not be the only one.' He looked up. 'Sire, the overriding priority now is no longer to defeat the Russians. It is my conviction that that is no longer possible. What matters is survival. That means we must save as many men, horses and guns as we can. They will be needed to hold our ground in Europe when this campaign is over.'

There was a silence around the table, before Ney laughed. 'Ever the optimist, Davout! Damn it, man, you paint the blackest of pictures.'

'Sometimes the picture is black,' Napoleon replied, glancing at the portrait at the end of the room. 'In any case, the decision is made. The army is to abandon Moscow, on the nineteenth. Return to your commands and prepare your men to march. Berthier will send each of you your orders for your place in the line of march.'

Napoleon sat on his mount, surrounded by his staff, as the column trudged by under a leaden sky of gathering rain clouds. The army had set out at first light, but the days were growing shorter and dusk was settling over Moscow before the tail of the huge column had cleared the city. Marshal Mortier commanded the rearguard, and his men were busy spiking the guns that had to be left behind in the city because there were no longer sufficient horses to draw them. Mortier's soldiers were also tasked with destroying any stocks of powder and weapons that might be of use to the enemy. Afterwards, they would set off, covering the rear of the army.

As Napoleon watched his men pass by, they still offered a cheer as they saw him, but they were no longer the men of the Grand Army that had crossed the Niemen nearly six months ago. They looked more like a procession of beggars in their tattered uniforms and the assortment of coats and jackets they had looted from Moscow. Many were laden down with the more burdensome spoils of war, and the route was already lined with discarded paintings, mirrors and laquered boxes, left in the mud.

In amongst the columns of infantry were wagons and carts filled with the wounded, whatever rations could be gleaned from Moscow, and yet more spoils. The vehicles, and the army's remaining guns, were drawn by skeletal horses and mules, their ribs clearly delineated under the loose folds of their hides. It was the same for the cavalry, Napoleon noted sadly. The gleaming mounts that had been spurred on across the steppes were now mere shadows of the finest cavalry in Europe. Thousands of troopers no longer had mounts, and marched as infantry, their carbines slung over their shoulders.

He watched them for a while, then took a last glance back towards the Moscow skyline. His heart filled with a bitter hatred for the Tsar. Tugging the reins, Napoleon turned his mount to follow the column snaking back the way it had come as the first cold drops of rain began to fall.

Chapter 31

Arthur

Madrid, 12 August 1812

The bells of the great church of Nuestra Señora de la Almudena rang out across the city, but were scarcely audible above the din of the crowd lining the streets down which the British troops marched as they made for the royal palace. Despite its being the hottest part of the year, the Spaniards had turned out in their tens of thousands to greet the liberator of Madrid. A battalion of the Coldstream Guards led the way, in carefully patched uniforms, fresh tripoli on their cross belts and buttons polished to a glassy shine. Next came a squadron of the German dragoons who had scattered the last division of Marmont's army the day after the battle at Salamanca. And then, together with his staff, came Arthur, mounted on his favourite chestnut horse, Copenhagen. He had dressed for the event and left his plain coat and hat at headquarters. Instead he wore his red coat, adorned with gold lace. On his left breast he wore the medals and stars of the titles that he had won over the years. A new bicorne sat on his head, with a plume of white feathers lining it from front to back.

'I feel like a damned stuffed goose,' he called to Somerset, who rode to his side and slightly further back. 'All done up for a Christmas banquet.'

Somesert laughed, doffing his hat to a group of Spanish ladies who were sheltering beneath parasols as they watched the procession from a balcony. 'Just as long as you look the part, my lord. After all, the Spanish government has conferred upon you the title of the supreme commander of all Spanish forces.'

'A measure that will be of supreme indifference to almost every Spaniard under arms, I can assure you.'

'Be that as it may, my lord, you have won their hearts, and the Spanish deserve to see a conquering warrior, not some chap in a coat who might as well be a country doctor when all is said and done.'

'Country doctor?' Arthur sniffed. 'Well, at least my appearance does not seem to concern our fellows unduly.'

He sat stiffly in his saddle as he rode with all the dignity he could muster, occasionally turning to one side or the other and raising a hand to acknowledge the crowd's cheers, which only prompted a further burst of wild cries and frantic waving of strips of cloth in the red and gold of Spain. It was an impressive reception, Arthur mused. The previous day, Madrid's population had greeted the army with hysterical joy, pressing bottles of wine and gifts of bread, pastries and dried sausage into the hands of the first soldiers to enter the suburbs. For their part the soldiers had grinned as they nodded their gratitude and responded with the few words of Spanish they had picked up. Today's procession to the royal palace was a much more formal affair, but had taken on the air of a wild public holiday.

The hated French had gone. As news of the crushing defeat at Salamanca reached King Joseph, he hurriedly packed up his valuables, and a heavily guarded convoy of French officials left the city a few days before the arrival of the allied army. A large column of Spanish collaborators left with them, to avoid the growing bloodlust of the mob. The French were heading south-east to Valencia, where Joseph sought the protection of Marshal Suchet.

Even so, the allied army was short of supplies, the men were tired and many of Arthur's senior officers were out of action due to injury and sickness. There was little more that could be achieved by pursuing Marmont, and the liberation of Madrid would be an effective blow to French prestige across Europe. It would also help to raise morale back in Britain, where the new Prime Minister, Lord Liverpool, was working hard to generate political support for Arthur's campaigns in the Peninsula.

Arthur felt his mind reeling with the possibilities that the victory at Salamanca had opened up for future operations. But that was work for later. For the present he was content to play the part of the liberator of Madrid, and as the royal palace came in sight along the avenue he raised his hat from his head and held it high as he swept it round towards the sea of ecstatic Madrileños, cheering as they waved their strips of cloth in wild abandon.

As soon as Arthur stepped inside the tall doors of the balcony he gestured towards a footman bearing a tray of glasses of water. The cheers of the crowd filled the room almost as loudly as they filled the plaza outside. The midday heat beating down upon Madrid had caused Arthur to perspire freely under his scarlet woollen jacket. Once he had removed his hat and wiped a dribble of sweat from his brow, he downed two glasses of the chilled water in quick succession. Then he allowed a servant to remove the ribbon across his shoulder and the other around his waist before unclipping his sword belt, undoing the buttons of his jacket and slipping it off.

'Thank God for that.' He breathed deeply. 'I believe I would have stewed in my own juices if I had been forced to wear that a moment longer.'

General Alava smiled. 'It seems that our climate suits no one but the natives.'

'There are more comfortable landscapes across which to wage war,' Arthur agreed. 'But for now we will rest the army for a few days. Let the men indulge themselves, and let the locals enjoy their freedom, while I decide what is to happen next.'

'And what will you decide, I wonder?' Alava cocked an eyebrow. 'You have Madrid, but taking the capital – while a great achievement in itself – will not rid my people of the French.'

'No, it won't,' Arthur admitted. 'But it has forced them to withdraw to the north and east of the country, and Marshal Soult will have to give up the siege of Cadiz and leave Andalucia, or risk being cut off.' Arthur took another glass of water and sipped at it thoughtfully. 'Now that we have our great victory, and have chased Boney's brother out of Madrid, it would be criminal to squander the favourable circumstances in which we find ourselves.'

He stretched his arms and then crossed to the huge oak table that dominated the middle of what had once been King Joseph's library. The most valuable books in the collection had been hurriedly packed into the convoy when the French had fled. Now there were gaps in the shelves, like missing teeth, and hundreds of volumes that had been pulled out and then rejected still lay where they had been dropped on the floor. Most of the rooms in the palace had been ransacked by the palace staff as soon as the French had left, and now the elegant halls and chambers were littered with broken vases and crockery.

Many of the maps and charts that had been stored in a large rack in the corner of the library had been left behind, and Arthur selected a large-scale representation of the Peninsula and unrolled it across the table, helping Somerset pin the corners down with some of the discarded books. Then he stared at the map thoughtfully. Less than two years ago his army had been crammed into a small sliver of land north of Lisbon, while the French had free range across the rest of the sprawl of land depicted on the map. Now, the French were pressed back into the north and east of Spain. While they still had over two hundred thousand men in their armies, the marshals were bitterly divided and treated Joseph with barely disguised contempt, according to the reports of Arthur's agents. Moreover, they had been largely abandoned by their master as he pursued his apparently limitless ambitions in Russia.

Arthur was still astonished by the news of the invasion, and the scale of the forces involved. Just half of the resources Bonaparte had deployed in Russia would have enabled him to settle his troubles in Spain very swiftly indeed. As it was, the soldiers of the Emperor were now forced to fight on two fronts, stretched thinly over hostile terrain with only the most rudimentary of road systems. Unless destiny was perversely over-generous in the favour it bestowed on Bonaparte, his empire was being stretched to its limits. Here in Spain, Arthur was determined to strike a mortal blow to French aspirations. If the Tsar could do the same in the depths of Russia, then surely this war of wars was drawing towards the final act.

Arthur focused his mind again. At length he put voice to his thoughts as Somerset and Alava stood either side of him. 'With Joseph having fallen back on Suchet's army at Valencia we are faced with the prospect that Soult will at some point come to his senses and join forces with them, in which case we will, as so often before, be outnumbered. However, I believe that we might still be able to hold the centre of Spain if we can be sure that we have contained what is left of Marmont's strength as far north as the river Ebro. That means taking Burgos.' He turned to General Alava. 'What do you know of the fortress of Burgos?'

'It is on the main route between France and Madrid. Bonaparte must have recognised its importance, since he ordered a number of improvements to the defences.' Alava shrugged. 'Though nothing on the scale of Badajoz.'

'I'm glad to hear that. Might I ask if you have actually seen the fortress since these improvements were made?'

'No,' Alava replied frankly. 'But I have heard enough from my sources to know that Burgos will not present you with much difficulty, my lord.'

Arthur stared at him for a moment and then nodded. 'Very well. Now then, if Joseph and Suchet advance on Madrid then our Spanish allies must do everything in their power to disrupt the advance. The army of Andalucia must strike into the flank of the French, while the irregulars harry them every step of the way. If they can be delayed until autumn then the rains will have swelled the Tagus and I will be able to cover the handful of crossing points that will be left.' Arthur paused and stroked his chin. 'What do you think, gentlemen?'

Somerset puffed his cheeks out and shook his head. 'Sir, you're pinning your faith on things falling into line.'

Arthur shrugged. 'I have no alternative. That is the hand I have been dealt. I intend to hold Madrid for as long as possible. It may not achieve much for us tactically, but we must look to the wider strategy that determines this war. Every day that we can stay here delivers another blow to the Bonapartes' rule over Spain. It will give heart not only to the Spanish, but to all Europe.'

Somerset thought for a moment, then nodded. 'I understand, sir. I just hope we don't spread ourselves too thin to prove the point.'

'Spread ourselves thin?' Arthur repeated with a wry smile. 'My dear Somerset, where on earth have you been these last years? Thanks to our government, if we were any more thinly spread then the enemy would see right through us.'

'They may do that yet, sir.'

Arthur turned to Alava. 'General, I want you to head south. You will speak for me. Tell every resistance leader and every regular officer you find that I have been given command over all allied forces in Spain. My orders are simple. They are to attack the French wherever they find them.'

Alava grinned. 'That will be a pleasure, my lord. And what of you? What will you do now?'

'Me?' Arthur reached across the map and tapped the name of a town far to the north of Madrid. 'I'll take half the army and seize Burgos.'

Chapter 32

Burgos, 4 October 1812

The summer seemed reluctant to loosen its grip on Spain and every day the sun beat down on the parched landscape as the army marched north, driving back the small French force that had been scraped together after Salamanca. Then, as Arthur commenced his siege of Burgos, the weather changed as autumn swept in with unseasonal ferocity. The landscape of Castile was lashed by rainstorms which flooded the trenches and batteries that had been painstakingly cut out of the ground by Arthur's men. The engineers had suffered heavy losses at the two previous sieges and had been reduced to a mere sixteen officers and other ranks. Nor was there sufficient siege artillery to end the task swiftly. By the time the army had reached Burgos along the heavily rutted and broken-up road that led north from Madrid, only three eighteen-pounders had survived the journey. The rest had suffered broken wheels or splintered gun carriages and had to be left behind while repairs were attempted.

'So much for Alava's sources,' Somerset commented bitterly as he gazed at the fortress sitting atop a steep-sided hill. It was separated from the rest of the town by a ravine and linked to the town by a narrow spur of rock. A powerful battery covered this approach and rendered any frontal assault suicidal. Moreover, the fortress was constructed in concentric tiers so that the defenders would be able to continue their resistance even if the outer wall was taken. Somerset stared sourly at the fortress. 'The place is all but impregnable, sir.'

'Nonsense!' Arthur snapped and then, cross at his fraying temper, continued more quietly, 'We have one of their outworks, thanks to Major Somers-Cocks. It is just a question of time and steady effort and the fortress will be ours.'

Somerset glanced at him and then back at the fortress without saying a word, but his doubt and frustration were palpable. Arthur could understand his sentiment easily enough. There were thirty-five thousand men camped around the fortress. According to the local people the garrison amounted to little more than two thousand men, but their commander, General Dubreton, was every bit as wily and spirited as his comrade Philippon had been at Badajoz. Memory of that terrible siege had been preying on Arthur's mind ever since the army had arrived before Burgos and he was determined not to repeat the bloody assault that had cost him so dearly. There would be no massed assault this time. Burgos would be taken piece by piece.

'My dear Somerset,' he said patiently, 'I have seen many hill forts like this when I served in India and I managed to break into them readily enough. We will have Burgos in due course.'

'I trust you are right, sir.'

'How are the preparations for the mine proceeding?'

Somerset gestured towards the narrow trench zig-zagging up the slope towards the outer wall. A short distance from the base of the wall the trench disappeared into a tunnel. 'Captain Perkins says that it will be ready to detonate at dawn tomorrow, sir.'

'Very well. Pass the word for Major Somers-Cocks to see me at headquarters at three in the morning. I will give him his orders in person.'

The major, like so many who had bought their way up through the officer ranks, was young, fair-haired and fresh-faced. But Arthur knew the man had a fine combat record. As such he was just the kind of man Arthur needed to lead the assaults on the defences of the fortress. He seemed to court danger with impunity and had been one of the handful of officers who had volunteered for the duty. It was as well for England that she produced such fine soldiers, Arthur reflected as he briefly examined the man standing at attention in front of his desk in the early hours.

Arthur cleared his throat and began the briefing. 'Have you completed the preparations for your assault party?'

'Yes, my lord,' Somers-Cocks answered with a slight Scots burr. 'The men are already waiting in the approach trench. Two hundred and fifty volunteers, as you ordered.'

'I hope it will be enough.'

'It will suffice, my lord.' Somers-Cocks smiled. 'After all, my orders are not to take the whole fortress. Merely take and hold the breach.'

'If you are successful, the support wave will reach you quickly enough. But understand, they have strict orders not to advance unless you give the signal that the breach is in your hands.'

'I understand, my lord.'

'Good.' Arthur nodded, and then softened his formal tone. 'Did you have any difficulty finding the volunteers for the assault party?'

'Most came willingly.'

'Most?'

'Och, you know how it is, my lord. Some men never know that they want to volunteer until they receive the right kind of inspiration.'

Arthur arched an eyebrow. 'That being?'

The major pursed his lips. 'The choice between fifteen minutes in the breach and a week of fatigues in the latrine generally has the desired result, my lord.'

Arthur laughed and stood up, offering his hand to Somers-Cocks. 'Good luck, my boy.'

'Thank you, my lord.' He shook Arthur's hand, then stepped back, saluted and turned to leave the tent. Arthur stared after him for a moment, wondering if he would see the man alive again when the next day had dawned. Then he shook his head. Somers-Cocks was one of those individuals who was fated to survive.

'Four o'clock, sir,' Somerset said quietly, his boots squelching in the mud as he stepped forward to Arthur's side.

'Yes.'

All was still. Overhead a bank of clouds had blocked out the stars and added to the pitch darkness that enveloped the fortress. Torches on the wall picked out some of the details of the defences and occasionally one of the French soldiers on watch. The only sounds came from the allied camp where a handful of drunken soldiers from two battalions were engaged in a brawl. The provosts would soon sort that out, Arthur reflected, but for now the noise would help to divert the attention of the defenders while the assault party edged as close to the mine as they dared.

'Five past four,' Somerset muttered. 'The engineers are late.'

Arthur was about to reply when a jet of flame blasted out from the entrance to the tunnel leading under the wall, followed by a roar that echoed off the walls of the nearby town. After the sound died away there was a stunned silence before Arthur heard the crash and rumble of masonry as a section of the wall above the mine collapsed. At once there was a cry from Somers-Cocks. 'Forward! Go forward!'

There was no cheer from the men of the assault party as they burst from the shelter of their trench and scurried up the slope towards the breach. A few muskets fired down at them from the nearest tower of the outer wall, but they charged on, clambering up the debris slope and into the breach. The sounds of fighting carried back to the command post as Arthur strained ears and eyes in an attempt to try to discern how the attack was progressing. Then there was a sudden lurid flare of white sparks as one of the assault party lit the small pot of powder that had been taken forward to act as the signal that the beach had been taken. At once the waiting support brigade rose up from where they had been concealed in the approach trenches and rushed towards the breach. The sounds of musket fire continued for the next half-hour before dying down to the occasional exchange of a handful of shots.

As the first light gathered on the horizon a runner came panting up the trench to the command post, his boots slipping in the glutinous mud that filled all the trenches.

'My lord.' He breathed heavily as he stood to attention. 'Major Somers-Cocks begs to report that the breach has been taken, and his men are holding the flanks while the brigade invests the defences around the breach.'

'Very good,' Arthur felt the burden of anxiety lift from his shoulders. 'Pass on my congratulations and my thanks to the major.'

'Yes, sir.'

Once the man had slithered back down into the trench Somerset spoke. 'Well, that was fairly straightforward, thank God.'

Arthur rubbed his aching eyes briefly. 'We have the breach, Somerset. That is all. You can be sure that Dubreton is already planning his counterstroke.'

As the morning passed the assault party took cover around the breach and continued to exchange shots with the defenders in the upper level of fortifications. Meanwhile the follow-up brigade, under the guidance of the engineer officers, hurriedly built up a breastwork inside the breach and began to clear away the debris to make the passage through the gap easier. At noon, Arthur sent forward a company of Portuguese troops to relieve Somers-Cocks and his men, while another company took over from those widening the breach.

It was slightly overcast and a chilly breeze was made yet more uncomfortable by a steady drizzle that began mid-morning. Arthur made his way along the approach trench to inspect the breach. There was already a foot of water lying in the bottom and the soil beneath was muddy and slippery so that he had to tread carefully. In places the sides of the trench were crumbling away and small parties of men, drenched and covered with mud, were shoring up the banks of earth with wicker baskets filled with rocks. As the trench began to climb the slope the puddles ceased and instead the water gushed down the floor like a small mountain stream. Arthur paused to look up at the fortress looming overhead and there was a soft zip as a plug of mud exploded into the air near the edge of the trench.

'Keep yer bloody 'ead down!' a sergeant bellowed at him.' 'Less you want it blown orf!'

Arthur ducked and then turned towards the sergeant. At the sight of his commander's distinctive hooked nose the sergeant blanched. 'Beggin' yer pardon, my lord. Just that we've already lost two men today to some bleedin' Frog marksman up there.'

'I thank you for your wise advice, sergeant.' Arthur smiled at him, and keeping low he continued up the trench, making sure he kept close to the most sheltered side as he climbed up to the breach. Captain Perkins of the engineers saluted him as Arthur emerged into the small open space in front of the gap. A section of wall fifteen feet across had collapsed and the soldiers were busy removing the rubble and using it to build up two low walls linking the end of the trench to the breach.

'How is the work progressing, Captain?'

'Well enough, sir.' Perkins was another Scot, short and thickset, with a broader accent than Somers-Cocks, and he was as covered with mud as his men. 'Once we have the breach cleared, I'll set the lads to work constructing the approach to the second wall, though it'll be hard work.'

'Oh? What's the problem?'

'Let me show you, if I may, sir.' Perkins did not wait for a reply but made his way through the breach and crouched down just inside the ruined masonry. He turned and gestured to Arthur to keep his head down. Arthur crouched beside him and quickly glanced round the interior of the fortress's first wall. A cobbled track ran between the two walls, and to its side there was a cliff of perhaps twenty feet in height before the foundations of the second wall rose up. The cliff was a good fifty feet from the breach. Perkins coughed and smiled apologetically. 'Caught a bit of a cold in all this damp, sir. Anyway, as you can see, there's open ground between us and the cliff. In order to mine the second wall we will need to cut into that rock and tunnel up towards the foundations. It's going to be a tough job.'

'But you can do it?'

'Given time, sir. Yes.'

'Time is something we are a little short of, Perkins. My scouts to the north report that a French army is gathering to relieve Burgos within the month. The latest word from Madrid is that Soult is marching to join Joseph. When that happens they will make for Madrid. We have to take Burgos as soon as possible and join forces with Hill if we are to hold the centre of Spain. Do you understand?'

'Aye, sir, I do. We will carry out our duty as swiftly as we can, but before we can start mining we have to get the lads across the open ground. A trench is no good because the Frogs have the ground covered by the bastion to our right, and the angle of the wall to the left there. At the moment the Portuguese boys have the wall covered' – he nodded towards the brown-uniformed men crouching amid the rocks at the base of the cliff on either side of the breach – 'but to get men and equipment up to the cliff we are going to have to build a covered gallery across the open ground. Dangerous and time-consuming work, sir.'

'I see. How long will it take?'

Perkins pursed his lips. 'Two days to erect the gallery. Two weeks to tunnel up through the rock, a day to prepare the mine, and then it's up to the infantry to storm the fortress, sir.'

'Two and a half weeks, then,' Arthur mused. 'That's cutting it fine. Do whatever you can to speed things up, Perkins.'

'Aye, sir. I've had the necessary tools brought forward and I'll set the lads to work as soon as the breach is cleared.'

'Very well.' Arthur clapped him on the shoulder. 'Keep me informed.'

He was about to turn away when there was a sudden crackle of musket fire from close by. The two officers looked towards the sound. To their left the Portuguese were firing along the cobbled road as it bent round the corner. More shots were fired, this time to their right. Then there was a shout and the sound of boots echoing off the fortress walls and Arthur saw the first of the Frenchmen appear along the road. More came, filling the gap between the walls as they charged forward, pausing only to fire at the Portuguese troops in their way.

Perkins cupped a hand to his mouth and bellowed, 'To arms! To arms! The Frogs are sallying!' He turned to Arthur. 'You'd better go, sir. Get back to the support trench and order some reinforcements up here.'

Arthur shook his head as he stood up. 'No.'

Perkins reached inside his coat and pulled out a pistol. 'As you will, sir.'

All around the breach, the men who had been working to clear the rubble scrambled for their weapons and rushed forward, past Arthur. There was a brief skirmish as the Portuguese company tried to hold their ground, thrusting their bayonets and clubbing the butts at the Frenchmen, but there were too many of the enemy and they were quickly swept aside and cut down before the French closed in on the breach from both sides. Perkins and his men rushed forward. Most had muskets, but some had snatched up shovels instead and now wielded them like hatchets. It was close work, and bloody, with no time for mercy. Arthur saw Perkins raise his pistol and shoot a Frenchman in the face, blowing out the back of his skull in a shower of blood, brains and bone fragments. Arthur felt a surge of fear as he realised he was unarmed. Looking round he saw a musket leaning against the outside of the wall and scrambled across the rubble to snatch it up, hoping that it was loaded. By the time he got back to the breach, his men were already being pressed back through it, as hundreds of Frenchmen surged forward. He saw Perkins double over as a bayonet plunged into his chest, piercing him through.

'Get back!' a voice called out. 'There's too many of 'em. Fall back!'

The soldiers gave ground, carrying Arthur with them. They reached the trench as the first of the enemy emerged from the breach, led by a huge officer with a thick moustache. He bellowed at them to charge, and kill all in their path. His men plunged towards the trench, driving the British back. Arthur had already been thrust some distance and turned to make his way down the slippery trench towards the camp. Then he saw a young lieutenant, wide-eyed with terror, pressed against the side. Arthur grabbed him by the arm.

'Lieutenant! Rally these men. You must fight back. Here!' He thrust the musket into the man's hand and pulled him into the middle of the trench, blocking the way of those still scrambling back from the breach.

'Stop there, lads!' Arthur held up his hand. 'Stop, I say!'

At the sight of their general the men drew up, unwilling to disobey him, yet afraid to turn and fight. Arthur pointed his gloved hand back up the slope. 'The enemy have the breach! If we let them hold their ground then we will have to take it again! I will not waste lives unnecessarily. You must turn round and take it back! Come, lads, 'tis the only way!'

The lieutenant nodded, and then pushed through the throng of men, holding his borrowed musket at the slope. 'After me, men!' he shouted, a slight edge of hysteria to his cry. 'Forward! For the King! For England!'

'For England!' echoed the sergeant who had urged Arthur to keep his head down. 'Let's gut those bloody Frogs, lads! Forward!'

The men let out a cheer and surged back up the trench. Arthur watched them go for a moment and then hurried back down the approach trench, slithering here and there in the mud. When he reached the flat stretch he splashed along until he came to the first of the assembly areas, where he saw Somers-Cocks and his volunteers.

'What's happening, my lord?' asked the major.

Arthur did not answer, but thrust his arm towards the breach. 'Take your men up there at the double. Clear the breach and hold your ground. Go!'

'Follow me!' Somers-Cocks bellowed, drawing his sword. He plunged into the opening of the trench, and his men ran after him, splashing through the muddy water that filled the bottom. Arthur turned and hurried on, making for the command post. There he found Somerset and gave orders for a brigade to be sent to support Somers-Cocks. Then, snatching up a telescope, he leaned against the sandbag parapet of the command post and braced his elbows to squint through the eyepiece. The French were hurriedly smashing down the makeshift walls on either side of the breach. Others were busy finishing off the allied wounded with their bayonets. An officer in a gold-braided uniform was directing some of his men to gather up the engineers' tools and carry them back into the fortress. Arthur's heart sank at the sight. The French defenders were as intelligent as they were brave, he thought bitterly. The capture of the tools would set Arthur back far more than the deaths of his men.

The French officer took a last look round the breach and then down the slope towards Somers-Cocks and his men, charging forward to join the survivors of the attack battling their way back up the final stretch of trench before the breach. With a wave of his sword the Frenchman ordered his men towards the gap and they withdrew in good order and disappeared from view.

'We lost ninety-four killed and thirty-two wounded, most of the tools that Perkins had brought forward, and twenty yards of the approach trench have been pushed in,' Somerset reported that night. 'The breach is back in our hands, and Major Somers-Cocks has established a permanent force of two companies of the Coldstream Guards to protect our foothold inside the fortress. Captain Morris has taken over the mining operation, my lord.'

'Very well.' Arthur nodded wearily. 'We'll proceed with the siege, for now. Did you read the latest report from our Spanish friends?'

The news was bad. The Spanish general charged with holding up any French advance from Valencia towards Madrid had taken umbrage at the appointment of Arthur to supreme commander and mutinied. Meanwhile Soult was marching to join Joseph Bonaparte. To the north of Burgos, General Souham had been confirmed in his appointment as

Marmont's replacement and had gathered nearly fifty thousand men on the far bank of the Ebro. Any day now, Arthur expected to hear that Souham had crossed the river and was making for Burgos. The final slice of misery was an intercepted message from the French Emperor to his brother announcing that he had won a great victory over the Russians at Borodino and was on the verge of capturing Moscow.

Somerset sat back in his chair despondently. 'Unless our luck changes, it may well be prudent to cut our losses and retreat.'

'From Burgos, perhaps,' Arthur agreed. 'But I fear that we may also have to abandon Madrid as well. What else can we do if this news is accurate? If I had the whole army here I could take on Souham and defeat him, at the price of leaving Madrid open to Soult. If I return to Madrid and combine Hill's army with mine that would give us sixty-five thousand men with which to face Soult with as many as a hundred thousand, while Souham closes on us from the north. We would be caught in a vice.' Arthur shut his eyes and forced his exhausted mind to think as clearly as possible. 'The best we can hope for now is to take Burgos and put in a strong, well-provisioned, garrison. That will hold Souham up while we return to Madrid. Then? All I can do is pray that Soult is delayed.'

Somerset watched his general closely for a moment, noting how sunken his eyes looked and how exhausted he appeared. The cold, miserable weather of the past weeks and the mud and depressing landscape of Burgos had added to his burden and for the first time Somerset began to wonder how one man could endure the strain of command for so long. The campaign had begun at the start of the year and now, ten months on, the officers and men were clearly exhausted and their morale was low. If they were close to the end of their tether, then by what greater order of magnitude was Wellington close to the end of his? Only one man could have led the army to achieve all it had in the Peninsula, and looking on that man now, Somerset feared for himself, and for the whole army, far from a home some had not seen for years.

'Sir?' he asked quietly. 'Shall I order you something to eat? Sir?'

There was no reply, just a deep, even breathing. Somerset smiled fondly, then rose to his feet and fed a few more logs into the campaign stove. After a moment's hesitation he picked up the mud-stained cloak lying across one of the chests in the tent and carefully draped it over Wellington's body.

'Good night, sir,' he said softly, and left the tent.

★ ★ ★

Four days later, the French attacked the sappers again, bursting into their works between the walls in the early hours. They killed the engineers who were cutting a small tunnel through the rock beneath the second wall; the men charged with protecting them had put up a short fight before fleeing back towards the breach. There they had encountered Major Somers-Cocks, barring their path. He was attempting to rally them and counter-attack the enemy's raiding party when he was shot through the heart. His men's spirit broke and they fled back down the trenches, leaving the enemy to seize yet more tools before they set a small charge in the mouth of the mine and blew it up, burying the entrance under tons of rock.

Later, when the first report of the attack reached headquarters, Arthur read through the details and then lowered the document, his face ashen as he turned to address Somerset. 'Somers-Cocks is dead.' Then he walked slowly outside to stare at the fortress where the tricolour flag was flying defiantly above the keep.

Major Somers-Cocks was buried that afternoon, in an icy downpour. As his body, wrapped in a length of canvas, was lowered into the ground the chaplain of the Coldstream Guards read out the service in the usual blank monotone. Arthur did not listen to a word of it. He had heard all the words before, read out in the same dry manner over the bodies of many such young men. Some had shown similar promise to Somers-Cocks, most had not. Some had been cheerful spirits, gamely entering the field of war, while a few had been nervous, fearful even, eaten up by the prospect of death yet forcing themselves on until death had claimed them by shell, bullet, blade or disease.

The chaplain closed his prayer book and bowed his head for a moment, and most of the officers and men followed suit. Arthur did not. He glared at the fortress for a long time, the rain running down the sides of his face in glassy rivulets. Then at last he turned to Somerset, cleared his throat and spoke harshly. 'I'm lifting the siege. The army is leaving Burgos and will march back to Madrid. Issue the orders, if you please. I'll be in my tent if I am needed.'

He turned and splashed away through the puddles, rippled by the heavy rain.

'Needed?' Somerset repeated quietly. 'Now more than ever, my lord.'

Chapter 33

Tordesillas, 31 October 1812

'So, he's done it then?' Arthur shook his head in frank admiration of the achievement.

'Yes, sir,' Somerset replied, glancing down at the captured bulletin. 'Bonaparte entered Moscow on the nineteenth of last month.'

'And does it say anything about the Tsar coming to terms?'

Somerset scanned the rest of the item and tilted his head to one side. 'Not exactly. It just says the Emperor is waiting for the Tsar to admit defeat.'

'Hmph,' Arthur snorted. 'If the Russians make peace then Bonaparte will be free to switch the balance of his power away from the east and towards us. At which point our goose will be thoroughly cooked. Well, we shall just have to hope that the Tsar continues to defy him. Now then, what is the latest intelligence on the enemy's movements?'

Somerset shuffled through his reports. 'It seems the French have seized a crossing over the river Douro at Toro.'

'Toro, eh?' Arthur frowned. 'That's bad news. They threaten to cut us off from Portugal. I had feared that they might be attempting to get between us and Madrid. Now it looks as if they might have designs on catching us between the Army of Portugal and Soult's force marching on Hill.' He paused and pinched the bridge of his nose. 'It seems that I am now in a worse position than ever, Somerset.'

The army had slipped away from Burgos a few days earlier, under cover of darkness. With the wheels of the guns and the wagons muffled by straw, they passed over the bridge at Burgos and then marched south-west towards Valladolid and the river Douro. It was Arthur's intention to put as much distance as possible between his men and the French Army of Portugal. Any hope that the enemy was still too demoralised to fight after the defeat they had endured at Salamanca was soon dashed. They pursued the allied army with all the speed they could muster and pressed forward with the sturdy confidence of those who had the bigger battalions on their side. As the month had drawn to a close it had become clear that the French were too strong for Arthur to risk battle and he would be forced to give up any hope of keeping his forces in central Spain ready to renew the campaign the following year. Now, it seemed that he was in danger of being trapped here.

He looked up at Somerset. 'There is no question over what we must do. Hill is to quit Madrid at once. I had hoped that we might join forces north of there, but it's too late for that now. Send an order to him to meet me at Salamanca. Meanwhile he is not to engage the enemy.'

Somerset looked surprised. 'It is your intention to allow the French to retake the capital, my lord?'

'What would you have me do? Hill cannot stand against Soult alone.'

'I agree, sir, but what will our Spanish allies make of this? They will say that we have betrayed them.'

'By God, they can say what they damn well like!' Arthur thumped his fist down on the table. At once he relented, furious with himself for having succumbed to the foul temper that had been brewing within him ever since the army had failed to take Burgos. He drew a deep breath and opened his fist, forcing himself to continue in a calmer tone. 'I am sure that our Spanish allies will pour scorn on us for this. However, that is the cross we must bear. After all, we owe them little. I have learned never to expect much from the efforts of the Spanish grandees, even after all that we have done for them. They may cry *viva*, and they are friendly towards us, and hate the French, but in general they are the most incapable of useful exertion of all people I have known, and the most vain. So in balancing the good of my army against the goodwill of the Spanish, there is no question about which side my sympathies lie, Somerset.' He looked at his aide, his eyes dry and sore from lack of sleep, and his head aching for the same reason. 'Now, will you please be so kind as to send the order to Hill?'

'Yes, sir, of course,' Somerset replied guiltily. 'I apologise.'

'Nonsense!' Arthur forced himself to smile. 'It is I who must apologise. The faults that provoke me into my present melancholy are not yours, Somerset. Be comforted by that at least. Now get that message off to Hill, quick as you can.'

Although the skies cleared early in November, the winter had begun to settle across the heart of Spain. The roasting landscape that the army had marched through the last time they had cause to make for Salamanca was now gripped by cold dawns and blustery days with a chilly wind that sought out every rip in a man's uniform and cut through to his skin.

'An army in retreat is never a happy thing,' Arthur said ruefully as he watched a regiment from General Campbell's division trudge along the muddy road to Salamanca. The men were in a sorry state. Unshaven, some in patched uniforms that barely justified the term, others, having discarded the remnants of the grey worsted trousers they had been issued nearly eleven months earlier, wearing an assortment of replacements. Their muskets, however, were well cared for and not a speck of rust disfigured the long, dark grey barrels.

Some of the men glanced at Arthur with surly expressions as they passed by, and there were none of the cheers that usually greeted him when the men recognised their commander. Their bitter mood had not been helped by the incompetence of Arthur's new quartermaster-general, Colonel Gordon, who had managed to send the supply wagons to Salamanca by a different road and so denied the army its rations for the last three days. The men had taken to eating acorns and chestnuts gathered along the way.

Arthur's own mood soured as he reflected on Somerset's recent discovery that Gordon had been sending back defeatist despatches to the newspapers in London. Arthur had long since grown accustomed to such 'croaking' from some of his subordinates. It was an inevitable consequence of a long conflict. But what he would not tolerate was incompetence, and he resolved to have Gordon dismissed, regardless of the man's political connections.

General Campbell helped himself to a pinch of snuff as his men marched past. When Arthur commented on their demeanour, he said casually, 'Oh, they're miserable beggars at the best of times, sir. Especially the veterans. But they'll be happy enough with a tot of gin in them and the prospect of a fight.'

'Then let us hope that the French don't disappoint us when we reach Salamanca.'

Campbell winced as he sniffed, blinked his eyes, and then turned to Arthur. 'It's your intention to offer battle then, sir?'

'Why not? It will be as good an opportunity as any, once we add Hill's strength to our own.'

'What will that give us?' Campbell paused to calculate the numbers. 'Sixty-five thousand men to set against perhaps a hundred thousand Frogs?'

'Fewer than that, I should say,' Arthur replied, 'if my intelligence is correct. There were reports that several of Souham's formations have been diverted to other commands. It is likely that we will be faced by no more than eighty thousand men.'

'They still outnumber us, especially in cavalry and guns, sir.'

'True, but I suspect that they will be unnerved by the prospect of fighting over the same ground where they were so soundly beaten last time. I dare say it will raise our fellows' spirits for exactly the same reason.'

Campbell looked at him with a grin. 'Why, you're a wily one, sir, that you are.'

'Perhaps.' Arthur frowned. 'I just hope I have not overplayed my reputation. It would be a bad business if Soult and Joseph refused to take the bait for want of confidence.' His attention returned to the soldiers marching past. 'I would be sorry to spare your men the chance to amuse themselves.'

Campbell laughed, and offered Arthur his snuff box. 'Like some, sir? Clears the head wonderfully.'

Arthur looked at the box with disdain. He had never liked snuff, nor could he understand the pleasure that could be derived from the sneezing it induced. He shook his head. 'I thank you, but no. With my nose, you would be sure to lose half your supply.'

Campbell stared at him wide-eyed, and then barked out a laugh as he tucked his snuff box away.

'Now, keep your men moving, Campbell. I'll need every one of them when we turn and fight at Salamanca.' He touched the brim of his hat and turned his mount to ride on to the next division in the line of march that snaked west across the bare landscape.

Hill and his force joined the army at Salamanca two days after Arthur arrived. A day's march behind Hill came the combined forces of Soult, Joseph and Souham. Arthur promptly had his army make camp, as before, on the reverse slopes of the Lesser Arapil. Just beyond the opposite ridge the French halted to make camp, posting a string of cavalry vedettes along the ridge to keep watch on the allied position. Arthur used the farmhouse where he had first spotted Marmont's out-flanking move as his headquarters. As the men scoured the surrounding countryside for firewood and made the best meal they could out of their remaining rations, Arthur summoned his senior officers to the farm to brief them on his plans.

He was pleased to see General Alava again. Alava had joined Hill's column on the retreat from Madrid and smiled faintly in response to Arthur's greeting.

'My lord, you have no idea how much animosity your quitting Madrid has stirred up. I had a difficult time of it persuading the Cortes to let me re-join you.'

'I apologise for your discomfort. However, I would hope that those who govern Spanish affairs would rather I had my army intact than have it remain in Madrid and be destroyed.'

Alava winced. 'I only wish they were so foresighted, my lord. There are some who are all for declaring war on England.'

Somerset was scandalised. 'You're not serious?'

'It was in the heat of the moment. It will pass,' Alava waved his hand. 'Fortunately, I was able to persuade cooler heads that this was a temporary expedient and that our allies would return to liberate Madrid, permanently.'

'Thank you.' Arthur waved Alava towards a seat around the tables the farmer had set up in his barn, the only space large enough to accommodate such a number of officers. Arthur rapped his knuckles on the board to silence them and get their attention. 'Gentlemen, it is my hope to confront the enemy tomorrow. Though we are outnumbered, we have a fine defensive position which will negate whatever advantage they may have in guns and cavalry. It also leaves us with a clear route to Portugal, should we need it. We have been in a similar situation before and if the French come on in the same old way, why then we shall beat them in the same old way. As we did at Vimeiro and Busaco.' He paused, preparing his officers for a change in tone. 'The truth is, this battle, if there is one, will be the last opportunity we have to squeeze some advantage out of this year's campaign. If we can defeat, or drive off, the French, then our retreat stops here. If they beat us, then at least we can retire to Portugal to lick our wounds and come back at them in the spring.'

'What if they choose not to fight?' asked Hill. 'The last time we occupied this position, Marmont proved reluctant to attack. It was you, my lord, who had to take the battle to the enemy.'

'Last time we were evenly matched, so I could afford to attack,' Arthur replied. 'This time, the odds are against us and it would not be prudent to do so. Besides, given the effort our enemies have made to scrape together every available man from three armies, I cannot believe that they will not offer battle. I assume that Soult, since he holds the senior military rank, will be in command. The last time we crossed swords was in Oporto. He will be thirsting for revenge. Soult will know that he must fight us here, or be obliged to follow us to the shelter of our fortresses in Portugal. Gentlemen, I am certain that we will have our battle.' He looked round the barn at his officers. 'All that remains is for you to do your duty.'

★　★　★

The sun rose out of a misty haze and bathed the two ridges in a warm glow that was welcomed by the soldiers, wearied of the wind and rain that had accompanied their march across the centre of Spain. While Arthur's men quietly filed into their positions on the reverse slope, his artillery crews prepared their guns, positioned on the ridge where they could savage any enemy columns advancing up the slopes of the Lesser Arapil. Arthur had considered garrisoning the Greater Arapil, but decided against it. He needed all his men in the main battle line, and was wary of starting a savage battle of attrition for control of the hill that would work in favour of the more numerous French.

On the far ridge, the French forces marched into line to the accompaniment of their bands, which struck up the usual stirring tunes to fill their troops with the appropriate sentiments of drama and patriotism. For nearly three hours the French host formed in an arc around the Lesser Arapil, a steady stream of infantry battalions standing behind their tricolour standards topped with the gilded eagles that Bonaparte had conferred on his army. On the flanks, dense masses of cavalry stood patiently, the horses scraping the ground, tails occasionally flicking, as their riders waited for the order to mount. In the centre, ready to pound the allied line, a great battery of more than forty guns had been hauled forward and the first racks of shot and handful of charges had been brought up to load them.

By ten, all was in readiness on both sides and the soldiers waited in tense expectation, ears straining for the sound of the signal gun that would announce the opening of the battle. Arthur and his staff had mounted their horses and ridden as far forward along the ridge as was safe, and there they waited. Every so often an officer would fish out his watch and mark the passing of time.

Then, at midday, the French skirmishers began to advance, stepping out across the valley, and then rushing to cover as the British riflemen opened fire, shooting down a handful of French officers and men. A desultory duel between the two screens of marksmen dragged on for another hour with little result, since the riflemen were content to stay where they were and the French skirmishers, armed with smooth-bore muskets, and therefore outranged, only dared to bolt from one cover to another, until they were within effective range to fire their weapons. As the exchange of fire continued, the clouds above thickened, casting a gloomy pall over both armies.

'Half past one, my lord,' Somerset said casually. 'No sign of any attack. What the devil is Soult up to?'

A sudden fear struck Arthur. What if Soult was biding his time while another element of his army was moving into position. 'Any word from the cavalry patrols?'

'Sir?'

'Any report of other enemy columns in the area? Or anywhere on the Portugal road?'

'No, sir.' Somerset had rarely detected such anxiety in his commander's voice and added, reassuringly, 'I am certain of it. I read all the reports first thing this morning. This is the only French army near Salamanca.'

'And you would wager your life on that?' Arthur asked curtly.

'I would.'

Arthur turned to look at his aide, his eyes filled with contempt. 'Then you are a fool, Somerset. Or a charlatan.'

Somerset swallowed his anger. Wellington was not himself and allowances had to be made, so he held his tongue as the general turned his attention back to the enemy, the fingers of his left hand tapping out an unconscious rhythm on his saddle holster. Arthur had a clear view of the enemy commanders and their staffs, crowded about the same position Marmont had occupied in the earlier battle. Raising his telescope, he trained it on the large group of horsemen and picked out the elaborate uniforms of Joseph and his senior commanders. They seemed to be locked in an animated debate.

As Arthur watched them he heard a faint pat on the brim of his hat, then another. Lowering his telescope, he saw that it had begun to rain. The pattering became more general, and then merged into a hiss as the rain fell in earnest, creating a steely veil between the two armies. Arthur glanced up at the sky and saw that the clouds had spread to the horizon. The most distant hills had already been blotted out and those only a few miles off had been reduced to grey outlines.

'Still no movement from the enemy,' an officer muttered.

Arthur nodded, and thrust his telescope back into the saddle bucket, fastened the buttons of his cloak, and sat stiffly as he considered his next move. The rain would handicap both sides. The French would have to advance across the muddy floor of the valley before mounting the slope leading up to the allied position. Infantry and cavalry alike would be hampered by the soft ground. At the same time, the rain would increase the number of misfires from Arthur's men, which would reduce the firepower of his line, a worrying factor given that he was already outnumbered. As he was thinking, Somerset rose up in his stirrups and pointed towards the far ridge.

'Sir, look there. The French are on the move.'

Arthur raised a hand to shield his eyes from the rain and squinted. Sure enough, the men of the enemy cavalry reserve, massed on the crest of the ridge, were mounting their horses. Then, one squadron at a time, they turned and rode away over the ridge. As the order spread to the other formations, the French army began to withdraw towards their camp.

'It would seem that rain has stopped play,' Somerset said.

Arthur nodded and sighed. There would be no battle today. Soult would not be lured into an attack on a strong defensive position. That left only one rational course open to Arthur. He tugged the reins and eased his horse round to face his staff officers. 'That is it then, gentlemen. The army is to fall back to Ciudad Rodrigo. Somerset.'

'Yes, sir?'

'Stand the army down. They are to return to camp for the night. Inform all divisional commanders that the army is to begin the retreat at dawn. They will have their written orders for the march during the night. That is all. Gentlemen, you are dismissed.'

The disappointment and dejected spirits of his officers were evident in their faces as Arthur watched them turn their mounts away and walk them back to the headquarters at the farm. He shared their sentiments. The army would have returned to the starting point of the campaign, and the failure to take Burgos, the abandoning of Madrid and the discomfort of the long retreat through the months of winter would weigh on the mind of every soldier. Many of them would voice their disgruntlement in letters home as they waited for the winter to pass.

However, Arthur reminded himself, soldiers were always inclined to complain about those things that caused them immediate discontent. In time, when they had rested, and fed well, and been issued with new boots and uniforms, they would recall the glory of Salamanca well enough. And the triumphant entry into the Spanish capital.

Arthur turned his horse back to face the enemy. Even though Soult had deprived him of the day's battle, he recognised the significance of this moment. Despite his advantage in men, Soult had refused to fight. Bonaparte's marshals had come to fear him, Arthur noted with satisfaction. They were no longer the masters of Europe's battlefields. He hardly dared to voice the thought, but in his heart he knew that the tide of the war was turning against France, and against Bonaparte.

Chapter 34

Napoleon

Maloyaroslavets, 25 October 1812

The rain petered out after the first two days of the march, and clear skies and mild weather meant that the French army reached the town of Maloyaroslavets, sixty miles from Moscow, by the end of the fifth day. Napoleon decided to head south-west, towards Kutusov, in the hope that the Russians would fall back, thereby opening up a clear line of retreat towards Smolensk. The news from the other elements of the army was grim. Marshal MacDonald, who had been besieging Riga on the Baltic coast, was facing ever greater numbers of Russians, and the loyalty of many of his own troops was suspect, particularly the Prussians. To the south of the Pripet, General Schwarzenberg and his Austrians were facing twice as many Russians and were being forced back.

Meanwhile, Murat's scouts were reporting that other Russian forces were closing in from the north, south and east to join Kutusov. There was no denying the danger: the trap was slowly closing around the Grand Army. If Kutusov could block the river crossings along the French line of retreat, then hunger and the cold would ravage Napoleon's army and Kutusov's men would finish them off.

The day before, Prince Eugène had forced his way across the bridge over the river Lusha at Maloyaroslavets and this morning Napoleon, his staff and a small escort of dragoons had ridden out to reconnoitre the western road. Two thousand men were holding the town while the rest of the army waited on the north bank for the order to advance. The sky was clear and the morning air crisp and chilly, so that riders and mounts exhaled steamy plumes as the small party trotted through a shallow vale. Bare fields and the occasional peasant hut lined both sides of the road before giving way to forests that sprawled into the distance in all directions.

Napoleon glanced up at the sky and then spoke cheerfully to

Berthier. 'If this weather holds for another two weeks we shall make good progress to Smolensk.'

'Yes, sire,' Berthier replied, but his tone was cautious and Napoleon turned to look at him as their horses sloshed through a patch of watery mud.

'You have doubts, Berthier?'

Berthier briefly scratched his stubbly chin. 'May I speak freely, sire?'

'Do.'

'Very well. I cannot help thinking that we should be taking the most direct road back to Smolensk, particularly as the weather is good. The sooner the army falls back on its depots the better.'

'I agree, my friend. But the biggest challenge facing us at present is to keep our army in being. If I had given the order to retrace our steps there would be no way of concealing from the men that we are retreating. You can imagine how that would affect morale. It is better that we chart a different course, one that allows me to present it to the men as an advance. If they believe that, then I am confident that they are ready to fight on. Do you understand?'

Berthier nodded.

'Good. Then let's see if we can find a high point to see the way ahead.' Napoleon looked round and pointed to a knoll a mile down the track. 'There.'

He was about to spur his horse into a canter when there was a shout to his left. Napoleon turned. One of the thin screen of dragoons riding fifty paces to the left was pointing to the woods. A group of riders, perhaps fifty men, clutching lances had burst out from amongst the trees and were racing towards the party of Frenchmen. They were dressed in flowing red cloaks and wore black fur hats. Their mounts were smaller and shaggier than the French horses.

'Cossacks,' Berthier muttered.

There was another shouted warning from the right and Napoleon and his officers turned to see a second party rushing from the forest on the other flank, angling out slightly to cut the Frenchmen off from the town. The dragoons had drawn out their carbines and were hurriedly steadying their mounts to take aim. There was a puff of smoke and a crack as the first dragoon fired. The shot went wide. As his companions joined in Napoleon saw one of the Cossacks' ponies tumble over, pitching its rider forward on to the muddy field over which they raced towards the French Emperor and his small party. As soon as they had fired, the dragoons holstered their carbines and drew their swords, spurring their mounts towards the oncoming horsemen. On both sides of the imperial party the Russians charged forward, shouting their war cry as they leaned low over their ponies and swung their lances down ready to strike. The dragoons were heavily outnumbered and swiftly overwhelmed. As the last of them was cut down the Cossacks charged on, straight for Napoleon and his staff officers.

'Draw your swords!' Berthier bellowed. 'Defend the Emperor!'

The ornately decorated blades rasped from their scabbards as the French officers drew out their light cavalry sabres and dress swords and formed a loose ring about Napoleon. A handful of them had pistols attached to their saddles and pulled them out of their holsters, cocked them and held them ready, aiming up at the sky in order to prevent any premature discharges from striking their own side. Napoleon watched the Cossacks race across the open ground towards him, close enough now for him to make out the long moustaches flicking out round each cheek as their lips curled back, mouths wide open as they cheered themselves on.

'Brace yourselves!' Berthier called out. 'Don't let them get through.'

One of the officers lowered his pistol, took aim, waited until the last moment and shot a Cossack in the chest. The man dropped his lance and toppled from his sheepskin saddle. A rapid succession of pistol shots followed and then the first of the Cossacks reached the cluster of gold-braided staff officers with their feathered and cockaded hats. He thrust out his lance arm and the point shot towards the chest of a young colonel on the topography staff. With a desperate slash the officer parried the head of the shaft and drew his arm back to strike as the Cossack drew level. The sweep of the highly polished blade hissed through the air, but the Russian swung his body to the side and hung low beside the saddle, and the sabre sliced harmlessly over his head.

Napoleon glanced round to see that all his officers were engaged now, locked in an uneven duel with the Cossacks as they jabbed their lances at any target that was presented to them. For their part the staff officers tried their best to parry the strikes and use the greater weight of their horses to force the enemy back, but they were outnumbered and were gradually driven into a tight knot around the Emperor. Napoleon had no pistols nor even a sword, and drew out his telescope, hefting it in his spare hand as he prepared to use it as a club. All around the air was thick with the scrape and clatter of blades on steel points and wooden shafts. The Cossacks had stopped their cheering and now focused intently on their hand-to-hand fight with their enemy, teeth locked in feral snarls. With a gasp, the first of Napoleon's officers went down, falling from the saddle as the tip of a lance ripped from his stomach a bloody, glistening tangle of intestines. Almost at once he was joined by the Cossack who had struck him down as a sabre cut deep into the Russian's neck, severing muscle and blood vessels and breaking through the spine. The man flung his arms out, spasmed in the saddle and fell.

'Sire! Look out!' Berthier yelled, urging his horse between Napoleon and the Cossack who had pressed through the ring behind them. Napoleon swung round to see the Russian's wild expression as he drew back his lance to strike. The point came forward, foreshortened and deadly, like a snake striking, and Napoleon swept out his telescope, just managing to knock the point aside. Then the pony slammed into the flank of Napoleon's mare, nearly knocking him out of his saddle. He swayed briefly before grimly tugging on his reins and clamping his legs round the horse's girth. Berthier struck back, slashing his blade down on to the man's shoulder, shattering the collar bone and shoulder blade with a sharp crack. The Cossack dropped his lance, snatched the reins aside with his good hand and raced away, barging between the men struggling around Napoleon.

'Thank you, Berthier,' Napoleon panted, his heart pounding with fear and excitement. Berthier smiled, then both men heard a distant trumpet note sounding across the fields. They turned and saw a squadron of Guard cavalry charging into view round a bend in the road.

'Hold on!' Napoleon shouted to his officers. 'Hold them back!'

The skirmish intensified as the Cossacks strove to cut their foes down before they were saved by the reinforcements. Another officer fell, pierced through the chest, the bloody point bursting through his back less than three paces from where Napoleon sat on his mount. He recoiled involuntarily at the sight, then the lance was yanked back and the officer swayed in his saddle, groaning in agony, before he began to slump forward. Another cried out as a lance pinned his arm to his side, passing on into the Frenchman's ribs. Napoleon quickly rose in his stirrups to see that the dragoons were spurring into a charge to save their Emperor, pounding down the road in a muddy spray, their swords held high and glittering in the sunshine.

A sudden shout behind Napoleon caused him to swivel in his saddle, just in time to see another Cossack making for him, lance ready to strike.

'No you don't!' a voice shouted back and an officer spurred his horse between the Russian and the Emperor. As the Cossack thrust the officer threw his sword into the man's face and grabbed at the shaft of the lance with both hands. The Cossack clung on but with a swift, powerful jerk the staff officer wrenched the other man from his saddle and sent him crashing to the ground. A savage thrust to the throat with the lance finished him off.

The approach of rumbling hooves drew Napoleon's gaze away from the officer who had saved him and he saw the Guard cavalry charging up to the mêlée. They were hand-picked men mounted on the best of horses, and they charged down those Cossacks who could not turn and flee in time. The rest disappeared across the field into the woods, pursued by the galloping Frenchmen.

'Who is he, Berthier?' Napoleon nodded towards the officer holding the lance. The man was no older than thirty, blond and with fine features.

'Colonel Eblé, sire. An engineer.'

'Then see to it that the colonel is promoted to general. A brave man, that.'

'We will need all of his kind in the weeks ahead,' Berthier responded quietly.

Napoleon frowned. He wanted to upbraid his chief of staff for his pessimism, but he knew that Berthier was right. Glancing round at the forests on either side, he could already see mounted figures stealing back towards the tree line, watching them. Abruptly, he turned his mount back down the road and a moment later Berthier fell in alongside him.

They were silent for a moment as Napoleon glanced from side to side.

'I think we may have to reconsider our route,' he said.

Back in the campaign wagon, Napoleon pulled a map of the Moscow approaches from its case and spread it out across the folding table. He leaned forward on his elbows and examined it briefly, then nodded to himself. He tapped his finger where the name of Maloyaroslavets was marked.

'We dare not take the whole army across the river using a single span. It would take too long, and if the enemy can bring forward sufficient strength to attack the bridgehead then we could be stuck here while Kutusov approaches from the east.'

'That is a possibility, sire,' Berthier agreed. 'But if the ground on the far side is held by a few bands of Cossacks and the remnants of the column that Eugène forced aside, then I would say it is worth the risk. If the army gets over the Lusha then there are few natural obstacles between us and Smolensk.'

Napoleon thought a moment and then shook his head. 'It would take only a few cannon to sweep the bridge and there would be a panic. We would lose thousands – men I cannot afford to lose. No, the army cannot cross here.' Napoleon traced his finger across the map. 'We'll head north, back to the Moscow–Smolensk road.'

Berthier sucked in a breath. 'But that will cost us six days, sire. We can't afford to lose so much time.'

'Time is irrelevant if there is no army left to make use of it.' Napoleon straightened up and rubbed his back. Even though he had slept little in recent days he felt something of his old energy returning. His stomach was no longer hurting, he realised.

He continued to stare at the map. It was possible that Berthier was right, he conceded silently, and the march north would cost him six days, but the danger of attempting to cross the Lusha outweighed Berthier's fears.

A sudden gust of wind caused the map to flap where it wasn't clipped to the table. Napoleon shuddered and turned to one of the orderlies waiting outside the carriage. 'Find me a warm coat.'

Several days later, the army re-joined the road to Smolensk and passed through the battlefield at Borodino. There had been no time to bury the vast number of dead men and horses when the Grand Army had pursued Kutusov in the direction of Moscow after the battle six weeks before. Since then the corpses had swollen, putrefied and been scavenged by packs of wolves that had been drawn from many miles around by the scent of death. Amid the ravaged bodies was the litter of war: abandoned muskets, shattered gun carriages, cavalry helmets and breastplates, cleaved by musket and cannon fire.

'Good God . . .' Berthier muttered as he gazed around the desolate landscape as the headquarters column passed through. He sat opposite Napoleon in an open carriage.

'An ugly scene,' Napoleon nodded, and then wrinkled his nose. 'And a foul stench, even now.'

He turned in his seat to look back along the column snaking across the battlefield. Although the men looked lean and ragged, they still kept hold of their muskets and packs. As Napoleon watched, he saw hundreds of them break ranks and hurry across to the rotting horses to see if there was any meat to be gleaned, no matter how rancid. It was a sobering sight and Napoleon turned away, settling himself down in his seat and shutting his eyes. He did not sleep, but anxiously reflected on the steady disintegration of the Grand Army.

Earlier that day one of Murat's troopers had brought the Emperor a report from the rearguard. The reports of conditions at the rear of the army were hard to believe. Davout's corps had taken over the rearguard, and he informed the Emperor that as many as thirty thousand stragglers and camp followers were clogging the road behind the main body of the army. Most had abandoned their weapons and the strongest formed bands and preyed on the weak, stealing their food and clothes and leaving them to die. Starvation was killing hundreds every day. Men dropped by the side of the road and stared into space, waiting for death.

Roving bands of Cossacks and peasants were happy to oblige and butchered any French soldiers they came across. The wounded on the remaining wagons were crushed in together, and when a man died, or was deemed to be beyond help, he was thrown over the side to die in the mud or be crushed under the following vehicles. The remaining horses were little more than skeletons, and the lame animals were butchered where they fell, to be torn to pieces by frenzied mobs. Some men were even unhitching the horses from the wagons of the wounded and leaving their comrades behind, ignoring their pitiful pleas not to be abandoned. And all along the line of march lay the abandoned spoils of the campaign, amid the discarded weapons, spiked guns, carts, wheelbarrows and wagons.

When the army reached the Dnieper river on the first day of November, Napoleon gave the order to halt to give the rearguard time to catch up. There was ominous news from further ahead. Russian forces were marching to block the crossings over the Berezina river, a hundred miles from the border with the Duchy of Warsaw.

As night fell the temperature dropped below zero and kept dropping. Having read the day's despatches and written his responses, Napoleon climbed down from the campaign wagon and strode over to the fire that had been lit for him by a section of guardsmen. They now stood around the perimeter of the light cast by the flames, muskets slung over their shoulders as they stamped their feet, trying to keep warm as they stood guard. A servant brought a bowl of onion soup and a small loaf to the Emperor, who sat on a campaign chair a short distance from the fire. As he sipped at the hot soup he saw hundreds more fires dotted across the surrounding countryside and trailing back towards the eastern horizon. A half-moon hung in the sky, providing a thin illumination of the dark bands of forests and cleared swathes of farmland that stretched out on either side of the army. In the distance there was a brief outbreak of musket fire, then silence, and finally the long low howl of a wolf, taken up by others, which continued until a fresh rattle of musket fire scared them off.

Napoleon felt something cold prick his cheek, and blinked. Then a pale fleck floated lazily past his face and settled on his thigh. Another followed, then more, and he looked up into the night sky to see a sudden swirling motion against a bank of clouds drifting slowly across the heavens, obscuring the moon and stars. A low wind began to blow, fanning the flames of the fire. Napoleon heard footsteps nearby and turned to see Berthier approaching, a worried expression on his face.

'I had hoped we might reach Smolensk before the snow came, sire.'

Napoleon took another sip of onion soup. 'So did I. Now all we can do is pray that it doesn't last.'

Neither man spoke as they watched the veil of snow close in across the landscape, slowly blanking out the fields and forests as it began to settle on the ground like a funeral shroud.

Chapter 35

6 November 1812

Berthier looked up from the despatch that Napoleon had handed him to read. 'It seems to have been handled efficiently enough. The Paris garrison has stamped down on the traitors, and, as you say, General Malet is clearly a lunatic.'

'Lunatic or sane, he deserved to be shot, along with the others,' said Napoleon as he shuffled his stool closer to the stove. Outside the barn a blizzard was blowing, adding to the snow of the previous days. The imperial headquarters had struggled on until after dark before reaching the barn and the handful of sheds that were the only shelter the scouts had been able to find for the night. A stove had been fetched from the imperial baggage and one of the carts was broken up for firewood, providing enough for the stove and a small blaze outside where the sentries drawn from the Old Guard were huddled.

As twilight settled over the snow, painting the winter landscape in a pale blue hue, the headquarters staff had encountered a messenger on the road to Smolensk. The sealed despatch bag had only been opened once Napoleon had eaten and warmed himself by the stove. There was a message from the Minister of Police marked *Most urgent*, which Napoleon read first.

The minister reported that there had been an attempt by some senior army officers to seize power. The ringleader was General Malet, a longstanding opponent of the Emperor who had been committed to an asylum. Somehow, he had managed to escape. Arriving in Paris with a forged army despatch, he had declared that Napoleon had died in Russia, and managed to persuade a number of officers to join his cause. It was only when the military governor of Paris refused to believe the news that the plot was foiled and the culprits were arrested, tried and shot.

'Well, it's over now.' Berthier folded the despatch and placed it in the document box of correspondence that had been read. 'From the sound of things it stood no chance of success.'

'You're missing the point,' Napoleon said wearily. 'I don't doubt that Malet and his friends would have failed. The soldiers in Paris would never have gone over to them. What worries me is that so many officials were prepared to believe that I was dead.' He looked earnestly at Berthier. 'Don't you see? It does not take long for my hold on power to slip when I leave Paris for any length of time.' He was silent for a moment, staring at the beaten earth between his boots. 'It seems that my presence is needed in Paris as soon as I have led the army to safety for the winter.'

'Sire,' Berthier responded with a warning glance, and then looked round at the other officers in the barn. Some were hunched over campaign tables, busy writing orders, while others collated the latest strength returns, a task that daily revealed the increasing peril of the Grand Army as the number of men in each corps dwindled. Satisfied that he would not be overheard, Berthier continued. 'You must remain with the army for as long as possible. While you are with us there is still some hope for the men. They trust you, sire. They know that you will lead them out of this frozen wasteland. But if you leave . . . if you abandon them, then whatever is left of their fighting spirit will die. The army will dissolve. We have to save as many of them as possible, else there will be nothing to stand between our empire and the forces of Russia when the next campaign season begins.'

Napoleon frowned at his chief of staff. 'You exaggerate the danger, as ever, Berthier. What makes you think these conditions affect the enemy any less than us, eh? The Russians are still men. They feel the cold. They grow hungry as they outmarch their supply lines. I dare say that, even now, Kutusov is sitting in his headquarters listening to a doom-mongering subordinate of his own. The Russians will be in no better condition to continue the war than we are when the spring comes.'

'You are wrong, sire,' said Berthier. 'The Russians are living within their supply lines. Their men have food when they need it, and are not obliged to try to carry it with them every step of the way.'

'Nor will we be when we reach Smolensk!' Napoleon snapped back. 'There are rations enough there for all the men. The city has strong defences. The army could winter there while I return to Paris, and when the spring comes we will be within striking range of St Petersburg. If the loss of Moscow does not move the Tsar to seek peace, then perhaps if we take his new capital he will begin to see reason. If that does not work we shall take his cities one by one, and burn them, until he comes to terms.'

313

Berthier shook his head. 'I am no longer sure that the loss of all his cities would weaken his will to resist. In any case, if the Grand Army, or what's left of it, remains in Smolensk then it runs the risk of being trapped there during the depths of winter. And all the time the enemy will be drawing on his reserves to increase the size of the armies gathering against us. Come spring they will be ready to close the trap around Smolensk and compel the army to surrender, or perish. There would be no army for you to return to, sire.'

Napoleon lowered his gaze and stared at the flickering orange rim round the iron door of the stove. Berthier was right. He could not afford to quit the army when the morale of the men was so fragile. Yet he was gravely concerned about the situation in Paris – and not only Paris. The Prussians could not be trusted, nor could many of the other lesser allies in the German Confederation. Then there was Spain, where French control of the country was slipping from his hands, as Wellington and the accursed Spanish rebels continued to run rings around Napoleon's marshals.

He felt the burden of it all weigh on his heart like a great rock. His empire needed him everywhere. He was fated to be either a ruler directing his wars from a distance, or a general leading his soldiers at the front, far from the capital. A man could not do both, he mused, and then smiled to himself. Perhaps not a man, but a Napoleon? Only history would tell.

'Sire?' Berthier interrupted his thoughts.

'What is it?'

'Your orders. Will the army halt at Smolensk?'

Napoleon was still for a moment and then shook his head. 'You are right. It is too exposed. We will fall back on the depot at Minsk. Meanwhile, send a message to Marshal Victor. His corps is still intact. Order him to advance towards us. He is to keep our lines of communication open at all costs. I cannot afford to be out of touch with Paris.'

'Yes, sire.'

Leaning towards the stove, Napoleon held out his hands and spoke softly. 'The campaign is lost, Berthier.'

'Yes, sire. I know.'

'Then all that remains to do is get as many men out of Russia as possible.'

The Emperor and the Imperial Guard reached Smolensk on the ninth day of November. The stock of supplies for the Grand Army was far lower than Napoleon had anticipated. Not nearly enough to feed his men through the winter, or even until the end of the year. As the following formations reached the city, they were issued with all the food they could carry. Many of the men had had hardly anything to eat for weeks, and ignoring the orders of their officers they gorged themselves, leaving little to sustain them as the army marched on, crossing to the south of the Dnieper and leaving Smolensk behind.

Napoleon and his staff attempted to reorganise what was left of the army. There were now less than forty thousand front-line troops. Murat's cavalry had almost ceased to exist and the officers were ordered to hand over their horses so that a small force could be scraped together to confront the menace of the Cossacks. The six thousand survivors of Ney's corps took over the rearguard and rested a few days in the city to allow the wretched column of stragglers to pass by, looting what little food was left in the depots and houses of Smolensk in the process.

Early on the seventeenth, the same day that Ney had been ordered to quit Smolensk, the vanguard came up against a strong Russian force blocking the road. The sky was the colour of lead above the thick gleaming white layer that blanketed the stark landscape. A mile ahead of the Grand Army was a low rise where the Russians waited, infantry and a handful of guns to the centre and thousands of Cossacks drawn up on each flank. Napoleon regarded them through his telescope and then conferred with Berthier.

'I would estimate perhaps twenty thousand all told.'

'Yes, sire,' Berthier replied a moment later. 'I agree.'

'They must be pushed aside.' Napoleon bit his lip. There was only one remaining formation in the Grand Army strong enough to complete the task. If they failed then all was lost. He turned to Berthier. 'Tell General Roguet to have the Guard form a battle line across the road. Here.' He stabbed a finger towards the ground.

As the faint glow of the sun climbed behind the clouds the men of the Imperial Guard marched up the road and then turned and filed across the snow to take up their positions. In front of them, the last of the artillery horses hauled twenty guns into place and the crews clumsily began to load the weapons with numbed fingers. As Napoleon watched the preparations he saw that his elite corps had suffered the same privations as the rest of the army. The guardsmen were bearded and filthy, their mud-stained uniforms in tatters, and strips of cloth had been tied round their boots and hands in an attempt to keep their feet and fingers warm. Yet they formed ranks as neatly as if they had been on parade in the courtyard at the Tuileries. Napoleon could not help feeling proud of these men, who had served him through many campaigns. This moment was what they had been saved for. At the Grand Army's darkest hour it would be the Imperial Guard who would fight to preserve them all.

A series of dull thuds from the Russian line announced the start of the battle, as the enemy cannon opened fire. General Roguet gave the order for his guns to reply as the last battalion of the Guard took its place in the line. For fifteen minutes the guns of both sides exchanged fire, their shot kicking up short-lived fountains of white as they grounded in the snow. Now and again a shot struck home, smashing a gun and striking down some of its crew. The men of the Imperial Guard artillery soon warmed to their task, grunting with effort as they laboured to load and fire their guns, and their superior training quickly showed as they silenced one enemy gun after another, while only two of their own were put out of action.

'That's the spirit!' General Roguet grinned as he sat on his horse beside Napoleon. 'First round to us, sire.'

Napoleon nodded, clasping his arms about his torso as he hunched his neck down into the muffler wound thickly about his neck. 'Tell your men to concentrate their fire on the infantry now.'

'Yes, sire.' Roguet spurred his mount forward through the snow towards his general of artillery. Moments later the first French shot began to fall into the dense ranks of the waiting Russian infantry as Roguet returned to his Emperor's side. Each time a ball struck home it caused a swirl of bodies, deep into the heart of the Russian lines. Yet they calmly closed up the gaps and held their position. For an hour they endured the punishment, until the general of artillery reported that his ammunition was running low. The Guard's dwindling convoy of supply wagons was still some miles further down the track leading to Smolensk.

'Then send the infantry forward, General,' Napoleon ordered. 'Order them to clear that rise and then push the enemy back to the south and open the route for the rest of the army.'

'Yes, sire.'

Shortly after the last of the guns had fallen silent the order to advance was given. The drums beat the rhythm and the leading companies of each Guard battalion stepped out towards the enemy, their boots making only a soft crunch as they broke through a thin crust of ice atop the snow. After a short delay the following companies rippled forward, following the tracks left by their comrades, until over seven thousand men were closing on the enemy. Napoleon heard the blare of a distant horn and then the note was picked up and repeated along the Russian line as the Cossacks surged forward, hooves kicking up sprays of snow as they brandished their lances and let out their war cry.

A moment later Napoleon saw the Guards halt. The flanking battalions steadily formed squares and then the entire formation stood its ground as thousands of Cossacks came charging across the flawless blanket of snow towards them. Up went the muskets, levelled at the oncoming riders, and the French officers held their fire, waiting as the shouting wave of riders surged closer, no more than a hundred paces from the guardsmen, then fifty. Napoleon felt his guts tighten in anticipation. Then the entire front rank of the French line fired with tiny stabs of flame and the sudden bloom of a band of smoke immediately to their front. From his position, Napoleon had a clear view over the smoke and saw the foremost Cossacks cut down, men and horses tumbling amid the snow. At once the front rank of guardsmen went down on one knee and angled their bayonets towards the enemy. The second line raised their weapons, paused, and then another volley crashed out as another wave of musket balls scythed down more of the enemy.

The horsemen facing the front of the French line drew up, hesitating as they saw hundreds of their comrades sprawled in the snow around them. On the flanks, however, they had suffered few casualties and they spilled round the corners of the French squares, only to be met by more volleys from the companies covering the flanks of the Imperial Guard's line. The charge broke, and the Cossacks turned their mounts away and galloped back to the rise. General Roguet ordered the squares to resume their original formation and then the Guards reloaded their muskets and continued their advance, halting as they came within range of the waiting Russian infantry. There was one exchange of volleys and scores of the leading battalions of guardsmen went down, and then the charge went in. The stolid courage of the Russians did not long endure as Napoleon's veterans cut through them, stabbing and clubbing their way forward. Within a minute the enemy broke and ran, tiny dark figures scattering across the snow.

Roguet's men took control of the rise, turning to the south to confront the clusters of Cossacks who had re-formed, and the two sides watched each other warily, just beyond musket range. Napoleon nodded with satisfaction. The road was open again and the army could make for the last crossing over the Dnieper at Orsha. After that, there was only one more river to cross before the final leg of the retreat to the Niemen.

For the rest of the day Napoleon remained with Roguet as the Guard continued to confront the Cossacks. Behind the guardsmen, the rest of the army tramped along the road. The snow was quickly compacted and the surface ice gleamed as the ragged French soldiers trod warily, trying to avoid slipping over. Behind the Guard artillery came the other battalions who had not taken part in the brief battle and a few hundred horsemen, all that remained of the thousands of finely mounted heavy cavalry that had advanced into Russia mere months before. Then came the gaunt figures of Prince Eugène's corps, some battalions reduced to less than fifty men still following the colours topped by the gilded eagles. No more than five thousand men remained of the forty-five thousand who had crossed the Niemen in June. Behind Eugène's corps came the ten thousand of Marshal Davout, who had led the largest formation on the campaign. Fewer than one in seven still marched behind their eagles. Following Davout was the long, ragged mass of stragglers, the wounded and the camp followers; women wrapped in cloaks, some clutching the hands of children who stared down apathetically as they staggered on. Some distance behind them, perhaps as much as a day's march, was the rearguard commanded by Marshal Ney.

Napoleon stared down his telescope for any sign of Ney's corps beyond the last dots of the final stragglers still trying to keep up with the army, but saw nothing but an almost empty winter landscape. With a feeling of anxiety he shut his telescope and turned to General Roguet.

'Have your men re-join the column. Close up the stragglers as best you can.'

'Yes, sire.' Roguet nodded. 'What about Ney? Do you intend to halt the army and let him catch up?'

'No. We must not stop. We have to reach Orsha before the enemy, or they will deny us the crossing.'

'Sire, I can leave a few battalions behind to hold the road open and wait for Ney.'

'The Guard are the very last of our reserves. I cannot afford to risk losing a single man of them unnecessarily.'

Roguet shook his head in protest. 'But, sire, if we abandon this position then the Cossacks will close the road behind us. Ney's corps will be cut off.'

'That's too bad,' Napoleon replied, and then forced a smile. 'My dear Roguet, if any man can survive this retreat, it is Michel Ney. You can count on it.'

Roguet looked back down the road to Smolensk. 'I hope you are right, sire.'

'Trust me. Now then, General, order your men to join the column.'

Roguet bowed his head wearily and walked his horse away from the Emperor towards the dark lines of his men still facing the distant clusters of Cossacks. Napoleon stared at the enemy with loathing for a moment. The Cossacks were like animals. There had been many reports of the atrocities they had perpetrated on stragglers or small groups of prisoners they had captured. Only the day before a group of foragers had been rounded up and forced into a barn which was then set on fire. As a consequence the imperial headquarters had issued an order that no prisoners were to be taken. In any case, Napoleon reflected, there were too few men to guard them and no food to feed them with. Literally no food. Already there were rumours that some had turned to cannibalism. Napoleon's expression turned to disgust at the thought. He did not believe the rumours, he told himself. Men did not do such things.

He shook off the thought and turned towards Smolensk one last time as the dusk closed in across the land, dimming the snowfields to ever darker shades of grey.

'Good luck, Ney,' he muttered, and turned his mount, spurring it into a trot in the snow alongside the column as he rode to catch up with his headquarters.

The vanguard marched hard, driven on by the knowledge that it was in a race to reach Orsha before the enemy could take the town and block the crossing. Two days after the battle the Imperial Guard reached the town and hurriedly set about fortifying the bridgehead across the Dnieper. Over the next days the rest of the main column trickled in and took shelter in the small town, crowding into the buildings and barns to get out of the bitter wind and snow. The small stocks of food in Orsha were soon exhausted and the rear elements of the Grand Army were forced to beg whatever scraps they could from their comrades. There was still no sign nor any word from Ney, and once the last of the stragglers had passed into the town the sentries kept an anxious watch for the first of the Cossacks that were sure to be close behind.

The staff of the imperial headquarters had taken over the town's corn exchange and were gathered in the main hall where a fire burned in a vast stone fireplace constructed from blocks of granite. The road to Warsaw had been cut once again and the latest reports from the cavalry patrols brought more bad news.

'The Russians have sent columns round our flanks to cut us off from the far bank of the Berezina,' Napoleon told his staff and senior commanders as they stood before him. He paused before delivering the next blow. 'They have taken Minsk.'

A groan went up around the hall. The supplies stockpiled at Minsk would be denied to the French army. Napoleon raised his hands and called for silence so that he could continue. 'It is clear that they will make for the bridges and fords around Borisov. If they can hold them in strength before we arrive then there is no question about the outcome. The Grand Army must surrender or face annihilation. Therefore, I must ask for another great effort from the men. We must cross the Berezina as swiftly as possible.'

He paused and his tone softened. 'I know how you must feel. We have been running from our pursuers for over a month now. It seems that there is always one more river we must cross to escape. I don't doubt that your men will despair when they hear the news. The ordeal is not over yet. A hard march lies ahead of us, but when we cross at Borisov it is only another week's march to Vilna where there is food enough for the whole army, as well as coats, boots and drink. Tell that to your men. Tell them it is there for the taking, if they can make the effort.' Napoleon paused and looked round the room. He was sad to see the resignation in so many of their faces. They were beyond calls to patriotism and appeals to the heart now. But they must still be open to reason, he decided. He drew a deep breath. 'Tell them whatever you like, as long as it inspires them to keep marching. When that fails, use force.'

He gave them a moment to let his words settle in their weary minds. 'We will have to do all that we can to increase the pace, gentlemen. To that end it is necessary that we leave behind all our heavy vehicles and any unnecessary baggage. We will keep the guns, limbers and ammunition carts only. Every wagon, carriage and cart is to be left behind. They will be burned, together with any supplies that we can no longer take with us.'

'What about the wounded?' asked Berthier.

'The walking wounded can stay with the army. The rest will be left here, together with any who volunteer to remain behind to look after them.'

There was a silence as the officers digested the order, then Roguet cleared his throat. 'Sire, that is a death sentence. We know what the Cossacks do to their prisoners.'

'Then we must hope that the Russian regulars enter the town first,'

Napoleon replied. 'But, just in case, we must ensure that every man is left with the means to escape captivity. The choice is theirs. There is nothing else we can do for the seriously wounded.'

Roguet shook his head, but kept his silence. Davout asked the next question.

'What about the engineers' pontoons, sire? Are they to be burned as well?'

'Yes.'

Davout frowned. 'But, sire, if the enemy take Borisov then we will need the pontoons to make our escape across the river.'

'They're not necessary,' Napoleon replied. 'The temperature has not risen above freezing for the last five days. It is likely to get colder still, in which case the river will freeze. Hard enough for us to cross the Berezina wherever the ice is thickest.'

'That is taking quite a risk, sire,' Davout protested. 'If the Borisov crossings are denied to us, and the ice cannot bear the weight, then . . .' He shook his head.

'That's why we need to move as fast as we can.' Napoleon clasped his hands together behind his back and concluded the briefing. 'Pass the orders on to all officers. All the vehicles are to be gathered in the market place. Half the remaining draught horses are to be butchered and the meat distributed to the men. Only our soldiers, mind you. Any civilians are to look to their own devices. The army will march at dawn.'

All through the night the wagons and other vehicles were dragged out of the town and pushed tightly together. Kindling was piled beneath the axles. The injured were carried into the buildings and made as comfortable as possible on beds, mattresses and piles of straw. Those who carried them tried to block out their comrades' desperate pleas not to be left behind. The weakest horses were led to the cattle market and slaughtered, and the army's butchers hurriedly stripped the carcasses of meat and placed the chunks in barrels to distribute to each surviving battalion of the army. An hour before dawn, as the men were roused from their billets in readiness to begin the next march, the engineers set light to the vast jumble of vehicles and the flames licked high into the sky as the first glimmer of the coming day lightened the eastern horizon.

It was at that moment that the alarm was raised. An officer from the battalion tasked with the last watch of the night came running into the corn exchange and breathlessly announced that a column was approaching Orsha. Napoleon quickly countermanded the order to begin the march and told Roguet to have the Guard ready to repel an attack. Then, with Berthier, he followed the officer through the streets to the eastern side of the town and climbed the tower of a small church. The officer commanding the watch battalion was already in the tower, gazing towards the sunrise. He turned and saluted as his Emperor panted up the steps and joined him.

'What is your name?' asked Napoleon, somewhat surprised to see a captain in charge of the battalion.

'Captain Pierre Dubois, sire.'

'And how old are you, Dubois?'

'Twenty-one, sire.'

'What happened to your colonel?'

'We lost him, and most of the other officers, at Borodino, sire. I took over command from Captain Lebel in the second week of the retreat.' Dubois paused and looked at Napoleon anxiously. 'I meant the second week of the march, sire.'

Napoleon smiled and patted his arm. 'Easy there, Dubois. It's all right to speak the truth to your Emperor. Now then, where's this column of yours?'

Dubois led the way to the tower window. The shutters had been bolted back and a light breeze flapped the corners of Napoleon's coat as he squinted into the half-light. The church was close to the river and as Napoleon glanced at the bridge, no more than fifty paces downstream to his right, he could see small ice floes gliding down towards the large stone buttresses. Dubois pointed to the road on the other side of the river. The handful of wooden houses on the far bank had been burned to deny the Russians any cover if they approached the town while the French were still occupying it. Beyond the charred ruins the road to Smolensk stretched out for a mile before it disappeared into a forested vale. A dark band slowly edged out of the vale, and raising his telescope to his eye Napoleon could just make out the figures of a column of infantry marching towards Orsha.

'Russians?' asked Berthier.

'Can't tell yet.' Napoleon rested the telescope against the side of the window frame to steady it and then squinted. It was most likely that it was the vanguard of Kutusov's army, hurrying forward to force Napoleon to turn and fight while the flanking Russian columns made for the Berezina. The tail of the column had emerged from the vale, and Napoleon waited a moment to see what would follow. But there was nothing. No more columns, guns or Cossacks. Just what appeared to be a strong battalion of infantry. The column marched steadily towards the bridge. Down below in the streets the first companies of the Imperial Guard were entering the buildings surrounding the end of the bridge and smashing open the windows and knocking rough loopholes in the walls with picks. Others dragged furniture out into the street to form a barricade across the bridge.

'Very strange,' Berthier muttered as he watched the column approach. 'They have to know that we are here, with all that smoke from the fire. But surely they would not dare to attack us on their own?'

'Assuming they are Russian,' Napoleon replied. He glanced through the telescope again. The head of the approaching column was now no more than half a mile away. At that moment, a small gap in the clouds opened on the horizon and sunlight flooded across the landscape, picking out a gleaming form at the head of the column. An eagle.

Napoleon felt a surge of relief and joy fill his heart as he lowered the telescope and beamed at Berthier. 'It's Ney!'

'Ney?' Berthier shook his head. 'Impossible. The rearguard was cut off. There must have been thousands of Cossacks between Ney and the rest of the army.'

Napoleon's smile faded. 'That explains why there are so few of them. But come on, we must greet him.'

They hurried down the stairs and out into the street. The stern expressions of the guardsmen preparing to defend the town turned to disbelief and joy when Captain Dubois shouted the news that Ney had survived. Napoleon and Berthier edged round the barricade and hurried across the bridge. They stopped on the far side as the head of the column came into view a short distance away. The men were marching in step, muskets resting on their shoulders: the very picture of military efficiency were it not for the rags holding their boots together. At their head marched Marshal Ney, a musket slung across his shoulder and a scarf wrapped over his feathered hat and tied under his chin. Several days' growth of red beard covered his jaw and cheeks. Twenty paces from the Emperor he stepped to the side of his men and bellowed, 'Rearguard! Halt!'

The column stamped forward a pace and stopped.

Ney stared at them a moment and then bellowed, 'Rearguard! Long live Napoleon! Long live France!'

They echoed his cheer with full throats, and as the echo of their cry died away Ney turned to Napoleon. 'Permission to return to main column, sire?'

'Permission granted!' Napoleon laughed. He strode forward and clasped Ney's arms. 'My God, it is a fine thing to see you again. How on earth did you manage it?'

'A moment, if you please, sire.' Ney turned back to his column and drew a deep breath. 'Rearguard . . . Fall out! Get some food and some rest. You've earned it!'

The men broke ranks and filed past Napoleon and the two marshals. Despite their bearing as they approached the town Napoleon could clearly see that they were at the end of their endurance. Ravaged by hunger and exhaustion, their eyes were sunken in dark sockets and their cheeks looked pinched as they walked stiffly over the bridge. The guardsmen cheered them as they entered the town, embracing their comrades and shoving their own meagre rations into the newcomers' hands.

'Just over nine hundred of them,' Ney said quietly as they passed by. 'All that's left of my corps and those that joined them at Smolensk.'

'What happened?' asked Berthier.

'We were pursued most of the way by Cossacks. At first we drove them off with musket fire, but two days ago we were down to three rounds a man. I had no choice but to close up and form square. We halted for the night, and they kept coming at us, racing in from the shadows to pick us off a few at a time. There was no chance to sleep, so I got the square moving. We marched through the night, and the whole of yesterday, under attack nearly all the time. I had to leave the wounded behind. I would have ordered them to be shot, but we needed the ammunition. The Cossacks only broke off towards dusk. We rested for the night in what was left of a village then started marching again at first light. Haven't seen a single Cossack since yesterday. Don't know why they let us go, but thank Christ they did. We're down to our last few rounds.'

Napoleon stroked his chin. 'They let you go because they had orders to get ahead of the main column. They'll be making for Borisov. At least that's my guess.' He looked up at Ney again and could not help smiling again. 'I knew that I had not seen the last of you. I knew it.'

'Well.' Ney shrugged. 'I have to say that I had my doubts.' He unslung his musket and stared at the weapon. 'It's been quite a while since I last fought as a ranker. Here!' He thrust the musket towards one of the last of the soldiers crossing the bridge. 'Take this for me.'

'Yes, sir!'

As the soldier hobbled on Napoleon punched Ney lightly on the shoulder. 'Marshal Michel Ney, Duke of Elchingen, I shall have to find a new title for you. But for now one will have to suffice. Ney, the bravest of the brave.'

Ney nodded his approval and then rubbed his hands together briskly. 'I thank you, sire, but right now I am Ney, the coldest of the cold. Where's the nearest bottle of brandy?'

Chapter 36

The skies cleared as the army marched out of Orsha and made for Borisov. For the first time in days the sun shone and the temperature rose above freezing. Meltwater dripped from the trees and the surface of the road gradually turned to slush that made the going a little easier for the soldiers and remaining horses of the army. The men's mood was lifted by the escape of Ney and his rearguard. After all, if they had survived their predicament and fought their way through the Russians, then there was something to hope for.

The army made its way across open farmland towards the Berezina without sighting any Cossacks on either flank, or behind them. For the first time in weeks, Napoleon was beginning to think that the worst was over. Marshal Victor and Marshal Oudinot had advanced from Vilna and joined the army with twenty thousand fresh soldiers and a convoy of supplies.

Then, towards the end of the second day's march, a dragoon came galloping up to Berthier with a despatch from the cavalry screen, some fifteen miles ahead. Berthier quickly read the message as his horse walked along and then trotted forward to Napoleon's side.

'Sire, the scouts sighted Borisov at noon.'

'Is the way clear?'

'No, sire.'

'The Russians have taken the town?'

'Worse than that. They've burned the bridges and have dug into the far bank.'

Napoleon reined in and took the slip of paper from Berthier to read it through for himself. Then he handed it back with a heavy heart. 'We needed those crossings.'

'Yes, sire.'

A hearty cheer interrupted their conversation as the remains of a battalion from Oudinot's corps marched past. Napoleon turned to them with a smile and raised his hand in greeting. The smile dropped at once as he turned back to Berthier. 'We keep marching towards the Berezina. The army is too weak to divert north or south. We must halt while an alternative crossing place is found. There's a village called Loshnitsa less than a day's march from the river, I recall. Give orders for the vanguard to halt there.' Berthier nodded. 'I'm riding ahead to see for myself. I'll join you at Loshnitsa.'

Escorted by one of the few remaining squadrons of Guards cavalry, Napoleon spurred his horse forward. They passed the Imperial Guard at the head of the column and then followed the road west. The thaw had brought some of the peasants out of their huts to replenish their stocks of firewood. As soon as they saw the small column of distant horsemen they ran for cover. There was still no sign of the Cossacks and as night fell Napoleon rode on until they came up to one of the cavalry patrols observing the distant fires of the Russian soldiers on the far side of the river.

Napoleon dismounted as the colonel in charge of the dragoons made his report. 'The enemy has invested the town, sire. Must be upwards of five thousand men. We've seen more of them up and downstream, patrolling the far bank.' The colonel turned to point to the north where a dim glow reflected off some low clouds scudding in from the east. 'See that? Camp fires. But there's no knowing how many of them are over there, sire.'

Napoleon nodded, then looked closely at the colonel. 'What regiment do you command?'

'Regiment?' The colonel looked surprised. Then he smiled ruefully. 'Sire, I command all that is left of Nansouty's cavalry corps. All the remaining horses have been allocated to the dragoons. All two hundred of us.'

Napoleon struggled to hide his shock as he glanced round at the handful of pitiful-looking mounts that were tethered to the back of a small hut where the colonel's men were sheltering for the night. 'Where are the rest of your men?'

'I have one troop to the south and one close to the bank to observe Borisov. The other two troops are scouting the river to the north, looking for any crossing points.'

'Good work.' Napoleon nodded towards the shed where a welcoming glow lit the door frame. 'I will spend the night with you.'

'Sire, we'd be honoured.'

Napoleon turned to the commander of the Guards squadron. 'You're dismissed. Find some shelter for you and your men, then report back here in the morning.'

The officer saluted and then wearily ordered his men to follow him as he trotted off into the darkness.

327

'That's the situation, gentlemen,' Napoleon concluded as he ended the briefing of his senior officers in the dacha on the outskirts of Loshnitsa. 'The cavalry patrols have scouted thirty miles upstream and every bridge and ford is defended by Russian guns and infantry. They also report that the recent thaw has caused the ice on the Berezina to break up.' He paused. 'We have to consider our options.'

He sat back and waited for his officers to respond. There was silence for a moment before Davout spoke for them.

'I will say what is on all our minds, then. The choice is between a long march to the north, until we can cut round the upper reaches of the Berezina, or negotiating an armistice with the Russians. It is more than likely that the Tsar will deny us an armistice. He will want nothing less than a full surrender of the Grand Army.' Davout nodded towards the Emperor. 'Sire, if that happens, then it is vital that you are not taken prisoner along with the rest of the army. I must ask if you have made any plans to escape in the event of a surrender?'

There was a silence as Napoleon looked round at his officers, men he had known for years. He nodded. 'I have considered the possibility, but not the precise details.'

'Then might I urge you to think on it?' Davout insisted.

'Very well.' Napoleon stirred and sat up. 'I don't think there is anything else to be said, gentlemen. I bid you good night. Oh, and Davout . . .'

'Sire?'

'It seems you were right about the pontoon bridges. I was wrong to give the order for them to be burned.'

'I know.' Davout nodded. 'Good night, sire.'

When the last of the officers had left the shuttered drawing room a sentry closed the door. Berthier remained seated at the table, having returned to his routine of updating the dwindling figures from the strength returns in his notebooks. Napoleon twisted one of the silver buttons on his greatcoat.

'What do you think, Berthier?'

Berthier replied without looking up. 'Think of what, sire?'

'My abandoning the army.'

Berthier lowered his pen and looked up. 'I think it may shortly become a necessity, sire.'

'And will it be a mistake? Speak honestly, my friend.'

'If you are captured by the Tsar, then you can expect little mercy from him given what happened to Moscow, and the other towns and villages we have marched through. Even if your life is spared, you can be sure that you will be humiliated, and France along with you. So, yes, sire. If it comes to it, then you must do everything in your power to avoid being taken by the Russians.'

'Everything?' Napoleon asked quietly.

'Yes, sire,' Berthier nodded. He had understood. 'Even that.'

'My surgeon has some phials of poison. I have always ensured that he carried them in case of such an emergency. I will keep one on my person from now on. As a precaution.'

'It would be wise, sire.'

Both men were silent for a while before Napoleon stirred. 'Of course, if I abandon the army, they will say I am a coward, my enemies.'

'You must expect that. But the people of France will understand that it was necessary. They will know that as long as you are alive France must be counted a great nation. While you live, you inspire our soldiers to acts of greatness, and you awe our enemies. Soldiers can be replaced. You, sire, can not.'

Napoleon searched Berthier's face for any sign of flattery or insincerity, but his chief of staff seemed utterly convinced by his own words. Napoleon smiled warmly at him. 'You, too, cannot be replaced, my friend. You are the word to my thought. It is through your words that my will is exercised and France has won its greatness on the battlefield. I should have thanked you before now.' Napoleon felt an uncomfortable surge of guilt as he recalled the numerous occasions he had slighted or insulted Berthier. He shifted uncomfortably and gestured towards the door. 'I must think, alone. Leave your books for tonight. Go and find something to eat, some wine to drink and a bed by a warm fire.'

Berthier hesitated, then nodded. He gathered up his notebooks, placed them in his large leather despatch case and quietly left the room. Napoleon rose stiffly from his chair, then carried it across to the remains of the small fire glowing in the grate. He carefully placed some more logs on the flames and sat back, closing his eyes, surrendering to the comforting warmth. He pushed troubling thoughts aside and pictured himself on the lawn at Fontainebleau, in the summer, playing with his infant son.

'Sire.' A hand shook his shoulder gently.

Napoleon woke immediately, eyes wide as he looked into Berthier's excited features.

'What is it?'

329

'Marshal Oudinot is here with me, sire.' Berthier stepped aside to reveal Oudinot.

'So?'

'It's best if the marshal explains himself.'

'Explains what?' Napoleon eased himself up. He glanced at the clock on the mantelpiece. It was three o'clock in the morning. He had been asleep for over five hours, he realised, angry with himself.

Oudinot stepped forward. 'I've come straight from my headquarters. sire. I'll come to the point.'

'Please do.'

'A column of reinforcements under General Corbineau joined my command this evening.'

'I know about that. He commands a brigade that was sent for from Vilna.'

'That's right. Corbineau intended to cross the Berezina at Borisov on his way to join us, but the day before yesterday he discovered the town was in Russian hands. So he questioned a local peasant to see if there was another place to cross the river. The peasant guided him to a ford eight miles north of Borisov, at the village of Studienka.'

'I know it, but there's no ford there.'

'None marked on the map, sire. But Corbineau crossed there.' Oudinot could not help smiling. 'He says the water was no more than waist deep.'

There were several flashes in the night as the firing on the far side of the river faded away. Corbineau and his men had succeeded in storming the two guns that had been left to cover the unmarked ford. They had earlier waded across the freezing river, muskets held high, and driven off a company of Russian infantry before turning on the guns. Evidently the enemy had also known about the ford, but since it had not been marked on any maps they had posted only a token force to protect the crossing place. In the distance, to the south, there was an occasional rumble of artillery as Oudinot's men carried out their diversionary attacks opposite Borisov. As Napoleon had hoped, the Russian forces strung out along the far bank had hurried south, marching to the sound of the guns.

As soon as Corbineau sent word back across the river that he had control of the far bank Napoleon gave the order for General Eblé's engineers to set to work. The plan called for two bridges to be constructed in the darkness and the army was to begin crossing the moment they were completed. Davout's and Victor's corps were to cover the approaches to Studienka while the rest of the army crossed over. The swiftness of the current and the unevenness of the river bed had ruled out any attempt to ford the river in strength. Half the army would have been swept away and the rest would have been frozen by the immersion in the icy water.

A handful of braziers were lit on the east bank to provide illumination for the engineers, and a short time later some more fires appeared on the far bank as a second team of Eblé's men began work from the other end, a hundred paces away. Napoleon strode down to the river bank to watch the progress. He found Eblé directing the work, a few feet from the edge of the icy current swirling downstream. Out in the river the dark figures of his men stood braced against the current as they held stout timbers in place while their comrades used a makeshift piledriver to ram the timbers into the river bed.

'How goes it, General?'

Eblé turned and saluted. 'The first trestle is in position, sire. We've been lucky with the frost.'

'Lucky?' Napoleon stared at the men standing up to their thighs in the river.

Eblé stamped his boot on the frozen river bank. 'It's hardened the mud. Makes it easier to get the materials down the bank.'

'I see.' Napoleon gestured towards the handful of wagons behind them. 'I thought I gave orders to have all the wagons burned at Orsha.'

'Yes, sire. However, I gave orders for my men to save a handful of wagons for our tools and nail barrels.'

'You disobeyed my order.'

Eblé stared at him and then shrugged. 'Evidently.'

'Good man. I wish half my generals showed such initiative.' Eblé looked relieved, but Napoleon pointed a finger at him. 'Just don't make a habit of it.'

Eblé laughed.

Napoleon looked round at the timber piled on the bank. 'Will you have enough material to complete the job?'

'That depends on Studienka, sire. The timber comes from the houses. My men are busy tearing the buildings down to get what we need. As long as the village is big enough, you can have your bridges.'

'When will they be completed, General?'

'Before noon tomorrow, if we are lucky. But the river is starting to rise, and there's ice in it. That may slow us down. I can't let the men work in these conditions for more than an hour at a time. I'll work them in shifts. An hour in the water, and half an hour resting by the fires. Still, we're going to lose many of them to the cold, sire.'

The sound of the engineers' hammers and piledrivers continued through the night. Meanwhile, the stragglers and non-combatants were arriving at the village and filled the streets of Studienka while they waited for the bridges to open. Napoleon intended to get the bulk of the army over the river before giving the civilians their chance. Last of all would come Victor and the rearguard, then the bridges would be destroyed.

As dawn broke, weak and pallid as clouds obscured the sun and threatened snow, a party of Cossacks was sighted a mile to the south on the far bank. They observed the bridge-building for a few minutes before turning and galloping away.

'They'll reach Borisov within the hour,' Napoleon muttered to Berthier. 'It will take the commander there an hour or so to form his men up and begin to march towards the ford. Give them three hours at the most to reach us, and another to deploy. We can expect them to start attacking our outposts early this afternoon.' He turned to examine the bridges. Trestles extended from both banks and the engineers were hard at work nailing support beams and planking in place. The smaller bridge, built for infantry to cross, still had a gap of some twenty paces between each end. The second bridge was larger, constructed to bear the weight of the army's remaining guns and the wagons that had escaped the fire at Orsha. It was going to take somewhat longer to complete.

'Shall I give the order for Oudinot to withdraw to the bridgehead, sire?' Berthier asked.

'What?'

'The Russians know what we are up to. There's no need for Oudinot to continue his diversionary action now.'

'Yes, of course. Recall him at once.'

The first bridge was completed just after one in the afternoon and the leading elements of Oudinot's corps which had just reached Studienka were the first to cross, hurrying over the bridge to advance along the causeway that stretched over the marshy land on the far side of the Berezina. It was the only means of escape and Napoleon had ordered Oudinot to keep the causeway open at all costs.

As soon as the first soldiers were marching across the bridge Eblé and his engineers concentrated their efforts on the larger structure. Already, a third of the engineers had been swept away, or were too weakened to work any further. Napoleon joined them by their braziers and did what he could to lift their spirits by praising them for their bravery and the sacrifice they were making for the army. The men listened in numbed silence as they shivered in their ice-crusted uniforms, struggling to keep their places close to the brazier.

Towards the middle of the afternoon, Eblé informed the Emperor that the second bridge was ready. Napoleon gave the order for the artillery and the Imperial Guard to begin crossing and then embraced Eblé.

'Your men have performed a miracle, General.'

Eblé was trembling with the cold and fatigue and he could barely stay on his feet. He nodded. 'Thank you, sire, but our job is not over yet. The river is still rising, and I don't know how long the trestles will withstand the pressure of the floes. It would be best to get the army over as swiftly as possible.'

Napoleon smiled. 'That is my intention. Now, you'd better re-join your men. Berthier, find the general and his men some brandy. I believe there are still a few kegs in the headquarters stores.'

'Yes, sir.'

As Berthier turned away to order one of his aides to find and distribute the brandy there was the crump of artillery to the east, adding to the faint sound of guns and musket fire from the far bank, where Corbineau and his men were holding their ground, steadily being reinforced by the troops crossing the first bridge. Napoleon strained his ears as he looked to the east. Soon the cannon fire from the rearguard action merged into an almost continuous rumble. The trap was closing on the French. Kutusov and the main Russian army would arrive from the east at any time. The survival of the Grand Army depended on Eblé's bridges, hurriedly constructed using scavenged timber from the village.

For the rest of the day and into the evening the soldiers, cavalry and guns continued to cross the river. As soon as the civilians had heard that the bridges were open they had made for the river, and a strong cordon of infantry with fixed bayonets was holding them at bay, keeping the bridges open to military traffic. During the night a section of the second bridge collapsed, taking a gun carriage with it. Two hours were lost as the exhausted engineers repaired the bridge. The following morning the bridge was open again and the army continued to cross. At noon Napoleon ordered his headquarters to move to the far bank, together with the remaining elements of the Imperial Guard. The sound of cannon fire behind them had died away during the afternoon and the latest report from Victor was that the enemy were manoeuvring to the south, as if they still expected Napoleon to attempt to force the crossings at Borisov. Napoleon was watching the steady flow of guns and wagons over the second bridge. He could not help smiling as he read Victor's report.

'It seems there is no overestimating the caution of our enemy. They have us in a vice and yet Kutusov fears to tighten it.'

'Lucky for us, sire,' Berthier responded. 'Fortune seems to be favouring you again. Oudinot's cavalry have taken all the bridges along the causeway without encountering any Russians. The road to Vilna is open.'

'Yes, fortune is with us, Berthier. Fortune, and sheer pluck, eh?'

Berthier was about to agree when there was a splintering crack. Both men turned to watch as one of the trestles in the second bridge started to collapse. Planks split and tumbled into the water. The rear wheels of an ammunition cart fell into the gap. For an instant everyone stopped to stare; the staff of the headquarters, the soldiers and civilians on the far bank. Then there was another crackle of shattering timber and a second trestle shivered and lurched to one side. The planking fell away and the wagon slipped back, even as the driver lashed his horse team to pull forward. The horses were weak and the heavy burden dragged them back towards the widening gap. Then the wagon tipped and fell into the river, dragging the horse team after it, kicking and whinnying in terror. There was a succession of splashes and the wreckage of the wagon, the debris from the bridge and the struggling horses were swept downriver.

'Did the driver survive?' asked Berthier, breaking the silence. 'Did anyone see?'

Napoleon stared at the bridge. Three trestles had gone, leaving a large gap in the centre. Already, Eblé and most of his engineers were running towards the bridge while other men grabbed long poles and rushed on to the smaller bridge to try to fend the wagon away from its slender trestles.

'Sire, look there.' Berthier pointed towards the huge crowd of stragglers and camp followers that had gathered beyond the second bridge. A great cry had risen up when they saw the collapse of the bridge. All at once they pressed forward, sweeping aside the cordon of soldiers set to contain them, and began to scramble along the bank towards the remaining bridge.

'What do those fools think they are doing?' Napoleon asked furiously. 'There'll be chaos. They'll destroy everything.'

The mob rushed the end of the bridge, sweeping aside the engineers. In amongst the press of people there were a few carts and wagons and their drivers lashed the horses on, trampling scores of people in their attempts to get on to the bridge. Already the first of the mob were on the planking, hurrying over towards the western bank. They were the fortunate ones. In a matter of moments a dense press was pushing forward on to the narrow strip. Everyone was acting for themselves and the merciless shoving was already thrusting individuals over the edge to splash into the river below. Napoleon could see the planking begin to bow under the pressure and knew that there was little time to save the bridge. He turned quickly and shouted an order to the captain of the company guarding the headquarters.

'Get your men down there now! Clear the bridge. I don't care how you do it, but clear that crowd away from the bridge!'

The officer ran towards the bank of the river, bellowing at his men to follow him. They ignored the broken stream of individuals that had made the crossing and now bustled past them, and stopped a short distance from the head of the tightly packed mob on the bridge. The captain hurriedly ordered his men into line, and they raised their muskets into the faces of the crowd bearing down on them.

'Get back!' the captain shouted. 'Get back, or we will fire on you!'

Those at the front of the mob tried to halt, but the pressure behind them was relentless and they were thrust forward.

'Front rank!' the officer cried out. 'Fire!'

The muskets spat out flames and smoke into the dusky afternoon and several bodies collapsed on to the planking.

'Second rank! Advance and fire!'

Another volley crashed out, cutting down more, who tumbled over the bodies of the first to fall. A cry of panic rose up from the front of the mob and they tried to turn and scramble back to the eastern bank, against the continuing pressure from those still desperate to escape over the river. Napoleon felt sickened as he saw a man in the greatcoat and shako of a *voltigeur* thrust aside a woman with a child bundled into her arms. She staggered to the edge of the bridge and screamed as she fell. Many more were being pushed into the Berezina as the Guards continued to fire at the unyielding mob.

Gradually, some awareness of the danger on the bridge began to filter back through the crowd and at last those still on the eastern bank began to draw back, slowly giving ground as they retreated towards the streets where they had been waiting shortly before. The captain ordered his men to cease fire and they advanced, bayonets lowered, keeping a short

335

distance from the retreating crowd. At length they reached the end of the bridge and spread out, forcing the crowd away. It was no easy task, as many had perished in the crush and their bodies lay heaped on the ground around the bridgehead.

'Sweet Jesus,' Berthier exclaimed as he stared ashen-faced at the scene. Below the bridge several bodies were caught up in the trestles. A few individuals were still alive, clinging to the posts, calling for help. Nothing could be done for them and within minutes the icy water caused the last of them to relinquish his grip. 'What a massacre. What did they think they were doing?'

'Panic,' said Napoleon. 'We can expect more of that in the hours ahead. Make sure that the ends of the bridges are well guarded, and the routes leading to them as well. See to it at once.'

As the light faded the engineers repaired the gap and began the grim task of dragging the bodies away from the end of the other bridge to clear the route leading on to it. Once the last of the soldiers had crossed the bridge and only Victor's corps remained on the eastern bank, General Eblé did his best to get some of the civilians and stragglers across. But night had fallen and there were flurries of snow in the bitterly cold air, and many refused to stir from the warmth of their fires.

In the early hours, Victor informed Napoleon that the Russians were beginning to push forward against his entire line. The sound of cannon fire increased in volume and soon even the distant sound of musket fire could be heard from the Emperor's headquarters. Dawn brought a fresh fall of snow with thick flakes swirling about the crossing and mercifully muffling the sounds of fighting from where the rearguard was struggling to hold back the enemy.

'How is the vanguard doing?' Napoleon asked Berthier.

'They have reached the end of the causeway and deployed to guard it from flank attacks, sire. Ney's men are holding the southern approaches to the crossing and the rest of the army is advancing along the causeway.' He paused. 'We've been lucky the Russians haven't pressed us more closely.'

'Indeed. Time to call in Victor. Inform Eblé he is to fire the bridge the moment the rearguard is across.'

'Yes, sir, and what of the civilians?'

'They will have to cross as best they can before the bridges are destroyed.'

Throughout the day, the engineers and the first formations from Victor's corps tramped over the bridges, together with a steady stream of non-combatants. The fighting drew ever closer to the river and as the light began to fade General Eblé took a speaking trumpet and called across the water to the silent mass still huddled about the fires on the far side.

'The bridge will be cut within the next few hours! I beg you to cross while you can!'

Napoleon shook his head as few seemed to heed Eblé's warning. 'They had their chance,' he told himself softly.

As the sun set into a blood-red haze on the horizon, Victor reported to Napoleon. He had not shaved or slept in days and looked haggard.

'The enemy will reach the bridge within the hour, sire. I have no horses left for my remaining guns. The crews have been ordered to fire off their remaining rounds, spike the guns and fall back. There are three battalions holding the edge of the village. They will follow as soon as the order is given.'

'You have done well, Marshal.'

'My men have done all they could, sire. But the Russian guns will be in range of the bridge at any moment.'

'I see.' Napoleon stared across the river into the gathering gloom. 'Then don't delay. Give the order now.'

'Yes, sire.'

As Victor returned across the river the engineers were hurriedly coating the timbers of the bridges with pitch, and the acrid smell made Napoleon's nose wrinkle as he waited for Victor and the last of his men to fall back. Then they appeared, trotting down the street and over the smallest bridge, a company at a time. The last battalion retreated facing the enemy, and then hurried over. Last of all came Victor himself, sword in hand until he reached the western bank and sheathed it.

A silence fell over the scene as the last of the engineers abandoned their brushes and pots of pitch, and then Eblé raised his speaking trumpet again.

'For the love of God! Escape while you still can!'

The civilians seemed to be too exhausted and lethargic to respond, and Eblé sadly lowered the speaking trumpet and gestured to his men to proceed with their orders. Torches were applied to the pitch and the flames licked out along the length of the bridges as the fire quickly caught and spread.

There was a drone through the air and a howitzer shell burst amongst the crowd in a bright flash. At once they struggled to their feet and ran for the bridges. More shells burst amongst them with lurid explosions of red and orange, the shell fragments cutting down scores of the tightly packed bodies at a time. The fugitives made for the bridges, trying to protect their faces from the flames as they ran towards the far bank. A few made it across, some on fire which the engineers hurriedly smothered. Others, blinded by the heat, stumbled over the edge and fell into the river. Some were desperate enough to plunge into the water, but few were strong enough to wade or swim across and the cold killed them before they reached the western bank. Flames reached high into the evening sky, reflected in the surface of the river, and the crackling and bursting of wood was accompanied by shrill screams of panic from the mob trapped on the far side.

Bit by bit, the planking and trestles collapsed into the water and, as the fire began to die down, the crowd fell silent and stared in numbed horror at the ruined bridges. The Russians had ceased fire as soon as they saw that most of the French had escaped and a terrible quiet fell over the scene.

The imperial headquarters had already set off down the causeway. Napoleon took one last look at Studienka and then climbed on to his mount. With a click of his tongue he urged the horse into a trot and made his way alongside the survivors of Victor's corps, heading towards Vilna.

Chapter 37

Molodetchna, 29 November 1812

The haggard remnants of the French army was stretched out along the road to Vilna. The snow fell steadily, drifting against the last of the abandoned vehicles, and the corpses of men and horses, until they were mercifully covered over, hiding the dead and the detritus of the army from those who still lived.

A handful of units remained together, mostly for self-protection rather than through discipline or any sense of duty. They marched with bayonets fixed, with little ammunition remaining in their haversacks, warily watching the surrounding countryside for any sign of the Cossacks who were following the column. Occasionally the horsemen would attack, with a sudden series of war cries as they dashed from concealment to rush any defenceless French soldiers, or civilians. They did not bother to discriminate between the two as they cut them down and then searched the corpses for anything of value. The Cossacks had learned to leave the formed units alone and often stood by, within musket range, letting them shuffle past.

Once again the snow had compacted and frozen so that the passage of the Grand Army was marked by a long, winding gleam of ice that was treacherous underfoot. The temperature continued to fall and had not risen above freezing since they had left the nightmare of the Berezina river behind them. The nights were bitter and dawn, when it came, was bleak. Any men, horses or equipment left in the open were covered in a heavy rime of frost. Increasingly, those who could not find shelter for the night did not survive to see the dawn. Only that morning, Napoleon had passed a peculiar scene by the side of the road. A soldier, a woman and two children were sitting around the remains of a small fire, built in the lee of a crumbling wall. They sat, cross-legged, wrapped in blankets, the children leaning into their mother with their heads resting against her, as if asleep. But they were unaturally still, and Napoleon stopped to look at them.

'Frozen to death,' he muttered as he stared into their white faces, wondering at the peaceful expressions on all four. 'Frozen to death,' he repeated in horror, before spurring his horse forward again.

That night, the headquarters staff and the Imperial Guard halted at Molodetchna. The soldiers found billets in the village and tried to scavenge some scraps of meat and vegetables to make soup, while the Emperor and his staff took over the village's one tavern. The Russian armies were mostly behind them and so now the battle was for survival. Regular communications had been re-established with Warsaw and an escorted courier sent by the Minister of Police had arrived in the village earlier in the day. In addition to the official messages, Savary had instructed his official to brief the Emperor on the dangerous situation in Paris.

Napoleon had retreated to the tavern's kitchen with Berthier to hear what the man had to say in private. A small cauldron was steaming over the cooking fire and the tavern's owner was peeling vegetables to add to the stock.

'Out,' Napoleon said to him, pointing at the door.

The tavern keeper shook his head and pointed to the cauldron. Napoleon clicked his fingers and then pointed to the hilt of his sword before he repeated his order. 'Out!'

Once the door had closed, he turned to the courier. 'What's alarming Savary so much that he has sent you all the way out here?'

'You already know about Malet's attempted coup, I take it, sire?'

'I know. Savary's last report was that he had rounded up the plotters and dealt with them.'

'That's right. The problem is that the rumours of your death have still been circulating around the Paris salons, and amongst the army officers in the capital. The situation is made worse by the reports that are starting to filter back from Russia, mostly letters from soldiers in the rear echelons who have heard rumours of a disaster befalling the army. Of course, the newspapers are continuing to put out the official line that all is well and that your imperial majesty has bested the Tsar. Many people still seem willing to trust the newspapers but it's clear that they need proof that you are alive, sire. Better still, they need to see you in person. They also need to know what has happened in Russia. It's the only way we can quell the rumours and cut the ground from under those who might be plotting against the regime.'

'I see.' Napoleon nodded and rubbed his eyes for a moment as he thought through the implications of the news.

Berthier coughed. 'Once the full scale of our losses is known, there is going to be trouble unlike anything we have seen before. There's hardly a family in France that won't be grieving over the loss of a brother, a husband or a son, sire. Your enemies in the capital will use this, and your absence, to call for your abdication.'

Napoleon opened his eyes and stared at Berthier. 'What do you think I should do?'

His chief of staff met his gaze firmly. 'I think you should return to Paris, sire. While there is still time to prevent the traitors and royalists from stirring up any more trouble. You have lost the campaign. There is no more reason for you to remain in Russia.'

'Lost the campaign,' Napoleon repeated. There was a time, only a month before, when he would have denied it. Now he felt completely worn out, and almost numbed by the scale of the disaster that had engulfed the Grand Army. The mistake was not in the plans that he had made. How could it be? Every last detail had been accounted for. No, the fault lay in the nature of the Tsar. He had not behaved as any rational ruler would have done. It was Alexander's inhumanity that Napoleon had failed to take into account. Only in that was Napoleon at fault. He drew a deep breath and nodded.

'It is over. I have done all that I can for the army. All that remains for them now is to reach the Niemen and cross to safety. I am not needed here.'

Berthier looked relieved, and so did the courier. The latter quickly took advantage of the Emperor's decision. 'The minister hoped that you would return to Paris, sire. He assumed that there would be some final matters that would require your attention before you left the army behind. In which case, he asked me to request that you issue a despatch stating that the campaign is over and that you are returning to Paris imminently. To allow us to hold our position while we wait for your arrival,' he explained.

Napoleon looked at him closely. 'Is it as bad as that?'

The courier looked down and did not reply.

'Tell me the truth,' Napoleon said firmly. 'There is nothing for anyone to gain by sweetening the message.'

'Very well, sire. It is the minister's opinion that unless you return to Paris within the month, he cannot guarantee that there will be a throne for you to return to. He needs a despatch from you to prove that you are alive, and also to put an end to the rumours concerning the fate of the army. It will shock the nation, sire, but even bad news is better than no news.'

'I see.' Napoleon nodded. 'Thank you.'

Once the courier had left the room, Napoleon sent Berthier for some paper and a pen. With a weary sigh, he dipped the pen into the ink pot and began to draft the despatch Savary had requested.

> *29th, Bulletin of the Grand Army. His imperial majesty, Napoleon, Emperor of France, King of Italy, is pleased to inform his people that the campaign in Russia is complete. The valiant men of the Grand Army, the largest gathering of allies ever to set out on such an adventure, has marched across the trackless expanses of Russia to humble the Russian Tsar and prove to him that the will of the Emperor, and all France, will not be denied. Defeated in battle, and having lost his most important city, the Tsar, against all the dictates of justice and humanity, refused to end the war. Accordingly the Emperor, having been refused the victory that all right-thinking men will agree should have been granted him, was obliged to order his army to withdraw to the territory of the Duchy of Warsaw.*

Napoleon paused, mentally composing the next section with care.

> *Due to the deceitful nature of the enemy the army was tricked into remaining in Moscow until the start of the autumn. Within days of setting out, the weather became unusually cold and the lack of sustenance derived from the lands through which the army marched, in concert with the swift onset of winter, has resulted in a considerable loss of men. The Emperor shares the grief of his people at the sacrifice of so many valiant soldiers. He trusts that their families will take some comfort from the knowledge that they died heroes, giving their lives for the glory of their countrymen.*

Napoleon continued by giving a casualty figure that was half the true amount. Even this would cause great consternation in France, but the full total must wait until he had returned and could break the news in person. He wrote about the dreadful climate and offered rousing descriptions of the battle at Borodino and the heroic crossing of the Berezina. He described the glorious achievement of Marshal Ney and the band of heroes in his rearguard as it fought its way through the Russian army to re-join the Emperor. Napoleon concluded with a final sentence to allay their fears. *His majesty's health has never been better.*

Setting down his pen, he called for Berthier to copy his draft into a legible hand and then signed and sealed the document before giving it to Savary's courier.

'Leave at once. Tell the minister I will follow you as soon as I can.'

★   ★   ★

A fresh blizzard blanketed the Russian landscape over the following days and the army grimly continued its retreat, heads down and leaning into the wind as it buffeted the shambling columns, as well as the civilians who had survived the Berezina crossing and had escaped the attentions of the Cossacks so far. Napoleon had ordered Berthier to make secret preparations for his departure for Paris, and when the foul weather lifted five days later, as the army crept into Smorgoni, he decided the time had come.

The marshals of the army were summoned from their billets into his presence that evening. They had been told that they were required for a briefing on the army's progress towards the Niemen, and slumped wearily down into the chairs set around a long table in the town's guild hall. Napoleon had given instructions for his last stocks of wine and brandy to be fetched and the marshals gratefully helped themselves as they waited for the last of their number to arrive. Ney was commanding the rearguard again and had the furthest to travel, and he did not reach the town until late in the evening. He unbuttoned his snow-flecked coat and slung it across a side table as he joined his companions, smiling at the sight of the brandy.

'Ah! Now there's a sight for sore eyes.' He poured a generous glass and downed it in one, then coughed to clear his burned throat. 'Needed that! Nothing like brandy to put fire back into a man's belly.'

Napoleon waited until Ney was seated and then rapped his glass on the table. 'Quiet, if you please.'

The marshals settled back into their chairs and looked at him expectantly. Napoleon was too weary to waste time with any preamble praising their efforts and promising rewards when they all returned to France. He drew a deep breath and began in a flat tone.

'It is my conviction that the army has made good its escape. Though it is hungry, there are more than enough rations at Vilna to feed the men and provide sufficient supplies to reach the Niemen. Therefore, I am no longer required here. I am, however, urgently needed in Paris where our enemies are trying to stir up sedition and revolt against all that we have fought for. With that in mind, I have decided to leave the army. A covered sledge, together with a small escort of Guard cavalry, stands ready to convey me to Warsaw. From there I should be able to continue the journey to Paris by carriage.' He looked round at them, waiting for a reaction.

'Bless my bloody soul.' Ney shook his head. 'I don't believe it. You're abandoning us.'

'I have no choice.'

'Really?' Ney smiled thinly. 'It seems to me that you do.'

'Then it is a choice that is forced on me by circumstance. Does that please you better?'

'Oh, it makes no odds to me, sire. It is you who will have to live with the decision.'

'I do what I must for France,' Napoleon replied testily.

'Who will take command of the army?' asked Davout.

'The King of Naples.' Napoleon nodded at Murat.

'Me?' Murat looked surprised, and then could not help smiling that he had been singled out from the other marshals, even if the command was little more than an empty title.

Davout puffed his cheeks. 'Might I ask your majesty why Murat is chosen for this honour? I would imagine he has enough responsibility already, co-ordinating the army's cavalry.'

'What's left of it!' Ney barked, then poured himself another glass of brandy. 'Shouldn't tax his mind too much, eh?'

Murat scowled at him as Napoleon explained.

'As King of Naples, Murat is the ranking officer. My decision has been made, Davout. You and the others will accept it.'

'As your majesty commands.' Davout bowed his head.

'That's right.' Napoleon looked round the room. 'Gentlemen, it is vital that you do not breathe a word of this to anyone outside this room. The army's morale is already as low as it can be. It would be dangerous to let them know that I have left. As far as the men are concerned I have fallen ill, nothing too serious, and am confined to my campaign wagon. The truth can be told only once the army has reached Vilna. By then it should make little difference. The Russians are having to endure the same hard conditions and I doubt they will be in any shape to attempt to bring us to battle. The only danger will come from the Cossacks. But if the men are fed and armed and stick together they will come to no harm. Those are your orders.'

He paused. 'Now the hour is late and I must prepare to leave. There is no time for any questions. It only remains to say that it has been an honour to be your commander, gentlemen. There is no finer body of officers in the world. I am sure of it. When the history of this campaign is written, you can be sure that your heroic deeds will be remembered long after the last of us is dead.' He stood up and raised his glass to them. 'My friends, I salute you. When I next see you, I hope it is somewhere warmer.'

The marshals rose from their chairs, and one after the other they came forward to grasp the Emperor's hand. Ney was last.

'I wish you a safe journey, sire.'

'And I wish you would take greater care of your life, Ney. On the battlefield you are my right hand. I have already lost too many friends. Don't give me further cause to grieve.'

'I will do my best to survive. I always have, sire.'

Napoleon could not help smiling. 'If only all the politicians in Paris shared your capacity for dishonesty, my dear Michel.'

Ney frowned until he got the point and then smiled back. 'Sort them out, sire. Then come back to the army. It's where you really belong.' He released the Emperor's hand, strode over to the side table to collect his coat and left without looking back.

The sledge was waiting at the edge of the village, in a private yard guarded by the ten-man escort. Napoleon left headquarters before dawn, dressed in a plain coat and wearing a thick woollen cap in place of his familiar bicorne. A scarf was tied round his face to conceal his features and he carried a large satchel as he followed General Caulaincourt through the dark streets, crunching across the snow. Napoleon had decided it was best if he travelled in disguise, posing as Caulaincourt's secretary. That way they would be able to pass through French units without arousing any undue attention. More important, if they passed by any allied troops of dubious loyalty they would not be tempted to take Napoleon prisoner and offer him to the Russians in exchange for some reward.

Capture by the enemy was a possibility, if the Cossacks were bold enough to take on the escort. In that event, Napoleon had resolved to kill himself. A phial of poison hung from a chain round his neck, and it would be the work of a moment to snap the top and pour the contents down his throat. The imperial surgeon had assured him his death would be certain, and swift.

Caulaincourt approached the sledge, a small cabin with glass windows perched on a heavy set of iron-rimmed runners. There was a small bench for the driver and six horses were harnessed to the pinion just below the front of the vehicle. At the sight of Caulaincourt the driver hurried to the door and opened it with a neat bow. Napoleon managed to stop himself from getting in first and waited deferentially as the general climbed in before him. The driver shut the door behind them and Napoleon found himself squeezed in beside Caulaincourt on an upholstered leather seat. There was a narrow-lipped shelf opposite and Napoleon placed his satchel on it. Caulaincourt pulled a thick bearskin from under the shelf and placed it over their legs, drawing the edge up to their chests.

'We won't be able to move much and we need to stay warm. One of the officers at headquarters told me it had dropped to twenty degrees below zero last night.'

Napoleon nodded, huddling down under the covering, trying hard to draw himself to the kernel of warmth that still remained in his torso.

Outside there was a sharp cry and a crack of a whip and the sledge lurched forward. Once it was in motion the ride was surprisingly smooth, and apart from a faint hiss from the runners the only noise was the soft beat of the horses' hooves on the fresh snow. The dawn was cold and the snow had a blue tinge. Already the leading elements of the army had set out. The lieutenant commanding the escort called out for those ahead to clear the way. Looking out of the window Napoleon could see the men lining the road, ice crusted on the scarves wrapped over their faces, as little plumes of exhaled breath swirled around their heads. Within the hour they had passed through the vanguard and the way ahead was clear. The sledge slowed as the horses struggled up a small rise and Napoleon leaned towards the window and opened it to look back down the road. A blast of freezing air knifed through his headgear and he narrowed his eyes.

Some distance behind the sledge was the head of the column, and beyond that a thin trail of figures which wound its way back to the east. The soldiers shuffled along in a motley collection of small bands, interspersed with handfuls of men and even the odd isolated figure. Napoleon shut the window and settled back down on to his bench, glad at last to be quitting Russia, the graveyard of the Grand Army.

Chapter 38

Arthur

Ciudad Rodrigo, April 1813

It was a fine spring day and the trees in the garden courtyard of the town's monastery were covered in new leaves. Though the air was cool, it was dry and refreshing and Arthur breathed it in deeply before turning away from the window to begin briefing his generals. He felt vitalised as never before since he had arrived in the Peninsula. He knew it was true of his men as well. Once in winter quarters they had begun to recover from the retreat that concluded the previous year's campaign. Their morale was further enhanced by the issue of brand new tents throughout the army, as well as a surfeit of food, wine and tobacco. More reinforcements had arrived to swell the ranks and every ranker and officer was fortified by the news of Bonaparte's crushing defeat in Russia.

'Gentlemen.' Arthur smiled as he looked round the table at his senior commanders. 'There has never been a more propitious time to take the war to the French. The balance of power in Europe has shifted decisively in our favour. Our ally, Russia, has now been joined by Sweden and Prussia in the crusade against the Corsican Tyrant. I suspect that Bonaparte's relations with his Austrian father-in-law may soon take a turn for the worse.'

The officers laughed and Arthur indulged their good spirits for a moment before he raised a hand to quieten them. 'With Bonaparte scraping together every man that can hold a musket so that he can take the field in northern Europe, our role in the Peninsula has assumed a new significance. My agents report that over twenty thousand of the enemy's best soldiers have been withdrawn from Spain to fill out the ranks of the Emperor's northern army. In addition, Marshal Soult has been recalled to Paris. By these measures, Bonaparte has made our task easier. At the same time, the French have been forced to abandon southern Spain, and their remit, such as it is, only runs through the eastern and northern provinces. Even then, tens of thousands of French soldiers are tied down suppressing local insurrections and chasing bands of resistance fighters. Over the winter we have been reinforced to over eighty thousand men, and our Spanish allies have promised twenty thousand more to swell our ranks.'

'Would that I live to see the day when the blackguards march with us,' Picton cut in with a surly expression. A number of officers grumbled in agreement.

'Then I am delighted that your wish should be granted with such celerity,' Arthur replied. 'Two Spanish divisions will be joining our army within the next few days.'

'I'll believe it when I see it,' said Picton. 'Bloody people have been more of a hindrance than a help ever since we fetched up on these shores.'

Arthur turned to Somerset and nodded towards the large easel standing to the side of the table. It was covered with a loose sheet, and Somerset carefully removed it to reveal a map pinned to a board. The map indicated the territory of northern Portugal and Spain, stretching from the Atlantic to the Pyrenees. Two red labels marked the positions of the allied armies that had been forming up in readiness for the coming campaign. One was based at Ciudad Rodrigo, poised to advance along the road to Salamanca, as had happened the previous year. The other was just south of the Douro, in the north-eastern corner of Portugal.

Arthur strode over to the side of the map and could not help smiling at his officers. 'I know that some of you are perplexed by the division of the army at the start of the coming campaign. You may be glad to know there is method in my apparent madness. The Russian campaign has changed everything. Before news of the scale of Boney's defeat reached me it had been my intention to advance towards Madrid once again. But now I believe it is within our power to put an end to French control of the Peninsula before the end of this year.'

The officers around the table exchanged surprised looks. General Beresford was the first to respond.

'Sir, while I am sure we all share the ambition, surely it is too early for such a result? The enemy has two hundred thousand soldiers in Spain. More than twice our number.'

'No more than half of which are available to concentrate against us,' Arthur countered. 'The key to the coming campaign will be to advance swiftly, before they can mass enough men in one place to out-number us. Moreover, we will not strike where Joseph and his senior commander, Marshal Jourdan, expect us to.' Arthur turned back to the map. 'First we must throw them off the scent. To which end, General Hill, with a third of the army, will advance from Ciudad Rodrigo towards Salamanca. I will accompany the army to ensure that the French think that we are attempting to retake Madrid. Meanwhile, General Graham will be leading the main force through the mountains in the north-east of Portugal and fetching up on the north bank of the Douro as he enters Spain.'

Beresford frowned slightly as he concentrated on the map. 'But, sir, that means taking the main force through the Tras Os Montes. I know the area, and the roads through the mountains are treacherous. I would even go so far as to say they are impassable.'

'I am sure that the French share your opinion,' Arthur smiled. 'Which is why General Graham will use the mountain roads to appear where the enemy least expect us. As it happens, our engineers have been at work over the winter removing the worst of the obstacles on the route. It will be hard going but there will be no opposition and we will have turned the enemy's flank. As soon as Graham has cleared the mountains he will march along the Douro to Toro where General Hill's column will join him, after leaving a small garrison at Salamanca. By the start of June we will have eighty thousand men ready to take Burgos and clear the north of Spain. In the meantime, Joseph will not know which way to turn. If all goes well we can shatter his formations before they have a chance to concentrate. Any questions?'

'Yes, sir,' Picton grumbled. 'This is all very well, but what if Joseph takes advantage of our position north of the Douro to strike west and cut our communications with Portugal? We have to protect our supply lines to Lisbon.'

'Not for much longer.' Arthur indicated the northern coast of Spain. 'I have given orders for our siege guns to be loaded on to a convoy that is already anchored off Coruña. Our new supply base will be Santander once we have taken the port.'

His generals grasped the significance at once, Arthur was pleased to see. He continued, 'With Santander in our hands we will dominate the north of Spain, cutting Joseph off from France. In that case, what choice does he have but to fight us? The alternative is to retreat from Spain altogether, which will not endear him to his brother.'

Beresford nodded approvingly. 'A fine plan, sir. Why, we could hold the line of the Ebro before the year is out.'

'The Ebro be damned! I fully intend us to reach the Pyrenees by then.'

'And after that?' Picton intervened. 'What? You intend to invade France?'

Arthur was aware that every general was hanging on his reply, but he simply pursed his lips. 'One thing at a time, eh, Picton? Even though I know you are in a hurry to reach Paris.' He cleared his throat. 'Well then, gentlemen, that is the broad plan. You will keep it strictly to yourselves. I will not tolerate any croaking to your friends and family back in England. We've had enough of that in the past, and it is my belief that by the time this year is over, the army will be the toast of our country, and any naysayers will look like complete fools. Now then, Somerset has your sealed orders. Take them back to your headquarters and prepare to march.'

The generals rose from their chairs and slowly filed out of the room, exchanging excited remarks as they collected their orders from the table by the door. Arthur watched them closely. Only Picton seemed to be unaffected by the high spirits, but then Picton was disposed towards seeing the worst in plans and men alike. But for his fighting qualities Arthur might have been tempted to dispense with his services long ago. Somerset closed the door behind them and returned to examine the map in silence for a moment.

'Penny for your thoughts, Somerset.'

Somerset turned towards him. 'It occurs to me that you might be thinking of ending the year's campaign on the far side of the Pyrenees, rather than the Spanish side, sir.'

'Really?' Arthur raised an eyebrow. 'And why is that?'

'If Joseph is forced to fight you in northern Spain and we defeat him, then the game is up for the French south of the Pyrenees. That's clear enough. But if we cross into France, in such force that we can remain on French soil through the winter, then it would be a devastating blow to French morale.'

'Yes. I expect it would.'

Somerset thought for a moment. 'Why did you not tell the others, my lord? It might have added to their inspiration.'

'I should have thought you would know my methods well enough to guess by now. You saw how they reacted to the prospect of reaching the Pyrenees. Some of them are certain that I am over-extending the army. Like the French, they assume I am wedded to waging war in a defensive manner. The time for that is past. This year we are strong enough to send the French reeling. The men have never been in better condition and in better spirits, in contrast to the enemy. Beresford would have us stop on the bank of the Ebro. By offering the Pyrenees instead, I have set them a challenge, but one that they can believe in. If I said France, then I would have planted the seeds of trepidation in their hearts. Besides, my generals are not my only audience in this little drama of ours.'

'Sir?'

'Our political masters in London would think me mad to advance so far. So I have told them even less than the generals know. It is always better to give people a lesser ambition to aim for, so that their sense of achievement is all the greater when they exceed it. If we reach France, then I am sure you can imagine how grateful our country will be to us, Somerset.'

'Indeed, sir. You are certain to be rewarded handsomely.'

Arthur looked hard at him. 'Is that what you think motivates me?'

'I did not say that, my lord.'

'You did not *say* it.' Arthur laughed drily. 'Oh, I have had my rewards. I was made a lord after Talavera, then an earl, and a marquess for Salamanca and now the Order of the Garter. Our Spanish and Portuguese allies have conferred dukedoms on me, and so our soldiers call me, though with some measure of jest. I dare say that in time I may even become a duke of England. But these are all baubles, Somerset. Baubles. What drives me is not a title, nor some ribbon, nor a bejewelled star, but the prospect of a Europe free from French tyranny. That is a cause worth fighting for, and dying for if need be. Do I make myself quite clear?'

'Yes, sir.'

Arthur stared at him for a moment and then clapped his hands together. 'That's that, then. Are there any other matters requiring my attention?'

Somerset could not help smiling. 'Just one thing, my lord. It arrived from London today. I shall fetch it.' He hurried out of the room to his desk in the anteroom. A moment later he reappeared with a velvet case the size of a large book. He set it down on the table, together with a small note addressed to Arthur in the unmistakable spidery writing of his wife Kitty. He broke the seal and opened the letter and read the brief message.

My dearest Arthur,

    I know how you dislike my intruding upon you when your mind is set on military affairs and the duty you owe to your country. It is some months since I last received a letter from you, and it seems I learn more about you from the newspapers and the gossip of the wives of your officers than I do from your hand directly. My Arthur, I know that I am not the wife you deserve. I know it more and more with the passage of each year. Yet I love you, and our children love you, and long for you to return to us. I know that you cannot before the war is over, and while we wait please know that we take the most intense pride in what you have achieved for our nation. In token of which, I forward the enclosed, sent to us from Windsor, and trust that it will remind you of the affection in which you are held by so many.

Your loving wife, Kitty.

Arthur refolded the letter and returned it to the table. He knew that he should feel guilty, but that sentiment refused to stir in his breast. Just a deadening certainty that Kitty spoke the truth, and that he would never be able to care for her in the way that she wanted.

For an instant, he wondered what would become of them when the war did end. Assuming he survived, then what would he do? For twenty years he had known little but war. He had refined his martial abilities to a fine edge and was proud of himself, his officers and his men. What did the prospect of peace offer to such a man as himself? A return to the ennui of life out of uniform, and Kitty . . .

'Aren't you going to open it, my lord?' Somerset broke into his thoughts.

'What?'

'The case, sir.'

'Yes, of course.' Arthur drew it closer, fiddled with the dainty catch and then raised the lid. Inside, cushioned on and pinned to white silk, were the insignia of the Order of the Garter, the most noble order of knighthood that England had to offer. Arthur could not help but be moved by the honour that had been bestowed on him. He swallowed, then touched the gleaming stones of the star.

'It is a fine thing, is it not?' he mused.

'Not just another bauble then, my lord?'

Arthur's eyes narrowed. 'If you do not wipe that foolish expression off your face you may find that I am obliged to bestow a very different kind of Order upon you.' He reached down and slapped the side of his boot.

His aide fought manfully to suppress his humour.

'That's better.' Arthur stood up. 'Then, if you're quite ready, I think it is time for us to join General Hill.'

Chapter 39

Towards the end of May Ciudad Rodrigo was turned over to a Spanish garrison and the southern wing of the allied army set out for Salamanca. Given the rough terrain that General Graham would be crossing to reach the north bank of the Douro, most of the army's guns, and the cavalry, marched with Arthur. In order to conceal his true numbers from the enemy Arthur sent over four thousand horsemen ahead of the main column, screening it from enemy scouts and at the same time impressing the French with the size of the effort being made to take Salamanca.

The French abandoned Salamanca to Wellington at the end of the month and the inhabitants of the city gave a guarded welcome to the allied army. Three days later that army abruptly left the city, marching swiftly north towards the Douro where they crossed near Toro and combined with General Graham's column. Having gathered his reserves in Madrid to meet the threat from the direction of Salamanca, Joseph had too few men north of the Douro to do anything but retreat in the face of the powerful allied army. Arthur drove his men on along the bank of the Douro as far as Valladolid and then turned north again, parallel to the great Royal Road that linked Madrid with France.

The first evening the army camped in the hills. Arthur was hunched over a map in his tent when Somerset entered in the company of a naval officer. Outside, the army was setting up camp in the cool evening air. Row upon row of the new white tents were being erected on the more level stretches of the surrounding slopes. An exhausting day's march had left the men quieter than usual and many had not bothered to light a fire, eating their rations cold before sorting out some bracken to lie on and promptly falling asleep.

Arthur was in a fine mood and he grinned as he looked up at his aide. 'Twenty-one miles today, Somerset! Fine progress, eh? We're advancing faster than the French can retreat.'

'Fine progress indeed, my lord. But progress towards what, exactly?'

'All in due course. Who is that with you?'

Somerset stood aside and ushered the officer into the tent. 'Lieutenant Carstairs, of His Majesty's Ship *Apollo*. He landed on the north coast and was escorted here by a band of partisans.'

Carstairs stepped towards Arthur's table and swept off his hat. 'I've been sent by my captain to find you, my lord. He commands the frigate squadron escorting the supply convoy from Southampton. We had orders to land your supplies in Oporto but found that you had left instructions to land them at Santander instead, and if the port was still in enemy hands we were to make contact with you for fresh orders. So, here I am.'

'Good work, Carstairs. I like an officer who takes the initiative. How was your journey?'

'Surprisingly easy, my lord. I have not seen a single French patrol between the coast and your camp.'

'I'm not surprised. Joseph Bonaparte is pulling every spare man back to the Ebro. The French are in a complete flap.' Arthur laughed, the customary whooping bark that Somerset had grown used to, but the naval officer looked at him in some alarm.

'Now then,' Arthur continued. 'As to the matter of my supplies, I want your captain to have the convoy heave to off Santander until such time as we have taken the port. I take it that will not cause the Navy any difficulty.'

'No, my lord. The escort squadron is provisioned for another two months. I am uncertain as to the arrangements of the merchant vessels, but we can feed their crews from our stores if need be.'

'Good. I would be obliged if you would ask your captain to advise the admiralty that all supplies and reinforcements are to be sent to Santander from now on.'

Carstairs looked surprised. 'Do you mean every convoy, my lord?'

'I do. We are cutting our communications with Portugal once and for all. Henceforth we shall be supplied from the north coast of Spain.'

'Forgive me, my lord, but from what I understand the admiralty has not been informed of such rerouting of the convoys.'

'They are not the only ones,' Arthur replied wryly. 'Be that as it may, my new instructions stand, and need to be passed back up the Navy's chain of command. See that your captain is informed as soon as possible, Carstairs.'

'Yes, sir.'

'Now then, I expect you would appreciate something to eat, and a bed for the night. Somerset, have one of the clerks take the lieutenant to the staff officers' mess.'

'Yes, my lord.' Somerset bowed his head and held the flap open for Carstairs. He returned a moment later and stood awkwardly by the entrance to the tent until Arthur looked up.

'Is there anything else?'

'Yes, my lord, since you ask. I am concerned by the supply situation. The men have rations for two days and we are already three days ahead of our supply convoys. They in turn are more than a hundred miles from our forward depot at Salamanca. We are already operating at the limit of our lines of supply.'

Arthur leaned back in his chair. 'You heard what I said to that naval officer. You are privy to my strategic intentions, Somerset. Therefore you know that we are shifting our lines of communication to Santander, and, in due course, San Sebastian. There is nothing for you to be concerned about.'

'Except that we have possession of neither of those ports, my lord.'

'Not yet. We shall just have to take them.'

'But we have no guarantee that we can take them,' Somerset replied. 'What if we fail to capture them, as we failed at Burgos, my lord?'

'We – I – failed at Burgos for want of adequate siege artillery. As you know, our siege train is aboard a convoy anchored off Coruña. When the time comes, we will have the firepower necessary to reduce both ports, and then we shall have a direct supply route to England. Does that satisfy you, Somerset?'

'Yes, my lord,' Somerset replied reluctantly. He saluted formally and left the tent.

Arthur sighed and ran a hand through his cropped hair before turning his attention back to the map.

The army was less than a day's march from Burgos and another two to the Ebro. The latest reports from the cavalry patrols revealed that the French were looking to defend the line of the Ebro. The enemy's chief difficulty was that they could not be sure where the allied army was. All that was before them was Arthur's cavalry screen and a division of Spanish troops. If the deception played out as Arthur hoped, then his army would be across the Ebro and threatening to cut Joseph and his army off from France before the French could react. The only course of action open to them would be to turn and fight. The decisive moment of the campaign would be attained, and all within a month of its beginning.

Despite his dismissal of Somerset's concerns, Arthur accepted that there were risks. He had marched the men hard, and they were weary and might yet go hungry for a short time, but what Somerset seemed to have missed was the desire to close with and destroy the French that simmered in their breasts. They had resented the loss of the second chance to fight the enemy at Salamanca, and now were set on crushing them.

During the night, the army was woken by the sound of a great explosion rumbling across the landscape. Shortly afterwards there was a red glow in the sky to the east that shimmered against the scattered clouds drifting across the starry heavens. Arthur watched from outside his tent, barefoot and dressed in breeches and a loose shirt. The glow continued for two hours before it began to fade, lost against the first hues of the dawn. Arthur returned to his tent to get fully dressed and was just emerging when Somerset reported to him.

'It was Burgos, my lord. One of the cavalry vedettes was close enough to see the explosion.'

'Explosion?'

'Yes, sir. The French set charges and blew the castle to pieces. They managed to burn down a sizeable portion of the town while they were at it.'

'Well, bless my soul,' Arthur muttered in surprise. The French were clearly panicking more than he had thought. That in turn introduced a new anxiety. What if the enemy's experience of the previous years had so cowed their spirit that they dared not stand and fight? If that was the case then Arthur's plan had to be adapted so that when the chance of battle came there would be no avenue of escape for the French. Joseph and his army would have to be caught in such a way that they would be forced to surrender, or be annihilated.

The leading division of the allied army quit the barren hills two days later and entered the Ebro valley. The change in the landscape was striking and for the soldiers, so used to tramping across the dusty, dry plains and hills of central Spain, the lush valley watered by the river was a vision of abundance. The roads along which the army marched were lined with fruit trees and vineyards and the soldiers, when their officers were not looking, filled their haversacks with cherries, oranges and apples to supplement their dwindling rations. They continued a short distance to the east before turning south towards the crossroads at San Millan.

Late in the afternoon an excited young lieutenant from the Ninety-fifth Rifles galloped up to Arthur with a message from General Alten. 'My lord! We've sighted the enemy!'

'Lieutenant, that will not do,' Arthur admonished him. 'Start again and deliver the message properly.'

The ensign nodded, and forced himself to speak in a calmer manner. 'I apologise, my lord. General Alten begs to inform you that his skirmishers have seen a French division marching along a road a mile to the south of the road the general is advancing along. The two roads intersect a short distance ahead. He asks your permission to attack the enemy column, my lord.'

Arthur's eyes glinted with excitement. 'Ah! This I must see for myself. Take me to Alten at once.'

The two horsemen spurred their mounts along the side of the artillery train that was rumbling along the rutted track. Beyond the guns they passed the infantry of the Third Division, where heads turned at the sound of approaching hoofbeats.

'It's Nosey!' a voice cried out.

'What's 'is bloody hurry?' another shouted. 'Ain't we marchin' as fast as we bleedin' can already?'

The nearest men roared with laughter and Arthur stifled a grin as he leaned forward and urged his mount on. Once they had passed the Third Division, they came up to the rearmost battalion of the Light Division marching down a straight section of road. To their right was a steep line of hills that gradually fell away. Nearly two miles ahead Arthur could see a small village basking in the afternoon sunshine. A faint haze of dust showed on the far side of the village as an enemy column marched east. At first Arthur thought that the French division had escaped, but then the ensign thrust his arm out and pointed up the hill. On the crest stood a small group of officers staring down the far slope.

'That's General Alten, my lord.' The ensign led the way as they passed between two infantry companies and began to climb the slope. By the time they reached Alten the horses were blown, and Arthur swung himself down from the saddle, heart pounding.

'Where is this enemy division of yours, Alten?'

'Over there, sir.' Alten gestured down the slope. Below, another road converged on the village. A long line of French soldiers and wagons was marching along at a quick pace. Hurrying down towards them were the green-jacketed men of the Ninety-fifth.

'What is your plan?' asked Arthur.

'The Ninety-fifth will open fire on them as soon as they are within range. The Fifty-second are double-timing down our side of the hill to get ahead of the last brigade and form a firing line. My Portuguese lads are marching to the right before dropping down the slope to the road to cut off their retreat. It's too late to catch the first two brigades,' he nodded towards the haze of a distant column beyond the village, 'but this one is in the bag.'

'Very good.' Arthur nodded approvingly.

Just then, the first of the riflemen opened fire on the French column, and the crackle of rifles spread along the slope. Several of the enemy were quickly struck down, and the others began to break ranks to look for cover. Their officers struggled to rally them and re-form their ranks ready to return fire at the Ninety-fifth. Just as they had been trained to, the riflemen targeted the officers and one by one they were cut down as they gave their orders. The survivors ordered their troops to fire a volley where they they could see the puffs of smoke, but the riflemen had plenty of time to take cover and the storm of musket balls tore up the stunted bushes and glanced off rocks and not one of the greenjackets was hit. As soon as the French lowered their muskets and began to reload they were steadily whittled down, falling in twos and threes, until, unable to bear the massacre any longer, the survivors broke and ran, streaming along the road towards the village. The riflemen continued to fire on the fugitives as quickly as they could reload and take aim, and soon the road was littered with dead and wounded men and a number of horses, shot in their traces, forcing the drivers to abandon their wagons.

'Glorious work!' Alten rubbed his hands together in glee. 'And now for the *coup de grâce*. Look there, sir!'

Ahead of the fugitives the men of the Fifty-second were crossing the road. They halted, and turned smartly towards the French. Up went the muskets and then a wall of darting flames and plumes of smoke briefly hid the redcoats. The volley cut down scores of the enemy, and the rest turned back, running into their companions and causing further chaos. Another volley crashed out, and the riflemen kept up their firing from the slope. Hundreds of bodies carpeted the road now, and blocked from two sides the French tried to flee back the way they had come, only to find a line of Portuguese troops filing down from the hill to close the trap.

Some of the French threw down their muskets and raised their arms in surrender, but others, with more heart, or fearing capture, turned and ran in the only open direction, clambering up the slope of the next ridge. The riflemen ceased fire and hurried down the slope and across the road, ignoring those who were surrendering, and then knelt at the bottom of the next ridge and started shooting down the Frenchmen toiling up the slope above them.

Within the space of ten minutes the brigade had been destroyed, suffering hundreds of dead and wounded, and leaving over four hundred prisoners. It had been a massacre, Arthur decided, but all the same he took pride in the effective performance of Alten's men.

'A finely executed ambush, General Alten. Ensure that you pass my congratulations on to your men.'

'Yes, sir. I will.'

'Make sure that your fellows escort the prisoners to the rear as swiftly as possible and resume the advance.'

Alten nodded and was turning to give orders to his staff officers when a major of the Ninety-fifth came panting up the slope clutching a leather satchel. Unusually for an officer, the major carried a rifle like his men, and he nodded a salute as he handed the satchel to Alten.

'Here, sir. We found this on the body of a French colonel.'

'What is it, Richard?' Alten asked.

'Orders, sir. From the divisional commander. I thought you'd want 'em as soon as possible.'

The major nodded and turned away to trot back down the slope to re-join his men. Alten drew the slim sheaf of papers from the satchel and scanned the contents. At once his eyes widened and he turned to Arthur.

'Orders from Joseph's headquarters, sir! Dated yesterday. He's called every available unit to fall back to a new position.'

'Where?' asked Arthur, his heart quickening.

'A town on the Royal Road not far ahead, my lord. A place called Vitoria.'

Chapter 40

21 June 1813

The clouds had lifted and the sky was clear, and the air barely stirred in the morning sunshine. There was a clear view of the valley through which the Zadorra river meandered eastwards towards Vitoria. The day before, Arthur had ridden round the hills to the north of the valley to survey the French positions and make his plans, and he was relieved to see that the French army was still camped in three lines between the river and the Heights of Puebla to the south. The enemy pickets had raised the alarm at dawn when they had seen the first of Arthur's men marching through the gorge into the valley, and now the French stood waiting. The dark lines of infantry and cavalry all faced to the west to meet the approaching threat.

Arthur smiled with grim satisfaction as he surveyed the enemy's dispositions from the hillside above the village of Nanclares. Marshal Jourdan had played into his hands. The French assumed that they would be facing a frontal attack and that the river and the Heights would provide adequate protection on each flank. As before, they had failed to account for the audacity of the allied army. Arthur's plan was simple enough, he reflected, as he trained his telescope across the valley. He had divided his army into four columns. General Hill's corps of English, Spanish and Portuguese troops would begin the battle by assaulting the Heights of Puebla, working their way along the ridge to threaten the left flank of the French battle lines. The main body of the army would be directly under Arthur's control and they would be tasked with making a frontal assault across the river. Two more divisions, under General Dalhousie, had set off before dawn to make their way round the hills to the north of the valley and then attack the enemy's right flank. The fourth column, commanded by General Graham, had the furthest to march, passing through the same hills but striking further round to cut off the French from any attempt to escape towards the frontier. A smaller Spanish column was tasked with blocking the final remaining route out of the valley. If all went according to plan the French would be trapped and forced to surrender, or be cut to pieces.

No plan was without its danger, Arthur knew, and this one depended on each column making its attack at the same time so that the French were disrupted by having to meet each threat. If the attacks were delivered piecemeal then Marshal Jourdan would be able to defeat each one in turn. If that happened then the allies would be forced to retreat, and Arthur had little doubt that he would be dismissed from his command by the politicians back in London.

He took a last look through his telescope towards Vitoria. The town was surrounded by thousands of wagons and carriages. His spies reported that many of the wagons were packed with valuables from the royal palace in Madrid: paintings, tapestries, gold, silver and jewellery. More important, a bullion convoy had recently joined the baggage train gathering at Vitoria. The allied army needed the gold to pay for supplies and it was Arthur's intention to capture the baggage train intact, before it could escape, or be ransacked by his victorious army.

'It's eight o'clock, my lord,' Somerset announced, breaking into Arthur's thoughts.

'Yes.' Arthur nodded. 'Then be so good as to have the signal gun fired.'

Somerset saluted and then raised his hat and waved it slowly from side to side. Further down the slope a single gun stood ready. As soon as the officer saw Somerset's gesture he cupped a hand to his mouth and ordered his gun to fire. Flame and smoke spat from its muzzle and a loud boom echoed around the valley.

That was it then, Arthur mused silently. He was committed now. All four columns would have heard the gun and begun to carry out their orders. Already he could see the leading elements of Hill's column climbing the western slope of the Heights of Puebla, towards the detachment of enemy soldiers on the crest. Within the half-hour the French had realised the danger to their flank and two battalions set off to climb the Heights and block Hill's progress along the ridge.

The faint crackle of musketry carried to Arthur's ears as he watched the brief skirmish between the Spaniards leading the attack and the French detachment. Then the tiny figures of the enemy soldiers broke away and began to retreat to the east.

'First blood to us, my lord,' Somerset remarked. 'Though I think General Morillo's men will find the next French position somewhat harder to carry.'

Arthur nodded as he looked at the enemy soldiers formed up across the ridge. Already, two more battalions from the second line had started to climb the slope to form another line to block the advance of Hill's column. 'That may be so, but Marshal Jourdan is doing as I hoped he would. Let him become preoccupied with his left flank and he will be undone in due course. Send word to Hill to extend his attack along the lower slopes. The more we can do to draw the enemy's attention towards Hill's column, the better.'

As the morning wore on the fighting along the Heights intensified as the men on both sides fought it out across the slopes, which were strewn with boulders and stunted bushes. The French steadily fed more men into the fight, weakening the centres of the first two battle lines. At eleven o'clock, Arthur saw the third line of the French army redeploying to face the north as it began to cross the river.

'See there?' Arthur raised his arm and pointed the movement out to Somerset. 'The French must have spotted Graham's fellows.'

Somerset tilted his head slightly and strained his ears for a moment. 'I cannot hear any sounds of firing to the east, my lord.'

'Nor I. That is to be expected. Graham's orders were not to begin his attack until after Dalhousie emerged from the hills.' Arthur frowned. 'Where the devil *is* Dalhousie? He and Picton should have reached the river by now.'

'Do you wish me to try to find them, my lord?'

'Not yet. They are sure to appear soon. Meanwhile, it is time that we attacked the front of the French line.' Arthur gestured to the wooded slopes to his left where the Light Division was waiting for the order to advance. 'Order Alten to move forward to the river. They are to take the bridge at Villodas and begin crossing to the far bank. Cole's division is to cross here at Nanclares.'

By the time that the orders had been given and the two divisions were advancing, the sound of cannon fire was echoing across the valley from the east. Through his telescope Arthur could see banks of powder smoke forming either side of the river as Graham's column began to contest the crossings north of Vitoria. He swept his telescope to examine the hills to his left and muttered a curse when he could still see no sign of Dalhousie's men. If they did not appear soon and divert the enemy's attention then Marshal Jourdan would be able to meet the attack of the Light Division and Cole's division with every available man and cannon.

'Somerset, send an officer to find Dalhousie. Tell the general to cross the river and engage the enemy at once. I'm riding forward to that knoll there, by Villodas.'

Somerset stared towards the village and saw that there were still Frenchmen defending the small cluster of houses that made up the village. Pairs of riflemen were rushing from cover to cover as they closed in on the Frenchmen amid a steady, uneven crackle of gunfire. Somerset cleared his throat. 'My lord, isn't that a little too close to the fighting?'

'Can't be helped,' Arthur replied as he grasped the reins and urged his horse forward. 'I must have a better view of the battlefield.'

He nudged his spurs in and the horse cantered forward across the lush green grass of a meadow, where a handful of goats that had evaded the French foragers scattered at his approach. He passed between two regiments of the Light Division and the men raised a hearty cheer as he rode by. Shortly before he reached the knoll he came across General Alten and his small staff.

'Good day, my lord.' Alten touched the brim of his hat.

Arthur returned the greeting and indicated the top of the knoll. 'Ride with me, Alten.'

They urged their horses up the slope and reined in at the top where they had a clear view of the village below and the old stone bridge over the Zadorra. No more than two hundred yards ahead the rifles were still duelling with the French skirmishers. At the sight of the two British officers a number of muskets were pointed in their direction and a handful of shots whipped through the air close by. Arthur felt the familiar tightening of his guts but forced himself to retain his calm facade.

'The Light Division will cross the river and form a line to the south, linking up with Cole's men once they have crossed at Nanclares. Then both divisions will advance on the French line.'

Alten cocked an eyebrow. 'Two divisions against the main French battle line? As you wish, my lord.' He scanned the dense enemy formations waiting less than a mile beyond the river. 'A frontal attack will cost us dearly.'

'It will, but there is no alternative. The French will have men and guns covering every available crossing point. We must cross here and prepare to attack.'

Alten puffed his cheeks and nodded. He was about to reply when the sound of hoofbeats from behind caused both men to turn. Somerset was galloping up the slope to catch up with his commander. A short distance behind him rode General Alava and another man, a Spanish peasant, on a small pony. Somerset reined in and saluted Arthur.

'Who the devil is that?' Arthur gestured towards the peasant as the other two riders joined them.

'My lord, if I may?' Alava broke in before Somerset could reply. 'This man is Jose Ortiz de Zarate. He owns a farm by the river over there, near the village of Tres Puentes.' Alava pointed to the north where the river curled round the slopes of a small hill on the far bank.

'Well, that's very nice for Señor Zarate, I am sure,' Arthur replied tersely. 'But what of it?'

'He says that the bridge there is undefended. There is not a Frenchman within a mile of it.'

Arthur stared at the peasant, and then looked towards the village, which was all but obscured by the hill. There was no sign of the bridge. Arthur felt a sudden thrill of excitement as he turned back towards General Alava. 'Ask our friend if that hill masks the bridge from where the French are positioned.'

There was a hurried exchange before Alava turned back to Arthur. 'He says it does. Or at least he could not see the French when he stood on the far end of the bridge less than an hour ago.'

Arthur fixed Zarate with a steely glare. 'He is sure that there are no French soldiers nearby? And that the bridge has not had charges set beneath it?'

'He says he is certain of it, my lord.'

Arthur's pulse quickened as he viewed the ground and the positions of both armies in his mind's eye. Then he nodded his thanks to the Spanish farmer. 'Tell Señor Zarate that if he is right, then he has done his people a fine service.'

The Spaniard stiffened proudly in his saddle as the words were translated, then Arthur continued. 'Ask him if he would be prepared to guide our men to the bridge. If he knows the lie of the land then we may need him once we gain the far bank. Tell him I will reward him greatly if we win the day.'

The farmer bowed his head graciously and then made a short speech.

'He says that he needs no reward. It will be enough to have played his part in defeating the French. However,' Alava could not help smiling, 'Señor Zarate would not dream of causing any offence by turning down your offer of a reward.'

'Hah!' Arthur barked out a laugh. 'Very well. Alten!'

'Sir?'

'I'll take Kempt's brigade over the river by Señor Zarate's bridge. If he's right then we will appear on the enemy's flank before the French can react. With Cole and the rest of the Light Division pressing them from the front there is every chance that we can break through the right flank. Somerset, I must know the moment we have any word of

Dalhousie's column. Meanwhile, order the cavalry forward to Tres Puentes. Let's be about our business, gentlemen.'

While Alten's men chased the French out of Villodas and began to cross to the far bank, Arthur and the three regiments of Kempt's brigade hurried north, following the river as it bent round the hill. General Alava and Zarate rode with him as he galloped ahead of the infantry, sweating as they double-timed towards the bridge. As they came round the bend and saw the bridge ahead Arthur felt a surge of relief to see that there was still no sign of anyone at either end. A short distance beyond lay the village of Tres Puentes, where a handful of figures had emerged from the shelter of their homes to stare across the river at the battle being fought along the Heights to the south.

'Come!' Arthur waved the other two on and they galloped to the bridge, and then a short distance beyond to a small rise by the river where Arthur had a clear view of the enemy line. He reined in and Copenhagen's flanks bellowed as the horse recovered its breath. The extreme right of the French line was less than half a mile away. Already they had been spotted by a French artillery officer, who gestured towards the three horsemen. A moment later the end gun was turned towards them. Arthur ignored the gun as he strained his eyes towards the Heights of Puebla. A pall of smoke indicated the extent to which Hill had pushed back the enemy, past the end of the enemy's left flank. Soon they would have to divert yet more men to hold their position, or fall back. To the east, the rumble of cannon indicated that General Graham was heavily engaged with the French forces holding the line of the river to the north of Vitoria.

There was a boom from the far bank as the French gun opened fire. Then a thud as a column of earth lifted up from the river bank, twenty paces to Arthur's right. Zarate flinched and then, seeing that Arthur and Alava seemed utterly unperturbed, he hastily straighted up and composed his expression to match theirs.

'That's the spirit.' Arthur smiled at him. 'Never show the enemy you are afraid, eh? General, ask our friend if he knows whether the other bridges along the river are in French hands.'

'He says that the next bridge to the east is guarded by some infantry and six cannon. Beyond that bridge he does not know.'

That would be the bridge that Dalhousie's column would be using to launch its attack on the flank and rear of the enemy line, Arthur reflected. He glanced to his left but there was still no sign of any movement immediately to the east. He was aware of a distant flash out of the corner of his eye as the French gun fired again.

'Ask Zarate if there are any—'

Arthur was interrupted by a wet crack and a splattering sound. He turned and saw the body of the Spanish farmer in the saddle, the hands tensed like claws. His head was gone, smashed apart by the second shot from the enemy gun. General Alava had caught the worst of the spray of blood and brains, which had spattered one side of his body and face. The corpse slowly toppled to the side and thudded on to the river bank.

'Good God,' Arthur muttered. 'General, are you all right?'

Alava had raised a gloved hand to wipe the gore from his face, and was staring at the vivid crimson streak on the back of his kid leather gloves. He looked round at Arthur and nodded.

'Then we'd best not continue to make a target of ourselves. Let's be off.'

'What about him?'

'What? He can be buried later. I'll see that his family has his reward. Come.'

They rode back to the bridge, where one of the battalions of the rifle regiment had already crossed and was hurrying up the hill as the rest of the brigade doubled over to the far bank. Arthur joined Kempt on the far bank and the latter looked anxiously at General Alava.

'Are you injured, General?'

Alava shook his head. 'We lost our Spanish guide. He was struck by a roundshot.'

'Poor fellow.' Kempt pursed his lips. 'Bad luck, eh?'

Arthur pointed to the hill. 'Have your men form up on the crest. It is likely that the enemy will see the danger to their flank and attempt to force your brigade back over the river. You must hold your ground until our cavalry crosses.'

'You can depend upon my lads,' Kempt replied grimly.

'My lord,' General Alava interrupted, gesturing towards the bridge where the infantry were pressing to one side as a mounted officer edged through. 'One of your staff officers.'

No more than a minute later they were joined by the officer, a young dragoon cornet whom Arthur recognised as one who had recently joined the headquarters staff.

'Williams, isn't it?'

'Yes, my lord.'

'Well?'

Williams swallowed and did his best to compose himself. 'My lord, I was sent by Somerset to find General Dalhousie.'

'You found him then?'

'No, my lord. I came upon General Picton instead. He was approaching the river a mile to the east of here. He asked me if you had orders for him. I told him that my orders were for General Dalhousie, to tell him to cross the river and make his attack, and that Picton's division was to support him.' The cornet paused nervously. 'Well, my lord, General Picton flew into something of a rage. He said that General Dalhousie had lost his way in the hills and would be delayed by as much as another hour before he could reach the river. He also said that he would be damned if the Third Division was going to support anyone. Then he gave me a message to deliver to you, my lord.'

'Did he, by God?' Arthur felt the familiar irritation that Picton so frequently roused in him. 'Then tell me. His precise words.'

The young officer swallowed and did his best to recall. 'Tell Lord Wellington that the Third Division, under my command, shall in less than ten minutes attack the bridge and carry it, and the other divisions may support me if they choose . . . That was it, sir. Then he sent me on my way and turned to order his men to advance.' Cornet Williams paused. 'I didn't know what to do, my lord. I had orders to find Dalhousie, but General Picton had given me fresh orders, and I thought it best to find you directly rather than continue to search for General Dalhousie.'

Arthur nodded. 'You did the right thing, Williams. Now report to Somerset and then go back to seek out Dalhousie.'

'Yes, my lord,' the cornet responded with evident relief, then turned his horse away and trotted back towards the bridge.

'Picton . . .' Arthur muttered the name through clenched teeth, furious at the man's petulant belligerence. That was the very reason why he had given command of the third column to Dalhousie, but with the latter not yet on the scene it would be best to let Picton lead the attack on the enemy flank before it could be reinforced enough to prevent any more British troops from crossing the Zadorra from the north of the battlefield. A burst of small-arms fire sounded from the east and Arthur pushed aside his ill humour and spurred his horse up the hill to the crest to get a better view. Kempt and Alava followed him, joined shortly after by Somerset who had given the orders for the main attack and now returned to his commander.

From the elevated position Arthur could see most of the valley. Further along the river he picked out the leading formations of Picton's division as they closed round the end of the bridge and engaged the small force posted to guard it. The fresh attack from a new direction had not gone unnoticed by Marshal Jourdan and already the right of the

367

French line was falling back so as not to present its flank to Picton's men, while a body of cavalry and a battery of horse guns galloped to support the men defending the bridge.

'Picton is going to be given a good pounding when he tries to cross the bridge,' said Arthur, 'unless he is supported. General Kempt, you must take your men forward and cover Picton's flank as he forces his way across the bridge. Have your riflemen do what they can to harass the enemy cavalry and those guns.'

'Yes, sir.' Kempt nodded. 'But what of this hill? Are we to abandon it?'

'It has served its purpose,' Arthur replied. 'It hid your brigade from view while you crossed the river. Now, get your men forward.'

Kempt bellowed his orders across the crest of the hill and the three regiments began to descend the far side and marched east, screened by two companies of riflemen. Arthur hurriedly assessed the positions of his forces to the south of the hill. Away in the distance the column on the Heights of Puebla was still grinding its way along the ridge, pushing past the left flank of the French line in the valley below. Closer to, from the crossing at Nanclares to the Villodas bridge, the men of Cole's division and the bulk of Alten's command had crossed the river and were forming a battle line across the gently rolling landscape between the Heights and the river. The allied army had won the advantage. Now it was time to press forward and deliver the decisive blow.

Kempt's riflemen hurried forward and taking shelter in folds in the ground they opened fire on the battery of horse guns that were, in turn, firing grapeshot at any of Picton's men who attempted to get across the bridge. From his vantage position Arthur could see that scores of men had already fallen along the approaches to the bridge. Now the tables were turned as the green-jacketed riflemen steadily shot down the French gunners. Behind the riflemen, the rest of Kempt's brigade stood in manoeuvre columns waiting for the command to advance, or form square if the enemy cavalry showed any sign of moving in their direction. With over twenty men and several horses down, the officer in charge of the French horse battery gave the order to fall back and his crews hurriedly limbered their guns and began to rumble back towards the main French line.

Once the guns had ceased firing, Picton's leading regiment hurried across the river and formed a line on the far bank. Arthur saw a shimmering ripple of steel as they fixed bayonets and then advanced towards the cavalry still barring their way. The line halted and a volley crashed out, knocking down several French hussars and many more of their horses. A second volley added to the enemy's losses and then the red line rippled forward, passing through the bank of powder smoke and charging home. Arthur felt a moment of anxiety at the rashness of the charge, but Picton had judged it well, and before the French could react the infantry were in amongst them, stabbing with their bayonets. In less than a minute the fight was over, and the French light cavalry were fleeing east, to the safety of the new line forming across the undulating ground just beyond the twin hillocks where the village of Arinez nestled.

As Picton pushed his men forward, driving back the remaining French soldiers either side of the hillocks, the first of General Dalhousie's men began to cross the river and follow up Picton's attack. Arthur beckoned Somerset to his side and pointed out the new line the French were hurriedly forming to repulse the forces pouring across the Zadorra.

'See there, where the French are massing a battery in front of the centre of their line?'

Somerset briefly glanced towards the enemy. 'Yes, my lord.'

'I want every available gun brought forward to form our own battery. While the other columns push in their flanks and threaten the enemy's rear, we can pound their centre to pieces. I doubt the French line will hold for long under such concerted pressure.'

As the allied centre formed and the guns rumbled forward, the attacks on either flank continued with Hill steadily pushing eastwards along the ridge. Picton and Dalhousie pressed on, but now their men came in range of the French cannon and the leading battalions suffered grievously as heavy iron shot ploughed through their ranks, cutting bloody lanes through the ranks of advancing redcoats. Arthur had ridden forward to the hills near Arinez, sending for his field headquarters to join him there, and felt sickened by the sight of so many of his fine men being cut down. However, severe though the losses might be, it bought time for the rest of the army to move up into position for what Arthur hoped would be the decisive attack on the French line.

Shortly after four, the allied army was ready and Arthur gave the order for Colonel Dickson's massed battery to open fire. Arthur had never before fielded so many guns in a battle and the seventy artillery pieces made a deafening roar as they belched fire and smoke and bombarded the French line, less than half a mile away, with heavy iron shot. Now it was the turn of the French formations to endure terrible destruction. Arthur watched with grim satisfaction as each shot tore through the enemy's battalions. Soon the guns of both sides began to target each other and the valley filled with the continuous crash and rumble of artillery as the men working the guns were whittled down, struck by shot, or by slivers of wood and metal when one of guns was hit, sending deadly splinters flying in all directions.

For a quarter of an hour the massed guns of both armies pounded each other, and so deafening was the noise of the barrage that Arthur did not hear Somerset address him and so was surprised to have his aide pluck his sleeve. He turned away from the spectacle as Somerset cupped a hand to his mouth and called out, 'We've had a report from Graham, my lord! He has been held along the north bank of the river, and Longa's division has been unable to cut the road to the French frontier.'

'Damn,' Arthur muttered. He had intended to block the enemy's line of retreat. At once he realised that it was vital that he attacked and broke the French army as swiftly as possible before it could withdraw from the battlefield in good order. Already, he could see the first vehicles of the baggage train heading east along the road to Pamplona. He leaned towards Somerset and spoke loudly into his aide's ear. 'The attack begins now. Tell Alten and Cole not to stop for anything. They are to keep pushing the enemy back and give them no chance to re-form and hold another line.'

'Yes, sir.'

As he waited for the line to advance Arthur saw that Hill's column was once again threatening to outflank the enemy. The surviving French guns fell silent and were hurriedly limbered up as Marshal Jourdan saw the threat and ordered his battered formations to withdraw. But before they could move, the centre of the allied army began their advance, pacing steadily across the open ground, their regimental colours swirling to and fro above their heads. Even as they approached Arthur saw the left flank of the French line give ground, and then form column before they began to march away to the east, leaving the rest of the French line to fight it out.

As the redcoats closed on the remaining French division holding its position, the British guns fell silent, and apart from the sounds of fighting from the Heights and away to the east, where Graham was struggling to fight his way over the river, a brief, dreadful quiet hung over the heart of the battlefield. The French were waiting in line, to bring every possible musket to bear as the British approached. Behind the infantry of Cole and Alten the cavalry trotted forward and deployed into lines, ready to charge and pursue the enemy the moment they broke and began to flee. There was a sense of inevitability about what was to come and the soldiers of both sides knew it. Arthur could not help admiring the courage of the Frenchmen waiting for their foes to strike the fatal blow. It was a terrible thing that it took war to bring out such a noble quality, he reflected.

His thoughts were interrupted as the French unleashed their first volley at the approaching redcoats. All along the front of the approaching line men staggered or fell to the ground under the hail of musket balls. Their sergeants bellowed the order to close up and the leading formations advanced another ten paces and halted, leaving a scattered band of red figures, dead and injured, in their wake. The British managed to fire their first volley an instant before the French replied with their second and a thick pall of smoke billowed between the two sides as hundreds of men were struck down. The soldiers of both sides reloaded and fired as quickly as possible, ignoring the cries of their stricken comrades and the sprawled bodies of the dead on either side.

After the fifth volley, the order was given to charge and the British surged forward, momentarily disappearing into the smoke before bursting out the other side, straight at the startled French. Arthur watched the two lines clash, the leading ranks merging into a bloody, merciless mêlée as the men fought hand to hand. More redcoats surged through the slowly dissipating cloud of powder smoke and the French began to give ground. The British pressed on, and then, as if caught by some herd instinct, the enemy broke and ran, streaming back across the open ground towards Vitoria.

Arthur turned to look expectantly towards the waiting cavalry. Unlike his previous battles in the Peninsula, when lack of cavalry had removed any chance of a successful pursuit, this time his mounted arm was a force to be reckoned with. Five cavalry brigades, nearly six thousand men, stood ready to be unleashed. As the French began to flee the regiments began to walk forward. The rear formations of the infantry line opened up to let the horsemen pass through and then the cavalry spread out again, picking their way over the bodies of those who had fallen in the exchange of fire shortly before. As the leading formations of the infantry saw the cavalry approach they hurriedly clustered together to avoid being trampled. The riders continued to advance at the walk until they had cleared most of their comrades in the infantry. Then the bugles sounded, the rising notes sounding thin and tinny from where Arthur watched the magnificent drama as they increased the pace from walk into trot, and then the canter, and finally the gallop as their riders spurred their mounts on and advanced their sabres with a throaty roar that drowned out the sound of the bugles.

Across the width of the battlefield the cavalry surged forward in a massive wave, their swords, and the helmets of the dragoons, glittering in the sunlight. Then the magic of the moment was lost as they surged amongst the French soldiers. Swords slashed left and right as the horsemen, caught up in the bloodlust of the charge, carved their way through their enemy. Here and there, small knots of men banded together around their eagle standards and tried to make for high ground as they held the British cavalry off at bayonet point. A handful of battalions in the French reserve line had the sense to form square and slowly made their way eastwards as the horsemen flowed round them.

Arthur gestured to his staff to follow him and galloped down on to the plain to follow the cavalry, ordering the infantry to join the pursuit as he passed them. Glancing towards the Heights he could see that Hill's column had taken the length of the ridge and was now descending towards Vitoria to join in the destruction of the French army. Towards the river the sound of cannon fire was fading away and as Arthur rode over a small hillock he could see the first columns of Graham's men marching on Vitoria. Beyond them, a host of French soldiers was retreating towards the rolling country to the east. All around Arthur and his party the ground was littered with dead and wounded Frenchmen. A number of guns had been abandoned as their crews had cut the horses free of the limbers and ridden off in a frantic attempt to escape the pursuing cavalry.

Ahead, as they approached Vitoria, Arthur could see the cavalry flowing round each side of the town. A short distance further on and he saw that the landscape to the east of the town was covered with wagons and carriages, their drivers whipping their horses on in a frenzied attempt to escape as the fleeing infantry caught up with them and hurried on. A few paused by abandoned or overturned vehicles to snatch up any easily available loot before running on, with terrified looks back over their shoulders. Behind them, the British cavalry came on, many of them forced to slow down as the riders threaded their way through the wagons to get at the enemy. Other units, commanded by cooler heads, had managed to direct their men around the sides of the wagons to avoid being caught up in the tangle of vehicles, soldiers and camp followers. Arthur reined in on a small knoll just to the north of Vitoria.

There was little doubt that his victory was complete. Aside from a few battered divisions fighting a rearguard action as they withdrew to the east, the bulk of the French army, its baggage, most of its guns and, most important of all, the war chest of King Joseph, would be taken. The last alone would provide the wherewithal for the army to operate for some months independently of the ports on the northern coast of Spain.

General Alava coughed. 'My lord, may I congratulate you on a most brilliant victory.'

Arthur looked at him coldly. 'You may, once the victory is in the bag, and not before.'

'But my lord, look there,' Alava protested, sweeping his arm across the panorama of abandoned vehicles between which the British cavalry pursued the enemy. 'There is your victory!'

As the officers paused to watch the final destruction of the French army Arthur noticed that more and more of his cavalry were breaking off their pursuit and heading for the baggage train. The first of the infantry had just begun to catch up with their mounted comrades and were dashing through and round the town to join the orgy of looting that was breaking out.

'Damn them!' Arthur cursed as he snapped his telescope shut and thrust it into his saddle bucket. 'The bloody fools are letting the enemy escape.'

Sure enough, the remnants of the enemy army were streaming away towards the low hills to the east, wholly unhindered as the allied soldiers began to break ranks and descend on the baggage train, desperate not to miss out on the plunder.

'Sir?' Somerset spoke quietly. 'What are your orders?'

'Orders?' Arthur shook his head. 'What is the point of giving orders to that rabble? The scum of the earth.' He drew a deep breath and sighed. 'Very well. I want every formation that has yet to reach Vitoria halted and sent back at least three miles. We must have some order established if there is going to be any kind of pursuit tomorrow.'

'Yes, sir. And where will you establish headquarters? Vitoria?'

'No. I have no desire to witness the spectacle of my army turned into a mob of thieves. I will be at Arinez. Find me there.'

'Yes, my lord.'

'One final thing. And do this at once. I want a company of reliable men. Men that can be trusted not to join in the looting. They are to locate the French army's pay chest. Once they have located it, they are to guard it with their lives.'

'I understand, my lord. I'll see to it.'

As Somerset rode away, Arthur took one last long look at the wagons and carriages, thousands of them, being systematically looted by his men. Then he turned his horse away from the spectacle and headed back east towards the village of Arinez, at the foot of the two hills rising up from the valley floor. He gritted his teeth and muttered again, 'Scum of the earth.'

Late that night Somerset reached the headquarters that had been set up in a tavern a short distance above the village. Arthur was sitting out in the open at a long wooden table by the light of a lantern. A folded map lay before him, together with a small notebook and pencil. He was staring out across the valley towards Vitoria and the blaze of torches and bonfires that defined the extent of the baggage train. He looked round as Somerset approached the table.

'You've taken a long time.'

'I apologise, my lord, but it took a while to locate the wagons with the enemy's pay chests.'

'You found them then?' Arthur's expression brightened. 'Well done!'

'I found some of them, sir. They have been placed under guard.'

'Some of them? How much exactly?'

'Difficult to say. At a guess I would imagine there is perhaps a quarter of a million francs in gold remaining.'

'A quarter of a million?' Arthur rubbed his cheek wearily. 'My spies reported that there was five million in those wagons. Now it's in the pockets of that rabble. And not just the gold. They'll be loaded down with every valuable they can find. Then there will be the drink and there are sure to be fights. I dare say the army will be unfit to continue the campaign for days.'

'That might have been true even if they had not given in to temptation, my lord,' Somerset suggested mildly. 'They have marched hard for the last six weeks, across some of the most difficult terrain to be found in Spain. The men are exhausted; they have to be rested at some point. Why not now?'

'Why not now? Because they have let the enemy escape. That should not have happened, Somerset. We should have pursued them to destruction. That was the entire purpose of my plan.'

'In which case, I would say that the plan was successful in almost every detail, my lord. Today's victory is sure to end French rule in Spain. The first reports say we have captured all but a handful of their guns. Why, we almost captured Joseph Bonaparte.'

'What?'

'One of our troops of hussars came upon his carriage a few miles to the east of Vitoria, caught up in a column of vehicles trying to escape. Apparently Joseph jumped out of one side of his carriage just as one of our officers was climbing in the other. He managed to reach some of his bodyguards and find another mount, and they cut their way free of the column and rode off into the night.'

'By God, that would have been some blow to Boney, if we had taken his brother prisoner. As it is, the episode hardly enhances Joseph's dignity.' Arthur smiled.

'He's not the only one whose dignity has been pricked.' Somerset fished inside the haversack he used to carry his notebooks and pencils and brought out a short rod, covered with purple velvet and encrusted with small gold eagles. He handed it to Arthur. 'Marshal Jourdan's baton, my lord. It was found in another carriage not far from Joseph's.'

Arthur held the baton up to the lantern and examined it. 'A pretty thing. I should imagine a bauble like this will amuse the Prince Regent. I shall send it back to England together with the victory despatch.'

'All Britain will be overjoyed by the news, my lord. And not just Britain. When word of your victory reaches the rest of Europe, it will fire the hearts of our allies to bring Bonaparte down.'

Arthur nodded slowly. 'That may be, Somerset. What is certain is that French interests in Spain cannot recover from this blow. All that is left to them now is a thin strip of land this side of the Pyrenees, and Suchet's army, bottled up in Valencia.'

'What are your plans now, my lord?'

Arthur tapped the map with the captured baton. 'Our work in the Peninsula is all but complete. The time has come to take the war to France. I aim to lead our army on to French soil before the onset of this very winter.'

Chapter 41

Napoleon

Dresden, 26 July 1813

Napoleon received the Austrian Foreign Minister in one of the Residenzschloss palace's smaller salons the night Metternich arrived from Vienna. Despite the season he felt cold and a fire was burning in the grate, creating a comfortable fug in the room which was enhanced by the rosy hue cast by the steady flames glowing on the candelabras. Ever since he had returned from Russia Napoleon had found that he was more sensitive than before to the cold and had developed a relish for being in the warm. The scars of that campaign had been borne across every sphere of life in France. Of the six hundred thousand men he had led into Russia the previous summer, scarcely ninety thousand had returned, and many of those had been crippled by frostbite. Others were broken men, unable to face the rigours of another campaign. Only the very strongest and the bravest had endured, and for a while they were all that stood between the forces of the Tsar and France's German territories.

In the months after his return to Paris Napoleon had been forced to scrape together every available man to rebuild his forces to face the threat from the east. The eighty thousand men of the National Guard were inducted into the army by imperial decree, as were tens of thousands of youths who were not due to be conscripted for another two years. Discharged veterans were recalled to serve under the eagles once again, and the marines and gunners of the navy were reassigned to fill out the ranks of the army's corps of artillery. Whatever their quality, there had been enough men to provide Napoleon with an army of a quarter of a million men when spring returned.

However, it was rather harder to find new mounts. Only a few thousand horses had survived the Russian campaign, and once Frederick William had switched sides and joined the Tsar the horse-breeding estates of northern Prussia were denied to France. Napoleon had felt their loss immediately when the year's campaign had opened. Murat's forces had been unable to adequately screen the movements of the French army. Nor had they been able to scout effectively, often leaving Napoleon in the dark as to the whereabouts of the enemy. Worse still, they were too few to prevent units of Cossacks from raiding the French supply lines.

As a result, despite winning two battles, the French had not been able to achieve a decisive result. After two months of exhausting marches across the plains and hills of the German states and the lands of western Prussia, Napoleon had been relieved by the Tsar's offer of an armisitice at the start of June. It had been agreed that the ceasefire would last until the end of July, while negotiations were conducted over the terms for a peace treaty. The Emperor of Austria, Francis, had offered to act as mediator and so Prince Metternich had spent the last weeks travelling between Napoleon's headquarters in Dresden and the Tsar and Frederick William in Berlin.

A sharp knock on the door broke into Napoleon's thoughts as he stood gazing into the heart of the fire, his hands clasped behind his back. He looked up as the door opened and Bertheir entered the room.

'Prince Metternich is here, sire.'

'Good. Show him in.'

Berthier bowed his head and left the room, leaving the door open. He returned a moment later and ushered the Austrian diplomat into Napoleon's presence. Metternich was accompanied by two members of his staff and they remained a respectful distance behind their master as he approached Napoleon and took the hand that the Emperor extended towards him.

'It is good to see you again.' Napoleon smiled warmly. 'I trust the accommodation for you and your staff is satisfactory?'

'Most comfortable, I thank you, sire. Though it would have been agreeable to have taken some refreshment and a rest before continuing our business.'

'I am sorry for that, but the peace of Europe comes before the comforts of the peacemakers, as I am sure you would agree.'

Metternich smiled thinly. 'Indeed, sire.'

'Good. You may wish to know that the Empress has written to me. She sends her warmest affection to her father, and trusts that he still regards France as a good friend and ally.'

'I will pass on her words to Emperor Francis,' Metternich replied flatly. 'He will be pleased to hear from his daughter.'

'I'm sure.' Napoleon smiled. 'And do reassure his imperial majesty that his son-in-law echoes the sentiments of his wife.'

'Of course.'

'Come then, and sit.' Napoleon waved his guests towards the oval table that had been set in the middle of the room. The Austrians waited for the Emperor to be seated first and then took their places, before Napoleon signalled to Berthier to sit beside him. When all had settled, Napoleon folded his hands together and addressed Metternich.

'So, my dear Prince, what terms have Alexander and Frederick William decided to offer me?'

Napoleon saw that Metternich was unsettled at the directness of the question, no doubt discomforted by the absence of the extended pleasantries that had been a convention of diplomatic negotiations in the days when Talleyrand had served as Napoleon's Foreign Minister. Metternich turned to one of his aides. 'The document case, please.'

The aide reached down for a small leather satchel, unfastened the buckle and opened it on the table before sliding it across to Metternich. The Foreign Minister picked up the top sheet of paper and looked up at Napoleon.

'Since you are determined to address matters directly, I'll just present you with the summary of their terms.'

Napoleon nodded.

Metternich held the document up close to his eyes and began. 'One: agreement to dismantling of the Duchy of Warsaw and the division of its existing territories between the central powers of Europe. Two: agreement to the disestablishment of the Confederation of the Rhine. Three: Prussia is to have its frontiers of 1805 restored. Four: the Continental Blockade is to be lifted and France is to respect the shipping of neutral nations. Five: all French troops are to be withdrawn behind the Rhine.' He lowered the document and looked up. 'There are other terms, but they are peripheral and can be negotiated once the main points are agreed to.'

Napoleon sat still and silent for a moment as he stared at Prince Metternich. Then he laughed contemptuously. 'Is that all they ask of me? There is no demand that I give up my territories in Italy, or that I abandon my brother in Spain?'

'The Tsar and the King are prepared to let you retain your possessions in Italy,' Metternich replied, and then allowed himself a slight smile. 'As for Spain, I suspect that the Peninsula will not be within your gift for much longer, sire.'

'Really? And what makes you so certain of that, I wonder?'

'The latest accounts of the war indicate that your armies there are exhausted and demoralised, and the population is almost wholly against the reign of your brother. And now General Wellington is marching across Spain with impunity.'

'What is Wellington to me?' Napoleon snapped. 'Just another over-cautious English general who will be thrown back into the sea the moment I deign to lead my armies against him in person. For the present, I am content to hold on to what can be defended in that country, but in due course the Spanish will be tamed and Wellington and his rabble of British, Spanish and Portuguese soldiers will be crushed. All Europe can be certain of that, at least.'

Metternich shrugged. 'I can only admire your formidable con-fidence, sire. However, Spain is not an issue for the present. We are here to discuss the armistice. I need to know if you accept the terms offered by Russia and Prussia, and if you have any counter-proposals to make.'

Napoleon stared down at his hands. 'You must realise that there is no question of my accepting the terms as they stand. France would be humiliated before the eyes of the world. *I* would be humiliated. How long do you think it would take the people of France to rise up and depose me, as they did Louis? What if there was another revolution? All would be swept away and the powers of Europe would be dealing with another popular tyranny bent on tearing down the institutions of the old regimes. I am all that stands between the thrones of Europe and anarchy. Alexander and Frederick William would do well to remember that before they seek to depose me.'

'They have not said that that is what they want to achieve,' Metternich responded carefully.

'Of course not. They just want peace,' Napoleon sneered.

Metternich did not rise to the bait and sat silently. Napoleon looked up and stared coldly at the Austrian. He noted the long nose and narrow face, and the same haughty air of superiority and condescension that Metternich shared with Talleyrand, and which so easily enraged him. None of these people, none of the rulers and aristocrats who held sway over the masses through an accident of birth, none of them would rest easy while a man who had fashioned his own destiny ruled France. He stirred slowly in his seat and leaned closer to Metternich.

'What does Austria hope to gain from this?'

'Sire?'

'Let us assume for a moment that I am not some naive simpleton who is happy to believe that Austria is playing the honest broker. So, what does Austria hope to gain?'

Metternich smiled. 'This is becoming the kind of conversation that is best conducted in confidence, sire.'

Napoleon nodded. 'Very well. Berthier, you others, leave us. At once.'

Berthier instantly rose to his feet, gathered his notes and headed for the door. After an enquiring glance at Metternich, and a brief nod from him, the aides followed suit, closing the door behind them.

'That's better, sire. Now then, you want to know Austria's position? I will tell you. But first you must know that this is what I believe, and while I cannot speak directly for Emperor Francis and his inner council I know that they have some sympathy with my views. Beyond that, they are, how shall I put it?' He smiled thinly. 'They are susceptible to a well-reasoned argument.'

'As you are susceptible to financial inducement,' Napoleon cut in. 'Or shall we speak plainly, Prince Metternich? You will take a bribe.'

'You mean to bribe me?' Metternich touched his breast and affected a hurt look. 'Sire, I would have you know that I am not Talleyrand. He raised corruptibility to an art form. I am not nearly so well versed in the craft.' He continued hurriedly as he saw Napoleon's brows begin to knit together. 'You ask what Austria wants from the present situation. It is simple. We want stability. Both within Europe, and between Europe and Russia. We need a real balance of power in Europe. France must give up some of her influence to Austria and Prussia. If we can draw Prussia into common cause with us, then Frederick William will have no need of an alliance with Russia. Every year the Tsar pushes his frontiers closer to Europe.'

'Closer to Austrian lands, you mean.'

Metternich nodded. 'True. That is why it would be better for Austria to be in alliance with France than with Russia. Yet that would only be acceptable to my Emperor if France reliquished its grip over much of the territory it presently controls.'

'I will not do that.'

Metternich sighed and closed his eyes for a moment before he continued. 'Sire, let me be brutally frank with you. You cannot win a war against the combined strengths of Russia, Prussia, Sweden and Britain. While this armistice has been in place your enemies have added new strength to their armies. You are outnumbered, and the odds against you will grow as each day passes. Our spies report that your men are weary, that Saxony cannot sustain your army for much longer and that your stocks of ammunition will be exhausted after another month's campaigning. Save your army, save your throne and make peace now. If you don't then I have to warn you that there is a good chance that

Austria may well throw her lot in with those powers allied against you.'

'Why?' Napoleon narrowed his eyes. 'Why would Francis do such a thing? You said it yourself, he has more to fear from the Tsar than from me. Austria should be fighting alongside France.'

'That is true, sire. But see it from our point of view. There are many in Vienna who are still smarting over the harsh terms of the peace you imposed after Wagram. They, and others, also point to the disaster that you involved us with in Russia. Now the nations of Europe are gathering their strength against France. If you are defeated and we are defeated alongside you then Austria can be sure that Russia will force peace terms on us even more unpleasant than those you imposed. So . . .' Metternich smiled. 'An alliance with France is not without its risks. If we remain neutral and you are beaten, which seems the most likely outcome, then we will be powerless to intervene when the peace terms are imposed. That will be to the Tsar's advantage. Therefore, as some of my compatriots argue, it would be better for Austria to be on the winning side in this war, even if that means being an unwilling ally of Russia. That is the real danger you face, sire. Your position is made more vulnerable still by any reverses you suffer elsewhere in your empire. If you would avoid disaster, then I urge you to make peace.'

'I see.' Napoleon folded the tips of his fingers together and fixed Metternich with a piercing stare. 'You make a good case. But you did neglect to mention one thing. The fact that England has offered to pay Austria half a million pounds in gold if you declare war on me, and another two million to support your war effort thereafter.' He smiled. 'You see, I have my spies too.'

'And they are well informed indeed, sire,' Metternich admitted. 'Yes, that is true. But I believe Emperor Francis would still prefer to have peace than to take a bribe and have war. However, if you refuse these terms then Austria will be compelled to act.'

'Am I to take that as an ultimatum?'

'Yes, sire.'

Napoleon's eyebrows flickered. 'I see. You have a copy of the detailed demands?'

'Of course, sire.'

'Then leave them here. I must have time to consider them.'

'Yes, sire. The Tsar has authorised me to offer you an extension to the armistice, by two more weeks.'

'That is generous. Please express my gratitude to him.' Napoleon stood up abruptly. 'Very well, I will discuss the terms with my advisors and we will draw up our own terms to put before Alexander and

Frederick William. Since the hour is late, I suggest we conclude this discussion.'

'Yes, sire.' Metternich hurriedly pulled out a copy of the peace terms and left it on the table as he swept the rest of the documents and notes back into his leather case and refastened it. Napoleon escorted him to the door of the salon and they exchanged a formal bow before Metternich left, summoning his aides to join him as he made his way along the corridor towards the stairs leading down to the main hall of the palace.

Napoleon stared after him for a moment and then snorted with derision. He returned to the table and carried one of the chairs over to the fire and sat down, leaning forward and resting his chin on his knuckles. After a moment he reached inside his waistcoat for the small locket he always carried with him. Clicking it open he gazed at the miniatures of the Empress and his infant son, gently caressing them both with his thumb. He had hoped that his marriage into the Austrian royal family might provide the necessary link that would prevent the two nations from engaging in yet another war against each other. Now it seemed that blood-letting was thicker than blood, he mused. He snapped the locket shut and slipped it back in his pocket. A short while later, Berthier entered the room.

'Prince Metternich has left the palace, sire.'

'Good.' Napoleon nodded towards the small door concealed in the wall of the salon that linked the room to a service corridor. 'Did you hear everything?'

'Yes, sire.'

'What do you think?'

Berthier carefully considered his response. 'Sire, the proposed terms are unacceptable. Our enemies must know that. I suggest we do what we can to prolong the negotiations and see what concessions we might win from them. Who knows, we could even have a peace agreement.'

'Peace? Do you really think the Tsar wants peace? He will not be content until France, the last obstacle to his ambitions in Europe, is brought down. There can be no peace between us.'

'Then let us use the negotiations to buy us as much time as possible, sire. Metternich knows some of the truth about the condition of our army, but not all.' Berthier waved a hand helplessly. 'More than half the army is in no condition to fight. We have too many boys. This morning I inspected some of the latest reinforcements. They had been given two weeks' training before being marched to Germany. When they left France only half of them had muskets and they had fired just two rounds of blanks during training. They haven't been issued with full kit and they haven't the slightest idea how to live off the land.' He shook his head in exasperation. 'Sire, we are sending lambs to the slaughter.'

'Nonsense! Boys become men as soon as they taste battle. And there are plenty of veterans in the Grand Army who will teach them the skills they need to live while on campaign.' He paused to look closely at his chief of staff. 'Perhaps the problem is that you are getting too old for this, my friend.'

'Sire?'

'You have worked tirelessly for many years, Berthier. Too many years. You are losing heart. It is is only natural.'

Berthier forced himself to stand stiffly, and shook his head. 'I am fit enough to carry out my duties, sire. I merely wished to point out that Metternich was right. This could be a war that we cannot win.'

'Cannot win?' Napoleon was astounded. 'Cannot win! You are defeatist, Marshal Berthier. I have never seen that quality in you before. And you are wrong. We can win. What our men lack in experience and equipment they more than make up for in their patriotism, and their devotion to their Emperor. That is why we shall win.'

'Sire, what if Austria joins the coalition? If that happens then our enemies can put over half a million men into the field against us. We will have to face them with little over half that number.'

'We have been outnumbered before, and won the day.'

'Not this time, sire.'

Napoleon frowned. What had happened to Berthier, he wondered. He searched the man's anguished expression, and saw as if for the first time that this, the most loyal and efficient of his officers, was close to exhaustion. Napoleon rose from his chair and approached him, touching him gently on both shoulders.

'My friend, you are weary. So are we all. Yet we must brace ourselves for one more effort. If we defeat the enemy then the coalition will collapse. This war is no longer about numbers of men, horses and guns. It is about spirit, and the will to endure. In that quality lies the secret of our success. I ask this one final effort of you, and all my soldiers. Then we shall have a great victory and we can rest. I swear it.'

Berthier looked at him, a spark of hope burning faintly in his eyes. 'You swear it?'

Napoleon nodded.

'Then I am your man, sire.'

Napoleon smiled warmly. 'I could not fight my wars without you, old friend. Now go, get some rest.'

Berthier bowed his head and turned to leave the room. After he had gone, Napoleon returned to the fire, stoking up the embers and adding some more wood before he resumed his seat. As the fresh wood cracked and hissed he reflected on all that had been said during the evening. He was certain that he could defeat the armies of Alexander and Frederick William, but if Austria did enter the war on the side of his enemies it would be the greatest military test of his career. He had no doubt that he would be able to meet the challenge, but the question that troubled him greatly was whether the officers and the men of his army would match him in the pursuit of glory.

The next morning dawned bright and clear, with not a single cloud to be seen in the sky as Dresden woke to a fine summer day. After he had taken breakfast Napoleon went for a walk in the Great Garden that stretched out to the south-east of the old city where the palace was situated. Some of the townsfolk were out, following the gravel paths that divided the ornate rose gardens, flowerbeds and clusters of trees. The half-company of guardsmen that screened the Emperor made certain that no one could get within pistol shot, and so Napoleon walked head down, deep in thought, oblivious of the curious faces that watched him pass at a distance.

He reached the far end of the garden and turned back, returning the same way he had come, consumed with thought over the planning for every eventuality when the armistice inevitably came to an end.

'Sire!'

Napoleon looked up and saw Berthier striding along the path towards him. He forced a smile and raised his hand in greeting.

'Did you sleep well, as I ordered?'

There was no smile in the marshal's face as he approached, and he spoke in a low voice. 'Sire, we have received a despatch from Marshal Jourdan. His majesty the King of Spain was defeated a month ago, at a battle outside Vitoria.'

'Another defeat?' Napoleon shook his head bitterly. 'Can none of my marshals teach Wellington a lesson?' He sucked in a sharp breath. 'No doubt Joseph's army will have to fall back to regroup.'

'Sire, there is no army to regroup. Two divisions escaped from the battle and retreated to France; the rest were routed. Only two guns were saved, and the army lost its entire baggage train.'

Napoleon stared at him, anxiety twisting in his guts. 'And my brother?'

'He escaped, sire.'

'Where is he?'

'Bayonne.'

'Bayonne,' Napoleon repeated numbly. He cleared his throat and faced Berthier sternly. 'Then he has abandoned his throne. From now, our affairs in Spain fall under military authority. Soult is in Paris. I will send him to take command. Joseph is to be kept away from Paris, out of sight, so that he cannot shame me.'

'Yes, sire.'

Napoleon pursed his lips for a moment, absorbed in the implications of the news Berthier had brought him. 'This is a harsh blow for us, Berthier. It will harden the resolve of our enemy. Emperor Francis will want to be on the side of the big battalions now.' He smiled sadly. 'It seems that there will be no rest for either of us for a while yet, eh?'

'I imagine so, sire.'

'Then we had better summon my marshals and make our war plans. It is only a matter of weeks, perhaps days, before Austria declares war.'

Chapter 42

Dresden, 26 August 1813

As Napoleon made his way to the city he nodded approvingly at the defences that Marshal St-Cyr had been putting in place since the armistice had ended. Napoleon had rushed to take command of MacDonald's embattled corps when news of a threat to Dresden had forced him to return to the Saxon capital. Several artillery batteries had been dug into the slopes on the right bank of the Elbe covering the south-eastern approaches to the old city on the far bank. The centre of the city was protected by a moat and rampart, and the entrances to the outlying suburbs had been blocked and the houses turned into stongpoints. Five enormous earthworks had been constructed in a wide arc to the south of the city and packed with field guns. Any attempt to assault the city from the south would have to run the gauntlet of a devastating crossfire even before it reached the defences of the suburbs. St-Cyr's preparations would be put to the test all too soon, Napoleon reflected.

The enemy was already driving in the French outposts and small groups of men were skirmishing with the enemy's light infantry and cavalry as they fell back towards the defences of the old city. Beyond the approaches to Dresden, dense columns of infantry and cavalry together with artillery trains were closing in on the city across an arc of six miles.

Napoleon frowned as he gazed at the enemy. The bitter sense of betrayal he felt towards Austria's cynical opportunism still chilled his heart. Once Austria had joined the coalition against France the peace negotiations had ceased abruptly. Now another quarter of a million soldiers were arrayed against the Grand Army. When the campaign was over, and his enemies were defeated, Napoleon resolved to make the terms he imposed so severe that neither Austria nor Prussia would ever be able to wage war on him again. Already, Marshal Oudinot was advancing towards Berlin to take the city, and if that did not provoke the enemy into suing for peace Oudinot was to burn the Prussian capital to the ground. As for Russia, Napoleon knew now that the Tsar could only ever be contained. The vast scale of Alexander's domain made conquest an impossibility.

As ever, the Austrians had advanced slowly, making their way through the hills of Bohemia towards Dresden. St-Cyr had already sent their vanguard reeling back, but now the full weight of the Austrian army, together with detachments of Russian and Prussian troops, was descending on the French supply base at Dresden. Some distance behind Napoleon marched Marshal Ney and the Imperial Guard, and behind them the corps of Victor and Marmont – recently returned from Spain – though they would not reach Dresden until the end of the day. St-Cyr and his garrison had to hold their position for the next twelve hours, Napoleon reflected.

The guards on the main gate recognised Napoleon from afar as his entourage cantered up the road, and let out a cheer of 'Long live the Emperor!' The cry spread across the city, and as he entered the gates and rode down the main avenues towards the bridge across the Elbe he was thronged by the excited, and relieved, men of St-Cyr's corps. Napoleon smiled back at them, raising his hat in greeting every so often, which brought forth a fresh crescendo of cheers each time. As he entered the old city Napoleon beckoned to the first officer he saw to guide them to the marshal's headquarters.

St-Cyr had occupied the cathedral, whose towers afforded a fine overview of the city's defences and the landscape to the south. The nave had been cleared to make way for a map table and the desks of the marshal's aides and clerks. Everyone immediately rose and stood to attention as the Emperor entered the building, thrusting his riding crop and gloves at Berthier before he removed his hat and handed that over as well.

'Sire, you do not know how glad I am to see you.' St-Cyr smiled as he bowed.

'There is no time for pleasantries,' Napoleon responded brusquely. 'What is your present strength?'

St-Cyr swallowed as he hurriedly collected his thoughts. 'A little more than twenty thousand, sire. Sixteen thousand deployed in the defences of the old town, and the rest in the new town.'

'Then pull your forces out of the new town at once. Every man is needed here.'

'Yes, sire.'

Napoleon approached the map table as he unbuttoned his coat. He leaned forward to examine the map. 'Your men will have to buy us time, St-Cyr. The Guard will reach the city about an hour from now. It will take perhaps another two hours for them all to assume their positions in the old city. Victor and Marmont will not reach Dresden before the end of the day, so we must hold out until then. Be clear on this: if Dresden falls, then the campaign is over and we lose everything east of the Elbe.'

'I understand, sire.'

'Then let me inspect your defences.'

St-Cyr could not hide his surprise. 'Now, sire?'

'Yes. Come.' Napoleon turned round and strode back towards the door, clicking his fingers at Berthier for his hat, gloves and crop, which Berthier had only just put down on a large chest. St-Cyr hurriedly ordered one of his aides to transfer the whole of the corps to the old town and hurried after the Emperor.

The party of senior officers followed Napoleon as he made a swift tour of the defences. The last of the outposts had been pulled back and a lull had settled over the battlefield to the south as the enemy formed up for a massed attack. Hundreds of cannon were brought forward and unlimbered to form great batteries to pound the defenders before the infantry was sent forward to assault the makeshift walls and strongpoints of the suburbs. The men of St-Cyr's corps watched the preparations with grave expressions as they lined the defences, peering over the walls and out of their newly cut loopholes. The imperial party finished the tour of the defences at the earthwork nearest to the bank of the Elbe: a large fort surrounded by a deep ditch. The side facing the enemy formed into a broad chevron so that the guns could sweep the ground before the city, creating a crossfire with the cannon from the neighbouring earthwork. St-Cyr had placed thirty guns in each of the forts, and the shot garlands sat by each weapon, with the main stores of powder dug into covered bunkers to protect it from enemy mortar shells.

Napoleon dismounted and then climbed up on top of a caisson so that he would be clearly seen by his men. Around him the gunners and a battalion of infantry eagerly crowded towards their Emperor as he addressed them.

'The enemy has decided to chance their arm in an attack on Dresden, even though they know that I am here with you, thanks to your announcing my presence so loudly!'

The soldiers laughed and smiled, and Napoleon raised his hands to quieten them. 'Even though we are outnumbered ten to one, reinforcements are on the way. By the end of the day we will match our enemy in strength and be ready to take the fight to them tomorrow.

This is the battle I have been looking for. So far our enemies have denied me the chance to fight, and now I understand their strategy. They mean to avoid a contest with Napoleon until they can mass sufficient men to make them confident enough to risk a fight. So even though they outnumber us by ten to one, do not be surprised if they lose heart and turn tail and run back to Bohemia, rather than face me.'

The men laughed again and someone shouted out, 'Long live Napoleon! Long live France!' The cry was taken up instantly.

Napoleon raised his arms and shouted with theatrical anger. 'Quiet, you fools, or you will scare them off! Is that what you want? Or do you wish to show those cowards how Frenchmen fight?' He paused a moment until every tongue was still. 'The great test of the campaign is upon us.'

He was about to continue when a cannon sounded from the massed formations of the allied army. An instant later there was a terrible roar as the enemy guns opened fire and the concussion ripped through the air. Spouts of earth lifted from the ground and a shot passed close overhead with a deep whirr.

Napoleon cupped a hand to his mouth and shouted, 'To arms! To arms!'

The gunners and the infantry rushed to their positions and a moment later the first of the French guns replied, crashing out as smoke billowed back through the embrasure. Napoleon climbed down from the caisson and hurried across to the rampart, and cautiously looked out through a wooden-framed viewing slit. An enemy column was quickly advancing along the side of the Great Garden towards the earthwork. Napoleon called over the captain commanding the nearest battery and pointed out the Austrians.

'See them? Let them have some case shot.'

'Yes, sire,' the captain grinned, and turned back to give the order to his gun crews. They adjusted the angle of their guns with handspikes and loaded the thin tin cases filled with iron balls. When the sergeants indicated that their weapons were ready the officer raised his hand, and then swept it down as he bellowed the order to fire. The guns kicked back with the recoil and the embrasures were briefly lit up by the jets of fire leaping from the muzzles. Then the view was obliterated. Napoleon hurried across to an empty embrasure where he could see, through a swirling veil of smoke, the damage done by the battery. For the first twenty paces of the column hardly a man stood. The rest had been mown down and lay dead and wounded, spattered with blood. An officer standing to one side waved the following men past the mangled bodies and the column rippled round them as it continued towards the defences. The smoke still hung about the battery so that they fired their next shots blind, but even though one gun merely succeeded in blasting the branches of some trees in the Great Garden into a shower of shattered twigs and leaves, the other guns struck home, carving more gaps through the oncoming column.

'Sire!'

Napoleon turned and saw Berthier approaching. He backed away from the embrasure and strode over to his aide. 'What is it?'

'The Guard has arrived, Sire. They are marching through the city now.'

'Where is Ney?'

'He is here, with Marshals Mortier and Murat, sire.'

'Murat? What is Murat doing here?'

'His cavalry is on the road to Dresden, sire. He rode ahead for orders.'

'Very well.' Napoleon made his way back across the interior of the fort to the entrance, facing towards the city, where the horses were being held for the Emperor and his entourage. The three newly arrived commanders stood waiting with St-Cyr.

'Gentlemen, we're in for some hot work,' Napoleon announced. 'The enemy have launched a full-blooded attack. St-Cyr, you take charge of the defences. Hold them off. Ney, Mortier, Murat, you will take one third of the Imperial Guard each and form a reserve, Mortier to the left, Ney to the centre and Murat on the right. You are to have your men ready to move at an instant's notice. But you are not to act without orders, unless the enemy break through the line in the suburbs. Then you may use your own discretion. But don't overreach yourself. Eject them from the city and fall back to your original position. We cannot afford to throw away any men unnecessarily. Dismissed.'

When the three men had mounted their horses and galloped back into the city, Napoleon took a last look around the largest earthwork and then, satisfied that it would hold the enemy at bay, he and St-Cyr led their entourage back to headquarters in the cathedral. The sound of artillery and the lighter crackle of musketry echoed along the entire length of the old city and Napoleon pointed up at the cathedral tower.

'I have to see what's happening. Where are the stairs?'

St-Cyr showed him to a small doorway in the corner of the nave and, telescopes to hand, the two began to climb the steep spiral steps winding up inside the gloomy stone interior. Breathing heavily and hearts pounding, they emerged into the belfry with its high arched windows affording fine views in every direction. To the south the city was ringed with banks of smoke as the guns of both sides continued to blast away at each other. In between the enemy batteries, and on either flank, the columns of enemy infantry advanced on the defences behind screens of skirmishers, who did their best to provide enough covering fire to keep some of the defenders' heads down and put them off their aim. As he slowly tracked his telescope across the line Napoleon was gratified to see that St-Cyr's men were holding their own.

As he watched the attack on the fort he had visited shortly before he saw the remains of the column that had been savaged by the canister fire struggling to get in through the embrasures. The ditch was littered with bodies and those who had reached the rampart were not carrying any ladders and were having to clamber up on to the shoulders of their comrades. Another column was sweeping round the left flank of the fort, hoping to make the most of the distraction caused by their comrades. A ripple of flames from the French guns on the far side of the Elbe announced their entry into the battle and roundshot ploughed through the column.

The assault reached a climax shortly after noon as the Austrians brought their guns closer to the city and attempted to blast gaps in the defences guarding the suburbs. The men in the forts took full advantage of the opportunity to lay down a devastating fire on the enemy batteries, blasting gun crews to ribbons, and smashing their gun carriages. The enemy endured an hour of the cruel punishment before withdrawing the cannon and continuing the assault with infantry. But without any scaling equipment all their discipline and courage came to nothing as they stalled in front of the French lines. St-Cyr's men held on grimly through the afternoon and as the cathedral clock struck five Napoleon decided that it was time to launch his counter-stroke.

Climbing down from the tower he emerged into the nave and summoned Berthier. 'The Imperial Guard's hour has come. Tell Murat and Ney to drive the enemy back. But they are not to lose their heads. The Guard is to advance no more than a mile from the outer works, and then fall back. Be sure that they understand that.'

'Yes, sire. And what of Mortier? Is he to be held in reserve?'

'What, and risk the wrath of his guardsmen?' Napoleon chuckled. 'I think I had better deal with them myself and put an end to their grumbling.'

'Be careful, sire,' Berthier said, in parting, as Napoleon hurried out of the cathedral to mount his horse. He rode east through the streets whose walls echoed the roar of the cannonade and shook under the reverberation of the artillery of both sides. Mortier was waiting at the head of his men, formed up in the confines of a large market square close to the edge of the eastern suburbs. The men, many sporting fine bushy moustaches and the gold earrings that had become something of a fashion amongst the elite corps, were called to attention as their Emperor came in sight. Napoleon slowed his horse to a walk as he made his way down the front rank, scrutinising the silent faces as they stared straight ahead, muskets held at the slope, the tall bearskins making them look like giants.

'Your men look as formidable as ever, Marshal Mortier,' Napoleon called out as he approached the commander of the corps. 'It would be a shame to sully such a fine turn-out by sending them into action.'

'Don't you dare hold us back!' a voice bellowed from the rear of the leading battalion. 'We've earned a chance for glory.'

'And you shall have it!' Napoleon called back. His smile faded as he turned to Mortier. 'The Austrian attack has failed. It is time to throw them back. The Guard is to retake the Great Garden.'

'Yes, sire.'

'And I shall be joining you for the attack.'

Mortier knew better than to question the Emperor's judgement and he nodded. 'It will be an honour to be at your side, sire.'

'Then let's be about it,' Napoleon replied. 'The Guard will advance.'

Mortier shouted the order and the drums began to beat the advance, a deep rhythmic rattle that echoed off the surrounding buildings. Then, at the command, the Guard began to march out of the square, down the broad avenue that led to the road leading out of Dresden towards Pirna. As they drew near to the edge of the old town, they passed the wounded being treated in the side streets and they cheered the Guard as they marched past. Now shots were flying overhead with a light zipping sound. The glass in the upper storeys of the houses was shattered and the masonry was pockmarked by musket balls. There were also gaping holes in walls and roofs where Austrian cannon balls had smashed through.

Then, as the avenue bent a little to the right, Napoleon saw that they had reached the edge of the town. A barricade lay across the road and a line of infantry, three deep, were taking turns to fire over it, then duck back and reload. Several bodies had been dragged to the side of the road so as not to encumber their comrades. A thick smog filled the open ground ahead of them, but little blooms of light marked the positions of the Austrians a short distance away, returning fire. A shot whipped by Napoleon's horse and one of the guardsmen bent forward under the impact, and then crumpled to one side of the column, dropping his musket as he clutched a hand to his stomach.

'Make way for the Guard!' Mortier bellowed, then he turned to Napoleon. 'Sire, if you please, wait here for the colour party. It will be the obvious place for the men to look for you.'

'And keep me safe, eh?'

'Yes, sire.' Mortier nodded sombrely.

'Very well.' Napoleon drew in his reins and urged his horse to the side of the avenue. Ahead, the lieutenant commanding the company on the barricade ordered his men to cease fire and clear the way. The enemy, unaware of the new danger, continued to shoot, inflicting several more casualties, and then the way was clear, just as the first guardsmen came marching up. They passed into the powder smoke and emerged on the other side, deployed into line and returned fire with two withering volleys, then lowered their bayonets and marched on.

Immediately behind the first battalion came the colour party, and Napoleon edged his horse alongside the standards and rode out of the town, through the dispersing bank of acrid smoke. On the far side the column passed through two lines of fallen bodies, one French, the other in the white uniforms of the Austrians. Ahead, two battalions of Austrian infantry stood in line, either side of a pair of field guns, but the guardsmen did not falter for an instant as they climbed over the rubble and steadily re-formed ranks. An instant later the guns boomed out and a spray of shot hissed through the leaves and struck down several guardsmen with a chorus of sharp thuds. Napoleon watched as they closed ranks and stepped out towards the enemy. Two times the guns fired, striking down more guardsmen. Then, as they closed to musket range, the Guard stopped, readied their muskets, took aim, and unleashed a volley before their colonel bellowed the order to charge, and Napoleon watched them disappear into the smoke as they swept the Austrians away.

Having endured hours of withering fire from the defenders and failed to break into the city, the enemy had little enough fight left in them, and they hurriedly withdrew in the face of the Imperial Guard's onslaught. By the time dusk fell, the enemy had been driven back as far as the line of villages where St-Cyr's men had established their original outposts. Napoleon had returned to his headquarters, pleased with the afternoon's work. There, Berthier reported that the first elements of Marmont's and Victor's corps were entering the city on the other side of the Elbe. Napoleon left instructions for his senior officers to join him at ten o'clock to be briefed for the next day's battle, and then ordered a hurried meal to be brought to him. Before the light faded completely, he climbed the tower one last time to survey the enemy's position. The camp fires flickered in a wide arc about the south of the city, but it was clear that the greatest concentration was on the line of hills the locals called the Racknitz Heights. Napoleon stared towards the dull loom in the clouds above the hills for a while and then nodded to himself.

'It is my belief that the enemy will launch another attack on Dresden tomorrow,' Napoleon announced to his marshals and senior generals as they sat on the pews arranged around St-Cyr's map table. 'They still outnumber us, but cannot be sure of our precise strength. The bulk of the two corps that arrived at dusk will not have been seen, so they will be confident of overwhelming us. However, we shall strike first, as soon as it is light. Since the centre is where their strength is, we shall feint there, and strike at their flanks. Every available man will go into our battle line tomorrow. Murat will command the right wing, Ney the left, and St-Cyr and Marmont will hold the centre. The enemy's centre and left flank are divided by a tributary river off the Elbe, here.' He indicated the map. 'The river Weisseritz. There is only one bridge across the river for several miles, at the village of Plauen. Murat, if you take that, then the enemy's left cannot be reinforced and will be at your mercy.'

Murat leaned forward and noted the village. 'Plauen will be mine within the hour, sire.'

'Good. Just make sure that you can hold on to the bridge.' Napoleon paused briefly. 'My intention is to force the enemy down the road to Pirna.'

'Pirna?' Ney frowned. 'Why Pirna?'

'Because Marshal Vandamme's corps crossed the river at Pirna this morning. He has cut the enemy's communications, and will block their retreat.'

The officers, except Berthier who already knew, stirred at this news and Napoleon was delighted to see the spirit that it had rekindled in their tired faces.

'If we succeed tomorrow, and Vandamme plays his part, then the Army of Bohemia will be eliminated from the campaign. That will leave only Blücher, and our friend Marshal Bernadotte, to deal with. Bernadotte has been tasked with defending Berlin, and Marshal Oudinot is advancing to deal with him even now. Blücher cannot hope to defeat us on his own. We are within a matter of days of ending this campaign and winning this war, my friends.' Napoleon smiled warmly, and then suddenly raised a finger. 'Ah! There is one further piece of intelligence I wish to impart to you. Earlier this evening, our pickets heard the enemy guns give the salute three times. It would appear that we are graced with the presence of not only Emperor Francis, but Tsar Alexander and King Frederick William as well. If they are taken in our trap, then the coalition is finished at a stroke. Questions?'

There was a pause before Mortier nodded. 'The plan is sound, sire. But there is one detail that concerns me.'

'Well?'

'Marshal Vandamme, sire. Is one corps enough to block the enemy's path?'

'I judge it to be sufficient,' Napoleon replied flatly. 'If we do our work well tomorrow then the allies will be a spent force and will surrender the moment they realise we have cut their line of retreat. Anyone else?' He stared round the table. 'Then it is settled. You know your roles, gentlemen. Now prepare your men for victory.'

Chapter 43

It rained heavily during the night, easing off just before dawn as the soldiers of the Grand Army, wrapped in their greatcoats and with oilskin covers fastened over their shakos, filed into their positions for the start of the coming battle. The ground was slick with mud and the Weisseritz stream had swollen into a swift current, too dangerous to attempt to ford. The last of the cavalry was forming up on the flanks as the first rays of dawn glimmered, dull and grey, above the hills to the east.

Napoleon had climbed the cathedral tower and stood with Berthier and a handful of other staff officers to watch the opening of the battle. As he had hoped, the thin light revealed that the enemy had been slow to prepare for battle. Unlike the French, who had been billeted in the town and slept in warm and dry conditions, the Austrian and Prussian forces had been camped in the open and the heavy rain had soaked them to the skin and made it almost impossible to sleep. As a result they stirred slowly and formed up in their battalions dispirited and tired.

As the cathedral clock struck six, the signal gun fired and the men massed on the French flanks rippled forward. To the left, they were opposed by the Austrian troops who had taken a mauling in their attempt to assault the city the previous day. Two divisions of the Young Guard led the way, marching steadily across the soft ground, pausing to deliver volley fire at any enemy units attempting to stand their ground. Further out, at the end of the French line, the cavalry picked their way across the muddy fields towards the forest that lined the banks of the Elbe and drove off the infantry who had tried to find shelter beneath the trees during the night.

Turning to the other flank, Napoleon watched the columns of Victor's corps striking out to the west, their left flank on the Weisseritz, while to their right Murat's cavalry formed line and waited for the order to begin their pursuit, once the infantry had broken up the enemy's formations.

Within the hour the bridge at Plauen had been captured and covered with a battery of horse guns, severing the link between the allied left and its centre. Thousands of the enemy, caught in the mud and unable to escape in time, were pressed back against the swollen stream and trapped. Victor's men stopped to deliver several devastating volleys at close range, and then the enemy began to throw down their muskets and surrender. A few hundred tried to cross the current, but lost their footing and were swept away, crying feebly for help before they disappeared from view and were washed down to the Elbe.

In the centre, St-Cyr and Marmont faced the greatest difficulty as they would be heavily outnumbered and the enemy had fortified every village and farmhouse that lay before the centre of the allied army. Sure enough, by eight o'clock they had been fought to a standstill and a thick bank of powder smoke lazily expanded for almost two miles as murderous volleys were exchanged at close range.

At midday the rain began to fall again and there was a brief lull in the fighting as the soldiers of both sides drew back a short distance to re-form their ranks, and steel themselves for the next onslaught. St-Cyr took advantage of the pause to bring his guns forward in readiness to blast his way through the enemy's front line.

Napoleon rested his elbows on the parapet as he gazed over the battlefield. He felt a peculiar sense of detachment and realised that it was down to the nature of the battle. Aside from a small force of the Old Guard, every man had been placed in the line and there were no reserves for him to send forward if they were needed. His subordinates had clear orders and the enemy lacked the initiative and the will to do anything but sit on the defensive, so there was nothing for Napoleon to do but act as a spectator as his marshals drove in the allied flanks and attempted to break their centre.

A staff officer brought him a basket of cold chicken and some small loaves of the dark German bread that Napoleon had little liking for. As he ate, the enemy guns began to open fire on St-Cyr's batteries as they unlimbered and soon a large-scale artillery duel had developed, the deep roar carrying across the battlefield.

'There has not been much progress in the centre,' Berthier observed. 'I fear the attack might be forced to a halt, sire.'

'It might.' Napoleon nodded, then jabbed a half-eaten chicken leg towards the Pirna road. 'Until Vandamme threatens their rear. Then the centre will break.'

'I trust it will, sire.'

'It will.' Napoleon took another bite, chewed swiftly and swallowed. 'Any news from Vandamme?'

'The last despatch was timed two in the morning, sire. He had run into the enemy outposts.'

'Then let us hope he had the sense to drive on through them and march to the sound of the guns here at Dresden.'

As the rain continued, the sound of musket and cannon fire began to dwindle. The left flank had been fought to a standstill, but over on the right Napoleon saw that Murat had unleashed his cavalry. The wet ground was making movement difficult and Napoleon slapped his thigh in delight as he saw large pockets of enemy soldiers trapped in the muddy fields surrounded by French cavalry and forced to surrender. By mid-afternoon the enemy's left flank had all but ceased to exist. But the centre still held, impervious to the frequent attacks that the French soldiers made at bayonet point.

At length, Napoleon took a deep breath. 'The army has done all it can for today, Berthier. This rain is bogging us down. Give the order to break off the attack. The men can spend another night under cover, and the enemy in the open, and we'll see how quickly their spirit breaks tomorrow.'

'Yes, sire.'

'And I want reports from every division. Butcher's bills, and the number of enemy captured and their casualties. By nightfall. There's another day of battle to prepare for,' he concluded irritably. 'Tomorrow we will finish this.'

The rain finally ended as dusk shrouded the battlefield and mercifully concealed the bodies and limbs stuck in the sprawl of mud churned up by the passage of many thousands of men, horses and heavy wooden wheels. The men of the Grand Army marched back to their billets, weary and wet but still in fine spirits, unlike the long column of prisoners that was escorted over the Elbe to spend yet another night in the open. Berthier collated the battle reports that came in from across the army and presented the final assessment to his Emperor as he sat wrapped in a blanket and close to a brazier set up in the nave. It had been several days since Napoleon had slept well, and exhaustion, together with the damp conditions, had combined to give him a slight fever. He trembled as he huddled over the fire.

'Sire, do you wish me to send for your surgeon?' Berthier asked anxiously.

'No. It will pass. Besides, I can rest after tomorrow.' Napoleon's face contorted for a moment and then he sneezed.

'Shall I order some soup for you, sire?'

Napoleon shook his head. His stomach was acutely uncomfortable and the idea of any food at all made him feel queasy. He glanced up at

Berthier and nodded towards the papers in the latter's hands. 'Are those the reports?'

'Yes, sire.'

'Give me the summary.'

'We have taken some twelve thousand prisoners, and after the body count, allowing for the usual proportion of wounded, the enemy suffered a total loss of over thirty-five thousand men. In addition, we have taken twenty-six guns, and thirty ammunition wagons.'

'And our losses?'

'No more than ten thousand, sire.'

'Good . . . good.' Napoleon concentrated for a moment. 'If Vandamme can keep pressing them for the direction of Pirna, then they will break when we renew our attack tomorrow.' He sneezed again, and then waved Berthier away. 'I will try to rest. You may wake me if there is any important news, or any sign of movement from the enemy.'

'Yes, sire.'

Once Berthier left him, Napoleon reached for some more wood to put on the brazier, and then wrapped the blanket tightly about him and shut his eyes. He felt truly wretched – his body strained beyond the point of endurance. His body had become weak, far weaker than it had been in the glorious early years when he had been lithe, and tough, and lack of sleep and long marches had been as nothing to him. The years had marked him, as had the burdens of being a ruler. As he leaned towards the fire he felt the pressure of his stomach on his thighs and was struck by a sudden sense of revulsion at the sorry state of his physique. The thin sallow face of the young general had become almost spherical, with an unseemly roll of flesh forming under his chin. He tired too easily, and the effort of climbing the cathedral tower had left him gasping for breath by the time he reached the top. The present campaign must end soon, he reflected, before his failing health incapacitated him. If not, then he in turn would fail the army, who depended on him to guide them to victory.

If ever there was an implacable tyrant in this world, he mused miserably, it was time. The remorseless army of time, in its serried ranks of hours, days and years, swept all before it. The greatest general was as powerless as the rawest recruit in the face of such an enemy, and all men were doomed to defeat.

Napoleon was bracing himself to climb the tower again when a message came in from one of the cavalry pickets. The allied army had withdrawn. Only a small rearguard remained, covering the line of retreat.

'Damn them!' Napoleon growled. 'They outnumber me and still they run. Cowards.' He turned away from the tower steps and went over to the map table. 'Do we know which direction they are headed?'

'Yes, sire. South, towards Bohemia.'

'Then we must effect a pursuit immediately. They have several hours' lead on us. The Grand Army must be ready to advance this morning. Murat can take the cavalry forward to harass them, and try to slow them down.' Napoleon quickly examined the map. 'We must send word to Vandamme. If he can reach Teplitz before the allies emerge from the mountains then they will be caught between Vandamme and us. The campaign is still ours to win.'

Berthier set the headquarters staff to work as they drafted the orders for the pursuit. Murat's cavalry were the first to move off, trotting south towards the Heights. Behind them the infantry of Victor's corps were forming up outside the city ready to march when a new message arrived at headquarters. The despatch was handed to Berthier by one of his aides and he read it quickly before he glanced up anxiously and hurried over to Napoleon.

'Sire, Marshal Oudinot has retreated to Wittenberg.'

'What?' Napoleon turned swiftly. 'What is he doing there? He promised me that he would be in Berlin four days ago. Why has he retreated?'

'He reports that he was defeated by a superior force outside Berlin on the twenty-third.'

'And he has run back to Wittenberg, rather than hold our northern flank.' Napoleon gritted his teeth. 'The fool has left the way open for the Prussians to march on Dresden. Damn him! Damn him!'

Everyone in the nave fell quiet as Napoleon shouted. They watched him nervously as he fought to control his temper, glaring at the map and balling his hands into fists. Berthier was silent for a while, then swallowed and cleared his throat.

'Sire, what are your orders?'

'Just a moment. I must think.' Napoleon closed his eyes and forced himself to concentrate. This news changed everything. The great advantage that had been won over the largest allied army would be worthless if the Grand Army was forced to abandon the pursuit in order to turn and face the new threat. Conversely, Napoleon could leave Dresden garrisoned and continue the pursuit, but if the city fell then he would lose his supply base and be cut off from France. He seethed with fury at Oudinot's incompetence.

'The army will continue the pursuit. There is still a chance of trapping the Army of Bohemia in the mountains. I will stay here with the Imperial Guard and wait for further news from Oudinot.'

Berthier nodded. As Napoleon looked round the nave he became aware of the silence and the stillness of his staff officers and aides. 'Well, what are you waiting for? Prepare the orders!'

At once the men bent their heads over their notebooks and despatches and carried on with their tasks, not daring to look up in case they caught the Emperor's eye. He stood, arms crossed, glaring at them for a while before turning back to the map. Coloured wooden blocks denoted the three main enemy armies, north, east and south of Dresden. Napoleon knew that he could defeat any one of them. But he could not be in more than one place at a time, and that meant he was compelled to delegate his command of scattered formations to his subordinates. They had failed him in this campaign. Perhaps they too were losing their touch, he thought. Fellow victims of the strains of age and weariness.

The pursuit continued for two more days, and then, on the evening of the thirtieth, a muddied dragoon officer arrived at headquarters with the news that Vandamme had been defeated at Kulm. Napoleon nodded calmly and bid the officer make his report in full. Vandamme, it seemed, had obeyed his orders with alacrity, driving his troops on as they marched round the hills to cut off the enemy's escape. On the twenty-ninth they had encountered the rearguard in the narrow valley at Kulm and fought an inconclusive battle. That night, another enemy column, in an attempt to escape St-Cyr's corps, had blundered into the rear of Vandamme's men, trapping them in the valley. Nearly ten thousand had managed to cut their way free, but the rest were either dead or had been taken prisoner, like Vandamme himself.

Napoleon heard the news without interruption, and then politely dismissed the officer before turning to Berthier and the other staff officers.

'It seems that the pursuit has failed. Recall the army to Dresden.'

'Yes, sire.' Berthier nodded. 'What are your plans now, sire?'

Napoleon frowned and shook his head. 'Plans?'

For a terrifying moment, he could think of nothing. His mind was numbed by lack of sleep and in any case every scheme he had devised to defeat the enemy had failed. It was becoming clear to Napoleon what the enemy's campaign strategy was. While they were content to fight his marshals when and where they could, they had resolved not to face Napoleon in person if possible.

'Clever, very clever,' he mused wearily. There was little doubt that the allies had finally hit upon an effective means of fighting him. Worse still, the fatal weakness that they had divined in the Grand Army was one of his own creation. For years now, Napoleon had exercised personal authority over every aspect of his army. His officers and men had come to rely on him utterly and had lost the ability to use their own initiative and trust their own judgement. So now, he was obliged to be everywhere, or concentrate all his men in one unwieldy host so large that it could not possibly survive for long off the land as it attempted to corner an enemy who was ever willing to trade time for space.

'Oh, yes . . .' Napoleon muttered under his breath. 'Very clever indeed.'

Chapter 44

Early in September Napoleon ordered Marshal Ney to make one last attempt to capture Berlin. Ney only managed to advance as far as Dennewitz before he was defeated and sent reeling back to the south. Meanwhile, Napoleon had taken the Imperial Guard with him to join MacDonald's army and crush Blücher, who he hoped would prove too impetuous to refuse battle. But, true to the allied strategy, Blücher fell back, and at the same time the Army of Bohemia advanced on Dresden once again, forcing Napoleon to race back.

For the rest of the month the enemy continued to probe towards Ney and MacDonald and each time Napoleon was obliged to force-march reinforcements to meet the threat, only for the enemy to withdraw again the instant they detected his presence. Napoleon was aware that Saxony could no longer feed his army. The supplies that had been built up in Dresden were steadily dwindling as the soldiers' daily ration issue was cut and cut again until the soldiers were being issued less than quarter of their usual allowance of bread. Forage for the horses was also running short and Berthier's daily report of the strength returns revealed a steady decline in the army's numbers.

'What do we do, gentlemen?' Napoleon asked his marshals at a meeting in Dresden towards the middle of the month. 'We have too few men to cover all the ground we are obliged to occupy. Those men that we do have are weak and weary and have lost the zeal that they showed when they fought here last month. And now there is news from our spies that the Russians have sent a fresh army from Poland to join the campaign against us.'

'We need to shorten our front, sire,' said Murat. 'Pull back to a more central position, behind the Elbe, concentrate our forces and wait for the opportunity to strike on our terms.'

'That is all very well, but what do we do about Dresden? We cannot afford to leave the city exposed to the Army of Bohemia. It will have to be defended, by at least one corps.'

'Why, sire?' Murat raised his eyebrows. 'Dresden has ceased to be of any real military value. It has all but run out of food, and the magazines are nearly empty. It would be better to have the garrison with the main army than cut off in Dresden and unable to affect the outcome of the campaign.'

Napoleon regarded Murat patiently. 'You are a fine soldier, Joachim, but you show poor political sense. Dresden is the capital of our sole remaining German ally, now that Bavaria is expected to declare for the coalition any day. If we abandon Dresden then we abandon any legitimacy for having French soldiers stationed on German soil. We cease to be allies protecting the interests of our friends, and become occupiers – invaders – instead. I can think of nothing more dangerous to our interests at the moment. The thought of every German peasant with a gun turning on our supply convoys is an alarming prospect.'

'Not if there are reprisals, sire. If we shoot enough peasants then I'm sure we will have no trouble.'

Marmont laughed drily. 'Have you forgotten your time in Spain? For every man we shot, five more took his place, filled with desire for revenge.'

'I remember Spain,' Murat replied. 'My only regret is that I did not shoot more of them.'

'Gentlemen, that's enough,' Napoleon interrupted. 'I have made my decision. We will leave a garrison in Dresden. St-Cyr, you are the obvious choice. I will leave you Lobau's division as well. You will hold out at all costs.'

St-Cyr nodded.

'That leaves us the question of where to make our new centre of operations.'

'The Elbe, then,' said Murat.

Napoleon thought briefly and shook his head. 'That is too much of a risk. Too long a front. We have to assume that the enemy will be able to get over the Elbe. If they manage to cross in more than one place then the front will collapse. What we need is a base from which we can concentrate our forces and then strike in any direction.' He leaned forward over the map, and pointed. 'Leipzig. It's a large city, connected to good roads, and will give us the advantage of interior lines if the enemy does advance from more than one direction. Thoughts, gentlemen?'

None of the marshals demurred and Napoleon nodded, the decision made. 'Very well, then the army will be ordered to concentrate at Leipzig.'

As the year moved into October the Grand Army's position grew steadily worse. Blücher and Bernadotte were operating in concert to the north, while General Bennigsen's Army of Poland was advancing from the east. The Army of Bohemia had bypassed Dresden and was forcing Murat back on Leipzig. As Napoleon read the reports he could not help but marvel at the scale of the coming struggle. A quarter of a million Frenchmen and a handful of allied contingents were facing nearly four hundred thousand Russian, Austrian and Prussian troops.

It was early in the afternoon as Napoleon entered Leipzig. The sound of cannon fire from the south told him that Murat was fending off the vanguard of the Army of Bohemia. The people of the city had learned that a great battle was imminent and were hurrying from their homes clutching whatever valuables they could carry. Some went east, but most went west, Napoleon noted. Clearly they judged that he would win the day and did not want to get caught on the wrong side of a pursuit once the battle was over.

His escort cleared a path for his carriage through the refugees, some of whom stopped to marvel at this glimpse of the great Emperor of France. The carriage and squadron of hussars trotted through the city, passing soldiers forcing their way into shops and houses to find food and secure a comfortable billet, and soon reached the Grand Army's headquarters in Leipzig's chamber of deputies. Berthier and his staff had arrived at dawn and occupied the clerks' hall, immediately settling down to work to ensure that the army's communications would flow efficiently once the battle was under way.

Napoleon greeted Berthier and then sat heavily in a chair beside his chief of staff's desk. 'Have the cavalry patrols located Blücher and Bernadotte yet?'

'Not yet, sire.'

'Even if they have joined forces, they are at least three days' march from here. That will give us a chance to tackle the Army of Bohemia before they can intervene. I intend to give battle in two days' time. The line of hills to the south of the city is ideal for artillery. That will be where we take up our position. The plan will be the same one we used at Dresden. Pin the enemy centre in place while we envelop their flanks. The army will use tomorrow to move into position so that the attack can begin the following morning.'

'Very well, sire. And what about our northern flank?'

'What of it?'

'If Blücher should appear, then we will need to block him, else he will cut the road to the west and fall on our rear.'

'We are safe from Blücher. He will not reach us until after the battle,' Napoleon replied dismissively. 'But you are right to be cautious.

Marmont's corps can guard the northern approaches until the battle is under way. If there is no sign of Blücher he can march south and add his weight to our right flank.'

'Yes, sire.' Berthier nodded, relieved. 'I will give the orders at once.'

Two days later the dawn was cold and misty and the soldiers of the Grand Army quietly took their places along the line of hills either side of the village of Wachau. Opposite them, across the rolling countryside south of Leipzig, the Army of Bohemia spread out across a wide front. Even before Napoleon and his escort reached his forward command post there was a deep roar of guns as the enemy opened fire.

'It seems that they have attacked first,' Napoleon said to Berthier. 'Very well, that serves our purpose. Let them expend their effort and then we shall take them with a counter-attack.'

The highest point along the line of hills was called the Galgenburg and it was here that the headquarters staff had prepared the Emperor's command point. The ground underneath his boots trembled from the exchange of artillery fire for the first half-hour and then the enemy batteries began to fall silent as the first waves of infantry advanced towards the French line. Vast columns of men marched forward beneath the national colours of Austria, Prussia and Russia, straight into the hail of case shot from the massed guns of the Grand Army. Gaps appeared in the enemy's leading battalions as men were smashed away, but the ranks closed up and the battalions came on without missing a step. Shortly before the waiting French infantry they halted to deploy into line, still under fire from cannon, and then began the deadly business of musket volleys as the two armies set about each other in earnest.

From his high position Napoleon followed the battle with satisfaction as the enemy attack made little progress. Here and there, the allies broke individual French battalions, but elsewhere their units crumbled away under the weight of French fire, and withdrew in disorder. The enemy took the village at Wachau at ten o'clock, and then it was retaken by French infantry after a bloody mêlée in the narrow streets which were left strewn with bodies, the neatly painted walls spattered and smeared with blood.

As midday approached it was clear that the enemy attack was spent and the battle had settled down into a deadly process of attrition.

Napoleon had seen no sign of the approach of Marmont's corps to take its place on the right wing of the French line, where it would be needed to swing the balance in Napoleon's favour once the time was right to launch the counter-attack.

'Berthier!'

'Sire?'

'Have there been any messages from Marmont?'

Berthier checked his log book. 'None, sire.'

'Then where is he? He should have reached his position an hour ago. Find out. Tell him I want him here, or he may cost us the battle.'

'At once, sire.'

At noon the French attack began as General Drouot, the commander of the artillery, gave the order to open fire on the enemy centre. The range was long and the gunners used round shot, but even so the heavy iron balls smashed deep into the enemy regiments formed up opposite the Galgenburg. On either side of the battery the French army began to advance, the infantry pausing to unleash volleys at close range before charging home with the bayonet. All along the battlefield Napoleon saw that the enemy was steadily being forced to retreat, giving up all their . earlier gains, and then more ground as they were pressed back towards their reserves. On the left flank, Murat unleashed his cavalry in a great sweeping arc intended to cut behind the enemy line.

As the attack drove forward, Napoleon heard more cannon fire, this time from the north. He became concerned as it rapidly intensified. Leaving the command post, he mounted his horse and galloped down the reverse slope of the Galgenburg and past the suburbs of Leipzig, making for the sound of the guns. Two miles north of the city was the village of Möckern, where the smoke from scores of guns was rising up in the still air. Spurring his horse on, Napoleon came across the first of the wounded, stumbling back from the battle raging to the north of Leipzig. It was Blücher, Napoleon realised. He had come up on them more quickly than Napoleon had calculated.

Marmont was directing his corps from a hill a short distance outside Möckern when Napoleon found him. The French still held the village, but the rest of the line had been forced to give ground. To the north Napoleon could see long columns of infantry and cavalry marching up to join Blücher's vanguard.

'Why the devil didn't you report this?' Napoleon barked in response to Marmont's salute. 'Did you not think the arrival of Blücher was a matter of some importance?'

'Sire, I was ordered to hold my ground by Marshal Ney. I assumed he would inform you that I had been attacked.'

'Ney?' Napoleon shook his head in frustration. 'Never mind. Can you hold Blücher back until tonight? You must buy me time.'

Marmont glanced over his line. 'I can hold them for two, maybe three hours, sire, but they are growing in strength all the while.'

'Do whatever you can to delay Blücher. Then fall back to the outer defences of the city.'

Marmont nodded. Napoleon stayed with him for another half-hour, until he was confident that Marmont's men showed no signs of breaking, then he turned his mount south and returned to the main battle. It was past five o'clock before he reached the command post. Berthier greeted him with a worried expression and made his report. 'The attack is stalling, sire. The enemy have more reserves than we thought. We have pushed them back the best part of a mile, but no further. We can't break through and our own reserves have been exhausted. Only the Imperial Guard remains.'

'Then why weren't they sent forward?'

'I didn't have your authority to give the order, sire. It was in the battle orders that they could only be deployed by you.'

Napoleon sighed with exasperation that he had been distracted by events at Möckern at the critical point of the main battle. It was too late to do anything now. The light was starting to fail and night would be upon them in little more than an hour. He clasped his hands tightly together behind his back and mastered his frustration before he could give the necessary orders to Berthier.

'Call off the attack. Order all commanders to withdraw. Once they break contact they are to retire on Leipzig.'

The Grand Army fell back on Leipzig under cover of darkness, forming a defence perimeter around the edge of the city. The strength returns sent in to headquarters indicated that the day's fighting had cost twenty-five thousand men, and it was likely that the enemy's losses had been somewhat higher, mainly due to the bloody failure of their initial attack. That was of little comfort to Napoleon now that the enemy's armies were closing in on Leipzig. There was no longer any possibility of fighting them one at a time, and no hope of defeating them en masse. Retreat to the Rhine was the only course of action lying open to Napoleon now, and the knowledge weighed heavily upon his weary mind.

The following day there was only skirmishing as the allied armies moved into position, preparing for a simultaneous assault on the city. Napoleon took advantage of the delay to send his baggage across the river that ran to the west of Leipzig. The ground on the far bank was composed of a low-lying marsh, crossed by a causeway, and it was clear that there was a danger that the army would be caught in a bottleneck if it collapsed under the coming onslaught. That night, Napoleon revealed his decision to retreat to his marshals.

'It seems that we have another Berezina, gentlemen.' Napoleon smiled thinly. 'We are outnumbered two to one. Our ammunition is running low. We must evacuate the city. We will start pulling men out of the line from midnight. MacDonald, Lauriston and Poniatowski will form the rearguard and keep the enemy at bay until the rest of the army is over, and then fall back themselves. In order for the evacuation to succeed, it is vital that the men cross the river and the causeway in good order. The rearguard will be covered by our guns on the far bank, and when the last men are across the bridge will be blown. Berthier will send you orders when it is your turn to cross the river.' Napoleon shrugged. 'That's all there is to say, gentlemen, except good luck.'

A light rain began to fall during the night, and it helped to conceal the sounds of the retreat as the horses, guns and men of the Grand Army filed across the river Elster. When dawn broke, half the army was still in the city, and in order to buy more time Napoleon sent an officer to the enemy to offer an armistice, spinning out the negotiations for as long as possible. Eventually the allies became aware of the ruse and sent the officer back, and began their attack shortly afterwards. There was little to gain from remaining in Leipzig and Napoleon mounted his horse and made his way through the streets to the crowded approaches to the bridge.

Once he reached the causeway Napoleon dismounted to observe the final phase of the evacuation as the soldiers pressed forward eagerly, despite the angry shouts of the engineer officers struggling to ensure that the men did not dangerously crowd the bridge. Napoleon approached the officer in charge of the demolition of the bridge as he supervised the laying of the fuses.

'You are certain that the charges are sufficient to destroy the bridge, Colonel . . .'

'Montfort, sire.' The officer smiled nervously. 'Colonel Montfort. Yes, indeed, sire. There's enough powder under the arches to blow it to pieces twice over.'

Napoleon nodded. 'That's good. You understand your orders?'

'Yes, sire. We light the fuse the moment the last of the rearguard is over.'

'That's right.' Napoleon regarded the man carefully. Montfort's left hand was twitching at his side. Napoleon patted him on the shoulder and smiled reassuringly. 'Just do your duty, Colonel, and we'll all be able to thumb our noses at the enemy, eh?'

The soldiers continued to file across the bridge as the last hours of the morning passed, until only the rearguard, some twenty thousand men, remained on the eastern bank. The sounds of fighting gradually drew closer to the bridge but Poniatowski reported that the rearguard was falling back in good order. Then, shortly before one o'clock, a party of Austrian soldiers appeared at the windows of a house overlooking the river. At once they opened fire on the men crossing the bridge. The range was long, and most of the rounds cracked into the stonework or zipped over the heads of the intended targets. Only a handful of men were struck, but it still caused a ripple of panic amongst those packed on the bridge.

Napoleon saw the danger at once and hurried over to the nearest gun covering the bridge, close to the position where the engineers stood by their fuse.

'Sergeant! You see that house there?' Napoleon pointed across the river, and a moment later there was a flash and a puff of smoke from one of the windows.

'I see 'em, sire.' The sergeant nodded.

'Then traverse your gun and put some case shot through those windows,' Napoleon ordered.

'With pleasure, sire.'

As soon as the gun was laid, and the elevation screw adjusted, the sergeant ordered his crew back and touched the portfire to the fuse cone. The field gun kicked back as a short jet of flame stabbed towards the house. Glass shattered and plaster exploded from the wall, splashing down into the river below. As Napoleon had hoped, the enemy musket fire ceased for an instant, but then a musket barrel appeared at the window and a shot was fired. The ball smacked into the bridge close by Colonel Montfort and he cried out as a stone chip grazed his cheek.

'Sweet Jesus!' he shouted, eyes wide with fear. 'The enemy are on us!' He turned quickly to one of his men, no more than a youth, holding the smouldering taper. 'Light the fuse! Do it now!'

Then he turned and scrambled up the bank, brushing past Napoleon as he ran along the causeway. Another shot struck the surface of the river close to the young engineer and he ducked and lit the end of the fuse.

'No! Don't!' Napoleon shouted, thrusting out his hands.

There was a bright flare, and then the spark raced along the fuse, hissing and spitting like a demon as it followed the loops of cord towards the central arches of the bridge. One of the guardsmen escorting Napoleon grabbed his sleeve and hauled him away.

'Take cover, sire!'

They stumbled across the bank of the river, making for the shelter of a low stone wall. The guardsman heaved Napoleon over the wall and dived after him, just as there was a blinding flash that shot jets of flame and smoke into the air. The concussion hit them with a deafening roar. Napoleon glanced up and saw chunks of masonry, men and limbs blasted into the air, where they hung for an instant before tumbling back down. A slab of paving smashed through the tiled roof of the house adjoining the wall.

For a moment Napoleon sat on his hands and knees, stunned by the ferocity of the blast. Then he scrambled up and looked over the wall. The central arches of the bridge had gone and the water beneath was churning as the lighter bits of debris rained down. A gap nearly a hundred feet wide had been blown out of the bridge and on either end the stonework was scorched black. Further back the bodies of his men lay heaped on the cobbles of the roadway. Here and there a dazed survivor struggled to free himself from the bloody carnage. On the far bank a crowd of men stood and stared, aghast. Their only escape route from Leipzig was gone. A collective groan reached Napoleon's ears from across the river.

'Oh, shit,' the guardsman muttered. 'They're fucked.'

Napoleon nodded. Already he could hear the sounds of musketry increasing in intensity as the enemy pressed forward against the French rearguard. Some of the men on the far bank looked round anxiously and then the first of them threw down his musket and struggled out of his backpack. Stripped down to shirt, breeches and boots, he clambered down into the current and struck out for the opposite bank. More followed suit, some clinging to small kegs and other items that would give them buoyancy. Most made it across, heaving themselves up on to the grassy bank either side of Napoleon. Some, poor swimmers or injured, were carried away by the current, and thrashed for a moment before being dragged beneath the surface by the weight of their uniforms and equipment.

'Look!' The guardsman thrust out his arm. 'Look there, sire. It's Marshal Poniatowski!'

Napoleon scanned the far bank and quickly caught sight of the marshal, his left arm in a sling, urging his horse through the throng, accompanied by a handful of his staff officers. All around him the French soldiers were throwing down their muskets and waiting to be taken prisoner. Poniatowski reached the edge of the river and reined in, gazing down at the men attempting to swim across the current. He looked up, in Napoleon's direction. For an instant Napoleon stared back, his first impulse bitterness to see the capture of such a fine officer. Just when France needed every worthy man, to save her from her enemies.

Napoleon cupped his hands to his mouth and shouted, 'Swim for it!'

He saw Poniatowski nod and turn to his officers. The nearest shook his head and there was a heated exchange before Poniatowski waved his uninjured hand dismissively, grasped his reins and spurred his mount down the bank into the river. The horse slithered the last few feet and splashed into the water, kicking out for the far bank. Poniatowski leaned forward, urging it on as he clung to the reins with his good hand. Napoleon watched, willing them on. Enemy soldiers further along the river bank were busy firing at the hundreds of Frenchmen in the current, struggling to escape captivity. Spouts of water leaped into the air amid the splashing from flailing arms and legs. Just as the marshal reached the middle of the river his horse was hit in the neck. There was a welter of blood, and the animal thrashed wildly, rearing up in the water. Poniatowski was thrown from his saddle and Napoleon watched helplessly as the man's head surfaced a short distance downstream from the stricken horse. The Pole managed a few desperate strokes with his good arm, and then slid beneath the whirling eddies and splashes of the surface and was gone.

Napoleon desperately looked for any further sign of him, to no avail, and then took a deep breath. Poniatowski was lost to him, together with scores more of his most experienced generals and over twenty thousand men and all their cannon, equipment and stores.

The campaign was lost. The thought struck him like a physical blow, dazing him momentarily. This was the kind of crushing defeat he had inflicted on his enemies in the past. He had been humbled. Napoleon felt sickened by the realisation. There was nothing he could do to save his empire east of the Rhine. The Grand Army would have to retreat, leaving behind tens of thousands of men still holding out in the towns and fortresses of Prussia and the other German states.

He needed time to prepare for what was to come. The war to hold the French empire together was lost. Soon, very soon, Napoleon and his battered and weary men would be forced to fight for the very survival of France.

Chapter 45

Arthur

St-Jean-de-Luz, 10 November 1813

As he rode through the camp of the Light Division that night, Arthur could see the good humour in the faces of the men, lit warm and red by the glow of the camp fires. The week's fighting had gone well and Soult's line of forts barring the way into France had been successfully stormed with a combination of courage and audacity that had warmed Arthur's heart. The allied army had crossed the Bidassoa and Nivelle rivers and crossed the enemy's border. They were now settling in for the night on French soil, and the thought filled Arthur with pride. Even so, he was already planning the next stage of his campaign. Bonaparte was unlikely to tolerate the damage done to his prestige by the incursion across the border from Spain. The French Emperor would be sure to order his forces to hurl Arthur and his soldiers back across the frontier.

Arthur smiled to himself. What Bonaparte might order and what reality might permit were two very different things. His intelligence officers had picked up rumours from French prisoners that the Emperor had suffered a serious reverse at the hands of England's European allies. Since the rumours came by way of letters received by the soldiers opposed to Arthur, it was difficult to know how much store to place in them. The enemy's censors were well practised in concealing bad news from their people, and the French newspapers that had come into the possession of Arthur's staff officers carried no hint of any setback. On the contrary, the cheaply printed news bulletins spoke only of Bonaparte's continuing mastery over the hordes of the Tsar and his incompetent allies. Arthur had grown used to the lies, as indeed had most Frenchmen, he noted with a smile. It had even become a catchphrase amongst the French – *to lie like a bulletin*.

If Bonaparte had indeed suffered a serious defeat then he would be hard pushed to reinforce the army under Marshal Soult that was facing

Arthur. Which was just as well, since Soult already had nearly as many men, and more artillery and cavalry, than Arthur. A few years before, Arthur would have been far more cautious about taking the war on to enemy soil before his lines of communication were securely guarded. As things stood, the enemy still held Pamplona, and Marshal Suchet and his army were still in the field in the region of Valencia. However, Suchet showed little sign of stirring from what had become his personal fiefdom, and the garrison of Pamplona was under siege by a Spanish army. Accordingly, Arthur felt the risks were acceptable. In any case, his political masters in London had allowed the allied army's swift advance and spate of victories to go over their heads and had insisted that Arthur proceed with an invasion of France.

Thus it had always been during the war in the Peninsula, he sighed wearily as he crossed the bridge and entered the town gate of St-Jean-de-Luz, touching the brim of the oilskin covering his cocked hat in response to the salutes of the sentries. His caution and careful planning had ensured British success, so far. His country was grateful to him, and his army trusted him, the latter being by far the more valued by Arthur. No amount of titles, spoils of war and parliamentary votes of thanks ever made a better general of a man, nor a better man of a general, he reflected.

He stopped a civilian for directions to the *mairie* where Somerset had been sent to set up the army's headquarters. The man briefly registered a look of surprise when Arthur addressed him in French, but he seemed almost unconcerned by the presence of so many English soldiers in his town. He turned and pointed towards the end of the street, where it appeared to open on to a small square. Arthur thanked him and walked his horse on. As he clopped into the square he noted with approval that a number of provosts were patrolling the area, keeping a watchful eye on the soldiers to ensure that they did not breach Arthur's orders concerning respectful treatment of French civilians and their property. More than ever he was dependent upon the goodwill of the locals. The allied army was no longer liberating a people from an invader. Now the allies were the invaders and Arthur knew it was vital that his men did nothing that might provoke the French civilians.

Arthur entered the mayor's reception chamber and handed his coat and hat to a corporal standing at the door. As soon as he saw that his commander had arrived Somerset rose from his desk and hurried over to greet him.

'The battle reports indicate we have taken every one of our objectives, sir. The first news from our cavalry patrols is that Soult is retreating towards Bayonne.'

'So we have won our foothold in France.' Arthur nodded. 'Which is as well. The army could never have survived for long in the Pyrenees. Now we shall have comfortable quarters for the winter, eh?'

'Yes, my lord.' Somerset could not resist a small smile. 'That is, unless you give orders to continue the advance.'

'I would, but first the men must be rested. Besides, there is no sure news of how Bonaparte is faring. For all we know he could have defeated his foes and be marching on us at this moment.'

Somerset pursed his lips and shook his head. 'That's not what our agents are saying. There is a wealth of rumour and scores of letters found on prisoners, or taken from the enemy dead, that make reference to a great defeat.'

'Rumours, that is all. Would you have me gamble the outcome of this campaign upon the thin vapour of these rumours of yours? Well?'

'No, sir.'

'No. Then until we have more definite proof, we shall assume that the army may need to fight a battle, or fall back, at a moment's notice. The men must not be allowed to become too comfortable.'

Somerset was chastened, but made one last effort. 'What about the newspaper reports?'

Arthur shook his head. 'I'd sooner trust the words I read in an English newspaper than a French one. That is how little stock I put in your newspaper reports, Somerset. We need intelligence from a more reliable source. Speaking of which, have we taken any prisoners of note?'

'Yes, sir. Several colonels, and the commander of a brigade, General Lapessière.'

'Good.' Arthur tapped his fingers lightly on his lips for a moment and then nodded to himself. 'Very well, I shall entertain Lapessière here tonight. I want Beresford, Hill and Picton to join us. Have the best cook in the port prepare the meal, and make sure there is ample wine.'

'Yes, sir,' Somerset nodded. 'Is that all?'

'For now.' Arthur hardened his expression. 'Bring me the butcher's bill, and the enemy losses, as soon as you can.'

'Yes, sir. Where shall I find you?'

'The mayor's suite. I take it he has a bath?'

'Indeed, sir.'

'Then I shall bathe.' Arthur scratched his cheek. 'And shave. I shall not provide General Lapessière with a poor model of an English gentleman. We have standards to uphold, Somerset. As much before the enemy as before our own men. I will not have some damned Frog looking down his nose at me, by God!'

415

Somerset looked up as Arthur entered the office, late in the evening. 'How did you get on with our guest, sir?'

'He was amenable to a somewhat indirect approach, once he was well into his cups,' said Arthur. 'He told us what we needed to know. It seems that the rumours are correct. Bonaparte has received a bloody nose and we have him on the run. Better still we know that he will not interfere with our operations here in the south of France. Indeed, it is likely that he will denude Marshal Soult of forces in order to build up his main strength to face the advance of the Russians, Austrians and Prussians. That leaves us a free hand against Soult. Just as well, since we have but a small numerical advantage over him. If he continues to fight defensively then it is likely that we shall suffer casualties at a higher rate than the French.' Arthur thought a moment and shook his head. 'I do not wish to become drawn into such a process of attrition.'

'Then what do you propose, sir?'

'We hold our ground for the most part, and take what small gains we can until the spring. If we can coincide our advance with that of our northern allies, then what is left of Bonaparte's forces will be stretched to breaking point.'

There was a loud knock at the door, and an officer entered. He looked nervous and strode quickly towards the table. By the light of the candles flickering in the candelabra Arthur saw that it was Colonel Whitely, the commander of the army's provosts. Whitely was a thickset officer, one of the rare men who had risen from the ranks. He cleared his throat as he addressed Arthur.

'Begging your pardon, sir, but I think you need to come with me.'

'Why, what on earth has happened? Out with it, man.'

'Yes, sir. It's the Spanish troops. They're looting one of the local towns. Their officers are doing nothing to stop them, and I don't have enough men to restore order. It's turning right nasty, sir, so it is.'

Arthur sighed heavily. He closed his eyes briefly and then stood up. 'Come, Whitely, you'd better take me there directly.'

The streets of Ascain were crowded with Spanish soldiers as Arthur rode into the town, accompanied by Whitely and twenty of his men. Several of the houses were on fire, and nearly all the rest had been broken into and plundered. The ragged Spaniards had taken the opportunity to gorge themselves on food and wine, and now helped themselves to gold, silver and any other items of value that they could find. Some of the local people had clearly tried to resist and several bodies lay stretched out on the cobbled streets, beaten or bayoneted to death. As the small party of Englishmen rode into the town square Arthur saw a jeering mob gathered to one side. A shrill scream cut through the cold night air and he caught a glimpse of a woman trying to break through the soldiers surrounding her. One of them grabbed the torn dress she had clasped to her chest and wrenched it away, baring her breasts. There was a cruel cheer and then someone knocked her to the ground, out of sight.

'Like I said, sir,' Whitely muttered. 'They're out of control.'

Arthur reined in and looked round at the Spaniards. 'It's only to be expected. After enduring the depredations of the French invaders for so many years they now have the chance to turn the tables. The fact that the locals are blameless is irrelevant to them. Besides, their own government rarely pays or feeds them. They see this as their hard-won right, no doubt.'

Colonel Whitely looked warily at his commander. 'Nevertheless, sir, your standing orders are that no looting is to be permitted, nor any violence to the locals.'

'I know.' Arthur sucked in his breath. 'Where is the divisional commander, General Longa?'

'He's settled himself and his staff in the local hotel, sir.' Whitely raised his hand and pointed at a large, neatly whitewashed building fronting the square. 'Over there.'

They rode across the square and dismounted. Leaving their horses in the charge of Whitely's men, Arthur and Whitely entered the hotel. There were two soldiers guarding the entrance. One was already asleep, head slumped on his chest as he stood wedged into a corner to one side of the door. The other man brought his musket up to the salute, wobbling slightly as he fought to stay on his feet. He stank of wine, much of which had been spilled down the grubby white facings of his jacket. Inside the entrance hall they saw the torn remains of a tricolour on the floor, and a large painting of the French Emperor hanging above the counter had been slashed by swords. The sounds of shouting came through one of the doors leading off the hall and they made for that, entering a large dining room. The tables had been pushed together along one side of the room and General Longa and his officers were feasting from plates of cold meats and cured sausages, accompanied by wine poured into beer mugs. Some had already passed out, heads slumped on the table in front of them, but Longa, a tall, handsome man with thinning grey hair, was holding court at the head of the company.

He smiled brilliantly as he caught sight of Arthur and rose to his feet so that he could bow elegantly in greeting.

'My dear Duke, will you join us?'

'Alas, no,' Arthur replied evenly. 'My duties do not permit me to take pleasure at the moment. May I speak with you, alone?'

'Alone?' A frown flickered across Longa's face before he nodded. 'But of course.'

Arthur gestured to Whitely to stay where he was and led the Spaniard to the far side of the dining room where there was a window overlooking the square. Arthur gestured to the men outside, their drunken expressions lit up by the impromptu bonfires they had made from furniture taken from the townspeople. 'Your men are out of control, General Longa.'

'They are celebrating our victory, sir.'

'They are committing theft, rape and murder.'

Longa stared at them and shrugged. 'Spoils of war.'

'I gave orders that there was to be no mistreatment of French civilians. Why are you permitting your men to indulge in these atrocities?'

'They will not obey their officers, sir. I will not put the lives of my officers in danger by asking them to confront the mob.' Longa turned towards Arthur with a cold expression. 'Besides, my men are entitled to revenge for what the French have done to our people.'

'Indeed they are, but they must exact their revenge on the battlefield. They have no grievance against civilians. Now, General, you must bring them under control. Use force if necessary, but put an end to this disgraceful display.'

'As you did at Badajoz?' Longa shook his head and did not try to hide the tone of contempt that crept into his voice. 'There, your troops treated my people as if they were a conquered enemy. As spoils of war. I do not think that I need a lecture from you on how my men should behave, sir.'

Arthur felt a surge of rage as he stood before the Spaniard. He would not tolerate such insubordination from one of his officers and the urge to put the fellow in his place was almost overwhelming. He fought down his anger and took a calming breath before he responded.

'Look here, General Longa, it profits us little to discuss past deeds, however regrettable we may find them. We have to look forward. Every battle we have fought, every sacrifice we have made, has been to bring us to this point. We are on the cusp of defeating our enemy. The enemy is not France, but Bonaparte. We are here to liberate France from tyranny, the same tyranny that threatens the rest of Europe. If you allow your men to mistreat the French people, then you will drive them into Bonaparte's arms. That is why you must put a stop to this, before you and your soldiers ruin us all.'

Longa stared back at him, then out of the window, and waved a hand in a helpless gesture. 'Sir, I understand what you say, but I doubt that *they* will.'

'Then I will be obliged to have a provost officer restore order by force.'

'Would you really do that? And risk a divided army?'

Arthur gritted his teeth. General Longa had a point. Such division might pose an even greater threat to the allied army than the alienation of the French population. He was caught between two impossible situations. The thought tormented him. Here, at the very hour of ascendancy over Bonaparte, having won great victories, the allied army might be the cause of its own downfall. Not for the want of courage or perseverance, but for the lack of sufficient discipline far from the battlefield. As he considered the wretched difficulty Longa's soldiers had placed him in, a third course of action occurred to Arthur. He nodded to himself. There was no question about what he must do, no matter the disadvantage it imposed upon the allied army. He cleared his throat and addressed Longa.

'You are right. There is nothing we can do to stop this. However, at first light, I want your division to withdraw from Ascain and await further orders.'

'Yes, sir,' Longa replied with a relieved expression. 'It is for the best.'

'Yes, I suppose so.' Arthur turned towards the door and beckoned to Colonel Whitely. 'Come, we must leave this place.'

'Are you certain there is no other way, sir?' asked Somerset as he lowered the draft order Arthur had penned for him.

'I have made my decision,' Arthur replied firmly. 'The only Spanish division that we can rely on is that of Morillo. The rest will be sent back across the border. If the Spanish government refuses to see to the sustenance of their own soldiers then I am damned if I will do their job for them.'

'But, sir, this will reduce the army by twenty thousand men.'

'That is so,' Arthur conceded. 'But I must have men I can rely on. Men who will do as they are ordered. Otherwise we provide a rod for our own backs, Somerset. If you had only borne witness to the scenes in Ascain you would have no doubt that we cannot afford to have such men march with us. They must be sent home. At once.'

Somerset puffed out his cheeks. 'As you wish, my lord.'

Left alone in the mayor's office, Arthur turned to stare out of the window. Outside, the sky was covered with dark grey clouds and an icy sleet was falling on the port. At a stroke he had reduced his numerical advantage over Marshal Soult to parity, and there would be a hard fight before the French were compelled to surrender.

Chapter 46

Villefranque, 10 December 1813

The right flank of the allied army had crossed to the east bank of the river Nive at Ustaritz with little trouble, brushing aside a small force of infantry. After the exchange of a few shots the enemy had hurriedly retreated north towards the main body of Soult's army in camp close to Bayonne. By nightfall five divisions had crossed the river using a hastily repaired bridge and advanced four miles downriver towards the enemy. After a detailed inspection of the French defences to the south and west of Bayonne in the last days of November, Arthur had quickly realised that a frontal assault on the town would be too costly. Instead he had decided to shift his main strength across the Nive and attempt to trap Soult against the sea. There was a risk that the enemy might attack the allies as they crossed the river, so Arthur had tasked his remaining three divisions with making a feint along the west bank to distract Soult.

Arthur had given command of the right flank to General Hill and had joined Hill at dusk to survey the enemy positions in front of Bayonne. It had rained hard during the early days of December and the ground was waterlogged, quickly turning to mud as the allied columns trudged through the glutinous slop that covered the surfaces of the roads and tracks crossing the countryside between the sea and the Nive.

General Hill fastened the clasp at the top of his coat as a fresh shower spattered down around them. 'This is foul ground to manoeuvre an army over.'

'True,' Arthur conceded. 'But it applies to both sides. Soult and his men are as mired in this as we are. There will be precious little chance to spring any surprises on each other. If we can push him back and contain him in Bayonne, then the army can go into winter quarters while the French are besieged. Even if we don't starve them out, they'll be in poor shape once spring arrives.'

'I trust you are right,' Hill said gently and then turned to one of his aides. 'Pass the word to the leading formations. We'll halt here and camp for the night. Have strong outposts sent forward to keep an eye on the enemy.' He turned back to Arthur. 'If you'll excuse me, sir, I must make arrangements to establish my headquarters.'

'Of course,' Arthur nodded.

The two men touched the brims of their hats and then Hill and his staff wheeled away and made for a cluster of farm buildings a short distance away. Arthur sat for a while, watching as Hill's columns began to spread out across the countryside. Half a mile in front of them stood the rearguard of the French army, formed up and ready to ward off any attacks that their enemy might make before night closed in. A cough to his side distracted Arthur's attention.

'What is it, Somerset?'

'Might I ask what your plans are for tonight, sir? Are we to stay with Hill, or return to General Hope's side of the river?'

Arthur thought for a moment. General Hope had only recently arrived from England and Arthur had yet to form an impression of his abilities as a field commander. As long as Hope carried out his orders and did not pursue his feint too far, and then withdrew and dug in, he and his men should not come to any grief on the other bank of the Nive. In any case, the latest reports from Arthur's cavalry patrols indicated that the bulk of Soult's forces were east of the river, facing Hill.

'We shall stay here tonight. I wish to observe Hill's attack towards Bayonne in the morning.' Arthur turned towards Somerset and in the failing light he saw that his aide was shivering. 'If you feel the need for some shelter, I suggest that you find us some accommodation for the night at Hill's headquarters.'

'Yes, sir. I'll make arrangements directly.' Somerset turned his horse away and spurred it after Hill and his staff. Arthur turned back towards the north and watched the enemy long enough to see them begin to light their camp fires. The French rearguard fell back over the brow of a low hill and left a thin screen of sentries to keep an eye on their enemy. There would be no fighting for what little was left of the day, and on into the night. The men on both sides were tired after months of campaigning, and the uncomfortable conditions of the winter months quenched any ardour for battle.

Satisfied that his army was secure for the night, Arthur tugged his reins and trotted his horse towards the farmhouse. All around him in the thin light of dusk many of the men of his army searched for firewood while their comrades set about finding shelter, or erecting tents where the ground was dry enough to hold a tent peg in position. The rain was falling steadily now, short steel-grey rods plunging down from the dark sagging bellies of the gloomy clouds overhead. Already the wagons and artillery teams of the army were struggling to a halt in the thick mud, despite all the whip-cracking and curses of the drivers.

Once he reached the farm buildings, Arthur dismounted outside the house and handed his reins to a groom with instructions to feed the horse and find it a dry barn for the night. Then Arthur climbed the short flight of steps to the door and entered. Inside he was greeted by a comforting wave of warmth and light and saw a small crowd of officers clustered round a large fireplace in which the farmer had lit a cheery blaze. As Arthur came in, he was offering his guests the chance to buy wine and food at premium prices.

Having taken off his coat and hat, and scraped his boots, Arthur joined the others for a dinner of stew and then retired to the farmer's best bedroom for the night, leaving Somerset with orders that he should be woken if there was any important news, and in any case an hour before dawn. As he settled beneath his warm coverings he let his mind dwell on the comforting prospect that the defeat of Soult and the fall of Bayonne would mark an end to the long years of campaigning that had begun in Portugal and Spain before finally extending into the enemy's own lands.

'Sir.' A voice broke into his slumber and Arthur grumbled and turned away, until a hand took his shoulder and shook it gently. 'Sir, it's Somerset. You asked me to wake you.'

Arthur blinked his eyes open and then rolled on to an elbow, facing his aide. 'What is it? What has happened?'

'Our outposts report that the French have gone, sir.'

'Gone?'

'Their sentries have pulled back, and when some of our lads followed them up they saw that there was no one left around the camp fires. Nor any sign of wagons or cannon.'

Arthur swung his legs over the side of the bed and reached for his boots, giving his orders as he struggled to pull them on. 'Tell Hill to send some cavalry patrols out to find the enemy. Soult may have fallen back to Bayonne, or he's trying to get round our flank and cut us off from the bridges over the Nive.'

'Yes, sir.'

'Is there anything else?'

'Shall I send word to General Hope about these reports?'

Arthur thought a moment and then shook his head. 'No. There's little point. Whatever Soult is playing at, his attention is sure to be firmly fixed on Hill's divisions. They're the main threat. We can inform Hope once we have a more certain grasp of Soult's intentions.'

'Yes, sir.'

Once Somerset had left him, Arthur stood and pulled on his dark blue jacket and fastened the buttons. The rasp of his stubble on the collar reminded him that he needed a shave, but he decided that there could be no delay in finding out what Soult was up to. Snatching up his hat, he left the sleeping chamber and strode downstairs to join Hill and his staff in the main reception room. The officers were gathered about a map table, illuminated by candles as it was still dark outside.

'What is the position?'

Hill glanced up from the map table and nodded a greeting as he replied. 'There's no sign of the Frogs, aside from a few patrols a short distance from Bayonne.'

'Any activity inside the town?'

'Hard to tell. We'll know more when dawn breaks.' Hill stroked his chin anxiously. 'Frankly, sir, I don't like it. We've lost contact with the enemy and our army is divided by a river. It could be a dangerous situation.'

Arthur nodded. He felt a sick sense of dread in the pit of his stomach. Soult had slipped away and Arthur cursed himself for not pushing Hill's men forward the previous evening, despite the muddy conditions of the road and the cold and weariness of the soldiers. The allied army might pay a bloody price for his complacency, Arthur realised.

As the first light crept into the sky he waited for news of Soult. One by one the cavalry patrols reported in and confirmed that the enemy had successfully broken contact. The only indication of the direction Soult had taken was the churned mud along the road to Bayonne.

'Why would he fall back to Bayonne?' Hill wondered. 'That would give us a free hand along the entire south bank of the Adour. Why abandon the attempt to contain us?'

Before Arthur could respond there was a dull rumble away to the west. Several of the officers looked up and exchanged worried glances.

'Cannon?' someone suggested.

'Of course it is,' Arthur replied with forced calmness as he realised, all too clearly, what had happened. 'It seems we have discovered where Marshal Soult has taken his army, gentlemen.'

'Good God!' Hill explained. 'He's gone after General Hope.'

Arthur nodded. 'It makes sense. I have underestimated Soult. Still, General Hope should be able to hold his ground well enough while we return across the river.' He spoke calmly, belying his cold anger at himself for handing Soult this opportunity to attack the allied army in detail. 'Hill, leave two of your divisions here to cover Bayonne. Send the rest back to reinforce Hope. I'll ride there directly to take charge.'

'Yes, sir.'

Arthur glanced round at the other officers, noting the nervous expressions. 'Gentleman, Soult may have stolen a lead on us and now we must catch up with the old fox and wring his neck. We can do it if we just keep our heads and move swiftly. Is that clear? Good. Now, Somerset, come with me.'

The bugles were calling the men to arms across the surrounding countryside as Arthur and Somerset rode out of Villefranque and galloped south, along the bank of the Nive towards the bridges at Ustaritz. To their right the sounds of cannon fire steadily increased in intensity and now there was a faint crackle of musketry that told of a sizeable engagement a mile or so to the west. From his personal reconnaissance of the country to the south-west of Bayonne Arthur knew that there were plenty of minor ridges and ravines breaking up the landscape. Thanks to the waterlogged ground Soult would be forced to advance on the two roads leading south from Bayonne. Arthur fervently hoped that the left wing of his army had obeyed the orders he had given and fortified their positions at Barroilhet and Bassussarry, blocking the roads. The scattered copses and hedgerows of the region would provide fine cover to conceal an advance and Arthur had little doubt that the enemy would have achieved a measure of surprise against Hope's divisions. However, if they could hold on until they were reinforced then the situation could be retrieved.

They crossed the repaired bridge, clattering over the cobbles. A handful of engineers recognised their commander in chief but he had galloped on before they could raise a cheer. Once on the far bank they took the road north towards Bassussarry, the sounds of battle growing louder as they approached. A few miles short of the village, they came across a small column of wagons hurrying south. Arthur reined in and spoke to a supply officer.

'What is going on?'

'French attacked at first light, sir. Thousands of 'em. General Alten ordered all wagons to the rear.'

'Where is the Light Division?'

The officer turned and pointed back down the road. 'I heard they were making a stand at Arcangues, sir.'

Arthur tugged his reins and urged his horse on, along the column of wagons, then back on to the road, increasing his pace to a gallop as the horse's flanks bellowed with each ragged breath. Ahead the sound of guns boomed out and as the road emerged from a large copse Arthur saw a low ridge ahead, perhaps a thousand paces in length. At one end stood a small but solid-looking church, at the other a country house. Both structures had been garrisoned. In between, the rest of the Light Division was drawn up, two deep in the front line, with a reserve line on the reverse slope. As Arthur and Somerset rode up the slope they came across the first of the wounded, sitting on the damp grass as they tended to their wounds, while those too badly stricken to help themselves had to wait for a member of the division's corps of bandsmen to treat their injuries.

A colonel of the Fifty-second Foot hurriedly directed them to General Alten's headquarters in the church tower before turning his attention back to his battalion as a fresh shot from the enemy guns smashed two of his men down before ploughing a muddy divot in the ground a short distance from the colonel's horse. From the vantage point of the crest of the ridge Arthur could see the entire length of the Light Division's battlefield. Before the front rank the ground sloped down for four or five hundred paces before flattening out. Rough lines of blue-uniformed bodies marked the extent of the earlier French attacks, while a few score men of Light Division lay sprawled in the trampled and muddy grass. The French columns had halted at the foot of the slope while behind them a dozen guns continued to fire on the defenders of the ridge. There were only two British guns on the ridge, light mountain guns, whose puny bangs were all but drowned out by the regular blasts of the enemy batteries.

General Alten was in the church tower, calmly watching the artillery exchange, as Arthur and Somerset came panting up the narrow spiral staircase into the belfry.

'How goes it?' asked Arthur, straightening up and discreetly rubbing his buttocks, numbed after the hard ride.

Alten pursed his lips. 'Oh, they caught us napping right enough. Started drifting forward in ones and twos, and then made a dash at our pickets. I had my fellows pulled back at once to this position.'

Arthur glanced along the ridge and noticed the boggy ground protecting the flanks at each end. He nodded approvingly. 'A fine choice. They'll not get through the Light Division in a hurry.'

'I should think not,' Alten replied stiffly. 'In any case, as you can see, we have already thrown back one attack. The Frogs have been resorting to guns ever since, mostly trying to reduce our strong points.' Alten patted the masonry. 'They'll not pound this to rubble in my lifetime. Mind you, their roundshot has played merry hell with the stones in the cemetery.'

Arthur leaned forward and peered down. Several of the headstones had been smashed to pieces. As he looked up he saw movement to the rear of the French formations lined up opposite the ridge. Three columns had broken away from the force and were marching west, towards the other road. He pointed them out.

'D'you see? I suspect that Soult has decided to press his luck against our left, having failed to break through here. It is a pity, though, that you had to abandon your fortifications and fall back at all, Alten.'

The general looked at him with a puzzled expression. 'Fortifications?'

'As per your orders. Make a feint towards Bayonne, halt and fortify.'

'We were given no such orders, sir,' Alten protested. 'Just told to push the Frogs back and keep 'em busy. That's all.'

'I see. Would you happen to know where I might find General Hope?'

'Yes, sir. He is headquartered at Bidart, with a Portuguese brigade.'

'And where is the First Division?'

'Last I heard, they were billeted at St-Jean-de-Luz.'

Somerset started. 'But that's almost ten miles from Barroilhet! Good God, what are they doing so far to the rear?'

General Alten shrugged. 'Best ask Hope, eh?'

Arthur felt an icy dread grip the back of his neck. The left flank of his army was far too extended in depth. If Soult threw his men into the attack they would roll up the allied formations and then turn on the Light Division, cutting Arthur's left flank to pieces before Hill could intervene. Such a defeat would wreck every success that Arthur had achieved since the campaign began. He turned hurriedly to Somerset.

'Ride to St-Jean-de-Luz. If the First Division isn't already on the road to Bayonne then get them moving, on my express orders. If they are marching, then hurry them. They must reach Barroilhet before our position folds. Go now.'

427

Somerset nodded and hurried down from the tower as Arthur gave orders to Alten. 'Hold your position here. If Soult breaks through to your left, then you may fall back on Hill. Keep your men closed up, in square if need be. Inform me at once if you are obliged to shift your position.'

'Yes, sir. Where will you be if I need to send word to you?'

Arthur took a deep breath. 'I am going to find General Hope.'

He reached the ridge behind the small village of Barroilhet at noon, just as a single brigade of redcoats rushed into line to reinforce the Portuguese soldiers who had been holding off a series of French attacks all morning. The enemy had already gained possession of the village and were pouring forward, ready to assault the ridge. Arthur found General Hope sitting on a bench outside an inn giving orders for the defence of the new position. A bloodstained dressing had been tied round his left calf and his uniform jacket and hat had been shot through by musket balls. He rose stiffly to his feet to greet Arthur as he dismounted.

'Glad to see you, sir.'

'Lucky, more like.' Arthur gestured to his wounded leg.

'Indeed, sir. I went forward to Barroilhet the instant I heard the French had attacked. They were on us in a trice. My staff and I had to fight our way out.'

Arthur was tempted to comment that such an escape would not have been necessary if Hope had obeyed his orders. But there was no time for recrimination, and at least Hope had thrown himself into the fight the moment he recognised his peril.

'What strength have you available to counter Soult?'

'The remains of the two Portuguese brigades holding the village, and Aylmer's brigade. I sent for the First Division at once. They should reach us before two in the afternoon.'

'Good.' Arthur nodded. 'Until then, we will have to make do with what is here. At least the ground favours us.'

As at Arcangues the French were obliged to attack on a narrow front. Half a mile either side of the muddy road lay two small lakes, surrounded by bogs. If the line could be held long enough for the First Division to arrive then Soult could be contained and his audacious plan would fail. For an instant Arthur felt his heart warming to the enemy marshal. It must have been sorely tempting to attempt an attack on the stronger half of the allied army as it crossed the Nive. But Soult had seen that his foes were playing into his hands by straddling the army across the river. Instead of fighting, he had lured Hill's column away from the crossing, and then marched his forces across the bridges at Bayonne to achieve an overwhelming advantage against the allied soldiers remaining on the west bank of the Nive.

'Clever,' Arthur muttered under his breath. 'Very clever. Soult is a man who knows how to wait.'

Then Arthur dismissed his opponent from his mind as he scrutinised the scene before him. The arrival of Aylmer's brigade had put fresh heart into the Portuguese troops, who had been fighting valiantly all morning but had been close to being overwhelmed. Now they closed up in front of their colours and braced themselves for another French onslaught. The enemy infantry had moved aside to make way for a brigade of cavalry: dragoons, in heavy coats with flowing crests atop their gleaming helmets. They walked their horses forward and slowly spread out across the muddy ground in front of the ridge. Arthur was relieved to see no sign of the enemy's guns, no doubt still stuck in the mud beyond Barroilhet.

'Not the best conditions for cavalry,' Hope commented.

'And no need for your men to form square,' Arthur responded. 'I doubt that those dragoons will make any speed over that mud. A few volleys will see them off long before they pose any danger to our line.'

Hope stared at the ground and nodded before turning to one of his staff officers. 'Campbell, ride down our line. Tell the colonels that their men are to remain where they stand.'

The officer saluted and then spurred his horse away to relay the order.

It took over half an hour for the French cavalry to deploy, and when at last the advance was sounded the heavy mounts struggled through the mud as they picked their way towards the bottom of the slope.

'What I'd give for a battery of nine-pounders,' Hope commented bitterly. 'Case shot would make short work of 'em.'

Arthur turned his gaze away from the dragoons towards the nearest of his men. They stood their ground and waited, with not a backward glance. As Arthur had expected, the poor ground slowed the cavalry to a walk, and they were still moving no faster when the order to make ready to fire echoed along the allied line. The muskets were advanced, and then there was a brief pause before the order to cock the weapons was bellowed and a light clatter filled the air.

'Take aim!'

Up came the muskets, and each man pulled the butt in tight against his shoulder, anticipating the savage kick as his weapon was discharged.

Arthur saw that the dragoons were perhaps seventy or eighty yards away. A longer range than he would like, but the large targets would be easy enough to hit when the volley was unleashed.

'Fire!'

The volleys of each company of British and Portuguese troops crashed out along the line, spitting over a thousand musket ball into the oncoming formation.

'Reload!' a sergeant cried out. 'Reload your weapons, blast yer!'

Some of the men had paused to see what damage they had caused as the smoke slowly began to disperse, but now lowered their weapons, reached for a fresh cartridge and began to reload. From his position on the crest Arthur could see that scores of dragoons and their horses had gone down, some of the animals kicking and thrashing wildly in blind pain and terror. Their comrades picked their way past, edging closer to the thin line of men defending the ridge.

A second volley spat flame and lead at the dragoons at under thirty yards, point-blank range, and this time even more went down, collapsing into the mud where they were caught like wasps in jam, struggling futilely.

'That's the way!' Hope cheered, breaking into a beam as he watched his men punish the enemy.

A third volley cut down yet more of those who had managed to find a path through the bodies, and they now added to the tangle of men and horses, dead and wounded, caught in the mud. The dragoons were brought to a standstill, and the fourth volley decided the issue. The strident notes of bugles sounded the recall and the horsemen turned their mounts round, not without difficulty, and headed back down the slope, rather faster and with less order than they had ascended it. The Portuguese brigades, down to a handful of rounds, held their fire, but Aylmer's men fired two more volleys before the order to cease fire was bellowed out.

Arthur guessed that over a quarter of the enemy brigade had been cut down and now the survivors picked their way back through the lines of infantry to the rear. There was a short pause as the walking wounded struggled out of the mire and made their way down the slope, buying the defenders more time. Arthur turned round and scanned the countryside for any sign of reinforcements. Then he saw it, the dull gleam of red as a column of British soldiers emerged between two copses and headed down the road towards them, still a mile and a half away. The slender line of men on the ridge must hold their position for a while yet, Arthur realised.

The deep rumble of drums drew his attention back to the enemy. The French skirmishers were already moving forward in pairs, warily stepping out over the open expanse of churned mud. There would be no cover for them as they approached the waiting Portuguese and British infantry. Behind them three brigades of infantry advanced in column, urged on by their officers and the insistent rhythm of the drums. Hope had recalled his light infantry earlier and his men stood their ground as the French sharpshooters halted and opened fire, steadily picking men off. As each fell, dead or wounded, his comrades closed up to the right and stood firm. They did not have to endure the skirmishers for long, as the French columns steadily climbed up the gentle slope, boots weighted down by the clinging mud.

As the columns came up to the allied line the skirmishers fell back, and for a moment the sound of firing ceased. The French halted and discharged a ragged volley, striking down a score or so of the allies. An instant later Hope's men returned fire in a massed volley. As the range was close and almost every musket could be brought to bear against the heads of the French columns the effect was devastating. Men toppled down and staggered back all along the leading ranks of the columns. Then there was a pause, filled with the hurried rattle of ramrods as each side reloaded.

'Interesting,' Arthur mused aloud. 'Do you see how the French remain in column instead of forming into a firing line? Those men are clearly poorly trained. Their officers don't trust 'em with battlefield manoeuvres.'

'They don't need to, as long as the enemy outnumber us as they do,' Hope replied.

'Not for much longer.' Arthur pointed out the approach of the First Division. 'Nevertheless, I think that quality rather than quantity will win the day.'

He turned back to the battle just in time to see his men fire their second volley a few seconds before the enemy, and more men fell on both sides. Powder smoke wreathed the air between the line and the columns, slowly merging into one mass, illuminated from within by the orange flash of each volley as the soldiers fired blind. This was the test of each army's mettle, thought Arthur. The side that took such punishment longest would win. As he watched, he noted with cold satisfaction that his men were firing three volleys to the enemy's two. Before long the French were no longer firing volleys but in a constant rattle of musketry as each man reloaded and fired at a different rate.

There was a pounding of hooves as Somerset came galloping up. He reined in and dismounted, cheeks flushed from his exertions in the cold air. He touched his hat to Arthur and General Hope.

'The First Division had already set out from St-Jean-de-Luz when I arrived, sir,' he reported. 'Caught 'em up on the road and been chivvying them on ever since.' He turned and surveyed the battle lines, and then the massed formations of Soult's army half a mile to the north. 'Good God, we haven't got a chance.'

'You think so?' Arthur smiled wryly. 'We shall see.'

The figures of the lightly wounded trickled back down the sides of the French columns, and those in the ranks shuffling forward to take the place of those who had fallen glanced at them nervously. Then Arthur saw one of the men at the rear of the nearest column turn and creep away from his formation. More followed, brushing past an enraged sergeant who was shouting at them to return to their position. The men at the head of the column were starting to fall back, no longer filling the gaps of the fallen. Slowly, the French columns retraced their steps, away from the thick bank of powder smoke, leaving a tide mark of dead and injured lying in the mud. For a while their officers and sergeants tried to halt them, but there was no will to advance back towards the withering fire of the allied troops.

As soon as the British and Portuguese officers became aware that there was no longer any enemy fire they ordered their men to stop, remove casualties to the rear and re-form their ranks. While the smoke dispersed Arthur watched the battered French brigades re-forming at the foot of the slope. A figure on horseback, his coat richly embroidered with gold lace, rode down the line haranguing his men and pointing his arm at the ridge. Arthur smiled to himself. He could imagine Soult's fury. The day had begun well for the French, but the drenched ground, the natural bottlenecks along the roads down which he had chosen to advance, and the steadfast courage of the allied troops had halted his attack in its tracks.

The beating of the drums began again, and this time Soult himself rode forward with his men, shouting encouragement as he drew his sabre and waved it forward. The muddy slope, already churned up by the cavalry and infantry of earlier attacks, was a glistening quagmire and the men had trouble keeping their footing as they struggled forward. Behind Arthur the leading brigade of the First Division had reached the ridge and was taking up position on the reverse slope. The succeeding formations were already breaking away from the road to form up on the flanks.

Arthur turned to General Hope. 'Have them advance to the crest. They'll be safe enough as there's no enemy artillery on the field. Let Soult's men see 'em.'

'Yes, sir.'

The faltering French attack struggled up the slope a short distance while more and more British troops appeared on the crest of the ridge. Soult reined in, sheathed his sword and surveyed the growing number of the defenders. Then he turned away and plodded back towards the rest of his army, calling an order out to the nearest officers as he passed. A moment later the drums stopped, and the French brigades halted. Arthur and the other officers watched and waited, in tense silence. Then the French began to turn about face and tramp back down the slope.

A chorus of whistles and jeers rose up from the men on the ridge and Hope snapped to one of his aides, 'I'll not have such damned indiscipline! Get along there and pass the order for them to be silent.'

'No,' Arthur interrupted. 'Indulge them. They've earned it. Besides, it can only add to the enemy's discomfort. Indulge your men, Hope.'

'Yes, sir,' he replied reluctantly.

As the rest of the First Division formed up on the ridge, the French began to fall back beyond Barroilhet, leaving a screen of skirmishers to defend the village. Arthur told Hope to send pickets forward and then stand his men down.

'You might consider fortifying your position this time,' he added drily. 'I'm prepared to forgive a man his mistakes, provided he learns from them immediately. I trust I make myself clear?'

'Perfectly. I will do all that is necessary, sir,' Hope replied, momentarily chastened. Then he cleared his throat and continued in a bluff tone, 'That was a close run thing. Soult is a fine commander. Almost a match for you, sir.'

'If you say so,' Arthur replied dismissively. He was irked by the comparison, and by Hope's effort to pass the blame for his incompetence to his commander. Even so, Arthur relented. Hope's brave example had steadied his men at the critical moment. 'But let me tell you the difference between Soult and me. When he gets in a difficulty, his troops don't get him out of it. Mine always do.' He paused and continued under his breath, 'Even if their officers don't.'

General Hope nodded contentedly, grateful to have saved his reputation. Then he turned away to issue orders to his staff. Somerset stared towards the last of the French troops pulling back through the village ahead. 'Is it your intention to pursue Soult?'

Arthur was silent for a moment. 'No. It will do us no good. There is little to be achieved in this weather. Soult will retreat to Bayonne and settle into winter quarters. Our men are weary and need time to rest and re-equip. The issue will be decided next year. Both here and in the north.' He smiled thinly. 'The days of Bonaparte are numbered, Somerset. Make no mistake about it.'

Chapter 47

Arthur slid two five franc pieces across the desk towards Somerset and then leaned back in his chair.

'Tell me which is the forgery.'

Somerset pursed his lips as he stared at the two silver coins, then he picked them up, one in each hand, and examined them closely, sensing their even weight as he did so. Both carried a minting date of five years earlier. The only distinction was that one was slightly less worn-looking than its companion. Somerset lowered the other coin and raised the shinier one up. 'This one.'

Arthur slapped his hand down on the table and laughed. 'Wrong!'

He was delighted with Somerset's error. Earlier, he had been presented with the two coins by Wilkins, a sergeant in the Rifles, but formerly a resident of Newgate prison, who was in charge of the small team of conterfeiters. Wilkins had asked him to choose between the two coins and Arthur, like his aide, had failed to pick the forgery, and now took pleasure in passing on Wilkins's explanation of the deception to Somerset.

'You see, the coin has been stained with coffee. It gives the illusion of wear and will last long enough for the coin to pass through several hands before arousing any suspicion.'

Somerset picked up the coin and examined it again. 'Very clever. Sergeant Wilkins and his men have done a fine job. We're damn lucky to have such men with us.'

'Lucky?' Arthur raised his eyebrows. 'In this instance, yes, but I have never been convinced of the wisdom of the army recruiting its men from the scum who infest our prisons.'

Somerset smiled. 'Newgate's loss is our gain, sir.'

'True, but I shudder to think what use such fine skills might be put to in peacetime. In any case, Wilkins reports that he and his men have minted enough French coins for us to buy supplies for the next month at least. By which time, I hope that the promised gold arrives from England.'

Somerset puffed his cheeks and looked doubtful. His scepticism was probably justified, Arthur reflected. Almost every promise made to him by the government over recent years had been subject to alteration, delay or denial. The lack of gold posed the most serious threat to his campaign at present. The mule drivers who carried most of the army's supplies had not been paid for over three months, and the soldiers for even longer.

Marshal Soult had his own problems, Arthur discovered from the locals. Unable to feed his army of sixty thousand and the population of Bayonne, Soult had been forced to leave a garrison and move the bulk of his army further inland. As the two armies settled into their winter quarters the civilians crossed freely between them, carrying wine, bread, meat and cheese from Bayonne and returning with sugar and coffee that arrived on the first English merchant vessels to enter the port of St-Jean-de-Luz. Even so, it was a seller's market and the high prices charged by the peasants were made more aggravating by their refusal to accept the silver dollars the army had been using in Spain. Hence the small counterfeiting enterprise Arthur had set up in a closely guarded warehouse in the port where Wilkins and his men melted down the Spanish currency, added in a small measure of base metals, and then cast, finished and aged the French coins. As soon as they were mixed with the other French coins in the army's war chest they would be ready to go into circulation. Arthur had managed to supplement his supply of French currency by trading coins for British treasury bills with some of the banks in Bayonne. He had been mildly surprised by the bankers' willingness to enter into such deals with an enemy power, but then the venality of bankers surpassed their sense of patriotism by a considerable measure.

He put the coins in his drawer and turned to the next item on the list of administrative tasks that he and Somerset were working through. 'Uniforms. Well? How is the replacement programme going?'

'Slowly. Only a few consignments have arrived in the port. The winter seas are delaying the convoys from Southampton. So far we've been able to issue new kit to two of Hope's divisions. He is sending one regiment at a time into the port to collect their new uniforms. What they leave behind is being laundered and issued to Hill's men to use for patching.'

'Good.' Arthur nodded. Hill's men, being positioned furthest from the port, were the last to get any kind of supplies, since the roads across the country were largely impassable. The mules used to carry supplies were short of forage and soon wasted away due to the exertion of struggling through the mud to reach the right wing of the allied army.

'See to it that some of Hill's reserve formations are recalled to the port to get some new kit. Best not let the men get some fool idea that one formation is being favoured over another.'

'Yes, sir.' Somerset bent his head to make a quick note.

'Now then, on to the requisition of shipping for the Adour crossing. How is Major Simpson faring?'

The engineering officer had been tasked with securing sufficient vessels to construct a pontoon across the mouth of the Adour river. Once the bridge was in position General Hope's men could encircle Bayonne when better weather returned and the campaign could be continued, while the main column of the allied army drove Soult east.

'Simpson sent requisitions to the ports as far as Santander, and to some of the nearest French ports. There's no shortage of interest amongst ship owners. The only difficulty is that they want paying in gold or silver.'

'No surprise there,' Arthur replied ruefully. 'Tell Simpson we can offer them a third now, a third on arrival and a third on completion of the bridge.'

Somerset looked up and sucked in a breath. 'Can we afford that, sir?'

'We can afford the initial payment. That will be enough to get them here. Then they'll have to wait their turn for money, like the rest. Once the ships are under our guns there's little they can do about the situation in any case. Not very ethical, I know, but needs must.' Arthur shook his head wearily. 'Is that all this morning?'

'Yes, sir.'

'Then we'll finish this. You may go. Tell Wilkins to have his men complete their work as soon as possible. The army needs to be provisioned. It may be on the march before long, depending on events.'

'Events, sir?'

Arthur nodded at some French newspapers that had reached headquarters that morning. 'Even Bonaparte's bulletins admit that he is falling back towards the French border. If we are approaching the endgame, then it is vital that we do our duty here in the south of France, and prevent Bonaparte from drawing any reinforcements from Soult.' Arthur fixed his aide with a determined expression. 'The end is near, Somerset. Bonaparte cannot stave off the combined armies of his enemies. The war will be over before the end of the year.'

'And then, sir?'

'Then? Then we go home.' Arthur waved a hand. 'Now then, off with you.'

When the door had closed behind Somerset, Arthur rose from his seat and walked over to the window. It looked out over the port's rainswept quays, now packed with shipping, much of it British, free to come and go thanks to the Royal Navy's domination of the French coast.

What would become of Bonaparte when the war was over? Arthur knew that his army, almost to a man, would be happy to see the French Emperor dethroned and 'decapitalised' as they put it. For his part Arthur knew that there was little desire for a return of the Bourbons amongst the French people, and so he was prepared to countenance Bonaparte's remaining on the throne, as long as his army and his ambitions could be safely contained. Arthur smiled to himself. Whatever he might accept, he doubted that England's eastern allies would be quite so merciful.

The wet weather continued throughout the rest of December and into the New Year. Most of the allied soldiers had been billeted in the port and the small villages south of Bayonne and the Adour river. Some battalions were not so fortunate and had to make do with barns and whatever shelters they could find. The rest slept in their tents, now worn and leaky after months on campaign. Yet if their comforts were few, their days were filled with a familiar range of pleasures. There were many amenable women amongst the camp followers ready to serve their carnal appetites, rough games of football to be played across muddy pitches, and for the literate rankers too the chance to read whatever they could find, and write home to their families, and to those of the illiterate on their behalf for a small fee. The officers put on plays and recitals and hosted meals, each brigade trying to outdo the next as they acted as hosts. Christmas was celebrated with the fervent enthusiasm of men who knew that they might well never see another, and the carols that were sung around the camp fires carried a kind of warm melancholy to Arthur's ears as he toured his army to present the season's greetings to his soldiers.

While the men made the most of the enforced break in the campaign Arthur worked long hours at his desk, cajoling his supply officers into making sure that they prepared his army for the next, and he hoped final, campaign of the war. In addition to such burdens, he also had to send increasingly terse messages back to the government in London, explaining why he had been obliged to halt. Politicians seemed to have no understanding of the logistical handicap that mud presented to an army. To them mud was little more than the unsightly accretion on footwear that obliged a man to hand his boots to his servant for cleaning.

It was early in January, while Arthur was wearily drafting yet another

438

reply to his political masters, that a message arrived on the regular mail packet from Southampton. The commander of the vessel, an excited young lieutenant, brought the message to him in person. After handing over the official sealed message he could not help himself from speaking.

'Wonderful news, sir. It's all across England and no one speaks of anything else.'

'Really?' Arthur replied drily, and then tapped the message. 'Do you mind?'

'What? Oh, yes. I apologise, sir.'

The lieutenant stood stiffly, biting his tongue, as Arthur casually broke the seal, unfolded the document and began to read. Somerset, sitting at a smaller desk in the corner of the room, could barely contain his curiosity. When Arthur had finished he looked up.

'Good news indeed.' He turned to Somerset. 'It seems that our eastern allies crossed the Rhine three days before Christmas. They have begun the invasion of France. Bonaparte has too few men to do anything but mount a fighting withdrawal.' Arthur lowered the letter. 'The time to act is upon us, and our allies urge us to renew our offensive. However, we cannot advance while the weather and the ground are against us. In the meantime, then, we must prepare the army to break camp and march against the French. No later than the middle of February.'

'What about the roads, sir? What if they are still impassable?'

Arthur considered the possibility for a moment. 'When the finishing line is in sight, then damn the mud! We shall have to advance in any case.'

The following month Hill's corps left their winter quarters and advanced to screen the activities of the rest of the army. At the same time a flotilla of hired boats and small ships made their way up the coast from St-Jean-de-Luz to the mouth of the Adour. The weather had moderated, clearing the sky and adding to Arthur's good humour now that the campaign was under way again. Under the cover of the guns of a frigate and a battery of cannon on the south bank of the Adour, the engineers began to anchor the craft side by side in the estuary and lay down a wooden road across their decks. The far bank was lightly defended, and the enemy fell back the moment the first roundshot came their way.

Towards the end of the first day the bridge was nearly complete and a Portuguese brigade had been landed on the far shore, together with a handful of guns and a rocket battery. Arthur had crossed the river to oversee the establishment of the bridgehead when there was an exchange of musket fire from the road to Bayonne. A moment later a soldier came trotting back to warn that an enemy column was approaching. Colonel Wilson, the commander of the brigade, immediately formed his men up across the road ready to defend the small party of engineers constructing the landing stage on the north bank. The guns and the rockets were in place on a small mound overlooking the river and Arthur gestured to Somerset to follow him and rode up to the two batteries for a better view.

To the east the road snaked between undulating ground, and Arthur could see tiny puffs of smoke as the Portuguese skirmishers exchanged fire with the light infantry advancing in a line in front of the main French column.

'A division, I should say.'

'And cavalry, there, towards the rear, sir,' Somerset said quietly. 'Could cause us some difficulty.'

Arthur looked towards the boat bridge. There was still a gap of a hundred yards between the anchored boats and the river bank. The last of the vessels still had to be edged into position and then the bridge would have to be laid across the decks. It would be at least another three hours before the first troops could march across the Adour. That meant standing and fighting, or giving the order to abandon the bridgehead until a larger force could be landed by boat to drive the French away. If the north bank of the Adour was lost it might take days to retake it. Arthur saw Colonel Wilson glance back at him, and he composed his face and remained still to give Wilson the chance to make the right decision. There was a pause, then Wilson turned back towards the enemy and ordered his men to advance to where the ground was more open and they would have the space to deploy into a line long enough to bring every musket to bear on the approaching enemy.

No more than ten minutes later the Portuguese skirmishers came trotting back down the road and took up their position at the left of the line. From his position Arthur could see the French skirmishers now, steadily advancing across country until they came within range of the Portuguese line. They had little time to harass Wilson's men before the rest of the French column came up, marching swiftly. The commander of the leading brigade halted his column and began deploying opposite the Portuguese.

'This should be interesting,' Somerset commented. 'Let's hope our allies can stand their ground alone.'

'They will,' Arthur replied firmly. 'They are seasoned men, as good as our own line infantry. Besides, they are not entirely alone.' He gestured towards the guns and rockets. A moment later the artillery battery fired its first rounds. The range was short, and the ground wet enough to absorb much of the energy as the solid iron balls struck the earth, kicking up wedges of turf before coming to a stop just short of the enemy. The captain in charge of the battery, Mosse, instructed his crews to increase the elevation and the next shots fell on target, carving their way through the French line.

Arthur turned his attention to the rocket battery. Their launch troughs were supported by a simple iron A frame which could be quickly raised or lowered by means of a sliding bolt to change the angle at which they were fired. The crews had loaded the first rockets and now stood back, the sergeants holding the cords that triggered the flintlock firing mechanisms.

Turning back towards the battle lines Arthur saw that the French had made no attempt to advance yet.

'What are they waiting for?' asked Somerset.

'Their cavalry. Once they reach the head of the column I should imagine they will attempt to get round Wilson's left flank. If that happens, then his brigade will be forced to form square. That's when their infantry will advance. This could turn to the enemy's advantage, unless something is done.' He tugged his reins and walked his mount over to the rocket battery's commander.

'Hughes, isn't it?'

'Yes, sir.'

'Your rockets can fire up to two miles, I believe.'

'That's right, sir. Of course they will not be accurate at such a range.'

'They are not accurate at any range,' Arthur replied tersely. 'So we should be thankful the enemy are providing us with such a large target. Now then, you see the enemy's cavalry?'

Lieutenant Hughes glanced to the east and nodded.

'Then aim for them, if you please. Let us see what your contraptions can achieve.'

The officer grinned and touched the brim of his hat before turning away to order his men to align their launch troughs towards the distant target. When all was ready he gave the order for the first rocket to be launched. The sergeant gave his firing cord a sharp tug, the flintlock snapped shut with a spark and the short fuse sputtered for a few seconds before the charge was ignited. With a harsh, hissing roar the rocket leaped from its trough with a brilliant jet of fire and cloud of smoke.

Arthur watched the spiralling path of the rocket as it rose to the top of its arc and then curved down towards the French column. It exploded with a flash and white puff some distance above the enemy. Arthur saw several of the soldiers struck down by shrapnel, while others ducked, forcing the column to stop.

'Very good!' Arthur grinned at Hughes. 'That's put the wind up them. Kindly continue your good work.'

'With pleasure, sir.'

The second rocket went wildly astray, over the river where it slammed into the water close to the boat bridge. Hughes looked sheepish before he turned back to supervise the next rocket. He had better fortune with the following two, which burst on the ground, the first into the infantry column, the second right in the middle of the cavalry regiment, striking down at least a dozen and scattering a hundred more as the horses bolted from the unfamiliar weapon. At the same time the artillery battery had continued to punish the French line which still had not moved, and was standing waiting for the cavalry. A distant boom drew Arthur's attention to the southern bank of the Adour where more allied batteries were positioned. The range was long but the enfilading fire was soon doing great damage as each shot ploughed into the enemy's left flank.

Somerset was enjoying the spectacle and slapped his thigh with glee each time one of the rockets exploded just above or amongst the enemy. The effect on the enemy's morale was far in excess of the damage caused and soon the column had been stopped in its tracks as men and horses scattered as each rocket corkscrewed towards them with a shrieking roar.

Arthur reached into his saddle bucket for his telescope and trained it on the disrupted ranks of the French column. He sought out the enemy general and could not help smiling as he saw him shake his fist and shout at his men. Each time he began to reassert control a fresh rocket undid his work and in the end he snatched off his hat and threw it on the ground in frustration. After enduring half an hour of the bombardment he finally gave in and the column turned about and hurried back down the road towards Bayonne. The Portuguese troops could only see the line of men in front of them, and they let out a great cheer as soon as the enemy re-formed their columns and hurried after their comrades.

Arthur lowered his telescope with a satisfied smile. 'Well, that's that. I shouldn't think we'll have any further difficulty with the bridgehead. You may tell General Hope that his blockade of Bayonne can begin the moment his corps completes the encirclement of the city.'

'Yes, sir.'

'As for us, we'll re-join Hill.' Arthur's smile faded as he considered the next phase of the campaign. 'Then it's back to hard marching. This time, we'll run Soult down and defeat him once and for all. With the south of France in our hands and the north falling to the allies then our friend Bonaparte will be caught in the middle. Let us hope the man has the sense to admit defeat.' Arthur stared at the French bodies littering the road to Bayonne and continued quietly, 'By God, Somerset, I want nothing more than to see the end of the slaughter that has been carried out in his name.'

Chapter 48

Napoleon

Paris, 24 January 1814

A cold blue hue covered the city as dusk gathered. Napoleon stood back from the window of his office in the Tuileries and looked over the public square in front of the gates. Only a handful of people still wandered across the cobbled expanse in ones and twos, huddled into their coats as a chilly wind blew across the city. Several beggars squatted outside the gates, hoping to get a few coins from those who passed by, trying to catch sight of the Emperor. There was little chance of that, Napoleon thought bitterly. The risk of some madman taking a shot at him was too high. After his return to Paris, three weeks after the disaster at Leipzig, Napoleon's police minister, General Savary, reported that he had uncovered a number of conspiracies.

Most were harmless enough – coteries of disgruntled aristocrats sending letters denouncing Napoleon and declaring their loyalty to the Bourbon cause. They were kept under watch and any contacts they made duly noted. Other plots were more dangerous. Groups of army officers planning to compel the Emperor to sue for peace, or have him forced from power. The minister's agents were busy compiling evidence against them in readiness to make arrests. Such officers were destined for a dank cell in a far-flung prison, or to be placed up against a wall in the cool light of dawn and shot. Then there was the minority of traitors who planned to kill Napoleon, and his heir too if possible. There was little common cause between the groups. Some wanted the restoration of a Bourbon monarchy. Others wanted a return to the values and institutions of the early years of the Revolution. And there were those who merely wanted revenge for a past grievance.

Whatever their causes, Napoleon did his best to ensure that he was protected against them all and did not expose himself to danger any more than was necessary. Since his return he had seldom ventured outside the Tuileries, save for visits to St-Cloud to see the Empress and his son. There was a beleaguered air about the palace, and the Parisians no longer gathered in vast crowds to acclaim their Emperor. Most of them were already looking to the future, making sure that they did not openly support a regime that might well fall at any time. Yet the grip of Napoleon's reputation, and the optimistic pronouncements of the newspapers, ensured that the people dared not openly question whether the Emperor's days were numbered.

He turned slowly away from the window and crossed the room to his desk. Tomorrow he would be leaving the capital to return to the army, or what was left of it, he mused bitterly. After Leipzig the exhausted soldiers had been forced to make one retreat after another, pressed back by the allied armies who clung to their heels like hunting dogs scenting the kill. By the end of the year France had a mere eighty thousand men to hold off nearly four times that number across a front that stretched from the North Sea to the Alps. In Italy Prince Eugène, also outnumbered, was holding on. In the south Soult was struggling to contain the recently promoted Field Marshal Wellington, who had crossed the frontier into France.

Napoleon smiled briefly. Soon Wellington would be taken care of. Two months earlier he had signed a treaty with Prince Ferdinand, returning the Spanish crown to him in exchange for an alliance against Britain. Once Ferdinand's grip on power was assured, then his soldiers would turn on the British and Wellington would be compelled to retreat. That would free Soult and his army to march north.

Even so, more men were needed to fill out the ranks of the Grand Army and Napoleon had issued an edict calling for over nine hundred thousand men to defend the motherland. Scarcely a tenth of that number had answered the call, Napoleon mused angrily.

'What do they want?' he muttered. 'A fat Bourbon king on the throne? Aristocrats to bleed them dry? The priests of Rome claiming their tithes? Why won't they fight to save themselves?' He thumped his fist down on the desk and repeated loudly, 'Why?'

Those who had joined the army were poorly equipped due to shortages of muskets and uniforms. The cavalry regiments were the worst affected of all, as there were so few remounts available in France.

The door to the office clicked open and a clerk nervously looked in.

'What is it?' Napoleon barked.

'I – I thought I heard you call for me, sire.'

'No. I was just thinking aloud. Go away . . . No! Wait. Have my brother and generals Savary and Berthier arrived yet?'

'No, sire.'

Napoleon frowned. 'Well, send them in the moment they reach the palace. Is that clear?'

'Yes, sire.'

The clerk bowed his head and backed out of the office, closing the door quietly behind him.

Although Joseph and General Savary knew the reason why they had been summoned, Napoleon wanted to ensure that they had a full grasp of his intentions for the governance of France, in case anything happened to him. Berthier would take over the management of the war in the absence of the Emperor. The years of constant warfare and the exhausting task of translating the Emperor's commands into orders and providing him with the minutest details of the strength and location of every unit in the Grand Army had exacted their toll on Berthier. After Leipzig he had returned to France a broken man and had only just returned to light duties. Some of the other marshals were still recovering from wounds received at Leipzig. Those still serving in the army were tired of war and some had openly urged Napoleon to sue for peace. Murat had withdrawn to his kingdom in Naples and was ominously silent, not having replied to a single request from his imperial master for help in the defence of France.

The door to the office opened again and the clerk entered. 'General Savary, Marshal Berthier and his highness Joseph are here, sire.'

Napoleon stared at him. 'They arrived together?'

'Yes, sire.'

'In the same carriage?'

'I don't know, sire. They were together when they entered the anteroom.'

'I see.' Napoleon felt a sudden stab of suspicion. If they had arrived together then it was obvious they had travelled to the palace together. Why? What reason could they have for meeting before attending their Emperor? Napoleon breathed out slowly. He was in danger of seeing conspiracies everywhere.

'Sire?'

Napoleon realised the clerk had been waiting for his response. He nodded. 'Show them in.'

The clerk disappeared and a moment later there came the sound of footsteps. Joseph led the way. Savary wore a plain dress jacket as he had since taking the post of Minister of Police. Berthier was also wearing civilian clothes. Napoleon had grown so accustomed to seeing him in uniform that it came as something of a surprise. Berthier looked pale and thin and his hair was streaked with grey. Napoleon nodded towards the chairs lining one side of the room. 'Bring them over and be seated.'

He waited until the three men had taken their places and settled before he continued. 'I have done all that I can to prepare the army for the present campaign. France has provided me with all that she has left to defend her sacred soil, and I will find and defeat our enemies and send them reeling back across the Rhine. Let no man be in doubt of that.' He glanced at each of them, daring them to defy his will. 'Tomorrow, at first light, I will ride to join the army. While I am gone, you, my brother, will be appointed Lieutenant Governor of my realms. That is why I have recalled you to Paris.'

Joseph nodded steadily. 'You may rely on me, sire.'

'As I did in Spain?'

Joseph flushed but kept his mouth shut to prevent any expression of his hurt and anger. Napoleon felt no desire to offer his brother any comfort. The situation was too perilous for forgiveness.

'This time, you will confine yourself to civil affairs. General Savary will act as your eyes and ears in the public and private salons of Paris. If there is any dissent, or open opposition to the regime, then the general will deal with it, using whatever powers and force are required. General Savary's authority in maintaining order and quashing my enemies is absolute, is that clear?'

Joseph nodded.

'Good.' Napoleon turned to Berthier. 'I require you to take charge of recruiting soldiers for the campaign, and making sure they are equipped. Do you accept?'

'Of course, sire,' Berthier replied quietly. 'I have never failed in my duty to my country. However . . .'

Napoleon's brow tensed. 'However?'

There was a brief pause before Berthier cleared his throat and leaned forward slightly. 'Sire, I have followed events as best as I can during my convalescence. The war is going badly for France. Two days ago I heard that Ney, Victor and Marmont had been forced to retreat beyond the Meuse.'

'That is correct,' Napoleon admitted. 'It was expedient to do so. They are retreating on to their lines of supply, while the enemy is extending theirs with every pace that they advance. I would prefer to have taken the offensive, but strategic exigencies prevent it. So, we lure them into a trap. At present they have divided into three armies, each of which can be defeated, provided that I can keep them apart and deal with each in turn.'

Berthier shut his eyes and shook his head gently before he responded. 'But, sire, you will suffer attrition with each battle, and the odds of winning become less favourable. Besides, many of the regiments in the army are under strength. To stand any chance of defending France you must find far more men.'

'Which I am in the process of doing,' Napoleon replied defiantly. 'Once King Ferdinand ratifies the peace treaty between Spain and France then tens of thousands more men will be available. And more, as soon as Murat sends reinforcements from Naples. Meanwhile, there are two divisions forming at Lyon. They will march north to reinforce me the moment I call on them.'

'They are merely boys and invalids, sire. Many of them have still not been issued full uniforms, or muskets. They cannot be considered as front line units.'

'We are all in the front line, Berthier. Every soul in France has been in the front line from the moment the enemy crossed our border. But rest assured, I will only fight delaying actions until the moment I can attack each of their armies at an advantage.'

'Even if that means retreating as far as Paris, sire?'

'Even that,' Napoleon conceded.

Berthier slumped back in his chair. He sighed. 'Then we must make ready the capital's defences, sire. The people need to be prepared for the worst. We must lay in rations to feed the population and the garrison, mount every spare cannon on the walls and in the forts.'

'No.' Napoleon shook his head. 'If the people think that Paris will be attacked then it will only result in panic and strengthen the hand of those traitors who seek to bring France low. There will be no attempt to prepare any defences. As far as the people are concerned, they are safe from the enemy. Is that perfectly clear?'

'Yes, sire,' Berthier replied patiently. 'But if, for the sake of argument, the enemy are able to advance far enough to attack Paris, what then?'

'Then there will be no attempt to abandon the city. The garrison and the people will resist the invader to the last breath, and if necessary we must bury ourselves under its ruins.'

There was silence in the room as Berthier stared at the Emperor, then exchanged brief glances with the others. He cleared his throat. 'Sire, that is not a strategy. There is no honour, or purpose, in a ruler dragging a civilisation down to destruction. After what happened to Moscow we can be sure that the Tsar would happily destroy Paris in revenge. We cannot risk the capital, or its people, in this way. Either you give the order to prepare Paris for a siege, or, if you decide that it cannot be defended, it must be declared an open city.'

Napoleon stared at his subordinate, momentarily surprised by his boldness. If Berthier, of all people, dared speak to him this way, then his power over his followers was not as firm as he had supposed. It would be best to affect a conciliatory aspect, he concluded.

'It is possible that the enemy may advance as far as Paris,' he conceded. 'It might be prudent to avoid giving battle in the streets, if there is an advantage to be sought from doing otherwise. But you are right, my dear Berthier, it would be better to avoid unnecessary civilian casualties. After all, they pay taxes.' He chuckled, and the others smiled thinly in response. 'You have your instructions, gentlemen. I place my complete trust in you to keep order during my absence. Savary, Berthier, you are dismissed.'

The two officers rose from their chairs and left. When they had gone, Napoleon eased himself back with a sigh, and then smiled at his older brother. Joseph returned the smile hesitantly.

'It is a comfort to me to know I can rely on you, Joseph. I can trust you with my empire while I go to fight the enemies of France. Can I also trust you to take care of my wife and son?'

'Of course.'

Napoleon scrutinised his brother. 'We are so unalike, in many ways. You are a man of considered opinion, and of gentleness. I was wrong to impose the crown of Spain upon you. It was too heavy a burden. I see that now. I should have used your talents more wisely.'

'I have served you as well as I could, whatever you asked of me.'

'I know. I have always been grateful to you for that.'

'Even when you have not shown it?'

Napoleon smiled sadly. 'Even then.'

The injured note in Joseph's tone was clear and for a moment Napoleon could not look his brother in the eye. Instead he reached for the decanter of wine and poured two glasses, carefully sliding the first across the table towards his brother. 'Tell me honestly, what do you advise me to do?'

Joseph stared at him for a moment and then shrugged. 'The war is lost. The allies have offered you terms — generous terms under the circumstances. Why don't you accept them, while there is still time to keep your throne?'

Napoleon stroked his brow. It was true that some, at least, of his enemies were prepared to discuss peace on fair terms. Both England and

Austria had offered to end the war if France accepted the frontiers that she had at the outbreak of the Revolution. Napoleon would be permitted to retain his throne, but would have to renounce his authority over the Confederation of the Rhine, as well as all his lands in Italy. He shook his head.

'No. If I accepted such a peace the people of France would never forgive me. Besides, the Tsar and the King of Prussia would not accept peace on those terms. They want my head. In any case, you are missing the vital point.'

'Oh?'

'The allies are divided into two camps: the interests of England and Austria are inimicable to those of Russia and Prussia. That is why they are keen to offer peace. They need France — they need *me* — to keep the balance of power in Europe. That is their weakness, which I intend to exploit. Don't you see, Joseph? If I can keep the war going long enough then the alliance against me must break. They will turn on each other and I shall be saved. Then I can make peace with whom I choose. On my terms.' He smiled coldly. 'When I have won, history will judge that I am right.'

Joseph shook his head. 'I fear that you are mistaken. You are chancing everything on the hope, the faint hope, that your enemies will set upon each other before they defeat you. It is madness to take such a risk when they offer you peace.'

The burden of the last months of frantic activity weighed heavily upon Napoleon, and the prospect of a bitter dispute with his brother made him feel weary and heavy-hearted. He sighed. 'I have made my decision. My plans. I will not change them now. I do not deny they may go awry, but I do not feel that destiny has abandoned me yet. So, brother, I will go to war, and you and the others will govern France in my stead. Can I depend upon you?'

Joseph nodded wearily.

'Then the matter is settled. Save one final duty I ask of you.'

Joseph's eyes narrowed. 'What is it?'

'It is possible that I may be defeated. That I may even be killed on the field of battle. In either event I could not bear the thought of my son being raised as an Austrian prince. I would rather his throat was cut. Do you understand? Under no circumstances is he, or his mother, to be allowed to fall into enemy hands, alive.'

Joseph could not hide the look of revulsion that instinctively rose up in response to the request. 'I am not a murderer.'

'It is not murder. It is mercy that I ask of you. If the worst happens, then spare my son, my flesh and blood, the indignity of denying his true identity. I ask you to promise me this. Swear to me that you will give the order. On your honour.'

'No!' Joseph raised his hands. 'Ask anything of me but that.'

Napoleon glared at him for a while, then slumped back into his chair. 'Very well. I shall have to ask another. But it pains me that you of all people should deny me this comfort before I go to war.'

'It pains me that my brother, of all people, should ask me to commit such a monstrous act.' Joseph stood up abruptly. 'Now, if you no longer require my presence, sire, I will leave.'

Napoleon stared up at him coldly. 'Then leave.'

His brother turned and strode towards the door, opening it swiftly and closing it loudly behind him, without once glancing back at Napoleon. The room was silent, save for the low moan of the wind outside as it gusted over the darkened city.

Chapter 49

Arcis-sur-Aube, 20 March 1814

The engineer officer approached Napoleon and Marshal Ney and saluted. 'The bridge is repaired, sire. The army can cross as soon as you give the command.'

'Well done, Captain. You and your men have pleased me. Pass on my thanks to them.'

'Yes, sir.' The engineer's pleasure at the compliment shone from his face. He swallowed nervously. 'And . . . and I'm certain they wish you a swift victory, sire.'

'That may take somewhat longer to achieve.' Napoleon smiled thinly. He turned to Ney, instantly banishing the other man from his thoughts. 'Send Sebastiani and his cavalry across first. They are to press forward and screen the bridgehead. The Guard can cross next.'

Ney bowed his head to acknowledge the order, then replied, 'We still can't be certain what strength we face to the east, sire. What I wouldn't give to have Murat and his men with us now. Such fine cavalry . . .' Ney glanced quickly at his Emperor and the latter's dark expression instantly stilled his tongue.

'Then it is a shame for us both that Murat has decided to deny us his good services,' Napoleon responded bitterly. It was only two weeks before that the news had arrived from Italy. Marshal Murat, the Emperor's brother-in-law, whom Napoleon had gifted the kingdom of Naples, had defected to the allies. There had been little of the rage that Napoleon might once have given vent to when he first heard of Murat's treachery. Anger had swiftly given way to contempt and disgust. Napoleon fervently hoped that he lived long enough to have his revenge. Not just on Murat, but on the newly recrowned Ferdinand of Spain as well. Despite the treaty he had signed with Napoleon at Valençay, Ferdinand had failed to keep one of the promises he had made so earnestly and Spain was still at war with France.

Revenge would have to wait, he reflected. That was a luxury he must deny himself, until the invaders had been driven from French soil. The allied armies remained divided, advancing boldly across northern and eastern France, confident in the strength of their numbers. As a consequence he been able to strike at their overextended columns several times since he had taken command of his forces at the end of January. Although the snow, and the subsequent mud, had hampered the movements of both sides, Napoleon held the advantage of support of the French people, who turned out to help heave the guns through the mud, or sabotaged bridges and obstructed roads to delay the enemy wherever they could. If they no longer showed unrestrained joy and loyalty in his presence, then at least he could rely on them to hate and resist the enemy.

At present, Napoleon needed every shred of assistance that could be mustered for his outnumbered soldiers. While he marched with Ney against the Austrians of General Schwarzenberg, Marmont was attempting to hold the approaches to Paris against two Prussian armies. Napoleon was already contemplating the need to abandon the capital to its fate and concentrate all his forces for one bold, massed attack sweeping across the lines of communication of his enemies. It would be a desperate measure, but there was no hope for any other strategy – military or diplomatic – should Paris fall to the enemy. The allies had just announced that they were resolved to agree a single peace with France and there was no longer any question of reverting to the pre-Revolution borders, under the rule of Napoleon. His reign was forfeit, and the allies would dictate their terms to France, if they were victorious.

Napoleon cleared his throat and addressed Ney calmly. 'Sebastiani's patrols reported that the main Austrian column is twenty miles to the north. We are facing their rearguard. If we can advance quickly enough to force a battle then we shall overwhelm them. There is nothing for you to be concerned about.'

'I'm not concerned for myself, sire,' Ney responded testily, and gestured towards the columns of guardsmen waiting for the order to advance. 'But we cannot afford to risk the few men we have left to face the enemy.'

'We will lose some,' Napoleon shrugged. 'The trick of it is to make sure that they lose more, far more, than we do.'

'They can afford to, sire.'

'Not indefinitely. As long as we are resolved to fight the invader, we have the advantage of interior lines of supply, and a unity of resolve and purpose, something that no alliance ever truly has. So we shall continue to drive a wedge between them, until their alliance shatters.'

'And if it doesn't?'

Napoleon forced a smile. 'Come now, my dear Michel, surely the bravest of the brave has not lost the desire to fight?'

'Do not doubt my courage, sire. But I am a man of sound judgement too and I question what we are doing here.' He paused, then shook his head wearily. 'You should have accepted their offer of peace.'

Napoleon looked at him coldly. 'It is too late for that. We must do what we can with the tools at hand. Now, order your men to cross the river.'

Ney's lips compressed and he stared at his Emperor briefly before tugging his reins and spurring his horse over towards the leading formation of Friant's guardsmen.

Early in the afternoon Napoleon crossed the bridge and re-joined Ney and the Guard as they approached the village of Torcy-le-Grand, nestled in rolling farmland. Ahead of them, dotted across the countryside, rode the cavalry patrols, ever watchful for a sign of the enemy. From the east a distant crackle of small arms carried on the chilly air and Napoleon pointed in the direction of the sound.

'Have that investigated at once. The enemy is supposed to be in the south.'

'Yes, sire.'

While Ney sent an order forward to Sebastiani, Napoleon turned his attention to the men of the brigade he was riding alongside. They were soldiers of one of the recently raised units. There was a leavening of veterans, denoted by the chevrons on their sleeves, but most were new recruits, selected from the training camps to join the Imperial Guard directly. The only battle experience they had was the last few weeks of campaigning. A few men raised cheers for the Emperor as his horse trotted by, but most either just glanced at him, or stared at the ground in front of them as they tramped on, bending under the burden of their muskets and backpacks. The strain of forced marches through the cold days and nights of winter was evident in their grim and numbed expressions. These men must endure the hardships of the campaign better than their enemies if they were to win victories and save France, and their Emperor's throne.

Never had the odds been so heavily weighted against him, Napoleon reflected. And yet he felt the thrill of the conviction that he must somehow win. Sheer force of will had led him to dominate Europe, and he would die rather than bow to lesser men.

The sound of firing increased and Napoleon looked to the east, where a regiment of Sebastiani's hussars were galloping towards a low ridge in the direction of the guns. Beyond them, silhouetted against the overcast sky, were the vedettes who had fallen back. A twinge of anxiety clenched in the pit of Napoleon's stomach. There was not supposed to be any threat from the east, according to the intelligence reports. Yet something had caused the cavalry screen to fall back, and Sebastiani to concentrate his cavalry.

With a dull clop of hooves Ney trotted up and reined in. 'Seems like the patrols missed an enemy column, sire. It's only to be expected, given how little cavalry we can field.'

'Don't make excuses for your officers,' Napoleon snapped. 'Someone will answer for this incompetence.'

Ney looked at him sourly. 'Then let it be me, sire. The men are only as good as their commander.'

'Do not dissemble with me, Ney. Why, if I took your line of argument to its absurd conclusion, then I should be the man ultimately responsible.'

Ney said nothing for a moment, then looked back towards the ridge and spoke quietly. 'Those responsible will always be held to account, one way or another.'

Before Napoleon could reply the sounds of bugles cut through the chilly air. As the last of the French vedettes and patrols trotted back towards the main column the first of the enemy appeared. They wore the plumed helmets of cuirassiers, and the heavy coats that covered their breastplates made them seem large and formidable. Squadron after squadron appeared along the crest, and reined in.

Marshal Ney immediately halted his column and turned them to face the threat as Sebastiani's cavalry retired to the wings of the line of infantry. The artillery was still stuck in mud on the far side of the river and Napoleon cursed the lost opportunity to give the Austrian horsemen a savage pounding. His bad mood increased as a battery of horse artillery joined the enemy on the ridge, and soon the stubby barrels of howitzers were presented to the Frenchmen.

'Now we're in for it,' Ney muttered, and glanced down the line. 'I pray that the men hold firm.'

A moment later there was a brief series of flashes and puffs of smoke, and after a short delay the sound of the enemy's howitzers carried down the slope, sharper than the bellow of cannon. There was a burst of orange and red just above the heads of a company of infantry a hundred paces to Napoleon's left, and several men collapsed as if slapped down by a giant hand. More shells burst above the men, or slammed down into the muddy ground, fuses sputtering before they detonated, sending a spray of mud and fragments of iron slicing through the surrounding men. As the Austrian gunners reloaded and fired as quickly as they could, the casualties mounted along the French line, and Napoleon noticed that the men were slow to close up and fill the gaps as they stared fearfully at the howitzers.

'They'll not stand much more of this,' said Ney as he watched the men of the nearest battalion waver, some already edging away.

There was a loud splat nearby and Napoleon glanced sharply towards the noise. A shell had landed right in front of the nearest men, a company of grenadiers. The men flinched back, terror in their expressions as they tried to push away from the fiercely fizzing fuse burning on top of the spherical iron casing. Napoleon kicked his heels in and jerked the reins savagely. With a shrill whinny his horse turned towards the shell and galloped forward. It took seconds to reach the shell, but Napoleon was only aware of a serene stillness of mind that seemed to slow the passage of time as he took in myriad details of the line of soldiers reeling back, the impressions of boots and hooves in the soft ground, and then the ugly protrusion of black metal and sparks.

'Sire!' Ney shouted in alarm. 'What the hell are you—'

Then Napoleon's horse was directly over the shell, there was a flash and a roar that he felt as a blow, transmitted through the body of the horse beneath him. There was smoke in his eyes and mouth and his ears were numbed, and the saddle fell away beneath him as the horse collapsed, killed instantly by the explosion. Napoleon dropped the reins and struggled to rise up from the saddle. Hands grabbed his arms and pulled him away from the horse and held him up. Ney was staring anxiously into his face. 'Sire? Sire, are you injured?'

Still dazed and with his ears ringing Napoleon looked round and saw that the blast had torn the belly and legs of his horse to shreds. Intestines, organs and blood lay spattered either side of the animal's body. But the hapless beast had absorbed the full force of the explosion, and no one else had been hurt. Napoleon shook off the hands that supported him and adjusted his hat.

'I'm all right,' he announced. 'I'm not wounded.'

Ney glanced over him and then shook his head. 'What did you think you were doing, sire?'

Napoleon had to concentrate hard before he could summon a reply. 'The men were breaking. Besides, if I hadn't then we'd have both been killed. It was the logical thing to do. Now get me another horse.'

'Logical?' Ney frowned, and then barked a laugh. 'Sire, I swear, you have balls of steel!'

The men whom Napoleon had saved joined in his laughter, then one called out, 'Long live Napoleon! Long live the Emperor!'

The cry echoed down the line as the men cheered to see that he was alive. Napoleon climbed into the saddle of the mount one of Ney's staff officers hurriedly gave up, and raised his hat aloft, waving it towards the ridge.

'There is your enemy! Here is your Emperor! Providence is with us! Advance and drive them back!'

Ney bellowed the order and an instant later it was carried down the line and the French infantry began advancing towards the ridge, cheering Napeolon's name at the top of their voices. The Austrian cavalry had formed into lines, ready to charge, and still their guns lobbed shells towards the approaching French formations, causing further casualties. But the men's blood was up now, and they came on, bayonets angled towards the enemy, shouting out their battle cry, heedless of the violent flashes of fire as the shells burst over and amongst them. As his men approached the enemy, Napoleon saw the gun crew hurriedly limber the howitzers and then withdraw down the far side of the low ridge. The cavalry remained, as if the enemy commander could not make his mind up what to do. Finally courage won out over caution. When the two sides were no more than two hundred paces apart, the Austrian bugles sounded the advance.

The horses stepped forward, and then moved swiftly through a trot into a canter, bits jingling and hooves thumping down in a rumble that could be clearly felt through the ground. Ney halted his line, and ordered them to prepare to receive a cavalry charge. The front line went down on one knee, bracing the butts of their muskets firmly against the ground so that the points of their bayonets faced the oncoming cavalry in a thicket of pointed steel. The rear ranks thumbed back their firing hammers and took aim.

'Fire!' Ney roared and the order was repeated at once as flame and smoke spat at the enemy. From his saddle Napoleon saw scores of them topple from their mounts and tumble into the mud. The rest spurred on, thrusting their straight heavy blades towards the French as they attempted to charge across the muddy ground. The second and third ranks changed places and then another volley crashed out as the Austrians drew within fifty paces of Napoleon's men. Horses and men tumbled down, forcing others to swerve round them or draw up, creating yet further confusion as the charge was forced to halt, a scant twenty paces from the waiting infantrymen.

'That's it, lads!' Ney bellowed, as he punched his fist into the air. 'Hit 'em hard!'

They fired another volley. This time the range was so close that hardly a shot missed and over a hundred more of the enemy cavalry went down. Napoleon rode forward to join his men, and saw that the rearmost Austrians were already breaking away, urging their mounts back up towards the ridge. The panic leaped from man to man and soon all the surviving cavalrymen were falling back. A handful of officers, with their guidons, tried to rally the men on the ridge, but they flowed past and carried on.

The French line continued forward, picking its way over the heaped bodies of men and horses, with a handful of shots as injured horses, lashing out in agony and terror, were put out of their misery to prevent them from causing injury with their iron-shod hooves.

Ney reined in alongside Napoleon, his expression flushed with excitement. 'Did you see 'em? Ha! They bolted like rabbits. That'll do our lads a power of good.'

Napoleon returned his grin. He felt his heart beating quickly and the familiar thrill at the prospect of victory, and, beyond that, the hope that he might yet overcome his enemies.

'Press the attack, while their cavalry is disordered.'

'Yes, sire.'

'That'll be one enemy column less to deal with.'

Ney's expression became more sober. 'One, yes. But how many more are there?'

'Be assured, my friend, however many there are, as long as they serve them up to us one at a time, then we must win in the end.'

'And if they are not so foolish as to do that?'

Napoleon turned away and made no reply as he stared ahead. Ney was right to fear that the enemy would learn from their mistakes and concentrate their forces. Napoleon hoped that he could inflict enough damage to cause the allies to pause, and possibly retreat. In that event he could present himself to the French people as their saviour and might yet buy enough time to rebuild the army so that it could engage the enemy on more even terms in the following year.

The rational part of his mind mocked him for his hopes. So much of his strategy depended on the enemy being utterly foolish, and his own men performing like the finest soldiers he had ever commanded. There was not one chance in ten of winning the present campaign, he told himself. And yet . . . what else could he do?

Napoleon's thoughts were interrupted by Ney, who had pulled a little further ahead, and had now reached the crest of the ridge. On either side the line had halted and the men stared before them in silence. Napoleon dug his spurs in and cantered forward to join Ney, ready to bitterly rebuke the soldiers who were throwing away the chance to charge down the disordered enemy.

Instead, the words died in his mouth as he beheld the sight before him. Thousands of enemy infantry and horsemen were advancing across the countryside towards the slender French line. Dense columns rippled along lanes and over fields. Long trains of field guns and their wagons trundled amongst them. This was no rearguard they had encountered, but the vanguard of the main Austrian army itself.

'My God,' Ney muttered. 'There must be sixty thousand of them. At least.'

Napoleon nodded.

Ney scrutinised the approaching horde for a moment. On either side, the French soldiers, who had been cheering loudly a moment earlier, now stood in silence, aghast at the horde marching towards them. The cavalry that they had broken was already rallying at the foot of the slope, and more columns of horsemen were cantering forward to reinforce them.

'Sire, we cannot stand and fight. We must fall back. At once.'

Napoleon turned to inspect the ridge. The slope was steeper on the far side. He thought aloud. 'We have a good position here. If we can get our guns up here, then—'

'No, sire,' Ney said firmly. 'We cannot stand here. We will fall back across the river at Arcis and blow the bridge.'

Napoleon stared at him. 'You dare to give the orders?'

'I am the commander of these men,' Ney replied defiantly. 'I will not order them to go to a pointless death.'

'They are soldiers. They will do as their Emperor commands. As will you.'

'No. I will not. I am in command here, and my order is that they retreat. You may stay and fight if you wish.'

Without waiting for Napoleon to respond, Ney pulled his reins and steered his mount forward towards his staff officers. 'Fall back! Form column and march for the bridge at Arcis. In good order. This is not going to turn into a rout.'

Napoleon glared at him, speechless. His heart was filled with bitter outrage that Ney had defied him so forcefully to his face. Then he felt a stab of fear and anxiety. What had happened to his authority? Why did his presence no longer seem to effortlessly command the opinions of others? He watched Ney sidelong and wondered how much trust he could afford to place in his marshals any more. He felt a strange tingling in his arm and looked down to see that the hand holding his reins was trembling. He stared at it for a moment, then tightened his fingers and turned his mount towards Ney.

'Take command here,' he ordered flatly. 'I'm returning to headquarters.'

'Yes, sire,' Ney replied with a curt nod.

'Report to me later.' Napoleon turned his horse about and spurred it into a gallop, back down the slope towards the river.

Napoleon remained at his headquarters for the next four days, anxiously reading reports from his patrols and the commanders of the hard-pressed armies struggling to delay the advance of the allies. After the skirmish near Arcis there had been no more reports of isolated allied columns small enough for Napoleon to risk attacking. The enemy had adapted their strategy, he realised grimly. On the evening of the fourth day there was a message from Marmont informing the Emperor that he was powerless to prevent the allies from taking Paris. At once Napoleon summoned Marshal Ney and thrust the despatch towards him. 'Read.'

He settled into his chair by the fire and waited while Ney concentrated on the message. At length the marshal handed it back to Napoleon, who tossed it on to the fire. 'I want as few men aware of the situation as possible. Clear?'

'Yes, sire. What do you intend to do?'

'There is nothing I can do to save Paris. The Prussians will reach the capital at least three days before we could.' Napoleon paused a moment and then shrugged. 'Paris will fall. Therefore it makes sense to order Marmont to gather every man that he can and abandon Paris and combine forces with us.'

'And then?'

'We march east, and strike towards the Rhine. If we cut the enemy's supply lines, then there is still a chance to force an armistice on them and buy some time.'

'For what?'

Napoleon looked at him in surprise. 'Why, to continue the fight, of course.'

Ney sighed. 'Sire, the war is lost. You are defeated. France must come to terms.'

'Damn France!' Napoleon slapped his hand on to his breast. '*I am France. Me. And I will not surrender. Not while I yet draw breath.*'

Ney returned his glare with a calm, almost pitying expression. 'If Paris falls, then I will conduct my own negotiations with the Austrians.'

'How dare you?'

'Because I will do what is right, sire.' Ney stiffened his back and bowed his head. 'Is there anything else, sire?'

Napoleon's lips pressed together in a thin line as he regarded his subordinate. Then, when his temper had subsided, he shook his head. 'This is treason.'

'No, sire. Treason is committed when a man betrays the interests of his nation. Any man.'

'I see.' Napoleon sneered. 'Then I had better leave, and find myself a commander who still has the courage to fight.'

If Ney felt any anger at this slight to his bravery he showed no sign of it. Napoleon pointed towards the door. 'Now get out of my sight.'

After Ney had left, Napoleon slumped down into his chair and gazed into the fireplace. He watched the languid flames slowly die down into a failing glow as the night drew on, and then, at midnight, called for his horse to be saddled and a cavalry escort to be made ready to ride within the hour.

Leaving Ney and his men behind, Napoleon and his escort rode south-west, to ensure that he did not run into any enemy cavalry columns scouting deep into the French countryside. They stopped briefly to rest the following night, and then crossed the Seine and turned west and north towards the capital. Villagers and townsfolk stopped in surprise to see their Emperor pass through, and even though some cheered Napoleon rode on heedlessly. He dared not stop now, not when a royalist, emboldened by the approach of the allies, might make an attempt on his life.

As evening drew in on the last night of the month, Napoleon reached Essonnes, twenty miles from Paris, and sent for the commander of the garrison to arrange for food and forage for his escort before they began the last leg of the journey. A portly officer with grey wispy hair came puffing up to Napoleon as he entered the garrison headquarters, and bowed low.

'Sire, it is an honour to receive you.'

'Later. My men and horses need feeding before we take the Paris road.'

'Paris?' The colonel frowned. 'Then you have not heard?'

'Heard? Heard what?'

The colonel licked his lips nervously. 'Paris has fallen, sire.'

Napoleon stared at him, and then shook his head. 'No. Not yet. Marmont said he could hold on for a few more days.'

'Sire, Marshal Marmont surrendered the capital in the early hours. Paris is in the hands of the Prussians.' The colonel saw the stricken expression of his Emperor and then glanced down, refusing to meet Napoleon's eyes. 'I have a copy of the official proclamation, sire. Do you wish me to fetch it for you?'

'No . . . no. That is not necessary. If it is as you say, then there is nothing left for me in Paris. There is only one place left for me now.' Napoleon steeled himself. 'One place where I can summon my men, and make a stand.'

Chapter 50

Fontainebleau, 4 April 1814

The grounds of the chateau, once the preserve of the imperial court, were covered with tents. Most were makeshift arrangements hastily sewn together by veterans who knew the value of any kind of shelter from the elements. The others belonged to officers and varied in size according to rank. Thankfully the winter had passed and the early days of spring brought clear skies and slight warmth to comfort the weary men of the French Army. Inside the chateau the splendours of the décor were largely lost on the staff officers and couriers, coming and going, trailing mud across the finely tiled floors and expensive rugs. The mood was sombre and a wary quiet embraced the men whenever the Emperor emerged from his study.

Looking at them, Napoleon could see that many had already accepted defeat and were performing their duties merely from force of habit, waiting for the order to finally stop. He could hardly blame them, even though they stood at the heart of an army of sixty thousand men. Every last available soldier and gun had been concentrated around the chateau and the engineers had thrown up earthworks to cover the approaches to the camp. Yet the allies had three times that number in Paris alone, and another army was cautiously advancing from the east. Marshal Marmont, having agreed the armistice, was still in camp a few miles south of Paris, but had refused to respond to Napoleon's order to join him at Fontainebleau.

After a hurried breakfast of which he ate little, Napoleon had requested his marshals to attend him at the chateau. From the window of the private dining room set for the meeting Napoleon watched as they arrived, noting their grim demeanour as they dismounted and climbed the steps, which were lined by the men of the Old Guard standing to attention. At least there was still plenty of fight amongst the rankers, Napoleon reflected. When he had toured the camp on the previous two evenings they had cheered him as heartily as ever, as if encouraged by the prospect of making a last stand against the invader.

MacDonald was the last of the marshals to arrive, and as soon as he had passed within the entrance Napoleon sent a clerk to summon them to his presence.

They filed in, silently, and took their seats. Napoleon glanced from face to face, scrutinising their expressions and appearance. They looked as tired as their men. Some had found fresh uniforms to dress in for this meeting but most were stained with splatters of mud and Victor had one arm in a sling from a wound he had taken a few weeks earlier. Napoleon cleared his throat and stretched his hands out on the table.

'There is no need for any preamble, my friends; you know our situation. The question is, what should we do now? The army is still in being, the men's morale is high and the people of France will not endure the presence of an occupying army for long. There is still everything to fight for. I need to decide whether to risk a battle on the streets of Paris itself, or attempt a wider strategic manoeuvre round the enemy's flank. So, gentlemen, I need your advice on which course of action would best profit us.'

No one responded. Some exchanged looks, while others looked down or stared fixedly at some feature of the room.

'Come, gentlemen, speak freely.'

'Very well then, sire,' Ney responded, half turning in his seat so that he could face his Emperor directly. 'I speak for most of the marshals here, including those who were . . .' his lips curled into a brief look of contempt before he continued, 'unprepared to face the truth and say what needs to be said.'

'And what would that be?' Napoleon asked.

'That France has fallen. Its armies are defeated. Its treasury is empty. The people want peace. There is no hope of overcoming the allies. It is plain for all to see. Even you, sire, must recognise the hopelessness of the situation.'

'It is not hopeless,' Napoleon replied, forcing himself to keep his voice calm. 'Does your memory fail you? Our position was far worse at Marengo, yet we snatched a victory from the enemy by the end of the day.'

'Marengo was a long time ago, sire. We were different men, fighting on foreign soil. If we had lost the battle, we would still have had a chance to win the campaign. Now? Paris is lost. There is nothing left to save. There is no reason to continue the war.'

'There is every reason! While the army exists, and you and I still live. While either of us can still hold a sword in our hand and spit defiance at our enemies, there is a reason to continue the fight!'

Napoleon stared at him, wide-eyed and enraged, but Ney refused to give way and steadily returned his glare. 'That, sire, is the counsel of a man who no longer regards war as a means to an end, but embraces it purely for its own sake.'

Napoleon was stunned. Ney had defied him before, in private, where such words could be forgiven and in time forgotten. But this? In front of his peers, the highest-ranking officers of the empire? What he had dared to say could never be retracted.

'Marshal Ney, I dismiss you. Your rank and titles are forfeit, and you are banished from our presence for ever. Leave us now, and never return.'

Ney could not help a faint smile. 'No.'

'No?'

'No. The war is over. I speak for all of us.' He waved a hand round the other officers seated at the table. 'Does any man deny it?'

There was no response. Napoleon leaned forward and pointed at MacDonald. 'You have sworn an oath to obey me. Would you betray me now, at the hour of my greatest need of you?'

MacDonald glanced at Ney and received a nod of encouragement before he replied. 'Sire, I also swore an oath to serve and protect France. I cannot honour both oaths. My duty to my country outweighs my duty to you, sire.'

'Pah!' Napoleon turned to Victor. 'And you?'

'I share the opinion of Marshal Ney, sire.'

Napoleon looked round at them. 'Is there no man with honour here? Well?'

His words hung in the ensuing silence, then Napoleon sneered. 'Cowards all. If you will not obey me, then damn you. I shall summon Marmont to command the army under me.'

Ney shook his head, and reached into his jacket to pull out a folded piece of paper. 'I have been in contact with Marmont since I arrived at Fontainebleau. He shares my views, sire. Indeed, he goes further. I received this at dawn. Marmont has gone over to the allies with his men. Talleyrand has established a provisional government and issued a decree that your reign is over.'

'Give it to me!'

Ney slid the message across the table and Napoleon snatched it up, unfolded it and scanned the contents. His lips pressed together as he read the details for himself. He tossed it back and glared at his marshals with contempt.

'So, not one of my marshals is prepared to fight. Very well, then I shall do without you, and promote more worthy men from amongst those officers who still know the value of loyalty and patriotism. At least I have no doubt that the rank and file will still obey me.'

'No, sire. They will obey their marshals. Did you think we should confront you without first having talked this through with our subordinates? Sire, if you force the issue, the army will turn on itself – the officers against the men. Is that how you wish this to end?'

Napoleon gritted his teeth. He felt trapped, and clenched his fists in his lap as he stared at his officers defiantly. At length he slumped back into his chair and cleared his throat. 'What would you have me do, then?'

'Abdicate,' Ney replied at once. 'Go into exile.'

'What?'

'Abdicate, on the condition that you do so in favour of your son. At least that way, we spare France from any return of the Bourbons.'

Napoleon considered the idea, even though it pierced him to the soul. Defeat was one thing, humiliation quite another. The prospect of being reduced to the status of a prisoner, exiled to some European backwater for the rest of his life, was unbearable. He would be mocked by his enemies and pitied by his former friends and subjects, condemned to a life of lingering insignificance. The thought made him sick. On the other hand, as long as a Bonaparte was on the throne, then there would be a means for Napoleon to exercise his influence, and one day resume his powers. He looked at Ney, wondering if the man understood that such an abdication would only curtail his power temporarily. He took on a resigned air and nodded slowly. 'You are right, my dear Michel. I must sacrifice my throne for the good of my people. They would expect nothing less of me.'

The current of relief that rippled through his officers was palpable. Even Ney's stern demeanour melted momentarily as he could not help smiling at the outcome of the confrontation between the marshals and their Emperor.

'Sire, your people will be eternally grateful to you for this.'

'And so they should,' Napoleon replied. 'We'd better draft a proposal for our enemies.'

'It is already done, sire,' Ney admitted. 'I had Caulaincourt draw it up as soon as I had the news from Marmont. It only requires your signature and then the Foreign Minister and Marshal MacDonald will depart for Paris.'

Napoleon smiled coldly. 'It seems that you have planned this well.'

'If I have, it is because I learned from a good master.'

The compliment was a poor palliative that fooled no man in the room. Napoleon rose from his chair. 'Then it is done. Make your offer to the allies and let me know the outcome. I will remain in the chateau. You, gentlemen, are dismissed.' He looked round at them. 'I just hope that you have made the right decision. If not, then France will never forgive you. Think on that.'

He turned away and strode towards the door, leaving Ney and the other marhsals to arrange the details of the negotiations with the enemy.

Caulaincourt and MacDonald rode out towards the allied outposts later that morning. For two days they negotiated with the commanders of the armies that had conquered Paris and were now closing in on the remnants of the Grand Army. Then they reported back to Napoleon, informing him that the allies would only accept an unconditional abdication. The decision on who should succeed him would be theirs alone.

In the days that followed, as the details of his fate were discussed in Paris, Napoleon fell into deep despair. He could not eat, and sat in a chair by a small fire, brooding in silence as his servants silently came and went, serving and removing meals that lay cold and untouched on their trays.

At length, Napoleon's hand slipped inside his shirt and felt for the small pouch of belladonna and hellebore that he had kept hanging from his neck since the retreat from Moscow when he had so nearly fallen into the hands of the Cossacks. His fingers gently cupped the pouch and he pressed the soft leather, feeling the deadly powder within. There was little deliberation over the decision. His death would cheat the allies of their prize, and there was comfort and satisfaction to be had from that small victory.

Slipping the thin silk cord over his head, Napoleon withdrew the pouch and steadily untied the binding. He eased the leather open, and stared a moment at the powder, pallid as ground bones. Then he tipped it into a glass, taking care not to spill any of it, before pouring in some of the watered wine left on a meal tray. He stirred the mixture with his fork, then lifted the glass. He avoided smelling it, in case it caused him to hesitate, and provided the least excuse to reconsider his decision. He raised the glass to his lips and drank swiftly, setting the glass down with a sharp tap. Then he sat still, staring into space, shocked by the enormity of the deed. He smiled as he recalled his coronation, how he had taken the imperial wreath from the hands of the Pope and placed it on his own head, announcing to the world that none but Napoleon was worthy of crowning Napoleon. Now the same principle of greatness applied to his death. Only his hand was worthy of the act. That thought calmed his fear of the oblivion into which his mind would be cast, if not his fame. He coughed and then called for his servant.

'Fetch Caulaincourt. Bring him to me at once.'

'Yes, sire.'

'He is to bring pen and paper with him.'

The servant bowed his head and hurried away, leaving Napoleon to mentally compose his final testament.

By the time Caulaincourt appeared, Napoleon could already feel the poisons working upon him. Despite the fire, he felt cold, and shivered. His skin began to feel clammy and sweat pricked out on his brow. Inside, his guts clenched painfully, and an aching nausea tightened his throat.

'Sire, you're ill,' Caulaincourt said the moment he sat down opposite his Emperor. 'Let me summon your surgeon.'

'No. There is no need. It's too late for that. I am dying.'

'Sire! I will get help.'

'No!' The effort of raising his voice caused a spasm of pain and Napoleon's features twisted for a moment, until the worst of it had passed. Sweat trickled down his cheeks. 'I have taken poison. This is the end.'

The Foreign Minister looked horrified. Napoleon touched his hand. 'I want you to take down my final statement. I don't know how much time is left. So we must begin. Quickly, Caulaincourt.'

'Yes, sire.' He nodded, and swiftly took out his notebook, rested it on his knees and poised the tip of his pencil on the paper.

'I will give you the sense of it, then you will compose it for general consumption. Be faithful to my intent, but ensure that what is left is clearly expressed and well crafted.'

Caulaincourt nodded.

'Very well. I wish it known that I was never the warmonger my enemies would depict me as. All I desired was peace and order amongst the peoples of Europe, even if that could only be achieved by subordinating their will to mine. I trust that my enemies will be as magnanimous in victory as I was when I triumphed over them. Therefore, all those who prospered under my reign should not be disgraced and punished under whatever rule is imposed hereafter. That includes my family, my heir and those gallant officers who have sacrificed so much for France. Their glory must not be denied, however much my fame is impugned and denigrated. They have rendered good service to France and France should honour them accordingly.' He paused to make sure that Caulaincourt was keeping up, then, collecting his thoughts, he continued. 'If my son, the dearest being on this earth, is not to reign after me, then I wish that he is at least raised a Frenchman and given the opportunity to learn of his father's achievements, without rancour. His mother, my beloved wife, Empress Marie-Louise, is free to return to her native Austria . . .'

A sudden surge of nausea swept through Napoleon and he leaned over the side of his chair and vomited. Caulaincourt started to rise, but Napoleon waved him back. He vomited again, and again. Each time it felt as if an iron fist was squeezing his insides like a vice. Then, when his stomach was empty, he continued retching, letting out tight groans as his head hung over the acrid stench rising from the glutinous puddle below. Finally the spasm passed and Napoleon lay back, shivering violently. His eyes flickered open and he looked at Caulaincourt.

'I can say no more. I leave it to you to craft my testimony as elegantly as you can.'

Caulaincourt swallowed anxiously. 'I will not fail you, sire.'

'Good.' Napoleon sat up and rose to his feet unsteadily. 'Now help me to that couch.'

Caulaincourt laid aside his notebook and supported the Emperor's weight as best he could as they made their way over to the couch. Napoleon collapsed upon it with a sigh. 'My thanks. For this, and all the services you have done me.'

'Sire . . . I . . .'

'Say nothing. Just leave me now. Tell the servants no one is to enter the room, for any reason. You can come back tomorrow and see . . . what has happened.'

'Yes, sire. I understand.'

Napoleon took his hand and squeezed it. 'Goodbye then. Now go.'

Caulaincourt hesitated for a moment, then returned to his chair to retrieve his notebook before walking steadily to the door and leaving the room. Once he had gone, Napoleon let out a groan and clutched his hands to his stomach. A fierce stabbing pain throbbed through his guts, and his entire body felt as if it was in the grip of some fever. The physician who had prepared the poison had told him it would be quick and relatively painless. Napoleon cursed him for a liar as he curled up on his side and waited for the end, the steady tick of a clock and the crackle of the fire marking the agonisingly slow passage of what time remained to him. The torment of the poison robbed him of the calm state of grace he had hoped would accompany his death. It occurred to him that this was what it must have been like for Lannes, and all those others, who had gone to their deaths slowly and in agony. There was no glory in this death, no sense of destiny, just the wretched writhing of an animal in its death throes, begging for an end to it all.

The hours passed, and death did not come, just more pain. As night gave way to dawn, and pale light crept through the gaps in the curtains of the study, Napoleon realised that he was not going to die after all. The poison, two years in the pouch, had lost its potency and had only served to deepen the humiliation to which he had been condemned. Gradually the fever passed, he stopped sweating and the agony in his stomach subsided, leaving him in despair.

At the eighth hour the door creaked open and Caulaincourt quietly entered the study, causing Napoleon to stir.

'Sire, thank God!' Caulaincourt exclaimed as he rushed over. 'You live!'

'So it seems,' Napoleon whispered miserably.

'Then I'll summon the surgeon.'

Napoleon did not protest. If he was not to die, then what point was there in prolonging this suffering? 'Call him then.'

'Yes, sire.' Caulaincourt jumped up, then sensing his master's disappointment he paused. 'Sire, you still live for a reason. Destiny must have a purpose for you yet.'

'Really?' Napoleon shook his head. He did not care any longer. He was too tired. He rolled on to his back and stared at the ceiling as Caulaincourt's footsteps hurried away. If he had cheated death, then death had cheated him also.

'Those are their final terms, sire,' Caulaincourt reported to the Emperor three days later, handing over a sealed document. 'The allies will allow you to retain the title of Emperor. You will be given the island of Elba to rule. The French treasury will provide you with an income of two million francs a year. You will be permitted to take a thousand soldiers with you, and any additional servants you may require. The Bonaparte family is to renounce all its other crowns in exchange for pensions provided by the French government, and the Empress will be granted the Duchy of Parma.'

Napoleon stared at the document in his hand, but did not open it. His pale skin still looked faintly waxy, as if it was stretched over his skull. The poison had left him feeling weak and apathetic and he could only stomach the lightest of meals. He lay, wrapped in a thick blanket, on a chaise longue in his study. He looked up. 'In exchange for my unconditional abdication?'

'Yes, sire,' Caulaincourt nodded. 'It was the best I could do. The Prussians were all for having you shot. I played on what was left of the regard the Tsar once had for you after the Treaty of Tilsit. It was the Tsar who offered you Elba.'

'Nevertheless, I am to be exiled.'

'Yes, sire. You will be required to remain on the island until the time of your death. You will not be permitted to enter into any treaty with another kingdom and you will accept a resident appointed by the allied powers through whom you will communicate with them.'

'While this resident spies on me.'

Caulaincourt nodded.

'I see.' Napoleon cradled his forehead in one hand as he continued to stare at the document. 'How long have they given me to consider their offer?'

'You are to sign it at once for me to return to Paris. If they do not have your agreement by midnight tomorrow then the offer is withdrawn and a bounty will be offered for your capture.'

Napoleon's lips curled at the insulting prospect of being treated like a criminal, but there was no time and no choice in the matter. He must accept.

'Very well,' he sighed wearily. 'I thank you for your efforts, Caulaincourt. Now fetch me that inkwell and pen over there.'

While Caulaincourt crossed the study to the Emperor's desk, Napoleon broke the seal and opened the treaty document. The clauses were simple and direct and a space had been left at the bottom for his signature. Caulaincourt returned and held out the pen, then removed the lid of the inkwell and offered it to Napoleon. 'Sire?'

Napoleon gazed at the treaty with malevolence. Every point had been calculated to diminish his glory and that of his entire family. It was strange, he mused, that even offended as he was, there was no desire in him to continue the fight at this moment. Exhaustion and his recovery from taking the poison conspired to rob him of the urge to resist his enemies. Flattening the paper on the surface of the couch, Napoleon dipped the pen into the ink and tapped off the excess. He hesitated momentarily before hurriedly scratching his signature, and handing the pen back to Caulaincourt.

'There.'

'Yes, sire.' The ambassador delicately took the treaty and wafted it in the air to speed the drying of the ink. 'I'll away to Paris immediately.

When you receive confirmation that they have the treaty, you are to leave for Elba.'

'So soon?' Napoleon eased himself back down and pulled the covers over his chest. Elba? He recalled the island, a miserable nonenity off the coast of Italy. The allies had found him the smallest of possible kingdoms to rule. But not one person in the whole of Europe would fail to see that in reality Elba was nothing more than a prison. Napoleon closed his eyes and Caulaincourt quietly left the room.

'Elba it is, then,' Napoleon whispered. 'For now.'

Chapter 51

Arthur

Toulouse, 13 April 1814

'Do you think it might be a trick, sir?' asked Somerset as he stood at Arthur's side, squinting through his telescope towards the gates on the eastern side of the town. They had been opened some twenty minutes earlier, and now a small party stood a short distance in front of the defences. Through his own telescope Arthur could see that they were mostly civilians, clustered together under a white flag.

'I think not. It seems that they want to parley,' Arthur said. 'After all, Soult has abandoned them. They have nothing to gain from defending the town.'

Even before dawn, Arthur's cavalry patrols had discovered the French column, picking its way to the south-east under cover of darkness. General Hill had immediately set off in pursuit, with orders to observe Soult and not engage him. Toulouse was a valuable prize and the army needed to rest and recover from the previous day's battle for the Heights of Calvinet which dominated the town.

'Hm.' Somerset slowly trained his telescope along the walls. 'There are still plenty of cannon on the walls, and I can see some soldiers.'

'That may be,' Arthur muttered, then snapped his telescope shut. 'However, there's no harm in talking to them. Ride down there and see what they want.'

Somerset lowered his telescope and nodded. 'And if they want to discuss terms, sir? What shall I say?'

'They are to surrender, without conditions, else we will sack the town.' Arthur paused, and then smiled thinly. 'You might mention that we have a division of Spaniards with us who are inclined to show little pity to the French.'

Somerset looked shocked. 'That's hardly fair, sir. Morillo's men are as disciplined as any in the army.'

'Yes, but they don't know that,' Arthur replied patiently as he nodded towards the waiting Frenchmen. 'Now then, don't tarry, Somerset.'

Arthur watched as his aide mounted his horse and cantered down the slope to cross the canal that separated the Heights from the town. The Spanish corps and Beresford's two divisions were stretched out along the Heights, on either side of Arthur's command post, and their sullen mood was evident in the slowness with which they had roused themselves at dawn and apathetically set to digging the earthworks Arthur had ordered constructed in case Soult decided to counter-attack. Even though the French army appeared to have quit Toulouse, Arthur thought it prudent to continue the work. If nothing else, it gave his men something to take their minds off the bitter fighting of the previous day. It had cost the allies over four thousand men to take the Heights, and across the slopes, raked by roundshot and canister, were clusters of freshly dug graves. With the war all but over, Arthur felt such losses ever more keenly. Even so, all the news from the north was encouraging. Paris had fallen and Bonaparte and what was left of his army must surely be compelled to surrender soon.

The distant figure of Somerset had reined in before the small crowd in front of the gates and was engaged in conversation with a man who had emerged as their spokesman. Arthur raised his telescope to follow the exchange more closely. A moment later, Somerset dismounted and the Frenchman rushed forward to embrace him, kissing the British officer on both cheeks. A light breeze lifted the white flag behind them and now Arthur could make out a design that had been hidden in the folds, a blue fleur-de-lys, the emblem of the Bourbons.

So that was it, Arthur thought with relief: the royalists had taken over the town. A moment later Somerset was in the saddle again and galloping back across the canal and up the slope towards Arthur. His face was flushed with excitement as he reined in and swung himself down.

'Sir, I have the honour to report that Toulouse is ours.'

'Yes, I gathered.'

'The mayor asks me to convey his fraternal greetings to you.'

'That's very fine of him, I'm sure.'

'He asks if you will do him the honour of addressing him, and the other worthies, before entering the town.'

'Not for the present.' Arthur shook his head wearily. 'There will be time for that. Tell the mayor that I would be grateful if he permitted me to set up my headquarters in his offices. When that is done I will be pleased to celebrate the liberation of Toulouse.'

'Yes, sir,' his aide replied, somewhat deflated. 'As you wish.'

Arthur looked at him sternly. 'Now then, Somerset, the war is not over, and the army must be commanded and its needs catered for. Is that clear?'

'Yes, sir.'

'Good. Once we have attended to our duties, you will be free to enjoy the hospitality of Toulouse.'

'Yes, sir.' Somerset glanced down towards the Frenchmen waiting outside the gate. 'What about them? They seem quite keen to greet their liberators, sir.'

'Oh, damn it, then send Beresford. Let him enjoy the mob's adulation if he likes.'

'Yes, sir.'

Arthur stared towards the small crowd at the town gates. 'I'll take my turn in Paris, when the time comes, if that makes you feel any better, Somerset.'

'It does, sir.' The aide smiled warmly.

While General Beresford and his officers, accompanied by several companies of grenadiers, basked in the adulation of the French townsfolk, Arthur and his staff officers entered by a smaller gate further along the wall. Somerset had arranged for one of the mayor's clerks to lead them through the back streets to the town square. Every so often the thin young Frenchman would turn and grin and call out, '*Vive le Roi et vivent les anglais!*' and curious faces would appear at the windows and doors of the houses the small party passed by.

'If that fellow keeps this up, we shall attract a crowd of our own,' Arthur hissed testily.

'You can hardly blame him, sir,' said Somerset. 'With the prospect that Napoleon will be forced to make peace any day now.'

The man cried out again and Arthur glared at him, to no effect, and let out an exasperated sigh. His officers read his expression and kept their silence for the rest of the short ride to the *mairie*. When they were shown to the suite of offices assigned to them they began to arrange the desks while they waited for the wagon carrying the army's records chests to arrive. The sounds of the cheering carried to the heart of the town and every so often a small cluster of excited civilians would hurry by on their way to join the celebrations.

Early in the afternoon the mayor arrived, somewhat drunk, to invite Arthur and his officers to a special performance of patriotic songs and recitals to be held at the town's theatre that evening, followed by a banquet. In the interests of cementing the friendship of the people of

Toulouse, Arthur accepted, and grudgingly made arrangements to have a bath and shave while his baggage was collected from the camp. So it was that he was standing before a mirror, face lathered in soap and razor poised above his throat, when the door to the washroom was unceremoniously opened and Somerset rushed in, accompanied by another officer whom Arthur recognised as Colonel Ponsonby, from the army outside Bayonne.

'What the devil?' Arthur growled, lowering the razor. 'You surprise me like that, and it won't be an enemy bullet that takes me. I'll die by my own bloody hand!'

'Sorry, sir.' Somerset thrust Ponsonby forward. 'But you must hear the news.'

'Ponsonby?' Arthur frowned. 'What are you doing here?'

'I was sent to find you directly General Hope received the officers sent from Paris.'

'Officers? What officers?'

'Colonel Cooke, and Colonel St-Simon of the French army, sir.'

'Well?'

'Sir, I have extraordinary news for you.'

There was no mistaking what the man would say. Arthur held up his hand to silence the colonel. 'It's peace. I knew that we would have it.'

'Aye, sir, we've all expected it. But there's more. Napoleon has abdicated.'

'Abdicated? It's time indeed.' Arthur replied without thinking. Then the full truth of it struck him. Napoleon was finished. With no throne, he would no longer be able to threaten the peace of Europe. At once his severe expression was split by a wide grin. Tossing his razor down into the basin, he clasped Ponsonby's hands. 'Abdicated! You don't say so?'

'I do, sir.'

'By God . . . by God, this is wonderful!' He turned to Somerset and could not help laughing. His whole mind and body was seized by the most pure and irresistible delight. 'Hurrah! Hurrah!' Releasing Ponsonby's hands, he snapped his fingers and hopped lightly from side to side. 'That I should live to see this!'

'Just what I was thinking,' Somerset chuckled as he stared at his superior's unprecedented display of jubilation.

The night's banquet was a raucous affair as British, Spanish and Portuguese officers celebrated with their French counterparts from the town's garrison. Just as the main course was cleared away the two

476

colonels sent from Paris arrived, bearing the official despatch. Arthur read it through, then stood to announce to the hushed audience that Bonaparte was to leave France for ever before the end of the month. Louis, the brother of the previous king, was to be returned to the throne. As the cheers echoed round the banqueting hall he sent for champagne to toast King Louis. As the glasses were recharged General Alava, who had recently re-joined the army from Madrid, quickly stood up and raised his glass towards Arthur.

'To Field Marshal the Marquess of Wellington, *el liberador de España!*'

A great roar of approval went up from the assembled officers and they downed their champagne. Then one of the Portuguese commanders made a new toast. '*El Douro* – saviour of Portugal!' There was another cheer before the mayor of Toulouse staggered up and toasted Arthur in broken English. 'To Monsieur Wellington. He save France!'

This time the cheering did not end. The officers thumped their fists down on the table in a deafening rhythm that set the remaining cutlery and glasses trembling. Arthur slowly rose at their acclamation. He bowed his head to each side, and tried to make his thanks, but it was impossible. At that moment, as he looked round at his men, it was not joy, nor triumph, that filled his heart. It was gratitude, and an almost paternal affection for those who had become closer than family to him.

Slowly the cheering subsided and then there was a respectful but expectant silence as they waited for him to speak. Arthur smiled nervously, then lowered his head and shook it gently, afraid his voice would betray the emotions that gripped him. Somerset saw his difficulty and hurriedly rose to his feet, leaning towards his commander.

'Shall we have coffee, sir?'

'What's that?' Arthur mumbled.

'There's been a deal of champagne drunk tonight. Some of the officers will need sobering up before they go back on duty.'

'Yes. Coffee.' Arthur nodded. He raised his head, and cleared his throat. 'I, ah, thank you all, most humbly. And much as I hate to break up the night's celebrations, it is time for coffee.'

Some groaned at his words, but most were just bemused, and happily cheered and clapped the suggestion.

As he sat down, Arthur turned to Colonel Cooke and his French companion. 'Do you have a copy of the despatch for Marshal Soult?'

'Yes, sir.'

'Then you must find him at once. Ride on, to the south-east. He cannot have more than a day's start on you.'

'Tonight, sir?' Cooke replied, surprised.

'Yes, tonight. Hill's men are pursuing him, and I'll not have one more life lost through any avoidable delay in getting the news through to Soult. Go now.'

'Yes, sir,' Cooke said, and gestured to Colonel St-Simon to follow him as he strode from the banqueting hall.

Most of the French soldiers in the south were eager to believe the news, but Soult refused to accept that his master had fallen until he received confirmation from the hand of Berthier. Having allowed his men to celebrate the victory, Arthur soon began to issue the orders for their withdrawal to Bordeaux, from where they would be shipped home to Britain in due course. While the men were excited by the prospect of returning home, their officers were less sanguine once the initial delight over the great victory had faded. For many of them peace would mean half-pay and no chance of further promotion.

While the army began to adjust to the prospect of peace after two decades of war, Arthur travelled to Paris to take his place amongst the victors as they led the parade through the streets towards the Tuileries. There, the new King of France would review the soldiers and offer his gratitude for the sacrifices made by the allies in ridding Europe of the scourge of the Corsican Tyrant.

On 3 May, the day before the parade, Somerset presented Arthur with a letter from the Prince Regent as he sat eating his breakfast in his rooms in the suite provided for him and his staff in the Tuileries. Arthur lowered his knife and fork and finished chewing a morsel of lamb chop as he broke the seal and read through the contents. At length he lowered the letter on to the table and picked up his knife and fork to continue his breakfast. Somerset let out a low sigh of frustration.

'Well, sir?'

Arthur cut off another chunk of lamb and glanced up. 'I have been offered the embassy here in Paris. Oh, and it is confirmed that I am officially gazetted as the Duke of Wellington.'

Somerset beamed. 'And not before time. May I be the first to offer my congratulations, your grace?'

'I thank you, Somerset. It is, as you say, overdue, in as much as it honours all those who have served under me these last years.'

It might have sounded like a platitude from another man, but Somerset knew his commander well enough to know that the sentiment was heartfelt. For his part, Arthur felt a pang of resentment that this recognition of the army's achievement should have been delayed by the enemies of his family in Parliament. The wretchedness of petty political intrigue had constantly threatened to undermine him and his men throughout their campaigns in the Peninsula. Well, it was better that reward came late than not at all.

Somerset looked out of the window, across the public square outside the palace, and saw that the crowds had already begun to mass along the route of the procession. 'You'll have quite an audience today, your grace. All come to see the general who trounced Bonaparte's marshals.' Somerset paused. 'It is a shame that you never had the chance to face him in battle.'

Arthur shook his head. 'No, I am glad that I never did. I would at any time rather have heard that a reinforcement of forty thousand men had joined the French army, than that he had arrived to take command.'

'Be that as it may, I have every confidence that you would have beaten him, your grace. You are the better general.'

'Well, we shall never put it to the test. In any case, I'll not be appearing before Paris as a soldier. The war is at an end, and as I am to be ambassador, then I shall dress as a diplomat. A plain coat, white stock and breeches and round hat will give the right impression, I think. Now then, if I might finish my breakfast in peace?'

'As you wish, your grace.' Somerset bowed his head and left the room.

Popping another chunk of lamb into his mouth Arthur chewed quickly. It was a strange quirk of fate that while he had beaten the cream of Bonaparte's marshals, and Bonaparte had beaten most of the allies' finest commanders, the two of them had not clashed. It was inevitable that the Corsican's apologists would for ever claim that their hero would have mastered the British commander had they met, Arthur mused.

The parade of the allied leaders and their finely turned out soldiers was greeted by cheers of joy by the vast majority of the crowd. Only a handful watched with sullen resentment, Arthur noticed as he rode beside Castlereagh, returning the crowd's acclaim with a curt nod of the head or brief wave of his gloved hand.

Castlereagh leaned towards him. 'Odd, ain't it? You fight the French for over twenty years, and then they greet you like a hero.'

'Peace and deliverance from tyranny are apt to make one cheerful,' Arthur replied drily.

'Indeed.' Castlereagh waved to the crowd, and drew a fresh cheer from them as they waved hats and coloured strips of cloth in a shimmering frenzy. His expression hardened briefly. 'Then 'tis a shame that the new King of Spain has failed to learn the lesson. You have heard of the troubling situation in Spain, I take it.'

Arthur nodded. On his return from exile at Valençay, Ferdinand had immediately set about imposing his authority in the harshest possible manner. All the reforms that had been instituted by the Cortes had been overturned and those who protested were thrown into jail. It was a hard thing for the Spanish people, who had fought one tyrant for so long, to have another imposed upon them.

'Very well, then,' Castlereagh continued. 'I shall need you to go to Madrid as soon as possible and try to talk some sense into the King.'

'Me?'

'Why not? You are the man who liberated them from the French, after all. You have more moral authority there than any man I could send, and, I dare say, more than even their new King.' Castlereagh paused to smile brilliantly at a distinguished-looking woman watching the procession from a balcony. 'Madame de Staël. A brilliant mind, that woman. You must look her up when you return here to take charge of our embassy. Speaking of women, you must be looking forward to seeing that wife and those sons of yours, eh? First time in years. By God, your boys must have been infants when you left.' Castlereagh glanced at him with a kindly expression. 'I fear you shall be as a stranger to them all.'

Arthur thought a moment. The prospect of returning to Kitty troubled him. He had been a soldier for far longer than he had been a husband, and he feared that peace would make the strains of their marriage unavoidable. He cleared his throat. 'I will see to my men at Bordeaux first. I owe them my thanks, and I must see that they are returned to Britain as swiftly as possible. Then I shall return home to my family.'

Castlereagh looked surprised, and then shrugged. 'As you will. Though I dare say that your nation will want its share of you before you can be allowed to enjoy the privacy of family life. You must know that all England holds you in far higher regard than even these people.' He gestured at the cheering crowd. 'Best get used to being the darling of the public, Wellington.'

Arthur nodded, but inside he felt himself shudder at the prospect. The affections of the mob were as changeable as the winds, and just as lacking in substance. So much had happened in the space of a month, he reflected. It was hard to measure the passage of days when each was so filled with events. The pace had been delirious, yet Arthur knew that he had an obligation to his soldiers to ensure that they were able to reap the profits of peace as soon as possible.

Once the celebrations in Paris were over Arthur returned to the army's new headquarters at Bordeaux to oversee the dispersal of the soldiers who had served him, and England, so well during the war in the Peninsula and southern France. The British regiments were bound for a variety of destinations. Most would return to Britain, but some were destined for Ireland, the West Indies and the ongoing war in the American colonies.

The first formations to leave the army were the remaining Spanish troops, and then the Portuguese, setting off towards the Pyrenees, cheering Arthur as they marched past. The only ticklish business was what to do with the small army of camp followers, especially the 'soldiers' wives' – the women who had attached themselves to many of the British soldiers, and borne them children. Very few were allowed to accompany their men back to England, and not a few of the soldiers simply refused to accept responsibility for them. So it was that Arthur watched a third column, weighed down by misery and the fear of an uncertain future, as it tramped away towards the border along with a motley collection of mules and carts.

It remained for Arthur to draft the last of his General Orders before the army was broken up. As he wrote, late into the evening of his last night with his soldiers, Arthur was well aware that he had honed the finest army in Europe and his men would have marched anywhere and done anything at his command. For all the desire for peace that burned in his heart he could not help feeling regret over the loss of such a formidable body of soldiers. Soon, all that was left to them would be the memories of their campaigns, the slowly dwindling impressions of battles that had shaped history. These would be tales recounted by stooped veterans to generations yet to be born, few of whom would ever grasp the significance of what Arthur's men had achieved, outnumbered and far from home.

While he was certain to have won his place in the memory of his nation Arthur was saddened to think that those lesser in rank who had fought at his side were destined to slip into his shadow. He paused a moment to collect his thoughts before penning the last paragraph.

Although circumstances may alter the relations in which the Field Marshal stood towards his men, so much to his satisfaction, he assures them that he shall never cease to feel the warmest interest in their welfare and honour; and that he will be at all times happy to be of any service to those to whose conduct, discipline and gallantry their country is so much indebted.

Arthur lowered his pen and read through the order. The words seemed a poor vehicle for the sense of affection and obligation that filled his heart. He could only hope that the men understood him well enough by now to see beyond the words. He called for Somerset to take the order for duplication and distribution throughout the army. Then he made his way up to his sleeping chamber. The hour was late, well past midnight, and at first light he would be leaving his men, his comrades, and returning home.

Chapter 52

London, 24 June 1814

'By God, I've had enough of this,' Arthur muttered wearily as the carriage and mounted escort halted yet again as the crowd blocked the way ahead. Ever since he had landed at Dover the previous day, Arthur had been thronged by his countrymen. Word of his return had spread along the road to London well ahead of his carriage and excited mobs of men, women and children, of all social stations, waited to catch a glimpse of the man who had delivered them, and Europe, from the clutches of the French Emperor. At first Arthur had been happy to rise up and lean out of the window to return their greetings, but as each occasion caused further delay, he settled back into his seat and merely nodded or waved as they approached the capital.

Now they were stuck in a street not far from Westminster Bridge. Outside, the cheery faces of the people contrasted with the grimy brickwork of a tannery from which smoke and stench curled into the warm air of a summer's day. Turning to look through the small window under the driver's bench, Arthur could see that a large man had stopped the carriage and was gesturing to his friends to take the reins of the six horses that had pulled it from the last posting inn.

'What the devil is he doing?' Arthur muttered.

'Do you wish me to go and see, your grace?' asked Somerset.

'By all means. Tell the fellow to clear the way and let us through.'

Somerset nodded, and opened the carriage door. Immediately there was a deafening cheer from outside, which swiftly fell away as Somerset looked up and the people could see that it was not their hero. He stepped down on to the road, shutting the door behind him. 'Let me through! Out of my way there!'

Arthur settled back into his seat and stared at the rear of the carriage, ignoring the faces pressed round the small windows of each door. Outside he heard a voice calling out above the din of the crowd.

'Beggin' your pardon, sir, we don't mean no 'arm. Me and these others are just wantin' ter drag 'is grace's carriage to 'is 'ome. Back to the arms of 'is good lady wife.'

Arthur hissed a sigh. This was the traditional way that the mob paid their respects to English heroes. They had done it for Pitt and Nelson, and now him. Five years earlier, during the Cintra inquiry, they had been bellowing for his head. He had no wish to humour their fickle mood. Besides, the spectacle of being dragged through London by this baying mob would be demeaning. As Somerset attempted to reason with the man, Arthur slapped his hand down on his thigh.

'Damn it!' he growled. 'I'll not stand for it.'

He rose from his seat and opened the door, dropping quickly to the ground. Those closest to him were stunned into silence by his abrupt appearance and Arthur pressed through them towards the six men from the Life Guards who had been sent to Dover to escort him. He clicked his fingers at the nearest rider.

'I need your horse.'

'Your grace?' The rider looked at him in surprise.

'Be so good as to dismount,' Arthur said evenly. 'I require your horse. I shall ensure that it is returned to you when I have finished with it.'

As soon as the man had slid down, Arthur climbed into the saddle and quickly took the reins. The nearest people in the crowd looked on curiously, while up ahead others continued to unharness the carriage, oblivious of what was going on behind it.

'The escort can return to barracks,' Arthur instructed the sergeant commanding the six men. He had no wish to attract undue attention as he made his way through London to the house in Hamilton Place. As the sergeant saluted, Arthur turned the horse towards a side street and waved his hand.

'Make way!'

The horse clopped forward, and the crowd parted. Arthur trotted into a side street lined with small shops. Many of the windows were decorated with coloured ribbons and several had crude prints of a soldier whose uniform was gaudily hung with medals and stars. With a mental wince Arthur realised that these were depictions of him and he gave thanks that he was dressed in his blue coat. Doing his best to avoid the eyes of anyone he passed, Arthur followed the street and then turned right towards the Thames and emerged on to the embankment. Glancing downriver towards Westminster Bridge, he could see that the bridge and the approaches to it were packed with people, so he turned away to find another crossing.

It felt strange to be back in England again, after four years of campaigning in foreign lands. For almost all that time his companions had been soldiers. Now he was surrounded by civilians who had carried on with their lives largely untouched by the war that had been fought on the sea and over foreign lands, Arthur was not sure which felt more unreal, the world he had just emerged from, or the one into which he was returning.

He passed by familiar, and yet somehow not familiar, landmarks with a growing sense of trepidation as he entered Piccadilly. His heart began to beat faster, and he slowed his horse as he approached the entrance to Hamilton Place. There he stopped, looking down the houses lining the wide street towards the door where Kitty and his children awaited him. The news of his return to England would surely have reached them by now and Arthur wondered if they were sitting inside, watching the street for the first sign of him. He edged his mount over to the corner, to keep out of sight.

What was holding him back, he wondered. It was almost as if he dared not continue. For a moment he was tempted to ride on, and report his return to Horseguards, and perhaps visit Richard. Anything but face Kitty and two sons he barely knew.

'Damned fool!' he muttered to himself. This was how wars ended. No man could or should fight for his entire life. War was a necessary evil, as Arthur had frequently pointed out to his officers, and its sole purpose was the restitution of peace and the return of soldiers to the arms of their families. And yet here he stood, on the threshold of his return, reluctant to cross it.

With a quick kick of his heels and a tug on the reins Arthur turned the horse into Hamilton Place and trotted along the row of neat steps rising to imposing columned entrances. He drew up outside the house and eased himself down from the saddle. Hitching the reins to the railing, he took a calming breath and climbed the steps to the front door. Before he could reach it, the door opened, and there stood Kitty, in a plain muslin dress, drawn close beneath her bust as if she were still a young girl at the court of the Viceroy in Dublin. She squinted slightly and her bottom lip trembled until she bit down on it gently.

'Arthur?' She raised a hand to her face. 'Arthur.'

He stood still and stared at her for an instant, and then nodded. 'I've come home.'

He felt a fool as soon as he said it, and then stepped up and took her hands in his. Any more words he might have said dried in his throat as he looked down at her. She seemed older than he had thought she would. There were faint creases around her eyes and the eyes themselves had lost the sparkling lustre he had recalled whenever he had thought of her in the Peninsula. Yet there was still the same small nose and fine lips that had first caught his attention.

Then she smiled, shyly, and Arthur could not help a nervous laugh, relieved that his pleasure at seeing her felt genuine. 'By God! I've come home!' He laughed and drew her to him, kissing her on the forehead, then again on the cheek and lastly on the lips, until she pulled back with a surprised look.

'Arthur! People will see.'

'Let them.' He cupped her cheek and kissed her on the lips again. Now Kitty laughed, and tugged his sleeve, pulling him inside the door. A servant stood to one side, staring at the opposite wall as he reached for the door and began to close it.

'Wait,' Arthur intervened. 'That horse needs returning to its master.' He turned to the servant. 'Might I know your name?'

'Jenkins, your grace.'

'Well then, Jenkins, I have an errand for you. The horse belongs to a trooper of the Life Guards. I'd be obliged if you returned it to him at once.'

The servant glanced at the animal with little enthusiasm, and then bowed his head. 'As you wish, your grace.'

He left the house, closing the door behind him. They were alone, and he kissed Kitty again, closing his eyes and breathing in her scent, as if for the first time. Then he pulled back and arched an eyebrow. 'I believe I have two sons somewhere?'

She grinned and gestured towards the open door of the front parlour. Arthur walked slowly towards it, seeing a mental image of the two infants he had left behind years before. Sunlight was pouring in through the tall sash windows and seated on a window seat, looking out into the street, sat Arthur and Charles. They looked round as he entered and stared at him.

'Oh, come now!' Kitty beckoned. 'You know this is your father. He has returned home.'

They rose up obediently and stepped across the room, stopping two paces in front of Arthur and bowing their heads nervously.

'How do you do, Father,' the older boy said formally, as he had been taught to do.

Arthur gazed at them, his heart filled with a profound melancholic ache. These were his sons. His flesh and blood, whom he had come to love in the abstract. He felt that he should show them some affection. He should do what any father would in the same circumstances. Yet something held him back. Both boys were unable to conceal their nervousness as they looked up at him warily. There was a pause, then Kitty touched Arthur on the sleeve.

'You have had a long journey. I expect you might like some refreshment.'

'Yes. Yes, I would. Some tea, if you please, Kitty.'

She smiled warmly as he spoke her name. Then she looked at him and cocked an eyebrow. 'No baggage?'

'It is on the carriage. It will come shortly.'

'Good.' She smiled again. 'I'll leave you with our boys.'

Arthur felt a stab of panic but before he could reply Kitty had left the room. He turned back to his sons and cleared his throat. 'Hah. Hm. Well then . . .'

They stared back mutely, and the silence was painful and awkward. Then the youngest, Charles, looked down at his feet and spoke quietly. 'Did you really beat the French tyrant, Father?'

'Yes, I did.' Arthur cocked his head to one side. 'That is to say, I beat his minions. Alas, I did not have the chance to beat the tyrant himself.'

'Oh . . .' The boy looked so surprised and disappointed that Arthur could not help chuckling.

'But the war is over, isn't it, Father?'

'Yes, it's over. Bonaparte is defeated and we shall have peace, and with luck you two shall never have to go and fight an enemy for as long as you live.'

'But I want to be a soldier,' the older boy said. 'Just like you.'

Arthur looked at him fondly. 'A soldier you may be, but I pray that you shall never have to fight in such a war as I have. Come.' He reached out to them and they hesitantly let him take their hands. Arthur squeezed them lightly. 'Let's go over to the window seat and we shall talk all about it.'

The celebrations that had begun in Paris continued in London with equal extravagance. Tsar Alexander and King Frederick William, together with their courts, joined the great pageant. Once again the focus was upon Arthur as the foremost man amongst the ranks of those who had opposed Bonaparte. The flow of rewards and honours laid at his feet seemed endless. He entered the House of Lords bearing the titles of Viscount, Earl, Marquess and Duke. He was presented with the freedom of towns across England while Oxford awarded him an honorary doctorate. At the service of thanksgiving in St Paul's Cathedral, Arthur carried the sword of state. The leading politicians of both the Whig and the Tory persuasion courted him relentlessly, entreating him to name his political office in return for his allegiance. Arthur turned them down with as much politeness as he could muster.

While Arthur was the darling of the social world, his domestic situation troubled him. Within weeks of his return Kitty's shortcomings, overlooked in the first flush of pleasure at being reunited, came back to the fore. Though earnest and eager to play her part as the wife of the nation's hero, Kitty lacked the sophistication, and indeed the beauty, of many of the women Arthur encountered in society. It pricked his heart to make such unfair comparisons. Her short-sightedness condemned her to squint or stare blankly at balls and dinners, and she quickly fell victim to the suspicion that she was being spoken about or mocked by those she could not clearly see. She would fall quiet, retreating into the safety of silence, while the world paid court to her husband.

Nor was it easy to step into the role of a father. All that Arthur and Charles knew of him was refracted through the public adulation that had greeted his victories. So the boys had come to know him as a distant hero and were inclined to regard him with awe, finding it difficult to accept him as merely a father. Arthur tried to spend as much time with them as possible, but that summer his public life all but consumed every day, and they became an extended part of his audience, looking on from a distance.

Gradually the celebrations died down. The foreign dignitaries returned to the Continent and minds turned towards adapting the world to peace. Less than a month later Arthur and Somerset were in Brussels inspecting the British army placed under his command before he went to take up the embassy in Paris. A handful of the officers or men were veterans and the army was too small to mount any kind of intervention in France. The King of the Netherlands, though an ally, was wary of showing too much favour to the foreign troops on his soil. His newly acquired Belgian subjects were still loyal to France, and many of them had served Bonaparte faithfully during his last campaigns. So the British soldiers were denied access to the forts and towns along the border and remained in camp around Brussels.

True to his military training, Arthur ensured that his officers were aware of the need to be ready to march at short notice. He also spent several days riding across the countryside, noting its potential uses for his army. On the last day before leaving Belgium to ride to Paris, Arthur and Somerset trotted out along the road from Brussels that passed through the forest of Soignes before heading towards the border. They reined in on a low ridge overlooking the ground to the south. Behind them the woods opened out a short distance beyond the bottom of the reverse slope.

'See there, Somerset.' Arthur indicated the ground behind them. 'Enough cover for a large army.'

Somerset glanced round and nodded.

'And there, on the forward slope: a number of walled farmhouses that could easily be fortified to break up any attacks made on the ridge.' Arthur scrutinised the landscape for a moment longer and clicked his fingers. 'Mark this ground.'

'Yes, your grace.' Somerset fumbled with his saddlebag and pulled out his map case. Unfastening it, he took out the map and found the location, then folded the map and rested it on the leather case. He picked up a pencil and held it poised. 'There it is. Mont-St-Jean, your grace.'

'Mont-St-Jean,' Arthur repeated quietly. 'And that village a mile or so back, what was it called?'

'Waterloo, your grace.'

'Very well, make a note. Good ground to fight on,' he said approvingly. 'Damned good ground. Should the need ever arise.'

He urged his horse forward, and Somerset hurriedly packed his materials away before spurring his horse after his commander as he clopped down the road. On either side fields of wheat grew chest high, and a light breeze caused the heads of the crops to sway in a gently shimmering ripple. For a moment Arthur felt his spirits lift as he put his concerns aside and gazed out across the peaceful countryside.

Chapter 53

Paris, November 1814

A fine drizzle filled the air as the men of the King's bodyguard paraded in the great courtyard of the Tuileries. Arthur was standing beside the Duke of Angoulême reviewing the soldiers as they marched past the platform. Many of them sported the whiskers that had been the fashion of the former Imperial Guard, and there was something in their eyes that chilled Arthur even more than the cold weather of late autumn.

'How many of these men are veterans of the Old Guard?' he asked quietly.

The French aristocrat smiled. 'We inducted more than half of them.'

'You compelled them?'

'It was not necessary. They were pleased enough to have the chance to continue wearing a uniform. It was that, or return to the streets and go hungry.'

'And you trust them?'

'Why not? They would be nothing without the new regime. Their Emperor is gone, the war is over. They have had to adjust, along with the rest of the people.'

Arthur watched the next company march past before he replied. 'I hope you are right.'

'Of course I am. The Corsican Tyrant is no longer a danger to Europe. I understand that he is busying himself on Elba with improving the lot of his new subjects. But then I am sure you are better informed of his activities than I am.'

'Our resident sends regular reports of Bonaparte's activities,' Arthur admitted. As part of the treaty which had provided for the French Emperor's exile the British government had appointed a resident on Elba, Colonel Campbell, to keep a close watch on Bonaparte and keep track of those who visited him on the island, mostly former admirers and those curious to see the great man in his gilded cage. As a matter of course his former commanders were barred from speaking to him, but there was no preventing third parties from carrying messages.

'What does your resident say in his reports?'

'That Bonaparte reads the newspapers avidly, and is engrossed in writing his memoirs, and that he abides by the terms of the treaty. He presents no threat to the peace of Europe, as you say.'

'Perhaps,' the French aristocrat mused. 'All the same, it was a shame that he was not put to death. Then we might have finally quashed Bonapartist sentiment in France.'

'If he had been put to death, I fear the streets of Paris would have run with blood as his supporters and yours tore each other's throats out.'

The Duke of Angoulême glanced coldly at Arthur. 'Sometimes blood is the price of peace and security.'

'And sometimes it does not have to be,' Arthur replied firmly. 'More than enough blood has already been shed.'

The Frenchman turned back to watch the soldiers with a dismissive grunt. After a moment Arthur reached up and adjusted his stock to keep as much of the drizzle from his neck as possible.

While the review continued his mind turned to the wider situation in Paris. He had taken up his position as ambassador nearly three months earlier, and at first he had been gratified by his reception into Paris society. The British government had purchased the mansion of Pauline Bonaparte to serve as an embassy and the accommodation was as comfortable as anything Arthur could have wished for; it had pleased Kitty too when she joined him in October. Since his arrival Arthur had been welcomed into the Parisian salons, and Madame de Staël had proved a useful ally in assisting him to promote his government's case for the abolition of the French slave trade. He had even met many of the marshals and generals who had once served Bonaparte and was pleased by the cordial, and often friendly, mood which had accompanied their discussions of their experiences during the recently ended war.

But as the weeks passed and Arthur came to better know the general mood of the French capital, he began to grow concerned. The Bourbons might well be back in power, but the public enthusiasm for the return of peace and the restoration of the monarchy had swiftly given way to discontent. On several occasions Arthur had witnessed small gatherings of men in cafés toasting their former Emperor. Then, only the day before the review of the royal bodyguard, stones had been thrown through the windows of the embassy.

Nor was the news from Vienna any more encouraging. Castlereagh's coded despatches revealed that a formal alliance between Russia, Prussia and Austria was still a very real danger. Both he and Talleyrand were striving to draw Austria away from the others in order to maintain an equilibrium in Europe. Otherwise, a new war might be unavoidable.

The Duke of Angoulême leaned towards him. 'Time for the finale, my dear Wellington. Look there.'

He pointed across the courtyard to where the bodyguard was forming a line, two deep, facing the review stand. The Frenchman glanced at Arthur and smiled. 'Now for a small piece of theatre. Shall we see how the audience reacts?' He gestured subtly to the officers and aristocrats and their wives watching the review on the platform behind. Across the parade ground the colonel in charge had drawn his sword and now bellowed the order to make ready to fire. Up came the muskets.

There was an anxious murmur from behind Arthur and he glanced round and saw that the Duke of Angoulême's party were stirring uneasily, forgetting the discomfort caused by standing in the cold and damp. The Duke laughed lightly as he spoke softly to Arthur. 'Nothing to worry about. They're firing blank rounds. I thought it would be entertaining to give our guests some idea what it might be like to be on the receiving end of a volley.'

'Really?' Arthur replied flatly. 'I can assure you that there is a world of difference between mere smoke and noise, and the actuality.'

The Duke shrugged, and fixed his attention on the line of soldiers as they aimed their muskets across the parade ground towards the reviewing platform. The colonel barked an order and an instant later fire and smoke burst out, obscuring the line of soldiers, an instant before the deafening crash echoed off the walls of the palace. Arthur sensed rather than heard the faint whip through the air, almost lost in the din of the volley. A sharp crack came from behind and he turned quickly. Two panes of glass in the windows of the palace had shattered, just above the heads of the audience, and in line with Arthur and the Duke. Some of the guests turned to look and gasped in alarm, instinctively edging towards the steps at either side of the platform. Others gazed up, aghast, and then turned anxiously back towards the soldiers. The colonel was continuing to give orders, oblivious of those on the platform, and the bodyguards shouldered their muskets and began to march away, through an arch, as they returned to barracks.

Arthur turned back to the Duke of Angoulême who stood rigidly, hands clenched into fists at his sides. 'Treason,' he muttered. 'Treason. I'll have the culprits found and shot with their own weapons.'

His jaw was trembling as he finished speaking, whether from fear or rage Arthur could not tell. Arthur shook his head. 'I don't think there's much hope of finding the men responsible. Even if anyone knew which men took the shots, the chances are that they will close ranks and keep their mouths shut.'

'Then they're all in on it,' the Duke continued. 'Traitors all. I'll flog the truth out of them.'

'You do that, and they will turn on you,' Arthur warned him. 'By all means find the culprits, but do it quietly, and do it later. For now you must act as if nothing had happened.' He indicated the guests. 'Or you will alarm them.'

'Yes. Yes, of course.' The Duke nodded as he fought to steady his nerves. He cleared his throat and forced a smile as he waved towards the doors leading into the palace. 'My friends, now that the review is complete, refreshments await within!'

With Arthur at his side, he led the way down the steps and across the gravel towards the doors, which were hurriedly opened by footmen. Behind them the rest of the audience followed, muttering in muted tones as some of them took a last glance across the courtyard in case the soldiers returned.

'Not a word to my wife about this, do you understand?' Arthur said to Somerset as he related the attempt on his life later that afternoon back at the embassy.

'Of course, your grace. But are you certain you were the target?'

'There were two shots fired; there could have been more.' Arthur recalled the scene briefly as he stood, several paces back from the window of his office, and looked down into the boulevard where a steady stream of Parisians trudged past in the rain. He continued grimly, 'The shots were aimed at me, and the Duke. I have no doubt of it. They intended assassination. And it's not the first time that England's enemies have contemplated the act.'

Somerset nodded. There had been other reports of such plots from local agents, in the pay of the embassy. These had been passed on to London, and the Prime Minister, Lord Liverpool, had informed Arthur that they were reconsidering his appointment as ambassador.

Arthur puffed out his cheeks. 'Now then, we must think on the implications of this afternoon's attempt on my life. Pass the word to our agents, that they are to keep their eyes and ears open for any hint of another plot. I want to know everything. Also, the embassy's officials will need to be aware of the threat. They will need to be diligent about their safety whenever they leave the embassy. I will take an escort with me from now on. Pick four good men. They are to ride behind my carriage when I go out. They are to dress plainly and keep their weapons out of sight. Is that clear?'

'Yes, your grace. And what of your wife's excursions?'

'My wife?' Arthur stroked his chin. 'I'll speak to her first. At dinner.'

'I don't understand, my dear.' Kitty shook her head. 'If there is nothing to fear, then why should I curtail my social rounds?'

'It is just a precaution,' Arthur replied gently. 'You've seen how it is in the streets. The Bonapartists are more open about their grievances than ever. Now is not a particularly good time to be English in Paris. But it will pass. The new regime will not tolerate them for much longer.'

Kitty cheerfully sawed into another piece of beef as she replied, 'My dear Arthur, I have not seen anything to discomfort me when I am abroad. But if it is your wish that I exercise caution, then I will.'

'Thank you, Kitty.'

She popped her fork lightly into her mouth and chewed the meat before she spoke again. 'And what of the children? Are they to join us at Christmas, as we planned?'

Arthur had already considered this, and nodded. 'Let them come. I am sure there is no danger. Besides, if they did not come our French hosts might be offended.'

'Oh?'

'Kitty, we must show them that we are not fearful. We must continue as normal.'

'You said there was no danger.'

'Nor is there. No real danger.'

Kitty paused and narrowed her eyes as she stared across the table at her husband. 'You are not telling me the whole truth, are you? What has happened, Arthur?'

'Nothing that need concern you, my dear,' he replied, with what he hoped was a comforting smile. 'Perhaps I am being over-cautious.'

'And perhaps you are endangering our sons.'

Arthur stared at her for a moment. 'I would never do that. Believe me. They will be safe enough in Paris, I give you my word.'

'Safe enough?'

'By God, Kitty, I tell you they will be safe!' Arthur snapped. 'Arthur and Charles will join us here. It is decided.'

Kitty lowered her knife and fork and sat back in her chair, her expression nervous. 'There is no need to raise your voice, my dear. I bend to your will in all things. You know that, and I know that you think less of me for it. I am not such a fool as you sometimes think.'

'Kitty, I never—'

'Hush. I know you would never say it to my face. But I ask you, what kind of father places his children in a position of lesser safety for the sake of his country's reputation?'

Arthur stared at her in silence for a moment before he responded flatly, 'We do what we must for our country. All of us. It is as simple as that. It is the duty that comes with our rank, even for the youngest of us.'

Arthur and Charles arrived late in December, escorted by a maidservant and three footmen, one of whom turned out to be a government agent carrying a despatch for Arthur. After greeting his children he withdrew to his office to break open the seal and read the contents. Lord Liverpool had given much thought to the deteriorating situation in Paris and was anxious that Arthur be preserved from the dangers of assassins since his country may have need of his services as a general once again. Therefore Castlereagh was to be recalled from Vienna and Arthur would represent Britain's interests in his place. Somerset would remain in Paris to run the embassy and Arthur was advised that Kitty and the children should also remain, to reassure King Louis that Arthur intended to return to Paris once the Congress had concluded its business.

Although the diplomatic situation was still grave there was some good news. A peace had been agreed between Britain and the United States. That, Arthur was reassured, would mean that the government's attention could focus on Europe. It would also mean that more soldiers would be available for deployment in the army under Arthur's command in the Netherlands.

Christmas passed peacefully and Arthur and Kitty did their best to entertain the two boys by showing them the sights of the French capital. Even as he tried his best to play the role of a dutiful father, Arthur's mind was distracted by the burdens of wider affairs. He had urged the French King to order Talleyrand to co-operate with Castlereagh in Vienna, and early in the new year a secret treaty was signed, binding Britain, France and Austria in a pact against the other two powers if war broke out.

Arthur left Paris in the last week of January, travelling by carriage to Vienna where he arrived on the evening of 3 February. Despite the late hour he sought out Castlereagh at the fine mansion that had been allotted to the English representatives at the Congress. Castlereagh looked grey and exhausted when Arthur was shown into his study by a servant. The other man rose, smiled wearily and came across the room to take Arthur's hand.

'Good to see you again, Arthur. How was the journey?'

'Long and wet.'

'Loquacious as ever,' Castlereagh chuckled. 'Still, reticence will serve you well here in Vienna. Despite civilised appearances – there seems to be a ball, banquet or ballet happening almost every hour of the day – the place is a nest of vipers.'

'So I gathered from your letters.'

'Talleyrand and Metternich are the most devious scoundrels I have ever encountered, forever doing the rounds of private salons and offices proposing secret deals and selling confidences. Why, they have turned such practices into a virtual industry. I suppose I should be grateful at least that they happen to be "our" scoundrels. At least for the present.'

'I take it that you have had to offer them disbursements to support our position?' Arthur asked as he sat down. Castlereagh resumed his seat and nodded.

'I probably did not need to have offered such inducements, but the situation is such that I was not prepared to take the risk. Now that we have the treaty signed and sealed, I hope that you will not have to pay them another penny.' Castlereagh smiled faintly. 'I know you have a pronounced distaste for bribes and back room chicanery.'

'That is right,' Arthur replied firmly. 'I believe that men of honour can achieve more lasting good through being patient and observant than through politicking.'

'Then you will be something of an oddity at the Congress.' Castlereagh paused and looked at Arthur shrewdly. 'Though I dare say such an approach might win much favour after the deviousness of recent months. Besides, your reputation goes before you. The Tsar considers you to be the greatest hero of the age, to the chagrin of his own generals, of course.'

'Tsar Alexander is inclined to be generous in his praise,' Arthur recalled from his meetings with the Tsar in London the previous summer.

'Don't be fooled, Arthur. Alexander is as absolute a ruler as Bonaparte ever was, and just as keen to expand his domains. He has managed to dupe the King of Prussia into supporting his claims and paid him off with the promise of a few sops from Poland as well as a free hand as far as the other German states are concerned. If that is permitted then there can be no question of a just equilibrium in

Europe, and war will be inevitable. That is what you must prevent at any cost.' Castlereagh paused briefly. 'At least with the treaty, you will have a stick to beat them with if Alexander and Frederick William continue to push for more advantages in the final settlement.'

'It is good to have the treaty,' Arthur agreed. 'But I shall use it only in the last resort.'

'As you will,' Castlereagh bowed his head slightly. 'It would be most gratifying to see reason prevail, rather than veiled threats. I wish you the best of luck, Arthur. I shall be glad to quit this place.'

As Castlereagh had warned him, there were two distinct worlds at the Congress. With the gathering of so many rulers and statesmen and their entourages it was inevitable that grand social occasions should be given such prominence. In between such events the negotiations continued in the suite of rooms in the vast sprawl of the Schönbrunn palace. The fires were continually built up by servants, and the delegates from the great powers discussed the terms of the European settlement in sweltering heat. The uncomfortable atmosphere was made more taxing still by the Tsar's worsening hearing difficulties, which obliged the other delegates to strain their voices as they conversed in French, the common tongue of most of the royal courts on the Continent. Arthur's refusal to enter into any secret meetings and his forthright discussion of the need to reach agreement and the dangers of not doing so quickly won him the respect of the other powers, and the Tsar began to give ground on his demands.

A month after he arrived, the morning dawned clear and crisp and Arthur rose early to dress for a hunt that was to take place in the vast park that stretched out across the landscape to the west of the palace. He breakfasted, and was waiting for his horse to be saddled and brought to the courtyard at the rear of the British delegation's mansion when there was a sharp rap on the door of his private dining room. Arthur lowered his coffee and called out, 'Come!'

The door opened and a tall, thin-faced man entered. He wore a thick coat, spattered with mud. It was unbuttoned and revealed the gold braid across the red jacket of a British army officer. He strode across the room, halted in front of the breakfast table and saluted. Arthur frowned.

'Who the devil are you?'

'Colonel Sir Neil Campbell, your grace.'

'Campbell?' Arthur repeated, then his eyes widened. 'The resident in Elba?'

Campbell nodded anxiously. 'Yes, your grace.'

'What are you doing here?'

'Your grace, I beg to report that Napoleon Bonaparte has escaped from Elba.'

'Escaped? Where to?'

'I know not. All I know is that when I returned to the island he was gone.'

'You left the island?' Arthur frowned. 'In God's name, why?'

'I – I was invited to Florence for a ball, your grace.' Campbell's gaze faltered. 'I was gone for a matter of days. Nothing seemed amiss when I left. When I returned, Bonaparte had vanished, together with his men. I made for Italy at once and sent a message to London, and now I have come to Vienna to inform the powers at the Congress.'

Arthur glared at the man. The monster of Europe was loose again, thanks to Campbell's lack of diligence. 'Stay here. I will question you more closely when I return.'

'Yes, your grace.'

Arthur rose from his chair and strode towards the door. He walked quickly to find one of his aides waiting in the hall to join Arthur at the hunt. 'You can send the horses back to the stable.'

'Your grace?'

'Another has bolted,' Arthur responded. 'Run to the other delegations. Tell them we must meet at the Schönbrunn at once, on a matter of the gravest urgency. Run, man, as if the very devil himself were at your heels!'

'Escaped?' Metternich shook his head, and then laughed. The other delegates in the room joined in, though their laughter was more nervous than humorous, Arthur noted.

'Where does he think to hide?' the King of Prussia snorted. 'He is the most notorious figure in Europe. Who would dare harbour him?'

'I do not know where his ships were headed, your majesty,' Arthur replied. 'But I suspect that he would most likely make for Italy.'

'Why Italy? Why not France?'

Talleyrand shook his head. 'He would be arrested, or assassinated, the moment he set foot on French soil. I agree, he will go to Italy. He has friends there, and family. Napoleon will go to Murat.'

'Even though Murat betrayed him last year?' Metternich queried.

'I imagine he will ask his brother-in-law for asylum,' Talleyrand suggested. 'I know him, I know his strength of will. He is a hard man to refuse. Murat will take him in. Then, when the moment is ripe,

Napoleon will seize power. The kingdom of Naples will be his new base of operations.'

It made some sense, Arthur reflected. Murat's domains would provide him with an army large enough to threaten the rest of the Italian kingdoms.

The Tsar cleared his throat and leaned towards the conference table. 'The question is, gentlemen, what shall we do about this?'

Talleyrand looked at him with a faintly surprised expression. 'Do, your majesty? Why, we should organise an army to march on Napoleon and crush him, before he has time to prepare. That much is obvious. Meanwhile, the Congress must continue. The peace settlement is more important than the pursuit of a criminal, however notorious.'

The other delegates nodded their agreement, but Arthur was not so certain. He had witnessed the strong loyalties that Bonaparte still commanded in Paris. If the former Emperor raised his banner in Naples, then many thousands would flock to join him, and those who remained would be sure to unsettle the new regime in France.

Over the next few days messages were sent out from Vienna to mobilise the allied armies. The audacity of Bonaparte's escape had shocked the delegates, but there was little sense that he posed an immediate danger to Europe, and the powers continued their deliberations as they awaited confirmation of his location. It was four days after Colonel Campbell broke the news of his disappearance that the truth was learned. One of Talleyrand's aides entered the chamber just before the midday recess and whispered urgently in his ear. Arthur watched as the French Foreign Minister's face drained of blood. Metternich was speaking, reading verbatim from notes, and had not noticed the little drama.

Talleyrand rapped his knuckles sharply on the table and the Austrian minister looked up irritably, stopping his address mid-sentence.

'Pardon my interruption,' said Talleyrand as he looked round the table, 'but I have just been informed that Napoleon landed on the coast of France six days ago. He has declared that he has come to reclaim his throne and is marching on Paris.'

There was a moment's stunned silence, then Arthur spoke. 'Did the local authorities oppose him?'

'On the contrary. I am told that they went over to him without a shot being fired.'

'By God, that's bad news. Others will surely follow. If he gathers them up en route to Paris, I fear he will not be stopped.' Arthur cleared his throat and spoke as clearly as he could, to ensure that the Tsar caught every word. 'Your majesties, ministers, delegates, this changes every-thing. The peace of Europe is once more endangered. Every available soldier must be made ready to fight. If Bonaparte makes good his claim, then he will have the armies of France at his back again. We must face him on the battlefield once more.'

'We must do more than that,' Talleyrand interrupted. 'We must ensure that he never troubles Europe again. I beg to move that before the Congress is suspended to deal with the threat it passes one last resolution. That Napoleon Bonaparte is declared an international outlaw. In the event that he is taken, then the powers gathered here shall jointly decree that he is beyond the protection of the law.'

'I cannot agree to that,' Arthur protested. 'It would be nothing less than an incitement to assassination. Murder. Regardless of the ethical issues, it is a game that two can play. I would urge you to reflect on that.'

'Nevertheless, it is a step we must take,' Talleyrand countered. 'Speaking for France, I propose the resolution.'

'And Prussia supports it!' King Frederick William blurted out. 'Death is exactly what that tyrant deserves.'

'Very well,' Talleyrand turned to Metternich. The Austrian nodded, and Talleyrand fixed his gaze on the Tsar. 'Your majesty? What do you say?'

Alexander did not respond immediately, and raised a hand to touch his forehead. His lips pressed together in a tight line, and then he drew a deep breath and nodded. 'I support the resolution.'

'Four to one,' Talleyrand faced Arthur again. 'Will Britain unite with the other powers, or will you still extend the protection of the law to Bonaparte?'

Arthur stared back coldly. He was being forced into a position he had no wish to be in. The disposal of Napoleon was in the interests of every man, woman and child of Europe, yet Arthur could not bring himself to cast aside the civilised values England had striven to preserve throughout the long years of the struggle to free Europe from tyranny. Nor would the British government he anticipated. Yet Talleyrand was right. If Britain failed to declare Bonaparte an outlaw then he would be sure to seize on that as an admission of his legitimacy. Worse still, he would see it as a schism in the ranks of his enemies and would exploit it to divide them. With a weary sigh Arthur nodded reluctantly. 'Very well. I support the resolution.'

At once Talleyrand turned to one of his aides. 'Have that drafted for the delegates to sign. Now, I suggest that the Congress goes into recess. Are we agreed? Yes?'

The delegates rose and began to file out of the room. Arthur felt a hand touch his shoulder as he reached the door and turned to find the Tsar looking at him gravely.

'Your majesty?'

'What will you do, my dear Duke?'

'I must send word to my family to quit Paris as soon as possible. Then I will conclude our business here as swiftly as I can and make for Brussels to take up my command.'

'Ah. Then it is for you to save the world again.'

'That is the burden of us all, your majesty. The great test of our age is upon us.'

'And if we fail?'

Arthur stared at him for a moment and shook his head. 'We dare not.'

Chapter 54

Napoleon

Laffrey, near Grenoble, 7 March 1815

'Why have your men stopped?' Napoleon demanded, as his carriage rattled to a halt on the rough track.

General Cambronne, the commander of the company of guardsmen leading the advance, pointed down the track in the direction of Grenoble. 'We ran into a battalion of infantry shortly after we set off this morning, sire.'

'There was no shooting, I take it?' Napoleon asked sharply. He had warned Cambronne against spilling any French blood when he had given him his orders to lead the vanguard of the tiny force Napoleon had brought with him from Elba. The former Emperor had landed near Antibes with just over a thousand men, a squadron of lancers and two cannon. It was a minuscule army with which to reclaim his throne, Napoleon mused, but he had advanced from the coast at once. Given the royalist sympathies of the people of Provence, he had chosen to avoid the easiest route towards Paris in favour of the road leading through the hills to Grenoble. So far he had been received with muted enthusiasm in the towns and villages he had passed through. Even though the enthusiasm for the Bourbons had waned, the people were anxious to avoid reprisals if Napoleon's outrageous gamble failed. So they waited to see the outcome of his latest venture.

General Cambronne shook his head. 'There was no violence of any kind, sire. As soon as we encountered their leading company I told our men to greet them warmly, and share some wine. Their captain would have none of it, though. He ordered his men to fall in and march back to join the rest of the battalion. I was told not to follow him, or he would order his men to open fire.'

'Very well,' Napoleon scratched the bristles on his cheek. This was the moment he had been fearing. So far, no one had stood in his way. Now he was confronted by armed men, whose officers were clearly determined to oppose his progress. The question was, would the men follow their orders when the crisis came?

Napoleon sat in his carriage and thought carefully about the situation. Throughout the ten months he had remained on Elba he had followed events in France closely. In addition to regular scrutiny of the newspapers he had been receiving secret reports from sympathisers, and even from Fouché, who had been shrewd enough to keep a foot in both camps. Napoleon, and most Frenchmen, had been surprised when King Louis had appointed the arch-schemer as his Minister of Police, the post he had once held under Napoleon.

It was Fouché who had informed him that the Comte d'Artois, the next in line to the throne, intended to reverse the liberties gained by the common people in the years following the Revolution. D'Artois was also planning to reverse the land reforms that had transferred many aristocratic estates to the peasantry. The mood in France was poisonous, Fouché wrote to his former master. The common people were suspicious of the Bourbons and their followers. The sentiment was echoed by the demobbed soldiers who were struggling to find a place within the new regime, and looked back on the days of empire with increasing fondness.

As Napoleon read the reports, he resolved to quit his tiny kingdom of Elba at the earliest opportunity. No island of twelve thousand inhabitants could satisfy his ambitions, or sate his boredom, and he began to make preparations in secret. His small army was regularly drilled and his one warship, a small brig, was supplemented by five other small vessels sufficient to carry Napoleon and his men to France. All of this had to be carried out under the gaze of the British resident. Colonel Campbell was a kindly officer, much in awe of his host, and Napoleon was careful to speak with enthusiasm about his plans for improving Elba whenever the two had occasion to talk. Campbell seemed satisfied that Napoleon had accepted his new, minor station in life. Such was his confidence that Napoleon no longer presented any danger that he had announced he was making a brief visit to Florence.

Napoleon concealed his delight at the news as he enquired the date by which Campbell might return, on the pretext that he was planning a ball and did not want the Englishman to miss the event. As soon as Campbell had departed, Napoleon and his followers hurriedly loaded stores and equipment aboard the flotilla of small vessels and departed mere hours before the return of the Royal Navy brig that had conveyed Campbell to Italy.

Luck, as ever, had favoured him, Napoleon reflected. But now he faced the great test of his new adventure. The road ahead was blocked by regular soldiers, sent by the royalists to confront and arrest him.

'Sire, what are your orders?' Cambronne interrupted Napoleon's thoughts. 'Should I deploy the men?'

'No. Have them form up in column, lancers to the front. You and I shall ride at the head of the column. How far ahead is the road blocked?'

Cambronne turned to look up the track. It inclined gently down towards the side of a hill and then turned along the shore of a small lake, the end of which could just be seen. To the left steep hills rose up sharply, creating a narrow defile through which Napoleon and his men must march to reach Grenoble.

The veteran pointed towards the place where the road disappeared round the side of the hill. 'Just beyond the hill, sire, close to the far end of the lake.'

'Very well, let's proceed.'

Cambronne hesitated. 'Shall I have the guns moved close to the front of the column, sire? If there's any trouble, they can clear the way with a few rounds of case shot.'

'There will be no trouble,' Napoleon replied flatly. 'If there is, then our cause is as good as lost. Now, give the order for the men to make ready to advance. Make sure every man understands that they are not to fire a shot without my express order. If anything happens to me, then you are to lay down your arms at once. Is that clear?'

Cambronne nodded reluctantly, then turned away and strode over to the men who had fallen out alongside the track, bellowing at them to re-form their ranks.

A few minutes later the column started down the track. Napoleon was now riding a white horse, and he wore the old grey coat and battered bicorne that was familiar to every soldier who had campaigned with him over the years. As the track rounded the hill he felt his heartbeat quicken. To his right the small lake stretched out, the calm waters reflecting the wooded ridge on the far side. At the far end of the lake there was a stretch of open ground, perhaps a hundred paces across, between the hillside and the shore of the lake. A body of soldiers stood waiting, formed in line, with fixed bayonets that glinted in the afternoon sunshine.

'What unit is that?' asked Napoleon.

'The first battalion of the Fifth Regiment of the Line, sire.'

Napoleon nodded.

The column advanced in silence, marching along the side of the lake. Napoleon glanced back, past the flickering pennants of the lancers, and saw the grim expressions fixed on the faces of the guardsmen. If it came to a fight, the veterans would make short work of the men opposed to them. But the instant the first blood was spilled, France would be bitterly divided. Even if Napoleon survived such a struggle, he would be forced to deal with the other European powers with almost no chance of success.

As the gap between the hillside and the shore began to widen, Napoleon raised his hand to halt the column.

'Have the Guard form line. They are to shoulder arms. The lancers are to fall back and dismount.'

Cambronne sucked in his breath, but saluted and turned away to give the orders. As the guardsmen trotted out on either side of the track and formed ranks, Napoleon stared at the line of infantry barring his way. They stood silently as their commanding officer sat on his horse and raised his telescope.

Once the men were in position Cambronne resumed his place at Napoleon's side. 'What now, sire?'

'It's time you announced me,' Napoleon replied.

Cambronne edged his spurs in and trotted forward towards the waiting soldiers. Their commander lowered his scope and watched the solitary rider approaching. When Cambronne was no more than fifty paces away the other officer cupped a hand to his mouth and called out. 'Stop there!'

Reining in, Cambronne raised his hat and replied. 'Comrades! Our Emperor has returned! Join us!'

'Silence!' the officer shouted, then ordered his men, 'Advance your muskets!'

The bayonets angled forward, cold gleaming tips pointing towards Cambronne.

'What is the meaning of this?' he barked. 'How dare you threaten me? What do you think you are doing?'

'I have orders to prevent you proceeding,' the officer replied firmly. 'You will hand over the outlaw behind you, and tell your men to lay down their arms.'

'I shall do no such thing!'

'If you do not surrender within ten minutes, I will give the order to open fire.' The officer pulled out his fob watch and looked down at it.

'If you fire on the Emperor you will be responsible to all of France!' Cambronne responded. 'Come now, we are all Frenchmen.'

He sat in his saddle and waited for a response. Eventually the officer looked up from his watch and spoke. 'Nine minutes . . .'

With a muttered curse Cambronne turned his mount round and trotted back towards Napoleon. 'You heard him, sire?'

'Yes.'

'Do you think he will give the order?'

Napoleon stared at the line of soldiers for a moment. 'There's only one way to find out.'

He dismounted and handed his reins to Cambronne. 'Stay here. If anything happens to me remember your orders.'

'Sire, you can't put yourself in danger. France needs you.'

'Quiet,' Napoleon said. He drew a long deep breath and started walking slowly towards the soldiers. As he did so he unbuttoned his coat to reveal the green jacket of a colonel of the Guards. His heart beat quickly as he gazed steadily at the row of bayonets angled towards him. He knew that he was placing his reputation in the balance against the discipline of these soldiers. If he was mistaken then it would be likely that he would be dead within the next few minutes. Although it was spring, he felt cold and had to clench his fists behind his back to stop them trembling. They must not see my fear, he thought fiercely.

He continued to approach them steadily, taking in the details of the expressions of those men closest to him. It was impossible to tell whether they meant him any harm. Behind them, the officer on horseback glared defiantly at Napoleon as he stopped, no more than twenty paces from their bayonets.

'Soldiers of the Fifth! Do you not recognise me? Am I not your old general?'

His words echoed off the side of the hill and then there was silence until he spoke again. 'If there is a man amongst you who wants to kill his Emperor . . . then here I am!' He pulled back his coat and presented his breast to them.

'Present arms!' the officer called out, and the men in the front rank raised their muskets.

'Take aim!

Napoleon pressed his lips together and widened his eyes as he stood his ground and stared into the muzzles of the muskets pointing directly at him.

'Fire!'

Napoleon felt an instant of icy terror, then the moment was past. There was no crash of a volley, no flame and no smoke. Nothing but a strained silence.

'Fire, damn you!' the officer shouted angrily. 'Obey the order!'

Before the sound of the words had died on his lips, another voice cried out, 'Long live the Emperor!'

The soldiers lowered their muskets and cheered, almost as one, as they broke ranks and surged towards Napoleon. Some clasped his hand, while others, more awestruck, satisfied themselves with touching his coat. But all cheered his name again and again. Cambronne and his men joined in and ran forward to greet the other men as comrades. Napoleon smiled at those around him and then began to pace forward, the throng parting to let him pass. He stopped before the mounted officer, a young major.

'What is your name?'

'Lansard,' the man replied through gritted teeth. His face flushed with bitter shame over the failure of his authority. He ignored his men as he fixed his eyes on Napoleon. He took the handle of his sword and drew it from its scabbard, and then tossed it on to the ground at Napoleon's feet. He glanced down at the sword and then gestured to one of the soldiers next to him. 'Pick that up and hand it back to the Major.'

As the officer reluctantly replaced the blade in its scabbard Napoleon smiled at him. 'Lansard, you are no more a prisoner than I was. Now, your men are mine, and I ask you, will you join me?'

The officer was silent for a moment, and then nodded curtly. At once there was a fresh burst of cheering and Napoleon had to raise his voice so that Lansard could hear him. 'You and your men will join my column. Take up position between the Guard and the lancers. Clear?'

'Yes . . . sire.' Lansard saluted and Napoleon turned and made his way back towards Cambronne and the Guard.

'Cambronne!'

'Sire?'

'Send one of your officers, together with one of Lansard's, to Grenoble. They are to tell the people, and any other units they find there, what has happened. Tell them to announce the arrival of their Emperor.'

'Yes, sire.' Cambronne smiled with joy and relief.

Napoleon smiled back. 'The crisis has passed, my friend. Once others receive word that this first battalion has come over to us without a shot being fired, then the rest of the army will follow suit. Until this moment I was just an adventurer. Now? Now I am a great prince of Europe once again . . .'

Chapter 55

The Tuileries, Paris, 8 April 1815

Napoleon slowly crumpled up the proclamation of the Congress at Vienna and continued to crush it between his hands. 'So this is how they would treat me,' he said in a low voice that the others sitting around the table could hardly hear. 'They brand me an outlaw.' He sighed bitterly and tossed the small ball of paper aside. 'You can be sure this is Talleyrand's doing. This is his revenge for the indignities I heaped on him over the years. So what if I did? He deserved every slight. Every insult.'

His council of ministers and generals sat in silence. They had been summoned to hear the Emperor read out the allies' proclamation and discuss the appropriate response. Napoleon looked round at them. There were many familiar faces, recalled to service when Napoleon had returned to Paris. He had been greeted by an hysterical mob who had swept him off his feet and carried him through the streets, into the palace and up into the throne room, abandoned only the day before by King Louis. Napoleon had closed his eyes as they carried him, relishing the feeling of power he had over the affections of so many. Not just the people of Paris. At every stage of his march from the coast, the people had come out to greet him with cheers. The Bourbons had sent soldiers to oppose him, then armies, and in spite of their orders the soldiers had gone over to him. Even Marshal Ney, who had boasted to Louis that he would bring Napoleon to Paris in an iron cage.

Although the people and the army had acclaimed him, and demanded that he take back his throne, the more influential elements of French society had regarded his return with studied caution. The Chamber of Deputies, which had voted to depose him the previous year, hurriedly retracted their decision and welcomed the Emperor back to his capital, beseeching him to maintain the peace of Europe. Much as he would have liked to respond to their about-face with scorn, Napoleon realised that he needed their support. Without their co-operation, and that of officials and lesser assemblies across the nation, it would be almost impossible to build the support his regime needed.

The Emperor re-established his reign with caution. He had answered the calls for peace by sending messages to the other rulers of Europe assuring them of his desire to avoid conflict. He had even issued an edict pronouncing the end of France's involvement in the slave trade. That at least should have garnered some good opinion in Britain. But his offers of peace had been either ignored or curtly rebuffed. Now the allies had signed a treaty pledging to send over half a million men to defeat Napoleon. They sought to divide the Emperor from his people by claiming that their war was not against France, but only Bonaparte, whom they had pronounced an outlaw.

'You have all borne witness to my efforts to prevent war,' Napoleon addressed his council. 'I offered them my hand in friendship and in return they have spat in my face and offered me, and France, only threats. It is clear to all right-thinking men that Russia, Austria, Prussia and England are the aggressors.'

Marshal Davout, who had accepted the post of Minister of War, spoke up. 'Sire, they could be playing into our hands by refusing to declare war on France. It places them in a difficult position. If they invade France, then they can hardly avoid uniting the nation behind you, particularly as you have offered them peace. Therefore, they must wait, and hope that you will attack them, and thereby justify their declaration of war against you in person.'

'That is true.' Napoleon nodded thoughtfully. 'And what do you advise me to do?'

'Bide your time, sire. Make no attempt to provoke military action. At the same time we can build our strength and be ready to defend our borders if the allies become impatient and decided to invade. That is my advice.'

'I see.' Napoleon regarded him for a moment, then shook his head. 'We cannot risk such a strategy, Davout.'

'Why is that, sire?'

'At present there are two armies in the low countries, one under Marshal Blücher, the other led by Wellington. Each commands over a hundred thousand men. Schwarzenberg has another two hundred thousand men poised to cross the Rhine, and another hundred and fifty thousand Russians are marching to join them. They will be in position to invade France by the end of July. And what do we have to face them? Louis left us with no more than two hundred thousand men to guard our frontiers. I have ordered another seventy-five thousand veterans to be recalled to the army, as well as eighty thousand volunteers. Even after they have been trained, we shall still be massively outnumbered. Lack of manpower is not the only problem. We are short of horses, equipment, ammunition.' He paused. 'So you see, time is not on our side.'

'Then what do you propose, sire?'

Napoleon folded his hands together as he contemplated the answer he had already prepared. He knew that it would dispel any chance of portraying France as the victim of aggressors, yet he could conceive of no other course of action.

'There is only one chance of success, gentlemen. If I give the order for France to mobilise for war today, then by June I can form an army of perhaps a hundred and thirty thousand men on the border with Belgium. That is where the allies' two weakest armies are positioned. If we can surprise them, before they can concentrate, then I am confident that we can defeat each in turn. If we can annihilate Wellington and his army, then we may force England out of the coalition. Without English gold the other powers will be hard pressed to keep their armies in the field against us.' Napoleon paused as he saw the uncertainty in the expressions of his subordinates. 'Gentlemen, I assure you that I have fully considered the alternatives. If we wait, and allow the enemy to concentrate all their armies, then we must surely lose. If we attack while our troops are fresh and their morale is high, we can destroy a third of the enemy's strength at one stroke. The rest will surely hesitate. My aim is to make them offer us peace. That is the limit of my ambition, I assure you. The old days of conquest are over. You have my word on it. We will have peace, but first we must fight for it.' He looked round the table. 'Does anyone wish to speak? No? Then I take it we are agreed.' He paused briefly before continuing, 'Marshal Davout.'

'Sire?'

'I want the order to mobilise our forces issued before the end of the day.'

'Yes, sire.'

For the rest of the month, and into May, Napoleon worked tirelessly to prepare the country for war. At the same time, he was more mindful than ever before of the need to secure the loyalty of his war-weary people. The repressive measures imposed by the Bourbons were reversed. Political prisoners were set free and those officers who had served the Bourbons were freely pardoned and many offered commands within the reconstituted imperial army. At times this caused friction, especially when hard-line Bonapartist officers were denied promotion in favour of those who had served King Louis. But Napoleon knew that he could take the loyalty of his ardent supporters for granted, while the loyalty of the former Bourbon officers had to be bought. Thereafter they would be watched with suspicion by their subordinates and would be keen to prove their newfound allegiance to Napoleon.

Davout swiftly organised the production and supply of equipment for the rapidly expanding army. Mills and factories turned out thousands of uniforms and tens of thousands of cartridges. New cannon were cast and pinioned to freshly constructed gun carriages. Horses were requisitioned across the country. All the while a steady flow of soldiers marched north towards the Sambre river where they camped across a wide front, waiting for the order to concentrate. Napoleon remained in Paris for as long as possible. He had sent a private message to the Emperor of Austria, begging for the return of his son and his wife. But there was no reply and his heart hardened towards the Austrians, and he vowed that he would avenge this cruel silence.

As he made a show of dealing with his civil obligations, all the time Napoleon's mind was focused on planning the coming campaign, selecting his officers carefully. Murat's request to serve under him was brusquely declined. Murat had foolishly declared war on Austria as soon as he heard of Napoleon's escape from Elba and was defeated shortly thereafter and forced to flee to France. After his earlier treachery Napoleon could not trust him.

His uncertain hold on power meant that he must leave Davout to control Paris in his absence. Berthier would have been his first choice as chief of staff of the new Army of the North, but early in June came news that Berthier was dead. He had fallen from a window of his home in Bamberg, but it was not clear if it was an accident or something more sinister. In his place Napoleon appointed Soult, despite Soult's protest that he lacked the ability to run the Emperor's general staff, and was better employed on the battlefield.

On 7 June Napoleon ordered that the frontier with Belgium be closed. As a further security measure no mail or civilian traffic was allowed on to the roads, while the soldiers of the Army of the North began to concentrate on Philippeville less than a day's march from the border. A week later Napoleon's carriage and cavalry escort trundled into the small town of Beaumont where the headquarters for the army had been established. The usually quiet streets of the town were filled with soldiers and they jumped to their feet and cheered the instant they were aware that their Emperor had joined them. Napoleon, though exhausted by the preparations for the campaign, forced a smile and waved to them. Even amid the wild celebration his mind was coolly assessing their morale and he was pleased to see that there was no hint of the dull mood of resignation that had characterised the soldiers he had led a year ago. They pressed round the carriage, following it through the streets until it turned into the coachyard of the inn where Soult and his staff were waiting.

The officers had been alerted to his approach and were already lining the short walk to the entrance of the inn. As the carriage rumbled to a halt on the cobbles, Soult strode across the yard and bowed his head while a footman helped the Emperor down.

'Is everything ready?' Napoleon asked curtly.

'Sire, I have the honour to report that the Army of the North awaits your orders.'

'Very good, Soult.' Napoleon smiled and patted the marshal on the shoulder. 'Then it only remains to settle the final details of my plans.' He gestured towards the entrance. 'Inside.'

The two passed between the lines of staff officers, who bowed their heads as the Emperor passed. Napoleon noticed a few familiar faces, but most were unknown to him.

'I take it that you had difficulties reassembling my old headquarters staff?'

'Indeed, sire. Some had accepted service under the Bourbons, others were exiled or had left France. I have gathered the best men that I could find at short notice. They seem capable enough.'

'Soult.' Napoleon lowered his voice. 'The fate of France will be decided in the next few days, a few weeks at the most. I am depending on you, and your staff. You shall not fail me, in any detail, is that clear?'

'Yes, sire.'

They entered the building and proceeded through a small hall into the dining room. Every table had been pushed together in the centre to provide a map table for Soult and his staff. Small campaign desks and stools had been set up along the walls, and were presently piled with paperwork. There was little sense of the order that Berthier had insisted on, Napoleon reflected as he removed his jacket and slung it over the back of a chair. The weather in the last few days had been warm and the room was sweltering.

'Open some windows,' Napoleon ordered as he spread his hands on the table and leaned forward to inspect the main campaign map. While Soult unfastened the latches and thrust the windows open Napoleon took in the details of the Army of the North's deployment, as well as the forces of Blücher and Wellington.

'How accurate is our intelligence on the enemy's positions?'

Soult joined him at the table. 'As good as it can be, sire. We have many sympathisers amongst the Belgians and they have been feeding us with regular reports on the enemy. As you can see, their forces are still widely dispersed. I estimate that it will take them a minimum of three days to mass their armies once the order is given.'

Napoleon considered the map for a moment. 'Let us assume the worst and say a maximum of three days.' He paused for a moment and then smiled faintly. 'There is something else that works in our favour. See how their lines of communication are routed in opposite directions: Blücher's east towards the Rhine, while Wellington's stretch to the coast, at Ostende. Let's play on that. Have a cavalry brigade detached from the army and make a feint towards Wellington's communications. That should distract him. When we strike, their natural impulse will be to close up on their supply lines, and that will create a weak point at the junction of their armies, here.' Napoleon reached forward and tapped the map, indicating the road leading from Charleroi on the border straight to Brussels. 'That is where we must strike, Soult. The Army of the North's main thrust must be along this road. We shall divide them and crush each in turn.'

'Very well, sire.' Soult nodded approvingly. 'Which first? Blücher or Wellington?'

Napoleon was silent for a moment before he responded. 'Blücher, I think. He is the more aggressive of the two. We can rely on Wellington to conform to his usual caution. He will wait for us to come to him. And while he waits, we will deal with Blücher.'

Soult stirred uncomfortably. 'Do not underestimate Wellington, sire. He is more bold than you think.'

Napoleon looked at his chief of staff and shook his head. 'You overestimate his abilities because he has beaten you, Soult. Just the same as the other marshals he humbled in Spain and Portugal. You walked into the traps that he set, all of you. I will not be so easily fooled.'

'Sire, you are wrong. If you had faced Wellington last year then you would know. He is a man to be reckoned with, and his soldiers would follow him to the ends of the earth.'

'It is you who are wrong, Soult. I know how to beat Wellington. Besides, he does not command the same army any more. Wellington has a pot-pourri of nationalities fighting under him. Less than half of his men are British, and he dare not trust his Belgian units. While he faces such difficulties he need not concern us unduly. Is that clear?'

Soult stared defiantly at his Emperor for a moment, then gritted his teeth and nodded. 'Yes, sire.'

'Good.' Napoleon turned back to the map and examined the disposition of his army. 'Marshal Grouchy has been notified that he is to command the right wing, I take it?'

'Yes, sire.'

'Then I intend to appoint Marshal Ney to command the left wing, while I remain with, and command, the reserve.'

'Ney?'

'You question my decision?'

'Of course not, sire,' Soult replied hurriedly. 'It's just that Ney was the commander in chief of France's armies under Louis. Can you trust him?'

'Can I afford not to?' Napoleon responded. 'You know his reputation. The soldiers love him. He has great influence over those officers who served under the Bourbons. If Ney serves me, then we may be sure that those officers will follow his example. So, Ney commands the left wing.'

'Very well, sire. When will Ney be joining the army?'

'I sent for him shortly before I left Paris. Have him brought to me the moment he arrives.'

'Yes, sire.'

Straightening up, Napoleon rubbed his haunches, which were aching after the long journey by carriage from the capital. 'What is the strength of the army?'

'As of this last night's returns we have eighty-nine thousand infantry, twenty-two thousand cavalry and three hundred and sixty-six guns.'

Napoleon frowned. 'I had expected more.'

'A division was diverted to the Vendée to suppress the rebels there, sire. On your orders.'

'Ah, yes. A pity. Well, I am confident that we have enough men for the task. In any case we shall have the advantage of surprise and that is worth more than any division, eh?'

'Yes, sire.'

'So it only remains to decide the time and place of the attack,' Napoleon mused as he returned his attention to the map. 'We will strike here, at Charleroi, in the early hours of the fifteenth of June.'

Soult's eyebrows rose. 'So soon?'

'We cannot attack soon enough. Issue the orders. The cavalry is to screen our approach to the frontier tonight. No fires are to be lit until the campaign begins and every man is to be as quiet as possible. The enemy must not guess our intentions. Now, I am tired. I need sleep.'

Napoleon turned and headed back towards the door. 'I trust that you have arranged quarters for me?'

'Of course, sire.' Soult hurried after him. 'I'll have a clerk show you the way.'

The room was spacious and a comfortable breeze cooled the air as Napoleon lay on the bed, stripped down to his shirt and breeches. Even though he was exhausted by the frenzied activity of the last three months, no sleep would come. He lay still, staring at the ceiling, as orderlies and officers came and went in the rooms below. Beyond the walls of the inn he could hear the faint hubbub of the army; shouted orders, the occasional rattle as a recently recruited drummer boy practised his beats, and the high-spirited cheers and laughter of men on the verge of a great adventure. Napoleon's restless mind grappled with the supreme challenge posed by this latest campaign. Despite what he had said to Soult he knew that the odds were against him. Each of the allied armies matched his in size. Unless he could force his way between them there was little chance of victory, and without a decisive victory there was no hope of breaking the will of the vast coalition gathering to overwhelm him.

A large bee came into the room, its droning buzz growing louder while it flitted from side to side as it approached the bed. Napoleon's eyes sought the insect out and he smiled faintly as it landed on the bedpost by his feet. A bee, the symbol he had chosen for his emblem. It was a good omen.

That night, under cover of darkness, the army crept as close to the frontier as it dared. The soldiers on picket duty patrolled the bank of the Sambre, exchanging good-humoured insults with their unsuspecting Prussian counterparts on the far side of the river, just as they had done for many weeks. As each formation reached its position the men were ordered to fall out and settle down in silence. They had been issued with rations for five days, and as dawn broke over the gently rolling countryside the men chewed on bread and cheese, as they had been forbidden to light fires to cook the stew that they usually ate.

Even though he rose at first light, Napoleon did not leave headquarters to ride through his army to offer encouragement, as had been his custom on the eve of battle. As far as the allies knew, he was still in Paris, and it would be foolish to risk being greeted by cheers that might be overheard by the enemy pickets.

Marshal Ney arrived late in the afternoon. His coat was covered in dust and his cheeks flushed from the exertion of the ride from his estate outside Paris. Napoleon stared at him frostily as the marshal presented himself in the small office that had been commandeered from the owner of the inn.

'You are late, Ney.'

Ney sucked in a deep breath. 'I might have been given more warning, sire. I came immediately I got your summons. What is it that you require of me?'

'I need you to command the left wing of the Army of the North. Do you accept?'

'Yes, sire,' Ney replied without hesitation. 'When do you expect the enemy to attack us?'

Napoleon could not help a small smile and glanced at the timepiece mounted on the wall. 'It is we who will be attacking, Ney, in less than twelve hours from now.'

Ney's eyes widened. 'Sire, I know nothing of your plans. I need time to take up my command.'

'Your officers have already been briefed. Your chief of staff can provide you with all the details that you need. Do you still accept the command, or do you consider yourself unfit to meet the challenge?'

Ney glared back. 'I will do my duty, sire. I will lead the left wing of the army, wherever you command me to go.'

'Very well,' Napoleon stood up and held out his hand. 'My dear Ney, I have never needed you more than at this hour. You have no idea how much it comforts me to know that I will have the bravest of my marshals fighting at my side when we face the enemy.'

Ney puffed out his cheeks at such brazen flattery. Yet he took the emperor's hand and shook it firmly. 'I can think of no higher honour, sire.'

'Then it is settled.' Napoleon releaed his grip. 'Given the time we have left before the advance begins, I suggest that you collect your orders from Soult and ride to join your men.'

'Yes, sire!' Ney stood stiffly and bowed his head, then turned and strode out of the office.

The soldiers of the Army of the North spent the remainder of the day, and the first part of the night, resting in the fields and woods close to the peaceful flow of the Sambre. Then, at midnight, the sergeants and corporals quietly crept down the lines of sleeping men and shook them awake. In the cool night air the dark figures formed into columns and moved forward to their start positions. Elsewhere, in the artillery camps, the gun crews harnessed the horse teams and limbered the cannon before they too rumbled forward. Ahead of the dense columns of infantry and artillery the cavalry mounted and fanned out along the bank, and then waited for the order to cross the frontier. At three in the morning the sentries silently fell back and on the far bank the Prussians were puzzled when there was nō reply to the usual greetings they called across the water.

At headquarters Napoleon sat with his staff. Some of the officers conversed in low tones, but most sat in silence, glancing at the hands of a large clock perched on the mantel above the fireplace in the map room. The orders had been sent out to every formation hours earlier and the desks, stools and document chests had been packed on to the wagons allocated to Soult and his officers. There was a lull in the frantic activity of the last few days as everyone waited for the army to be unleashed against the allies. The hour hand of the clock crawled towards three and then, finally, Napoleon eased himself on to his feet, and his officers scrambled up from their chairs and faced him expectantly.

'Gentlemen! The attack begins. God willing, this time in a week we shall be celebrating in the streets of Brussels.'

Soult raised his fist and punched the air. 'Long live France! Long live the Emperor!'

His officers repeated his cry, again and again, while out in the night tens of thousands of men and horses rippled forward, advancing across the frontier.

Chapter 56

Arthur

Brussels, 15 June 1815

' 'Tis a damned disgrace,' Picton grumbled as he took his place at the table. 'The government has sent us not much more than half the troops your grace requested. And most of the beggars are green. Much of the army is foreign and nearly half the men speak German.'

'It is an infamous army, to be sure,' Arthur agreed calmly. He had invited his senior officers to an early dinner so that they might discuss their preparations for war before attending a ball that evening. Arthur had arrived to take up his command barely two months earlier and had been horrified by the lack of readiness evident in the lowlands. The failure of the British government to provide him with enough soldiers was only one of the difficulties he had had to contend with.

Faced with the new threat, Arthur had sought the services of as many as possible of the officers he had commanded in the Peninsula. Most had answered the call, but others had been imposed upon him, like his cavalry commander, the Earl of Uxbridge. It was the same with many of the staff officers who had been appointed by the Duke of York before Arthur arrived from Vienna.

Then there was the dubious quality, and loyalty, of the allied troops that made up two-thirds of his army. King William of the Netherlands had at first refused to agree to place his men under Arthur's command and had reluctantly consented only after intense diplomatic pressure from London, and the payment of a large subsidy in gold. Arthur had decided to distribute the most unreliable of his allied troops amongst his redcoats to lessen the impact of any treacherous sentiments. Picton was right to complain, Arthur reflected as the other officers took their seats. But that was the hand that he had been dealt and he must do the best he could.

At least Kitty and his sons were safe. Somerset had escorted them back to England before joining Arthur in Brussels. They had left Paris only a few days before Napoleon had arrived and Somerset had taken the commendable precaution of burning all the embassy's records before leaving. Unfortunately, the Bourbons had failed to show the same good sense and Napoleon had discovered the secret treaty that had been signed between Austria, France and England at the start of the year. When the details had been published in the French newspapers the Prussians and Russians had been outraged, and many of the officers in Blücher's army were hostile and suspicious of their English allies in consequence.

When the soup had been served, Arthur leaned towards Uxbridge and asked quietly, 'Any fresh reports of enemy activity on our right flank?'

'Nothing new. The Frogs seem to be there in strength, judging by what they show us along the frontier. Of course, if I had permission to send patrols into France we would have a far clearer picture.'

'Out of the question. My orders are to hold the army in readiness until war is declared. If we cross the frontier we become the aggressors.'

'Something of a nicety,' Uxbridge said dismissively. 'It is hard to believe that war can be avoided at this stage.'

'Nevertheless, we have our orders. In the meantime, I am concerned that Bonaparte may attempt to strike to the west of Brussels, and cut us off from the sea. The army must be ready to concentrate against an attack from that quarter. So, we must have adequate warning from your cavalry patrols, Uxbridge. They must stay alert.'

'I have them in hand, your grace. You'll be amongst the first to know if Boney goes for the coast, or takes the Mons road to Brussels.'

'That is well.' Arthur paused a moment. 'Blücher's chief of staff is demanding to know where I intend to concentrate my army in the event of an attack. I cannot tell him until I know where the main weight of the French army is positioned.'

'Damned Prussians,' Uxbridge muttered before he raised his spoon and took a sip. His eyes lit up. 'I say, fine soup.'

Arthur suppressed a sigh. He had been trying to keep up the morale of his army, and that of his Belgian hosts, by insisting that the social life of Brussels continue as if there were no threat of war. The difficulty of that was that many of his officers were playing their part too well and appeared to have scant concern for the presence of a French army gathering on the other side of the border.

He forced himself to make inane conversation with Uxbridge, until the end of the first course. Then, as the dishes were cleared away, a staff officer entered the dining room and hurried to Arthur's side and leaned towards his ear.

'Your grace, there is a Prussian officer waiting in the hall. He says he has an urgent despatch from Marshal Blücher's headquarters.'

Arthur nodded, and smiled apologetically to his guests as he rose from his seat at the head of the table. 'Pray continue the meal, gentlemen. I shan't be long.'

He followed the officer outside to where the mud-bespattered Prussian waited. Despite his anxious expression, the Prussian snapped to attention and bowed stiffly before speaking in heavily accented English.

'I come from General Gneisenau, your grace. The chief of staff begs to inform you that the French attacked our position at Thuin at eight o'clock this morning.'

'In what strength?'

'Enough to drive in our outposts and then take the town, your grace.'

'Are the French attacking anywhere else?'

'I don't know.'

'Very well.' Arthur nodded his thanks. 'Tell General Gneisenau that I am concentrating my army. I will send word of my position as soon as I can.'

The Prussian bowed his head again and turned to stride back towards the entrance of the house Arthur had rented in the heart of the city. Arthur turned to the staff officer. 'Get to headquarters at once. Tell Somerset to issue orders to every formation. The army is to form up and be ready to march as soon as orders are issued.'

'Yes, sir.' The officer turned away and increased his pace.

'Walk, my boy, don't run! We must appear calm in front of the local people.'

'Yes, sir,' the young officer replied, chastened.

Arthur returned to the dining room and sat back down. Picking up his fork he rapped the side of his glass. 'Quiet, gentlemen.'

The officers turned towards him.

'The French have crossed the border,' he announced. 'They attacked one of Blücher's formations.'

'At last.' Uxbridge smiled. 'Where was this?'

'At Thuin. The question is, does this constitute the main thrust of their attack, or is it a feint?'

'A feint?' Picton growled. 'Are you saying that Boney's trying to lure us towards the Prussians? That makes no military sense to me.'

'It does, if he means to break through on our right and sever our communications.' Arthur paused. 'That is what I believe his intention to be, for the present. To guard against that possibility, the army will concentrate to the west of Thuin. If there is any indication that this is not a feint, then we will adjust our position accordingly. I have given the order for the army to make ready to march. I will also send an order to General Dörnberg at Mons to probe for any sign of the enemy to his front. Meanwhile we shall wait until the situation becomes clear. Now, gentlemen, you know my policy with regard to the local people and our own civilians. We will attend tonight's ball and there is to be no mention of this attack. I suggest you make the most of the entertainment, since it may be the last such occasion for a while.'

Shortly after ten o'clock Arthur was talking to Uxbridge when he saw the guests stir by the entrance to the ballroom as a figure in a riding cloak entered and scanned the room. Arthur recognised him at once – General Müffling, the officer assigned to liaise between the headquarters of the two allied armies. As soon as he caught sight of Arthur the Prussian hurried through the crowd towards him.

'I fear the game is up,' Arthur muttered as the dancing stopped and the orchestra fell silent. All eyes were turning towards him.

'So it seems.' Uxbridge nodded.

Müffling had been riding hard and his cloak and boots were smeared with mud. 'Sir, Marshal Blücher sent me.'

'Come.' Arthur placed an arm on the Prussian's shoulder. 'Let us converse somewhere quiet, and I shall have refreshments brought to you.'

He led Müffling through a door at the side of the ballroom. Beyond, lit by a single candlestick, lay a small room used to store chairs. Arthur gestured to catch Somerset's attention and pointed towards the orchestra before closing the door behind him. As the music struck up Arthur turned to Müffling.

'What news?'

'Blücher has advanced to Ligny to confront the French army. He asks if you will move to support him.'

'How does Blücher know for certain that the French army lies before him?'

'We have been fighting the enemy throughout the day, sir. Our cavalry patrols report large columns marching through Charleroi. They even heard the enemy soldiers cheering for their Emperor. There can be no doubt that this is their main line of advance.'

Arthur was silent for a moment as he considered Müffling's words.

Then he nodded slowly. 'Very well, General. I hope that this is no ruse; I still think that the main attack will be along the most direct route to Brussels.' Arthur reached for the handle of the door and nodded towards the ballroom. 'Shall we?'

As they emerged back into the brightly lit ballroom Arthur saw that many of the officers had already left and more were taking their leave and making for the exit. There was nothing he could do to stop them, not without creating a scene. Müffling strode away and Arthur beckoned to Uxbridge and the other senior officers present to join him so that he might pass on their brief exchange. As the officers left to join their commands, Arthur saw that the remaining guests were hurrying to quit the ballroom, fear in their eyes.

The streets of Brussels were filled with soldiers hurrying from their billets towards the regiments forming up outside the city. As Arthur's carriage rattled over the cobbles he saw the first of the civilians loading their valuables into carriages and carts as they prepared to flee. Just before midnight the carriage reached General Müffling's house and Arthur was quickly shown through to the study where the general was waiting.

'I have given orders for the army to march east to support Marshal Blücher. We shall march through the night and hope to reach him by way of Quatre Bras tomorrow afternoon. Ride and tell him.'

'I will, sir.' Müffling reached for his coat. 'I only pray that it is not already too late.'

Arthur nodded. Every hour counted. If the French took the vital crossroads at Quatre Bras then there would be little chance of uniting the allied armies – and all that stood between Bonaparte and possession of the crossroads were two Dutch brigades.

THE WATERLOO CAMPAIGN JUNE 1815

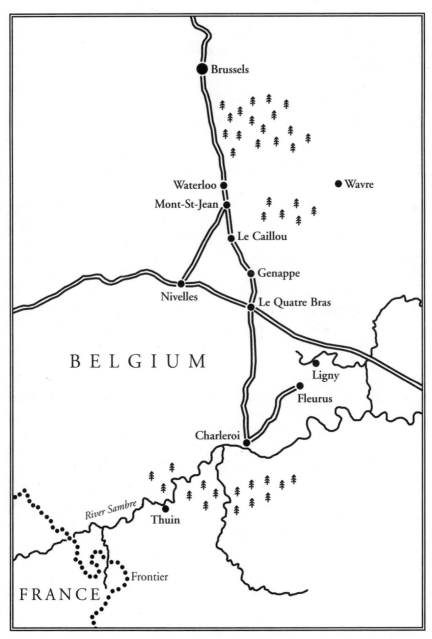

Chapter 57

Fleurus, 8.00 a.m., 16 June 1815

The order to Marshal Ney to seize the crossroads at Quartre Bras had just been sent when a report from Marshal Grouchy arrived, announcing that the Prussians were massing their forces near the village of Ligny, on the far side of the stream that gave the village its name. Napoleon felt his heartbeat quicken as he saw the opportunity that Blücher was foolishly extending to him. He looked up at the staff officer who had brought the message.

'Are you certain it is the main Prussian force?'

'Yes, sire. There is no question of it. They are forming up on the sloped ground on the far bank, in clear view.'

Napoleon smiled and then turned quickly to Soult. 'We will attack Blücher with Grouchy's wing and the reserve. Order them to advance on Ligny immediately.'

'Yes, sire. And what of Marshal Ney? Shall I send fresh orders for him to march and join us?'

Napoleon quickly considered the positions of his forces and shook his head. 'No. We must have the crossroads. But tell Ney that he is to report the moment he has won control of Quatre Bras.' Napoleon rose from his chair and strode towards the door of the hotel that Soult's headquarters had occupied. He gestured to the officer who had carried the message from Grouchy. 'Come! You are to take me to your marshal at once.'

The Emperor and his escort hurriedly mounted, and led by Grouchy's staff officer they pounded out of the village. Ahead of them stretched the rear echelons of the right wing of the army, battalion after battalion of infantry together with artillery columns. As the small party of horsemen galloped up the side of the road, the soldiers glanced round and let out a great cheer as Napoleon passed by, his grey coat-tails whipping out behind him.

An hour after he left headquarters Napoleon reached Marshal Grouchy's command post at a windmill on a small hill overlooking the stream and the high ground beyond. The soldiers and guns of Vandamme's corps were already deploying on the French side of the stream. Opposite them stood the Prussians: dense formations of infantry in their blue and black uniforms, spread out along the slope. Napoleon dismounted and hurried towards Grouchy and his staff.

'It seems that fortune favours us, gentlemen,' he said, gesturing towards the enemy. The officers smiled, and then Napoleon turned his attention directly on Grouchy. 'What do you know of their strength and dispositions?'

'That's Zieten's corps over there, sire. My skirmishers captured some prisoners at first light. I had them interrogated. They said that the enemy is concentrating at Ligny. Our cavalry patrols report that two more Prussian corps are approaching from the north. There is no question of it. Blücher intends to fight.'

'Then we may face as many as ninety thousand of them,' Napoleon mused. 'Very well, we need to bring every available man into line as swiftly as possible. You may start siting your guns opposite the Prussians. When the battle begins, they will make a fine target.'

'Indeed, sire.' Grouchy nodded.

Napoleon felt a surge of satisfaction flow through his body. His plan had called for the Army of the North to break through between the allies and then seek and destroy them one at a time. Now it seemed that Blücher had saved him the job. It was only a question of assembling his forces more swiftly than Blücher and attacking the instant he had the advantage.

As the hours passed and the sun climbed into the sky more infantry, cavalry and artillery swelled the ranks on either side. The Prussian infantry occupied all the buildings along the far bank of the Ligny and set about fortifying them, knocking loopholes in the walls to harass the French when they made their attack. While both sides prepared, Napoleon rode forward with his escort to inspect the battlefield more closely. The ground either side of the stream was marshy for some way and it was clear that any attack would be forced to use the bridges and fords scattered along the length of the stream. There would be heavy losses, Napoleon realised as he returned to the command post and waited for the rest of his forces, and Soult's headquarters, to reach the battlefield. It steadily became evident that the enemy were arriving in greater numbers than the French, and towards noon Napoleon sent a message to Ney instructing him to attack the Prussian right flank as soon as Quatre Bras was in French hands.

By two in the afternoon Napoleon had decided on his plan.

Standing over Soult's map table, he briefed his officers. 'The enemy has spread their forces thinly along the stream, over a considerable distance. The situation could hardly be better for us, gentlemen. While our cavalry contains Blücher's left flank, the guns massed in the centre of the battlefield will pound the enemy line, and then we shall attack frontally. When the moment is ripe, the Imperial Guard will smash through their line and cut their army in two. It will only remain for Ney's wing to fall upon their right flank and rear and the Prussians will be shattered. After that, we will turn on Wellington and end this campaign.' He smiled as he stared round at his officers. 'A few days from now France will have triumphed and our enemies will have no choice but to sue for peace.'

Half an hour later, the signal gun announced the opening of the battle, and the French batteries thundered out. At first they concentrated their fire on the defenders in the villages along the bank of the river, and then, as the order was given for the infantry to advance, they shifted their aim to begin wreaking terrible destruction in the ranks of the Prussian reserves drawn up in full view on the slope behind the stream. Roundshot smashed into the formations, leaving a trail of bodies and limbs to mark their passage. Despite the losses, the iron discipline of the Prussians held up, and the battered battalions closed up the gaps and stood firm.

Through his telescope Napoleon watched the progress of the attacks across the stream as his men fought to gain control of the villages covering the bridges and fords. The enemy fire was withering and the soldiers following the tricolours were being scythed down as they advanced. Yet their morale never faltered and the cheers for their country and their Emperor carried back faintly but clearly to Napoleon as he watched the bloody struggle.

Soult was at Napoleon's side and muttered, 'Our men are taking heavy punishment, sire.'

'As are the enemy,' Napoleon replied. 'We just need Blücher to commit his full strength to the fight, and the Guard and Ney will deal the decisive blows.' Napoleon lowered his telescope and focused his mind on the surrounding landscape once again. It would be as well to spur Ney on, to ensure that his men reached the battlefield in time to strike as hard a blow to the enemy as possible.

He turned to Soult. 'Send a message to Ney. Tell him the battle is in full swing. He is to manoeuvre immediately in such a way as to envelop Blücher's right and fall upon his rear. Tell him the fate of France is in his hands.'

Soult nodded as he finished scribbling down the message in his notebook and then hurried over to his aides to have the note rewritten in a fair hand. A moment later a despatch rider spurred his horse into a gallop and headed west towards Quatre Bras. Napoleon turned his attention back to the vicious struggle along the banks of the stream and noted with satisfaction that the first of the villages had fallen into French hands as a tricolour appeared in the tower of the church.

'Sire!' Soult called out as he trotted over from where his staff sat hunched over their campaign desks, dealing with the constant flow of reports and orders. He held up a scrap of paper. 'From Ney.'

'Well?'

'He reports that he is engaging Wellington at Quatre Bras. He estimates their number at twenty thousand, with more sighted approaching the crossroads.'

'Damn.' Napoleon pressed his lips together. This was unexpected. 'Tell Ney to continue to fight for control of the crossroads, but detach d'Erlon's corps to make the attack on Blücher's flank. I need every man here. Every man.'

'What about Lobau's corps?' Soult asked.

'Lobau?'

'At Charleroi, sire.'

Napoleon turned on his chief of staff. 'What the hell are they doing at Charleroi?'

'They have no orders, sire,' Soult explained. 'You made no mention of them this morning.'

'I made no mention?' Napoleon's face drained of blood as he raged, 'You fool, Soult! You idiot! What use is Lobau's ten thousand in Charleroi? Send for them. At once, do you hear? Now get out of my sight.'

He turned away from his chief of staff before he gave in to the temptation to strike the man. An entire corps of his army was sitting uselessly as the decisive battle of the campaign was being fought. Lobau had little chance of arriving in time to make a difference. The outcome of the day rested on Ney's shoulders. Napoleon turned and stared west for a moment, in the direction of Quatre Bras. If he could not have Ney, then at least d'Erlon's corps would swing the balance here in Napoleon's favour. There was still a good chance of destroying Blücher and his army.

Quatre Bras, 3.00 p.m.

The Prince of Orange greeted Arthur and Somerset with a cheery wave as they galloped up to his line. The 'Young Frog', as he was known to Arthur's officers thanks to his bulging eyes and thick lips, had drawn his two brigades up on a rise half a mile in front of the crossroads. The rolling land surrounding Quatre Bras, and the high crops of rye, obscured the view of the allied troops, and that of the French to the south. So far it had worked in the allies' favour, as the enemy could not have realised how few men stood before them. Otherwise, Arthur realised, they would have swept the two Dutch brigades aside.

'My dear Duke!' The Prince grinned. 'A pleasure to see you, sir.'

'And you too, your highness.' Arthur touched the brim of his hat. 'What is the situation here?'

'Calm enough. The French had left us alone until an hour or so ago. Then we heard their drums. Since then, they have contented themselves with sending forward some skirmishers to take those farms.' The Prince turned and indicated two small clusters of buildings to the south. 'They're also fighting my light infantry in the woods, to our right there.'

As Arthur and Somerset followed the direction indicated a fresh crackle of muffled musket fire sounded from the trees. In the distance the dull thunder of artillery at Ligny could be heard. The Prince cocked his head towards the east. 'I take it that Marshal Blücher has engaged the enemy?'

'Indeed.' Arthur agreed. 'I spoke to him less than two hours ago, just as the battle began. Unless we are attacked first, it is my intention to march the army to his support.'

'Bravo!' The Prince nodded. 'The Corsican pig will soon be on the run, eh?'

'That is my fervent hope, your highness. But first we must secure control of the crossroads.'

They were interrupted by a fresh exchange of musket fire in the woods, far closer this time. Figures emerged from the treeline, running back towards the Prince of Orange's position. Some had lost their hats, and others had abandoned their muskets. They disappeared into the rye and only the swirls of the tall stalks marked their passage. Behind them came the first of the French skirmishers, advancing out of the woods towards the right of the Dutch brigade. To the south, approaching through more of the crops, Arthur could make out another line of skirmishers, and behind them a shimmering mass of bayonets. A moment later the crested helmets of cuirassiers appeared to the left, working their way towards the vital Namur road that linked the two allied armies.

'We are in some difficulty, your grace,' said Somerset as he watched the enemy approach.

'I have eyes,' Arthur snapped. He turned in his saddle and stared up the road leading to Brussels. A British column was approaching, at its head the unmistakable figure of General Picton in his black coat and top hat, looking for all the world like an undertaker. 'Ride to Picton. Tell him to send one of his officers back down the road. He is to tell every formation he encounters that they must march for Quatre Bras as swiftly as they can!'

Without waiting to salute, Somerset spurred his horse into a gallop and raced towards the oncoming British soldiers. By the time he had returned to his commander Arthur was watching the steady progress of the French as they emerged from the wood and began to drive back the Dutch brigade on the right. On the left the French cavalry were forming a line to charge. Arthur could see the first of the Dutch troops beginning to waver as they saw the danger. Some of the men began to step back, disordering the line, and then the first abruptly turned and ran, dropping his musket and then wriggling out of the straps of his backpack as he fled. Arthur glanced back to see that Picton's leading regiment, the Ninety-second, Highlanders, were deploying into a line a few hundred yards behind the Prince of Orange's position. More regiments were advancing to extend the line, and over to the left another column, in the black uniforms of the Brunswickers, was striking out towards the left, to support the wavering Dutch.

'This is going to be a close fight,' Arthur muttered.

'Oh, you need not worry, sir,' the Prince of Orange responded cheerfully. 'My men will stand their ground.'

'I hope so.'

The shrill cry of bugles sounded and an instant later the French cavalry advanced, crushing the rye stalks under them as they closed on the Dutch brigade. A few shots rang out as a handful of men were too nervous to wait for the order to fire, then more followed, and a long ragged volley consumed the Dutch soldiers in a bank of powder smoke. For a moment they could not see the approaching cavalry, but they could hear them well enough and feel the vibration of hooves through the ground beneath their boots. It proved too much for the inexperienced soldiers and the brigade broke, streaming back towards the crossroads.

The French bugles sounded the charge and the cuirassiers let out a roar as they spurred their big horses on. They swept through the dispersing smoke, swords and breastplates gleaming in the sunlight, and then slashed left and right as they cut down the fleeing Dutch soldiers. A short distance beyond, Arthur saw the Brunswickers halt and try to deploy, but they were thrown into confusion as the Dutch rushed amongst them, swiftly followed by the French cavalry, and then the Brunswickers were fleeing as well.

'Your grace!' Somerset shouted a warning and pointed as one of the cuirassier squadrons began its charge down the length of the remaining Dutch brigade. Arthur saw the danger and called to the Prince of Orange. 'Your highness, follow me!'

The three officers turned their mounts and spurred them down the rise towards the line formed by Picton's division. The remaining Dutch troops, caught between the infantry emerging from the wood and the cavalry charging their flank, turned and ran. The air was filled with the sound of horses' screams and the irregular pop of muskets as Arthur urged his mount on. Ahead lay the Highlanders, two deep, front rank kneeling as they advanced their bayonets to receive the cavalry charge. With an icy stab of realisation, Arthur saw that he and the others were in immediate danger of being impaled on those bayonets.

Cupping his hand to his mouth he bellowed as loudly as he could, 'Ninety-second! Lie down!'

Even though the order was not in the manual, the nearest men had sufficient presence of mind to throw themselves flat, and the horses of the three officers leaped over the Highlanders. As Arthur reined in and turned his mount round the men rose to their feet to face the oncoming cuirassiers.

'Hold your fire until I give the order!' Arthur shouted, ignoring Picton's angry expression at his commander's presumption. 'Wait . . . Wait . . .'

The men held their muskets tightly into their shoulders, stilling their breath in anticipation. The enemy, having cut down the Dutch, now pounded on towards the redcoats, so close that their savage expressions were clearly visible. At no more than thirty yards Arthur shouted the order. 'Fire!'

The volley crashed out and from the saddle Arthur saw the leading Frenchmen and their mounts pitch forward in a tangle of arms, legs and horseflesh. Those behind had to swerve aside or rein in and the impetus of the charge was broken. A second volley cut down another score of cuirassiers and then they turned and cantered away, back towards the rise where the Dutch brigades had once stood.

Arthur glanced round and saw that the arrival of fresh troops had stabilised the allies' position and the French cavalry were in retreat. But already another danger was evident as the first French guns unlimbered to his front. Within fifteen minutes the first cannon balls were pounding the allied line.

For the next two hours the French made several more attacks. But all the time more allied units and guns were arriving from the direction of Brussels and gradually the battle swung in Arthur's favour. In the approaching dusk the allied line pressed forward, retaking the ridge and farmhouses while the light infantry cleared the French skirmishers out of the woods. As night fell the final shots were fired and then the battlefield was quiet, save for the groans and cries of the wounded.

While more formations continued to arrive, including his headquarters staff, Arthur was growing increasingly concerned by the lack of news from Ligny. The last report from the Prussian headquarters, received at five o'clock, had informed him that Blücher's men were holding their positions.

'In that case,' Arthur told his aide, 'we shall be in an advantageous position tomorrow. Once we combine with Blücher we are sure to overwhelm the enemy.'

'Assuming Blücher has held them off.'

'Of course. But we must be certain.' Arthur called over one of his staff officers. 'Colonel Gordon! Over here, if you please!'

The colonel trotted over as Arthur mentally composed his orders before he spoke. 'You have a fresh horse?'

'Yes, your grace.'

'Then I want you to ride to Marshal Blücher's headquarters at Sombreffe, north of Ligny. Tell him that we have the crossroads and by dawn the army will be here in sufficient strength to march to join him. Also, I would appreciate a report on his engagement today.'

'Yes, your grace.'

'Then off you go. You may find me here when you return.'

Colonel Gordon disappeared into the night, galloping along the road to Sombreffe, and Arthur stretched his shoulders for a moment before settling down by one of the camp fires of the Ninety-second to await his return. The long hours of the night passed without incident as more soldiers arrived at the crossroads and were led to their positions by staff officers. At first Arthur's spirits were high. It had been touch and go the previous afternoon, but his men had bested the enemy. Even if Blücher had not won at Ligny, he would be near enough for the armies to combine in the coming day. However, there was no sign of Gordon during the night, and as the first light appeared on the horizon a building sense of foreboding began to gnaw at Arthur's heart. The sun rose, bathing the rolling landscape in a warm rosy hue. From the south came the faint sounds of trumpets as the French stirred, but there was no attempt to renew the previous day's fighting.

Finally, at half past seven, Colonel Gordon returned. His horse was blown, its bridle covered in foam, and Gordon's face looked gaunt as he dismounted and strode up towards Arthur.

'Well?'

'If you please, your grace, might we speak out of earshot of the others?'

Arthur frowned, but paced a short distance away from the headquarters staff, who exchanged a mixture of curious and anxious expressions.

'Blücher was defeated yesterday, your grace.' Gordon spoke softly. 'Many of his formations were routed. The rest were forced to retreat.'

'I see.' Arthur felt his heart sink as he digested the news. 'Then I take it he is no longer at Sombreffe.'

'No, your grace. He has pulled his army back to Wavre. That's why it took me so long to find them.'

'Wavre?' Arthur was momentarily stunned. 'But that's nearly twenty miles from here. By God, we are undone,' he continued in a hushed tone as the full implication of the news struck home. Blücher was powerless to intervene if the French attacked Arthur's army at Quatre Bras. Taking a deep breath, Arthur patted Gordon on the shoulder. 'My thanks to you. I suppose in England they will say we have been licked. I can't help it; as the Prussians have gone back, we must go too.' He shook his head sadly. 'Find yourself some refreshment. But first, send General Müffling to me.'

'Yes, your grace.'

While he waited for the Prussian liaison officer Arthur glanced to the south and east, as if expecting to see the leading formations of the French army already advancing to attack him and seal their victory.

Müffling came up, hurriedly fastening his jacket buttons. 'You sent for me?'

'Yes. It seems that your countrymen were defeated yesterday.'

The Prussian's jaw sagged in dismay. 'I had not heard.'

'That is because we were not told,' Arthur responded coldly. 'Blücher has retreated to Wavre. Yes, Wavre. More than a day's march from here. And his chief of staff did not think to inform us of his reverse at Ligny. For what reason, I wonder? A suspicious mind might conclude that we had been left here, unaware, in order to cover the Prussian retreat.'

Müffling froze and then shook his head. 'That is an ignoble suggestion, your grace.'

'Perhaps. And if I am mistaken, then I apologise,' Arthur replied flatly. 'But the fact remains, my army is in an exposed position. I will have to withdraw. I want you to ride to Blücher at once. Tell him that I will fall back to a position parallel with his at Wavre.' Arthur closed his eyes and imagined the map of the surrounding landscape. He nodded. 'Tell Blücher I will make my stand at Mont-St-Jean, if he can promise me the support of at least one of his army corps.'

'Mont-St-Jean?'

'The ridge across the road to Brussels. Just before the village of Waterloo.'

'I know it.'

Arthur clasped his hand. 'If I am defeated by Bonaparte then I fear that England may never forgive Prussia. In that event the coalition will fail, and the shadow of Bonaparte will descend upon Europe once again.'

Müffling nodded. 'I understand. I will do whatever I can to persuade Marshal Blücher.'

Chapter 58

Ligny, 7.00 a.m., 17 June 1815

Napoleon was at breakfast when the first report came in from General Pajol. He had taken his cavalry forward at first light to scout for the Prussians and discover in which direction they had retreated. Pajol's officer informed the Emperor that a large body of the Prussians had been spotted on the road to Liège. There were signs that some more of the enemy had headed in the direction of Wavre, but Napoleon dismissed that. If Blücher was retreating, then he would be sure to fall back on his supply lines and make for Liège.

Napoleon nodded with satisfaction as he dismissed the messenger and turned his attention back to his breakfast. He had been joined by Grouchy, Soult and some of the headquarters officers. Despite heavy losses, the victory of the previous day had left the Emperor in a good mood, and his subordinates were grateful for that.

'All is proceeding according to plan,' Napoleon declared as he cut into a rasher of bacon. 'The Prussians are on the run, and Ney controls the crossroads at Quatre Bras. Wellington and his rabble will be withdrawing towards Brussels.' He popped a large piece of meat into his mouth, chewed quickly and swallowed. 'We have driven the enemy apart and it only remains to complete their destruction.' He smiled at his officers. 'This may go down in history as the swiftest campaign I have ever fought. Think on that, gentlemen. In years to come you will be sure to tell the tale to your grandchildren, eh?'

Soult and some of the others chuckled, but Grouchy's expression remained sombre.

'What is it, Grouchy?' Napoleon frowned. 'Why the long face?'

'Sire, we should have launched our pursuit of Blücher last night. If we had, then his army would have been scattered. As it is, we have lost contact with the Prussians. They could be anywhere. Rallying even as as we sit here and eat.'

'You heard the report. Pajol saw them on the road to Liège.'

'He saw some Prussians. They could be deserters. I'm not convinced that our cavalry have located the main body of the Prussian army. Sire, we have to find them.'

A fresh knock at the door interrupted Grouchy. A junior officer entered and handed a slip of paper to Soult. The chief of staff read through it quickly and then cleared his throat. 'From Ney, sire.'

'Yes?'

'He, er, says that he was not able to complete the capture of the crossroads yesterday. Wellington is still holding the position.'

Napoleon lowered his knife and fork and licked his lips as he considered this new information. What was Wellington playing at? He must know that his ally had been heavily defeated.

Soult leaned forward with an excited gleam in his eyes. 'Sire, the reserve could reach Quarte Bras in a matter of hours. If Ney can pin Wellington to the crossroads, then we can force him to give battle.'

'Wellington will not fight. He will retreat. In fact, I would be surprised if he had not already abandoned the position. He is not so foolish as to try to remain there now that Blücher cannot support him.' Napoleon drummed his fingers lightly on the table as he considered the situation. Then he looked up. 'As I see it, there are two possible courses of action. First, we leave Ney to keep Wellington occupied, and press on with the rest of the army to find Blücher and complete the destruction of his army. Second, Grouchy pursues Blücher with the right wing of the army, while Ney and the reserve take on Wellington. What are your thoughts?'

His officers were silent for a moment and then Soult spoke up. 'Sire, as we have lost contact with the Prussians any pursuit that we mount now entails the risk of marching in the wrong direction. If Blücher is making for Liège and we follow him, then we will have to extend our supply lines. If Wellington manages to elude Ney then he could cut our communications.'

'If. If. If!' Napoleon shook his head and continued acidly. 'Thank you for your advice, Soult.'

'Soult is right to point out uncertainties, sire,' said Grouchy. 'We should have remained in contact with the Prussians and destroyed them at the second attempt. Now it is too late. We know where Wellington is, so we must strike at him, as soon as possible.'

Napoleon was angered by the slight on his judgement, yet there was truth in Grouchy's words. It made sense to fall on Wellington. Yet there were other considerations. 'Wellington's army is still intact, whereas Blücher's is battered and in retreat. Blücher was always the bigger threat.

If the Prussians are annihilated then we will only have to face the weaker of the two allied armies.' Napoleon stared at Grouchy.

Grouchy gritted his teeth and sucked in a breath before he responded as calmly as he could. 'You are right, of course, sire. But the longer we spend looking for Blücher, the greater his chance to rally his troops and co-ordinate his efforts with Wellington. Whatever we do, we must do it quickly.'

Napoleon was still for a moment. Despite what Grouchy said, the prospect of the destruction of Blücher was too alluring and too valuable to dismiss. 'I will give General Pajol a little longer to confirm the location of the main body of Blücher's army. If there is no definite sighting, then we shall move on Wellington. Breakfast is over, gentlemen. Marshal Grouchy, you and I will ride to your command. I wish to congratulate your men on their efforts yesterday, while we wait for word of Blücher.'

For the next three hours Napoleon, Grouchy and a cavalry escort toured the battlefield. There were still thousands of bodies littering the ground about the villages where the fighting had been hardest. On the slopes lay the lines of the Prussian units torn to pieces by French artillery, and further up the scattered corpses of those who had been cut down by the cavalry charges with which the battle had concluded. Many of the French regiments had suffered grievously in the opening attacks, and Napoleon was careful to offer the survivors his praise, and hand out promotions and the promise of reward once the campaign was over. At his side, Grouchy did his best not to fret and surreptitiously checked his pocket watch whenever he could. Eventually he could bear it no more.

'Sire, it is almost eleven, and no further word from Pajol. You must decide.'

'Damn Pajol,' Napoleon muttered. 'What is he playing at? Why doesn't he report?'

'We have to assume he has not found the Prussians, sire.' Grouchy leaned towards him and spoke in a low urgent tone. 'For pity's sake, sire. We must act now.'

Napoleon stared at him for a moment and then nodded. 'Very well. Take your men and pursue Blücher. Keep your sword in his back. Meanwhile I will use Ney and the reserve to deal with Wellington.'

'Yes, sire.' Grouchy bowed his head with a relieved expression. 'I will set out at once.'

Napoleon nodded his consent and then abruptly turned his horse back in the direction of headquarters and spurred it into a gallop. The decision was made and now he must strike at Wellington as swiftly as possible, before the Duke could retreat out of danger. He returned to Soult just long enough to give the order for the reserve to move on Quatre Bras and then rode towards the crossroads to join Marshal Ney and his men.

The day was warm and the air quite still. To the east the sky was obscured by a dull haze. Directly above him only a handful of clouds floated serenely across the lush green of the Belgian countryside. Yet it was the very peacefulness that concerned Napoleon as he urged his mount on. There was no sound of cannon fire from the direction of Quatre Bras. If Wellington was still there then surely he should be hotly engaged by Ney's forces?

As the road crested a rise Napoleon saw the sprawling camp of the left wing of his army. There was no sign of any formation ready to advance and do battle. Ahead, astride the crossroads, he could see the thin red blocks of Wellington's army, interspersed with artillery batteries as they stood ready to defend their position. Beyond, in the distance, he could see more columns, moving in the direction of Brussels. Napoleon felt his stomach knot in fury as he beheld the scene, and he dug his spurs in sharply as he galloped on.

A mile later the road passed through an infantry regiment. The men were sitting quietly around their camp fires where pots of stew simmered, suspended beneath the iron cooking tripods. The pounding of hooves drew the attention of the closest men and they sprang to their feet as they recognised the Emperor, but the first cheers died in their throats as Napoleon reined in and shouted at them. 'What the hell is this? What are you doing here? To arms, you fools! You there!' Napoleon thrust his finger towards the nearest sergeant. 'Find your colonel. You tell him the Emperor wants this regiment formed up and ready to march in ten minutes. If it isn't I'll have him shot. And pass the word on to other units!'

'Yes, sire!' The sergeant saluted stiffly then turned to bellow orders to his men. Napoleon rode on, ignoring the other regiments he galloped through as he sought out Ney's headquarters. By the time he reached the farm a mile south of the crossroads his mount was blown, and its flanks heaved like bellows as Napoleon climbed down from the saddle and walked stiffly to confront Marshal Ney.

'Why are you not attacking the enemy?' he snapped.

Ney's face flushed red, and he opened his mouth to respond angrily, but controlled his temper just enough to growl back, 'I have not had any fresh orders to attack, sire. Not since I sent you my report of yesterday's action.'

'Orders? You do not need orders when you can see for yourself the need for action!' Napoleon clenched his hands tightly. 'Dear God, Wellington is all that stands between us and victory and you sit here on your arse and give him every opportunity to escape. Are you mad, Ney?'

'No, sire.'

'Then you must be a fool.' Before Ney could respond to the insult Napoleon continued bitterly, 'Form your men up to attack. We can only hope that we can still catch Wellington before he slips away. Get to it, Ney. There is not a moment to waste!' Napoleon turned away from his marshal, and found that he was facing General d'Erlon.

'France has been ruined,' Napoleon said bitterly. 'Go, General. Place yourself at the head of your cavalry and make ready to pursue the enemy's rearguard.'

It took nearly an hour for Ney's forces to prepare for battle. In that time the haze had spread across the land and now dark clouds were closing up on the crossroads. The air felt hot and clammy and made Napoleon's mood worse. He could only watch helplessly as, one by one, the regiments of Wellington's line pulled back and joined the retreat.

Quatre Bras, 2.30 p.m.

'Looks like we're in for quite a storm,' Uxbridge commented as he looked up at the dark clouds edging overhead.

Arthur nodded absent-mindedly. His attention was fixed on ground to the south of the crossroads. He had been expecting the French to renew their attack all morning, and yet nothing had happened. The army had started to withdraw towards Mont-St-Jean long before midday and now only the rearguard remained. Uxbridge's cavalry, together with Mercer's horse artillery and the rocket batteries, were all that stood between the crossroads and the enemy. At last, a few minutes earlier, he had heard the sound of bugles coming from the direction of the French and the men of the rearguard waited in tense expectation for first sight of the enemy.

A sudden breeze had picked up, swirling through the heads of the remaining clumps of rye in the fields that had been trampled the day before. The wind was cool and refreshing after the close stillness of the morning and early afternoon. A shadow engulfed the rearguard's position and swallowed them up in its gloom. Then Arthur felt the first drop of rain strike his cheek.

'Now we're for it,' Uxbridge muttered. '*Après ça, le déluge.*'

'Very funny,' Arthur commented. 'But I suspect we're in for a storm of a different kind any minute.' Half a mile to the south there was a rise in the land where the Prince of Orange's brigade had been mauled. The ground there and beyond was still bathed in brilliant sunshine. As Arthur watched, a lone figure on a white horse galloped on to the rise and halted to survey the British position. The grey coat and bulky bicorne hat were unmistakable and he heard Uxbridge take a sharp breath beside him.

'By God, that's him!' Uxbridge exclaimed. 'That's Boney.'

'Indeed,' Arthur replied, struck by the drama of the vision before him. The contrast in light made the French Emperor seem much closer than he really was. Arthur watched as Bonaparte scrutinised the rearguard and then looked, it seemed, directly at Arthur, though he knew he must be virtually indistinguishable from his men in the gloom. More horsemen appeared, in gold-embroidered uniforms, and halted just behind Bonaparte as they too surveyed the silent men defending the crossroads.

'Your grace!' a voice called out, and Arthur turned to see Captain Mercer waving a hand to attract his attention.

'What is it?'

Mercer pointed towards the distant horsemen. 'I believe they might be in range for case shot, your grace. May I have your permission to fire?'

'Why not?' said Uxbridge eagerly. 'Strike him down and the war is as good as over.'

Arthur stared at his enemy. Uxbridge was right. But there was the danger that Bonaparte's death might well turn him into a martyr and provoke his men into a furious desire for revenge. He shook his head.

'Save your powder to cover the retreat.'

'Sir?'

'Do as I order, Captain!'

Mercer turned away from his commander with a shrug and stared towards the enemy. Arthur was aware of a dull rumble and then he saw the flicker of red and white pennants as a squadron of enemy lancers appeared a short distance to the Emperor's right. More lancers appeared, and then cuirassiers, as the rise filled with horsemen. At that moment there was a dazzling burst of white, followed instantly by a metallic crash of thunder, and the horses started in panic. Raindrops, small and hard like fowlshot, lashed down from the sky. The darkness abruptly engulfed the French cavalry and swept on as the storm burst over the country-side.

Arthur cupped a hand to his mouth. 'This will serve us well.

Uxbridge, give the order to withdraw. Horse artillery first, then the rockets and then your cavalry.'

'Yes, your grace.'

'I'll see you later,' said Arthur. 'Find me at Waterloo.'

Tugging on his reins, Arthur turned his horse and urged it into a canter as he rode up to the crossroads and joined the road leading to Brussels. The rain was already pooling on the surface of the road and glistening amid the grass on either side. If the downpour continued for any length of time it would turn the ground into a muddy morass, Arthur realised. So much the better, as it would surely hinder any pursuit that the enemy attempted. The flat thuds of Mercer's battery caused him to turn back one last time and a moment later the first of the rockets hissed through the storm and burst over the enemy cavalry. Arthur watched a moment longer, and then spurred his horse down the road to re-join his army.

Chapter 59

Le Caillou, 9.00 p.m., 17 June 1815

The storm continued without let-up for the rest of the afternoon and on into the night, swiftly turning the surface of every road and track into thick mud that sucked at the boots, hooves and wheels of the Army of the North. Napoleon had continued his pursuit of the enemy at the head of Ney's cavalry. The afternoon had been spent in a series of running skirmishes as the British mounted a staggered retreat to protect their guns, and slow down the French. As dusk fell, Napoleon had reached the farmhouse and called a brief halt while the long tail of his army struggled to catch up. When the first elements of the imperial headquarters arrived and started to prepare the Emperor's quarters, Napoleon gathered some cavalry together and continued a short distance down the road. Ahead lay the dark mass of a low ridge. Napoleon squinted into the downpour and turned to the cavalry commander at his side.

'Milhaud. It is imperative that we know if Wellington has halted for the night, or if he is using the cover of darkness to continue his retreat. Take your men forward and see what you can find.'

'Yes, sire.' General Milhaud saluted and then called out for his men to advance. Napoleon and his escort waited at the side of the road as the dark figures of the mounted column splashed by and disappeared into the night. There was no sound for nearly ten minutes, then all at once a bright flare of light appeared on the ridge, followed by the boom of a gun. More jets of flame stabbed out along a line bestriding the road and Napoleon nodded with grim satisfaction. Wellington was there all right. Close enough to be forced to stand his ground and fight in the morning. Napoleon turned his horse back and returned to the farmhouse. The headquarters servants were still preparing the accommodation, so he rested on some straw spread in a wide trough in one of the barns as he waited.

His fury at Ney had hardly abated. The opportunity to force a battle on Wellington at the crossroads had been lost, and now the arrival of the storm had hampered the army's attempt to close up on their enemy. The men were exhausted, and strung out along the road towards Quatre Bras. It would be many hours before they caught up with the vanguard, ready to continue the pursuit once the storm had passed.

Napoleon knew that some measure of the blame attached to him as well. Too many hours had passed that morning before he had grasped the need to move on Wellington's army. Exhaustion had played its part. He had not slept properly for many days and the normal heightened alertness of his mind was dulled. But there was something else, he mused. He had been so certain of his assumptions that Blücher had deserted his allies, and that Ney would have taken Quatre Bras. That was an error of judgement. The breathless speed with which he had recovered power in France, together with the hysterical joy that had greeted his return, had made him feel invulnerable and infallible. Today had been a rude reminder of a commander's need to constantly adapt to circumstances.

As soon as the farmhouse had been prepared for the Emperor and his staff, Napoleon summoned his senior officers. Over the next hour, the marshals and generals of division arrived, in drenched coats and splattered with mud. There was only one room in the farmhouse large enough to accommodate them all and most of the officers had to stand as they crowded about the Emperor, who was himself perched on a stool.

'It is my intention to attack Wellington tomorrow. He has chosen the very worst of positions to defend. Behind him lies the forest of Soignes. If his army breaks, they will not be able to retreat and we shall annihilate them. The opportunity we lost earlier today will be set right.' He shot a cool glance at Ney and the Marshal pursed his lips angrily. 'It is therefore vital that as many of our men as possible are in place before dawn. I have no time for excuses, gentlemen. You will do whatever you must to ensure that your formations reach the field in time. Questions?'

'Sire.' D'Erlon raised his hand. 'Will Grouchy be close enough to take part in the battle?'

'I don't know. I am still waiting for him to report his progress. We must assume that he will not reach us in time to intervene. That need not concern us. We are strong enough to carry the day.'

'And what of the Prussians?' asked Prince Jérôme. 'There is a danger that they might intervene, sire.'

'Not if Grouchy contains them. Besides, as far as we know, their line of retreat will take them away from Wellington. I think we can discount the prospect of the Prussians' causing us any difficulties.'

Jérôme shook his head. 'I am not so certain, sire.'

'Really?' Napoleon raised his eyebrows as he looked at his younger brother. 'Why is that?'

'Two hours ago I had a meal at an inn at Genappe. A waiter told me an interesting story. He claimed that Wellington and his staff ate there this afternoon. He overheard one of the staff officers say that Blücher was at Wavre, and that he might move to support Wellington tomorrow.'

The other officers stirred at this news. Napoleon was silent until they settled down again. 'I thank you for that intelligence, Jérôme. But let us wait for Grouchy's report. Then we shall know for certain.'

'What if the waiter was telling the truth, sire?' Jérôme persisted.

'I don't see how Blücher can present any danger, as long as Grouchy is forcing him back, away from Wellington.' Napoleon waved his hand dismissively. 'Blücher is of no concern to us. All that matters is the army waiting for us at Mont-St-Jean.'

Waterloo, 10.00 p.m.

Colonel Frazer was standing stiffly before his commander in chief, trying not to show any expression as he endured the tirade.

'It is bad enough having to contain the foolihardiness of my cavalry without my artillery blasting away at every shadow they see in the darkness,' Arthur said bitterly.

'Begging your pardon, your grace, but it wasn't shadows my boys were shooting at. It was Frog cavalry.'

'I don't give a damn. It's the job of the vedettes and the pickets to deal with such things. Not the damned artillery. Now Bonaparte knows where your batteries are sited, thanks to your gunners' overeagerness. I've a damned good mind to break every sergeant back to private over this, d'you hear?' Arthur leaned across his table, bearing his weight on his knuckles, and tried to moderate his tone. 'Now then, Frazer, you will have to see to it that the guns are repositioned. Perhaps a little hard work in the rain and the mud might help to clear the heads of your men, eh?'

'Yes, your grace. I'll give the order at once.'

'I'd rather you oversaw the repositioning in person.'

'Yes, your grace. Will that be all?'

Arthur nodded and his senior artillery officer turned smartly and marched to the door of the cottage. The sentry opened the door for him and Frazer disappeared into the rain. Once the door was closed, Arthur eased himself back down into his chair and gently rubbed his eyes.

There was little doubt that Bonaparte knew that his army was in position on the ridge. Uxbridge's cavalry patrols reported that more French troops were massing opposite the ridge with every passing hour. There was no question of further retreat. The position at Mont-St-Jean was the last decent defensive ground before Brussels, and there Arthur must stand and fight. His best hope was that Blücher would respond to his request and send some portion of his army to support Arthur. As yet there had been no answer.

Le Caillou, 4.00 a.m., 18 June

Napoleon stamped the mud from his boots as he handed the oilskin cape to a servant. He had just returned from a visit to his outposts to try to see if there was any sign that the enemy were withdrawing. The ridge was quiet and the sentries patrolling in front of the allied army were clearly visible against the dull hue of a multitude of camp fires burning on the reverse slope. Reassured that Wellington remained in position, Napoleon had returned to his headquarters. As he entered the dining room of the farmhouse Soult approached him.

'Sire, a message has arrived from Grouchy.'

'Ah, at last. What does he say?'

'He has determined that the bulk of the Prussian army had retired on Wavre, and not towards Liège.'

'Wavre?' Napoleon's brow creased as he concentrated on the implications of this news. It seemed that there was some truth in the story told by the waiter in Genappe after all. If Blücher was at Wavre then he needed to be watched closely to ensure that the Prussians did not intervene in the day's business. 'Does Grouchy say what his intentions are?'

'Yes, sire. He intends to follow them in order to prevent them from reaching Brussels, and joining Wellington.'

'Good. That is the right thing.'

'Shall I acknowledge his message, sire?'

'What? No . . . No, it's not necessary.' Napoleon shook his head and then crossed the room to sit on a bench by the rain-streaked window. He leaned his head back against the plastered wall and shut his eyes.

The rain finally stopped just before dawn and as the first glimmer of light stretched across the landscape the sodden men of the Army of the North stirred from beneath their drenched blankets and coats and built up their fires with whatever wood was left. Then, huddled round the blaze, as they tried to get warm and let their uniforms dry out, they quickly ate some of their remaining rations before packing their kit and forming up in their companies.

At the army's headquarters Napoleon was having breakfast with his staff. Despite the hardships and lack of sleep in recent days the mood around the Emperor was light-hearted. One of the allied armies had been beaten and now another would share its fate. The only issue to spoil Napoleon's mood that morning was a report from General Drouot that the ground was too wet for the artillery to be moved forward to a position where they would have the enemy line in range. The wet ground would also lessen the impact of any artillery fire since the shot would not be able to ricochet off the ground and would simply bury itself in the muddy soil. Therefore Drouot requested that the attack be delayed until late in the morning. After brief consideration Napoleon consented. He had a clear superiority in artillery and it would make sense to use that to best effect.

'Well, then,' he announced. 'It seems that the army will be at leisure this morning.' A distant bell began to toll. 'Of course, it is Sunday, the day of rest. Most propitious, this rain.'

His officers smiled. Even Soult, whose usual energetic demeanour had been somewhat dampened by the burdens of his new position as chief of staff, relaxed a little. He waited a moment and then coughed before he addressed the Emperor.

'Sire, since the start of the engagement is to be delayed, might we recall Grouchy and put the result of the battle beyond doubt?'

'Doubt?' Napoleon was taken aback. 'You doubt the outcome? Why, we have ninety chances in our favour and not ten against. We do not require Grouchy. Soult, just because you were beaten by Wellington does not make him a good general. If he was, then he would surely not have chosen such poor ground to defend. His difficulties are compounded by the poor quality of his troops. I tell you, this will be a brief battle, not much more effort for us than eating this breakfast.'

'Truly, I hope so, sire.'

'What about you, Reille?' Napoleon turned to another of his commanders who had faced Wellington. 'Do you share Soult's anxieties about the quality of our opponents?'

Reille recognised the change in his master's mood and answered cautiously. 'Wellington knows how to defend, sire. Attacked from the front his troops are all but impregnable. However, we have the advantage in cavalry. If we manoeuvre on his flanks, then he must surely be defeated.'

'Rubbish!' Napoleon barked. 'A frontal attack is all that is necessary to break his line. You shall see. And this we can achieve,' he turned back to Soult, 'without Grouchy.'

Soult bowed to his master's will. 'Very well, sire. But may I at least communucate with Grouchy your desire that he should close up on the Prussians at Wavre?'

'As you will,' Napoleon replied carelessly. 'Tell him to keep pushing the Prussians back before him. Now then,' he rose from his chair, 'since there is time, I will inspect my soldiers. Soult, you will establish the command post at that inn . . .' He clicked his fingers.

'La Belle Alliance, sire?'

Napoleon nodded. 'It will provide a fine view of the destruction of Wellington's army.'

Mont-St-Jean, 10.00 a.m.

Arthur had joined his army soon after dawn and ridden along its length, to make sure that his men were in position and prepared for the coming battle. As he passed by the men cheered him and Arthur, true to the cool demeanour he had imposed on himself for many years now, occasionally favoured them with a curt nod. There was a constant crackle of muskets as the men fired into the air to clear the barrels of any moisture or grit washed in by the previous night's deluge. The rain had also had another peculiar effect that amused the men. The dye from their jackets had run and the white cross belts were stained red. Arthur hoped it wasn't an omen.

He had decided to ensure that his right flank was where his main strength would lie, in case Bonaparte attempted to hook round the army's position. The left, in the direction of Blücher, was far less formidable, and Arthur knew that he was taking a gamble on the timely arrival of his ally. The artillery had been sited along the crest of the ridge, where it could pound the French columns as they advanced to attack. Behind them, sheltered by the reverse slope, the infantry waited in a staggered line while much of the cavalry was massed behind the centre. A handful of farms lay scattered across the front of the allied line and these had been fortified, ready to act as strongpoints to break up the enemy's assaults. On the right was the small country estate of Hougoumont where Arthur had placed the Foot Guards, the cream of his infantry, and in front of the centre, on the road to Brussels, stood the large farmhouse of La Haye Sainte, defended by a battalion of the King's German Legion.

Arthur completed his inspection of his battle line and joined his staff officers on the ridge a short distance above the chateau and grounds of Hougoumont. 'Good morning, gentlemen!' he called out cheerfully.

They returned the greeting and touched the brims of their hats in salute. A figure at the rear of the press of officers edged his mount through and Arthur saw that it was General Müffling. He trotted forward to Arthur's side.

'Sir, I have been looking for you this last half-hour. I have received a message from Marshal Blücher, sent at seven this morning.'

Arthur composed himself before he responded. 'Well?'

'He promises to support you with at least two corps of his army. And he will lead them in person.'

Arthur felt a lightness of spirit fill his heart and he allowed himself a faint smile as he spoke to Müffling. 'I thank you, my friend. That is the very best of news.'

Arthur tugged on the reins and Copenhagen, his favourite mount, edged round to face the enemy, less than a mile away. As he surveyed the French, clearly massing for a frontal attack, Arthur realised quite how small the battlefield was. No more than three miles by two, within which the best part of two hundred thousand men were preparing to contest the ground. The French were manhandling the last of their guns into position, in the middle of their battle line.

'There's Napoleon, your grace,' a voice called out.

Arthur glanced to his side. 'I'll thank you not to get carried away by your enthusiasm, de Lancey.'

His young quartermaster-general flushed. 'I apologise, your grace.'

Arthur turned to gaze across the vale separating the two armies. Napoleon was clear to see, mounted once more on his snow-white horse, and escorted by a squadron of Polish lancers. As he made his way steadily between the massed formations of infantry his soldiers cheered wildly, some raising their shakos up in the air on the end of their muskets.

'They put on quite a show,' Uxbridge mused. 'Doubt we'll ever get the damned battle started at this rate.'

Arthur said nothing as he continued to watch his opponent. He was quite content for the French to waste time. Every minute that passed bought more time for Blücher's soldiers to reach the battlefield. Bonaparte seemed wholly unconcerned by the passage of time as he paraded through the formations of his army for the best part of an hour before returning to his command post beside the Brussels road. A few minutes later a signal gun boomed from close by the Emperor's position.

There was a faint click as Somerset opened his fob watch. 'I make it close on eleven thirty, your grace.'

Arthur nodded. 'Note it down.' He cleared his throat. 'The battle has begun, gentlemen. To your positions!'

Before the sound of his last words had faded the air was split by a terrible roar as the massed batteries of French artillery opened fire.

Chapter 60

A mixture of shot and canister rained down on the allied positions and from his command post Arthur could gauge that the enemy's fire was concentrated on the flanks of his army. Hougoumont in particular was being subjected to a pounding. Branches and leaves leaped from the small wood and the orchard that lay to the south and east of the chateau. Roof tiles exploded into fragments as a handful of French guns aimed too high. Through his telescope Arthur could see that the men defending the walled orchard had crouched down to take shelter from the bombardment. Even so, an occasional shot would smash a hole in the wall, sending lethal fragments of brick and flint flying through the air.

On either side of Arthur the allied guns were firing back at the enemy. The artillery was under strict orders not to engage in any counter-battery fire, and took aim on the massed formations of infantry and cavalry instead. As he had chosen to follow his usual tactic of keeping the bulk of his army on the reverse slope, Arthur knew that the French guns would not be the greatest danger on this day. The real test would come when Bonaparte launched his foot and horse against the allied line.

Even though the main weight of the French artillery was battering the flanks, the rest of the line was still being subjected to fire. The skirmishers were scattered amid the pale green corn and wheat across the allied front, rising to take aim and fire at their opposite numbers before ducking down again to reload. Every so often the crops around them would swirl as a ball, or a blast of canister, cut through the stalks, and one or more of Arthur's men would be plucked from sight as they fell.

The drone of a shot passing close overhead caused some of his staff officers to flinch and Arthur looked round. 'Steady, gentlemen.'

Glancing to his right he saw that one of his regiments, the Fifty-first Foot, was closer to the crest than was healthy, and even as he watched a roundshot hit the ground just in front of the flank company, smashing two men to bits as it bounced on.

'Somerset, order that regiment to lie down.'

'Yes, your grace.'

As Somerset galloped off, Arthur saw that his staff officers, over forty in all, were clustered together behind him. 'Uxbridge, it strikes me that our generals are rather too thick on the ground.'

Uxbridge nodded. 'I'm sure we make a tempting target.'

Turning Copenhagen, Arthur cupped a hand to his mouth to address his officers. 'I'd be obliged if you gentlemen would disperse. I will ride to you if you are needed.'

As the staff broke off into smaller groups Arthur saw that more regiments were following the example of the Fifty-first and going to ground, where they would be far less exposed to enemy fire. Turning his attention back to the situation around Hougoumont, he could see a French division forming up in front of the woods, ready to attack the moment their artillery ceased bombarding the chateau and its walled garden. Once the French infantry moved forward the allied guns on the ridge would be unable to fire on them for fear of hitting their own men.

The enemy artillery fire on Hougoumont gradually began to slacken and when the last of the guns ceased fire there was a brief pause before the French drums began to roll, beating an insistent rhythm, signalling the advance. The leading battalions of the division positioned in front of the chateau's woods began to pace forward.

'There are too few men defending Hougoumont, your grace,' said Somerset. 'They should be reinforced.'

Arthur shook his head. 'They are adequate for the task.'

Somerset shot him an anxious look but Arthur did not react, and fixed his attention on the action beginning down the slope. The leading French formations disappeared from sight as they entered the trees and an uneven crackle of musketry followed as the British skirmishers fell back towards the chateau. A moment later the first of the enemy reached the garden wall and began to clamber over. The defenders, spread thinly along the wall, did their best to hold the perimeter, but were forced to give way as the French climbed over, or scrambled through the gaps smashed through the wall by artillery fire. The blue-coated attackers quickly spread out across the gardens and approached the chateau and its outbuildings. Sparks of fire and puffs of smoke erupted from windows and loopholes as the defenders opened fire on the French infantry pressing in from two sides.

The enemy had reached the chateau more quickly than Arthur had anticipated and he feared that Somerset might be right. Nudging his spurs in, he trotted over to the commander of a battery of howitzers of the Royal Horse Artillery that stood limbered up and ready to move.

'Major Bull, isn't it?'

The battery commander saluted. 'Yes, your grace.'

'I need the services of your battery. Follow me.' Arthur turned and trotted down the slope towards the chateau. Bull and his howitzers followed, the gun carriages rumbling over the ground. Arthur drew up a hundred yards from the chateau. From the far side the din of the desperate struggle filled the air. 'Have your howitzers fire over the chateau. We must take the pressure off the defenders. But be sure to get the range right, Major.'

'Yes, your grace. I understand.'

Arthur watched as Bull's men swiftly unlimbered the howitzers and loaded the fused iron spheres into the stubby barrels. Bull carefully ensured that each gun's elevation was adjusted so that the shells' trajectories would clear the chateau by a safe distance. The battery opened fire and Arthur looked up to follow the faint smears of the sputtering shells as they arced over the chateau towards the wood beyond, bursting amid the branches and blasting the attackers with small iron shards.

'Very good,' Arthur called out to Major Bull. 'Remain here to support the chateau as long as you can.' He turned and galloped back up to his vantage point to watch the attack. Hundreds of French soldiers were crowded about the chateau and its walled courtyard, but as far as Arthur could see, none had succeeded in gaining entry. The relentless fire from the defenders was cutting the enemy down in droves and bodies steadily piled up around the building. Further back, those still in the woods were being savaged by the howitzer shells. The attack raged for ten more minutes before Arthur saw the enemy begin to fall back, fading into the trees before they retreated over the field beyond the wood. The firing in the chateau ceased and a moment later Bull's battery followed suit.

Arthur nodded with satisfaction. 'First blood to us, I think.'

La Belle Alliance, 1.00 p.m.

'What is Prince Jérôme doing?' Napoleon snapped as he watched fresh troops advancing towards Hougoumont from a second division. 'He is only supposed to be making a feint against the chateau. He was supposed to force Wellington to draw on his reserves, not me.'

'Sire, do you wish to order the Prince to cease his attack?'

Napoleon watched as the fresh wave began to enter the woods. A moment later the air above them was dotted with the white puffs of exploding shells. He shook his head. 'No. Jérôme may still force Wellington's hand, and if the Duke does not take the bait then we shall take the chateau, and use it to harass the allied line.'

Once again, Hougoumont was shrouded in powder smoke as Napoleon's men made their assault. He watched the ridge for any sign of movement and then pointed triumphantly as a column of redcoats doubled down the slope towards the chateau. 'There! I knew Wellington would have to send in more men.'

Soult watched for a moment and then said quietly, 'I make that no more than four companies, sire. Prince Jérôme has committed the best part of two divisions so far.'

Napoleon glared at him a moment and then turned his attention back to the battlefield. The smoke from the cannon of both sides was eddying above the landscape in dense clouds, threatening to blot out the view of the surrounding countryside. A sudden anxiety caused him to raise his telescope and sweep the horizon from the south round to the north-east. Fields, farmhouses and small woods glided past the eyepiece, and then a dark shadow just beyond the edge of a treeline caused Napoleon to stop. He blinked his eye and called one of the headquarters staff to stand in front of him so that he could use the man's shoulder as a rest to steady the telescope. Soult, and a handful of others, had seen his worried expression and now turned in the same direction and scrutinised the dark line that was gradually emerging from the trees.

'There is a column of soldiers over there,' Napoleon announced. Then he lowered the telescope and hurried across to the map weighted down on a table outside the inn. He scanned the map and then stabbed his finger down. 'The woods near Chapelle-St-Lambert.'

Soult exchanged a worried look with the other staff officers gathered about the map. One of them swallowed and asked, 'Could it be Grouchy? Marching to the sound of the guns?'

Napoleon shook his head. The distant column was coming from the direction of Wavre. 'Prussians. There is no doubt about it.'

There was a brief silence as the staff officers digested the information and then Soult raised his telescope towards the distant woods and spoke quietly. 'I can see more columns, sire.'

Napoleon stroked his chin. 'The Prussians are still two hours' march from the battlefield. They cannot support Wellington for a while yet. There is time enough to win the day.'

'And what of Grouchy, sire?' asked Soult. 'Shall I send for him?'

'By all means.' Napoleon shrugged, as he considered the last known position of Grouchy's thirty thousand men: advancing towards Wavre from the south. 'Though I fear that he is too far away to intervene, even if he were to wheel towards us at once.'

Nevertheless Soult hurriedly wrote the order and thrust it into the hand of one of his aides. 'There. Take that to Marshal Grouchy. Tell him that the fate of France in is the balance.'

As the officer swung himself up into his saddle and spurred away Napoleon sighed. 'The fate of France will be decided by those who are already on the field, Soult.' Turning his attention back to the ridge in front of the French battle line Napoleon pointed to the stretch of the slope to the right of the Brussels road. 'We cannot delay the main attack any longer. Soult, tell d'Erlon to prepare his corps to advance. It is time to see if these Englishmen you are so afraid of can really stand before our columns.'

Chapter 61

The Ridge of Mont-St-Jean, 1.30 p.m.

The massed guns of the French had been firing for the last half-hour, tearing up the hedge that ran along the road stretching across the ridge. The British skirmishers had lain down and pressed themselves into the earth as roundshot whirred overhead and canister hissed through the rye stalks like a sudden squall. Just in front of the ridge, spread out in line across the slope, were the Dutch soldiers of Bylandt's brigade. Arthur had not ordered them to withdraw to the reverse slope for fear that Bonaparte might think that the allied centre was retreating, cut short his bombardment and order his infantry forward. The brigade would have to be sacrificed to buy time. Word had reached Arthur that the Prussians had been sighted, but would not reach the battlefield for some hours yet. Arthur's heart was heavy as he watched the Dutchmen stand their ground and endure terrible punishment as the French guns tore bloody gaps in their ranks again and again.

Beside him, Somerset watched the sickening slaughter and turned to his commander. 'Your grace, I beg you, allow me to recall Bylandt.'

'No. They must stand and take it.'

Somerset shook his head. 'They will not endure it much longer. No men could.'

'They must. We must snatch at every chance for delay, until Blücher arrives.'

The French fire began to slacken and in less than a minute the last of the guns had fallen silent.

'What now?' Somerset wondered. 'Cavalry or infantry?'

His question was answered by the faint rattle of drums. Arthur trotted forward towards the large elm tree that grew close to the junction of the Brussels highway and the lesser road running across the ridge. Below, perhaps six hundred yards away, a dense bank of powder smoke obscured the French on the other side of the valley. The surviving British skirmishers were cautiously rising to their feet and peering into the smoke. Behind them the remains of Bylandt's brigade closed up and advanced ten paces to clear the shattered bodies and limbs of their fallen comrades.

Arthur strained his eyes, trying to penetrate the smoke as the sounds of the French drums drew closer. Then he saw the first of them, dim figures edging through the smoke as the skirmishers advanced ahead of the main columns. As they emerged into clear sight Arthur saw that the line stretched from in front of La Haye Sainte to his right for over half a mile across the battlefield towards the farmhouses of La Haie and Papelotte on the left.

'This is no feint, Somerset,' Arthur decided. 'They mean to break our centre at one stroke. From the frontage, I would think Bonaparte is sending three divisions against us.' He looked to his left, where the men of Picton's division were standing in battalion columns on the reverse slope. 'Three to our one. Not good odds.'

'If Picton breaks, then the enemy will cut our army in two, your grace.'

Arthur nodded, and then gestured towards the cavalry reserve. 'Ride to Uxbridge. He is to order his cavalry to make ready to charge.'

Somerset wheeled his horse and galloped away and Arthur turned back towards the enemy. There was a steady crackle of muskets as the skirmishers began their one-sided duel. The outnumbered British fired and fell back before the onslaught. Here and there, a red-coated figure was struck down and stumbled out of sight. The French columns continued their inexorable advance: one great mass of men who toiled up the muddy slope towards the ridge. They continued to emerge from the smoke, rank after rank, seemingly without end, and Arthur gazed upon the spectacle with a cold heart. It was a magnificent sight, he thought, more than ten thousand men boldly advancing to do battle. Magnificent, but those fine regiments must be destroyed.

The British artillery crews on the ridge took aim on the French line and opened fire, over the heads of the skirmishers, so that the roundshot plunged down amid the rear ranks, sweeping away files of ten or fifteen men at a time. The air was filled with the crash of cannon and the concussion shook the very air about Arthur. As he sat in his saddle and watched, the allied officers recalled their skirmishers and the men trotted back up to the ridge and through the gaps in the hedge to rejoin their regiments. Only Bylandt's brigade stood before the oncoming mass. The persistent rattle of the drums was accompanied by the cries of the French officers as they urged their men on, and the soldiers cheered for their Emperor in a deafening roar.

The British guns were now firing canister directly into the face of the columns, felling groups of men in an instant, but the gaps closed up and they continued forward relentlessly. At fifty paces, Bylandt gave the order for his men to make ready. Their muskets came up and a moment later the order to fire was lost in the crash of their volley. Directly before them the leading rank shimmered under the impact and men crumpled to the ground. Those following quickened their pace, but before they could close the distance the Dutch troops, shaken by the terrible losses they had already endured, gave way, falling back through the hedge. Their officers did their best to rally them on the far side, and for a moment most of them stayed with their colours and began to reload. There was no attempt to fire a volley and individual soldiers shot at the enemy as soon as their muskets were ready, then turned and fled after their comrades.

Arthur ignored them as they ran past his position. A moment later the last of the gun crews in front of the oncoming columns discharged their cannon and trotted back to safety through the gaps between the regiments of Picton's division.

Somerset had passed the orders on to Uxbridge and came galloping back to his commander's side. 'Your grace! You must move back; the French are almost upon us.'

Arthur nodded and turned Copenhagen away, and the two riders trotted towards the rear of Picton's division. A hundred yards away Picton spied his commander and raised his top hat in greeting before turning his attention to his men and bellowing an order to his Highlanders. 'The Ninety-second will advance! All in front of you have given way. Be brave, my boys! Forward!' He drew his sword and waved it above his head.

The leading ranks of the French columns had reached the hedge and now some of the battalions halted to fire, while others pressed through the hedge and halted a short distance the other side. Arthur could not help holding his breath as the French muskets came up and a voice called out, '*Tirez!*'

Flashes lit up the line and the volley tore through the Highlanders running forward to engage the enemy. As scores of kilted figures tumbled down, the line staggered and almost came to a halt. Picton spurred his horse forward and called to his officers. 'Rally! Rally the Highlanders!'

At that moment his head snapped backwards. His fingers spasmed and the blade fell to the ground. As the horse trotted on, Picton slumped to one side and fell from his saddle, rolled across the trampled grass and lay still.

'Good God,' Arthur muttered. 'Poor Picton.'

A groan passed through the ranks as they became aware of their commander's death, and then the Highlanders let out an angry roar and plunged towards the waiting French. It was a valiant charge, but Arthur knew that the weight of numbers was on the enemy's side and that Picton's men could not hold the centre of the allied line unaided.

From behind came the call of a trumpet, three blasts ending in a long, higher pitch, again and again. Uxbridge had ordered his heavy cavalry to attack. Two brigades edged forward. There was too little space to launch into a gallop and they could only trot through the gaps in Picton's division as the infantry hurriedly closed up to let the horsemen by, cheering their mounted comrades on. The horsemen cantered forward, into the massed ranks of the French infantry, hacking and slashing with their heavy blades. For a moment the enemy's nerve held, but as more British cavalry flowed round their flanks and loomed above them like giants in the thick smoke, their courage left them. The leading ranks turned and pressed into those behind, desperate to escape the swishing sword blades, and the panic communicated itself through the entire formation in moments. Thousands of infantry turned back down the slope and ran, desperately wriggling out of their cumbersome packs as they sought to escape.

'By God, that was well timed!' Somerset said as he rose up in his saddle and cupped a hand to his mouth. 'Ride, men! Ride! Run 'em into the ground!'

Arthur turned to frown at him, about to tell his subordinate to show some restraint, when he caught sight of Uxbridge dashing past, sword drawn and urging his men on at the top of his voice. Then Uxbridge's mount leaped a low stretch of hedge and thundered down the slope in pursuit of the enemy.

On the ridge the battered lines of Picton's division re-formed their line and Arthur let out a low sigh. The centre had survived the first great test of the battle.

La Belle Alliance, 2.30 p.m.

Napoleon stared in silence at the fleeing mass, borne towards him like confetti. Surging forward through the fleeing figures were the riders of Wellington's cavalry, closing up on the line of cannon stretching across the middle of the battlefield. The gunners dared not fire for fear of slaughtering their own men and could only watch in dread as the danger swept down the slope towards them. As the first of the British horsemen reached the guns some of the crews tried to defend themselves, using ramrods, handspikes and short swords. It was a brief, unequal struggle and the gunners were quickly driven away from their cannon, hurrying back to find shelter amid the limbers and under caissons. The horsemen pursued them, sabreing any man who came within reach. They also slashed at the tendons of the draught horses to disable them, and the helpless animals collapsed in their traces, whinnying in agony and terror.

Around the Emperor, his staff officers watched the cavalry charge aghast. Only a short time earlier, it had seemed that nothing could stop d'Erlon's corps from smashing its way through the heart of the allied army. Now all three divisions were scattered and the slope was covered with thousands of bodies.

'Sire, what are your orders?' asked Soult. 'Should we move the headquarters to safety?'

'There is no need,' Napoleon said wearily. 'The counter-stroke is already under way. Look there.' He gestured to their right where General Jacquinot's cavalry had emerged from the broken ground on the east of the battlefield. The force was made up of cuirassiers and lancers and they swiftly deployed to charge into the flank of the British cavalry, many of whom were still engrossed in the destruction of d'Erlon's men and the artillery train behind the grand battery, and so carried away by their exuberant spirits that they failed to realise the danger, or respond to the desperate recall signal sounding from the top of the ridge.

When his men were ready, Jacquinot led the charge himself, steadily building the pace until he unleashed his cavalry a short distance from the enemy. The charge crashed through the British horsemen, who were cut down as they struggled to meet the attack. Their horses were blown, and many who gave up the fight and turned back towards the ridge to try to escape were overtaken and killed.

Napoleon watched with grim satisfaction as his cavalry avenged their comrades, riding down and killing one enemy after another and leaving their bodies in the mud alongside those of d'Erlon's men. Both sides had suffered a bloody reverse, Napoleon reflected, but the allies still held the ridge, as well as the strongpoints that lay before it.

'We can only win this battle if we break Wellington's centre,' he announced. He looked towards Hougoumont, shrouded by smoke, not all of which was caused by the furious exchange of musket fire. A billowing column was rising into the sky from amongst the buildings, and flames glittered along the roof of a barn. With luck the fire might spread and force the defenders to fall back. That left the smaller farmhouse of La Haye Sainte, directly in front of Wellington's centre. Napoleon had observed the withering fire that had been poured into the flank of d'Erlon's division by the defenders of the farm. Clearly, La Haye Sainte must be taken, if any attack on the ridge was to have a chance of success. He turned to Soult.

'Tell Ney we must have the farm if we are to win the battle. He must take it at any cost.' He pointed to the stretch of ridge behind La Haye Sainte and Hougoumont. The slope there seemed more gentle than where d'Erlon had made his advance. It was also less muddy, and would not be such a hindrance to any attack on the ridge. 'That is where we must strike next. Tell Ney to use every available gun to pound the allied centre before he sends in an attack.'

Soult nodded and made a quick note. As he wrote, a courier galloped up to the inn and dismounted from his exhausted horse. Spotting Soult he hurried over and handed him a despatch. Soult quickly finished his order to Ney and read the report. Then, with a grim expression, he approached Napoleon and spoke softly so that the other officers would not overhear.

'A message from Grouchy, sire.'

'Well?'

'He is still advancing on Wavre. He will not be able to reach us until late this evening.'

Napoleon pursed his lips. 'Then we must forget about Grouchy.'

'And what of the Prussians, sire?'

'We must delay them. Send Marbot's hussars towards Lasne, and alert General Lobau to have his corps ready to move to guard our right flank.'

Soult finished his notes and strode across to the officers sitting at the table set up outside the inn to have the orders copied into a fair hand and sent off. Meanwhile Napoleon's attention fixed on La Haye Sante. It was far smaller than Hougoumont and there would be fewer men defending it. Ney should be able to take it with ease.

Chapter 62

There was a brief lull across most of the battlefield while as many French guns as possible were positioned between Hougoumont and La Haye Sainte. All the time, the assault on both continued. Napoleon could see his men right against the walls of the latter, snatching at the muzzles of any muskets that appeared through the loopholes and trying to wrench the weapons from the hands of the defenders. The door of the barn was missing and a ferocious mêlée was being fought out at the entrance. As they pressed forward in a desperate bid to overwhelm the defenders, more of the enemy fired down on the French from the wall beside the barn. Some even hurled bricks on to the heads of the men below.

Once again the attack failed and the French fell back, passing through the shattered trees of the orchard out of range. As soon as they had retired to a safe distance a battery of howitzers resumed their bombardment of the farm and the shells burst over the tiled roofs with a flash and puff of white, or landed before exploding and briefly illuminating the interior of the farm's walled yard in a lurid red glow.

To Napoleon's left there was a rumble of hooves and he turned to see the cavalry reserves moving forward to form up behind the line of guns being trained on the ridge. Regiment after regiment of cuirassiers, lancers and dragoons came forward until the floor of the shallow valley was a mass of horsemen, sitting silently in their saddles as they awaited the order to attack. Ney took his place at their head and raised his feathered hat to signal the guns to open fire. With a staggered roar the bombardment began. Each gun spat flame and smoke as it jumped back a short distance with the recoil.

Wellington's gun crews stood to, but did not return fire, and Napoleon realised that they must be conserving their ammunition for the French cavalry, when they began their advance. Napoleon saw one of the British gun carriages above Hougoumont disintegrate as it was struck by roundshot. Splinters exploded in all directions, felling the crew. The axle collapsed and the barrel canted up at an angle towards the sky. All along the ridge columns of earth tore into the air, but the lines of soldiers still stationed on the forward slope and the ridge itself stood their ground as roundshot, canister and shell decimated their ranks.

'They cannot take such punishment for long,' Soult commented.

Napoleon nodded. But even as he took grim satisfaction from the destruction being dealt out by the French guns, he was aware that time was slipping away. Every minute brought the Prussians closer to his right flank. The battle could still be won, he calculated, but the odds were no more than sixty to forty in his favour. Victory depended on breaking the centre of the allied line. Napoleon reached down and took out his fob watch, and glanced at the hands. Wellington's soldiers, scraped together from the forces of Europe's minor powers, had defied Napoleon for over four hours.

'Their nerve will break at any moment, Soult. I am certain of it.' Napoleon gestured towards the waiting cavalry. 'And then nothing will stand between Ney and the streets of Brussels.'

The elm tree, 4.00 p.m.

Even though Arthur had given the order for the battalions on the ridge to lie down the casualties were still fearful. Heavy shot, angled low, smashed through the prone figures, leaving bloody smears and tangled bodies to mark their passage, and there was no shelter from the shells that regularly exploded overhead, sending fragments of iron slashing through the men below.

'We endured nothing like this in Spain, your grace,' said Somerset as they watched the bombardment to their right. Even though the French guns were targeting the stretch of the ridge between the two strongpoints of Hougoumont and La Haye Sainte, occasional shot smacked into the slope or whirred through the air close to Arthur and his small party of staff officers. Once there was a dull roar behind them, and Arthur turned to see a column of smoke swirling into the sky from the shattered remains of a handful of ammunition wagons, now ablaze as several dazed figures around the wreckage rose to their feet and staggered away from the flames. Scores more men and horses lay on the ground, unmoving.

'Lucky shot with a howitzer,' one of Arthur's aides muttered.

'Lucky?' Somerset snorted.

The officers turned their attention back to the furious bombardment. It seemed to Arthur as if it had reached a climax. He turned to look at the men of the nearest regiment, one of those composed of new recruits fresh from their training battalion in England. There was no mistaking the fear in their expressions. Arthur knew that they had to be moved back, before their spirit failed.

'Somerset, pass the word. The centre of the line will retire a hundred paces.'

'A hundred paces? Yes, your grace.'

The aide spurred his horse away and conveyed the order to every unit defending the ground under fire from the French guns. One by one the battalions stood up and formed ranks before turning about and pacing back down the reverse slope, out of sight of the French gunners. Within quarter of an hour the only men still visible to the enemy were the gun crews. Some of the batteries, overcome by the exasperation of enduring losses without responding, ignored Wellington's order not to engage in counter-battery fire and had started to blaze away.

There was no time to ride over to the gunners and berate them, as at that moment Arthur realised that the enemy bombardment was slackening. The last few guns fired and then the French crews reloaded their guns and closed up to them to create as much space between each gun as possible. The reason for this was at once obvious to Arthur, who spurred his horse forward, down the reverse slope towards the infantry regiments sheltering there.

'Prepare to receive cavalry! Infantry will form square!'

The order was relayed from battalion to battalion and each of the lines of infantry steadily manoeuvred into blocks, three ranks deep. The front rank knelt, each man resting the butt of his musket against a boot so that the bayonets angled out to present a bristling line of steel points on each face of the formation. Soon the reverse slope was covered in a patchwork of red rectangles, loosely staggered like elongated squares of a chessboard. Arthur and his staff took their place in the middle of a battalion close to the ridge, and waited. Above them the British artillery fired away at the advancing cavalry as long as they dared, then abandoned their guns and rushed for the shelter of the nearest square, throwing themselves flat beneath the outstretched bayonets. A handful of crews had the presence of mind to remove a wheel from their guns and run it down the slope with them, leaving their gun immobilised.

'Here they come,' Somerset muttered as the ground shook beneath the impact of four thousand cavalry ascending the forward slope. The sharp notes of bugles sounded an increase in pace and then the first of the enemy appeared on the ridge, wearing the crested helmets of dragoons. They came on, sweeping past the abandoned guns, their front extending for a thousand yards, charging towards the squares in a deadly wave of gleaming swords and deadly lance points.

'Hold your ground!' the colonel of the battalion bellowed to his men. 'For England!'

Arthur watched a squadron of cuirassiers swing towards the square, their gleaming breastplates shimmering as their mounts stretched their necks and galloped down the gentle slope.

'Fire!' the colonel shouted and the view of the enemy was obliterated by smoke. Arthur heard the thud of the bullets impacting on horseflesh, and the clatter as they struck the cuirassiers' breastplates. The smoke eddied away revealing horses and men strewn across the flattened crops.

'Fire at will!' the colonel ordered.

On all sides now the first volleys blazed out and enemy cavalry tumbled to the ground. Then they were in amongst the squares, flowing between the rows of bayonets, like a wave crashing against rocks and forced to channel its flow between immovable obstacles. The most fearless of the cavalry steered their mounts up to the lines of bayonets and then attempted to lean out and slash their blades down at one of the kneeling men. But, almost to a man, they were shot out of their saddles before they could strike.

As Arthur watched he nodded with satisfaction. His men were holding firm, and as long as they did, the French cavalry would be sacrificed to no purpose. The only anxiety Arthur had was that while his infantry was preoccupied, Bonaparte might be ordering up infantry and artillery to support the attack. If that happened then there was little that could be done to save the allied army. Threatened by cavalry they would be forced to remain in square, and thus provide perfect targets for the enemy's cannon.

His train of thought was broken as one of his aides was thrown to the side by the impact of a bullet. With a groan the young officer fell from his saddle.

'Get him to the dressing station!' Somerset ordered a passing drummer boy, and the wounded officer was dragged away, towards the colours where the other members of the battalion's band were treating the injured.

Some of the Frenchmen had realised the futility of trying to break into the squares and had sheathed their blades and taken out their horse pistols to fire at the infantry who had defied their initial charge. The last of the volleys had been fired and now the air was filled with a constant crackle as individual soldiers reloaded and fired. The smoke hanging over the squares was soon as dense as the thickest London fog and the enemy horsemen were little more than shadows. The bloom of muzzle flashes lit up the smoke all around, and above the sound of gunfire Arthur could hear the desperate cries of officers of both sides encouraging their men, as well as the cries of the wounded and the terrified whinnies of crippled horses.

For fully twenty minutes the enemy cavalry attempted to break into the squares, but each time one of Wellington's men fell the body was dragged inside the square and the gap closed up and the formation remained as impregnable as before. Then Arthur was aware that the fire was fading away, and a voice cried out, 'They're going! The Frogs are on the run, boys!'

A cheer went up, and spread from square to square. Arthur gestured to his staff to follow and trotted out of the square that had sheltered him, the infantry moving aside to let him by. He cupped a hand to his mouth and called out, 'Gunners to your pieces!'

Passing out of the smoke, he rode forward a short distance to gauge the situation. A handful of the enemy were still retreating over the ridge, and those who had lost their mounts struggled across the churned field, hampered by their heavy boots and cumbersome breastplates. Hundreds more were sprawled on the ground with their mounts, many writhing feebly as they groaned. The artillery crews paid them no attention as they dashed forward and manned the waiting guns. Not one of the guns appeared to have been spiked, Arthur noticed in surprise. A foolish oversight on the part of the enemy, and one for which they would pay dearly. He headed across the slope to join the battery of Captain Sandham. His nine-pounders and howitzer were in action as Arthur rode up and acknowledged his salute.

'Pound 'em, Sandham.'

'I will, your grace,' the captain grinned.

Two hundred yards away, the French officers were struggling to rally their troops and Arthur recognised Marshal Ney wildly haranguing the men before him. Suddenly the marshal's horse lurched as a roundshot smashed into its neck. The animal collapsed beneath Ney, but as Arthur watched he calmly rose from his saddle and strode a few paces to the nearest horse, took its reins and ordered the rider to get down. Once in the saddle of his new mount Ney continued his impassioned address.

'They're coming again!' Mercer yelled.

'Get back to the squares,' Arthur ordered. 'You too, Somerset.'

Sandham's crews fired their last rounds and made off. Arthur waited a moment longer, then reached for his telescope and trained it on smoke rising up from a village away to the east, no more than two miles from where he stood. There was fighting there, and there could be only one explanation for it – the first of the Prussians had reached the battlefield. A French bugle sounded the advance and Arthur snapped his telescope shut and turned Copenhagen back towards the squares dimly visible in the slowly dissipating smoke.

The next charge suffered the same fate as the first and then the attacks became piecemeal as each enemy regiment broke off, rallied and came back again. During the intervals between the attacks, the French artillery opened fire and the shot arced over the ridge before plunging into the densely packed squares, causing far more casualties than the cavalry attacks. Arthur rode from square to square to show his presence and encourage his men.

'Heads up, lads, they will not break us! . . . Just a while longer, now . . . The Prussians are coming!'

The men took heart from his words and shouted their scorn at the enemy as they returned again and again, stopping their tired mounts within pistol range and hurriedly discharging their weapons before trotting away to reload. As the smoke cleared before the face of one of his squares Arthur saw a French officer standing by one of the abandoned guns venting his enraged frustration by raining frenzied sword blows on its barrel.

At length Ney must have realised the futility of attacking without the proper support. Shortly before six o'clock the sound of drums was heard on the reverse slope and Arthur muttered to Somerset, 'This is what I feared. Come, we must act at once!' He galloped over to the brigades commanded by General Maitland and General Pack and pointed towards the right of the line, the ridge above Hougoumont.

'I need your fellows there at once. They are to form line.'

'Line, your grace?' Maitland looked anxious. 'With cavalry present?'

'It's not cavalry that is the danger now. Lead your men forward directly.'

The two brigades doubled across the slope as the gun crews hurried back to their weapons and reloaded with canister. From the crest of the ridge Arthur was not surprised to see that the enemy cavalry had pulled back to allow their infantry to advance. They came on as before, in dense formations that quickly fell prey to the allied guns raking the slope with canister, and those that approached the ridge were suddenly caught in the flank by the volleys of the two brigades that had been ordered forward. Leaving hundreds of their comrades strewn amid the bodies of horses and riders left from the cavalry attacks, the rest fell back towards the French lines.

Arthur took stock of the situation. His squares, though unbroken, had suffered heavy casualties from the enemy's artillery. The battalions of his Dutch allies were badly shaken and their officers and sergeants now stood to the rear ready to pounce on any man who fell out of line and thrust him back into position. Already one of his cavalry units, the Cumberland hussars, composed of inexperienced gentlemen, had turned away and was disappearing in the direction of Brussels.

'We'll not survive another such attack,' Arthur muttered soberly. 'In any case, look there.'

He pointed towards La Haye Sainte and his aides followed the direction indicated. A handful of men, the survivors of the garrison, were trotting back towards the ridge above the farmhouse. Emerging from the buildings behind them came the first of the French soldiers, cheering as they fired shots at their retreating enemy. The men of the King's German Legion did not stop to fire back.

'They're running for it,' an aide said coldly.

'Their ammunition must be exhausted,' Somerset suggested. 'They had to quit the farmhouse, or die there.'

'It might have been better if they did,' Arthur responded. 'Anything to delay Bonaparte.'

The officers were silent for a moment as they watched a figure appear on the roof of La Haye Sainte's stables, waving a tricolour from side to side in triumph. As Arthur stared at the fallen strongpoint, and the French forces gathering behind it, he knew that Bonaparte was preparing for one last assault on the allied line. Arthur's reserves had been thrown into the battle. The men that remained had been under fire since noon.

'What shall we do, your grace?' asked Somerset. 'Shall I order a fresh brigade to retake La Haye Sainte?'

'Yes, we must do that. It will be a bloody business but we can't afford to lose the farmhouse. If it remains in French hands then all we can do is hold the ridge, or die where we stand.'

'If we fail to retake it, what are your orders?'

'There are no more orders,' Arthur replied flatly. He stared towards the east where the first gloom of dusk was gathering on the horizon, partially obscured by the smoke of battle from the direction of the village of Plancenoit. 'The night must come,' he said softly. 'Or Blücher.'

Chapter 63

La Belle Alliance, 6.30 p.m.

'Ney has taken the farmhouse!' Soult exclaimed. 'Sire, we have La Haye Sainte. Look.'

Soult pointed to the French flag waving above the barn. Ney had already ordered some guns forward and they had begun to scourge the redcoats on the crest of the ridge, less than three hundred paces away. Soult held out Ney's scribbled report. 'He asks for reinforcements, sire. Wellington is beaten. One more attack and the day is ours, he says.'

'Ney says so?' Napoleon sneered. The ground around the farmhouse was carpeted with French bodies, as was the slope between the farmhouse and the end of the walled garden of Hougoumont. 'The proof of Marshal Ney's wisdom lies there for all to see. He has squandered our entire force of cavalry on his useless attacks. And then thrown Foy's division away. So you'll understand why I might begin to question the good marshal's judgement.'

Soult looked across the valley to the ridge, where spouts of earth leaped into the air as more of the French guns resumed their fire on the allied line. 'Perhaps Ney is right this time, sire. He needs more men.'

'More men?' Napoleon threw his hands up bitterly. 'Where do you expect me to get them from? Do you want me to make some?'

Soult closed his mouth and looked down, enduring his master's wrath.

'Ney has undone us. Just as he did at Jena. Besides, we have other matters to deal with.' Napoleon turned to the map table and indicated the eastern half of the battlefield. Lobau's corps had attacked the head of the Prussian column and been forced to fall back, giving up the village of Plancenoit. Napoleon had immediately sent in the Young Guard to drive the Prussians out. Shortly before Ney had taken the farmhouse, news arrived that Plancenoit was once more in Prussian hands, no more than a thousand paces from the road to Charleroi. Unless Blücher's soldiers could be halted, there was a danger that the Army of the North would be surrounded. Only the six battalions of the

Middle Guard and eight of the Old Guard, eight thousand men in all, remained in the army's reserve.

'We must stop the Prussians first,' Napoleon announced. 'Keep two battalions of the Guard back as a final reserve. Send the rest to form a line in front of Plancenoit. Have them form square in case the Prussians send cavalry forward. Then order two battalions of the Old Guard to retake the village.'

'Two battalions?' Soult shook his head. 'Duhesme estimated that there were over ten battalions facing him at the village.'

'That may be, but two is all I can spare. They know what is at stake and they will do their duty. See to it.'

Soult nodded reluctantly and dictated the order to one of his aides. As the officer rode off, down the road beside which the finest soldiers of the army stood waiting, Napoleon examined the map again. The recapture of Plancenoit would give him a reprieve only. If it was done, then there might still be time to beat Wellington. If he was routed then the remnants of the French army could wheel east and hold the Prussians at bay while Grouchy marched on their rear during the night. Napoleon felt a nervous sickness in his stomach at the great peril that threatened to engulf him. He tried to thrust it from his mind, turning away from the map and clenching his hands together behind his back as he stared towards Plancenoit.

Within half an hour of the order the sound of firing from the village intensified and Napoleon and his staff waited anxiously for news of the outcome. They were not kept long as one of Duhesme's officers came galloping up. He reined in and bowed his head to Napoleon. 'Sire, I have the honour to report that the Old Guard have driven the Prussians back. Plancenoit is back in our hands.'

'Very well.' Napoleon turned to Soult. 'Recall the reserves and have them formed up to the right of the inn. We have one last chance to finish Wellington. There.' He pointed to the ridge, where the cavalry had charged earlier. The artillery that Ney had brought forward had annihilated two brigades of Dutch troops sent forward to retake the farmhouse of La Haye Sainte, and were now tearing into the nearest British formations.

'Order every available man forward,' Napoleon ordered. 'Turn every gun on to the enemy.'

The weary men of d'Erlon's corps and those of General Reille who had rallied to their standards cheered the nine battalions of the Guard that had been ordered to advance. With drums beating the veterans stepped out proudly, the grenadiers in their tall bearskins leading the way, while four batteries of horse guns followed the formation. Napoleon strode to his horse and a groom helped him up into the saddle. Taking the reins he spurred his mount into a trot and made his way down the road before cutting across to take up position ahead of the Guard. His heart filled with a defiant pride as he approached the bottom of the vale and began the approach to the ridge.

A drumming of hooves to his left made Napoleon turn to look and he saw Ney galloping across towards him, followed by the handful of staff officers who had survived the earlier charges.

'Sire, what are you doing?' Ney frowned as he reined in beside the Emperor.

'I am doing what I should have done from the start of the battle. Leading my men from the front.'

'You will be killed, sire.'

'It is possible.'

'You must not fall here, sire. For the sake of France. While you live, there is hope.'

'Hope? What hope?' Napoleon asked blankly.

Ney leaned over and took the reins from him. For an instant Napoleon was tempted to snatch them back, but he hesitated. Then his resolve to lead the final attack of the day, perhaps the final attack of his life, faded.

'Take the Emperor back to the inn,' Ney ordered, handing the reins to one of his aides, who led the horse back through the gap between the two leading battalions of the Guards. One of the veterans raised a cheer. 'Long live Napoleon!' and the others joined in at once, and continued until he had passed through the formation. Then they set their faces towards the ridge and fell silent as they marched forward.

'Stop,' Napoleon ordered Ney's aide. 'I command you.'

The aide paused uncertainly, then bowed his head and handed back the reins. At once Napoleon wheeled the horse about to watch the cream of his army cross the floor of the valley, slowly disappearing into the dense cloud of powder smoke that had gathered as a result of the French batteries' bombardment of the ridge throughout the day. Ney halted the formation and ordered them to form square, then the Guard continued their advance, five battalions to the front, and four behind, in reserve.

Soult had taken a horse and now rode up to the Emperor. He pointed towards the line of the ridge as it turned to the north-east of the battlefield. The dark shape of a distant column was approaching

Wellington's left flank, and clearly visible to the men of d'Erlon's corps.

'Sire, those are Prussians.'

'Quiet, Soult!' Napoleon snapped. Glancing round, he saw that none of the soldiers seemed to have overheard. He turned back to his chief of staff. 'I know what they are. But you will ride down the line and tell our men that it is Grouchy, come to save us.'

'Sire?'

'Our fate hangs by a thread, Soult. Our men need to believe they can win, or we are finished. Now go, tell them!'

Soult nodded as he grasped the necessity of the lie. He took a deep breath and spurred his horse along the front ranks of d'Erlon's corps. Snatching off his hat he waved it from side to side and then thrust it towards the distant column.

'Men! See there! It is Marshal Grouchy! Grouchy is coming! Wellington is beaten!'

His words were seized on eagerly and the men cheered wildly, and then began their own advance to the right of La Haye Sainte. The roar of their voices carried across the valley to where the Imperial Guard continued their relentless approach to the ridge. Marshal Ney paused at the rear of the column. He glanced back towards Napoleon, waved his hand, and then turned to the front as he drew his sword and urged his horse forward, disappearing into the smoke.

The allied centre, 7.30 p.m.

'Heads up!' a soldier from Halkett's brigade shouted. 'Here they come again!'

Arthur had just led two battalions of Brunswick infantry forward to the ridge. The inexperienced young men looked ahead nervously as they heard the shout and guessed its import. Even though the French guns had continued to fire on the ridge, there had been no attacks for nearly an hour and Arthur had used the opportunity to pull in his flanks and concentrate what was left of his army astride the road to Brussels. Halting the Brunswickers, he rode ahead with Somerset and Uxbridge as far as the hedge on the crest and looked down the slope. The sound of drums drifted through the smoke.

'Infantry again,' said Uxbridge.

'Then we shall send them on their way.' Somerset forced a smile. 'The same as we did before.'

They waited a moment longer and then saw the heads of what

appeared at first to be five large columns of infantry. There was no mistaking the uniform of the men approaching the ridge.

'By God, Boney's sending in the Guard,' Uxbridge muttered. 'In squares. Well, they need not have bothered. I've too few men left to mount a decent charge.'

Arthur turned to Somerset. 'I want every gun turned on them. They must not get over the ridge. Ride the line and tell every battery commander.'

'Yes, your grace.'

As Somerset galloped away Arthur took a deep breath. 'Here it is, Uxbridge, the deciding moment.'

He looked along the ridge and saw the smoke-grimed faces of his weary men. The artillery, who had been exposed to enemy fire longer than any other arm, had suffered badly. All that remained of some batteries were the smashed fragments of their weapons, while others had lost guns, men and horses. Those still on their feet had been serving the weapons for eight hours and moved with the leaden stagger of men on the verge of collapse. As Somerset went along the ridge warning of the approach of the enemy, those units still in square hurriedly wheeled their sides out to form a line facing the ridge. The surviving guns blasted away, shooting canister into the faces of the French squares. Napoleon's veterans instantly closed up the gaps, dressed their ranks, and continued forward, as if they were executing a parade-ground manoeuvre. With a rumble, some batteries of enemy horse guns trundled up between the squares and halted to unlimber. The crews had their weapons trained on the ridge and ready to fire in less than a minute.

'Never seen guns moved so well,' Arthur marvelled.

They opened fire, targeting the English guns with canister and cutting down their crews. For as long as they could Arthur's gunners poured their fire into the advancing imperial guardsmen. The two battalions on the right of the French line were marginally ahead of the others, and as they came up to the crest of the ridge Arthur and Uxbridge cantered over to the safety of Halkett's brigade. The infantry could not see the Frenchmen yet, but the sound of the drums carried to them clearly and they tightened their grip on their muskets and stared grimly ahead.

The tops of the bearskins appeared first, and above them the gold of an eagle atop its standard.

'Make ready to fire!' Halkett bellowed and his men advanced their weapons and pulled the hammers back to half-cock.

The front ranks of the first two French squares halted, raised their muskets and quickly fired a volley. Bullets zipped past Arthur and Uxbridge and a dozen or so of Halkett's men fell.

'Take aim!' Halkett held his sword aloft, and then swept it down as he bellowed, 'Fire!'

From his saddle Arthur could see that the British volley was far more effective than the enemy's, and the front rank of the two squares seemed to collapse en masse. He turned to Halkett and called out, 'Charge your brigade! Now!'

Halkett nodded and repeated the order in a clear bellow. His men let out a roar as they advanced their bayonets and plunged through the smoke. Ahead of them the guardsmen stood their ground for an instant, uncertain and afraid, and then backed away.

'They're running! After 'em, lads!' a sergeant called out.

A handful of the French veterans stood their ground, and were quickly cut down by Halkett's infantry. The redcoats plunged down the slope, the guardsmen fleeing before them. Arthur touched his spurs into Copenhagen's flanks and galloped along the line to Maitland's brigade, lying down on the reverse slope. The next two squares of the Imperial Guard were just appearing over the crest and Arthur cupped a hand to his mouth. 'Now, Maitland! Now's your time!'

Maitland nodded and gave the order. 'The brigade will rise!'

In a few seconds some fourteen hundred men, in four ranks, appeared in front of the French guardsmen, who only a moment earlier had thought nothing stood between them and victory. The surprise and shock on their faces was unmistakable as they stumbled to a halt.

'Take aim!' Maitland ordered. 'Fire!'

Arthur saw the deadly impact of the massed volley, and the charge of Maitland's men did for these squares exactly what Halkett's had for the first two. The Imperial Guard, the finest body of soldiers in Europe, broke and fled back down the slope. Maitland spurred his horse after his men and followed them a short distance down the slope, until he saw the last square to his right. Turning to the nearest companies, still bunched together as they headed down the slope, he halted them and formed a line facing the side of the last French square in front of the allied line. The redcoats quickly reloaded their weapons and took aim. Ahead, and to the other side of the square, more allied soldiers did the same. There was a moment's stillness, then the first of the volleys crashed out. Others followed, and the French soldiers were felled in waves. The survivors stared in terror at the bodies around them and then turned and ran.

A cheer rose up from end to end along the allied line at the sight of the elite French infantry pouring down the slope. Arthur stared at the sight, not quite believing his eyes and not immediately grasping what it meant. It was Uxbridge who reacted first.

'Boney's beaten! By God, he's beaten!' He grasped Arthur's arm. 'Your grace!'

Before Arthur could reply the sound of a cannon ball passing close by filled the air with its drone, and he felt Uxbridge's fingers suddenly dig into his sleeve.

'I'm hit . . .' Uxbridge looked at him, wide-eyed. 'I'm hit.'

Arthur reached over and grabbed his shoulder to steady him. 'You there!' he called to a gun crew who had retreated to Maitland's brigade. 'Help me. Get this officer to the rear!'

The gunners eased Uxbridge down from his saddle and laid him on the ground. Arthur saw that his knee had been smashed by a roundshot and was now a bloody mess of bone and muscle. The artillery crew picked him up and Uxbridge let out a deep groan as they moved off. Arthur turned back towards the battle and looked down the slope. There were still four battalions of guardsmen formed up, but they were now slowly falling back, covering the retreat of their stricken comrades. Over to the right, the garrison of Hougoumont still held on as they fought to contain the fire that had broken out earlier. To the left, the French were abandoning La Haye Sainte and retreating down the road to Charleroi. Over to the east Arthur could clearly see the columns of Prussians pushing back the remnants of the Young Guard.

'By God,' he muttered to himself. 'We've done it . . . We've won.'

Somerset came riding up, his face alight with excitement. 'Your grace, d'you see? The French are broken. They're retreating!'

Arthur could not restrain himself a moment longer. The strain and anxiety of the terrible contest was lifted from him and he felt a wave of elation course through his body. Somerset was grinning at him.

'What are your orders, your grace?'

Arthur took off his hat and waved it above his head, in the direction of the enemy. 'Give the order to every man you can find – general pursuit.'

As the word spread swiftly through the ranks of the men who had held the ridge all day the army swept forward, infantry mixed with cavalry as they chased after the French. Arthur rode with them and at his approach his men cheered him for all they were worth. The French spilled out across the landscape as they desperately tried to escape, abandoning their guns, caissons and wagons along with their wounded. Arthur searched for sign of Bonaparte, but the Emperor's distinctive white horse was nowhere to be seen. He reined in briefly at La Belle Alliance, where men from one of the Dutch cavalry regiments were busy ransacking what was left of the French headquarters in the gathering dusk. A hundred yards further down the road he came upon the first of the Prussian soldiers. They were busy bayoneting wounded Frenchmen and glanced up at him suspiciously until they realised from his beaming smile that he could hardly be an enemy. A short distance further on he saw a cluster of Prussian officers on horseback. At their head was a stiff-backed, elderly man with a fabulous growth of silvery hair on his cheeks.

'Marshal Blücher!' Arthur called out at once, raising his hand.

The Prussian officers turned towards him and as he reined in Blücher recognised Arthur in turn, edged his mount over and embraced him. Neither man spoke the other's language, and Blücher blurted out, '*Mein lieber Kamerad!*' And then, in a guttural accent, '*Quelle affaire!*'

Arthur laughed and clapped him on the shoulder. 'Bonaparte is beaten. Once and for all.' He paused and shook his head. 'But it was a damned close run thing!'

The pursuit continued after nightfall. Arthur's troops were too exhausted to go far and gradually abandoned the task to the Prussians. A pale moon rose over the battlefield and cast a ghostly silver-grey hue over the fields of death where the bodies of tens of thousands lay stiffening in the cool air. The ride along the road back to Waterloo filled Arthur with a numbing sense of unreality. The air over this same ground had earlier been filled with the deafening roar of guns, the crack of muskets and the rhythmic signals of bugles and drums.

It was quiet now, but far from silent. Many of the wounded lay groaning, crying out or simply talking to themselves. Some babbled incoherently, driven mad by pain or the trauma of the day's experiences. Here and there small parties of soldiers searched for wounded survivors of their regiments to carry back to the dressing stations behind the ridge and in the village of Waterloo. The defenders of Hougoumont had emerged from their strongpoint and left the fire in the barns to burn itself out, the flames still casting a glow across the bodies piled around the house and gardens.

Arthur shivered as he reached the shattered limbs of the elm tree on the ridge. He looked back across the battlefield one last time and then spurred Copenhagen into a trot as he made for the inn that served as his headquarters at Waterloo. Somerset had arrived shortly before him and could not hide his relief that his commander was unhurt. Supper had been prepared by the innkeeper and the headquarters servants had laid the table for Arthur and his staff officers with the best silverware and china. He sat down at the head of the table, and Somerset took the seat to his left.

'Where are the others?' Arthur asked. 'My aides?'

'They will be along directly,' Somerset replied, then frowned. 'At least, some will, I'm sure.'

Weariness had set into every bone in Arthur's body and he managed to eat little of the cold meat and bread that was put in front of him. Servants came and went and a few officers arrived with messages, which Somerset took and read, only handing on the most important to Arthur. Midnight came, but no more of his staff officers returned to headquarters. Arthur turned to Somerset.

'Thank God I do not know how it feels to lose a battle, but few things can be more painful than to win at the cost of so many fine officers, and friends.'

'Yes, your grace.' Somerset nodded. 'It is a hard thing to take.'

'I must sleep,' Arthur said quietly. 'Then I will write my report. England must know the result. Wake me at the third hour.'

Somerset nodded.

Arthur rose stiffly from his seat and winced. He stood for a moment, staring at the empty places along the table and feeling a terrible emptiness within him. 'I pray that I have fought my last battle.'

Then he smiled bleakly at Somerset and crossed the room to one of the wooden pallets that had been covered with straw-filled mattresses to serve as beds. He was too tired to take off his boots and eased himself down, lying on his back. His eyes ached terribly, and he closed them for a moment, and was deeply asleep shortly afterwards, his snores filling the room.

'Your grace, wake up.'

Arthur stirred, blinking his eyes open. Somerset was leaning over him.

'What time is it?'

'Just past midnight, your grace.'

Arthur sighed. 'I was to be woken at three.'

'Yes, but we have a visitor, your grace.' Somerset turned and gestured to a figure standing just inside the door of the inn. By the light of the lantern hanging above the table Arthur saw that he was wearing the uniform of a French officer. Arthur swung his legs over the side of the makeshift bed and stared at the man. He was tall and thin, some years older than Arthur and dark-featured. A bloody rag was tied around his head.

'Who the devil are you?'

'Colonel Chaumert, of the Imperial Guard, your grace.' The Frenchman bowed his head.

'What are you doing here?'

'I have a message for you.' He glanced at Somerset. 'It is for your ears only.'

Arthur rubbed his jaw. 'Leave us.'

Somerset hesitated. 'Are you certain, your grace?'

'What harm could befall me now?'

Somerset shrugged, and then left the room, shooting a warning glance at the Frenchman as he went through the door and closed it behind him.

'Now then.' Arthur gazed directly at Colonel Chaumert. 'Explain yourself.'

Chapter 64

On the road to Charleroi, 4 a.m., 19 June 1815

'You must understand that this meeting must remain a secret,' Chaumert said as they passed by the company of guardsmen blocking the road.

'If the meeting serves no purpose I have no intention of ever admitting to it,' Arthur replied coldly.

'Good,' the French officer nodded as the small column of riders passed through the moonlit countryside.

Despite the defeat a number of units of the Army of the North had remained intact and had been avoided by the Prussian pursuit, who had preferred easier pickings. Arthur and his small escort of Life Guards had ridden with Chaumert as far as Genappe, and then Arthur had continued with the colonel and a squadron of lancers to the final destination, following side roads to avoid the French soldiers fleeing towards the frontier. Now they turned off the road on to a narrow lane, at the end of which was a small farm. A carriage sat in the farmyard. By the light of the moon, Arthur could see a perimeter of sentries surrounding the building. Chaumert reined in and slipped down from his saddle. He tethered his horse to a post outside the door and looked up at Arthur.

'He's waiting inside.'

Arthur hesitated. He wondered if he should have heeded Somerset's advice not to leave his headquarters with the French colonel. But there was little to fear, and something might yet be salvaged for the good of all by his agreeing to come. He dismounted and handed the reins to Chaumert. Then he lifted the latch and entered the farmhouse. A small fire glowed in the hearth of the main room and by its flickering light Arthur could see the dim figure sitting on a stool to one side. He turned at the sound of Arthur's footsteps.

'Good evening, my dear Duke,' Napoleon said without a smile. 'I

579

should say that it is a very good evening for you. I congratulate you on your victory.'

Arthur stared at him from the shadows by the door, and replied, in French, 'There has been too great a loss of life for me to accept any congratulations.'

'For the moment, yes. But in time the dead are forgotten and such a victory is remembered for ever.' Napoleon waited for a response, and when it did not come he gestured towards a plain wooden chair on the opposite side of the fireplace. 'Come and sit.'

Arthur crossed the room and eased himself down. Napoleon's features were dimly visible by the light of the fire: heavy jowls and sunken eyes beneath a broad brow and short, dark hair.

'Your officer said that you wanted to discuss surrender terms.'

'That is what I said, but I have other reasons.' Napoleon stared at Arthur curiously for an instant.

'I am not interested in them,' Arthur replied. 'I am here to discuss surrender, or I leave at once.'

'Very well, we will discuss surrender. But first, let me say how kind the years have been to you.'

'What do you mean?' Arthur asked suspiciously.

'You don't remember?' Napoleon's brow rose a fraction. 'Ah, but I do. I never forget . . . Angers. The School of Equitation. Twenty-nine years ago. You played the violin.'

Arthur felt his blood turn cold. Though his mind was tired he recalled the happiest year of his youth, spent away from his mother, and brothers whose academic ability far outshone his own. A year when he had been released from the burden of his family to enjoy the company of his peers, under the kind patronage of the school's aristocratic director. The Comte de Pignarole had perished in the Revolution. Arthur recalled a day when the school had entertained some young officers from a French artillery regiment. As the memory crept back he looked searchingly at Napoleon.

'I see that you do remember.' A smile flickered on the weary features. 'The world has changed so much since then, eh? And we have changed with it, and become great men.'

'As I recall, we did not have much in common that day,' said Arthur. 'There was a disagreement.'

'That's right. You were all for the rights of the aristocrat, and I argued for the rights of the common man.'

'And now you are a tyrant, and I am the one fighting to restore liberty.'

'Liberty?' Napoleon sneered. 'You want to restore the Bourbons, and they want to restore the corruption and privilege that drove the people to revolution in the first place. You mark my words, the Bourbons will not last. None of the ruling houses of Europe will survive. The Revolution opened people's eyes. It will take some nations longer than others, but revolution will come to them all.'

'I am not here to listen to this,' Arthur interrupted. 'We will talk of surrender, or I leave now. What are your terms?'

Napoleon stared coldly at him. 'I am not accustomed to being spoken to in such a manner.'

Arthur shrugged.

'Whatever the outcome of today's battle, I am still Emperor of France.'

'Your title means nothing now. Your army is crushed, and the people of France will not forgive you for leading them to defeat again.'

'I have other armies. Grouchy is still in the field. I can retreat on Paris, gather my soldiers to me and make a stand.'

'There is no hope of resisting the coalition,' Arthur said wearily. 'It is over.'

'There is always hope,' Napoleon replied vehemently. 'When I was exiled to Elba you all thought I was finished, admit it! And yet I came back. It took me less than a month to have France back in my grip. What is to stop me doing it again?'

'There will be no Elba this time. You have been declared an outlaw. If the Prussians take you prisoner then you will be shot. I doubt if the Austrians or the Russians will be inclined to be any more merciful.'

'And what of England? Would my oldest enemy do the same?'

'I cannot speak for my government, but I would prefer not to see another ruler torn from his throne and executed like a common criminal. It disturbs the natural order of things. So, perhaps I should state my terms first.' Arthur lowered his head for a moment to order his thoughts. 'Tell your soldiers to surrender. Every man in your service. Then declare your unconditional abdication. In exchange, I will take you into custody. I offer you no guarantees for your protection. I will abide by whatever decision my government makes concerning your fate.' Arthur looked up. 'Those are my terms.'

Napoleon was silent for a moment before he responded. 'Those terms would not dignify a dog. What can I do but refuse and fight on?'

'With what? You have nothing to fight with, except a dwindling number of followers who only want a glorious end. I have seen enough of war to know that it has little glory. It is an ugly, cruel thing, and it would be better to put it behind us as soon as we can.'

'Yet you have known no other life but that of a soldier at war,' Napoleon said shrewdly. 'Do you really think you can be comfortable with peace?'

'I do not know,' Arthur replied. 'But I do know that I no longer want to live in a state of war. I feel that with all my heart. I ask you . . . I beg you, put an end to this conflict now. Spare the lives of your people. Spare the lives of your enemies. Take this chance to be remembered for having done the right thing when you could still choose to. Agree to that and I will do all that is in my power to find you a respectable place of exile in which to end your days. It will not be Elba. Make no mistake, it will be a prison, and you will be closely guarded. If you refuse then you must take your chances with England's allies.' Arthur looked at the Emperor earnestly, hoping that he would see the futility of continued resistance.

Napoleon folded his hands together and leaned forward to rest his chin on them. He stared back into Arthur's eyes with the penetrating stare that had so intimidated his generals and ministers. The Englishman did not flinch.

'I cannot accept such terms. I am Napoleon. What will history say of me if I flinched at the end?'

'If you fight on, beyond the point of reason, and have more men die for nothing, then history will surely brand you a tyrant. . . and a monster.'

'I wonder?' Napoleon smiled.

Arthur felt a surge of anger at the other man's preoccupation with his place in history. How many more men would be buried in the foundations of such posterity? He stood up and looked down on Napoleon. 'There is nothing more to say. This meeting did not take place, as far as I am concerned. I had hoped to save the lives of my men, your men, even you. But I can see that you will not let that happen.'

Napoleon shook his head. 'I have not given you permission to leave.'

'Permission? I do not need your permission.'

'I can order my men to prevent your leaving.'

'I was given your word that I would be allowed to pass freely.'

'Is that what Colonel Chaumert said?' Napoleon smiled thinly.

Arthur felt bitterly sad that it had come to this. There was no end to Bonaparte's lack of integrity. He looked squarely at the other man. 'If you don't care for your own reputation, that is one thing, but would you dishonour Colonel Chaumert too? And to what end? Even if you refuse to let me go, your defeat is assured. And you would add the weight of eternal shame to that of eternal tyranny. That will be what you are remembered for.'

Napoleon breathed in deeply and was silent for a moment. 'Go then. We shall not meet again.'

'I have no desire to,' Arthur replied. He made his way to the door, opened it and stepped out into the moonlight. Colonel Chaumert looked at him expectantly.

'My horse, if you please.'

Chaumert handed Arthur the reins and offered his hands to help Arthur up into the saddle. Arthur ignored him and climbed into the saddle unaided. Chaumert mounted his own horse and the two men rode out of the farm, back up the road towards Brussels. As they reached the place where Arthur's escort was waiting, he turned to Chaumert.

'Before I go, tell me something.'

Chaumert shrugged. 'What is it?'

'You are a good man, I take it.'

'I have tried to be.'

'Then what is it that makes a good man prepared to follow a tyrant to the very end?'

Chaumert thought for a moment. 'Even tyrants have the seeds of true greatness in them. A good man sees that, and he serves in the hope that one day the greatness will out.'

'And if it doesn't? What do you do then?'

'Then I am wrong, in which case I deserve oblivion, for all those who suffered at the hands of the tyrant I served so faithfully.'

'Then why stay at his side?'

'Because there is still time for some measure of redemption.'

Arthur held out his hand. 'I fear you will be disappointed.'

'And I fear you may be right.' Chaumert smiled as he clasped Arthur's hand. 'Sir, in another life, I would rather have found a man like you to serve. But then what man ever truly has the chance to choose his own fate?'

Arthur stared at him and then nodded sadly. 'Goodbye, Colonel.'

'Farewell, sir. I hope you, of all men, live to enjoy the fruits of peace.'

'The fruits of peace?' Arthur paused as he considered the future. Home. Kitty and his unknown sons. A return to the flummery of social life, and the poison of politics. The war had made him, furnished him with the closest friends he had ever known. It had shown him the heights of human endeavour, as well as the depths of depravity. He smiled. 'For men like us the fruit of peace is the absence of war. Little else. It's over. All over.'

Then he turned his horse in the direction of Waterloo and galloped away as the first rays of a new dawn seeped across the worn, torn continent.

Chapter 65

Plymouth, 30 July 1815

As Napoleon emerged from the companionway the lieutenant of the watch gave a quick nod to the midshipman standing by the blackboard easel. The youngster snatched up a rag and hurriedly erased *Eating Lunch*, and then chalked up, in big letters, *On deck*, for the benefit of the thousands of spectators aboard the swarm of small boats bobbing on the sea surrounding HMS *Bellerophon*. As those aboard the boats turned to read the new notice some stood and scanned the deck of the warship for the first sign of the great man. For the last week the harbour had been packed with local people and those who had travelled some distance just for the chance to catch sight of the Frenchman who had threatened to humble Britain for the last fifteen years.

Napoleon straightened up as he emerged on deck and nodded a greeting to the lieutenant. Behind him came his small coterie of staff officers, and the party climbed the short flight of stairs on to the quarterdeck of the seventy-four-gun warship. At first Captain Maitland had tried to insist that the French officers stick to the port side of the quarterdeck, leaving the starboard side free for the ship's captain and his officers. However, Napoleon had ignored the instruction and wandered where he willed, asking endless questions about the operation of the warship of those officers who spoke French. Maitland was not on board today. He had gone ashore and taken a room in an inn favoured by naval officers to await fresh instructions concerning his prisoner. Ever since Napoleon had arrived on the deck of the ship, surrendering himself to the protection of his most inveterate enemy, the British had not known what to do with him. Maitland had reported Napoleon's presence to the senior admiral on station, who had ordered him back to England to refer the matter up the chain of command. Now Napoleon's fate was being decided by the government in London.

Crossing to the side of the warship he gazed down over the thousands of spectators who had come to see him. He smiled and raised his hat in greeting and there was a ragged chorus of cheers from his audience.

De Las Cases, Napoleon's secretary, shook his head. 'The English make strange enemies, sire. You seem to be as popular with them as their own monarch.'

'Well, I must ensure their continued good will,' Napoleon replied quietly as he raised his hat again and waved it at a party of young women aboard a small yacht that had somehow slipped through the screen of guard boats which were rowing swiftly to cut the yacht off. 'I have no desire to be handed into the custody of my enemies on the continent.'

Few doubted that he would be put to death if he were returned to France, which left his English captors with a dilemma. Of all his enemies, Napoleon had calculated that England would treat him the most leniently. That was why he had given himself up to Captain Maitland. In truth, he had little choice in the matter.

After the defeat at Waterloo, he had raced back to Paris to take charge of the situation and prepare to gather all available forces to stem the advance of Wellington and Blücher. Such was his exhaustion that he allowed himself several hours' rest once he reached the Tuileries. By the time he awoke his enemies had made their move. Led by Fouché, the Chamber of Peers and the Chamber of Deputies had passed motions declaring that they could not be dissolved without their agreement, and called on the National Guard to defend them. Fouché had then called on Napoleon to abdicate for a second time. Weighed down by fatigue and despair Napoleon had given way. As a last favour to his former master Fouché had placed a French frigate of the Rochefort squadron at his disposal and requested that he leave France once and for all. Napoleon had delayed in Paris for a few days, offering to serve his country as a mere general to help stem the allied invasion. His offer was curtly rebuffed. As the first exchange of cannon fire echoed across the city Napoleon and a small band of close followeres had fled to Rochefort, only to discover that it was closely blockaded by the Royal Navy. Napoleon had hoped to escape to the United States, and waited in the port for the chance to slip out to sea under cover of a moonless night.

As he waited, a report came from Paris that the capital had surrendered to Wellington and Blücher. The Bourbons were to be restored once more, and had already issued orders for Napoleon's arrest. To wait any longer was foolhardy, and so, on 15 July, Napoleon had commandeered a lugger to carry him and and his party out to the nearest British warship.

'What becomes of us now then, sire?' de Las Cases wondered. 'I mean, if the English decide not to return us to France.'

'They will treat us as honoured guests,' Napoleon replied confidently. 'That is their nature. They baulk at extreme acts and would not have my blood on their hands. I expect that Lord Liverpool and his government are even now deciding on a small estate, somewhere in the heart of the country, where we may be kept under close supervision.'

'And in the longer term, sire?'

'Once it is felt that I no longer pose a threat to peace, I shall be free to leave.' Napoleon turned to his secretary with a glint in his eyes. 'I am finished in France, but I am sure that my talents can be put to good use in another sphere. You'll see. Perhaps I will even be permitted to resume my rule over Elba.'

'I hope so, sire.'

'In the meantime, we must create a good impression on our hosts. Wave, man. Show them they have nothing to fear from us.'

The pair returned the waves from a number of the nearest boats. Even as he put on an act for his captors, Napoleon's heart seethed with bitterness. At the end, he had been betrayed by Fouché and his marshals, who had refused to rally to his side.

'The next time I have the chance to exercise any power, I will be certain to be more careful about those I trust,' he muttered. 'I tell you, if I had hanged just two men, Talleyrand and Fouché, I would still be on the throne today.'

'Deck there!' a voice cried out from above and Napoleon turned and leaned his head back to see one of the sailors pointing towards the shore. 'Captain's returning!'

The lieutenant of the watch nodded his acknowledgement and hurriedly gave orders for one of the mates to assemble a sideguard to greet Maitland. Looking out across the water Napoleon could make out the *Bellerophon*'s launch, stroking neatly across the calm surface. Maitland sat stiffly in the stern, with a civilian at his side. The launch picked its way through the crowd of small vessels and made for the side of the warship. A short distance away the sailors raised their oars and the man in the bows caught on to the ship's chains with a boathook and drew the launch up against the side. Captain Maitland climbed up the rungs on the side of his ship and as his head drew level with the entry port the mates blew their whistles and the side guard of marines and sailors stood to attention.

Napoleon nodded approvingly. 'They are well drilled. Like clockwork, as with everything else on the ship.'

The civilian rose unsteadily in the stern of the launch and had to be helped up the warship's side by two of the sailors. As he clambered on to the deck and joined Maitland the captain was talking to the lieutenant on watch in a low urgent tone, and he nodded briefly at Napoleon before striding towards the entrance to his cabin, followed by the civilian.

'Looks like he's had some news from London,' de Las Cases suggested.

Napoleon nodded, feeling relieved that his fate had been decided. The sooner he got off the ship and back on dry land the better, he decided. Maitland had allocated the first lieutenant's quarters to the Emperor and Napoleon found the cabin cramped, damp-smelling and dingy. He longed for the comfort of a warm salon with a large fireplace and relief from the limited diet of boiled meat and vegetables offered aboard the *Bellerophon*.

'Sire.' De Las Cases nodded towards the lieutenant of the watch who was crossing the deck towards them. The English officer stopped in front of Napoleon and touched the brim of his bicorne.

'Sir, the captain wishes to see you in his cabin at your earliest convenience.'

'Ah.' Napoleon smiled. 'Then he has news from London, eh?'

'I couldn't say, sir.' The lieutenant gestured towards the companionway. Napoleon turned briefly to de Las Cases. 'Stay here. This shouldn't take long.'

Then he followed the lieutenant below decks as the midshipman by the blackboard rubbed it down and reached for the chalk once more.

The lieutenant paused outside the captain's door and knocked, then opened the door and stood aside to let Napoleon pass inside. Maitland was sitting behind his desk and rose up carefully to avoid bumping his head on the deck above. He bowed his head.

'General Bonaparte, may I introduce Mr Jacob Waterman, from the Cabinet Office. He has come directly from the Prime Minister.'

Napoleon had been surprised by the captain's mode of addressing him. So far he had been pleased to use the imperial title, but now 'General'? He frowned for an instant before he forced himself to smile a greeting and advance to offer the civilian his hand. Waterman made no attempt to reciprocate, and stood, hunched beneath a wooden beam, hands clasped behind his back.

Captain Maitland cleared his throat uncomfortably. 'Er, Mr Waterman is here to convey the decision concerning your fate that has been decided by his majesty's government.' He nodded to his companion. 'If you would be so good?'

He sat down without waiting for a reply and the government's representative addressed Napoleon coldly.

'General Bonaparte, after careful consideration of the obligations of the government and nation of Britain, the Prime Minister and his cabinet have resolved to convey you, and a limited number of your followers, to a place far enough from Europe that you shall not again disturb its peace. You will be placed under guard, and all communications and visitors shall be at the discretion of the government.'

Napoleon raised a hand to stop Waterman. 'I take it that you have decided not to return me to Elba then?'

'Elba?' Waterman looked surprised. 'Certainly not.'

'Then where will I be taken?'

'The government has chosen the island of St Helena.'

'St Helena? I have never heard of it.'

'I am not surprised, sir. It is a small British colony in the south Atlantic ocean, thousands of miles away.'

Napoleon felt his heart sink at the prospect of a long sea voyage. Worse still was the thought of being held captive on some primitive rock far from decent civilization.

'How long does your government propose to keep me there?'

Waterman and Maitland exchanged a brief look before the former replied. 'For the rest of your life, sir.'

'What?' Napoleon felt a stab of desperation at the prospect. 'Surely the Prime Minister can't mean it? Let me write to him. Better still, let me make my case in person. I swear that if I am granted a comfortable exile in England that her people need never fear for my actions again.'

'I'm sorry, sir,' Waterman shook his head. 'There's no time for you to present your case. A fast frigate, the *Northumberland*, will convey you to St Helena as soon as she is provisioned. You are to select no more than six of your companions to join you in exile. You may take whatever possessions are left to you. Do you have any questions, sir?'

Napoleon was momentarily stunned by the swiftness with which his fate had been decided. There would be no semblance of a kingdom for him to rule this time. Only a dreary life eked out on an island prison far from Europe.

Waterman sniffed. 'You seem surprised, sir. What did you expect? You are an enemy of peace. Because of you a multitude have suffered. Europe will bear the scars of your influence for a generation, or more. You have proved to be too dangerous to be allowed to remain in

589

proximity to Europe. Of course, should you wish to return to France, then I am sure that his majesty's government would be inclined to look favourably on such a request.'

'That would be a death sentence, and you know it.'

'Quite. And as far as I am concerned, it is no more than you deserve.' Waterman paused. 'However, the choice is yours, General. You might find some comfort in a martyr's death if you return to France and face your enemies. Or you live out the rest of your days, and end your life in unregarded obscurity. Which will it be?'

Napoleon glared sourly at the official. For a moment he was seized by the fire of defiance. Let him return to France. Let him face his enemies and show them how a soldier dies. Who would ever forget the name of Napoleon Bonaparte then? His fervid imagination pictured the scene of his execution. Firing squad or blade, each prospect filled him with a cold dread that he had never known on the battlefield. A glorious end would be denied to him for ever now. He did not want to die the death of a common criminal. He was afraid to, and that insight sickened him. He swallowed and looked down at the deck as he made his reply.

'I will accept exile on your terms.'

'I thought so,' Waterman replied with a hint of scorn. 'Very well, then I am done here. Good day, General. We shall not meet again.'

He did not wait for any reply, but made his way out of the cabin. Maitland was still for a moment, and then rose up from his table and left to make arrangements for the transfer of his prisoner to the *Northumberland*. Napoleon stood alone in the cabin staring blankly at the outside world through the grille of the leaded stern windows.

Paris, August 1815

Arthur lowered the copy of the despatch that Somerset had brought him a few minutes earlier. He did not respond immediately, but stared out of the window of the Tuileries palace into the gardens. Scores of Parisians were walking along the gravel avenues stretching out between the flowerbeds and neat lines of trees, enjoying the cool of the early morning. In the afternoon, Arthur knew that the gardens would be almost deserted and he decided to take his exercise then. There had been little chance to take a break from his duties since the allied army had accepted the surrender of Paris at the beginning of July. Despite the defeat at Waterloo, the French had put up a stiff fight outside their capital before giving in. Within days Louis was back on the throne, but everyone in Paris knew that the real power in France was now the Duke of Wellington. His word was law. The newly-returned King did not dare protest against Arthur's instruction to reappoint Fouché as Minister of Police, even though Fouché had fixed his signature to the death warrant of the previous monarch. Even so, Arthur knew that his authority would be severely tested in the months to come. The Royalists were openly calling for revenge against those officials and army officers who had gone over to Bonaparte during his brief resumption of his throne. Arthur was determined to do what he could to prevent the thirst for revenge leading to unnecessary bloodshed. His task was complicated by the desire of the Prussians to make France suffer for the indignities that Bonaparte had heaped on Frederick William over the years. General Müffling had requested yet another meeting with Arthur to state the demands of Blücher and Gneisenau, and Arthur sighed wearily at the prospect of facing Müffling within the hour.

He puffed out his cheeks and turned back to Somerset as he tapped a finger on the despatch. 'Boney should be comfortable enough on St Helena, I suppose. I have been there, you know.'

'Really?' Somerset raised his eyebrows.

Arthur nodded. 'On the return voyage from India, the best part of fifteen years ago. As I recall, the climate was pleasant and the uplands attractive. There are worse prisons.' He paused and frowned. 'It is a shame that Bonaparte did not perish on the field of battle and spare us all the burden of his incarceration. As it is, he has dealt us a tricky hand.'

'How so, your grace?'

'While he lives he must be guarded closely. The world cannot afford to let him escape again. At the same time, it will be politically inexpedient to hand him over to those in Europe who clamour for his blood. There are too many English Whigs and radicals amongst his admirers.'

' 'Tis true,' Somerset agreed bitterly.

'Still, while he is on St Helena, he can do no harm,' Arthur concluded. 'Now then, it is time to face General Müffling, I fear.'

Somerset smiled thinly. 'Shall I send for him, your grace?'

Arthur nodded. 'Let's get it over with.'

While Somerset left the study to fetch the Prussian emissary, Arthur glanced round the room, reflecting with some wonder that this had been the room where Bonaparte had dreamed his plans for the fate of Europe less than two months before. Now the dreams had crumbled and other nations could begin to hope that a lasting peace had finally dawned.

The door clicked open and Arthur hurriedly composed his mind as he stood up and nodded a greeting to the Prussian officer. Müffling smiled back as Somerset closed the door and left them alone.

'Your grace, it is good to see you again,' Müffling began.

'And you. Please take a seat.' Arthur gestured to the chairs on the other side of his desk as he sat down himself. 'I imagine Marshal Blücher has sent you to demand that England hands Bonaparte over to suffer Prussian justice.'

'Indeed, your grace.' Müffling pulled out a copy of *The Times* from inside his jacket and laid it on the desk. 'It seems that your government is considering offering shelter to the Coriscan tyrant. No doubt that would be a pleasing outcome for those of your countrymen who still admire the enemy of peace. My superiors wish me to convey to you their outrage at such a prospect.'

'I would share that sentiment, if it were true that England had decided to shelter Bonaparte. The Prime Minister has decided, however, to send Bonaparte to the island of St Helena, some three thousand miles from Europe, where he will be kept under close guard.'

'To what end?' Müffling shook his head. 'So that he may be used, by England, as a diplomatic bargaining counter?'

'No,' Arthur replied firmly. 'He is too dangerous a creature to be played with. Bonaparte will remain on the island, isolated from the world, and there he will live out the rest of his days.'

'Why should he be permitted such an end? After all the death and destruction that he has dealt out to the people of Europe? Marshal Blücher demands that he be handed over, tried and executed. This, he richly deserves.'

'Oh, doubtless.' Arthur nodded. 'We must, however, consider the wider context, my dear Müffling.'

'Wider context?'

Arthur took a brief moment to form his argument. 'What is the point of executing Napoleon now? What good would it do? It would only satisfy the desire for revenge, that is all. That is not a good enough reason to shed any further blood. It is not . . . civilised.'

'Forgive me, your grace, but that is an easy thing for the English to say. They have been spared the presence of French soldiers on their soil. I wonder how reticent your countrymen would be if England was not set apart from the rest of Europe by the sea?'

It was a fair point, Arthur conceded. He had seen at first hand the cruelties inflicted by the enemy, and could readily understand the rage of those who had suffered under French occupation. He cleared his throat and spoke.

'Be that as it may, the execution of Bonaparte will not serve any of us well once revenge has been satisfied. His death at our hands would outrage many in France, and beyond. I dare say there will be people who will say that he did not deserve to be defeated. There will be others who will seek revenge. Then neither I, nor you, nor Marshal Blücher, will sleep easily in our beds as long as allied forces occupy Paris. It is far better to let Bonaparte fade into obscurity. Then when he dies it will not be an event of note, but a mere detail, as the rest of the world lives in peace,' Arthur concluded.

Müffling was silent for a moment as he stared back at Arthur. Then he nodded faintly. 'Obscurity? I wonder if that will really be his fate.'

'I hope so. As I hope that Europe will learn never to endure another such.' Arthur stroked his jaw. 'If he is not to be cast into obscurity, then let him at least be remembered as the first general in all the world.'

Müffling looked surprised. 'Surely you, or Blücher, might assume that title with just cause, in the wake of Waterloo?'

'Perhaps. It is customary for the victors to write the history, and on the day I outfought Bonaparte.' Arthur turned to gaze out of the window. 'Yet I cannot easily believe that so singular a genius, and so cruel an ambition, will ever release his grip on posterity . . . For my part, I am not sure that I care. I have played my role, served my country, and now I am done with soldiering. Whatever history eventually makes of me, I know that I have earned my peace.'

Author's Note

It has been an epic tale and, having followed the lives of two of history's greatest figures, I imagine that many readers will want to know what became of Napoleon and Wellington after their titanic struggle came to an end.

For Napoleon, there remained less than six years of life. He spent these at Longwood House on St Helena, a meagre accommodation for a former emperor. Napoleon continued to be bitter about his imprisonment, perpetually complaining to the governor of the small colony, and writing letters to the British government to demand better conditions and relocation to a less desolate place of exile. When he was not protesting about his captivity, Napoleon set about writing, or rather dictating, his memoirs. These were fabulously partial and depicted Napoleon as an heroic, moral and infallible figure. That his empire had collapsed he put down to the betrayals and incompetence of his subordinates. His enemies were portrayed as foolish and corrupt, and he regarded Wellington with increasing resentment. This was partly because he blamed the Duke for the decision to send him to St Helena (wrongly, since the location was suggested by a civil servant) but mostly because Wellington had beaten Napoleon, as he had beaten the emperor's best marshals, and thereby demolished their reputation of invincibility.

When he put aside his protests, and his rewriting of history, Napoleon occasionally walked about the small island, always under the watchful eyes of his captors. He ate excessively and put on a great deal of weight. His health began to fail and in 1821 he complained about a sharp pain in his stomach which grew steadily worse as the weeks passed. Napoleon died on 5 May and was buried with full ceremonial honours four days later. His grave was covered over with a plain cement slab and there his body lay until 1840, when it was returned to France and entombed in Les Invalides. The funeral procession was attended by the surviving veterans of the Grand Army, tearfully following their former master to his final resting place.

There is still a debate about the cause of Napoleon's death. At the time it was said to be cancer, the same fate that had befallen Carlos

Buona Parte, Napoleon's father. More recent tests on samples of Napoleon's hair revealed the concentrated presence of arsenic, however, and certainly the symptoms noted at the time are consistent with such poisoning. It is possible that the arsenic had been administered in small doses for as long as two years prior to his death and the accumulated affect was fatal. The identity of any poisoner is unknown. Some argue that it was an assassin acting on behalf of the British government, but it is equally likely that it was an agent within Napoleon's small household, paid to do the deed by the Bourbons.

The report of Napoleon's death was received with a degree of equanimity in Europe. Despite some hysteria amongst those still loyal to Napoleon, it is Talleyrand's characteristic response that best sums up the real significance of his death. Tallyrand is said to have been playing cards when word reached the house of his hostess. The lady was silent for a moment before exclaiming, 'What a momentous event!' Talleyrand shook his head and responded. 'No. It is only news.'

The principal victor of Waterloo (in terms of the rewards garnered, if not the absolute responsibility for bringing about Napoleon's defeat), lived a long and prosperous life. Prize money and the rewards awarded to him by parliament amounted to over three quarters of a million pounds – a staggering fortune by the standards of the day. On his return to England, Arthur insisted on the creation of the Waterloo medal – the first such to be issued to all ranks. Although he was never again called upon to serve in the field he did briefly become commander-in-chief of the army, an honour usually reserved for a member of the royal family. Following the death of Prime Minister Canning in 1828, Arthur reluctantly accepted the premiership and was immediately embroiled in a political crisis. For many years, reformers had been pressing for legislation to relieve Catholics of some of the oppressive restrictions they were forced to live under. Fearing that there might be a civil war unless the restrictions were lifted, Arthur steered the legislation through parliament and even fought a duel with a staunch opponent of Catholic relief. Luckily, both men were sensible enough to shoot wide and settle the affair with some measure of honour.

Embittered by his experience, Arthur opposed more reform, this time to permit more people to vote for their members of parliament, and his government fell. After some years in opposition, he served as foreign secretary before retiring from politics in 1846.

On his return from the war Arthur's marriage to Kitty steadily soured. He felt no love for her, and was constantly frustrated by her lack of sophistication and common sense. For her part, Kitty lived in hope of restoring just a little of the affection he had once genuinely felt for her in the early days of their courtship, before the outbreak of the French Revolution. She died in 1831, never realising that hope. Arthur's disappointment with his wife extended to his two sons who were for ever burdened by living in the shadow of their father. Arthur's relationship with his grandchildren was far happier and he took great pleasure in their company as he grew old and infirm.

Arthur died in 1852 and his body was placed in a tomb in St Paul's Cathedral after a spectacular funeral procession. Ten thousand soldiers accompanied the coffin, together with Queen Victoria and the leading statesmen of the age. Over a million people turned out to line the route and pay their respects to the man who had provided two decades of the finest service to save his country from a foreign dictator.

For those readers who want to pursue their interest in the Duke of Wellington, there are a large number of histories, as well as an interesting history of his heirs, written by his descendant Jane Wellesley. I would also heartily recommend a visit to Apsley House in London. Number 1, London, as it happens, though such a singular address, does not seem to attract quite as many visitors as you would imagine. It is a fascinating experience to tread the halls and chambers of the Duke's London home. There you can see some of the treasures awarded him by the grateful Spanish after the battle of Vitoria. Best of all is the huge statue of Napoleon, represented as a classic nude, which stands as a permanent trophy from the wars that shaped the destiny of Europe, and much of the rest of the world besides.

My parting thought is to remember the words of a noted historian I heard when he was replying to a question from an undergraduate. He had been asked what was the main significance of the French Revolution, and the rise of Napoleon. The historian was silent for a moment before he replied, 'I think it is too early to say.'

He is right. Even now echoes from the world that Napoleon and Wellington fought over and fashioned are still with us, and their names will doubtless resonate with subsequent generations, long after we are gone.